In Wilder Lands

The Fall of Eldvar

Jim Galford

Edited by Chris Galford

Cover art by Danijel Firak

First edition 2011. Published by Amazon Press.

Table of Contents

Chapter One

"Altis"

Whenever I dreamt, time seemed to lose its meaning, but the story remained the same. It would always start with that peaceful warm feeling that just seems to belong in any state of near-sleep. I could feel people close—my parents—while my mind was adrift. My mother would whisper to me as I lay there, telling me that she loved me. These are the things every mother tells her child, I've been told.

What made my dreams unique was where things went from there and how vividly I could remember them every time I woke. Dreams based on your own memories can be brutal like that. I could choose to ignore my own history while awake, but my dreams would never fail to remind me of every painful detail.

After a time—how long was debatable, as it felt like hours, but could have been mere minutes of sleep—I would feel my mother leave my side. I was aware of her departure, though I did not fully wake either in the dream or real life. She was gone for a while…too long in my childhood's mind.

Each time I reached this point in the dream, I could feel a chill creep down my spine, knowing what was coming but unable to change it.

It was then that the screams would begin. Distant at first, but still clear. Voices I should have known, mixed with so many I do not remember anymore. They were probably my neighbors, maybe even the other young I played with, though the dream blurs so much and my own memory could not identify them. They have become nameless and faceless, which only makes their deaths that much more difficult for me to accept.

If I was lucky, this was all I would remember when I woke.

Estin woke, his heart pounding as it did nearly every morning. He shook as his limbs tried to run for a moment, the dream continuing into wakefulness. When he did finally free himself of its hold, he groaned and relaxed as best he could.

As he pried his mind from the horrible memories, Estin collapsed back onto the cobblestone street and covered his eyes against the bright noon sun. The cloth sheet he had draped over his corner of the alley must have blown away during the night, he realized, not particularly happy about that.

He started to drift off again. Estin had never been one for daytime. He was a creature of the night and the sunlight would give him headaches after too long. He much preferred to sleep through at least until early evening.

A sound nearby—a little scratching on the stones—made Estin's ears twitch as he bolted upright, fearing that he had been found by the town guard. They were decidedly disapproving of any of the homeless, driving them off with kicks or even swatting them with sticks. Given their dislike for Estin's people, he would be lucky to get just a sound beating. He had heard of others like him who had been thrown into the city dungeon or even just dragged off by the guards to the slave auctions and never seen again.

He rolled onto his feet, partially crouched as he sniffed and looked around for the danger. Instead of a group of armed soldiers, he realized that he had been startled by nothing more than a small rat, which was snatching pieces of rotten food he had stolen from a cart two days prior. The little rodent stared unblinking up at him, twitching its whiskers as it slowly grabbed another piece of bread with its teeth and backed cautiously away, dragging the food.

"We aren't much different, little guy," Estin said softly, watching as the rat escaped to a tiny hole in the brick wall of the north side of the alley, taking the bit of bread with it.

Estin was hardly being symbolic with his statement and he knew it. He looked down at his hands on the cobblestones and knew that he was viewed in the same light as the rat that had escaped. While the town may have been run by an amalgam of races, his kind were not welcome.

He dragged his claws across the stones, feeling the scraping of the nails against the ground all the way up into his shoulders. What angered him at times, was having to live among the other races as an outcast. Frustrated, he held his hands in front of his face and scowled at the animal-like paws he had been born with. Thick pads covered the inner-side of his hands and his feet, giving him an incredible grip and the ability to climb out of harm's way with ease. His father had once told him that his people had lived in trees at one time, but he had long since learned that his hands and feet would scale buildings as easily as any tree. In his life he had spent more time in the slums than near any trees, as he was far less likely to be found and hunted under the noses of those who would trap his kind.

Sitting back against the wall, he stared broodingly at the people passing by the end of the alley. They were all legally-allowed here. There were the elves with their pointed ears—Estin noted dryly that his own ears were no less pointed, but that was no excuse to be in the city. Humans were everywhere with their stocky builds that made them far larger than himself. Every so often, one of the dwarves would pass by, far shorter than even

Estin, but every one of them likely outweighed him.

Estin had even heard of other people from other lands being welcomed in the city. Even barbarians had been cautiously given entry for a time during attacks by another city's army—a place called Lantonne. That had been a rough time for Estin and the few others of his kind hiding in the city.

Many of the barbaric people believed it a proof of adulthood to kill the largest animals they could find—that would be Estin and kin. By the time the tribesmen had moved on, he had seen no less than four of their members wearing pelts that were nearly man-sized.

When he had first come to the city looking for food and shelter, he had feared being seen all the time. Now, he knew that there were certain places that the others did not care to look. Alleys were a wonderful place for him, despite the stink, occasional mugger, and various vermin. The rightful residents would never look down the alley, no matter how obvious he was, for fear of seeing something they did not want to know about. This made hiding almost too easy at times.

As he thought on this, a human youth came racing through the alley, nearly stomping on Estin's tail as she ran past. In passing Estin, the young girl threw a bag in his lap and kept going, breaking out into the crowds at the far end.

"What was that all about?" Estin started to ask, glancing back the way the girl had come. There, he saw five human guardsmen, clad in chain armor and bearing long pikes.

The guards stepped into the alley, looked at Estin, then down at the bag in his lap.

"Thief!" one shouted and they charged into the alley.

Cursing under his breath, Estin quickly knotted the bag onto his belt and looked at the walls on either side of the alley. The south was useless, almost smooth stone that had been properly fitted. East was a mass of humans in the main street. West were the guards. He shifted and scanned the north wall's bricks, finding many misplaced and uneven ones that he was sure would bear his weight.

Estin grinned back at the guards, then leapt to the wall, scrambling swiftly straight up, his long claws clicking into the spaces between the bricks or locking onto the edges of others. This was what he had learned to use his half-inch claws for in the city. It was something he had gotten quite good at. He hopped vertically, catching another uneven brick, but realized that he was running out of handholds. Just as he thought he was making good headway, rough hands grabbed his tail.

Estin struggled against the bricks, trying not to lose his grip and still move upwards. The next tug on his tail nearly ripped him from the wall and sent stabbing pains through his back. He looked down and saw that one of the guards must have leapt and was hanging precariously from Estin's eight-foot long black-and-white striped tail.

Though the guard weighed far more than Estin, he dragged himself upwards, his fingers numbing with the effort. The pain in his lower back and hips would force him to let go soon if the guard did not release him. Luckily, as he moved steadily hand over hand, the guard let go and fell to the ground, apparently convinced Estin could keep it up.

Not one to question good fortune, Estin practically ran up the rest of the wall and up over the edge to the roof. Once he knew they could no longer see him, he collapsed, pulling his tail tight to his body and clutching it in agony. He had a strong tail, capable of lifting himself off the ground, but it was not built for picking up armored humans.

Tears stun Estin's eyes as he lay there, trying to catch his breath. Slowly, feeling was returning to his tail and he flexed it slowly to make sure nothing was truly injured. As he did, his ears twitched and he became aware of grunts and clanks of armor as the guards climbed one of the ladders that allowed access to the roofs from certain spots in the streets. He likely did not have much time before they found where he was hiding.

He rolled to his feet and surveyed the nearby buildings. The one he was on was shorter than most of its neighbors, which gave him no clear avenue of escape. As he searched for anywhere else he could go, the first of the city guards hopped off a ladder and out onto the roof, followed by several more.

"Nowhere to go, vermin!"

Estin scurried to the edge of the roof and studied the distance to the nearest rooftop. Twenty, maybe twenty-five feet of open air, then a difficult grab on the stone trim of the clay-shingled building. It would be pushing both his luck and ability to jump, but at least it did not have pikemen waiting for him there.

He checked behind him and found that the guards were close now. Any of them could easily strike him with their pikes at this range. As he watched, one was setting down his weapon and pulling a length of cord from his belt.

"That's a good…," the man stopped and looked at the others, "what the hell is it, anyway?"

"A housepet or a good field worker, that's all that matters," replied another, making a very fake lunge in Estin's direction, probably to keep his attention off the man with the rope. "Get him leashed and let's get out of here."

Estin's eyes narrowed and he felt his heart begin beating louder as he saw the man tie the rope into a noose-like lasso. He had seen ropes put around others' and had no intention of letting someone drag him by his throat. Nothing made him more determined to flee than seeing someone with a leash.

Snarling at them and baring his fangs, Estin grabbed the edge of the rooftop and threw himself as far out as he could. Without a running start, his leap was less than perfect and he barely caught the lip of the far roof. Even so, his claws scraped and slid, letting him dangle off the edge from just the tips.

"Did you see that thing jump?" asked one of the guardsmen.

Another snorted loudly and replied, "Don't care. It's still dangerous to kids and other pets running around the streets like this. Someone could get hurt."

Grunting as he rocked side-to-side, Estin tried to get his foot up on the roof's edge. On the third try, the claws on his feet caught the lip and he managed to roll fully onto the steep roof. Then he allowed himself to look back at the sulking city guardsmen. He gave them a small wave, then checked the roof for a good way down, but there was none.

He was not about to waste any more time and so dashed up and over the roof, coming down the far side and leaping for the next building. Estin kept moving from one roof to the next, until he could no longer see the guards and knew that they would be hard-pressed to track him down. With that bit of confidence, he continued two more roofs and then stopped to catch his breath.

They would be after him again soon enough. Once the guards became aware of one of his kind, they would hunt them tirelessly until they had lost the trail or the poor unwanted creature was dragged off by its throat. Estin had no intention of being one of the latter. Not this day. Not any day if he had any say in it.

He took a moment to get his bearings. The building he was standing on was one of the abandoned structures in the poor section of town. Still, he reminded himself, the residents of the poorest part of the Grinder—the nickname of the slums—were wealthier than he was, and far more welcome in the city. At least an empty building would be a good place to hide out for a few hours, while the guards searched for him.

Estin checked both sides of the peaked roof, leaning over the edge of the loose and shifting shingles to see if there was a nearby window. At last, he found one window within range of the roof's edge, though it was boarded up. He studied the boards a moment, then decided that they looked to be rotten enough to open.

Taking a deep breath, Estin flipped on the edge of the roof, hanging down by the lip. He could feel the old and cracked clay shingles begin to break under his weight and so quickly swung himself toward the wall of the building. He let go as he got as close as he could, digging his claws into the wooden walls to keep from tumbling to the ground far below. Once he had a good grip on the wall, he knew he could take the time he needed to get inside.

Working slowly, he picked at the soft wood of the boards over the window with his claws. It did not take long before he was able to pull the boards away and slip into the dark interior. As he did, he checked outside along the street below for anyone who might have seen him, but there was no one who appeared to be interested or aware.

Estin collapsed inside the room, sighing happily as his eyes adjusted to the deep darkness. He sniffed at the air, squinting at large bundles throughout the room.

"Trash. Lovely," he muttered, his nose twitching. "Why is every abandoned building filled with trash?"

Not quite ready to abandon the safety of the room, he untied the mysterious bag from his belt and set it on the floor in front of him. As he unfastened the bit of leather that held it closed, he caught a sharp whiff of fruit. His mouth watered immediately—he was fairly starved, but any form of fruit was also his greatest weakness in life. The various city fruit vendors were likely the ones most willing to pay a bounty for his hide.

Within minutes, Estin had his face covered in sticky juice from the first two oranges he yanked out of the bag. By the time he was stuffing the last bite of the third into his long mouth and realized just how much juice was matted into his fur, Estin realized he heard voices from the floor below. He froze for a while, listening to be sure they were not guardsmen looking for him. Instead, it sounded like calm conversation.

He got to his feet—tucking the bag of fruit under an arm—and cautiously moved between the bags of trash, taking care each time his paws came down to be sure that he did not squeak a board and give away his presence. Moving out into the hallway, he found a staircase nearby and though it looked to be badly rotted, a few pokes with his foot convinced him that it would hold for one more day.

With nervous curiosity, Estin reached the bottom of the staircase, finding himself in another nearly-identical hallway as the one above. The difference here was that a single door was closed and candlelight flickered from beneath it.

Estin snuck up to the door and put an ear to it.

"But daddy, I'm hungry!" whined one voice. Female, he noted, and probably very young. The voice was certainly human—all the races had their particular accents.

"I already told you, dear, I couldn't get any more food today. That loaf of bread is all the baker could spare."

Estin frowned and looked down at the bag that he held in his left hand. There was still a lot of fruit in there and his own stomach had stopped growling, at least for the moment.

From the other side of the door, Estin heard two large shapes move and the voices he heard next were the man again, as well as a woman's voice. They were talking quietly near the door, now.

"Lester, if we don't get some real food soon, she's going to get sicker."

"You think I don't know that?" snapped the man. He sighed loud enough that Estin could clearly hear it. "There's no work to be had. I'm doing what I can."

A muffled sob from the woman made up Estin's mind.

Balling up his black-furred hand and hesitating only a second longer, he rapped on the door and waited.

The door creaked open loudly and the man—a stocky human with an unkempt beard and long hair—stared out at him, holding a long wooden broom in front of him defensively. He took a quick step back when he got a good look at Estin.

"We don't have any food for you!" the man bellowed, waving the broom at Estin. "Get out! Get!"

Slowly, so as not to draw any rash actions from the man, Estin opened the bag and poured out the remaining oranges into the doorway, letting them roll into the room.

"For you and your family," Estin told the human, looking past him at the exhausted-looking woman and young child, who certainly did appear to be ill. The woman clutched the child protectively, both of them staring wide-eyed at Estin. "You need it more than I do."

Turning the broom over, the man swept the fruit into their hovel of a home, without taking his eyes off Estin. Once the last of the oranges was behind him, he flipped the broom over again and jabbed Estin in the chest with the bristles.

"Ow," Estin exclaimed, a bit surprised. "I'm just trying to help."

"Get!" the man snapped, swatting Estin on the bridge of the nose with the broom. "Get outta here! Shoo!"

"I can talk, you know," mumbled Estin, backing into the dark hallway. "Maybe I can help…"

The man smacked him again on the nose with the broom's bristled end and Estin stumbled back, nearly sneezing.

"Would you please stop doing that?" he asked the human, rubbing his nose. "It really stings."

Stepping back into the room, the man slammed the door. The sound of a bolt being locked gave Estin no doubts about whether the human would be back.

"You're welcome," Estin told the dark hallway, his long tail drooping disappointedly.

He wandered off to find somewhere to sleep for the day, preferably where humans would not find him. They were just too unpredictable and weird for him to put up with any more that day.

*

Later that night, Estin woke up, feeling much better for having slept through most of the daylight hours. He stretched out his limbs and tail, smacking his jowls as he licked away the last of the juice that had dried, matting down his whiskers.

Rolling over, Estin got a good view of the rising moon and open sky beyond the lip of the perch. This hiding place was halfway up the city's walls. He sat up, hanging his legs off the edge of the block he sat on. Above him, there was about twenty feet of wall and below him a sheer drop of about fifty feet. This particular wall was not facing any of the roads and so he would never be seen, allowing him to relax.

Years before, a catapult had severely damaged this particular section of wall, creating the perch he was enjoying. It was one of his favorite spots to hide when the weather was not too awful.

"Is pretty, yes?" asked a female voice directly above him, her accent very thick and foreign.

Estin nearly fell of the ledge in surprise. Hanging from a rope harness was a young human girl. One sniff and he knew it was the one that had thrown the fruit in his lap earlier, effectively framing him for the crime.

Dark-skinned and thin, the girl wore clothing that even Estin could recognize as an odd fashion. Multi-colored—though mostly blue or brown—and patterned loose-fitting pants and shirt were accented by jingling metal bits on a cloth veil that covered much of her face. She wore a series of pouches fastened to her sashes. Sandals and a light leather vest were the remainder of her outfit, aside from the harness that kept her from falling.

"You weren't so well-dressed earlier," Estin noted dryly, still trying to figure out how the girl was hanging over him, let alone why. It looked as though she had tied off on a battlement stone above and managed to climb down without him hearing. "If I didn't recognize your smell, I wouldn't know who you were."

The girl shrugged and laughed, swinging slightly side-to-side, then stopped herself so that she was standing on the side of the wall.

"Clothing gives us away to the city-folk. I must blend in, yes? They suspect me far less if I look like to be one of them. But perhaps you do not know this?"

Estin glared and bared his teeth for a moment, then flopped back down on his perch.

"You're one of the gypsies," he observed. The sparkle in the girl's eyes above the veil hinted that she might be smiling. "You're about as disliked around here as my kind. Right now, I like you less than the city-folk."

"I am what you say, but is not why I am hanging off this wall, risking a fall on my quite-crushable head." She pointed at the rope, as though to remind him. "Perhaps you still have what I rightfully stole? It would be most disappointing to have come all the way down here otherwise."

"All gone," he said grumpily. A fly was starting to buzz around his face, annoying him—just like this girl. He swatted at the fly with his tail.

"You ate them all? I think you eat more than my brothers, if this is true."

Estin gave her a dark glare.

"I gave them away to a starving family."

The girl laughed and clapped softly.

"You are more generous than most who live here. Sadly, you have taken what was not yours and given it to someone without permission," she told him, sounding genuinely disappointed in him. "You will of course be indebted to my clan."

It took a moment for Estin to register what she had said, but when he did, he sat up and demanded, "What do you mean? They weren't yours, either!"

The girl was already almost to the top of the wall, having climbed the rope back up almost as fast as he could have climbed the wall. When she reached the battlements, she leapt out of sight, then stuck her head back out to look at him.

"Details, my friend." She waved at him, revealing many gaudy rings that Estin had not noticed before. "We will worry about who owns what another time. You will make it up to me another time. Do not worry about it. We can make this right."

With that, the girl vanished. Seconds later, Estin heard the marching of a patrol pass by.

"I really hate dealing with gypsies," he lamented to himself, leaning back against the wall. "Can this day get any worse?"

His stomach growled, as if on cue.

"Right…that whole starving homeless outcast thing."

Estin sniffed at the damp evening air, testing for any scent of the patrol, but they had passed beyond his section of the wall. Once he was sure that there were no humans nearby—gypsy or otherwise—he picked his way up the smooth wall and over the top ledge. From there, he had to move quickly, scrambling down the inner-side of the wall until he was low enough to freefall onto the stone roof of the guard barracks.

After getting his footing, Estin froze for a minute, making sure no one had heard his landing on the barracks. Beyond the normal noise of the city, he heard nothing and so made his way to the ground. Once he had dirt under his feet, he took off into the city proper, making sure to get some good distance from the barracks before relaxing.

The slums that he was in were probably the safest for him, at least at night. Every lowlife and criminal wound up in the Grinder. For the most part, the guards turned a blind eye to the area, though it was somewhat patrolled during the day.

This early in the evening, the Grinder was just waking up, with prostitutes wandering out from their homes, rubbing their sleepy eyes. In other areas, rather shady-looking gentlemen were dragging boxes to the street corners, where they would undoubtedly sell stolen goods to anyone who wandered past.

"You lookin' for some love?" barked a heavyset human woman, barely looking at Estin.

"Not tonight," he answered, holding up his hands defensively. "Besides, I'm probably not your type."

A massive green-skinned orc stepped out from the alley near the prostitute, puffing on a cigar.

"She's anyone's type for the right coin," he offered, laughing at himself. "Ain't that right, Marigold?"

The woman grunted and looked past Estin at another passerby, trying to get his attention.

"You're named after a flower?" Estin asked, somewhat surprised.

Snorting, the woman answered, "You never heard of a stage-name?"

"Sorry I asked," he replied, moving along quickly. The orc was making him more uncomfortable than the prostitute. The man could likely break Estin over his knee without exerting himself.

After the various prostitutes—and one horrible offer after another that left Estin wishing he could afford a trip to the Grinder's bathhouse—he made his way to a suspiciously abandoned building at the end of a dead-end street. Though most of the buildings around here probably should have been abandoned, this one truly looked it.

Near the end of the alley, a middle-aged female dwarf was staggering drunkenly, her traditional braids cut short in the dwarven sign of dishonor. She stumbled past Estin, nearly thumping her forehead into his chest—for she was far shorter than even he was—when she lost her balance yet again.

Past the dwarf, Estin had to step over an unconscious elf, who smelled even more strongly of booze than the dwarf, if that were possible. Immediately beyond the elf, he stopped at a door that hung precariously on its hinges.

"You two are the guards tonight," he stated, before touching the door. Behind him, he could hear the elf and dwarf snickering. A glance over his shoulder confirmed that they were right behind him now and appeared to be stone-sober.

"You don't belong here, wildling," the dwarf said hoarsely. "The Grinder's no place for woodland animals."

"And yet you let the elf stay?" Estin noted with a smirk. They both laughed, but did not move.

"You know why I'm here," he told them next, motioning at the door. "I still owe him some jobs and I need the coin to eat. I'm guessing I'm still on the list of people who don't get stabbed for coming by."

The elf nodded grimly and pointed at the door. "Then go, little beastie. He won't wait all night for you."

Estin backed into the hovel, knowing he probably should not turn his back on either of the two thugs until he had the door closed. Even then, he guessed there were many more in the dark interior of the house, though in all his visits he had not seen them. His sense of smell was no help here either, as the rank odor of garbage covered up any other scents.

He moved by memory through the mess of rotting furniture and random discarded items—he had been warned long ago that a trap would go off if he made a misstep—to the back of the house, where a broken desk lay.

Grabbing the front of the desk, Estin lifted it up. All of the pieces of the desk, including the chair, came up with the floorboards they were attached to, revealing the secret staircase below. He headed downstairs, letting the desk fall back into place behind him.

The light began to get brighter as he neared the bottom of the steps, where the passage soon opened into a larger room. As he had expected, Nyess—the owner of the building and master of the thugs—was sitting at a little table, counting silver and gold coins carefully. The rat-man eyed each coin with suspicion, as though it would trick him into losing its value.

Nyess was a wildling—an animal person—just like Estin, though he bore little similarity. Slightly smaller in stature, Nyess looked just like a large rat, whereas Estin had somewhat more of a humanoid body shape. The only non-animal thing about Nyess was his thin shirt and pants, as well as the tiny top hat he always wore to make himself appear more professional. The man really only cared about being able to manipulate other beings into projects that furthered his hoarding of coin.

To that end, Nyess had built quite the underground empire within the city of Altis. While most of their kind were considered a burden on the city, Nyess had somehow managed to make connections and elicit favors from so many people in all walks of life that he managed to keep himself out of harm's way from any guard in the city, even as he ran a well-established thieves' guild, hiring many who, like Estin, were willing to perform any job that did not involve bloodshed, if it meant a full stomach.

"You failed on your last task," Nyess mumbled, placing another silver coin on a pile and noting it in a ledger beside him. "I have yet to receive that necklace I sent you to get. I've half a mind to turn you back in to the guards…I think the slave auction still has your name on file. I hear that laborers are going for about ten copper these days, though if I convince them that you're worth breeding, I might be able to get a silver."

Estin resisted the urge to bump the table. "It's hard to steal something that isn't in town."

"Excuses do not change the fact that you promised to get that necklace," the rat answered, still not so much as glancing at Estin. "Just because the owner left town before the task was given to you, doesn't mean you are free to wander off without chasing it down."

"She was halfway to Lantonne when I found out about it," he objected, pointed at a map on the wall. Altis was far up in the mountains and Lantonne was several hundred miles to the southeast. Nyess seemed not to even notice or care.

"You owe me, Estin."

"I hear that a lot lately."

Nyess finally gazed up at Estin with his beady black eyes, emotionless as always.

"Do you think I care what you do outside of my employ? I don't care if you owe half of Altis a debt or have a hundred children to feed," he said, still holding a silver coin over the pile it would go on. "You can either make up for your mistake by doing another job, or you can go play with those two furless idiots upstairs."

Estin gave Nyess his best sad-face, but the rat-man's expression never wavered.

"Fine," Estin conceded, "I'll do another job, if the pay's the same."

"Though I would normally let you burn slowly over a fire for questioning what I would pay you, I prefer to be more professional in front of the one who has signed this contract."

Nyess waved at the back of the room, where boxes of collected artwork and other valuables had been labeled and stacked in orderly rows. From behind one of them, the gypsy girl stepped out, grinning broadly as she gave Estin a playful bow.

"This is Warra," explained Nyess, apparently unaware that Estin had met her already, though he hesitated with the introduction, squinting at Estin. "That sour look…either you have eaten something that is upsetting your bowels, or you know this human."

"This one knows me," explained Warra, touching Nyess' shoulder as she passed him. "We have much history. This is why I request him."

Nyess shrugged.

"I really don't care who you want doing the job, as long as your family pays."

"As promised, my cousins will repay you when they arrive in town."

"And I get to keep everything but Estin's payment, in addition to what your cousins are bringing?"

Warra bowed her head slightly in agreement.

"Then take the giant squirrel with you and get it done," ordered Nyess dismissively. "If this weren't such a big heist, I wouldn't even consider your offer. Make sure you do not let me down."

Estin glowered, resisting the urge to bear his teeth. He hated being called a squirrel, a rat, or a monkey. Those seemed to be the most popular choices that people went with in describing him.

"I am not a squirrel and you know it, Nyess."

"Yes, I do," Nyess noted as he documented another coin on his ledger. "It infuriates you so, I cannot help it. We're all vermin here, Estin. Learn to accept it."

Warra tapped Estin's arm and headed for the staircase.

"Until next time, Nyess," Estin said, trying to be polite. The rat-man just grunted something and kept counting.

Turning and hurrying to catch up with Warra, Estin asked her, "So what is this job you're dragging me into and why are you determined to keep tabs on me?"

Warra raised her veil as she smiled at him, putting a finger to where her lips would be. She pointed at the staircase and made a "wait" motion with her hand.

Biding his time, Estin followed her up into the hovel, then out onto the streets, where they passed the dwarf and elf, who were both back to their drunken acts, stumbling about and looking harmless. It seemed every time he came here, the guards of the secret door were different.

Once they reached the main street, Warra slowed her pace and fell in beside him. The young gypsy girl seemed as spry and untroubled in the slums as she would at a party in her honor. Estin had to assume it was just something about the mindset of the gypsies, as all the ones he had met in his short life had been like this, whether they were human, or another race raised by the gypsies. Always enthusiastic and overly outgoing.

"We must…how do locals say…set ground rules." The girl casually held her veil to her mouth and nose as they passed a manure cart being hauled from a stable out toward s the city gates. "You will follow my instructions, or we will both be in trouble. And what I mean by trouble, is that we will both be quite dead."

"Danger understood," he replied, "but why would you want the help of a wildling, Warra?"

Warra glanced at him and turned them north towards the spires of the duke's keep at the center of town.

"Before we discuss that, we get my name right. My name is Warra."

"That's what I said."

"No…Warra."

Estin stopped walking and stared at her.

"Seriously, is my accent wrong?"

Giggling at him, Warra nodded, saying, "Yes, your accent is wrong, but that is a failing of your upbringing. My name is wee, eh, ar, ar, eh."

Estin started to snap at her, but stopped with his mouth open, changing pace in his thoughts. "Wait…vee?"

"Yes, this is what I say over and over, wee!"

Blinking at the woman, Estin was reminded how foreign the gypsy accent was everywhere they went. This drove that idea home for him.

"So your name is Varra?"

"Yes!" Varra exclaimed and began walking again. "Now, what we are doing is reclaiming something that is ours, plus an appropriately-sized apology for having taken it in the first place. The man of bad clothing has this something and I wish it back."

"The…duke?"

"Yes, that man. We will be going into the tall house and taking it. To do this, I needed someone who climbs better than I do and will be unpredictable if they catch us. The wilder-folk are the only ones I would expect to do both and be willing to take this job without too many questions. I have watched you and I think you can do this. Without this job, Nyess will stay angry about the necklace. So is good for us both."

Estin nodded.

"Probably right. I've just never known a gypsy with more money than I have, let alone enough to pay off my debts like that."

"Ah yes, about this." Varra gestured grandly, as though trying to pull the correct words to her from the air. "I do think someday you will meet one of my cousins who has wealth…maybe I will, too. For now, Nyess will have to wait."

"You don't have a cousin coming with the money?" Estin asked, incredulously. "He'll kill us both."

"Yes, is likely," she answered, taking a right and heading up another street, still meandering towards the keep. "I am thinking that if my life is in danger and my cousins cannot save me, perhaps I will give him the necklace he wants so badly. Is rather ugly and does not go well with my clan colors. I have found no shade of our blues and browns that can match the stone in it. I look better in brass than gold."

"You have the necklace?" demanded Estin, feeling the hair on his ears stand up. "How did you steal it, when the owner left town before Nyess even contracted the job to me."

"She left town because I told her a thief was coming for it," answered Varra, slyly. She giggled again. "I followed her and switched out the necklace for fake before she left the mountains. Perhaps she made it to Lantonne before she realized the loss, yes?"

Estin closed his mouth and shook his head. This girl had put his life in danger, used that angle to gain his help, then used the act to save him. He could not even think straight about why any human would be so unpredictable—let alone one who seemed to think he would be the unpredictable member of the party.

At length, they reached the wealthier homes as the sun was about to come up. This made Estin twitchy and alert for any citizens who might notice him and call for the guard, but apparently at this hour no self-respecting resident would be out of their home.

"Up here," Varra told him, pointing at a gorgeous home that was larger than any inn

Estin had ever stayed in…or on. "We will wait on the roof until tonight. From there, it is short walk to the keep's outer wall."

"So your plan is to scale the wall?" he asked, lifting his head and gazing up the incredible structure's walls. It was easily as tall as twenty houses, stacked one atop another. The first window was about thirty feet up the walls or higher. "Where is the item we're taking?"

Varra tapped his shoulder, then pointed at a spot near the top of the wall.

"The badly-dressed man keeps it in his gallery, as though it were prize. We go up near the top, where only the man and his friends may go. You will climb the whole way, then let me in. I will walk up so many stairs I will be tired and cranky when we meet at top."

Even Estin wondered if his arms would let him climb that far. It was going to be a long time getting up there and far longer coming back down. It was far taller than the city walls, which he knew for a fact were difficult for him to climb.

"Do you think we can do it in one night?"

Varra frowned and studied the wall.

"No," she replied softly, squinting at the sheer stone. "We may have to stay inside and escape the next night. I had not thought about the time it would take."

She perked up and slapped Estin on the shoulder, exclaiming, "This is why I bring you, yes? You are thinker."

"Yeah, that's me," he muttered, staring at the window far above the city. "We are definitely going to die."

*

For most of the daylight hours, Estin dozed off atop the roof, occasionally waking to the sounds of an overly-loud youngster or an overzealous merchant announcing their wares. He generally was able to sleep through nearly anything that was not right next to him—or at least that did not sound like something coming to eat or chain him—so the day passed quickly between the times he opened a drowsy eye to double-check on his surroundings.

Just past midday, he popped an eye open after hearing the snarls of a dog somewhere nearby and realized that Varra was gone. Some of her bags were still there, letting him know she intended to return, but he had no idea how long she had been gone or how much longer she would be away.

Sighing and rolling over to put his head in the shade of a tall chimney, he went back to sleep. He could only hope that when he woke the next time, she would be back. If not, he would think about how to escape Nyess' debts and whether that meant leaving town for a while.

Estin was woken by close noises again as the sun began to drift towards the horizon. He checked the roof, but Varra had still not returned, making him start to wonder if he would have to leave on his own. The noise that had woken him was a man making announcements in a voice that carried for far around. The sounds of many other people created a blanketing din that made it difficult to think.

Scooting up to the edge of the roof, Estin peeked into the streets to see what the commotion was about. Up against the keep's wall, an elven royal herald—Estin recognized the red and white standards of the city's duke—was glaring at the crowd, while holding up a large parchment he had apparently been reading from. Once the crowd quieted down slightly, he continued talking.

"…as per the Duke Harlin's orders, we have begun looking into other ways to keep the city safe, with the defeat of our army. Our lord is committed to ensuring that the sacrifices of those drafted or enlisted will not be in vain and he hereby pledges that there will be no further drafting, despite the recent decimation of our military, defending this land against the incursion of Lantonne's forces."

"If there are no troops, how the hell does he expect to protect us?" shouted a dwarven woman, shoving several humans aside so she could be seen, her braided hair slapping at the people near her as she spoke. "We demand that something be done to keep us safe!"

A cheer went through the crowd and the herald gave an incline of his head to acknowledge the woman, waiting for the chance to speak.

"Our lord has not abandoned us," he advised the crowd, though boos and derisive cries indicated many did not believe him. "As he has said many times, he will do anything to protect this fair city, even if it is unpopular. In this case, he has heard your pleas and will send no more of your sons to war. A new plan is in motion."

Disgusted muttering drifted throughout the crowds and people began to disperse, several stopping by the herald first to spit at his feet. The man just stood there regally, staring straight ahead as though he were alone. Once the streets were mostly clear, the elven herald seemed to relax and his shoulders hung weakly. He stalked off towards the entrance to the keep, appearing as though he had been beaten, which Estin had to think was very close to having happened.

"They do not wish to be forced to fight, yet they fear having no soldiers," noted Varra, lying beside him on the roof. She had somehow snuck right up next to him. "City-folk do have strange ways."

"I didn't even know we were back at war," Estin admitted, sliding back from the edge so that he would not be spotted by people on the ground. "Thought that ended a while ago."

"Oh yes, this you are. What hole have you been hiding in, my furry friend?"

Estin gave her an annoyed growl. "The slums mostly. Lantonne's armies could be inside the city before we knew anything was happening."

"Ah, this I do see." Varra shifted a large sack that Estin was sure was new, using it to sit upright. "You know of Lantonne?"

"Yeah, a little. Not sure how much is true. Crazy city to the southeast, outside the mountains. They say it's ruled by a council of humans and dwarves and that they use magical war machines to decimate other nations. The rumor is that we only have held this long because we're so far up in the mountains that they can't bring their war machines up here."

"No, no," laughed Varra. "This is hardly true. Lantonne is a beautiful place, though they make my people stay outside of arrow range from the walls. They have defeated many armies, but always to defend farmlands that they claim. Like so many city-folk, they think they own dirt, yes?"

Estin just shrugged. "I've never owned anything myself, so I can't say I understand that, either."

Waving away his comment, Varra continued, "They do have great machines for war, as you say. It was these that let them destroy Altis's entire army as the sun set. This they did from within the mountains, maybe a mile or two down the road. Rather than invade, they have retreated, announcing that they do not wish to harm the people of Altis, though the badly-dressed human in the tall building will not say that, I am sure."

"Any idea what the great plan to defend the town is, then?"

Varra shook her head, her various jewelry chains jingling softly.

"The army lies dead and no one collects them. The badly-dressed man's scholars walk the fields of the dead, talking about what to do about it, while they do nothing. This is a shame my people would never allow, but the city-folk have their own ways, yes?"

"How do you know all this?" Estin asked, glancing at the large sack again.

Varra laughed.

"This is where I went while you spend the day sleeping. Dead men have no use for many things that we, the living, must regretfully take and put to good use."

She slid the sack between them and began emptying it, surprising Estin with each item she pulled out. First came several swords and daggers of varying styles and sizes, all stained with dried blood…sometimes on the blade and sometimes on the hilt. Next, she drew out a bag that gave a metallic rattle that sounded like a few coins. Lastly, she took out several belts, pouches, and leather armor accessories.

Varra was smiling to herself as she looked up at Estin, then frowned.

"You do not approve? I collect things to help us. This should be a good thing, no?"

Estin shook his head slightly as he picked up a short sword and some of the leather bits that he thought might help keep his arms and legs from getting too torn up on the climb up the keep walls. If he had to risk his life foolishly, he hoped at least to mitigate the damage to his hide.

"Stealing from the dead wouldn't be my first choice of ways to get the gear we need."

Varra shook her head vigorously.

"First, the city-folk say we are thieves for taking things that they do not need or have left lying around, uncared for. This my people just cannot abide, letting things go to waste. I learn from my error and try to do the right thing and take only from those who will not be deprived by the loss, but now you think this is bad, too? I am saddened that your people have so little respect for their dead…they no longer need these things and would want them used. I only honor that."

Estin snugged the straps on an armguard as he stared with annoyance at Varra.

"Ok, so I make that up. These things were left, so I took them. There is no harm…and some were quite pretty."

She held up a copper necklace as evidence.

"Whatever makes it okay in your mind," Estin told her, tying a belt around his waist to hold a sword and dagger he had picked up from the pile. "I just want to be done with this job before you get me into trouble with the law."

"Ah, the law. Is it still a crime if we do not get caught?"

"For once, an idea I can agree with. You do know you're rationalizing theft with a street urchin?"

"And this is why I bring you here, yes?" laughed Varra. "You are urchin from these streets, where I am urchin from any streets that come along. You are more familiar here."

"Girl, I want to live to see tomorrow. Helping you just barely fits that hope." He inclined his head towards the wall, perhaps twenty or so feet away from their position, asking, "Do you have a plan to make this work? We'll need to start climbing in a few minutes as the shadows hit the wall."

"We do, but you will not like it."

Varra pulled a thin rope from the canvas bag that had held the weapons and other stolen goods. The rope would hardly hold a child's weight, let alone the two of them.

"Even if that could hold us, there's nothing we can get a grappling hook onto," he observed, studying the wall again. "I can probably make the jump to it, but you'll need to get to the ground to climb it."

"No, I have a much more foolish plan. If we went down there, the guards would catch us before we made it even as high as we already are. Best time to climb is also when most guards are out. If you are ready…?"

Estin nodded and tightened his belt over the weapons he had taken from her. They dug into his back where his thinning shirt met the small of his back, but he needed the belt tight to ensure the sword in particular did not slip as he climbed and catch on his legs or tail.

"So what is this plan?"

Varra nodded grimly and took out the rope. She uncoiled it, revealing two runs that were about thirty feet each.

"How much do you know of magic, Estin?" asked Varra, pulling a small crossbow from the canvas bag, which she then began loading. Her dark skin seemed to take on a nervous pallor that made Estin truly begin worrying.

"Not enough to even be dangerous to myself," he admitted, wondering if all the guards and shopkeepers trying to kill him for years would be outdone by a little gypsy girl. "No one teaches my kind to read, let alone use magic. Why?"

After tying the thin rope to a metal bolt, Varra aimed at the wall across from them. The other end she stepped on, to keep it from flying off the roof. She then lowered the crossbow slowly and fired. The bolt whizzed through the air, then made a sharp 'chink' as it embedded itself in the wall, leaving a drooping line of rope between their roof and the wall.

"This will not be the wise magic of wizards that the tavern singers speak of," she noted, affixing the second rope to another bolt. As she aimed, she added, "This will be foolish magic, based on the ramblings of a cousin who has had much too much to drink."

She fired again, placing the second bolt just to the right of the first. Then, she pulled the ropes taught and put a brick on their ends, keeping them from dipping at all. With both relatively straight lines in a slight descent towards the wall, Varra sat down on the lip of the roof again.

"The magic I will use is designed to create walls, for closing off rooms you do not want sneaky sneaky thieving people entering. It is dependent on having lines that it follows, such as the frame of a door. This type of magic has little use to my kind, as we are often in the open, traveling with only our wagons. It took a very smart and very drunk cousin to find another use for it."

For a moment, Varra's left hand glowed faintly, tracing patterns in the air as though drawing symbols that Estin could not even visualize. Varra then spoke a faint word and touched the space between the ropes. The air rippled and seemed to solidify, appearing like glass between the roof and the wall.

"Now, the reason that this is foolish," she explained, tugging at the ropes until they pulled free of the bolts. The barely-visible ramp remained as though anchored to the keep, "is that the wall is like the most smooth ice you have ever walked on. If I have gotten the angle wrong...well...we shall meet those soldiers below the hard way, yes?"

Contemplating the risks he was taking, Estin leaned out over the roof's edge and tapped the magical wall with his finger. It appeared solid, but his finger's claw slid right off it. He tried again and could not press against it without his hand sliding away.

"I should go first, yes?" Varra asked him sheepishly, standing up and brushing her silk garments with her hands nervously. She pulled out two metal spikes, the likes of which Estin had seen before, usually used for letting humans climb walls or rocky surfaces. Over her shoulder, she draped a ten foot loop of heavier rope, also designed for climbing. The girl looked to be genuinely terrified of trying this, taking one breath after another. "I just slide down, stop on the wall, then climb. Should be easy enough."

Estin put an arm in front of her, blocking her way onto the magical wall. He stood slowly, eyeing the angle of the slide and looking for any handholds he could get once he reached the wall.

"I've got this, Varra," he told her, stepping up to the edge. "I don't have great balance for my people, but it's still better than most humans. If I fall, you can be gone before they're done slapping chains on me. If you were caught, they would look for more gypsies."

"This is true."

Varra stepped away and motioned grandly for him to go ahead.

Estin stepped out onto the magical platform, hoping he would be able to reach the wall without falling first. If he could just get his fingers onto the rough stone, he was sure he could cling to the wall with ease and likely help Varra get a good starting grip.

The moment his paws touched the glass-like barrier, Estin began sliding uncontrollably, gaining speed quickly as he raced across the gap towards the keep's wall. His stomach lurched, and panic overtook him as he lost his balance, tumbling forward and slamming his muzzle into the very surface that was hurtling him towards the stones ahead.

Dazed and disoriented, Estin continued trying to get up as the keep got closer. He simply could not get his feet under him and kept falling, sometimes forward, but just as frequently onto either side. Despite the haphazard movement and disorientation, he swung his tail in the air, using its weight to shift his direction and facing. He soon realized that his right arm and leg could feel the edge of the slide and he was drifting quickly off that side. The magical wall was not level.

Several feet before the keep's wall, Estin flew off the edge of the magic wall, feeling himself airborne just before he crashed into the keep's wall. He flailed, rolling as he fell to get himself facing the stones. Even once he did so, his claws dragged across the stone for several feet before he slowed and then stopped, his fingers and toes nearly numb with the strain.

A glance down revealed two guards, smoking trollsbane cigars not far below him. Their conversation or the din from the streets had somehow covered his noise. In his own mind, he had sounded like a stampede, but their lack of reaction let him know that he had been relatively successful in remaining quiet.

Once Estin was sure he would not fall again, he turned and checked on Varra. The girl was in a full panic, staring at the wall in utter terror. After several seconds, she looked at him, but her fear was just as plain.

"Come on!" he mouthed, waving her over with one arm as he hung from the other and one foot. "I'll catch you."

Varra shook her head vigorously and took a single step away.

Estin glared and pointed at the tower, then at the wall. Varra seemed to take the hint and stopped backing away.

Tightening her hands on the metal spikes she still held, Varra closed her eyes for a moment, then hopped onto the slide with both feet. Somehow, she managed to just barely keep her balance, though she was struggling to stay upright, right up until she rammed into the keep's wall even harder than Estin had, just above him. Unlike him though, she had the presence of mind to drive the spikes into the wall as she hit, keeping her from falling at all.

"Are you alright?" he whispered up to her, but she just nodded, dangling from the wall. She was gasping for air and likely could not answer him.

After more than a minute of silence, Varra let go with one hand and reached over to touch the magical slide. It vanished instantly, leaving only open air. There was nothing left to show how they had gotten to the keep, other than the small crossbow bolts, which likely would never be seen except by someone climbing the wall.

Pulling out a length of rope, Varra tied off to one of the spikes on one end, and the other to herself, allowing her to hang much like she had the night they had met. She dangled this way as she stretched her arms and rubbed at her jaw where she had hit the wall particularly hard.

"I think I am ready now," she told him finally, her voice barely audible. "I had the breath driven from my chest, but now can go. Meet me at the first window. We can rest there. It should be quiet this time of night."

With that, Varra pulled the untied spike free and rocked herself sideways until she was able to stab it into the next seam between stone blocks above her. She looped the rope around this spike and kicked the one below her free, pulling it up by the rope. Varra repeated this process over and over, making slow progress up the wall.

Estin only had so much patience when it came to climbing—which was to say very nearly zero patience—and so began picking his own way upwards. His claws hooked onto tiny crevices and cracks, allowing him to make rapid progress, passing Varra after a few seconds. He continued up, but kept his ears perked and listening for the girl, to be sure she was alright...not that he could have done much if she did fall.

It only took him a minute or two to reach the window, as it was less than twenty feet up from where they had started. He peeked over the edge into the room beyond, but in the darkness, could see very little without letting his eyes adjust. Instead, he sniffed the air and could not pick up any nearby humanoid scents, other than his own and Varra's.

Assured that the room was empty and had been for at least a little while, he pulled himself over the windowsill and onto the floor.

The room was completely unlit and filled with elven-style furniture—lots of embroidered cloth and carved woods—and the far door was closed. Another sniff confirmed that an elf had been here that day, but just not recently. Judging by the scents, this room was normally occupied by a man, though there were a lot of different female scents, not even all elven.

Estin just rolled his eyes, never quite understanding the ways of the other races.

He knelt by the window, listening to the sounds of the keep and waiting for Varra. As he waited, there were nearby footfalls from the hallway, where he could make out at least three people passing the room he was in. Soft conversations drifted through the door, but Estin was unconcerned unless they were coming to his hiding place, which it seemed this group was not.

Estin turned his ears somewhat, listening to the steady 'clink' noises of Varra getting close. Her pace would put her at the window in a minute or two. He cocked his head, tilting an ear in the direction of the door to listen for anyone approaching, but now the hallway was silent.

Looking around instead of using his ears, Estin saw that he had landed in front of a full-length mirror, probably worth more from the silver behind the glass than his life would fetch on the open slave market. He stood slowly, touching the frame and judging whether he had any way of sneaking it out of the keep.

Estin shoved at the side of the mirror and found it incredibly heavy, dashing his hopes of stealing it. His second thought was to possibly smash the glass and take the silver, but that would be too loud. With a sigh, he stepped back and admired the ornate wooden patterning around the edges of the glass, as he waited for Varra. He soon found himself looking himself over—something he rarely allowed himself to do. His appearance was something he was deeply insecure about.

Estin was well aware that he was still very young—even for his people—at six years old. That made him an adult by two years or so, but still young enough to make at lot of mistakes. Those mistakes showed in his appearance, as did the tattered once-white shirt and dingy brown pants he wore. He knew that he looked far older than he should, but living as an orphan in a city that considered his kind to be little better than pack animals did not help him any.

Though Estin stood straight like a human, he bore little resemblance to one. His long arms and legs were covered in fine grey fur, as was his back and most of his head. His face was visibly lined with stress and cold nights outside, even noticeable through the black muzzle and fur by his eyes, as well as the thicker white fur of the rest of his face. Even his white and black ears drooped more than he remembered his father's, even at three times the age. His orange eyes were far more pale than he thought his father's had been, too. That could have been untrue, as five years of memories could be quite inaccurate, but he had to believe that his life was taking a toll on him, even if that lifestyle was what he needed to be able to survive.

Estin held up his hands and examined the black fur that covered them. Patches were bare, exposing rough black skin, where he had scraped himself climbing. Unlike the humans, he could not wear gloves or boots, given the long claws he bore on both hands and feet. Despite all the other visible differences between his kind and the other races, he considered the claws to be the defining trait that made him truly different.

At that thought, he swept his tail around into view. It was longer than he was tall, measuring not quite eight feet from hip to tip and almost as wide as his fist. Black and white stripes alternated every few inches down its length. This, he knew, was what the other races saw more than the rest of him. His parents had been prideful of the tails their breed bore, but Estin saw it as just another liability, drawing attention to him that he could not hide. No cloak would cover a tail as large as his and he had never found any other way to hide it and blend in.

"You admire yourself while I climb?" chided Varra, now hanging on the window-ledge. "You are a handsome boy, now get over it and help me up."

Estin snagged one of her hands and pulled her up over the ledge, then grinned as she clapped softly for him.

"We have made first hurdle," she told him, seemingly quite happy with them both. "Now is easy part, I wish to think."

"You mean the next twenty floors?"

Varra rapped him on the bridge of his nose, snapping his attention back to her face.

"Is not right to be so negative. If your ears drooped more, I would have to pick them up off the floor. We have made good start, yes?"

Estin winced and tried to move towards the door, but Varra hopped in front of him.

"We are okay, yes? I am sorry. No more will I hit you on the nose. Is this good?"

Nodding and refraining from telling her how much he distinctly hated humans resorting to smacking him on the nose, Estin moved back to the door, popping it open an inch or two so he could peek out. Seeing nothing, he began to move out, but Varra tugged at his shirt, yanking him back. She practically slammed him into the wall, pressing herself against him to hold him there.

Estin began to object, but Varra was vigorously pointing down the hall in the opposite direction that Estin had been looking. He followed her gesture and saw a robed figure—the build suggested a human—moving their direction. This man walked in the dark hallway with no torch, his heavy cloak sliding softly along the stone floor, making little noise.

As the man passed, Estin sniffed, trying to identify the man's race or where he had come from—the act was mostly instinctual, giving Estin far more information than simply staring at someone—but all he smelled was dirt and a faint scent of mildew. The regular odors of the humanoid races were badly muted and he could only hazard a guess that the person was indeed human, though his build could have been elven as well, he realized.

"What was that?" he asked once the man had disappeared.

"That," Varra said, her voice shaky, "was a necromancer of the Turessi tribesmen from the far north. I had heard they were to visit this area, but I did not believe. For this I was foolish."

"A necromancer?"

Varra nodded vigorously, then spat on the ground. She peeked around the door one more time, verifying that the man was out of earshot.

"Most tribesmen believe in the spirits, the elements, totem animals, or even their ancestors. These particular tribes believe that the dead hold no value, revering the death of their kin. They try to keep their dead serving the tribe until their bodies have crumbled to ash from age. To my clan, that is the worst heresy we can imagine to perform on your ancestor. Worship whatever dark god you wish, but leave your ancestors' bodies alone."

Estin felt a cool chill right down to his tail at the idea of an entire tribe of death worshipers and decided to keep his distance from them. He made a mental note of the man's aroma, hoping to never encounter it again.

"We avoid Turessians…I like this plan. Shall we move on?"

With a curt nod, Varra inched out the door and checked both directions repeatedly, squinting in the dark hallway. Somehow silencing the jewelry she wore, the girl moved off to Estin's right, heading quickly away from where the Turessian had gone.

Estin watched until Varra had disappeared around a corner, then went back to the bedroom window. Taking deep breaths to calm himself before the long climb, put one foot up on the sill in preparation for his lengthy climb, when he heard the door open behind him.

Light and voices filled the room abruptly, forcing Estin to rush out the window, barely having the presence of mind to be careful of his grip on the sheer surface. He swept outwards, catching the stone edge of the frame with his claws and swung himself back against the wall on the outside. As fast as he was able, he pulled his tail out as well, hoping that no one had seen it darting into the darkening sky beyond.

"Nolen, this room is freezing!" exclaimed a female voice. Dwarven, by the scent.

"We just close the window shades and start a fire," stated a man's voice, the tone indicating a distinct desire for the female, Estin thought. "Much cozier."

Estin thumped his head against the stone wall as the window was closed behind him, wondering for at least the thousandth time in his life why humans and elves claimed that wildlings like Estin were "breeding like rabbits" and needed to be thinned. This had been the common justification for enslaving his people even moreso than the debtors of other races. From what he saw and heard, quite the opposite was true, with his people becoming more scarse, even as the "accepted" races bred with anything at their disposal.

Estin wondered if the other races realized how crude their breeding habits seemed to everyone else. Somehow he doubted it.

He hugged the wall, keeping his body and tail flat against the wall as he looked up to gauge just how far the climb would be. Though he had tried to study the wall when he had been on the neighboring building, staring straight up twenty or more floors was far more intimidating.

Clenching his jaw and fighting back an image of throttling Nyess for putting him up to this just to pay off debts, Estin began moving upwards. He knew he could move faster if he wanted to, but with each floor of the building, he had less desire to risk losing his grip. Not only that, he was quickly becoming nervous about whether his arms would support that long of a climb. He was very good at climbing buildings, but this was many times taller than any building in the town. His mother had claimed she could climb the mountains for fun, but living in a city, Estin had only really needed to scale one or two stories at a time. This, he could do quickly, but endurance was not needed for such a task.

Estin continued slowly but steadily upwards, trying to ignore the increasing numbness in his fingertips and toes from supporting his weight. Nine more floors up, he clung to the wall again, trying to calm his muscles for a moment. He looked up, unhappy to see he was only nearing halfway up.

Just as he convinced himself to begin climbing again, a sharp gust of wind off the mountains swept his precarious grip with his feet away, nearly shoving him right off the wall. Estin clung for dear life by his fingertips, getting a quick view of the ground far below as his body flapped out from the wall, then slammed back into it. Aching and now terrified, he flattened his face against the stone, trying to block out the panic before it made him make a mistake that would certainly kill him. He pressed himself as solidly to the wall as he could manage, closing his eyes as he struggled against a full panic.

"Just a little farther," he whispered to himself, but he barely could hear himself over the cold winds. "No more climbing ever again after this."

His heart slowed soon and Estin swallowed hard, trying to steel himself for the rest of the climb. Slowly, one trembling hand at a time, he began climbing again, getting more steady with each handhold that did not drop him to the cobblestones below. That last section of the climb seemed to take hours, until at last he checked above him, only to find the windowsill he had been trying to reach only a few feet away.

Scrambling through the last section of the wall, Estin gave himself one last push upwards and caught the sill with one hand, pulling himself up slowly so as to peek into the room beyond. This room's wooden shades were closed, but there was no light coming around it, giving him hope that he could at least get inside without alerting anyone.

With his free hand, Estin tugged at the shades outwards, grumbling as he found them barred. As he had learned in many thefts for Nyess, he flicked one of his claws through the gap between the shades, lifting the bar that held them closed, pulling them quickly open. He crawled up onto the sill and over into the room, collapsing onto the stone floor as quietly as he could manage.

The moment Estin's weight was off his arms and legs, muscles began knotting painfully and his fingertips and toes throbbed. Even in the dark he could tell that they were bleeding badly, but there was little he could do about it, other than lay where he was until the pain became manageable.

Estin slowly stretched the trembling muscles until he could focus on his surroundings without feeling like he was going to scream. He must have lain there for an hour before he felt whole enough to sit up, knowing he was likely leaving bloody paw-prints on the stone floor, but not especially caring.

This entire floor of the keep was visible from his location. There were no dividing walls on the floor, just one large open room with a staircase along the far wall, leading both up and down. Within the massive room, waist-tall shelves and cabinets were every few feet, covered and filled with objects that he could not identify in the dark. A few were obvious, such as armor or weapons, but much of the detail was lost even to his eyes, given the darkness.

Getting slowly to his feet, Estin began padding through the room, poking at the various trinkets. This was clearly a gallery of pride to the duke, though most of the items were a mystery to Estin and he could not fathom any reason the duke would find value in many of the collected goods. Some were clearly valuable—a golden idol from some foreign land would certainly be worth more money than Estin had dreamed of in his lifetime—while others were not. He roamed around, exploring and getting an idea what all was in the room.

Estin passed dozens of shelves filled with gemstones, some of which he shoved into his belt pouch, barely thinking as he did so. Their worth far outweighed any consideration of discretion.

He walked past long rows of ornate weapons and armor that likely were significant to someone with military background—which was certainly not Estin, who barely knew how to swing his weapons without hurting himself. He poked at several pieces of art that he knew he could not possibly carry out, paining him to think that no one besides himself and the duke might ever see them. The way human excluded others sometimes bothered him, especially when it came to art and beauty.

As he neared the staircase, Estin glanced through a pile of tribal-looking jewelry. One particular piece—a leather choker made with dye-stained bones and dangling feathers—caught his eye and he fastened it around his neck, before examining several delicate rings near it that he was fairly sure were engraved ivory. Those went into his pouch without a second thought.

Faint rapping from the direction of the steps told him that someone—hopefully Varra—had arrived and he hurried over, finding the heavy door that blocked the stairs locked with three different types of lock, all of which he could open easily from the side he was on without any need for skill. He popped all three and swung the door open.

"Ah, is you," Varra exclaimed as the door opened, jumping slightly as she looked at him, moving her hand away from a dagger he had not noticed she possessed earlier. She unshuttered a small lantern she was carrying, lighting the staircase brightly. "I was worried you had fallen and smashed your furry head, my friend. Is good to see you are here!"

"I wasn't sure you'd make it this far, either," he admitted, waving her inside. In the lantern light, he now realized just how much gold and silver was glittering in the room. It took his breath away.

Turning around in place to survey the wealth, Estin let out a very soft whistle. Varra nodded, her eyes wide as she too scanned the room. She appeared to be mesmerized, as though she were trying to decide where to start.

"What does the item the duke stole look like?" he asked Varra, taking mental note of many priceless objects that could have been the gypsy girl's lost belonging. Some, he decided would not be what she sought and he quickly stuffed into his pouches.

"This, I do not know," admitted Varra, unfastening her veil and pulling back the silk hood she wore. A deep frown marred her face. "I did not think the badly-dressed man had quite so much hidden from sight. Will take more time than I had thought."

Estin turned on her, annoyed.

"You don't know what it looks like?"

"No," she conceded, smiling at him and flicking the necklace he had taken with her fingertip. "This suits you. Is a little odd for wearing around town, yes? Perhaps you should move to the wilds. This style is in fashion among the tribes there. Some barbarians might think you belong."

"Stop changing the topic," Estin cut in, getting genuinely flustered as he stuffed the necklace under his shirt. "We climbed all this way and don't even know what for?"

"Oh, this is not so. I know what we are here for, just not what it looks like." She seemed to finally notice his anger and waved it off dismissively. "Do not worry. The ancestors will guide us, in time."

"In time?"

Varra laughed, shrugging away his annoyance.

"You do not think that a bunch of dead gypsy elders would be able to focus on timeliness with all this wealth to stare at? They will let me know when they are ready and sober enough to help."

"Are all human gods so…distracted?"

Varra's smile vanished instantly and she turned to him with a stark anger in her eyes that shocked him, even as he saw her hands reach for hidden folds in her garments, likely where she hid her weapons.

"The ancestors are not gods, Estin. They are our fallen, who have moved on and still guide us. They advise, teach, direct us, but they are not to be worshiped. Please keep your mythology off my people. We will not be mocked."

"I didn't know, Varra," he admitted, backing away. "I'm sorry."

"This is good!" exclaimed Varra, happy once more, her hands reappearing without any weapons. "The ancestors do not like being laughed at and I would hate to have had to be their vessel for slapping sense into you."

"That makes two of us."

Varra turned and walked away from him, wandering the room. Though Estin rarely saw her hands move, jewelry and small objects vanished in her passing. By the time she had reached the window he had entered through, her pouches were looking rather stuffed.

"The item…," she began, her eyes distant for a moment. She pointed towards the south end of the room. "…is over there. My great-grandmother just told me she had seen it once and told me what it looks like."

Estin scratched his ear, watching Varra, but not really sure how he could help. He was not even sure she was sane, but he had nothing to lose by letting her talk to her deceased relatives.

Wandering towards the area she had indicated, Varra's hands passed over many objects, as though testing each for familiarity. She set the lantern down and kept walking, closing her eyes as she moved through the aisles.

"Here," she observed, picking something up. She went back to the lantern and brought the object over to Estin. "This is what we are here for."

Clutched firmly in her left hand, Varra held a copper goblet, with intricate engravings along the entire surface of the bowl portion. Though beautiful, Estin had doubts as to its value.

"This is worth breaking into the duke's keep?" he inquired, cocking his head. "Nearly everything in here could fetch a better price."

Varra rolled her eyes and tucked the goblet into her belt.

"Not all value is in the materials, Estin. This, my people owned at one time. Now, is ours again. We do not worry about losing little things, but that which belongs to family, must stay with the family…even if it means climbing a human's keep."

"As you wish," Estin answered dryly. He honestly could care less what she wanted out of the place. The gems and trinkets in his pouch would pay off any debts he had left with Nyess and likely still be enough to get him out of town.

He had always wanted to travel south, where he had heard that the rulers opposed slavery, no matter the race. Maybe the west would be better, far beyond the mountains, where there were deserts that had never seen occupation by the various races of man. Either way, he had choices now, for the first time in his life. He just needed to get out of the keep.

"We will stay the night, somewhere hidden, yes?" Varra asked, leading towards the stairs. "I have found a good place. It will be a short way out of the keep from there and there are no guards at this time."

"How far away is it?"

Varra shrugged and answered, "Is down in the main section of the keep, near the ground floors. Is late enough now, the halls are mostly empty. We just need to avoid guards on the way down. Most others should be sleeping. It was remarkably easy to get this far up without being seen. If we could leave by the front door, this hidey place would be near there. Sadly, we will rest there, then come back up a floor or two to climb down the outside."

"Are you sure we can't get out yet tonight, rather than waiting here until tomorrow night?"

"You have lost your track of time," she chided, pointing towards the window.

The sky beyond was turning a violet as it began to lighten. Estin blinking hard, not realizing it had taken so long to climb the wall, or that they had been in the room for so long. He likely had another hour, maybe more, before the sun rose, but the climb down would take nearly twice as long as the climb up. There was a chance they could make it, but it would likely be quite light by the time they reached the bottom.

"Lead the way. I'll hide wherever you say as long as it keeps me from being beheaded."

Motioning for him to follow, Varra hurried down the stairs to the floor below. They moved very quickly, down one floor after another, pausing only briefly at the junction into each floor to listen for guards. In a little more than an hour, they were nearing the bottom of the tower, having only needed to dart off the main halls once for a passing patrol.

At this point, Varra turned down another hall, taking them farther from the outer walls. They moved through these living quarters swiftly, sometimes running right past servants, who paid no mind to the intruders. Most of the servants seemed to be barely awake and just beginning their daily routines, giving vague greetings to anyone who passed them.

"This way!" Varra hissed as they ran down a long paneled hallway, lined with paintings and sculptures. "Quickly!"

Varra dove through an ajar door on their right, just as a pair of guards began to come around the corner at the end of the hall.

Racing after her, Estin threw himself into the opening as well, collapsing onto a narrow staircase. He rolled as he landed, pushing the door mostly closed, without slamming it. Laying there, he waited until he heard the clomping of the humans' boots as they passed the door, continuing down the hallway, somehow managing to have missed Estin.

"These may be the worst guards ever," he whispered to Varra, who was sitting several steps above him. "It's like they're not even trying."

"This is the thing about city-dwellers," Varra answered him, sounding as though she was repeating a story she had heard over drinks. "City-dwellers spend their time worrying about people coming into their large stone and wood boxes…afraid that those people will take their things, which they may have taken from other people. They are so concerned about anyone getting in, that they hardly know what is inside their big homes. The very things they are protecting could sprout legs and walk away and they would never notice. They might not even notice a big fuzzy wildling and a jingling gypsy, yes?"

"Sounds like a good theory," he admitted, looking up the staircase as he eased the door the rest of the way shut. "Where do those of us from the city who don't own a house fit in?"

"This makes you more wise. You only use what you need and do not collect useless baubles like the humans so love to. Maybe you should come roam with the gypsies? We do not turn away those who would help our family and who will enjoy a good drink with us. You can drink?"

Estin snorted, saying, "I try not to. Just makes my stomach tingle. Never understood why the other races obsess about wine and such. Good flavor, but it makes humans and elves act foolish."

He padded up the stairs, exploring, while Varra just turned on her step and watched him.

"You never act foolish?"

"Not if I can help it. Mistakes around here would get me dead in a hurry."

Estin reached the top of the stairs, finding a dark hallway with even darker arched openings along the left side. There was not a sound or hint of movement ahead of him, or through the archways.

"Maybe you would make a bad gypsy, then," Varra offered sadly. "If you are unwilling to make mistakes, you will never learn what life is about and how to enjoy it. You will spend every day wondering what could go wrong and waiting for it to happen. This is not the gypsy way."

"Is this another bit of wisdom from the ancestors?"

Varra laughed and shook her head, jingling a bit.

"This is Varra talking, not a long dead relative. Their advice tends to be more practical and less helpful. If it sounds more dry, such as 'the black crow leads the way to a lost path'…this would be ancestors. When I say you are being foolish and missing out on life, that is Varra."

Estin chuckled in spite of himself and checked the upper hallway again, but the place was dead silent. Varra apparently had chosen their hiding place well.

"Estin, if you do not mind me asking," Varra began, climbing the stairs and passing him. She leaned on the windowsill of the hallway, her eyes wide in the dark—Estin could tell she was all but blind in the hallway. "I have wondered something."

"Ask away," he told her, coming up the last step and into the hallway. "We have all night to kill."

Estin glanced out the arched windows and realized that he was on a balcony, looking down into the duke's throne room. If he had to guess, archers might stand up here to ensure the safety of those in the room below.

"You act boring and dull," Varra began, seemingly oblivious that anyone might take her words as insults, "yet you do not seem as old as the rat-man. I do not know how to guess the age of your kind, so I must ask how old you are."

"Six."

Varra turned quickly, not quite looking directly at him.

"Six?! I have brought a child to this kind of danger?"

Estin grinned, but doubted she could tell.

"I've been an adult for some time, Varra. My kind reach maturity much faster than yours. By the time you're cursing your old bones, I'll have been dead and gone for a decade or two. Not that you should be questioning my age…you're young for a human. You couldn't have been away from your clan long. You're what...thirteen? Maybe fourteen?"

"Bah!" she snapped, making a rude gesture in his direction. "The city-folks say I am young, but my people know to make every year count. I have been running on my own to help the clan since I was ten and have been betrothed since eight. When I return with the cup, I will be honored as an adult and may be given a party in my honor. I might even let my betrothed get a kiss—or more—in celebration. This is a good life, yes?"

"Maybe for your people." Estin leaned over the balcony edge and studied the banners of the duke briefly. "Mine would be happy to be able to have a full belly and not be slapped in chains and sent to a warehouse to make things for the other races' homes. A meal, a warm place to sleep, and a mate are about all we'd probably hope for."

"A mate? So formal sounding. One can find someone to bed without so much formality."

"Not interested, Varra," he snapped. "We have our ways, you have yours. I'm not looking for a betrothed, either."

Varra giggled and stalked to a corner, where she curled up as though to sleep.

"We could feed your kind and there is always shelter in the wagons," she told him. "Is hard to recruit these days, no? Did not think even the wildlings were too good to help the gypsies."

"Not too good," Estin replied, sitting down with his back against the balcony wall, "just too different. I don't know about other breeds of wildlings, but I'd never fit in with gypsies. Too boring and dull, remember?"

Varra giggled yet again. "This is what I have said, yes. I am sorry for pushing you on this…my clan is very short on hands these days and one of the tasks for the young ones is to find others who might at least be willing to help the family. This was expected to be an easier task than finding this cup. Perhaps the elders misjudged the difficulty of their requests, no?"

Minutes passed in silence, other than the occasional jingle from Varra's clothing as she adjusted her position in the corner.

Finally, Estin asked her, "Why did you bring me?"

"The rat would have sold you to the slavers," she admitted. "He had already made the deal and was signing off on it when I arrived. My intent was to recruit a human—or some such—to blend in and let me into the keep. When I learned he was willing to sell out his own people, I could not allow it. Lucky for me, I found a way that you could help me."

She was quiet for another minute, then added, "I am sorry you were not my first plan. You did better than I could have hoped with my original plan."

"Honestly, I'm happy I was an option…I don't care if I was the last choice. Around the city, most people try not to acknowledge us, let alone include us in plans."

"Right now my plans are to sleep," she said dreamily. "I would hope you will also be part of these plans to not be awake…I do not wish to be kept up by your talking."

Estin sat quietly, closing his eyes and listening to faint sounds of the keep. He knew he would not sleep easily at night, especially in such a dangerous place. Maybe during the day, but not at night. He chose to rest and listen for danger until dawn, when Varra would be able to watch as he slept.

Wrapping his tail around into his lap to cover part of his body and keep him warm on the cold stone floor, he slowed his breathing and just waited. If he could stay awake, the dreams might not come.

Chapter Two

"What is Wild"

After the screams of our neighbors, the dream would become more personal, though I can never remember hearing any more screams from outside the home after this point. I believe I ignored them, being far more worried with what was happening in front of me.

I would always wake within the dream, but fear paralyzed me, keeping me in the little nest of blankets mother had tucked me into. Over and over, I would try to call to my mother, but my voice would just not come, out of fear. Perhaps this is for the best.

Despite knowing I was still asleep and dreaming, I can feel my chest tightening and it becomes hard to breathe as the dream continues.

The cries would melt into the sound of scuffles outside my room and the faint roar of flames somewhere beyond our home. It was then that, in the dream, I finally found the courage to venture from my bed and creep on all fours to the small opening that led to our family's main room. We only had three rooms—mine, which had once been my older sister Yalla's, my parents', and the entry room. It was looking into the entry room that would progress the dream. I had managed to resist looking in there for a short time in some of the dreams, but eventually I had to, as the worry over what I would see inevitably overcame my wish to avoid it.

My mother, unconscious I still believe to this day, had a long chain around her throat. She lay at the feet of a human who was rummaging through the room for anything of value. He was older than my parents and balding. The man wore makeshift armor of leather, with pieces of metal riveted on for extra protection in spots. He had not noticed me sitting in the hallway, I'm sure with eyes wide and tearful, though I honestly cannot remember how I had felt at that time, only what I saw.

The chain—the leash—has become a focus over the years for me. My own mother's face being twisted in pain is dwarfed by the terror I feel seeing that degrading collar around her neck. I would never allow myself to be treated like she was. I hoped dearly that I could find the strength to never allow another to be treated that way.

Mother was still not moving and it was then that I would first notice the gash on her forehead and the bloodied club at the man's side. I sniffed and could smell blood and not just mother's and certainly not just inside our home. She was hurt, but many others were, too. I did not know what to do, or how to help. I was just a child...how could I know how to *tend to an adults injuries?*

The sounds of fighting outside were getting closer and occasionally drew the attention of the human who was dragging mother behind him as he knocked over pots and decorations, pocketing anything that looked remotely saleable.

The man shuffled towards another of the home's shelves and the chain tugged at mother, thumping her shoulder against an overturned chair. She groaned and shifted, then choked softly and lay still again. The intruder never so much as glanced at her. She was of no more value than the trinkets he was stealing. She was not my mother to him...she was just another trinket.

Then, I finally understood that my mother was dying and became terrified.

After all these years, this part of the dream invokes both fear and rage. Someday, I promise myself in my dream, I will drag that human around by his own leash. If my mother is to die, everyone else will, too.

Estin woke abruptly from his nightmares to a sharp prod from Varra. She had grabbed his jaw and nose, holding his mouth shut to keep him from speaking even before he could have tried to do so. She looked genuinely worried and her veil was pulled up to hide her face again.

The hallway was still somewhat dimly lit, but when Estin turned, the throne room was bright. He shifted further and saw that a great shade had been drawn from a large window at one end of the throne room, illuminating everything but the archer balcony. The design would ensure that no matter how bright the room was, the balcony remained dark enough that no one knew if there were archers or not...luckily, at the moment there were not.

Varra motioned to indicate something in the throne room proper.

Flipping over onto his knees, Estin eased himself upwards, peeking over the edge. He kept his ears as flat as he could, hoping that the white fur along their edges did not give him away, even in the dark. He had made that mistake many times in the past, sticking his head out just enough to see, then realizing that his ears were sticking several inches farther out, giving him away.

Below, the room had filled with well-dressed people of many races. Estin would have expected only to see humans, elves, and dwarves, but in this room were many others that he had not even known were allowed into the city proper.

Among those standing in the tightly-packed room he saw a single man of fae blood—obvious with his hooved legs and pointed ears, but human otherwise. Estin had heard that the duke considered it fashionable to allow one of fae blood into court as some perceived blessing of the fae. This particular fae-kin looked bored and aware that he was out of place, but present at someone else's command or request.

Near the back wall, a black-skinned woman stood with an ornate parasol that she was using to shield her face from the sunlight entering the room. If Estin's guess was right, she was likely a dark elf, come from one of the nearby underground cities of their people. Though the dark elves were entirely untrusted by Altis, the duke had recently signed a treaty with them that would have mandated that someone from their people be present. It was more a pretense than anything else.

In a corner opposite the dark elf, he spotted a pair of heavily-robed Turessians, standing rigidly in the shadows. Had he not been looking for them, he might have assumed they were statues. Prior to Varra's warning, he might have ignored them completely. Knowing who they were, he watched these people the longest.

Atop the throne's platform, two hulking orcs stood guard, their dark eyes watching for any excuse to strike down those around them. Orcs were rarely allowed in Altisian lands, but in rare cases rich humans—such as the duke—would enlist their aid to intimidate peasants and enemies alike.

These two Estin was sure were not just for show, as both had black battle scars marring their green skin and one had a broken tusk at the end of a disfiguring slash in his cheek. They had seen more than their share of battle at some point.

The only race beside his own that he did not see were ogres. These were outlawed in Altis, despite their relatively peaceful behavior in the area. Many elves were terrified of the large grey-skinned beings, believing that ogres secretly ate elven children, largely due to their size and the dangerous-looking tusks and horns that all ogres grew. Estin had long believed this to be a tale told to elven children that had mistakenly gained acceptance among the older members of that race. Whether true or not, their paranoia had led to every ogre being driven from the nearby region.

Estin scanned the crowd, noting that the style of clothing among the races was almost identical—aside from the dark elf. This likely meant that they were all from Altis, as Estin had often seen the different cuts and colors the Lantonne people wore and those styles were the only ones in attendance.

At the head of the room, Duke Harlin sat on his throne. Harlin was a roundish man, buried under a pile of expensively embroidered cloth. The man was old enough to have plenty of grey in his beard and long hair, but Estin could not guess his exact age. Fifty, maybe a little older, Estin thought, but he knew his opinion of human appearance was usually off.

Varra leaned in uncomfortably close to Estin, whispering so softly in his ear that even he barely heard her.

"I heard the call to court. They are expecting an ambassador after a few more trials."

"So?" he asked in reply, sitting back down. "Human affairs hardly concern me, as long as we're safe up here. You woke me up for this?"

Varra gave him a glare, but sat down beside him, saying nothing.

"Ronald of the eastern farms," called out the herald. As he did, Estin could hear the doors of the great hall opening and footsteps coming somewhat in his direction.

"My lord," began a man's voice, though Estin closed his eyes and barely paid attention. "There have been raids on my farm by..."

"Why was this man let in here?" demanded Harlin to the laughter of many in the chamber. "Does he hold rank that I do not know of?"

As the laughter calmed somewhat, the sheepish-sounding human continued, "If you would just listen, my lord..."

"Get this man out of my sight. I am far too busy to be bothered by commoners who barely pay taxes."

Estin smirked as he heard a brief commotion down below, the human being dragged off without his grievance being heard. Not terribly surprising, he thought, deep-down amused by the humans' mistreatment of their own. He had heard that the duke had little pity for those who did not hold title within his lands, but this just served to confirm that.

Once the laughter at the expense of the farmer had died down, Estin distantly heard the call of the herald again, just as he was starting to drift back to sleep.

"Lady Feanne of the wilder animalfolk," announced the herald in a dull monotone.

This woke Estin instantly and he sat back up, looking down into the room. He stared in wonder at the idea of one of his people being in the duke's chambers and not hiding. Though he was awestruck by the idea, rude snickers filled the chamber as the woman marched in.

The female was nearly Estin's height, by his guess. She was thin, though her form was muted by the heavy oiled leather she wore. A long sheet of leather—a shin-length loin-cloth, as best Estin could name it—covered her lower body, leaving her legs free to move. Like the others of his kind he had met, she wore nothing on her paw-like feet. A vest of thick leather covered her top, forming to her body.

Bright golden and silver chains covered the female's leather, with rings of the same metals along the leather's edges and fitted to her wrists and ankles. A necklace of gleaming gold hung around her neck and earrings of silver hung from her pointed ears. She bore no weapons—an even more striking detail, given that she was standing in the house of what Estin would have considered her adversary .

Estin was immediately struck by the scents that entered the room with her, which were distinct enough to stand out with nearly a hundred humans, elves, and dwarves already stinking up the room. She brought with her a smell of the woods…the trees, flowers, and rain. Mixed with that, the aroma of the oils that coated her leather clothing, making it resistant to water. What he could not pick out was her specific scent, which surprised him, after so many years of being able to identify humans from nearly a block away.

Standing in stark contrast to the chocolate brown of the leather the Lady Feanne wore and the dark ruddy fur covering most of her, the female's tail tip and lower jaw stood out in snow white, drawing Estin's eye. He almost failed to notice her black-furred hands and feet, with their sharpened claws. She kept her hands at her sides and while not looking overtly threatening, Estin guessed she was more than prepared to defend herself in this place. As he watched, she kept flexing her fingers, as though preparing herself to claw at someone.

The lady stopped after entering, surveying those around her who sneered at her presence. Her reddish-brown muzzle and wet black nose twitched as she sniffed at the room, her ears twitching, as if she were looking for more beyond those who glared at her within the hall.

Estin found himself studying her far more than he cared to. She was, after all, the first wildling that he had seen since his childhood who was neither a slave nor on the auction block to become one…or was Nyess, he added. The regal demeanor of this female captivated him, after coming to believe that his people were as low as one could be on the social ladder of Altis. She was another breed—which his father had taught him meant they were no more kin than he was with the humans—but as a wildling, she was still somewhat more like a relative than he had known in a long time. Even a fox wildling was more kin than the humans, elves, and dwarves.

At last, the fox marched towards the throne, her paws clicking with each step as her claws tapped against the floor. She strode as though she and the duke were the only ones in the room, watching him intently the whole time she was walking. With a visible sense of purpose that Estin could only wish he could muster in his life, she walked right up the first step to the foot of the throne and bowed slightly, retaining a majestic stance that seemed somehow out of place even in a throne room.

"Your Grace," Faenne offered, though she somehow managed to make it sound like a greeting of equals, despite the derision around her. "My pack has asked me to come and seek a truce between our peoples."

"You see!" Varra whispered right in his ear. "Your people are not all slaves! This one understands what it is to be free. We need to get you to her people so you understand what we gypsies have always known about living free of the badly-dressed humans. Maybe she can teach you to dress better, too."

"A truce?" bellowed the duke, drawing a room full of laughter. "When did you last pay a copper in taxes, beast? Give me one reason that you should be allowed to stand before me without a leash."

The Lady Feanne glared at the duke, and Estin thought for a second that she might try to attack him. Instead, she smiled coyly, smoothing over the hostility easily.

"Your Grace, I have come here to pay any debts you believe that my people owe," she explained, motioning towards her necklace. "We only ask for the same respect that you show the other races. I would gladly turn over all this wealth in exchange for recognition as citizens of your fine city."

Estin watched nervously as the duke studied the fox-woman, his eyes roaming over the valuable jewelry she wore, while the rest of the room was quite silent.

"Your people, like many of the peasants, have no right to own anything," the duke finally answered. "By law, you are to be placed under our protection so that you do not harm yourself or others."

"Enslaved, you mean," Feanne answered, her face neutral.

"Your people are no better than animals and we are protecting you by bringing you in from the cold to be our servants. You would freeze in the woods without our aid. Why would we want to let you continue running amok in our fields, eating our cattle, and generally being a nuisance? I'm already being generous by not putting your people in the fields as livestock."

Lady Feanne glared at the duke with a ferocity that made Estin think of the wild animals that roamed the streets at night, even though he was not the target of the stare. The fox-woman seemed to bite back the anger in her demeanor and bowed again, coming back up with a far more calm appearance. Though the other races might not notice, Estin could feel the tension in the female's stance and knew she was struggling not to attack the duke.

He doubted he had that much self-restraint himself, though his reaction would have been to run away.

"My people are as well educated as most of your peasants," she argued, keeping her voice level. "I would seek nothing more than the same respect you show the other citizens. It is a small price for our willing involvement in your city's prosperity. My people ask for nothing more."

"Get this foreigner out of my sight," demanded the duke. "Strip her of the silver and gold as back payment for her taxes."

Feanne seemed undeterred, continuing to talk, even as armed guards began to mass around her.

"You have taken people from my pack for the last year through violence and threats," she told the duke, somehow making it not sound as though she were criticizing him. "This will end. My people are weary of fighting with the city of Altis. As such, I and the wealth I bring are a payment for our freedom. Accept either and leave my people to live their lives in peace. I am to be the last from my pack to risk themselves over your whims."

The chuckles and insulting comments through the hall died away as many appeared to be waiting to see how the duke would react, or were watching the guards that now stood in a full circle around the wildling female. The duke seemed to be contemplating the offer, studying the gold and silver that Feanne wore.

"Why do you claim the title 'lady,' when you are not of noble blood?" demanded the duke, gesturing to one of his orcish guards to lean closer. He whispered something, then waved the large green man away. "You demean those of true nobility through this claim. Some might be executed for such a claim above their station. You cannot even claim citizenship, yet you use a title above your station."

"I asked your crier what the appropriate title for my position among my people would be," she replied calmly, dark eyes watching the edges of the crowd carefully. "Among my own, I am known as Keeper Feanne, or simply Feanne. This title 'lady' is as appropriate as any human title might be for my kind. I would expect the same respect I show you shown to me."

The orc rushed at Feanne, striking her so hard across the face that Feanne tumbled backwards into the aisle leading to the throne, sliding on her back a foot or two. Clearly stunned, she struggled to sit back up.

Estin watched this in horror, wondering how this wildling had thought things would end up, even as he hoped that she would keep her mouth shut in vague hopes of avoiding death or slavery.

"You will kneel before your betters, beast!" roared the orc, returning to his place beside the duke. "Stand in the duke's presence again and you will be leashed!"

Estin felt his own temper rising, wishing he could do something before matters got any worse. He looked over to Varra, but the girl did not even notice him, glaring darkly at the orc.

"That one will suffer a most uncomfortable rash in places he would never admit to," she noted dryly to herself. "This I pledge to my ancestors. Rudeness like this is not to be tolerated."

Down below, Feanne had finally gotten back to her knees, shaking her head and stumbling as she got her legs under her. At first it looked as though she were trying to get into a proper kneeling position, but then abruptly, she pushed herself to her feet and raised her head triumphantly…if somewhat groggily.

Estin could hardly believe that anyone would be so bold, risking their life to remain noble, when they had not been granted such a title. Part of him thought this Feanne was crazy, even as another part was impressed and adored her for trying.

"As I was saying, Your Grace," Feanne began again, fixing the duke with a stern gaze. Her left eyelid was swelling badly, closing the eye as she spoke. "I have come to negotiate a peace, not to challenge your rule or engage in a fight with your pets. I have shown you no disrespect, so please treat me accordingly."

Estin very nearly thought the orcs would leap on her, but somehow they restrained themselves…barely. The one that had struck Feanne earlier began casually scratching his inner thigh uncomfortably.

"I think this circus is over," stated the duke, waving a hand dismissively. "Put the dog in the kennel and dispatch troops to collect her 'pack,' before they try something foolish and get themselves killed. If any other peasants or foreigners want an audience, throw them in chains as well."

Soldiers rushed in on Feanne, grabbing her arms and wrestling her to the ground. She went down hard, but did little to resist the attack, making it easy for them to pin her to the ground.

With a knee on Feanne's neck, one guard pulled out a length of leather cord and tried to fasten it around the wildling's neck like a leash. This, Estin watched in fear, wondering if the first truly memorable person of his kind was about to become another emotionless slave to the city.

Though she had been relatively docile in letting them manhandle her until then, as soon as the leather strap was placed near her head, Estin watched as Feanne exploded into a flurry of claws and teeth. Everything said to her had rolled off without reaction, but attempting to place a leash on her did even more to upset her than it did Estin. She seemed to go insane in that moment.

Claws grabbing for any exposed flesh, Feanne ripped into the guards, slashing faces and crippling hands anytime they came near. More than once in the tussle, Estin thought he saw her tackle a guard and try to bite his neck or shoulder. Seconds into the fray, the soldiers were trying to scramble away, as she dragged them back and continued to maul them.

Blood flew everywhere as the wildling tore at her captors. With the blood came chaos as the hall emptied in a rushed panic, with screams and a stampede for the door. The room cleared quickly, while Feanne continued tearing at the guards, even as they tried to get weapons drawn on her. One managed to get his sword out, only to have the female rake his hand with her foot and kick the weapon away. She was on him instantly, her hands tearing at the man's face until Estin could not even recognize him.

Then, just as abruptly as the fight began, it ended swiftly when the orcs reached the melee. Both waded in, kicking and punching at anything that moved, then tossing bodies aside that were human. When they reached Feanne, they both kicked at her until she stopped moving and just curled into a fetal position, even pulling her tail to her body to keep from being stomped anymore. They kicked her a few more times after that, then one dragged her to her feet and wrapped the leash around her neck. Feanne barely seemed aware of the leash, her eyes unfocused as she tried to get her feet under her and failed.

With only the two orcs, the duke, and three guards who were not severely bleeding left in the lower hall, Estin found himself halfway over the rail of the balcony before Varra grabbed his arm and dragged him back.

"No!" she hissed, nearly pulling him over backwards onto the balcony. "You will be leashed too if we go now...and maybe me too, which is unacceptable. No leash on gypsy!"

The orc threw Feanne to the floor of the room, looking up to the duke for direction, while holding the leash tightly.

Lying on the floor, Feanne crawled to her knees, trying to get up, only to have the other orc punch her in the back, driving her to the floor again.

The duke looked around his empty hall and uttered a short but profane rant to several gods that Estin had not even heard of before, before standing up.

"Get her out of here. Do not ever allow another non-citizen into my hall under pain of execution," the duke demanded, then turned and stormed out of the hall via a hallway near the throne.

The orcs glanced at each other, then down at Feanne. Without another word, they dragged her from the room by the leash, with her choking and attempting to get onto her feet as they disappeared from Estin's view.

Until the moment Feanne was out of sight, Estin watched in terror, staring not at her, but at the leash that choked her. He could see his own mother being treated similarly, making him feel as though he had just failed her all over again. The feeling made him sick to his stomach, wanting to vomit, run for safety, or fight for Feanne out of principal.

"Why would you stop me?" Estin snapped, glaring at Varra, feeling like he was as guilty as those who had beaten the female. "I might have been able to help her."

"You do not know her and she does not know you…do not throw away your life for a stranger," Varra chided, then raised a finger to her lips, pointing towards another section of the balcony, where it wrapped around the throne room.

Squinting at the area she indicated, Estin realized that there was a figure standing there, as well as another farther down that side.

"Archers?" he asked more calmly, trying to see how many of them were over there. "Do you think they saw us?"

The faintest scratch of leather sole on stone caught Estin's ear and he spun in time to see a large human with a crossbow approaching them from the steps they had come up. The gruff older human froze as Estin turned on him, raising his crossbow to fire.

Varra must have seen the man too, stepping between Estin and the crossbowman. She spoke words Estin could not understand—though vaguely familiar from atop the building where she had created the magical bridge—and swept her arm across them both in a shielding motion. As she did, the crossbow fired loudly and the bolt flew true, but struck an invisible barrier and clattered aside on the stone floor.

"Run!" Varra urged Estin, drawing her daggers from her belt. "Get to a window and get out! I will exhaust my magic far too quickly if we stay to fight."

Drawing the sword he had brought with him, Estin started to rush at the crossbowman, but the man flew backwards down the stairs, tumbling to a stop at the bottom. Estin glanced back at Varra, who was now sweating, but waved him on.

"Just go! I can hold the others. Get out of the keep! I meet you outside town."

Estin could see the other crossbowmen now, racing around the balcony to get to their side for a clean shot at them. Trusting that Varra knew what she was doing, he dashed down the stairs, keeping his sword close to his body to block any attack that might surprise him as he entered the hallway at the bottom of the steps. As he went, he drew his dagger as well, knowing any extra weapon would be handy if he were found out.

Finding the hallway empty, Estin took off to his left, remembering vaguely a window one floor up and at the end of another passage. It would be a short run and he was sure he could make it before reinforcements could arrive.

As Estin ran, he heard shouts behind him, along with the 'twang' of crossbows. Seconds after that, he could make out the din of weapons clashing, but this faded rapidly as he reached the next floor. With his bare feet pounding against the cold stone tiles, he raced towards the nearest outer-wall room, which was farther down the hall.

Estin reached the door, panting, and moved to shove the sword back into his belt for safekeeping, when he realized something out of place on his belt. Reaching back, he felt the cool metal lip of Varra's goblet hooked over one of his pouches.

Varra had been quite clear that she considered that goblet worth risking her life over. If she had sent it away with him…

"Damnit!" he growled, spinning on his heel to go back for the gypsy. He would not let another person die when he could at least try to help, let alone one who was key to him getting paid.

Nearly tumbling down the stairs, Estin arrived at the foot of the steps in time to see Varra facing off against a Turessian at the far end of the hall. The dark-clad human was facing away from Estin, blocking Varra's escape.

With remarkable speed, Varra slashed at the robed man, sending scraps of cloth flying. He advanced on her, never even attempting to block her attacks, even when she stabbed him squarely in the chest.

"Die already!" she cried, kicking the Turessian in the chest. The man barely rocked, then grabbed her by the wrist with his left hand.

"Varra!" Estin shouted, starting to run towards the conflict.

As he did, the Turessian twisted Varra's wrist sharply, breaking it with ease, the eerie crack echoing through the hall for the second before she screamed. The man seemed unmoved, twisting again to free her dagger from her limp hand. Turning the dagger over in his hand, he drove the blade into Varra's chest hard enough to thump her body against the wall behind her, before yanking it right back out, sending a spray of blood across the hallway.

For a moment, Estin stopped and stared as Varra staggered and the Turessian took a step away from her. Varra wavered briefly, looking past the Turessian at Estin, then down at the goblet on his belt. Without a word, she collapsed onto the floor in a heap, blood pooling around her.

The Turessian remained over her only a second, then turned and gazed back at Estin, faint red eyes glowing under his hood. Where Varra's weapons had torn at his clothing, Estin could see sickly grey skin and gaping cuts that did not bleed.

"What in the planes…," Estin mumbled, nearly dropping his sword. His fingers felt numb.

When the Turessian took its first step towards him, Estin's trance was broken and he took off at a dead run. He had no idea if the creature would follow him, but he knew he could not risk it, choosing random directions and stairs in the hopes that it could not track him through the keep.

It was almost an hour of running through the keep before Estin collapsed in a empty kitchen's corner, flopping between two bags of flour that he hoped might at least partially conceal him. He lay there gasping for air, seeing the flickering fireplace light through his eyelids as he tried to find the strength to run again.

Estin at last opened his eyes and looked around the room once his heart rate had slowed and he felt that he had escaped the Turessian for the moment. Painful sadness wracked him, thinking of what he had seen, watching the girl die to ensure his escape. He tried to hide from the feelings, burying his face in his hands for a little while until he was able to compose himself and remind himself that he was still being hunted.

This kitchen was vacant, despite it likely being almost noon. The size and type of pottery scattered about hinted to Estin that this might be used more for evening feasts, than for midday meals. If that were true, he only had a bit of time before the servants would arrive to begin preparing the evening meal for the duke.

Rolling onto his knees, Estin began to stand when he heard someone coming. Dropping back behind the bags of flour, he pulled one bag over him, keeping his sword between himself and the bag so if someone moved the bag, he could strike quickly.

"Savage little bitch," grumbled a deep male voice as heavy footfalls entered the kitchen. "Damn near clawed my eye out. Help me find a rag to stop the bleeding."

Another equally gravelly voice, "Let it scar. I wouldn't go to a healer to fix scratches from some little wildling whore."

Estin ground his teeth and peeked around the edge of the bag, verifying that it was the two orcs from the throne room. One was rooting around the kitchen, while the other stood in the middle of the room, grinning at the first one.

He turned as slowly as he could, noting which of the three doors they had opened to come into the kitchen.

"Bah, get me to the tavern. I'll pour some hooch on it until I feel better. Next time I see one of those fuzzy rodents, I'm breaking it in half."

The two left through the far door, still muttering.

Not about to waste another minute, Estin slid out from under the bag and made for the door the orcs had entered through. Once he was out into the darker hallway, he bent low to the floor and sniffed at the stones, picking up the scent of the orcs easily. He noted which direction they had come from, hurrying down one hallway, then another, until he came to a large window on his right and a descending staircase ahead of him.

Estin checked the window and found that he was only a little more than twenty feet from the ground and the window faced the outer wall of the city, where there would be fewer guards on patrol. It was a quick and sure escape.

The deep-throated barking of at least a dozen dogs pulled his attention to the staircase. He hated hunting dogs, having been chased by them far too many times in his life.

Not even thinking, he sniffed the floor again, picking up the odor of orcs, a dwarf, dogs...and oiled leather. All four scents came from the direction of the staircase.

Estin stood in the hallway, repeatedly checking for anyone approaching from either direction as he debated what to do. The window was the obvious answer. Varra was dead, some crazy glowing-eyed monster was chasing him, there were two hulking orcs looking for a good reason to stomp him, and his own punishment would likely be as bad or worse than Feanne's had been when all the wealth in his pouches was discovered. He did not know the fox and had no obligations to save her. Any obligations he had were to Varra and those had died with her.

He even went so far as to lean out the window, watching for any chance of being caught escaping there, but found none. He really had no reason not to run. It was the obvious choice...he really should just head out of the keep and never look back.

Still, knowing that one of his kind was nearby, likely being tortured or killed set off something inside him. Feanne had showed more backbone than he could have imagined possible for a wildling, standing up to the very people who would gladly sell her to the highest bidder. That should not have swayed Estin, but he found himself wondering if there were more like her, more wildlings like his parents who were still free.

Muttering, Estin turned back to the staircase and took a deep breath, knowing he was being incredibly stupid. The little voice in the back of his mind told him that he needed to get his priorities straight and save himself—but he ignored it and began down the stairs. Fighting himself each step of the way.

Halfway down the steps, Estin began to strongly smell the odors of a kennel. He proceeded more carefully, descending the spiral staircase as quickly as he dared, trying to be wary of anything coming up. As he went, the barking became louder and the smells grew overpowering—dog feces, wet fur, old straw bedding, and ever so faintly the two orcs and Feanne's clothing.

Estin reached the bottom of the steps soon enough, finding himself in a small entry room with an iron-bound exterior door. The scents were extremely strong now, coming through that door. He doubted it was more than ten feet between the door and the source of those aromas.

Evaluating the place he was in, Estin realized this was a defensible entry location for the keep, but otherwise useless to him. There were no hiding places, nowhere to climb, and no other way to get to where he could gather more information without risking himself. The fox wildling was somewhere past the door.

Lifting the latch on the door, Estin eased it open slowly, checking for anyone on the other side waiting for him. Outside, he saw the courtyard of the keep, with a large stable off to his left and a dog kennel on the right. The kennel was filled with cages built for reasonably-large dogs—the large brown mutts that the duke used for hunting. Those were the same dogs that had chased him at least twice when he had come near the keep and been seen.

At this time, every one of the fifteen dogs were outside their pens, standing in a tight circle around a single cage that had been dragged to the middle of the kennel area. A few passers-by glanced in at the dogs, but kept walking past.

The dogs were barking, howling, and biting at the bars in an effort to get at something inside, sometimes fighting each other for position around the cage. From where he stood, Estin had a limited view of the kennel area and he could not make out much, but did see a flash of blood as one of the dogs snagged something inside the cage.

Easing the door open slightly more, Estin could see a single dwarf leaning against the wall of the keep near the door Estin was coming through. The dwarven man was watching the mayhem with arms crossed over his chest, grunting and chuckling at the ruckus.

He quickly sized up the dwarf from a cursory look at the man. The dwarf's beard hung nearly to his knees, indicating age and a belief in his own skill. That might mean he was a dangerous fighter, but could also be merely a matter of ego. He also noted that the dwarf's beard was shaggy and unkempt, but he was not as sure what that could mean. From what Estin could see, the dwarf bore only a thin and slightly pointed stick as long as he was tall and no other weapons.

Just as Estin was motivating himself to step out and strike at the dwarf, the shorter man marched up to the cage, jabbing through the bars with his stick.

"No clawing me dogs!" he hissed, stabbing at the contents of the cage roughly. As he did, the dogs moved aside, giving Estin a confirming glance at Feanne inside the cage, the dwarf's stick leaving bloody spots on her fur as he jabbed her.

The wildling was wedged tightly in the dog-sized iron cage, which forced her into a kneeling position, huddled into a ball to keep her arms, legs, and tail far from the bars where the dogs could nip and bite at her. All of Feanne's jewelry was gone. Much of it appeared to have been torn from her, leaving bare patches where the fur had been scraped away, including a deep cut in her right ear, where an earring had been torn free.

Estin had had enough, rushing from the doorway up on the dwarf. He acted without thinking—at least not thinking about what he was doing. Instead, he was seeing Varra's death again, and somehow lashing out at the dwarf did some small part in redeeming his conscience for failing to save her.

His blade drove deep into the dwarf's back, deflecting off bone as the dwarf grunted and fell. The dwarf rolled when he hit the ground, gasping and whimpering as he clutched at his neck.

The dogs reacted immediately to the dwarf's cries, leaping on him like they would a rabbit. The original victim forgotten, the dogs tore into the dwarf as a pack, only making him scream more.

Estin had to move fast, knowing the dogs would realize that he did not belong there soon enough. He rushed to the cage, where Feanne remained curled up tightly, trembling as she buried her face into the dirt at the bottom of the cage. Her fur was torn in many places, matted with fresh blood. Tufts of hair were missing where the dogs had just barely caught her. All around her, the dirt was stained with droplets of her blood from her many cuts. Swelling down the length of her muzzle from her left eye had closed the eye completely, likely from the beating she had taken from the orcs earlier.

"If you are freeing me, do so now," she croaked, just barely raising her head. She was still shaking slightly as she looked up at him. "Otherwise, open the cage and let the dogs finish me while you run. I can at least be your distraction while you escape. I believe I have the strength to hold them for a time."

"Already lost one person today and I don't intend to lose another. You're coming with me."

Feanne raised her head slowly, revealing deep gashes he could not see before. Her good eye fixed him with a stare that made him feel cold as she studied him.

"Do you have a way to open this cage?"

Estin looked around, trying to find a key. His eyes fell on it…on the dwarf's hip, as he struggled to get the dogs off him.

"No," he admitted. There had to be some other way…

Feanne gestured towards a small fire in one corner of the kennel.

"Get me a coal, quickly," she ordered him, her eyes already on the dogs. "I can get myself out, but I need to be able to write."

Estin rushed to the fire, kicking at the ashes until he found a darkened piece of wood that was no longer aflame. Grabbing it despite the uncomfortable heat it still radiated, he darted back to the cage and shoved it through the bars.

Snatching the piece of wood from Estin's hand and putting it to the ground, Feanne began tracing symbols in the dirt.

"You may wish to run," she said calmly, though her hands were still trembling, forcing her to slow her writing almost immediately.

Estin looked back over his shoulder and found that several dogs were now eyeing him viciously. With the dwarf no longer struggling, they were looking for new prey.

"Even if I could, I'm staying until you get out."

Faenne glanced up at him, her voice cracking slightly, as though from pain, "If you're going to stay, then hold them off and I can help you shortly."

"Great…"

Estin pointed his sword at the dogs, who appeared unimpressed.

"Whatever you're doing, please do it quickly," he told Feanne, taking a step out into the courtyard with the dogs following slowly. Another two had joined in stalking him and they began to spread out in preparation for attacking. "I can probably stop one or two, but they're definitely going to eat me."

"The difference between breaking myself out of this cage," Feanne answered, still carefully tracing her odd symbols, now on the large lock of the cage, "and burning myself with acid is a small one. I prefer to get it right on the first try. Keep them busy for a little while without drawing attention to yourself."

"That's not really…"

Estin's words died in his mouth as a dog tackled him from the side, teeth snapping for his throat. He rolled with the impact, kicking it away, but then another was on him, its fangs digging deep into his leg, drawing blood.

Screaming, Estin tried to get away from the savage bites while swinging his sword where the dog had been, but it just darted out of reach as another raked his shoulder. When he turned to fight off that one, another bit his tail, eliciting a another cry of agony. He was being torn apart one bite at a time and realized that he was likely going to bleed to death in front of the very person he was trying to save.

Another dog leapt onto Estin and he dropped his sword and grabbed at its head, keeping it just barely from digging its teeth into his neck. Others were biting at his legs as he moved, trying to keep them from getting a solid mouthful of his flesh.

From the cage, a loud bang startled both the dogs and Estin, buying him a second he wasted looking around for the source.

The cage door now lay at a strange angle, its lock smoking and twisted. Feanne was slowly getting to her feet, stretching out her legs and neck as the dogs began baying at her again.

"I am done with this game," she told the dogs, making an idle gesture with one hand. Suddenly all of the dogs stopped attacking Estin or growling at her and instead walked over in front of her and sat down as though waiting for direction from a beloved master. "Stay."

Estin tried to get up, but his legs were in bad shape, with puncture wounds radiating pain up past his hips. His arms were barely usable with deep claw marks lengthwise down his left arm and several gaping bites that were pouring blood over his fur and onto the ground. He collapsed each time he tried to rise.

"You got me out of the cage, so the least I can do is get you out of here," Feanne said softly, leaning close to him. Her voice was still shaky, but she sounded stronger, or at least more confident. "Those beasts will wait for my command for a time, but I do not wish to be here when they come to their senses. Much as I'd like to skin every one of the little manmade monsters, we need to be gone."

Strong hands grabbed Estin's shoulders as Feanne leaned over him, muttering in a language not totally unlike the one Varra had used for her magic. This time, though, he felt the pain in his wounds ease gradually, until he thought he might be able to stand.

Estin looked back to Feanne and saw that she was even more badly injured than he had thought. Bites on her legs and arms looked nearly crippling, making him wonder how she was still standing. A series of long gashes down her left arm in particular was bleeding profusely. As though weakened by the very thought, she dropped to her knees.

Forcing himself to a seated position, Estin checked the courtyard and saw that soldiers were forming up at the far end of the yard. He turned back to Feanne, intending to warn her, when he realized that the wounds on her arms and legs matched his own. Though his were not feeling nearly as severe as before, hers looked much worse.

"What did you just do?" he demanded, pushing himself up to his feet. He felt dizzy and unsteady, but he thought he could run if he tried hard enough.

"I took your injuries on myself," the fox-woman answered, smiling somewhat. "They did not look so bad before. Perhaps I am a worse healer than I had thought. Give me just a moment and I'll be able to stand."

Feanne wavered and almost fell over even from her kneeling position, but Estin caught her, feeling blood begin to run over his hands from her injuries. The sight of so much blood made him want to yelp and run away, but he found that he could not leave Feanne, no matter how terrified he was. As an afterthought, he tucked his sword into his belt.

"We're getting out of here," he told her firmly, dragging her to her feet. She stumbled, but just barely managed to stay upright. "I won't leave you here to get eaten by dogs."

Estin suddenly felt foolish, glancing over at all the dogs who sat calmly watching Feanne for instructions. They wagged their tails happily, having forgotten the hatred they had possessed moments before.

"I appreciate the loyalty. Lead the way and I will find a way to make my body follow," answered Feanne at last, touching her hand to her head and trying to steady herself. Her balance appeared questionable at best, as she was clearly pushing herself to look healthier than she was.

"We can get out into the city by running that direction," he indicated an eastern path around the back of the kennels. "Once we get into the streets, I can find shelter for us until they get tired of chasing us."

"Less talk, more running."

Estin took off at a jog, going around the building's side that would block the other soldiers from seeing where he was going. He checked repeatedly as he went to be sure that Feanne was following, which she was, even if it was slowly, her feet coming down in an uneven line as she staggered after him.

They moved as quickly as they could manage, working their way past the side of the keep towards the main city streets beyond. Just as they reached the first section of city cobblestones, one of the duke's soldiers stepped in front of them, a crossbow readied and aimed at Estin's face.

"On your knees, beast."

Estin stumbled to a stop, raising his hands slowly. Wishing he had his sword already drawn, he put both hands on his head and waited for the chains to be placed on him. There would be no escape and Estin doubted he could have overpowered the human, even if he had been prepared.

"This will not do," Feanne declared, moving past Estin with a stubbornness that could only impress him. "Lower your weapon and leave us."

"Shut up, bitch," ordered the soldier. "On your knees!"

Estin lifted his head slightly and glanced at Feanne, who despite her injuries once again looked regal in her stance. She brought her hands up swiftly and before the man could loose his crossbow on them, a stunning flash struck him from the sky with a boom that made Estin's ears ring. Even as the soldier's scream died into the smell of burning flesh, the flash also washed Estin's vision, leaving only a burning white light.

He gasped, collapsing, holding his eyes. Midday sunlight had been bad enough, but this made his head ring with pain. "What in the planes was that?"

"Just lightning, so please do not call upon forces who have no place here," the fox told him, grabbing his hand and pulling him along. "We must not stop now. My strength will not last long and I doubt you wish to fight your way out of town without your vision. I will lead you."

Her hand tightened on his, dragging him along as she took off at a near-run. Estin struggled to keep up, blinking as occasional spots darted across his vision. When Feanne turned a corner, her sharp claws dug into his hand, but he held tight to her, trying not to get lost as they ran.

After Estin was yanked around another turn, he slammed into Feanne as she came to an abrupt halt. She said nothing, but something in the air told him that they were not in a good place. He tried to focus his eyes, but was still only seeing vague shapes.

"Soldiers?" he asked softly.

"Eight, who appear to be under orders to take us alive," Feanne replied, pushing him up against a stone wall. "Lie down and stay very still. I have a friend that will help us out of this. Do not move."

With that, her hand was gone and Estin found himself alone in the blurry prison of his own mind. He could hear the creaking of armor approaching them and the sharp rasp of blades being drawn. Estin felt around for his own sword, finding that he had lost it somewhere along the way.

Drowning out everything, Feanne spoke more words in her magical language, the sounds barely even discernable as a dialect. When she finished, Estin heard gasps and a man cursing, followed by the distinct sound of breaking bones and at least eight sets of booted feet rushing in on where he lay.

Within seconds, there were screams of agony and battle, the sounds of impacts on flesh, and of bodies hitting the pavement. Estin could smell blood everywhere and even the rank odor of a body that had been disemboweled nearby. Terrified at whatever Feanne had called to aid them, he clung to the wall, struggling to see at least enough to avoid being caught in the fray.

Clearer shapes slowly began to form in his vision, allowing him to see man-sized bodies being tossed about like ragdolls. The details were extremely vague and at least once he thought he saw Feanne in the combat, but he could not be sure. Given the ferocity with which she had tried to defend herself in the throne room, he was willing to bet she fought beside whatever beast she had called, though try as he might, he could not get a glimpse even of its shape. He knew it was there, as he saw one soldier stumble into his limited range of vision missing an arm.

The commotion soon died down, with several twitching bodies lying around Estin as he remained as motionless as he could manage, while trying to get a glimpse of what was rampaging around him. His vision continued to fade in and out, one moment allowing him to be able to identify the wounded or dying soldiers, the next he could not even see as far as his own hands.

Abruptly, strong hands grabbed his, their fur covered with warm blood, making him yelp and attempt to scramble away. The hands grasped his wrists firmly, keeping him from moving. After several frantic seconds, his vision drifted mostly back into focus, revealing Feanne kneeling in front of him, spattered head to paw in blood.

"It's gone. All gone," Feanne told him softly, pulling him to his feet. "I sent it away. We're safe now.

"How are your eyes?"

Estin blinked hard, trying to clear several dancing spots across his vision.

"Getting better," he answered her, pulling his hands away. Sticky blood clung to his wrists. "I can see some colors again."

He stared around them at the carnage. The soldiers were torn apart, with gaping wounds or missing limbs. It looked as though they had been gored and trampled. On the far side of the street were dozens of the town's citizens, staring in shock and disgust, much like Estin guessed he was doing.

"I had to…," began Feanne, but Estin raised a hand to cut her off.

"I don't think I need the explanation right now," he told her bluntly, watching as many more people were gathering to stare. Some were now bringing weapons with them. "We need to get out of here, fast."

Estin made a quick study of where they were within the city and realized they had actually gone far into the richer part of town, making it a longer trek to the outer gates.

Snagging one of the fallen soldiers' swords with his tail, he flicked it into the air and caught it with his hand. Motioning to Feanne to follow, he did the same with the next weapon they passed, then began running for the nearest alley to escape from the public eye.

"Why are we in here?" she asked, sneering at the piles of trash lining the alley. "There is no exit and we cannot hide in that filth."

Holding out the hilt of one of the swords, he answered, "We're not hiding. This is the best way to get out of town without the guards catching us again."

Feanne looked down at the sword and then back up at him with a disappointed frown.

"Why would you even offer that to me? You apparently need the weapons. I don't."

Estin hung his head and shoved the weapon into his belt.

"Fine, I'm guessing only one of us knows how to use proper weapons?"

"That would appear to be so," Feanne answered, something about her tone striking Estin as coy. "Now, how do you expect us to escape from here? I can smell burning tar…the pitchforks are likely not far behind. If you believe we can turn and walk back out of this row of brick walls without being hung, I do look forward to your ideas."

Estin checked the entrance of the alleyway. She was right, there were the smells of burning torches and he could hear a great many people gathering. It was very likely that he and Feanne would be lit on fire long before the town guard could even arrive.

"We go where they can't go," he told her, adjusting his clothing and pouches one more time, then pointed up at the wall. "Humans can't climb very well, so we go up the buildings and travel on the roofs."

For the first time since he had seen her, Feanne looked genuinely afraid as she stared wide-eyed at the sheer stone and wooden walls.

"And how do I escape?" she asked softly.

"You climb."

The fox shook her head slowly, still staring at the wall.

"I will run anywhere you say, but I do not climb. We need a new plan."

"No time," Estin said firmly, flicking his tail around her waist. He turned to the nearest wooden wall and dug his claws into the boards, bracing for the effort. "Please at least try to help."

"What…no!"

Estin began climbing, nearly losing his grip as Feanne's added weight dragged him down. Despite her objections, she soon began scrambling at the wall herself, at least lightening his load, even if she was doing little more than scratching up the wood in a blind panic.

His muscles trembling and burning, Estin advanced up the wall one hand and foot at a time, having to stop after each move to dig his claws in deeply to prevent them from slipping. It was very slow advancement, but by the time he heard the humans entering the alley, he had gotten Feanne above their heads.

Despite shouts from the people below, Estin pushed on, forcing himself to go even faster when he heard calls for archers to fire on him. The increased pace was not without its risks and his hands and feet kept tearing away from the wall as he moved, causing sudden lurches in the climb while he tried to reestablish his grip. Each time he slipped, he could hear Feanne let out a little cry as though she believed he would drop her.

Estin had to assume he had made good time when he reached the top and not a single arrow had been fired yet. With that in mind, he dragged himself over the lip of the roof's shallow slope and forced his aching and dulled claws into the shingles.

"You need to pull yourself over the edge!" he gasped, trying not to slide back off the roof. "My tail isn't strong enough to pull you over."

He looked back and saw Feanne pop over the edge several times as she tried to find something to cling to other than his tail. Finally, she got a handhold on the shingles and hoisted herself up beside him, collapsing on the roof.

"Never again do I climb for you," she told him grimly, panting and staring up at the sky. "That has to be the least dignified escape I have ever seen. Just let me die next time."

"I let one person die today. If another is going to die, I'm dying with them," said Estin, unwrapping his tail. Pain lanced through it as he attempted to straighten it out.

"The human girl?"

Estin turned and stared at Feanne.

"I saw you both on the balcony," she confessed, sitting up and glancing down at the people in the alley below. "I had thought she was part of the duke's guard at first, but when I saw you…"

"I know…too charming to work for the duke?"

Feanne stuck her tongue out.

"Too hairy."

An arrow whizzed past them and over the roof.

"I think we should hold the bragging until you find a way to get me back to the woods," Feanne noted, sounding a little annoyed. "Do the humans never give up?"

"Not until nightfall. Sometimes a little after."

Feanne got up first, hugging the shingles as she crawled towards the peak of the roof. She seemed terrified of slipping.

Estin on the other hand, got up onto his feet and walked past her, surveying the area around them.

"We can get to the wall in an hour if we go that way," he told her, pointing to the east. "They'll be able to track us the whole way. I'll take us south into the slums, where most of these people won't follow. We can hide there until near dawn when there are the fewest guards on the walls."

He began to stride across the roof towards the nearest one he could jump to, when he realized Feanne was very nearly paralyzed with fear as she looked around at the buildings…then back to the long climb down.

"I'll find a way that isn't too awful," he promised her, then began checking nearby buildings for attics or other easily-reached entrances.

Feanne crawled to where he stood not letting her hands or feet leave the shingles. Her existing injuries were bleeding badly again after being scraped on the way up the house and now rubbed against the shingles. She hardly seemed to notice the trail of bloody humanoid pawprints she left behind.

"I will make one jump if it gets me somewhere that I can't fall to my death," she told him, not looking up. "That's all you'll get out of me. I'm not about to start hopping from roof to roof, which is what I think you were planning."

"The thought had crossed my mind."

Estin spotted an open top-floor window that was about fifteen feet from the roof they were on. It was an easy jump for him, but he was not sure Feanne could make it. He honestly had no idea what a fox could or could not do.

"We need to find a way to get you over to…," Estin started to say, pointing at the window. As he did, Feanne stood up unsteadily beside him.

Feanne dug her feet into the shingles and then leapt past him, crossing the gap between the buildings and through the indicated window, as though she had been catapulted. Loud crashes sounded from the room beyond.

"Not the most graceful thing I've ever seen, but it works," he said to himself, wondering how she had made the jump. It would be a decently-long hop for him and he had always thought he was a good jumper.

Taking a step back, Estin ran to the edge of the roof and sprang across the gap between the houses. He caught himself easily on the far side, though he landed just below the window, grabbing at the sill to keep from tumbling to the street. With one good pull, he got himself up and over into the room.

The place looked as though a war had broken out and then been brought to a halt by stampeding elephants. Furniture was smashed and toppled and a black bearskin rug that he guessed had once been in the center of the floor was now flung to the far wall, marred by blood and torn in several places. Around it, most of the furniture and decorations that had been in a direct path of the window was piled up in disarray.

From beneath the rug and several other objects, Feanne unburied herself, looking—if possible—more battered than she had before.

"Ask me no questions," she growled, shoving the debris off her. "I will only say that using magic to augment your natural skills is dangerous…and at times, messy."

"Wouldn't even know what to say to that. Maybe we should just keep moving?"

He did not wait for her answer and began searching the upstairs of the house for multiple escape routes, just in case the people outside followed them inside, though he knew that was unlikely in the rich section of town. Rarely would the humans and elves willingly impose on another of their ilk without invitation, even if it would save the person's life. He was counting on that standoffishness to give them a lengthy head-start in escaping.

"You coming?" he asked as he stood at the top of the stairs. "We need to get moving. They will come after us eventually."

Feanne finally came out of the room they had entered through, the bear's skin draped over her shoulders as though it were a cloak.

"This I wish to keep," she noted, holding up a leg of the rug. "We do not get many bears in our part of the woods. At least few that I would skin."

Estin frowned at her, but she ignored him.

"It's a little warm for fur...extra fur," he added, reminding himself of the irony.

Feanne shrugged and walked past him and down the stairs.

"You live in the city. The woods are not nearly so comfortable at night."

"Whatever you want."

Estin hurried after her, then led the way down two more floors and finally to another staircase that was wooden and less well maintained. Cobwebs and dust lingered as they began descending. A damp chill made Estin shiver as the darkness of the cellar closed in around them. His vision faded from the bright colors of the upstairs to dull hues as his night-sight began adjusting. Individual colors faded into shades of grey, black, and white...the very colors of his own pelt, as well as his clothing.

"How will going into a hole in the ground get us out of this part of town?"

Turning to look back at her, Estin found that her own coloring had faded interestingly in the vision that only creatures of the night could see. Her leathers were almost pitch black, with all of the red and black of her fur dimmed to a near-black that blurred in the darkness. The only things that stood out where the white fur patches on her lower jaw and the tip of her tail. That, and her gleaming white eye that he realized was nearly as bright as his own orange ones. She likely could see as well as he could in the dark basement even with only one eye that could open. That was reassuring at least, given where they were going.

"Have you ever been in a sewer?"

Feanne's furrowed brows told him she had not and might not even know what he was talking about.

"The sewers reclaim all the water...and waste...from the houses in the rich part of town."

"And where does it go?"

Estin nodded, "That's exactly the point. We can't follow it too far, or we'll be taking a fast path down the mountains when it reaches a stream. If we only take it to the slums, we can come up in one of the buildings that connect to the sewers. I know most of them and where the entrances are.

"This won't be pleasant, but it's the safest way out."

Feanne nodded and gestured for him to continue.

"I have seen more unpleasant places than likely exist within the walls of this city," she told him. "Show me these sewers so that I can get away from anywhere else that you might make me jump around like a monkey."

"Then let's get going."

He led her down to the less-used sections of the basement, listening for running water. What he heard first was a door being kicked in upstairs, followed by many voices and the pounding of feet. Just after the mob broke into the first floor, he spotted what he was searching for—a grating near one corner to allow any excess water to drain away and for servicing the sewers if something were to get backed up.

"Down here," he said quietly, grunting as he tried to lift the heavy grating. With all the climbing he had done this day, his arms were in agony, but this was not the time to stop and worry about it.

After several seconds and the sound of nearing footfalls, Feanne stepped up beside Estin, grabbing onto the grating herself. She whispered something that Estin did not recognize, then hoisted the grating as though it were weightless.

"Pull it closed behind us," she told him, setting the grating alongside the hole, then slid past him and dropped into the darkness below with a faint splash.

Estin shifted himself under the grating, then dropped through, using his weight to yank the grating closed behind him as he fell.

He landed in about three inches of water, though from the smell of the place it was likely not exactly water. Estin winced as his feet sunk in and, as he had every time he had entered a sewer, he envied the other races with their thick boots. Bare paws in the muck was hardly something he enjoyed. A slick foul sludge had already begun to work its way in between his toes, burning on the scrapes and cuts that covered his feet.

"Not much worse than some of the swamps to the far south," Feanne noted, pulling the bear skin tighter over her shoulders.

"I'll have to trust you on that."

Estin began down the sewer tunnel as quickly as he could with his feet being sucked down into the mire with each footfall. The trip would not be long, but he wanted to get out of this place as fast as he could as he remembered how long it had taken for the stink to get out of his fur the last time he was down here. That time had been a profitable theft in a house not far from this location, giving him a good sense of where they were and how to get out.

"Down here," he announced, turning right and continuing through the darkness.

This area was far enough from the dimly-lit gratings of houses that the already-dim light faded to the point that he had to slow his pace and stare hard to make out the walls. A glance back confirmed that Feanne was doing no better, as she had a hand on the wall to ensure she was moving the right direction. Nonetheless, she did not complain or question , but followed along behind him.

Soon the passage grew brighter again as they neared several drain grates along the streets. At each of these Estin paused to check their location.

"We're close now," he promised, pushing on, even as the sludge rose above his ankles. "There will be a small hatch in the upper-right corner shortly."

Sure enough, about fifty feet on, he found the well-disguised patch of wood. It was placed such that anyone coming through with torches could not see the door, as the shadows from the torches would conceal it. Those who knew where it was, or could see in the dark would have little trouble locating it.

Estin had to feel around the door a bit to find the latch, which was inconveniently-placed at best. Once he got a finger on it, he felt the lock click open and he slid the panel away to reveal a dim room above.

"After you," he told Feanne, stepping aside.

She gave him a queer look, then tossed the bear skin up through the opening. She waited a moment, as though listening, then grabbed the lip of the opening and pulled herself through easily. Her white tail-tip vanished through the gap and she was gone.

Reaching up to the opening himself, Estin lifted himself through and collapsed inside the building, his arms trembling badly now. He casually shoved the hatch closed.

The room they were now in was barely lit by a thin ray of light from a boarded-up window on the south wall. Scattered through the old warehouse were boxes that had rotted, their decayed contents falling out into moldy piles. Estin had always wondered what they had been, but everything had been rotting so long that he could not tell if they were boxes of food or cloth.

Feanne had set herself to work immediately upon getting into the room, having found a steady leak of water from a pipe that may have once fed the building, but now just dumped its contents endlessly onto the floor, contributing to the decay. She had her feet under the stream, cleaning the grunge from her fur. Once that was less caked, she began rubbing the dried blood off her hands, claws, and the cuts on her arms, all the while leaning heavily on the wall, as if her strength were beginning to fade again.

"How do we get from here to the outside?" she asked him, somehow knowing he was watching her. She sounded extremely tired. "You said this was just until we could escape."

"There are ways through or over the walls once the sun sets," Estin explained, coming over to sit on the floor near the running water. He tried not to look at his sticky-feeling feet and tried even harder to keep them away from his tail or anything else he would have to clean. "I have someone in the next building over who might watch out for us until we can escape. Once we're past the wall, the only ones who would come after us would be the army. I'm hoping that they don't have any troops nearby."

"There are more than enough troops nearby," Feanne corrected, stepping out of the water, checking her feet one more time for sludge, then glancing at her tail for any filth. "I was escorted in from nearly a mile outside the walls."

"Really? I had no idea they were out that far."

"They have enough to harass the wilds," Feanne remarked, her tone dark and impatient. She put a hand to her heard again, steadying herself. "I will not talk further on this. Go find your person and plan our escape. I will rest while you do this."

She staggered to the nearest dark corner and flopped down, curling into a ball as she tossed the bear skin over herself, effectively hiding. If he had not known where she was, Estin doubted he could have spotted her in the dim lighting.

Estin kicked his feet through the water to clean up at least a little, then headed for the back of the warehouse. There he slid a more-intact stack of boxes aside to reveal hole just large enough for him to squeeze through that led into the abutting building. This was all part of the secret network that Nyess had built over the years, allowing him to escape raids by the town guards. Some routes had been shown to Estin in his service to the rat, but he doubted he even knew a fraction of what Nyess had available to him.

Once he was through, Estin sat up and nearly leaned right into a shining knife leveled at his throat. He raised his gaze and saw that it was another of the dwarves Nyess employed on occasion. This one's beard was trimmed down to a short mass of hair—a grievous insult among dwarves, but likely a mark of distinction among thugs and thieves. While most dwarves Estin had seen liked to be seen and heard, this one was dressed in mottled dark colors that blended with the dimly-lit setting. He also appeared as though he had not bathed in several days, his face sweaty and his odor reeking of ale.

"So good of you to come, monkey," growled the man, grabbing Estin's shirt collar and dragging him out of the opening to the warehouse and onto the floor of the room. The knife came right back to Estin's neck. "The boss was getting worried about you. I think he wants to talk to you."

"Saves me time looking for him," Estin said, trying to sound calm as he pushed the blade away from his neck slowly. "Lead the way."

Once he was on his feet, the dwarf shoved him hard to get him walking, nearly making him tumble forwards. As they walked through multiple rooms and floors, he continued to give Estin occasional pushes, apparently for his own amusement.

At last, they reached a dingy basement room with stark block walls and a single desk at the center. There sat Nyess, his beady eyes watching Estin from the moment he entered, as his furless tail whipped back and forth impatiently.

"Where is your employer?" demanded the rat-man. "This is bad for business to have our customers disappear."

The weight of Varra's death hit Estin again like someone had punched him in the stomach. Once again, he struggled to push down the memories and keep his calm. There was no place in the streets for someone who let their feelings run away with them.

"She was killed by a Turessian while we were escaping. The item she wanted stolen was left with me...I assume she wants it taken back to her people. I was not able to get her body out of the keep."

"A fine mess that is."

Nyess stood up—one of the few times Estin had actually seen him do that—and walked a slow circle around Estin, eyeing him up and down.

"The cup on your belt," noted Nyess, tapping the metal with his filed nail. "This is what she wanted stolen?"

"Yes, that was all she wanted."

Nyess sneered at the goblet as he leaned closer to get a look at it.

"It's not valuable, is it?" he demanded, poking it again.

"I think it's a family heirloom. Something about gypsy honor and people stealing from family."

Snorting, Nyess flopped back into his chair, making it creak dangerously.

"Your employer is dead, you came back with nothing of value, and I'm guessing you want something. Why shouldn't I have...what was your name, dwarf?"

"Finth, sir."

"Yes, whatever. Why shouldn't I have Finth stab you repeatedly for my own amusement?"

Estin swallowed hard. The first time he had met Nyess, a young elf had been being beaten in the back corner of the room for failing to pay a debt. His meeting with Nyess had lasted nearly an hour and when he had finished, the man was still being beaten...though he had stopped screaming by that point.

He thought about revealing the gems in his pouch from the keep, but realized without bartering, he might just be ensuring his death. Estin decided to use those as a last-resort to get out of danger if things went badly.

"I plan to take it to the gypsies," he lied, hoping it was sounding at least fairly genuine. In reality, he doubted they would want to see him if he was coming with news of Varra's death. "Varra said that they would provide payment at that time. I'll bring that back to you."

"That will work," Nyess said quickly. "How can I help facilitate the trade?"

Estin's mind raced, going over his options and which ones might well get him killed for requesting. In the end, he settled on the simplest and safest option.

"I shouldn't need anything more than some food, water, and a quick distraction at the south gate," he explained, thinking through what might slow Feanne and his escape from the city. "The duke has likely got people hunting us and we're not exactly able to blend in."

"I understand. I'll have some of my contacts make sure that the southwest corner of the wall is clear for about half an hour at dawn. You will need to cross there during that time, or your head will be on a pike and there is nothing I can or will do to save you."

"Thank you, Nyess," Estin said, watching Nyess' face carefully. The other wildling was entirely calm and seemed to be taking the whole problem in stride. "May I return to the warehouse?"

"Go, get out of my sight and don't come back until you have the payment."

Estin looked at Finth, who shrugged and waved back the way they had come. Forced to lead the way with occasional prodding from the dwarf, Estin made his way slowly back to the filthy warehouse where they had started. As he reached the hole through the wall, he glanced behind him and found that the dwarf was gone, having slipped away somehow.

Shivering at the idea of the creepy dwarf lingering around the area unseen, Estin hurriedly shoved the stack of boxes against the hole after he had gotten through it. As an extra precaution, he placed several metal bits from around the floor up against the boxes, hoping they would make a scraping noise to alert him if the boxes were moved.

Estin fiddled with the boxes for several minutes, until he was confident that no one would be able to surprise them. He then went back to the corner where Feanne had bedded down before he had left, but it was now empty and cold.

"I prefer if people cannot find me when I'm unable to see them coming," she said from somewhere behind him, her voice unsteady. "Sleeping is not the safest time in the wilds."

Turning sharply, Estin had to scan the warehouse for her. It took him some time to spot her, nestled among a pile of the fallen boxes. She had somehow gotten to the middle of a vast pile without disturbing the outer boxes, allowing the disheveled pile to conceal her. She watched him carefully with her good eye, though the other had swollen over onto the side of her jaw. If Estin had not met her already, he would have gauged her expression as challenging him or trying to scare him off.

Once he had spotted her, Feanne stood up among the boxes on top of the bear skin, then moved slowly through the garbage pile, carefully picking her way to the warehouse floor without knocking anything down. She hopped from the last section of refuse, leaving no indication she had so much as stepped on the soft trash. She hesitated as her toes came down, as if she had to work to keep her balance.

"You know my name from watching me shame myself in the court of the furless," Feanne said, her voice and stance abruptly switching from friendly to predator. "I would know who you are and what pack you guide before I let you leave my presence again. I must also know where the pack is, before we leave the city. My father will want to make contact with them."

"Pack? That I don't know anything about. As for who I am, I'm Estin."

"Estin," she repeated, stalking around him. "Just…Estin? No title? No pack?"

Estin felt he had just made a huge error, but doubted he could have guessed an appropriate answer. He turned to try to keep her from being behind him…something in the corner of his mind told him that his survival might depend on it. Though he had willingly allowed her to follow him most of the way to the warehouse, now he felt very nervous about allowing her out of his sight.

"No pack," he replied, trying to keep Feanne visible. He felt foolish turning around in circles, but she forced him to either do that or lose sight of her. "I run alone in the city. Most of the other wildlings are slaves here."

Feanne leapt with a feral snarl, bowling him onto his back as her fangs snapped near his throat. She pinned him quickly, slamming him down on the warehouse floor with enough force to knock the wind from his lungs and daze him as she sat down on his chest.

"You deceived me!" she growled, clamping one incredibly strong hand around his neck, her claws tapping dangerously against his throat. "Give me a reason not to rip your throat out!"

Estin thought of a dozen reasons instantly, mostly having to do with his own desire to keep breathing, but with her hand crushing his windpipe, he could manage no more than a croak. Spots began to dance in his vision as he struggled for air.

Abruptly, Feanne released him, but stayed atop him, keeping him from running as he desperately wanted to. He started to move his arms and found that she had those pinned under her thighs, keeping him from doing much more than speaking or breathing, the latter of which he was happy to be able to do now.

"Explain yourself," she ordered, digging a claw into his chest where the necklace he had stolen from the duke hung, though the dangling feathers and other decorations were tossed about on his neck. "If I do not like your answer, I will find my own way out of this city and you will be without a bottom jaw."

"I'll answer anything you ask, but I need to know what I'm supposed to be explaining!"

Feanne just stared at him for a time, making Estin worry more and more. She kept one hand close to his neck, claws at the ready, as a reminder that he was entirely trapped. Panic set in quickly at being pinned down by a predator. The fear continued to build, slowly overwhelming his ability to think, until at last Feanne spoke again.

"Do you think I am a fool and would follow a stranger through the city without question?" she asked, tapping the tip of her claw between his eyes. "I would have left you to die to those dogs, had you not been marked. You claim ignorance of what I speak."

Feanne eased her hold on him, letting him breathe somewhat easier, but he found his arms still pinned. She wavered atop him, putting a hand to her head again.

"You clearly have no idea what this is," looping a finger through the necklace as she spoke, letting the feathers fall into her palm. "Where did you get it?"

Estin finally made the connections and began talking, though much faster than he meant to and found himself unable to slow down.

"I found that in the duke's keep. Up on the top floor. He has all kinds of things stored up there. I didn't know what half of them were. I just…I took a few things that caught my eye. Varra said this looked appropriate for me. I should have left it. Maybe I should have left everything. Do you want the necklace? It's yours. Take it. I have some gems in my pouch…"

"Shut your mouth, Estin."

He nearly bit his own tongue as he clamped his mouth shut.

Feanne twisted the necklace around and pulled the knot out to remove it. With little ceremony, she tied it onto her upper-arm over the deep lacerations, then returned her attention to Estin.

"Now," she began again, her claw brushing the tip of his nose. At this distance, he could see that she had filed the claws, apparently for fighting. "You are very lucky that I am the one who caught you wearing that. My father would have been far less forgiving and likely would have killed you the moment he knew it did not belong on you."

"What is it? It wasn't like I was trying to pretend I was something else. It's just a necklace. I thought it was pretty. How could I know? Things like that just shouldn't be left…"

"Quiet."

Feanne slowly lifted herself up, letting him move out from under her, but kept her eye on him as he scrambled from her reach.

"You were wearing an elder's mantle," she explained, glancing down at the leather straps, beads, and feathers that now hung around her arm. "The colors of the beads have meaning within that pack. The feathers are a symbol of victories over one's enemies.

"Many of the pack elders and significant members of the pack wear these. It is a way for a traveler from another pack to recognize a leader or a healer if they are ignorant of that pack's ways. Sometimes the great warriors of a pack will also wear similar necklaces, but the style is different.

"When I saw you coming to help me, wearing one of these, I had to assume you were a revered member of a pack I had not been aware existed within the city walls. I placed my trust in you, solely because of this piece of jewelry, while ignoring my own instinct to run the moment I freed myself, using you as a distraction."

"That's just plain mean," Estin said, before thinking better of it.

"It is the way of the wilds. Trust your kin and trust your pack…no one else deserves your trust until they earn it."

"I saved you from a cage," he answered, trying to be jovial, "does that count for anything?"

Feanne lashed out again, clubbing him in the chest with her fist, knocking him over.

Rolling back onto his feet, Estin found her standing over her, her gaze deadly, even as her wounds bled freely again.

"You watched me beaten by guards. You let me be dragged off on a leash. You walked away and wandered the building for over an hour, while I was caged and tortured by dogs. Where in there do you think you earned anything from me? Have I pushed you around enough to compare to having my flesh torn and ripped by dogs?"

Easing back onto his haunches, Estin realized no amount of politeness was going to win him any ground in this conversation. He lowered his eyes and put up his hands defensively.

"I'm sorry that I misled you," he said, flinching just in case another blow was about to land, but it never came. "I honestly had no idea what I was presenting myself as. I did not suffer like you did, but I did lose someone who had been kind to me in that keep. It's not often people are good to me and though I didn't know her, I still feel like I lost a friend today. I was hoping not to make any extra enemies, after all that."

Feanne growled softly, kicking aside some debris that lay near her foot.

"I am sorry you lost the human," she admitted, stalking over to where she had left the bear skin. She snatched it from the old boxes, knocking several over as she stumbled. "My anger got the better of me. The fact that you found this necklace means that there is one less pack out there, thanks to this city. I do not like being hunted to extinction and will not go calmly."

"That much I had guessed."

Feanne flopped down on the bearskin again, this time with her back against the wall, so that she was sitting facing Estin. She wavered slightly, putting her hand to her head yet again, making Estin begin to wonder if she was in a lot of pain from her injuries.

"What is your friend's great plan to get us out from this city?"

Easing himself down into a sitting position, he faced her uncomfortably, feeling like if he misspoke he would get attacked. In fact, he was quite sure of that.

"He isn't exactly my friend," he noted, grimacing. "Nyess is a wildling, but that's about as far as our relationship goes. He sells his services and those of the people who owe him debts to the highest bidder."

"And you have bartered for our escape?"

"I did. But he's betraying us to the duke. There will be guards at the point he recommended for escaping. He wants us to go over the southwest wall, where I'm guessing an entire contingent of the duke's men will be waiting."

Feanne's eye widened.

"You know this and yet we remain here?"

Estin nodded.

"Yes. Nyess believes he's a lot more clever than he is. Since I didn't act like I knew he was selling us out, he'll carry through with his plan. We're entirely safe unless we actually go to the escape point. Once we don't show up there, then he'll send people after us."

"And how do you know he's betraying your trust?"

Estin chuckled at that.

"Mainly because he let me negotiate a trade where I pay him nothing up-front. Nyess does not do anything without payment first, unless he thinks he is bartering for the trust of a new client. To get his help escaping should have cost me dearly, but he just asked me to pay him later. That tells me someone else already paid him. The last time I saw someone try to get a favor this big out of him, he demanded that their eldest child serve him for a year…he asked me for nothing."

Feanne actually smirked at that…maybe it was a full smile, but Estin could not be sure with the swelling in her face. She was beginning to look very tired.

"Then how are we to escape, if not by the route your old friend has offered you? Also, should we depart now, rather than wait?"

"I'd rather not," he admitted. "We both did far more than is healthy today. I can't possibly climb another wall without some rest and you look like half the army has beaten you. If we push on, I'm afraid you'll bleed to death before we reach the woods. We have until dawn to rest."

Feanne held up her arms, inspecting the deep gashes that still oozed blood onto her brown-red fur. She looked over her legs next, checking each similar wound. Even her tail revealed a sizable tuft of hair missing.

"They are getting infected," she said somberly, touching her cheek as she spoke. "This one is already infected and there are broken bones. Resting for a few hours would be good, but much longer and I will not have the strength left to continue on. I believe that magic I used earlier to maintain myself is all that is keeping me going. Do not worry though, I will be strong enough after some rest."

They sat in silence a time, as the warehouse darkened with nightfall. Neither seemed to be quite able or ready to settle in for sleep, instead they both stared of in random directions, lost in thought.

"Feanne?"

She lifted her head and stared at him, her eye starting to show white as the light faded.

"You may ask."

It took him longer than he would have liked to find the words, especially without getting himself mauled again.

"Why did you go into the keep by yourself with all that wealth on you? Did you think the duke would do as you asked?"

Feanne laughed openly for the first time since he had seen her, the sound lightening the tension in the room instantly.

"No," she confessed, smoothing the bear fur with one hand. "The answer is not a short one, I am afraid. How much do you know about the packs out in the wilds?"

"Absolutely nothing. I haven't been outside the walls of the city for more than an hour at a time since I was two."

Feanne gave him a sad look, but hid it quickly.

"My father's pack was one of many in the area. We have dealt with slavers and furriers every so often, as every pack does. They come in the night and grab our young and our slower members, while the pack moves on to new parts of the woods, looking for a safer place to live apart from the cities of man. This is how it has been since my grandmother's grandmother was learning to walk.

"Several months ago, the packs began disappearing. It began with the ones closest to the city, but others vanished soon after. My father's scouts had reported seeing the first large armies leaving this city in the months leading up to the first of these disappearances, but we could not learn what the connection was for a long time.

"Eventually, the men came for our pack, raiding our camps with greater numbers than any slaver group. They came with horses and armored warriors.

"Our pack was one of the lucky ones. We managed to drive them off, then escape before they could regroup. We lost many that night."

Estin asked as she paused, "Did your father manage to keep the pack together, or did you all split up to stay safe?"

"More than that," explained Feanne, smiling. "He drew together most of those who had gotten away during previous raids on the other packs. They came together for safety, shelter, and a common desire to avoid being stalked by the city's men."

She shifted her weight, wincing as she tried to find a position where her wounds were not paining her. Finally she seemed to find a more comfortable angle and brought her attention back to Estin, though he could see a dark streak of blood on the wall where she had been leaning.

"We believed that we were far enough out from the city to be safe. This was incorrect. We were attacked again and again. Each time we would lose a few more of our people, as would the city's collectors.

"At first, we thought they were taking our people alive for the city's slave market. I was part of the group that was to attempt to free one particular convoy of our people that had been caught the night before. We followed them back to a camp not far from the same river we were using for water. The moment they arrived in camp, they killed every one of the wildlings they had captured."

"That makes no sense," Estin interjected.

"This is what we thought. We stayed out of sight that entire day, watching. At nightfall, one of the black-robed humans arrived at the camp. The ones who were at the back of the throne room this morning."

"Turessians."

Feanne shrugged the name off, "Whatever they are called, they were the ones who came. The dark man worked magic that I am unfamiliar with over the bodies. When he finished, the dead got back up. He gave them weapons and they left with the rest of the city's men."

Estin's jaw worked, but he struggled to find words. Memories of Varra's killer flashed across his mind.

"They are raising the dead? Why would someone do that?"

"The disbelief you possess is what I encountered back at our camp when I returned." She leaned back against the wall and closed her eye. "I was called a liar. Neither my father nor mother could convince the people of the truth and I am not sure that they believed me either."

"So why come here, knowing they would take you, too?"

"Several notable members of our pack demanded that we settle with the master of the city. They believed he was selling our people into slavery out of greed. Somehow, they came to the conclusion that if we delivered him enough gold, he would stop attacking us."

"That's incredibly stupid."

Feanne growled softly, but replied, "Not stupid...ignorant. Most of the pack has never dealt with the cities of man. They do not understand money or the hearts of those not from the wilds. Rather than just delivering a box of gold, I decided to make it clear to my people what the city's intentions were by sending in one of us, carrying the gold. If the duke took the one carrying the gold hostage, it would prove much about his motivations. If he killed that person, it would make them a martyr and convince every wildling in the region to either flee or fight."

"Why you?"

"Would you let another risk themselves in your place?" she asked, holding her head, but not letting go this time. She seemed to struggle to continue the conversation, as though she were distracted. "I knew that whoever was to make the delivery...they would be taken captive, or worse, and I would not put another through that, just to prove I was correct. The gold...um...gold would only make the duke more willing to strike at us, so I wanted to be sure that there were no trails leading back to the pack. I could trust no one else and...and would not risk anyone else. I came into the city knowing that I would die.

"When I...I came to the city...I...what was I saying?"

Feanne abruptly leaned back against the wall, seemingly dazed, then fell completely over, leaving a large streak of blood on the wall.

"I...," she looked around frantically, her eye out of focus, "...where am I?"

Scrambling over to her, Estin found that she was cold to the touch and all of her wounds were bleeding worse than he had realized. She barely moved as he touched her. He examined the injury over her eye and could feel intense heat radiating off of it, the only noticeable heat at all from her.

"You've almost bled to death," Estin told her gravely, looking around for something to tie off the wounds. There were just too many and several were in places he wasn't sure he could properly bandage with anything he might find around the warehouse. "We won't be going anywhere with the fever you've got. You'll be lucky to stand on your own. How did you even get this far?"

"Leave me here," Feanne replied, smiling absently up at him. She seemed to be half-asleep as she stroked the feathers of the necklace tied to her arm. "I came to Altis to die for my people. One way is as good as another. Have mother tuck me in..."

"Feanne," he prodded, giving her a little shake. Her eye focused for a moment, then began to glaze again. "Feanne, you need to stay awake. Can you magic yourself healthy again or something?"

She giggled, burying her face in the bear fur.

"No, my magic does not work that way. I am not a healer, Estin. My mother can do much more than I ever will be able to. Healing is hard work. Did you know she makes a nice rabbit stew? Rabbits are hard to catch..."

Estin winced, realizing that the fever was a lot further along than she had led him to believe. He suddenly wondered if she had hid among the warehouse boxes in order to die alone where she would not be found. He had heard of wildlings doing that, especially those from the wilds. Her agreement to travel again in the morning now stunk of delays so that she would no longer be a burden by the time he was ready to go on.

"Feanne, do you remember what you did for me back at the kennels?"

She stuck out her tongue and squirmed, wiping at her face as though swatting away flies. Feanne did not ever react when she rubbed at the swelling around her eye, the pain apparently not getting through the fever's stupor.

"That was silly magic," she mumbled. "Makes the hurt go somewhere else."

"Can you do it again and give me back my injuries?"

She rolled onto her back and stared at him, her eye drifting past him repeatedly.

"Maybe," Feanne replied, her face straining with concentration. "So tired. Can I have a blanket?"

"Just do it, please!"

Her hand shaking, Feanne reached up and took hold of the fur along his neck. She whispered the same words as earlier, though they were faint and breathy as she struggled with the spell, taking a long time to cast it, unlike the brief moment it had taken the first time.

Sudden warmth flared in Estin's neck where she touched him, then rushed out from there, chilling his body. Pain followed, as his flesh tore itself open in many places and he felt his head spin as a wave of nausea raced through him.

Estin gagged and collapsed, his heart racing and his body wracked with pain. He could barely think through the stinging and burning wounds and the sensation that the world was spinning. The next thing he saw was Feanne, kneeling over him. She had both eyes open now, though her left eye socket was still swollen and the eye was bloodshot.

"Can you hear me, Estin?" she asked slowly, trying to meet his eyes, but Estin found it hard to focus on her. "I believe that I may have overdone the spell. My fever is gone."

Estin nodded, though he really had no idea what she was talking about. He really just wanted to sleep. The stone floor under him felt cool, but he was getting terribly warm. He curled up, trying to make the world stop spinning.

"Sleep now, Estin," she said, touching his forehead. "I will make sure you live to see the dawn."

Estin really hated the dawn. Maybe she would wake him when it was dark. He could only hope.

Muttering to himself, Estin flopped his tail over his face as he drifted towards sleep. The pain was finally going away, though it was terribly warm in the warehouse. He wished someone would open a window, though at least his mother was being nice enough to pet his face as he drifted off.

At least his mother...

Chapter Three

"The Wilds"

Within the dream, after watching mother get dragged around by the metal leash, it was then that father would burst into the room, coming from outside. He was covered in soot and had cuts on his arms and chest, as well as bloody spots on his fur that told of other injuries that I could not see, or possibly just did not remember. With only a growling shout at the man, he launched himself at the intruder, struggling solely for the chain that held mother. His single-minded focus kept his attention off the man's club, which struck him hard across the brow.

Stumbling to his knees, father looked up into my eyes as a second blow to his back flattened him. He mouthed one thing, even as I saw the club coming down over his head.

"Hide!"

Everything in the dream becomes a blur then. I always faintly hear the wet cracks as the man murdered my father, but I was so confused, so lost, that I could not think clearly. It would take me years to convince myself of what I heard, but in the dream I would dive back into my part of the home and tuck myself into my blankets, cowering in the darkest corner of the room. It seems a foolish place now, but the man apparently did not see me, or he never looked.

Hours or days passed, both within the dream and when it originally happened. Time was a blur, but I knew I felt the warmth of at least one day pass. All I could see was the inside of that blanket, as I lay there trembling. It was not until I began to smell death around me that I knew I had to leave my corner—no one was coming to help me. Maybe they had decided to save themselves…maybe I was the last one alive.

Estin woke slowly, a strange bouncing sensation jostling him to consciousness. He could see sunlight overhead, though it was filtered, as though through a canopy. As his eyes were having trouble focusing on anything, he could not be sure exactly what was above him, other than that it appeared to be moving.

He tried to roll onto his side and found that he could not move. Snug straps were fastened over his chest and legs, holding him to what felt like a hammock draped between two supports on either side of him.

Panicking slightly, he struggled to see what was moving around him, only to realize that he was moving backwards through the woods. The sensation of sliding the wrong direction through an unknown location made Estin's stomach lurch.

"Are you awake?" asked Feanne's voice behind him. She sounded strained and exhausted.

"I think so," Estin answered, letting his head fall back onto the cloth that was holding him off the ground. A simple litter made from sticks and cloth, he quickly realized. Atop him was Feanne's bear skin, keeping him warm. "I feel sick and weak and I think I'm going to throw up."

He looked around, realizing that the bustle of the city was long gone. They were moving through the woods now, the massive older pines creating a canopy over them, while the trunks created the sensation of walking through an unending room of columns—though even with the close confines of the woods, Estin had a nerve-wracking feeling of being in a huge open space. It was not something he was used to at all.

The ground that his litter was being dragged through was coated with a thick layer of pine needles that left a trail leading back behind them, where the poles dragged.

"I doubt you could throw up again," she told him, grunting as she pulled his litter over several rocks, bouncing him. "Since we cleared the walls, I believe your stomach is more than empty. Still, we will be able to rest soon. Until we can get you to a healer or tend to your infection for several days, you will be dangerously ill."

"Where are we? How did we get out here?"

Feanne stopped walking and eased the litter onto the ground. She stepped around to the side so that Estin could see her without twisting his head around, sitting down beside him.

"Your fever…my fever, I suppose, got much worse." She placed a hand on his forehead briefly. "It seems to be down somewhat now, which is good.

"I took what you said about the ambush and used a strategy my father taught me. People who are looking for someone will always watch the place they expect them, as well as the last place the target should be. They rarely look in nearby spots. This was true today. There was a squad of dwarves on the wall, hidden and waiting for us in the southwest corner. I took us through the southern section—not very far from the gates—with no real resistance."

"Clever. You made it out without anyone seeing you?"

"That I won't claim," she corrected, tightening one of the straps that held him to the supporting poles of the litter. "There were two young elves who tried to shoot me with arrows. I must say that I am considerably faster than they were, now that I feel more alert."

"Are they dead?"

Feanne shook her head.

"I did not want any more reasons for them to send extra troops after us. I simply broke their bows and beat them with the remains."

"Simply?"

"Yes. Simply."

"Remind me never to draw a bow on you, Feanne."

She snickered and patted his neck.

"You would be wise not to draw any weapon on me, regardless of the reason. As I recall, I have gotten us past ten city guards, whereas you have defeated one dwarf who had his back turned."

"You mean you and whatever you called to help us back there in the street."

Feanne's smile fell away instantly and she stood back up.

"Yes, that is what I meant. We should move on."

She walked past where he lay and quickly padded fifty feet or so back along their path. Feanne then turned around and walked back towards Estin slowly, dragging her feet slightly to even back out the pine needles. If Estin stared hard enough, he could see where the lines had been, but he doubted he could find them otherwise. Somehow, Feanne made hiding their path look remarkably easy.

"We will go over rocks for a little while," she said as though answering a question Estin had not thought of yet. "They cannot track us there. Once we have crossed a nearby stream, we will be able to move more freely without fear."

She grabbed the poles of the makeshift stretcher and lifted Estin off the ground and began dragging him through the woods again. True to her word, seconds later she was yanking the litter over uneven rocks and hard ground that made his stomach leap with each bump.

"Stop, stop!" he begged, silently thanking the universe for its mercy when she did stop moving. "I'll find a way to walk. Just let me get off this thing."

Feanne grunted something that sounded derisive, but she did lower the poles to the ground again. She came around to his other side and hooked the straps with her claws and cut them one at a time. It was then that he noticed for the first time that he was weaponless, though he did still have his pouches and the goblet Varra had given him.

"Can you get up?" she asked, offering her hand. "As bad as the fever was this morning, I doubt this is a good idea."

"I'm fine. Much better now. Where are my weapons?"

"I threw them off the walls of the city for fun."

He honestly could not be sure if she was joking or serious, so Estin just closed his mouth.

Estin forced his aching joints to pull him upright out of pure stubbornness, but then the world began spinning and he stumbled, catching himself on a tree. Bile rose in his throat, threatening to make him vomit.

"We will move slowly," Feanne offered, draping the bear skin over his shoulders and taking his hand. She led him towards a creek that passed through the rocky soil nearby. "It will not be too much farther yet."

They walked across the uneven stones, with Feanne supporting far more of Estin's weight than he cared to admit. Before long, she had to put her arm around him to keep him from collapsing, but she did it without telling him he was an idiot, which he appreciated. He knew he was being foolish by trying to stay on his own feet, but hated to feel so weak when Feanne had been strong through far worse over the last day.

As they progressed, Estin sniffed the air, trying to learn what was around them, if only to distract him from the nausea he was suffering. He recognized the pines, but a thousand other scents confused him and blurred together. Some were likely flowers, some animal, some he simply had no idea. Having not left the city in so many years, everything out here was alien to him, drowning his mind in new scents that he had no way to sort out.

Struggling to make sense of all the things his nose picked up, Estin tried to center his thoughts and managed to pick out strong familiar aromas in an effort to piece things out one at a time. The rich smell of Feanne's heavily-oiled leather vest and loincloth was easy to latch onto as a singular point in the sea of scents. Once he smelled that, he separated her unique scent from that of the leather, making a note of it so that he could recognize her more easily. It was a heavy woody smell of fur, mixed with the oils of the leather that had stained her fur, along with the more bitter additions of blood and one other item that he could not quite pick out. He was sure it was animal, but it was distinct from the leather and from Feanne herself. It smelled vaguely fox-like, but could have just been another wildling, or even a different breed of fox.

"Are you mated?" he asked without thinking, trying to identify the other scent. "I smell..."

Feanne dropped him face-first on the stones, where he lay, too weak to roll over or stand.

"Estin, there are some things you have no right to even ask," she barked at him and for a moment he thought she would kick him, but she threw up her hands in annoyance. "I am not, though not for lack of trying by my father. There are no suitable males in the pack and we have more important concerns, such as survival, for me to be concerned with being bound to a male for breeding or bragging rights. You especially have no right asking as an outsider to the pack."

"I wasn't trying...not implying...," he stammered, still unsure if she would strike. "I just smelled another animal and thought..."

"You thought you smelled another wildling," she finished for him, her posture calming considerably. "Now I understand. No, that is not what you smelled. It was the helper that I called in to help us in the city street. It leaves a scent that most of our kind find disturbing. I had nearly forgotten about it."

Feanne quickly slid under his arm and hoisted him back to his feet.

"I am sorry, Estin. I fear I'm doing as much damage to you as the dogs did. Perhaps you should avoid traveling with me in the future."

He laughed at her, while trying to concentrate on putting one foot in front of the other.

"Feanne, I've spent six years in a city where I was barely more than cattle. I'd rather have you beat me on a daily basis than go back to living in a town that's killing people and turning them into undead for the army."

"I will ask if you still feel that way after several cold nights out here," chided the fox-woman, smirking at him. "Your walls stopped the wind quite nicely. Out here, your fur alone will barely keep you alive."

"You keep making this sound like a big mistake."

Feanne tilted her head slightly, as though considering.

"No, I think this was good for you. I just do not think you will find it all as wonderful in the future as you do right now."

She stopped them then, just at the edge of the water.

"Have you ever been in a mountain stream before?" she inquired, glancing over at him.

"No, but I've been in the sewers more than I care to. How much worse could mud be?"

"It is not the mud that will bother you." She eased one of her feet into the water, while holding him upright on the shore. "These waters come from snow higher in the peaks. I am afraid we must cross to get to the pack's camp."

Estin stepped into the water and very nearly went into shock. He had been out in the winter weather back in Altis each year, but when he had been cold enough, he could always find an abandoned building to hide in. This water, though, was as cold or colder than anything he had ever experienced, or at least felt that way after walking along in cool but pleasant air.

Flinching and fighting his muscles, Estin forced himself to take another step into the water, following Feanne's guidance deeper. They moved very slowly across the narrow creek, the fast-moving water rising steadily to his knees as his feet went completely numb.

Feanne was steady in her movements and strength, even as he shook violently. She seemed to notice this and promised, "You do get used to it eventually. It takes time."

"Not really believing right now," Estin answered with his teeth chattering.

Seconds later, she led him up onto the shore, where he tried to lay down. She stopped him, practically pulling him along as she kept walking.

"You will not want to rest just yet. The water will freeze once the sun sets, so we need to keep moving to dry out. Once we get to camp, there will be small fires and plenty of pelts to warm you."

He turned his head slightly to look at Feanne, her face only inches away. It was an odd feeling for him, not having been within five feet of another wildling for most of his life and now to be practically carried through the woods by the most remarkable of his people he had met. All the others he had seen were broken beings, their individuality destroyed by the leashes they had worn most of their lives. Feanne was so unlike that that he found himself wanting to know so much more about her.

"Are you seriously not cold from the water?"

Feanne smiled and kept walking.

"No. I can tell that my feet are wet and chilled, but I have spent my life running through the woods, whether it is wet, dry, or snowing. After a few winters in snow up to your hips, your feet stop caring about the cold, so long as you get back to warmth as soon as possible."

"You've lived out here your whole life?"

Feanne nodded, answering, "Born in the woods and I would prefer to die there as well, free of anyone's attempts to tie me down. You helped make sure that comes to pass."

"That's...cheery."

She gave him a quizzical glance and noted, "You have a very strange understanding of our people, Estin. Do you believe that the wolves wake up each morning, praying to whatever deity they serve that they will not come to harm for years? Would you expect the hare stops hunting for food just because there could be a mountain lion someday that kills it?"

"No..."

"Why should we be any different? Believe in whatever you want and work to make things better in your life, but never forget that you will die. We can only hope for a good death on the terms we set. Wanting or striving for anything more will lead to disappointment, which is truly sad when it is your last thought in life.

"I had an opportunity to die in a way that might save my people, no matter how awful my own end was. To me, that is a good death and worthy of the pain of meeting it. What would you consider a good death, Estin?"

He blinked a few times, trying to wrap his mind around thinking in those terms.

"Or rather," she corrected herself, "what would you need to do or experience for your life to be complete? Perhaps that is easier to consider."

"It is."

Estin pondered as they walked. They went some distance while he went over things in his mind, until he finally came to an answer.

"When you were hiding in the warehouse...you believed you were dying?"

"Yes. I knew I would die from my injuries without help. I had failed to meet my anticipated death for my people, so a lonely death was appropriate. No one else needed to see me suffer."

"I don't need to accomplish anything or even do anything day to day to feel like my life is full," he explained, thinking about the years running around the city, scrounging for food. "Surviving is enough for me in life."

"And to die well?"

"To not die alone," he said sadly, thinking of his mother. "I've had family that died brutally and I hid. I don't want to be abandoned while I die and I certainly don't want to feel like I did the same to anyone else ever again. I guess I want to help people before I die."

"These are decisions we all make." Feanne hugged him somewhat tighter for a moment. "If you hid, I doubt it was with the intention of abandoning them. How old were you at the time?"

"Around a year, give or take."

"Why did you not die as well?"

Estin felt the familiar weight of guilt settle into his shoulders. It was a sensation he tried to avoid, but somehow he felt he could not refuse Feanne's questions, especially while imposing on her to help carry him through the woods.

"My father asked me to hide, even as he was killed."

"Then how do you believe that you failed him? His wish for dying was not to allow his child to die beside him. You fulfilled that wish and lived. That would seem a good death for a parent."

The pain of memories haunting him, despite efforts to push them down, Estin snapped angrily, "He died, so we won't know if he appreciated it or not."

"And this is why we should not fear death for ourselves," Feanne told him, shifting his weight. "No matter what you may believe about gods, dragons, or whatever silly thing the city people believe in as a deity, one day you will die, too, and no force can stop that. Whatever place your father has gone to is where you will be...then you can ask him. Until then, why do you let it keep you from doing more with your life? Worrying about whether you did the right thing years ago is like throwing away all those years, which is the very thing your father was sparing you from."

"I don't want to talk about this anymore."

"Suit yourself, Estin. I will continue to believe that you will find your good life and death and I will feel no guilt in hoping for that."

"Do your people always spend so much time talking about death?"

"Not all of us," she admitted. "Much of my time is spent in contemplation of the natural order of things and how it relates to our pack. Death is a large part of that, especially these days."

Estin let the conversation lapse, which Feanne thankfully allowed him to do. They limped along quietly for some time, his pace becoming more uneasy as they went, with his head beginning to pound badly. Eventually, he could go no further, collapsing to his knees and retching, despite Feanne's efforts to keep him upright.

"I can't keep going," said Estin, once he could speak again. His stomach was certainly empty, but he felt as though he would vomit again at any moment, given the slow spin of his peripheral vision. "The fever's back. I can't get up."

"I could carry you for a short time," Feanne replied, kneeling beside him. "Either that or I can call to my people and see if they are close enough to hear. I have waited on that, for fear the people sent by the city might hear me as well."

Estin tried to sit up and instead fell over onto his side. He realized he was starting to tremble with chill. Even as he struggled to stand, he heard the distant barking of dogs.

"I cannot run and cover our trail at the same time," Feanne said quickly, apparently having heard the dogs too. "They will find us, whether we stay or run now."

"Then leave me here."

Ignoring him, Feanne stood up and raised her face to the sky—or what was visible of it through the canopy of trees—and let out a throaty wail that vaguely reminded him of a wolf's howl, even though it was very different. She maintained the call for far longer than Estin would have guessed she could, until finally she lowered her head, the sound of her cry still echoing faintly through the mountains.

"If the pack does not come in time, I have only allowed the dogs to find us faster."

She sat down beside him and checked his forehead again. Shaking her head sadly, she noted, "If the pack does not find us, the dogs will not shorten your life considerably. The fever is very strong again."

Estin barely could find the strength to lift his head from the ground. As Feanne seemed to be settling in for a wait, he rolled onto his back and stared up at the treetops and the filtered sunlight that flickered through the needles of the pines. The trees swayed wildly in the wind, or appeared to in his fever-induced haze.

"My father once told me that we were tree people," he said absently, only vaguely aware of what he was saying. "I barely remembered what the woods looked like. Does that make this a good death?"

"Death by mauling is one I do not recommend. If the dogs come, just keep watching the trees."

Estin felt Feanne's claws settle in on his neck, even as the barking of dogs became much louder. Her touch was gentle, but the sharp edges of the claws lay directly on the veins that ran down his neck. Were he more coherent, Estin knew this would have concerned him, but right then the trees swaying was far more interesting as he tried to stay awake.

Large hunting dogs broke around the nearby rocks, racing towards Estin and Feanne, snarling and yipping for their masters as they closed. As they did, Feanne's claws dug into Estin's neck painfully and even his delirium was not enough to put down the fear that grew with each bounding leap of the hounds.

"Watch the trees, Estin," Feanne reminded him, shifting her body between him and the dogs. She bent over him, shielding his body as she started to push her claws into his neck. "Tell your father I am sorry."

A sharp crack nearly deafened Estin and was enough to snap him out of staring at the trees. Even Feanne reacted, pulling her hand away from his throat.

Throughout the area, tree trunks exploded into splinters as huge balls of ice slammed into them, showering the dogs with wood, then scattering them as the damaged trees fell with ground-shaking crashes. The fallen trees boxed Estin and Feanne in, but by the sound of whimpering and howls, the dogs were already on the run.

"The only one I know who would make that howl was Feanne," called out a gravelly voice somewhere beyond the downed trees. "And every time I've heard you make that awful noise, things have been about to tear you apart, girl. Just once I would like you to bring back good news."

Estin watched as a dog-like face peeked over the nearest of the fallen trees, its animal-like eyes gleaming with intelligence. The male wildling's white and brown patterned fur was a match for some of the wolf pelts he had seen worn by nobility around the city. What stood out to Estin though, was that the wolf's fur was lightly frosted—though melting quickly. Water dripped off his hands as he moved from the ice.

"Ghohar, it is good to see you, as always," Feanne offered, lowering her head as a supplicant bow of thanks.

"You'd be thankful to see a raging horde of talking mushrooms if it saved you," he noted dryly, kneeling beside Estin. "Your thanks are appreciated, anyway."

The wildling's face came near to Estin's, as he inspected Estin's injuries. He touched Estin's forehead and prodded at his fur to survey the various cuts and gashes. He stopped when he reached the spot where Feanne's claws had been resting on his throat.

"So little faith in the pack, Feanne?" asked the wolf, but did not wait for an answer. "I brought along Ulra for backup, just in case. Sohan is out leading the hunters in circles.

" Ulra can carry him to Asrahn. She's expecting you to be the one half-dead, as usual. This might just be a pleasant surprise in a stupid sort of way."

Estin blinked slowly, trying to take in the newcomer's words, but they were slow to get through the fog he felt he was sinking into.

"What's an Ulra?" he asked the wolf lazily.

"That," replied Ghohar, pointing back by the trees, "is an Ulra."

Turning his head as best he could while being poked at by Ghohar, Estin saw a massive brown-furred being tromp over the fallen trees. Her feet were easily three times the size of Estin's own and she was nearly half again his height. She towered over the group, her ursine features wrinkling with anger.

"This one is hurt badly," the bear-wildling said with a voice that made Estin's prey-instincts kick in and make him want to flee. "Do we need to kill something to protect him, or just take him back?"

"Take him back. Sohan is dealing with those who are pursuing," Ghohar explained, getting up off the ground and dusting his knees off.

As Ghohar started to move out of Ulra's way, Feanne grabbed his wrist.

"Thank you," she said, looking near tears. "Thank you both. You know how I hate the humans' hunting dogs."

Ghohar nodded and chuckled, patting Feanne's hand.

"That I do, girl. I just hate how damned dumb they are. Two healthy wolves would tear that entire pack of dogs apart. Awful shame what breeding has done to them. Poor Ulra didn't even get to fight them before they were scared off."

Estin just stared at the group around him in dazed surprise at seeing so many wildlings in one place. Since he was a child, the only time he had seen more than one wildling anywhere was at the slave auctions and those were not really the same creatures at all. They had no personality, no emotions, no sense of self. For all he could tell, those on the slave block were dead inside, having given up on freedom entirely.

These were different. He had thought Feanne might be the only one like that despite her talk about a pack, but now, seeing Ghohar and the massive Ulra, he had begun to believe that his childhood memories might not be entirely fiction. Perhaps there were more wildlings like him.

His thoughts fell away in a panic as Ulra scooped him up as though he were a child, cradling him in her massive arms and began walking off into the woods. He struggled briefly, not wanting to be anywhere near a bear's jaws, even if it was a wildling, but she hardly seemed to notice his efforts and soon he was too exhausted to continue.

The trip through the woods was rapid, with Ulra tromping swiftly over the rough terrain, seemingly unaware of brambles and heavy brush that would have slowed-down or stopped most others. She charged through it all, while keeping Estin held just above the tallest of the bushes.

The pounding pace of the bear should have kept Estin wide awake, but as his fear of her faded, he began growing tired again. Pain radiated through his arms and his head pounded, but his mind was shutting down quickly. As almost an afterthought, he looked down at his arms and saw that the many rips in his fur from dog-bites were bleeding badly again.

His last thought as he fell asleep was about whether Ulra would be upset at all the blood he had left all over her fur.

*

Estin felt like he was dragging himself back from a dark place as he came to, his mind struggling to overcome the weight of sleep that seemed to press itself on his eyelids. When he finally did get his eyes to open, the first thing he saw was a felinoid face staring down at him.

The female was clearly elderly, with grey fur around her mouth and chin and somewhat whitened eyes. Long strands of leather with feathers, beads, and even several claws hung from a sort of necklace not terribly unlike the one he had found back at the duke's keep. Her arms were resting on the side of the mat he lay on and most of the fur on her hands was whitened, as well.

The more Estin studied her face, the more he realized that she was not a breed of cat he had seen before. Though clearly of some kind of cat lineage, her face was longer than he would have expected, with a reddish line of fur up the bridge of her nose that spread out along her forehead.

"Wake up, child," she hissed at him, tapping a nail between his eyes. "The fever is past. It is time to wake and get out of my tent."

"Where am I?" Estin asked, his voice cracking, due to his throat being painfully dry.

The female ignored him and raised a bowl of water to his mouth.

"You need water first. Drink and then talk. If you talk while you drink, you'll drown and I'll not change the order for you."

The water was very refreshing, cooling his burning throat and helping to further wake him up. When she finally took the bowl away from his mouth, he pushed himself up a little on the mat, sitting up slightly against a pile of rolled furs that had been just above his head.

"Is this the camp Feanne told me about?" he asked, trying to get a glimpse of anything outside the tent. The flap was closed and everything inside was hazy with smoke from a tiny fire in the middle of the room, which was at the center of a circle made of fine white stones.

"The question you ask first is, 'What are you called, oh great elder that saved me?' Next, I recommend, 'Would you like to know who I am?' After that, it would be polite to ask me questions about the rest."

86

Estin was not sure what to make of the old female, who just stared evenly at him.

"Very well, who are you?"

"Psh!" she answered, shaking her head sadly. "You do not ask even that nicely. What manners do they teach you in the city? You may be hopeless, child."

"I'm not a child," he countered, sitting upright, though his head started pounding.

"You are what, five? Maybe six?"

"Six. More than an adult among our people."

The old female chuckled.

"I had a life-mate by your age, but that does not mean you are wise, child." She jabbed his cheek with her first-finger's tip. "What do you know of our people?"

Estin shrugged and replied, "Only what I see at the slave markets, what my parents taught me as a child, and what little Feanne has told me about this pack on the way here."

"Asrahn," stated the elder, crossing her arms over her chest. "You asked for my name. Now that you answered my question, I answer yours."

"You cared for me?"

Asrahn laughed hoarsely.

"No, Feanne cared for you, which is why you lived long enough for me to finish the task, by tending to your wounds, which is very different from caring. They brought you in last evening, barely breathing. If you were not already warned, it is widely considered unsafe to travel with the Keeper."

Estin looked down over himself, surveying the damage. His shirt was long gone, no real surprise given how badly torn and stained it had been. His arms and legs still hurt, but the ragged bites had faded into thin pink lines that appeared to have mostly scarred over.

"The fur may not return," Asrahn noted, her eyes following his. "Deep wounds near death are the hardest to completely heal, even with magic. They become a part of you as surely as the memory of getting them."

"You healed me?" he asked, checking his hands. The scrapes and other damage to his fingers from the climbs were all gone and he flicked his tail behind him, finding no pain there from carrying Feanne. "This is more magic? Do all of our people use magic? Feanne mentioned her mother was also a healer."

The female laughed openly at him.

"No, there are only a few of us who do use magic. Very few, in fact. Feanne's mother is rather skilled at it, I hear. Ghohar commands the elements to strike at our enemies. These are the only decently-skilled users of magic in a pack of almost fifty adults."

"And Feanne," he added.

Asrahn's eyes narrowed slightly and she asked sharply, "You have seen the Keeper use magic?"

"Only a little," he admitted, noting the title again. Asrahn seemed genuinely annoyed at him, so he added, "She leapt farther than I can using magic. She used some kind of magic to move my injuries to her, then back to me. I think she also called in some kind of monster to kill soldiers who were attacking us. Oh, and she broke the lock on the cage she was in."

"A cage?" Asrahn demanded, squinting at him. "This rather surprises me. I doubted that child would let herself get caged. This pack has been trying to tie her down in a figurative sense her whole life, but this may be the first time someone was successful.

"The monster, as you put it," she continued. "Did you get a look at it?"

"No."

Asrahn seemed to relax.

"Consider yourself lucky, child. There are reasons the Keeper shares little about herself."

"You keep calling her 'the Keeper.' What is that title?"

Ashran cocked her head slightly, but kept quiet for a time.

"You will need to eat," she said at length. "Your body will weaken quickly, given how close you were to death."

"Was I really that far gone?"

She nodded grimly. "Your heart was faltering and the blood was barely flowing from your wounds. I doubt you would have made it another hour and that would have made things far more difficult for me."

"Being dead is a big deal for me too," he noted dryly, tracing the fresh scars on his arms. Some were simple bare patches of white skin, whereas some had created thin lines that looked almost like tattoos that the humans living in Altis had seemed so fond of. These often came in double or triple lines for several inches on his arms, where the dogs' claws or fangs had raked him badly.

"I could have fixed dead," the old female answered, rapping his fingers to get his attention. "You ignoring my orders to eat is harder to remedy."

Estin traced a double-line down his left arm again, the smooth scar leading down almost to his elbow. At least most of the scars would be hidden by a shirt, he noted.

"Will the scars fade?" he asked Asrahn, taking an offered bowl of soup from her. "I had not thought healing magic would leave so many."

"It was hardly healing magic," Asrahn said with a mild sneer. "Feanne is many things, but a healer is not one of them. She did what she could, which kept you both alive. A skilled healer would have been able to prevent the scarring as well, but that was beyond her ability. As for these scars, scars stay if they need to for reminding us of our mistakes. Some do fade, but many stick around. I think yours will remain a while yet."

Asrahn lifted the shoulder of her simple doeskin tunic and revealed a deeply-burned scar that looked to be decades old, emblazoned just above her elbow. The scar had been modified, as though new lines were added later to change its appearance.

"An old slaver's mark," she explained, covering it again. "When I took a mate, we had matching scars made from the old slaver's marks we both bore. The new mark was not that of either slaver, but rather something we both bore together. We took the brutality of our old masters and made it something that we owned.

"We all bear our scars, but some make for a better story. Were I younger with your scars, I would not fear showing them, child. Mine could have gotten me hung by anyone who recognized them in those lands. Yours will draw odd stares and certain unpleasant questions, but just remember that we are all marked in our own ways."

Estin's ears perked, waiting for more to her story, but Asrahn just stopped talking and stirred at the pot of stew in the middle of the room. He waited, hoping she would explain further, but she seemed unwilling to even acknowledge his presence.

He sipped at the bowl she had given him, passing time slowly as his stomach grumbled to speed him up in his eating. Much to his dismay, Asrahn stayed lost in her own thoughts, ignoring him.

"Can I go outside and see this pack that Feanne has made so much fuss over?"

Asrahn waved him away, as though she was unconcerned, but he did catch her watching him from the corner of her eyes as he got up.

Estin got up slowly, finding that he was rather dizzy yet. As his head cleared, he found that much of his clothing had been removed or destroyed in their escape from town. His shirt he knew was long gone, a victim of Asrahn's tending to his wounds, but his pants had been sliced open on either side. This let them breathe nicely, but he found that the open sides made them feel not far different from the loincloths many of the other wildlings wore.

Suddenly, he realized his belt and pouches were missing and looked frantically around them room, not seeing them anywhere.

"You have lost something?" asked Asrahn, raising an eyebrow.

"My pouches and a goblet."

"I believe they were taken by the Keeper," she noted with a snort. "You will need to barter with her for their return. I know that I cannot convince her to do anything she does not wish."

Estin hurried outside, stumbling as he emerged into blazing sunlight. He stood there a moment, letting his eyes adjust, but when they did, he barely believed what they showed him.

Wildlings were everywhere. Ulra and another bear were off to one side of the forest clearing, dragging dead wood the size of small trees in from the tree line, likely for firewood. Several wolves—including Ghohar—were scattered near the wood line, patrolling the camp's edges for intruders. He spotted several other breeds running around, but they were there and gone so quickly, that he had a hard time identifying them.

"You, you, you!" exclaimed an excitable ferret, racing up on him. The young male darted in circles around Estin, prodding him with a clawed finger as though checking on his previous wounds. Like many of the others around the camp, the ferret was dressed in little more than a loincloth. "Asrahn got you all fixed up, that's great! Where are you going now? Hrm? Say something!"

"I...I was looking for Feanne."

The ferret nodded rapidly, doing another loop around Estin. "No time to wait around. Yep, yep, yep. Want me to show you were she is? Or do you wanna explore? Me, I'd explore. So much to see when people don't tell you want to look for. Right, right?"

Estin very nearly grabbed the ferret to stop him from moving.

"Who are you?" he demanded, trying not to sound mean, but the ferret was definitely driving him crazy. "We haven't met."

"Right, right, right!" the ferret said, slapping his forehead. "What was I thinking? Nothing, I bet. Sheesh. Sorry! I'm Sohan. I was the one who got rid of your hunters. They were really nasty people and wanted you dead in a big way. How did you get them so annoyed? I mean, I must have run around them for half an hour before they were as mad at me as they had been at you. That takes talent. Usually hunters want to stab me right away, but not these ones! They just kept yelling and trying to get the dogs to find you. Very annoying really, when you're trying to get someone's attention and they just won't..."

"Please stop talking," Estin cut in, trying to get his mind around the ferret's rapid speech. "Were you able to get rid of them or not?"

"Yep! Got rid of all but one!"

"One?"

Sohan bounced up and down, then grabbed Estin's hand, dragging him towards a large grouping of tents.

"Angry dwarf just wouldn't give up. Really stubborn guy." Sohan's feet dug tiny trenches as he tried to run with Estin, who was having none of that. "Ditched the rest of the hunters...some off a cliff...but the rest ran for town, complaining about crazy rodents...not that I'm a rodent, mind you. This guy just wouldn't stop chasing me though. I thought he was gonna get tired, but every time I sat down to laugh at the hunters, there he was again!"

Sohan led Estin up to a wooden cage, made from heavy tree bows that had been driven into the ground, then strapped together at the tops. Inside sat Osrinn, the dwarf that Estin had met in Nyess' lair, glaring out at them venomously.

"Well, hello there, monkey," growled the dwarf, sitting still in the cage with his arms crossed over his barrel chest. "This wasn't exactly the side of the cage I meant to be on, but it will do for now."

"Why did Nyess send you after me?" demanded Estin, kneeling beside the cage.

"You?" Osrinn said, his eyes widening in surprise. "Really? You think we gave two troll shits about you? The duke set a hundred gold price on the fox's head—dead, not alive—after she made that showing in his chambers. I'm sure I could sell her pelt for more than yours, too. Better looking tail, you know.

"You aren't worth more than five gold, though I could likely pawn what you stole for more than your head and hide is worth."

Estin stood back up and looked down at Sohan, who was bouncing beside him.

"Feed him to something awful," Estin told the ferret as he began to walk away. "I don't want to see that dwarf or his master again."

"Nope, nope, can't do that," chittered Sohan, zipping around Estin. "Feanne said we keep him for information. She said he was from the city and we needed to know more about what the hunters were after. Can't kill him until she says so."

"Do you do whatever Feanne tells you to do?"

Sohan skidded to a halt and cocked his head, contemplating the question.

"No," he finally answered, darting back to Estin's side. "Sometimes her father gives commands that she disagrees with. The pack-leader wins when that happens. Otherwise, yeah, I do what she says. Why? Don't you do what she says? Seems kind of silly to me. Dangerous, too. I don't like dangerous."

Estin watched the younger wildling run around as though he were physically incapable of standing still for more than a few seconds at a time. Estin stopped walking and just stood patiently as Sohan hopped around and generally kept in motion, usually while talking to himself.

"…and when Lihuan tells me to do something, that's just like law or something. When Feanne says to do it, it's more like 'do it or else,' which is still important, but doesn't quite mean the same thing. You know what I mean?"

Estin just stood there until the ferret trailed off and wiggled his ears in confusion.

"You're awfully quiet," Sohan noted. "Is that a city thing, or you just don't like to talk?"

"Both." Estin resumed walking now that Sohan was paying attention again. "The city people don't talk to our kind, so I didn't get much chance to talk to anyone. Right now, I don't have a lot to say, as I'm trying to figure out what my place is here and where my stuff has gone."

"Your stuff? That I can help with!"

The ferret nearly bounced up and down, seemingly excited at the idea of finding things.

"Asrahn said Feanne took my bags. I really need those back and I would like to find some replacement weapons."

Sohan's nose twitched as he thought hard about the request.

"The bags we can get back anytime she agrees," he answered. "If Feanne took them, there's a reason and she won't let them go anytime soon. The weapons are more tricky."

He hopped over to a nearby canopy and motioned to stacks of rusted swords and other weapons that had been tossed into piles.

"We collect them from the hunters, until we get around to melting them down," Sohan explained, poking at a halberd with his fingertip. "Sometimes we make armor from them, but mostly we use them for tools or arrowtips. If you like some, just take them. Only a couple people use them."

Estin stepped into the shade of the canopy, amazed at the array of weaponry that had just been tossed into piles. He had seen fewer weapons in the duke's keep than the wildlings had stockpiled.

"None of them are quite what I was looking for," he said after inspecting the most recent-looking pile of steel, where there was the least rust. "Mine weren't any better than these, but they were at least a matching pair."

The ferret just stared blankly at him.

"Better for balance."

Sohan blinked slowly.

"So…you fight with them?" Sohan asked, his face unreadable.

"Not well," he replied, laughing. "It's what I was taught to fight with. What kind of weapons do you use?"

Sohan raised his hands, holding up his short claws.

"Really? Swords?" he asked Estin, sounding nearly offended by the idea. "Feanne can't be happy about that."

"Why would she care?"

Sohan's eyes nearly popped out as he screwed up his face.

"You really need to talk to her more before you hang out with this pack," Sohan told him, scooting back out into the sunlight. "Lihuan will want to meet you too, but maybe you want your bags first? Where to...um...you?"

"Estin."

"Right, right, right. Estin. What breed are you? I know what I am, but I don't know what you are."

Estin stopped and stared at the ferret, who was sniffing and cocking his head, inspecting Estin. Sohan's eyes studied Estin's long striped tail.

"I really don't know what they call my kind," he admitted, coming out into the sunlight beside Sohan. The sun was high overhead and its heat baked into Estin's brow immediately and his bare feet felt the warmth of the day through the dry ground. "I am what I am. Beyond that, I don't try to guess too much. In the city, we're all just animals."

Sohan nodded quickly, then spun in a circle.

"Feanne first, then? No more sad talk about cities?"

"Lead the way."

Sohan bounced again, this time sniffing the air before leading the way off towards another section of the camp. He led Estin past several dozen makeshift tents and canopies, each with a unique scent that made Estin wonder just how so many wildlings had ended up in this "pack." He did his best to check out each group of wildlings they passed, doing his best to not appear rude, but Sohan's pace made any effort to look around rather difficult.

They passed groups of many breeds that Estin had never seen, or had not seen closely. Coyotes, foxes, wolves, and the occasional bear wandered by, making Estin wonder whether anyone in the camp besides him was not a predatory breed. It made him more than a little nervous when he thought about it.

They neared the edge of the camp and Sohan skidded to a halt as massive booted feet stepped in his way. With a hiss, Sohan dropped into a crouch and snarled at the giant humanoid that now stood in their way. Estin could not really take the action seriously, coming from Sohan.

Nearly eight feet tall, the man had grey skin that seemed to soak up the sunlight as he stared at Estin and Sohan with a dull gaze. Large tusks protruded from his lower jaw and long curved horns—like those of a ram—gave him a monstrous appearance that made Estin take a step back in surprise. He had only seen an ogre once up close and he had heard more than his fair share of rumors about how dangerous they might be. He had dismissed them all, but now questioned that choice with one close enough to grab him.

Sohan was undeterred and raced circles around the giant man, trying to trip him up and get underfoot. The grey-skinned man seemed hardly impressed and just reached down and picked up Sohan by the scruff of his neck.

"Still trying to knock me down?" asked the ogre, his voice rumbling, but gentle. "You never tire of the game?"

"Never!" exclaimed Sohan, squirming and giggling. "Mom said giants fall the hardest. I wanna prove it!"

The ogre sighed and set Sohan back on the ground, patting him on the head with remarkable care.

"You bring another to see the Keeper," the ogre noted, his black eyes falling on Estin. "What do they call you, young ringtail?"

"Estin," he answered, shifting his weight so he could run if needed. Talking to an ogre had not been on his list of plans for the day. "I just came to see Feanne."

"So many do." The ogre sat down slowly, barely making a sound, despite his size. Somehow every action the giant took seemed to reflect caution and grace that Estin would have never expected from a being that looked as he did. "You are just older than most who willingly visit her. Please go into the grove and see her. It is not my place to keep anyone out."

"I thought this was a pack of wildlings...not ogres," Estin mumbled, trying to find words as he faced the ogre, who he had no doubt could break him in half easily. "I...I don't understand."

"Many things are out of place in our world," the ogre explained, leaning up against a tree that creaked slightly at his weight. "You are from the city and yet you do not belong there. I am from these very woods, but I do not belong in this company. Your friend here does not belong underfoot, but still he usually is.

"As you imply, I do not belong here. Perhaps someday I will, wildling. Then again, mayhaps someday you will belong whereas I do not. There is much to consider in this."

Estin felt as though he had been robbed of any possible words to answer the ogre with and just stood before the large humanoid, feeling foolish.

"Don't you worry about him," jabbered Sohan, popping in front of Estin. "He's been here longer than the camp. These days, he helps keep the young and old safe."

"This is true," the ogre said in his rumbling bass voice.

"What do I call you?" Estin asked the ogre, trying to be polite but feeling intrusive instead.

"I do not give out my name," replied the giant, smiling at Estin—though the smile felt intimidating with the man's tusks. "Names and words have power over each of us. For now, I am what I am and not a name."

Sohan stuck out his tongue at the ogre.

"He's always like that," explained the ferret, grabbing Estin's hand and dragging him along. "C'mon! We're almost to Feanne. Then you can get your bags back and I can see what's in them. Right? Right?"

Estin rolled his eyes and kept his mouth shut, knowing that the excitable Sohan would likely ignore whatever he said anyway, so it was likely better to take the ogre's advice and say nothing extra.

"Over there!" Sohan said, hopping over to the entrance to a grove of trees. "There, there, there!"

Estin followed Sohan's pointing, seeing that the grove of dense old trees was filled with more people. Unlike the last few groups he had seen throughout the wildling camp, who had been mostly older, the grove was filled with a mass of young cubs, all racing around in an effort to tackle Feanne, who was laughing at the middle of the clearing.

As a wildling wolf cub leapt onto Feanne's back, she collapsed with a playful yelp, rolling on the ground in play. Two rabbits jumped at her next, but she caught them with her hands, making the cubs giggle hysterically.

"Feanne!" Sohan yelled before Estin could grab his arm.

The laughter dying down in the grove, the various young wildlings hopped to their feet and stared at Estin. In seconds they swarmed him, poking at his hands and tugging his tail as they inspected him.

Helplessly, he let them check him out, even as Feanne rolled onto her stomach and watched with amusement. She wagged her tail and smirked as Estin struggled to free his limbs of the children.

"What breed are you?" demanded at least three of the six children at once, one pulling his tail again for emphasis. Their voices all seemed to blur together, making it hard for him to pick out which was saying what. "I haven't seen your kind before. Did Feanne bring you here? My mom owes Feanne her life...do you, too? You smell like humans! Your clothes are funny!"

"Please let the newcomer stretch out before we maul him anymore," Feanne interjected at last, drawing pouting looks from the children. "Run along. Most of your parents don't want you out in the grove anyway."

With a chorus of whines, the cubs scurried off into the woods, leaving Estin, Sohan, and Feanne alone in the wooded grove.

"So to what do I owe this visit?" Feanne asked, sitting up and pulling her knees up to her chest. "I thought you would be longer to recover."

Estin started to ask after his belongings, when he noticed Feanne's arms and legs. Long scars ran the length of her left arm—matching his own. Another set of smaller bare patches from bites marred her legs and right forearm, again matching Estin's scars.

"Are those...?" he asked, pointing at his own arm.

"I told you I was a bad healer," Feanne reminded him, giving Sohan a small shove when he bounced too close to her. "The wounds scarred us both equally. This is the price I pay for my magic. I am thankful to see that Asrahn was better at mending you than I was."

Estin came over and sat next to her, studying her face as he did so.

"Your eye looks much better."

Feanne smiled and nodded, looking at him with two bright eyes that gave no indication of the broken eye socket from just a day earlier.

"Yes, I'm healed completely. I may be bad at healing others, but if left to my own means in the woods, I can usually fend for myself."

She self-consciously brushed some of her fur over the scars on her arm and asked him, "You came out here for a reason? I doubt Asrahn sent you my way just to see if I had mended."

"I did," he admitted, nearly losing his train of thoughts as Sohan bounded past, chasing a butterfly. "I believe you took my bags when I was taken to Asrahn."

"That is true." Feanne stuck a thumb out towards a nearby tree. "Your things are in the crook of that tree. Should you wish to buy your way back into Altis, the items you brought out with you should go quite far. If you intend to stay with us, you will not need them, though I left the goblet in your tent, as I figured that at least had some use."

Estin considered that, eyeing the tree that she had indicated. He made no move towards it.

"Can I stay here?" he asked, his eyes still on the tree. The idea of going back to the city was appalling, but Estin did not know any other life. "Is there a place for me with the pack?"

"If we can keep an ogre entertained, you are the least of our worries." Feanne rocked up onto her feet and offered a hand to Estin. "You will need to ask my father for permission. I cannot give it to you. Be mindful of his bargains, though."

Estin took her hand and hoisted himself to his feet, somewhat startled at the strength Feanne carried in her light frame. He had to remind himself that she had practically carried him most of the way from Altis to the camp.

"What can I do to help around here?" he asked her, glancing around the field. "I'm guessing your camp doesn't let people just wander in and expect to be fed."

Feanne smiled broadly at that.

"You are learning already. My father's rule is that everyone needs to contribute. You will be taught to survive out here and provide like the others. If you cannot help the pack, you will be asked to move on.

"The jobs are often suited to the person. Thus, most of our tree-climbers gather food, while my own kind tend to bring back meat and defend the camp. Others spend their time cooking, making and mending clothing, or other chores. I do not know what role my father will find for you, but more hands are always needed."

Estin glanced back at the tree again, wondering if he should just take the wealth and leave, but another look at Feanne's coy smirk told him that he was going nowhere, at least not yet. He wanted to know so much more about this place and the people who were like him.

"Feanne, what is a Keeper?"

The smile was gone immediately and Feanne slammed Estin against the nearest tree, with Sohan squealing and darting out of the way.

"Do you wish to mock me, or is that a serious question?" she demanded, her claws firmly against his collar. "Few members of the pack are willing to call me that to my face."

Estin attempted to push her hand away, thinking that he would have the strength now that he was recovered, but he could not budge her fingers. He looked past her at Sohan, who was making a sharp gesture across his throat, that either meant Estin was going to die, or that he should not be asking the question he had.

"I heard the title used. I thought it was some kind of honor," he admitted, ignoring Sohan as the ferret threw his hands in the air. "What does it mean?"

Feanne released him, letting him fall to the grass.

"It means I failed the pack and they mock me for what I have done," she said, glaring down at him, her tail swishing aggressively. "That is all that you need to know. Go to Asrahn...she will teach you to work for the pack. I have more important things to do."

Feanne turned and padded away, but Estin sat up and called out to her.

"Would you have killed me back in the woods when the hunters were coming?"

Standing with her back to him, Feanne said nothing for a time. When she did speak, she said only, "You should go to Asrahn for guidance."

Back straight, Feanne strode from the grove in a hurry, leaving Estin on his knees and Sohan scrambling around, trying to help.

"Are you stupid?!?" demanded Sohan. "She hates that title. Never, never, never call her that!"

"I figured that out." Estin flopped down on his back, staring up at the sky. "Can you please tell me why she hates me so much?"

Sohan froze, then leaned over Estin slowly, his brow crinkled up.

"Hate you?"

"Yes. She's nearly strangled me every time I've seen her."

"Estin, this is more stuff that you gotta learn," Sohan chided, suddenly sounding mature and well-balanced. "Feanne has some anger issues. You seem to have a nack for poking at them. If she hated you, you'd probably end up like her last mate…did she tell you what happened to him?"

Estin sat up and shook his head.

"She actually told me she was unmated."

"True, true," agreed Sohan, glancing back up the trail to be sure Feanne was gone. "Not for lack of her father trying. Her father found her a potential mate a few years ago, back about the time the city of Altis was starting to hunt our kind.

"Hunters came to the camp that winter. Feanne was told to run away with her mate to escape the carnage. You know what she did?"

Estin shook his head again.

"She escorted the young and old to safety," Sohan went on. "Everyone who should have died got away that day. That is why the pack trusts her. What they don't like to mention is that she abandoned her mate, letting him die to the hunters so that she could save others. Most of us would have made the other choice. I think she'll choose the pack every time over her own life and family, which is great for us...sad for her and anyone who depends on her."

"Why do they trust her with the cubs then?"

"Why wouldn't they?" Sohan asked in reply. "She'll get herself killed to protect every one of them, but probably would ignore her own father getting skinned by hunters. The only complaint from the others' is that she spends so much time out here with the ogre."

Rocking onto his feet, Estin stood up and surveyed the grove again. The tree where his belongings were stashed called out to him, but he clenched his jaw and walked away from it.

"I'm staying," he told Sohan firmly. "You need all the able-bodied adults you can get to protect these people. You have my weapons to protect the pack...once I find some."

Sohan bounced along beside him as they made their way out of the clearing, somehow missing the ogre leaning against the trees, watching them go.

Chapter Four

"The Pack"

How long I waited under my blankets, crying and shivering, varied each time I had the dream, but I would eventually crawl out from under the blanket and glance around my dimly-lit bedroom. The fear I would feel was always so strong that I could barely think. Despite this, I would see that the man had torn my bedding apart and kicked over the small pile of clothing in the corner. Maybe he had thought I was hiding there? Even the little tin water bowl I kept by my bed was crushed.

I would scamper to the entrance to the main room. There no sign of mother or father. The smell of dried blood was painfully clear to me—even in the dream—but there were no bodies or family waiting for me...only a bloodstain where I had seen father fall.

In my childish panic, I would dart into their room hoping to see father and mother waiting for me, only to find it as tossed as my own. Everything they had owned was gone or destroyed.

I would then grab what little I could find. There are a few handfuls of bruised fruits in a basket that had fallen in one corner. These would always go into a sack I find near the fireplace. Next, I would find several knives father had used for cutting bread...these too go into the sack. I grabbed anything I could imagine a use for, though a child's thoughts of what is useful are sometimes comical at best and some of the items I left behind still bother me.

I would always struggle to think clearly at this part of the dream. Mother had mentioned that they were saving coin to move us somewhere safer...somewhere more friendly. I then sit in the ruined hovel, trying to grasp at what she had said. Abruptly, I remember her standing by the loose stone in the fireplace.

Tearing at the stone with my small fingers, I finally manage to pull it free, finding a tiny bag behind it with a dozen copper coins and a single silver one inside. This would not go far outside our village, but it would have to do. I tucked them into a little belt pouch.

Father had taught me from a young age that we were targets. We would always be seen as victims or outsiders—if not yet, then soon. He had stressed ways of disappearing and escaping when being hunted. These were the lessons that pushed themselves past panic, fear, and utterly hopeless sorrow that any child would have felt.

With what little I had, I raced into the painful sunlight, not stopping to survey the village. I had been taught to run and run hard if something like this happened. He had always repeated, "make for the trees. Safety is in the trees." This was the time to act on those warnings.

I ran harder than I thought I could bear, nearly collapsing as I reached the first of the dense trees. I had no idea if I was being followed, but that was not what I was focused on. Only the pounding of my feet and the painful banging of my heart were able to cut through that nearly feral desire to reach the woods. Beyond those woods, maybe the city would be safe.

Now, I was determined to learn to love the woods. The trees were integral to my breed, yet I feared the unknowns out there, having fled the woods for the city as fast as I could all those years ago. Ghohar had been adamant in teaching me to hunt and patrol the area, but it was not something I was ready for. Even after spending a full month having him drag me around the wilds, I felt as out-of-place as I ever had among the humans.

Estin woke to freezing rain that pelted his face as he lay among the trees. He cursed and curled up, trying to stay warm without success.

"Now this is a hunting trip!" exclaimed Ghohar, striding through the sleet as though it were a clear day. "A good brisk morning, eh, Estin?"

Glaring up at the older wildling wolf, Estin shivered violently in his leather jacket and thin furs. They had been out looking for food for almost two days and he had been unprepared for the sharp turn the mountain weather had taken. When they had left, it had been warm and sunny, but rain and now snow loomed.

"How do you stay warm out here?" Estin asked through chattering teeth.

Ghohar knelt beside him and raised a hand, which frosted over, then encased itself in solid ice. He made a slight motion and the ice fell away.

"Some of us just like the cold," he said with a hoarse laugh. "The pack may not be fond of elemental magic, but it has its uses. I'm not sure if Asrahn wanted me to teach you that or how to hunt this time. She just said to take you out to the woods."

"Maybe she wanted to freeze me to death."

"If she hated you, do you think Lihuan would have let you stay these last few weeks? He usually agrees with whatever Asrahn wants."

"Seems like everyone in the pack does that."

Ghohar laughed and helped Estin stand, though the chill kept Estin shaking violently.

"Asrahn's been around the area longer than anyone but Lihuan," Ghohar noted, pointing off towards the south as a direction to set out traveling. "She knows more than anyone else. Hard to argue with someone that knows your job better than you do."

They walked through the woods, feet crunching on the thin layer of ice that was starting to accumulate. After they had traveled a time, Estin stopped and decided he had to know more on a topic he doubted he could ask anyone but Ghohar, who likely could not be offended by any ignorant thing he might say.

"I have to ask, what is Asrahn?"

"Old, important, and willing to take off someone's head if it furthers her causes," Ghohar answered with a wry laugh.

"No," Estin continued, shaking his head, "I mean what breed is she. I don't recognize the features. I recognize some cat in her, but I can't make out what kind."

Ghohar stopped walking and looked back at Estin, genuinely confused.

"I'm guessing your parents didn't get around to the whole talk about making little baby wildlings before you were out on your own," answered the wolf, grinning. "She's a half-breed. Mix of two breeds, with some features of each. Some mixes get jumbled up like that...others look like one breed or the other. Probably a quarter of the folks in camp are at least partly of mixed breeds, even if it never shows."

That was actually news to Estin. He had never given thought to his kind—wildlings in general—mixing with other breeds. As a child, he had always seen same-breed pairs. Since growing up, this camp was his only example of his own people.

"Have you been practicing?" Ghohar asked, abruptly changing topics. He held out his hand to collect the falling snow. "Asrahn seemed quite adamant that you learn some magic from either her or me...I think she's making that a rule for every new person in camp. There aren't many of our kind with any training and I don't think she wants it to die out. Last eight people they sent out with me couldn't learn a damn bit of it. A few others seem to think it's best for entertaining a potential mate and not much else."

"Seriously? We're freezing to death in the middle of the woods and you're worried about whether I've managed to create light without tinder?"

Ghohar slapped him on the shoulder.

"A little magical fire might keep you from bitching about the weather. Think about that the next time you're shivering and whining about magic."

Grumbling at being forced to practice what he viewed as a useless skill yet again, Estin stopped walking and held up his left hand. He partially closed his eyes, trying to block out the bitter winds and focus instead on letting magic flow into his hand.

"Just ease into it," Ghohar reminded him, watching Estin intently. "A little bit goes a long ways...concentrate."

Estin's hand began to glow faintly, but he barely could manage to maintain the simple magic spell. The moment the magic faded, he felt sick to his stomach and weak. Ghohar had warned him that every spell would be taxing on his strength, but practice would gradually allow him to maintain more and larger magical effects. Assuming he could perform any, he mused.

"Ah well, another day, perhaps?" Ghohar said jovially, then froze, his ears shooting straight up. "Do you smell that?"

Estin sniffed the air, picking up a variety of scents, ranging from plants that were dying in the cold weather to the more specific aromas of their leather clothing and even the oils Estin had used to treat the blades of his swords to keep them from rusting.

"I smell meat," explained Ghohar, hopping up a nearby rock to get a better view of their surroundings.

"Meat as in a slab of steak on a plate or meat as in a deer?"

Ghohar laughed and kept looking across the woods.

"We're all meat," he explained, his cool blue eyes sweeping the woods. "When I say I smell meat, it means something I'll eat, whether that be a deer or something bipedal. As long as it doesn't talk to me when I'm seasoning it, I'm a happy wolf."

Estin sneered at the idea and told Ghohar, "You can truly be disgusting at times. You know that, right?"

"That's what mom always told me," he said, laughing again. "Right now, I think I need to take back that remark about meat though."

Estin watched as Ghohar became more tense and the hair on the back of his neck rose.

"What is it?"

Ghohar raised a hand at Estin, indicating that he needed to be silent.

"Do you smell that?"

Estin sniffed at the air, picking up a faint whiff of raw meat that Ghohar had likely been referring to. He raised his nose higher and took another breath, catching what smelled more like decay.

"What is that?" Estin asked, trying to identify the smell.

"Corpses," said Ghohar, pointing to the east. "Somewhere down there. We're still close to camp, so I want to find out what's going on out here."

Estin hurried along behind the wolf as they raced down through the foothills into a sheltered valley area below. Though covered by the same thin layer of slush as the rest of the woods, something about the area made Estin feel dirty, as though the woods themselves were oily.

Ghohar led the way, slowing as he reached a dense section of trees where they would be concealed from anyone beyond. He waited there a minute, likely making sure they were not spotted on the way down.

"There is a road that runs through this part of the woods," he explained to Estin, sticking his thumb towards the south. "Was an old trade route between Altis and Lantonne, before they started warring. I haven't seen anyone out this far in a long time. Can you see anything?"

Estin peeked around the rocks and trees, slinking along the ground as cautiously as he could manage, inching towards the road. Soon, he could see the packed dirt trail, along with a group of wagons that sat in the middle of the road as though they had been abandoned.

Moving more quickly as he approached the open where he might be seen, Estin hopped to his feet and raced to the edge of the nearest wagon, flattening against it as he listened for movement.

The trail was deathly quiet, aside from his own footsteps on the slushy ground. An occasional bird cry would startle Estin, but other than that, the wagons could have been no more than rocks for the amount of life around them.

Here, the smell of death was strong and unmistakable. Estin had to breathe through his mouth to keep from gagging on the stench of torn bowels.

From the edge of the woods, Estin watched Ghohar pick his way over, moving carefully, but unable to be as deft or stealthy as Estin. The elder wolf swept his gaze around the area, clearly expecting a trap at any moment.

"Check the wagons for supplies," he ordered Estin, shoving his deer-fur mantle off of his arms to keep them clear. "We need to be out of here quickly."

Unfastening the cords that he kept looped over the hilts of his swords just in case Ghohar was right in his nervousness, Estin hopped onto the wagon and began poking through the front seat area. There was little to be found there, aside from blood stains and several deep gashes in the wood of the bench.

From where he stood, Estin looked around and realized something was missing. Horses. The wagons had not been there long, but the horses or oxen were missing and there were no tracks in the fresh snow. He guessed that the attack on the wagons had been just before the dawn snows.

"Hurry up!" barked Ghohar, his fingers twitching as he watched the woods.

Estin dove into the back of the canvas-covered wagon, finding more blood and basic supplies for travelers. He grabbed a sack with clothing and rifled through a second that had various tools and cooking utensils. Near the back of the wagon though, he found a long thin mahogany scroll tube with emblems engraved in it with a large sturdy lock. This he grabbed and tucked into his belt, but then froze when he saw another bag beside it that was half-spilled on the floor of the wagon.

Silver and gold coins lay in plain sight.

"This wasn't a robbery!" he exclaimed, rushing outside of the covered wagon with the coins thrown in the bags he carried. Ghohar just nodded and continued to watch the trees. "They left a bunch of coin."

"I think it is time to go, Estin."

Estin hopped off the wagon and as his toes dug into the wet ground, he heard the first footfall. He froze in a partial crouch, his ears tense as he strained to make out the noise. Just as he thought it was gone, he heard another crackle of a twig. The stench of death had gotten stronger, if possible.

"Surrounded," said Ghohar, his ears flattening against his scalp. "This is not my finest moment, boy. I hear four, maybe five. I don't smell any of them, though."

Estin squinted at the trees, seeing nothing more than mud, snow, and brambles in any direction. He kept turning as he drew one sword, then the other, trying to catch sight of the enemy. Still swiveling on the ball of his foot, Estin froze as he realized that he was staring back at something in the trees that was unmoving in watching him.

"Ghohar..."

"I see it." The wolf shifted his stance, as though expecting the enemy to leap. "I've got two more out there. Can't make out what they are yet. Human-sized."

"Run or fight?"

Ghohar looked around once more, then made the decision for them, shouting out a word of magic and sending a blast of ice and freezing water into the trees where one of the figures stood. The shards of ice tore through the bark of the trees and shredded the plants there and when the frost and mist cleared, the figure was lying on the ground.

"We might be alright," Ghohar declared, starting to walk towards the fallen shape. He froze mid-step as the humanoid shape climbed off the ground and resumed standing in their path.

"Not good," said Estin, noticing that one of the other dark shapes had taken two slow steps in their direction. "Got another plan?"

Ghohar raised his hands and began pointing out each of the figures he could see, as though marking them as targets.

"Aside from running with my tail tucked, no. Let's go with that plan."

Estin was faster, rushing at the creature that Ghohar had already used magic against, hoping it would be weaker for his attack and Estin could bowl it over to provide an escape route. As he entered the shade of the trees, he nearly dropped his weapons as a frozen and battered human stood before him, her face shattered and jaw hanging limply around her collar.

"Undead!" he cried, slashing at the abomination with his swords.

The corpse took his slashes without reacting, but when he tried to go around it, the creature shifted and tried to block his path.

Crashing and deafening cracks of ice behind him let Estin know that Ghohar was fighting now. That was not much relief as his blades cut at the silent corpse and it continued to move in front of him.

"Kill the living!" hissed an airy voice somewhere in the woods.

Instantly, the corpse leapt at Estin, its broken jaw gurgling as it tried to bite at him, while its torn arms flailed at him like maddened snakes, trying to catch his weapons or arms. The creature had no concern for his attacks, throwing itself at him with abandon.

"Get out of here, boy!" Ghohar commanded, stepping alongside Estin and raising his hand at the undead monstrosity. The creature tumbled backwards, rolling to a stop just out of their way.

The moment the corpse stopped rolling, it began climbing back to its feet.

"We can't win this," said Ghohar, shoving Estin as they began to run. "I'm not that good of a wizard."

They raced through the trees, scrambling over rocks and running straight through brambles. At one point, Estin fell forward, crashing into icy water and stones. He had barely registered that he was hurt before Ghohar had him pulled back onto his feet and they were off again.

When the two stopped running, the sun had set and there was no sign of the undead creatures. They collapsed in the shelter of a low-hanging pine, gasping for breath, but still watching the woods for movement.

"How many of them were there?"

"No idea," Ghohar admitted, his voice weak with exhaustion. "I saw three wearing Lantonne military clothing and another in gypsy silks. Never saw the one controlling them."

"A gypsy? What was a gypsy doing with Lantonne soldiers?"

"Likely just another thrall of the necromancer. Didn't look to be old enough to be involved with either city's army."

Estin felt a terrible chill set into his chest. He dearly hoped that he did not know that walking corpse.

"I think we've circled around far enough that...," Ghohar began, then cut himself short as a shadowy figure moved into sight a little way back along their trail. "What have we here?"

The dark humanoid shape was alone, but did not move in the haphazard way that the corpses had been. Instead, it walked along at a brisk pace, then would stop and examine tracks. It was following them and doing a fine job of it.

Estin waited until the figure moved into a more brightly-lit patch of woods and realized that the heavy flowing robes were very familiar.

"Turessian," he told Ghohar, tapping the elder's arm. "The duke's court necromancers."

Ghohar leaned forward in their shelter to watch the Turessian.

"So that's our controller. Take him out and the others will wander aimlessly. It's not perfect, but they shouldn't be able to hunt us down."

Estin eased his swords into ready positions.

"I will open on him," explained Ghohar, keeping his voice low. "He will probably begin casting spells at me. Use that opportunity to attack. Necromancers aren't usually too tough without their minions. I'll be able to stop a few spells, but you need to be quick."

Ghohar did not wait for confirmation, slipping out the side of their shelter, then turning and marching towards the Turessian. The darkly-dressed human froze and lifted his head to watch Ghohar.

"Go home, necromancer," Ghohar ordered, motioning in the direction of Altis. "You do not belong out in the woods."

Estin raced around through the trees, circling on the Turessian as the man stood silently watching Ghohar's performance. From his vantage point, Estin could see that the human was unarmed, his gloved hands empty and still.

"Last chance!" shouted Ghohar.

The Turessian stood straighter, leaving its back to Estin as he neared it. He held his position, waiting for Ghohar's cue.

"Do you know what you are, dog?" whispered the Turessian, its voice somehow cutting through the trees like the mountain winds.

"Just another dog in the woods, necromancer," called out Ghohar, raising his hands at his sides.

Ghohar threw his hands at the necromancer with a sweeping gesture that sent waves of ice crashing into the Turessian. The human stumbled, even as a bolt of frozen water slammed into him, knocking him off-balance. A second later, a column of ice fell from the sky, smashing the Turessian flat onto the ground.

Estin leapt from his cover, driving his sword into the human's back before he could rise. Without hesitation, the Turessian drove his elbow back into Estin, sending him tumbling away without his weapon. The impact knocked the wind from Estin's lungs, but he maintained enough presence of mind to slide into the cover of a bush, hoping for a second to recover.

Climbing to his feet, the Turessian paused to examine the blade protruding from its chest, then motioned towards Ghohar, not bothering to so much as touch the sword.

Dark energy flashed and Ghohar swept the magic aside, while preparing another attack. He never got the chance as his muscles locked and he simply stopped moving.

"Nicely tried," stated the Turessian, his right hand in a clutching gesture towards Ghohar. His hood turned as he looked around for Estin. "You fared better than most. There is no shame in death."

The necromancer motioned with his left hand and Ghohar let out a scream that made Estin's blood run cold. From every inch of Ghohar's body, cuts began opening as his blood flowed freely from him.

"One more for the clutch," said the Turessian calmly. "Care to show yourself before your canine friend stops breathing?"

Estin reached for his other weapon, but realized it had been lost when he had rolled away from the necromancer. Without allowing himself to think through his plan, he leapt from his cover again, grabbing the hilt of the sword still stuck in the Turessian's chest.

With strength borne of panic, he wrenched the sword free, then spun, using his weight to come down on the Turessian's extended arm. The blade went through cloth, flesh, and bone, flinging a gloved hand on the ground before the robed figure.

"Is that the best you could think of?" asked the Turessian, turning on Estin. It moved its arm in the direction of the severed hand, which flew back to the outstretched wrist. Tauntingly, the Turessian flexed the fingers on the hand that had been severed. "We are not as fragile as you seem to believe."

"Nor are we mortals!" shouted a deep voice as grey-skinned hands grabbed the Turessian's head and slammed his skull against a tree.

The ogre repeatedly struck the necromancer against the tree, but turned to Estin, rumbling, "Get your friend out of here! I cannot hold him forever."

Estin scrambled for Ghohar, finding the wildling trembling on the ground in a pool of his own blood. Knowing he had little time, he hoisted Ghohar onto his shoulder and began moving as fast as he could towards the deeper woods. Ghohar did not struggle and soon did not even move as Estin ran through the woods, praying that his adrenaline would not run out too soon.

He crashed through the trees, trying to get distance between himself and the battle he was fleeing. Panicked blindness set in and all Estin could see was blood, the trees and the woods forgotten as he just kept running, right up until strong arms grabbed him, wrestling him to the ground. He collapsed, crying out of pain and exhaustion, but no attack came. Estin slowly opened his eyes and found that Feanne and Asrahn were standing over him.

"What was it?" demanded Feanne, clutching his shoulder. "What was out there?"

"A Turessian necromancer," he answered, gasping for breath.

Turning on his side, Estin watched Asrahn as she knelt beside Ghohar.

"He will likely live," she told him without looking up. "His body is already dead, but it can be mended. Coaxing the spirit back will prove more difficult. We will need to take him back to my circle before too much time has passed."

Estin grabbed Feanne's wrist, telling her in a panic, "The ogre is out there fighting it alone!"

"No," she told him, prying his fingers free. "The ogre has already fallen. I felt his death before we found you. Knowing him as I do, he would have gladly given his life to ensure the escape of someone who's time had not yet come. His death was not without merit."

*

Estin sat in Asrahn's small tent, watching nervously as she tended to Ghohar's body. She was meticulous in her preparations of the corpse, treating it with sweet-smelling herbs and arranging him in the middle of the tent as though he were just sleeping on the floor.

"The spirit will try to return if the body has recovered," she explained to him, placing Ghohar's hands over his chest. Asrahn's expression was one entirely of sympathy. "Using healing magic, I can repair the body and show the spirit the way back. This does not always work, depending on how long the body has been cooling."

Asrahn touched Ghohar's forehead and closed her eyes. She shook her head and sat down beside him.

"The spirit is weak and unsure about returning," she told Estin. "After what you two saw, he likely finds death a safer bet."

Sitting cross-legged on a thin mat within the stone circle at the middle of the tent, where she had arranged Ghohar, Asrahn motioned to Estin to come closer.

"You will assist," she told him, patting the mat alongside her. "Have you ever seen a spirit before?"

Estin shook his head nervously, taking a seat as she indicated.

Asrahn motioned to the stone circle.

"This place allows us to focus on those who have passed beyond the reach of healing," she told him, taking his hand in hers. "You have seen death before?"

"Too many times."

"Good." She held up a small cup of the same herbs she had been applying to the body. "Breathe in the scent of these. It will fog your mind for a time, but will help you understand."

Estin took the cup and sniffed at it, feeling his head spin the moment he took a whiff of the strongly-scented herbs.

"Keep breathing it."

Wincing, he did as ordered, taking a deep breath of the liquid. Slowly he began to calm down, the fear and sadness of the day fading, even as his mind spun, trying to cope with the scents that flooded his mind.

"Now," Asrahn said, taking the cup from him, "what do you see?"

"I see Ghohar's body. And you. And me. I have big feet."

Asrahn laughed at him, rapping him on the bridge of his nose to get his attention.

"Concentrate, child," she ordered, pointing a finger at the body. "Ghohar. What else do you see around his body?"

Estin stared at the corpse of his friend, feeling sadness begin to creep back in even past the concoction Asrahn had given him. His eyes began to water as he studied the raggedly torn flesh that had caked with blood. His whole body was brutalized and matted with blood.

"I see...," he began, choking on the words, then saw something else.

Hovering just over the body was another Ghohar, lingering in the air like smoke. This ghostly form drifted as though it could be blown away at any moment. Like Estin felt, the spirit looked sad, watching its own real body.

"Is that his spirit?" Estin asked, nearly falling backwards out of the circle. "How can I be seeing this?"

"It's the power of the circle," she reminded him, touching his hand. "The drink just relaxed you so that you would stop trying too hard. This is what I see whenever someone has died and their body has been brought in. If you were trained, you could see them any time.

"Some spirits are too weak to even try to come back, or they give up for some reason. These often do not come with the body. We may as well have a stone in the circle for all it matters in that situation.

"Ghohar is willing to at least try to come back if we provide the conduit. He is waiting for us to show him the way back, using the circle as the guide."

Asrahn reached over and stroked Ghohar's forehead. As she touched him, the wounds closed slowly, giving his body a more natural look. Soon he appeared as though he really could be sleeping.

"His body is as well as it can be," she noted, tapping Estin's hand again. This time, Asrahn shifted to the far side of the corpse, as though to watch Estin. "Now it is up to you. His spirit will come to anyone's calling if he desires it, but if it is you, it will relieve him of the fear that you both died."

"What do I do?"

"Speak to him. In there, he can hear you. He will not remember what happened, but he will know that he is dead. Ask him to return. He will know if he can and will likely step back into his body. Then, all I do is tend to him like any other injured."

Steeling himself, Estin gazed up at the floating transparent wolf-like figure. Ghohar stared back at him, as though waiting.

"I am sorry, Ghohar," he said to the ghostly shape. "Please come back to us. Everything is safe now. The necromancer is gone. Asrahn has healed you."

The spirit perched atop its own body, examining the corpse as though looking for remaining injuries. Apparently satisfied, Ghohar's spirit turned its attention back to Estin.

Floating as though walking, the spirit knelt in front of Estin. Though it was unable to speak, Ghohar's spirit reached up and pointed at his own face, gesturing to the heavy wrinkles around his eyes, then to the grey fur that lined his chin and whiskers. He then leaned forward and touched Estin's face, though Estin felt nothing more than a shiver.

Ghohar's spirit then turned to Asrahn, touching her hands gently as though in greeting. He then bowed low before her, then faded and was gone, even as Asrahn gasped.

"What just happened?!?" Estin demanded, rolling onto his feet, frantic as he checked Ghohar's corpse. It was still cold and lifeless. "What did I do wrong?"

"Nothing," Asrahn said sadly, shaking her head. "Ghohar felt that he had lived long enough. That was his way of saying goodbye."

"What was the point of all this then? Why did we try?"

"You cannot make a spirit come back against its will, child. Ghohar made his own decision. Taking that choice away from him is at the heart of what it means to be a necromancer."

Estin swore and kicked the cup of liquid away from him, spraying it across the room.

"How could you do this?" he demanded of Asrahn as he stood and grabbed the tent's flap. "How could anyone want to do this more than once? I just watched a friend die, not just to the necromancer, but at my own hands, while I was trying to save him. I have no desire to ever see that again."

Rushing from the tent, Estin very nearly ran into Feanne, lurking in the darkness outside.

"Out of my way," he snapped, trying to keep from tearing up in front of her. "I need to be alone."

"You missed the most important part of that in there," Feanne said firmly, pressing her hand on his chest to stop him.

"What?"

"You saw your friend die, yes," she told him, blocking his escape. "You also got to say goodbye to your friend, when you should have been denied that chance. Without Asrahn, you would have seen nothing more than his bloody remains."

"Is that better or worse?" he asked, wiping at the tears that he was losing against. "With him killed, I could be angry at the Turessian. Now, I just feel like I have failed."

"Which is better is up to you," said Feanne, lifting her hand off of his chest and lowering her head respectfully. "I cannot make that choice for you. What I will tell you is that if I cannot save my kin, I would give anything to say goodbye. That is not something I am able to do and have regretted it more times in my life than I care to admit."

Estin relaxed a little, seeing his own anger and fears mirrored in Feanne's eyes.

"How often have you gone through this?"

Feanne winced and turned away from him, walking into the night. Though uninvited, Estin followed her.

A short distance out from the tents, Feanne spoke again, though she had not looked up to see that he was still with her.

"My sister was killed by poachers when we were very young," she offered, taking them out of the circle of tents and into the woods. "Besides having watched her die, I've got the blood of many others on my hands. Every time, I watch Asrahn and others with the gift say their farewells, but I can only talk to the air and hope the person hears me. It is never the same. On occasion I can glimpse the spirit in the circle, but it's rare."

They stopped a short ways out in the woods, where the chill night was quiet, aside from bugs making their creaking sounds and the occasional crackle of the melting ice. Estin took a seat as he tried to figure out what to say.

"Do you ever wish to be a healer?" he asked her eventually, but even in the dark he saw the gleam of her teeth as she grinned.

"As much as it pains me to not be a healer, I am what I need to be, Estin. I've said before that we all need to learn what we must to survive out here. What I do for the pack is not popular, but it has saved us more times than I care to admit. My place is in protecting the pack, no matter the pain that causes me."

"Such as losing a mate?"

Feanne snarled audibly, but otherwise did not react at first.

"I lost no such thing," she finally answered. "May I ask what story you were told?"

Estin fidgeted in the dark, trying to remember what little Sohan had told him.

"They say that you let your mate die to save the pack. There hasn't been much more than that."

With an angry flick of her tail, Feanne knelt in front of Estin, grabbing his chin with her fingers.

"Please listen and listen well. A mate is more than someone else's declaration that you belong to someone you have not met. This is something that my father failed to understand when he gave me to another fox-breed when I became an adult. I was to be his, despite having other...plans...for my life.

"The goal my father had in mind was to bring together our pack with another group of wildlings from the far south. They wanted a life-mating to seal the deal. I was apparently the price of that pact. it was a good plan for everyone except me...but I was not asked."

"Why didn't you just run away, or refuse the arrangement?"

"Things are never that simple," she replied, flopping back into a seated position. "In most wildling packs, if an arrangement is made—usually only by the one to be mated, but there are rare cases like mine—then it may normally only be broken by someone proving themselves more worthy by combat for the female. I had no desire for any other male, so asking someone to fight for me was pointless. I did what I had to and accepted the arranged mating.

"The group that was bringing my mate to the ceremony was late that day. They had been attacked by bandits and foolishly led them straight to our camp. My father ordered me to go to my would-be mate and work with his people to save them, while our camp fended for itself.

"I must be honest, I had no feelings for that male's kin or for him...I never knew them. If you were given the choice of fighting to your death to save a stranger who would claim ownership of you, or letting that stranger die to save your own people, which would you choose?"

Estin leaned close to her face and whispered, "You were a stranger. Where would you be if I left you?"

Feanne snapped her head back away from him and stood up quickly.

"I made the choice that I had to. Many lives were saved, but I'll carry the guilt of every life I failed to save for the rest of mine. You need to decide what you will and will not put yourself through to be able to live with what we see out in the wilds."

"Or I could go back to Altis and be executed."

"Or that."

Feanne stood before him for several minutes, her face taught as she watched him. He gave her nothing to work with and soon she touched his shoulder and left, heading towards the woods, rather than the tents.

The cold and damp ground froze Estin's backside and tail as he sat there, staring up at the rising moon. He could not even put to words what he was trying to sort out, but he remained on the dirt hill, watching until the moon passed over him. The moon's passing seemed to prod him to get up and he, struggling with the emotional weight on his shoulders, began to slowly walk back into the camp.

He passed the few patrols the pack always had out in the woods, though he barely saw them out in the trees. They were far more stealthy than he was and better trained for the woodland environment. Beyond them, he moved through several armored warriors, including Ulra, all of whom were relaxing within the camp, but on duty in case a call came up from the outer patrols. These wildlings were the strong, the tough, and the most willing to go toe-to-toe with the enemy if the camp were attacked. Again, he reminded himself, he certainly did not fit in there.

All his life he had raised himself to run away and hide. Now, looking around at the dozens of wildlings, he found that there was something worth staying for. Something worth defending. He just had no idea how to do it and felt entirely helpless having watched Ghohar die without having any means to aid him. He had thought he could manage himself with a weapon, but twice he had failed his companions, first with Varra and now Ghohar.

Frustration and anger welled in him, both things that he had been forced to ignore growing up. Being an outcast who can be skinned by others without remorse tended to be mind-numbingly frustrating, but he had no choice but to endure and accept. He had learned to do so quite well, he felt, but the threats were always against his own person, not against others. Anyone else's plight was something he could easily ignore. Now, all of his nightmares—the hunters, the walking dead, all of it—was very real and hurting people that he had begun to care about.

Without realizing it, he found that he had wandered the length of the camp and now stood before the tiny tent that had been set up for him. He felt his shoulders sink as he lifted the flap and looked inside.

The tent was more than he had been able to call his own back in Altis. Ten feet of dry ground where no one was trying to stab him in the face with a sword was practically a mansion to someone from the slums, but this place had always felt empty. The city had been awful, but there were people everywhere, often in much the same position of life as Estin. The dry quiet of his tent had made him wonder many times what those others were doing now and what he should be doing.

These were not even people he particularly cared about—the pushy prostitute from the tavern district, the grocer near the temple who screamed and yelled about Estin being vermin but still left him food every night, and even one of the city guards that had "accidentally" let him escape more times than he could count. These were not good people, not even people he would help in a pinch, but they were the faces that came to mind. He remembered how they had looked, but his mind raced, showing him these same people with rotting flesh and that hateful blank stare that the walking dead had fixed on him right before it tried to rip him apart. Whether he cared about these people specifically, he could not in good conscience allow more to end up like those at the caravan. Possibly like Varra.

The thoughts made Estin's stomach churn and he knelt by the tent flap, retching with the image of desiccated corpses marching through the city, tearing the citizens apart. In each death, he saw Varra's face as the life left her.

Tapping his forehead against the dry ground, choking with anguish, he sobbed and went over the fight in the woods yet again in his memories, finding dozens of mistakes he had made. He found a thousand ways that he believed he could have saved Ghohar, but his rational mind kept reminding him that this was just not true. It was simply a miracle that either of them had survived, but guilt plagued him that he could have done something different.

Gasping for breath as he knelt, Estin raised his head and looked into the tent. There was nothing in there that would quench his heart's tears, aside from curling into blankets and drinking a small keg of ale that had been left for him. He knew neither sleep or beverage would help at this point.

Estin sat up, moving his sword so that he was not sitting on the blade, when his hand fell on the bag and scroll-tube he had taken from the wagon. The bag of coins and tools he threw into the tent, but he pulled the tube from his belt and turned it over in his hands.

The wood itself was engraved heavily with symbols and flowing patterns in a thick lacquer that had been painted many layers deep. He doubted that the wood would be easily damaged by rain or could be cracked even from a heavy blow, without destroying the contents.

Upon examining the caps and the intricate lock, Estin began to wonder what would be so valuable to protect in this manner. Even in the duke's keep, there were few individual items that he could picture being worth a case of this expense. It would have been far cheaper to simply hire more guards to protect it.

He pried at the caps, finding them sealed perfectly. Without opening the lock, he doubted he could find out what was inside and whether it had anything to do with why the Turessian had attacked the wagons.

Estin tipped the tube end over end, examining the lock from different angles. He had picked many in his fairly inept life of crime working for Nyess, but they had always been simple and poorly-made. This one made his head hurt to even figure out how the pieces fit together inside. He was certain that half of the pins he could see inside were misleading and intended to break off or jam the lock if mishandled, but it was far beyond his skill to determine how best to proceed.

He sat there for some time, staring at the tube and wondering if he really cared enough to find someone else to open it. At one point, he set it aside, finding his thoughts quickly sinking into sorrow for the deaths he had witnessed that night. It made him feel sick to his stomach and he grabbed at the scroll casing once again, trying to immerse himself in something, in the hopes that it would at least keep his mind busy.

Eventually, he knew it was beyond his ability to even guess at how to proceed and he was losing his battle against his thoughts. Estin decided that he needed to find someone else who might be able to work on it, both for the extra set of hands and for someone to talk to, other than his own dark thoughts.

Estin climbed to his feet and slowly walked into the quiet camp, hearing only occasional smatterings of conversation among those who were still awake.

At first, he was not sure where to turn for help. The majority of the residents of the camp were from the wilds and had little dealings with the cities. That meant their knowledge of locks was likely far less than his own.

A thought came to mind, giving Estin some direction. When he had first come to the camp, he had been instructed to present himself to the pack-leader Lihuan. At the time, Estin had been forced to wait an hour to speak with the man, as he had been in the middle of a lengthy tale about his escape from slavers when he was young. It had been dramatically embellished, including a young and gorgeous female, many elaborate battles, and travels over deserts and mountains. What stood out in Estin's mind was a section of the story where Lihuan had claimed that he had been forced to free himself and his lover from not only their own chains, but had also managed to free many of the elders of the camp who had been enslaved with them. That meant he might know how to handle a lock.

Estin had given little thought of Lihuan since his arrival, as the pack-leader was generally busy either entertaining the younger members of the pack with his tales, or on his way to deal with one reckless youth or another who thought they were better suited to leading the pack. Three times already, Estin had watched the old fox soundly trounce contenders as young as Estin, usually using trickery and manipulation, rather than strength. Once though, Estin had watched in shock as Lihuan had torn a young badger up badly, showing an agility that he never would have guessed of anyone his age—though Lihuan had made no public appearances for a day or two afterwards, likely to recover.

Before he had finished thinking through his few meetings with Feanne's father, Estin found himself already at the entrance to the tent, surprising himself.

Estin stood before the tent for longer than he meant to, debating whether this was worth intruding on Lihuan. He had no other idea of where to turn for advice. If anyone in the camp might have the knowledge to help, or might know a locksmith or skilled thief, Lihuan was likely the only one.

After finally getting up the nerve to go in, Estin stepped up to the tent's entrance and spoke up.

"Lihuan," he called out. "It's Estin. I need to talk."

"Let him in," said a calm voice inside—Lihuan's he recognized—sounding well awake and fairly unsurprised. Estin could only guess that he had been smelled as he approached.

"Kiss my hairy backside," muttered a deeper male voice, as the tent flap was thrown open.

The dwarf Finth stood in the opening, glaring out at Estin. His beard hung raggedly, and a thick collar was fastened around his neck, though it was just buckled and could have been easily removed.

"What by my jiggling ass do you want?" demanded the dwarf, crossing his arms over his chest. "His royal fuzziness is really busy."

"Let him in, dwarf," ordered someone farther in the tent where Estin could not see. "Don't make me repeat myself again, or I'll turn you over to the young rabbits. They did say that they needed extra hands with collecting firewood…and I hear they like to dress up their playthings in the same way human children treat dolls."

Finth glowered and shoved a thumb at the inside of the tent, muttering something unseemly under his breath.

"Get inside, monkey," he grumbled. "His lord high fur-bag has commanded it."

Glaring at the dwarf in passing, Estin stepped into the dimly-lit tent, where furs lay in piles throughout. At one end of the tent, Lihuan sat reclining against a rolled up stack of animal furs. Unlike Feanne, his fur had faded to a mostly-grey color around his face, though hints of red still appeared in the torchlight in places. He wore a motley collection of furs and hides, though a beaded necklace like the one Estin had found at the duke's keep adorned his neck. Several faint lines in his fur revealed ancient scars, likely from challengers.

"I believe you've already met my pet," Lihuan stated, gesturing towards Finth. "He refuses to give us information regarding his masters, so I have been forced to keep him as a servant. It was hardly my first choice."

"I think his first choice was to see if it really is possible to lick his own balls," noted Finth, who then acted shocked. "Oh, is that an insult among your kind? So sorry."

"I would be more offended if it were the first time you came up with that joke. I have asked you to at least be original."

The dwarf shrugged and sat down hard on a pile of furs.

"I don't have a lot of material to work with," Finth griped, crossing his arms over his barrel chest. "You people are boring."

"Ignoring our antisocial guest," Lihuan said, sitting up with a soft crackle of old joints, "how can I help you? I am guessing you did not stop by simply to see how well I was sleeping."

"No," Estin said sadly, sitting down in front of the pack's elder. "I am guessing you heard that Ghohar and the ogre died tonight?"

Lihuan's eyes seemed to flare with a younger male's fire, but he just said, "I had. I make it my business to know all the stories told in this camp. Despite this, Asrahn has not deemed it important enough to inform me yet. I would assume she is tending to the bodies before coming to me with this. I am no healer and often I am not told of these things until all has been arranged. Others prefer to take these duties on themselves."

Estin set the scroll case on the ground between them.

"I found this among several wagons that had been attacked. Those manning them I believe were taken by a Turessian and used to create more undead. These are what attacked Ghohar and I. This scroll was all I found in the wagons that might tell us why."

Lihuan leaned forward and picked up the case with his long claws, his eyes drifting over the paintings on the tube.

"You do not know much about the Turessians," he said, as much a statement as a question. "They turn their ancestors into abominations. They have no reason to be in these lands."

"I have seen them myself in the duke's court."

Lihuan looked up from the scroll tube, as though weighing Estin's response.

"I am not saying you are wrong. I am saying that what we know of them would not lead them here. You believe this contains information that may explain why death-worshipers might be in Altis?"

"I do." Estin glared at the scroll casing and then shook his head. "I cannot open it. Whatever is inside is all I have left that might tell me what Ghohar and the ogre died for."

"We die because that is the way of life," Lihuan explained, eyeing the lock carefully.

"What is in here will not give you peace."

Estin nodded.

"I know. I don't expect it to."

Prodding the lock with one of his claws, Lihuan glared at it briefly, then tossed the scroll tube in front of Finth.

"This design I have seen before," he explained. "If I were to make a mistake, the mechanism would destroy the contents of the tube and might also burst into flames. I have no desire to burn myself this evening."

Behind Estin, another person entered the tent quietly, taking a seat behind and off to one side of Estin. He sniffed instinctively, recognizing Asrahn.

"Asrahn, this youth has come to tell me of the deaths tonight."

The elder feline growled something, then replied, "Yes, Lihuan. We have lost two spirits tonight. I was unable to bring them back. Ghohar is ready for the pyre in the morning. The ogre's body is not accounted for, but we hope to find him by morning."

"We had no healer out in the woods with them, I presume?"

Estin felt the tension in the room grow until Asrahn answered with a bite in her tone that told him she was barely maintaining a respectful tone.

"Lihuan, you know as well as I do that we lack healers. Would you have me go out with every patrol? There are no others and I am hardly young enough to keep up with them all. The last few you sent to me to train were hardly worth my time. They had no pity for the spirits they faced and no desire to help others."

Estin turned and glanced at Asrahn, whose feline features were twisted in anger. He doubted anything more than respect for the pack leader was keeping her from clawing at him, even at her age.

"What about Feanne's mother?" Estin asked, watching for Lihuan's reaction. "Feanne said that her mother was also a skilled healer."

"Are you dense, child?" Asrahn asked, her anger lost in a quizzical glare. "I'm her mother."

Estin blinked and stared at Asrahn, trying to make out the animal features that made her look somewhat less like a cat.

"Well this is just damned awkward," blurted out Finth with a bellowing laugh. "The striped monkey didn't even recognize the girl's mom. That kind of thing makes one feel really stupid, eh dummy?"

"Ignoring our guest, this is true," said Lihuan, leaning back against the furs with a deep sigh. "Feanne is a half-breed, as are many of the young around here. It is not something we hide, but it appears it has been forgotten around the camp since Asrahn and I stopped being seen together. Times past, there were no packs, so it was often not possible to find another wildling of your own breed."

Asrahn shot Lihuan a glare, but then softened as she told Estin, "My mother was a lioness and my father a grey fox. Feanne took only the attitude from my mother's side. The looks she must blame her father for."

Nodding, Lihuan gave Estin a hopeless look.

Estin glanced between the two elders, but lost his train of thought as a loud click cut through the silence in the room. He turned to Finth, who had something under his meaty arms.

"Show it to us," ordered Lihuan, motioning to the dwarf.

Finth made a clearly fake look of surprise.

"Me?" he asked. "What do you mean?"

All three wildlings glared at him until he spit on the ground and pulled out the scroll case, the lock open and one end's cap removed.

"It was an accident?" he tried half-heartedly, then tossed the tube onto the floor. "Damn it all, just read it. I was getting sick listening to animal family drama."

Estin began to reach for the scroll, but Lihuan leaned forward and grabbed it first.

Sliding a single rolled piece of parchment from the rube, the elder fox examined it carefully, then checked the tube for anything further. He shook it and a flat piece of metal fell out into his palm.

"The king of Lantonne's crest," he noted, flipping the metal disc in his hand. "I would not have expected to find this within fifty miles of Altis' lands. These tokens are sent as proof of importance with official documents. That would mean that this parchment comes from Lantonne, as did the people on those wagons."

"The suspense is killing me," muttered the dwarf, rolling his eyes.

Lihuan shot him a glance, noting, "One can hope."

With care, Lihuan picked up the parchment roll with his claws, examining the outside and the large wax seal on it.

"Again, the king's crest." He tapped the wax seal. "The parchment itself is still dry. The casing was well closed, but as wet as it has been lately, the parchment would have still become damp if it were out there long. This was freshly abandoned."

Asrahn touched Estin's wrist, drawing his attention briefly. She motioned emphatically towards a leather strap that lay along the floor.

Estin grabbed the long leather strap to hand it to her, but the cord went tight suddenly. Following the length, he saw Finth at the edge of the tent, stopped with the leather cord taught against his neck.

"Almost got out that time," he muttered, stomping back over to sit with the others. "You're getting sloppy."

Lihuan smiled as he examined the scroll.

"No. I gave someone else the chance to choke you. Such joys should be shared."

With a flick of his claw, Lihuan broke the wax circle that held the scroll closed. He unrolled it carefully, as though the paper might crumble at his touch. His eyes were impassive as he began reading, but a twitch near the corner of his eye gave away his surprise.

"We may have issues," announced Lihuan, looking first to Asrahn, then to Estin. "This is a royal declaration of peace.

"At the beginning, the king of Lantonne admonishes Altis for their escalation of the recent war. You may or may not know, but this war is quite mutual and has been ongoing in some form for nearly three lifetimes.

"In this writing though, the king offers to pay Altis for all the damages they incurred in the course of the war, despite noting that Altis has been on the verge of falling for years. His request is simply a treaty of mutual peace, so long as Altis abides by one request."

"Which is?" asked Estin.

"Apparently," the elder answered, unrolling another section of the parchment, "Altis has signed another treaty. They have, according to this document, partnered with the Turessians to provide troops and security for Altis. Lantonne feels that they do not know the depth of danger in allowing the Turessians to act without limitation in their efforts to supplement the army. It would seem that Lantonne believes Altis is losing its identity to their guests."

"So the creepy corpse-lovers are giving Altis help, which everyone else in the realm considers a really bad idea. Who cares?" grumbled the dwarf, picking something out of his beard. "I couldn't care less, so long as they aren't in my house...tent...this place."

"That is where you underestimate," Lihuan replied, but also gave Finth's leash a tug, throwing him off-balance. "The last section of the missive reads, 'They will use you and your citizens for their own ends, as has been seen in other lands.' It even goes on to list eight other kingdoms that allied with the Turessians and are now considered their serfs. It would appear Lantonne would give up the war in favor of just having the Turessians leave."

The tent was quiet as they contemplated, with Estin wondering just how deep the hole he had walked into had become. One day he had no idea that Altis was in trouble, the next there were Turessian diplomats in the duke's halls, and now talk of necromancers overthrowing a government.

"How big of a threat are they?" Estin asked of whoever could answer.

Lihuan spoke first, his cool eyes studying Estin as he spoke. He seemed to do that to each person he addressed, sizing them up, as if he were contemplating many other things while speaking.

"If they just sent a few necromancers, it is troublesome, but the duke can easily send them away or execute them. The weakest link with necromancy is always the caster."

"That may not be accurate here," interrupted Asrahn. "This is not just someone protecting a business deal. The clans of Turessi would not wipe out a diplomatic caravan just to hide their business arrangements. While I was tending to Ghohar, Estin told me that the Turessian was still standing after wounds that should have killed it."

Lihuan appeared to consider this, though he kept his eyes on Finth.

"How grave were its wounds?"

Estin chilled at the memory, but related the various magical attacks from Ghohar, the sword through the Turessian's chest, and the severed hand. With each item, Lihuan's mood seemed to darken.

"Turessians do not change their own, except in honor of their service in life and even then, they remain with their tribe. If you fought one wearing their robes who is turned, that would be very strange and does not fit with what I know of the Turessians."

"Have you dealt with them much, pack leader?"

Lihuan regarded Estin coolly, then pointed out the slave scars that were just barely visible on his shoulder—a match for the ones Asrahn had shown him earlier.

"I know what it is like to live in their lowest caste and be delegated to working in a copper mine to pay off a debt for having stolen bread. That is not to say I know everything about them, just more than most in these areas."

Scraping from nearby drew their attention back to Finth, who was scratching his back with an ornately-carved walking stick.

"Do you seriously have no manners whatsoever?" asked Lihuan, as though talking to a child. "I honestly cannot tell if you are mad, or if you are trying to make me so."

"I'm sober and have no idea what to do with myself," he answered, tossing the cane aside. "Been almost a month sober. Do you have any idea what that does to a dwarf?"

"I know what your actions will do to a dwarf...Ulra, please remove him."

The back of the tent opened abruptly, as though the bear had been waiting for the command. She reached in and grabbed Finth with a large paw as he screamed and tried to scramble away.

"Bathe him and teach him to be less ignorant," Lihuan told her and the far larger wildling bowed her head slightly, then dragged Finth from the tent.

"She honestly has been hoping I would give him up soon," Lihuan explained to Estin. "She seems to think dwarves are a lot like her own children. Bulky, overbearing, and in need of a mother's firm hand. I protected him as long as I could."

Estin clenched his jaw, trying not to laugh at the idea of Ulra washing the dwarf and treating him like a cub. He figured that was the least that could happen to one of Nyess' servants.

"Now, what to do about all of this?" asked Lihuan in general, though likely as much to himself as to the others present. He paused as Finth's vague threats and curses drifted in, then continued without comment, "The duke is unlikely to listen to us, as evidenced by Feanne's attempts. We are much too far from Lantonne to advise them, not that they are more likely to accept us into their walls. Unless either of you has a better plan, I believe for now I would like to keep this secret and use the knowledge to prepare the pack and be ready for changes in the local mood."

Estin was unsure whether he really had any right to speak his thoughts to the pack's leader and glanced at Asrahn for support. She ignored him pointedly.

"I would ask something," she inquired of Lihuan, ears perking slightly.

Lihuan lifted a brow and cocked his head.

"It has been a long time since you did much more than disagree with me behind my back and give rise to challengers to my authority. This I wish to hear. Speak."

"You have the authority here to order anyone of the right mindset to take a profession. I have received requests from the gatherers, as well as several of the cooks to have Estin join their ranks. While useful, I feel it would be far more beneficial for the camp to have someone new studying healing magic. I believe this will be essential if we are to fight the Turessian undead, unless you expect me to lead the battle. Would you agree, my pack-leader?"

"Do not call me that, female," he snarled back at her. "I have been your mate for longer than most of the pack has lived and nearly a generation longer than there was a pack. You know as well as I do that we have had need of younger healers for years and our last attempts to train someone went badly. Those two that you trained last year can barely fix a sprained ankle. Have you a new plan for this one, I take it? Or are you just claiming each new member of the pack?"

Estin noticed Asrahn's glance at him and went immediately defensive.

"Wait, no! I'm a really bad warrior, but that's what I'm built for. Magic is not my thing. I can help the hunters…"

"No?" Lihuan asked, his face going stern and his eyes cold. "Did you just tell me...no?"

"I...sort of…"

"Estin Ringtail, you will either submit to Asrahn's decision and attempt to learn, or I will banish you from this pack. This was not a discussion. If you doubt whether I will do it, please say no again. If you fail to learn, we will find a new role for you, but so long as there is hope that you can learn anything, I am placing you under Asrahn's control. Understood?"

Working his mouth to try and argue, Estin could only stare at those cold eyes that seemed to bore through him. For a moment, he remembered a similar look his mother had given him when he had thrown a rock at his sister as a child...though his mother had been holding him off the ground by the scruff of his neck at the time.

"I'll do what I can," he finally gave in, letting his head hang. There was no sense in hiding how he felt. "I promised to help the pack as I'm able. If I can learn to heal, I will."

Asrahn practically cackled beside him, clapping her hands happily. She snatched a quill, ink, and a scrap of old parchment from a pile of miscellaneous items at one side of the tent and began scratching out something.

"Why do I feel like I've just written a death sentence for you?" Lihuan inquired, trying to see what his mate was writing. "Asrahn...dear...what are you doing? Do not make me go back on the pledge I just dragged out of this child."

"Now that you are bound to Lihuan's command," she mumbled, scribbling one final note, then folding up the parchment tightly, "I will use that to my own ends...though it rather was to begin with. Regardless, your first task as my apprentice will be to learn things from others in the camp. Each person I send you to will be able to educate you on something that will make learning magic from me far easier.

"You will take this note to each in turn, without reading it yourself. If you do, I'll find out. You will do what they tell you to do without question. You only need know that what you are doing is essential to the survival of the pack. I'll tell you how at a later time."

Estin took the offered parchment and looked over at Lihuan, who was rubbing his temples and suppressing chuckles.

"Yes, it's her way," he answered without looking up. "The tales of what she put me through at our mating ceremony would be the thing of legend. She really just enjoys doing this to people. Sometimes I believe I'm still pack-leader just because others fear that she would take over."

"Lies!" Asrahn snapped. "It's all to make you silly males better people. How is it my fault that you need this much work?"

"You see?" Lihuan noted, sounding broken. "We spend our youth chasing them, only to learn that this is why we grow old...to get away from them."

"I...where am I going with this note?" Estin asked, starting to feel awkward even being there any longer. He had the feeling that if he stayed, his tasks would only get worse.

Asrahn grinned, revealing sharp teeth.

"Go to Feanne first."

"Oh hells, female," groaned Lihuan. "Just drown the poor child. Training with her will kill any breed not built for violence…and likely some that are."

Asrahn just ignored Lihuan and shoved Estin towards the tent's flap, saying, "Head north out of camp. You can find her a short distance away."

"Estin, if you work with Asrahn on this, I will make it worth your while," called Lihuan. "We need healers badly, so I'll put up with her games, if you will."

"But I don't know where Feanne has her tent. Can you be more specific?"

"Not really," Asrahn admitted. "She does not have a tent, so her resting place changes often. This is part of your task."

With that, she pulled the tent shut and left Estin alone in the dark outside.

"She is insane," he whispered to himself, then turned and walked away, heading at first towards his tent in the southeast corner of the camp.

Halfway across the camp, Estin stopped and glanced down at the note she had given him. It was unsealed, untied, and just folded several times. He could easily check the contents if he desired.

He looked around at the sleeping camp, the badly-sewn canvas or hide tents swaying in the steady breeze that nearly always swept through the area. There were few awake and none that he was willing to talk this over with.

Sohan, he might talk to, but if he woke up the ferret, he would be stuck talking to him all night and well into the day. Ulra was awake...and he could hear splashing water and angry shouts from somewhere in the northeast part of camp. He honestly did not know many of the others well enough to seek advice.

Estin turned to head north, seeing no other options at this time, other than to leave the pack and not come back. Somehow that did not seem to be a real option, so he picked his way through the haphazardly placed tents, until he came to an open area in the middle of the village.

Situated on a bier of dry wood, Ghohar's body lay for display. From what he had heard of the funerary rights of the wildlings of the area, they would leave him until the next evening, giving everyone the opportunity to say their goodbyes. At that time, his body would be burned, thus foiling any would-be furriers or others who would despoil the body. In the meantime, a single guard was set to protect the corpse from carrion animals and birds.

The guard who was present was not someone that Estin knew. He was a wolf—like Ghohar—and likely much younger than Estin, but was standing at a rigid attention that implied extensive combat training that Estin lacked. The wolf's posture and self-confident appearance put Estin off-ease and slowed his approach. At a cursory glance, Estin could have mistaken the youth for Ghohar.

"Please continue along," the wolf advised him as he approached. "Night is not the time to deal with the dead."

Estin stopped a short distance away and studied the body. His friend already looked to have withered in death, despite Asrahn's attempts to heal the body. Now, he looked stiff and cold, which had seemed to be delayed by the initial mending. Though earlier he had looked to be still and sleeping, now it was apparent that he had passed beyond life.

Wordlessly, he continued past the guard, though he could feel the other's eyes on him until he was well away from the bier.

It took about ten minutes to pass the last tent, given how erratically spaced they were. This was partially due to the varying size of the wildlings here, but also their breeds played a large part in it. When he had first arrived, Feanne had explained that the southern section—where Estin stayed—was mostly filled with animal-types that were at least primarily herbivores, though a great many were omnivores. Those who ate flesh as their main sustenance were here on the north end, helping to cut down on instinctual fights that Lihuan had no desire to deal with directly.

From what Estin had heard, early in the pack's existence, one of Lihuan's brothers had killed a young elk wildling during an argument that had mostly escalated from a misunderstanding. The pack had all but written it off as the way that a predator-breed would act towards prey. Lihuan had ordered his own brother executed. Since then, there had been no more major breed-related fights that anyone could remember, but precautions such as the camp arrangement had been quickly put in place.

Beyond the last tent, the woods loomed dark and whispering with the sounds of animals that Estin could not always identify. He stopped there, staring into the dark trees and wondering why the dark was scary for a night-breed wildling, especially one who had run through the dark streets of Altis for years without any regard for safety.

"Undead."

The word leapt to his mind instantly, explaining away his fear. He knew what the bogeyman of his nightmares was, now. It was not a vague oppressor like the duke. Neither was it the omnipresent sense of being less than any of the other sentient races. It was fear of death...death that got up from its grave and clawed for your eyes. He had seen that embodied twice now and he knew that it was what would haunt him for some time. All other fears seemed irrelevant by comparison.

He took a deep breath and strode into the night, sweeping his attention back and forth across the trees to watch for anything that might strike out at him. Soon after losing sight of the tents, Estin froze and realized with dismay that he had left his weapon back at the camp. He had nothing to fight with.

Cursing himself for his foolishness, he moved more quickly, trying to find any indication of Feanne's passing. There was no scent that he could not find in any other part of the woods. He could see no tracks, aside from the occasional deer or rabbit prints in the wet soil. For all he could tell, no one had come this way in weeks. The recent freezing rains should have made any tracks very clear to him.

"Are you an idiot?" whispered a soft voice nearby, making Estin spin.

Hunkered down near the base of a tree trunk, white eyes stared at him, though the speaker's body was concealed by the overgrowth. The only thing beyond eyes that he could see was the white mist of breath in the cold air.

"Feanne?"

"Thankfully. There are darker things out in these woods at night, Estin. You do not belong out here. Anything north of camp is my realm. Go back to your tent."

He almost obeyed, but then stopped, fishing the parchment from his belt.

"Asrahn insisted," he explained, holding it out to her. He had no idea if her vision was good enough to read in the dark, but he assumed it was, as he could. "She wanted me to bring this to you."

"It could have waited until morning."

Feanne stood and walked smoothly towards him, snatching the note from his fingers. Without word, she unfolded the parchment and raised it close to her nose as she read whatever was written on it.

"There is a misunderstanding," she said firmly, refolding the paper and holding it back out towards him. "You need to go back to camp and tell Asrahn 'no.'"

"I can't do that, Feanne. Your father said he would banish me if I refused."

"You are not refusing...I am. Banishment is safer for you, anyway."

"Feanne, I need this. I have nowhere else to go. I want to do what I can to help the pack."

She stared at him longer than he felt comfortable with, then tucked the parchment into her leather vest. Silently, she spun and began walking north.

"Either come along or go back to your tent. I will not argue further," she told him as she faded from his vision in the dark. For a moment, he could see only the white tip of her tail swaying into the darkness, then it was gone, too. "If you follow me, I will not accept any guilt over your death."

"I'm loving the options," Estin grumbled, eyeing the sky. It was heavily overcast, giving him little chance of tracking her if she got very far. Already he was losing her scent somehow, though he normally could follow an identifiable scent for hours after the person had left.

"Should I grab my sword?" he called out after her.

"Do you really think that will protect you out here?" came the soft reply somewhere far ahead.

Estin ran to catch up, but found himself struggling to find where Feanne had gone. Mist was hanging low on the ground, covering any tracks. She left no appreciable scent and had seemingly not touched the trees or bushes, thus leaving no marks there. He froze, hoping not to get too much farther off-path.

"Feanne?"

The night was silent. Not even the random chatter of animals an bugs could be heard.

On a whim, Estin glanced back towards the camp, where the central torches had been visible for nearly a mile during his patrols with Ghohar if one knew where to look. He saw nothing back that way, only more trees and impenetrable darkness.

"What do you hope to gain from Asrahn's teaching?" whispered Feanne, as though in his ear, but when he spun, she was nowhere to be seen.

"I'm just hoping to keep from being kicked out of the pack."

"Would that truly be so bad?"

"Feanne, this is the only family I have left. I want to stay."

"You can cook. Tend to the young. I hear there is a dwarf who needs bathing. Perhaps you do not serve us best as a healer."

Estin spun in place, trying to figure out where the fox was hiding, but her voice moved each time she spoke. On a whim he looked up, but unsurprisingly, she was not in the trees overhead.

"I will not be just another set of hands in the camp," he told her, trying to calm himself. The night felt as though it were closing in on him. "I want to truly help."

"I help and yet I am no healer. Who do you think keeps the patrols from having to fight off humans nearly every night. Who do you believe provides more protection for this pack...you or I?"

"This isn't about taking a job from someone else. I want to be useful."

Sharp laughter seemed to slap him down.

"Do you understand what happened to the last healer Asrahn trained, Estin?"

He froze as he heard footfalls somewhere nearby.

"No..."

Gleaming waist-level eyes opened all around him, boxing him in. The scent of wolves washed over him all at once and a low growl from many throats began.

"I found another way," Feanne answered, stepping back into his sight. The other eyes blinked occasionally but did not move. "I found a proper way to protect my people. Healing them will never keep up with the harm that the city-folk can heap upon us. You wish to tend to cuts and bruises, while the forest burns around you. This will never work."

Estin listened, but kept turning, trying to get an eye on the other figures in the woods. There were at least eight wolves by his count, but for some reason they ignored Feanne and she them.

"When the soldiers march into the camp," she continued, stepping lightly as she circled him, her paws coming down silently, "and they will, what will you do? The best of Asrahn's teaching will let you restore one of our warriors who has fallen at a given moment. A hundred soldiers will come, maybe a thousand. It will not be a single warrior, but all of them. They will fall all at once, while you stand there wondering who to heal first. What will you do then, Estin?"

"I'll heal Asrahn."

Feanne stopped walking and regarded him with curiosity.

"Why? I thought you would say that you would heal me or even Ulra."

Estin felt, rather than saw, one of the wolves move and he turned to face it, which put his back to Feanne.

"I would heal her, because she can help me heal others. It only makes sense, if I were a healer, which I'm not."

"If you are no healer, then you will need to be able to fight."

Estin expected an attack from her as she growled the last word, but when he turned she was gone again. Instead, the wolves advanced.

"Can you fight off the army when it comes?" called Feanne from somewhere out in the trees. "These wolves will show more concern for you than many of the duke's men. My mother's teaching will not help you if you are dead before you can heal anyone. Prove to me that you can survive long enough to make a difference. I will not spare you."

Fangs and claws erupted from all directions and the wolves began darting across his path, first one, then another, quickly closing their ranks around him. One beast brushed against his tail in passing, making him spin, only to have another nip his shoulder as it went past him.

"Defend yourself!" commanded Feanne, her voice coming from another direction now. "I cannot call them off anymore."

Estin rolled as another wolf leapt past him, avoiding a nip from the animal, but wound up barreling into yet another wolf. This one reacted swiftly, trying to get its teeth into him, but Estin kicked as hard as he could, bowling the beast over onto its back. As he did, he heard the others rushing towards him, their paws pounding the dirt like a stampede.

"You have weapons, Estin, so use them!"

Frantic as he was knocked to his back by another of the wolves, Estin punched the animal in the jaw as hard as he could, but it just pulled back an inch or two, then lunged at him again, going for his throat.

Estin could feel the other wolves around him, but he could not look away from the one atop him as he fought to keep both his hands on its neck to hold it back. He was surrounded by the snarling beasts and could only think of how close he had come to a similar death when saving Feanne.

He remembered then that he had something this time that he did not have back in the keep. Trees.

Rolling hard to one side to shake the wolf, Estin leapt by shoving off of the animal towards the nearest tree. He hit it hard, but scrambled up and out of the reach of the wolves, who circled below, unable to reach him.

"That wasn't exactly what I had in mind," Feanne told him begrudgingly, stepping back into view. "A tree is not your weapon."

"Might not be, but it got me out of there alive."

Feanne made several motions with her hands and whispered something, then the wolves began to scatter, behaving all the while as though they could not even see her. She walked up to the tree and lay one hand on it.

"It may not be your weapon, but it is mine."

With a lurch, the entire tree swept from one side and then the other, as though trying to dislodge Estin. He clung tightly until the tree slammed into one of its neighbors, sending him tumbling onto the ground.

"Are you insane?" he shouted at Feanne, facing off against her. "Not even getting into how you did that, why did you?"

She smiled sweetly at him, then took a step back as a thick tree branch crashed between them, sending pine needles and loose soil in all directions. When the air cleared, Estin could no longer find Feanne.

"Asrahn requires dedication, skill, and someone who can fight for the camp, even if she thinks she needs another healer to lighten her load," she answered from yet another hiding place in the woods. "You are not the one, Estin. Run back to camp. I will keep this up until you run or die. We will find something else for you to do."

A slick black glob of oily tar slammed into Estin's chest, knocking him onto his back. He started to just get back up when he felt nausea wrack him and his head began to spin. In a hurry, he ripped off his shirt and tossed it away, along with most of the tarry goo. The small amount that remained on his fur still seemed to ooze some kind of noxious fumes, but he was able to push past the feelings of vertigo and sickness.

"You see what others can do," purred Feanne this time, her voice coming from a new direction with each word. "Ghohar, Ulra, myself...we have the strength to fight for our people. Would you give up the ability to fight and instead leave a battle to help the fallen?"

The nearby bushes lashed out, thin cordlike branches entangling his legs and arms, dragging him to his knees. They tightened, making him gasp in pain as his hands and feet went numb.

From the darkness, Feanne emerged again, this time calmly walking straight towards him. Wherever she stepped, the living bushes flinched away, clearing her path.

"We need warriors, Estin. You disappoint me."

Feanne lifted her hands from her sides, extending her fingers so that her claws were visible. As she did, her entire hands, claws and all, grew to obscene proportions. Her monstrous claws were larger than Ulra's and from their appearance, Estin guessed she could tear an armored soldier apart.

"That how we got through the soldiers in Altis?" he asked her. "You changed and killed them yourself?"

"At last you start to understand."

She stepped over him, raising one large claw.

"Surrender and I will send you back to the camp. You have this one chance. My way does not allow for weakness."

Estin studied her face in the dim moonlight and knew that she was not going to hesitate. There was no compassion, no question of what she was going to do. He lowered his eyes and looked around at the branches that still held him, which were wiggling and shifting to keep from being near her feet.

"Do it. I'm not going back, just to be banished."

The claws fell faster than he expected, but Estin did his best to fall sideways, letting his hands be in the way of the attack. As Feanne's claws neared his bonds, the plants snapped free and raced away, allowing him to slide out from under her, taking only one painful slice across the back of his wrist where one claw caught him.

"Now that," she told him, watching him from the corner of her eye, "was clever."

She turned to fully face him, her hands shrinking back to normal size. Raising her hands slightly, she displayed her claws to him.

"Can you fight me like this?"

Estin checked around in the trees for any other tricks, but saw nothing.

"I can try."

Feanne wasted not a second, leaping into him, bowling him over. She slashed his chest three times with her claws, then rolled backwards, raking him once more with her toe-claws as she escaped him. She stopped herself in a crouch just outside his reach, her grin making her white teeth look wicked in the moonlight.

Grunting in pain, Estin pushed himself back onto his feet, feeling blood warm and sticky in his fur. Raising his fists, he tried to face off against her again, but Feanne stayed in her low crouch, watching him move.

"You cannot fight like this if you expect to win," she teased, slowly easing herself to standing. "Walk up to me and strike me, if you can."

Estin approached cautiously, expecting her to strike. Not a muscle twitched and her eyes were calm. She gave him nothing.

He punched at her face, but Feanne leaned out of the way, grabbing a handful of his side's fur and flesh in her claws.

"Right now, we have a problem, Estin. If I wished, I could open your side and you would bleed to death before anyone from camp found you."

Twisted in a position that gave him no easy reach to strike at her, Estin gasped for air as her claws dug deeper into his side. He could drive his elbow into her arm, but that would only further the problem.

"Say it. Say that you will yield. Asrahn's whim is not worth your death."

Feanne's other hand clamped down on the back of his neck, claws finding his spine.

"This can only end two ways. You need to choose quickly."

Immobilized and feeling the tips of her claws cutting through his flesh, Estin was nearly delirious with pain. As he attempted to twitch his way free of either grip, his tail slid across her feet, which she appeared not to notice.

Summoning the last bit of strength he could muster, Estin hooked his long tail around her knees, throwing off her balance. As he had hoped, when Feanne began to stumble, she lost her hold on him, allowing him to backhand her and spin free.

Hitting the ground hard, Feanne lay where she fell, laughing. Estin, though, stood still, waiting for the next attack.

"Will that do, Asrahn?" Feanne called out loudly. "Or shall I beat on him again?"

The elder stepped from behind a nearby tree and glowered at them both.

"Not quite the trial I had in mind, child. I just wanted to know if he can be taught. What think you? Can he be a warrior and a healer?"

Feanne back-rolled onto her feet so that she was facing Estin again.

"I can teach him," she replied, her eyes on him and glittering with humor, "but I do not think he likes my teaching style."

"What is this?" Estin demanded, letting his guard finally fall. Pain screamed through his side and chest, dizzying him. "All of this was some kind of test?"

Asrahn approached him, eyeing his wounds as she told him, "When I was younger, I learned that there are two ways of a healer. The first is to wait for the injured and to heal them when they come to your, or are brought. That was what my father wanted of me. My mother was a warrior, always rushing into combat if she could find the excuse...something Feanne seems to have inherited."

Feanne looked up from licking her claws clean, but kept silent.

"I preferred the more active role in a battle," Asrahn continued. "I am old now and am relegated to that which I hated as a youth.

"You have the desire to be a warrior, yet you weep over the fallen. A true warrior cannot let themselves grieve. Ulra would not do so. She would rush into battle and kill as many as she could manage with no remorse. If her allies fall, she cares only that they died doing their duties. Beyond that, she will not allow herself to grieve.

"That is not who you are."

"No," he agreed nervously. "I can't shake the memories of every death I've seen."

"I wish you to learn to stand in the face of bloodshed and heal those who fall so that they can continue fighting right then and there," the elder told him, stepping nearly face-to-face with him. "You will fight alongside them, but ultimately will support them. This requires a different mindset, which I hope that you possess."

Asrahn set her hand on his shoulder, near his neck, then clamped her claws into his skin.

"There is also the matter of concentration."

Estin yelped, falling to his knees as she cut into his shoulder, her claws as sharp or sharper than Feanne's.

"If you cannot concentrate on the magic while being cut, burned, or beaten, you will never survive as this type of healer. You need to be able to focus on the magic while fighting. As such, I need you to answer two questions correctly while I will continue to hurt you. Answer by any means you can manage."

Estin was in tears as her claws cut into muscle.

"The walking stick that the dwarf scratched his backside with," she said calmly, trying to keep him looking her in the face. "What was the animal's fur on the head?"

His thoughts were a scattered mess as he tried to think past the pain. Blood was dripping off his fingers and his arm was limp, but he struggled to remember what he had seen back in the tent. The delicate carvings were easier to remember, but the head...

"Crow...feather...," he gasped.

"Correct."

Her claws tightened again and Estin swore he felt the grinding of their tips on the bones of his shoulder as he almost fell over. Her claws literally held his weight and he managed to stay on his knees.

"Next, you must draw me the slaver's mark from my shoulder. Here is a stick. Draw it. When it is drawn properly, we can move on."

She put a twig into Estin's usable hand.

Estin fought his memories, trying to sort out the lines that he had paid little detailed attention to. At first all he could see were the scar patterns down his and Feanne's arms and legs. Gradually, through the haze of pain, he began to vaguely remember the pattern, which he traced onto the ground.

"No, not quite. Keep trying."

The claws tore at him still more, eliciting a scream he had fought so hard against.

"I...don't...remember."

"That will not suffice, child. Find a way, or I will not train you, which in turn means that Lihuan will banish you. I'm afraid once I've convinced him of something, it is very hard to change his mind."

Estin groaned and looked around for any escape. In doing so, he realized that Asrahn's arm that held him in a bloody grip was the one with the marking. Unfortunately, her doeskin tunic covered the scars completely, keeping it from his gaze. Using his good arm in any way would require dropping the stick, which he did not want to risk.

"Think more quickly!" she snapped at him, getting her face closer to his. "Lives are lost during delays!"

Estin gasped for air as he glanced over at Feanne, who was watching intently, her legs folded under her. As he looked directly at her, she smiled and made a show of sweeping her tail around onto her lap.

His tail.

Estin felt like an idiot for having not thought of it sooner, but he flipped his tail up, flicking Asrahn's sleeve out of the way, exposing the thin bare lines of the mark. He quickly recreated what he could see on the ground with the stick.

"Well done."

Asrahn released his shoulder and Estin collapsed, clutching at the bloody wounds.

"Now," she said, kneeling with a groan beside him, "this is what it means to properly heal a fresh wound."

At her touch, Estin flinched, but felt instant relief of his pain. He was hesitant to let her touch him at all, but when he allowed her to lay her hand fully on his arm, he could actually feel the wounds begin to close. In seconds, every wound he had suffered that night was closed and even the fur had filled somewhat.

"He is all yours, Feanne," Asrahn announced, struggling back to her feet. "Teach him to fight. I will deal with him when you are done. A warrior-healer is rather useless if he cannot fight properly."

From where he lay, Estin swore he saw Feanne's malicious grin again, but he could not be sure.

Chapter Five

"Wildlife Divisions"

A new dream started that night. I cannot say it was marginally better, but it was certainly not as hopeless.

This time, after the screams of our neighbors, my waking within the dream, and the sounds of the burglar entering our home, things would begin to change. I knew, even asleep, that this was not really how it had happened, but it was as though my mind were trying to work around the pain of my lifetime to come up with a new answer.

I really was not good at it yet.

I found the courage to venture from my bed and creep on all fours to the small opening that led to our family's main room. As usual, I looked out into the main room.

My mother had that long chain around her throat...how I seethed with hatred at the foul thing. She lay at the feet of a robed man who was collecting bones from a meal that had not been cleaned up properly, giggling and holding up each little animal bone with glee.

I rushed out this time, long before my father would enter. In my mind, I would save her this time. Father would be so proud. The Turessian would fall and mother would live. That was how it all should have happened.

My claws hit the robed man and went right through as his body fell apart, the robe collapsing around me as I struggled to stand. When I finally got it off me, I was alone in the room with mother. She was so very still, with that chain wrapped around her neck.

I checked on her, knowing that I now had the knowledge and training to save her. I could heal at a touch, giving her back what the intruder had taken from her. It was to be my shining moment...the completion of my training as a healer.

As I reached for her, mother rolled over, staring up at me with cold dead eyes. She grabbed at me, trying to drag me down into undeath with her. I fought to get free, but her hands were stronger than mine, pulling me down into the floor, where I knew I could never escape. If I could not free myself, I would be just as dead as mother and no amount of training could save me.

I cried out for help and saw Feanne standing in the window of the house, just watching. I called again and again, but she just watched me as I was dragged down.

I swear I saw her smile as the grave took me.

Estin woke the next morning with a start, finding himself safe in his tent. His remaining sword lay beside him, along with the bags he had taken from the wagon the night before. Several collected or gifted trinkets lay strewn about as reminders of the good things he had found in the pack since his arrival, including a tiny silver earring that a mouse child had given him in passing the day after he had first arrived at camp.

He rolled over and sat up, gazing upon the stark emptiness of the tent. In doing so, he tapped his head on another gift—a clay sculpture from Ulra that vaguely resembled the sun. She had told him that all things are better when you have the sun overhead to warm you. He had happily hung the piece of clay from the center of his tent's "roof" so that the sun was indeed always over him.

"Good morning," said a female voice softly, just behind him, near the tent's entrance flap.

Estin nearly dove out of the tent's wall in surprise as he spun, finding himself facing a young deer wildling, who watched him with large eyes as she sat cross-legged against one side of the small tent. Estin could not remember ever having met her, let alone bringing her into the tent. His mind raced, trying to remember if he had done something rash and blocked it out of his memory, but nothing came to him.

He knew she was young, but probably three to five years, so somewhere around maturity. Aside from her breed's common brown fur, she had thin white lines of fur that ran up across her nose, around her eyes and up her forehead.

Unlike most of the more predatory wildlings who wore deerskin leather, she wore a simple shirt and loose pants of thin fabric—which somehow made Estin utter an internal sigh of relief at not having to justify her wearing her namesake breed's skin for clothing.

The girl's ears shot back nervously as he panicked.

"Sorry, sorry! Didn't mean to startle you," she cooed, raising her hands in what should have been a calming manner. "Lihuan asked me to check in on you and introduce myself. I'm one of the pack's tailors, but I hear that you're going to be the next pack healer. It's so good to have one of ours in an important job like that, so when I heard, I wanted to meet you right away.

"Oh, can I help you in some way? You look like I've done something wrong."

Estin did not feel particularly frightened of the girl, but stayed away anyway, trying to figure out what was going on, having apparently been fast asleep when she snuck in. He started to answer, when he realized he was undressed—having been alone when he bedded down—and tried to calmly shift his tail to cover himself. He had been told by the others that nudity was more of a human concept, but having lived among humans his whole life, it was somewhat of a concern for him.

"No...I think I'm fine. Who are you and why did you sneak in on me?"

"Alafa. Like I said, Lihuan asked me to come by. I forgot to ask him when he wanted me to come by, so I decided I should do it right away. You weren't awake and Lihuan did say you had a rough night, so I really didn't want to wake you up. Did I do right?"

The girl blinked at him and leaned forward slightly, as though hanging on his reply.

"You did...fine," he fumbled, sliding over his leather clothing from the corner of the tent. With a sinking feeling, he realized it was all deerskin and decided instead to slide it out of sight behind him.

"I'm sorry. You seem bothered about not having your clothes," she noted, tipping sideways a bit to see where he had slid the pile of leathers. "I don't understand the city customs...would it help if I was down to just fur, too?"

"No, not really," he snapped at her, trying to modestly shove her towards the tent entrance. "If you could just leave..."

"Did I upset you?"

"No Alafa, it's fine. Just wasn't ready for guests."

"Oh good. I'll see you tonight, then."

With that, the girl practically skipped away from his tent and into the eastern part of camp, her short white tail disappearing into the maze of tents.

"That was...different," Estin said to himself, pulling on his loincloth and jacket quickly.

"Busy night?" asked Feanne, who was leaning on a sapling near him, watching him through the open tent flap.

"Been standing there long?"

"Since she arrived an hour ago. I was coming to wake you for morning meals before Ghohar's passing ceremony, seeing as it's noon already, but it looked like the girl had everything in-hand. I thought I would wait it out. You have missed the meal."

Estin flinched at her words and grabbed his belt and sword, fastening them on as he climbed out of the tent. Sure enough, the sun was high in the sky. The night's fights had exhausted him more than he had thought.

"Feanne, she wasn't..."

"Old enough to take a mate? Wrong there, she turned four last month. She's an eligible adult now."

"No, I meant what happened in the tent..."

"Was not my business, Estin. What happens on the south end of camp is none of my concern. I barely pay attention to the north, where I belong."

Feanne turned and walked away, leaving Estin to catch up with her quick pace, but Estin did note her sharp swishes of her tail...she was annoyed with him. Not the way he wanted to start the day.

They navigated towards the center of the camp, where Ghohar's bier had been paired with a second, which held the ogre's body. Already, various villagers were applying oil to the wood that bore the two bodies. So far as Estin could tell, every member of the pack was present, including Alafa, who was watching him. He made a point of not acknowledging her.

"As you all know," announced Lihuan, who stood at the head of the biers, though he gave Estin a sharp look as he came into the gathering, "last night, two of our own fell in the woods nearby.

"Our community is made up of about every breed of wildling that walks the lands and for that I am proud. Despite that, today I must honor the death of one who was not of our kin, but stood with ours until his last moments, defending the pack as his own. For this, we will offer him the same passing as we give our own. We will miss the tender watchfulness of the ogre of the woods.

"Also, we have lost one who was with us from the time we first began calling ourselves a pack. Ghohar of the wolven people fell at the hands of the same foe that felled the ogre of the woods. Ghohar stood with me when we defended this pack through years of attacks and would be proud to have died patrolling on our behalf.

"Despite these losses, there was a survivor of the attack. For every life that is spared, there is reason to be thankful. The pack will continue on."

Lihuan took a torch that was offered to him and flung it among the wood, which lit instantly, rapidly growing into a blazing column of flames.

Estin stood there, watching in wonder as the flames raged and consumed the bodies, even as an elder squirrel wildling stood atop a tree stump nearby, waving her arms and guiding winds to scatter the smoke so that it was less visible at a distance. The whole assembly remained silent throughout, watching the fires burn.

"Are you ready for the gathering tonight?" asked Alafa, suddenly at Estin's side.

He nearly jumped, but tried to appear unsurprised.

"Gathering?"

"The feast of the fallen," Feanne said, her eyes on the flames. "When one of the pack's members dies, a feast is thrown in their honor. The unofficial hope is that a celebration will bring about at least as many new children as the number that was lost that day. It is an old and vulgar custom that most truly enjoy...perhaps too much."

"It's great," babbled Alafa, bouncing up and down, which reminded Estin suddenly of a female version of Sohan. "Everyone's trying not to be sad, so they have more fun than usual. It's always best for those who are unmated. Like us. Just saying."

Estin immediately grabbed Feanne's arm and just started walking away, not saying a word. They were well into the line of tents before Feanne stopped and pulled her arm free.

"Problem, Estin?"

"How does this affect my training?"

Feanne laughed and glanced back towards the fires, where Alafa was still standing, watching them and fidgeting. Giving the girl a little wave, Feanne grinned viciously as Alafa darted away.

"If you take a mate, it will slow down your training I am sure. As will children. Aside from that, it changes nothing."

"I am not taking a mate!" he snapped, more harshly than he intended. "The girl just showed up. Maybe if I knew her, but having some random doe drag me off to be mated just because your father decided I need something to do on slow nights is not what I was expecting after watching a friend die."

Feanne grinned that evil smile of hers and nodded, ushering him into a slow walk away from the fires.

"I am aware. My father's usual style, I'm afraid. He considers himself a matchmaker. If you ask the child, I'm sure she believes you fought off the Turessian on your own and should be lauded as the hero of the pack. No doubt she believes you to be well on your way to pack leader. My father wields such stories the way you wield swords in hopes of boosting the morale of the pack. This is one of the many reasons I enjoy living outside his reach."

"What do I do about it?"

"You have some fun tonight," she offered. "Other than that, there is little to be done. Enjoy the fame while it lasts. He may well have seeded several others in case she was not of your liking. Given that you are the only one of your breed here, he has probably picked an assortment that will pounce on you at various times in the hopes that one...or

142

several...catch your fancy. It is an easy way for him to keep our numbers high."

"That...that is sick, Feanne. I don't mind the attention, but I don't like the idea of someone breeding me."

"At least he has only attempted to find a female to bed you. Consider yourself lucky that he had not attempted to arrange a life-mating without asking you."

"Would I know if he had?"

Feanne hesitated and then shrugged.

"I will come for you after the gathering. I will give you plenty of time to find whatever enjoyment you wish in the meantime. Once it is well into night, I will return to camp and find you. Bring your weapons, if you desire."

She did not wait for him to answer, before turning north and taking off at a run through the tents. It took only seconds and she was gone.

Alafa appeared as though summoned in her place.

"What do you like to eat?" she inquired, ears twitching nervously.

"I...I eat mostly fruit, but sometimes bugs, frogs..."

"Thanks!" the girl exclaimed, then raced off in almost the opposite direction of Feanne.

Estin stood alone in the deserted section of the camp, looking back and forth between the two females. He was starting to understand why when he had once told his father, "Girls are icky," that his father had instead replied, "No, girls are not icky...they're just scary and eat souls." He had laughed at the time, but now he was regretting his doubt.

The remainder of the day Estin spent in his tent, mostly avoiding getting himself into further predicaments. He sat on the ground, rubbing oil onto his sword's blade, both for something to do and to strip the last of the blood from the weapon. Black tarry blood had stuck to it after attacking the Turessian the night before and wherever it had been left on the metal, small spots of rust now marred the blade.

His second weapon had been waiting for him in the tent when he returned, likely brought back by whoever had brought the ogre's body in. This too, was badly rusted and needed a great deal of care.

So focused was he on scraping off the nicks in the blade's edge and cleaning away every last little reminder of the fight with the Turessian, that he very nearly lost a finger when Alafa abruptly started talking behind him.

"They are starting to dish up soups, vegetables, and some fruit," she said, as thought there was no reason to announce herself. "You may want to hurry. The Keeper is threatening to mix meat into all the pots. Deer meat."

"Did she say that to everyone, or just you?"

Alafa snorted and Estin swore he heard her stomp her hoof behind him.

"She just told me. I was asking her to please move away from the stew pots. It's just common sense that you don't let one of them near our food."

"One of...them?

"Predators!" the girl said, going even more wide-eyed. "I've seen the way she pushes you around. It's how they all are. We're just lucky that Lihuan's so good to everyone. I've heard that some packs actually claimed they would let our kind in, then just killed everyone without fangs and claws."

Estin held up his hand, showing his thick claws.

"Those aren't the same. Those are for climbing. That's why you use that."

She tapped the blade of the sword, but flinched away at the ring it made.

"I suppose," he noted, wiping the loose oil off the weapon, then sliding it into the simple sheath that he had pieced together for it. He looped a knot in the belt he had fastened the sheaths to, then turned to follow Alafa out of the tent.

As she had said, it was nearing time for the gathering. The sun was disappearing behind the mountain peaks, casting long shadows in its passing.

Throughout the camp, the scents of many different foods being prepared lingered in the air, along with the hanging scent of basic stews that must have been in large abundance to not only feed the camp, but to occasionally overpower the smell of cooking vegetables and meats.

It all made Estin's mouth water, even more so as he realized that his last meal had been at dusk the night before. He had not even thought about eating. It had been a very hard day and food was rather low on his list of priorities. Given what random beatings Feanne had in mind for the night's training, he doubted he could risk not eating much longer.

"You look really hungry," Alafa said, giving his arm a tug. "Lihuan's making us all eat in the middle of the camp, so we'll just have to find a good spot where there's real food and not a big pile of dead things."

Estin felt as though he were being dragged around by an invisible leash as the girl grabbed his hand and practically pulled him off his feet towards the middle of camp. It took him most of the way to the gathering to begin to understand why Alafa was getting under his fur. Spending so much time in the city had taught him to depend on himself to survive...everything about the girl made him think that she was a hazard, likely needing the protection of the pack to survive, whether she believed it or not.

He did not have the heart to break it to her that after living in a city for most of his life, he had grown quite accustomed to eating beef and chicken, even if fruit and such were still his preferred meals. He guessed that Alafa not only would not be happy about the idea, but might well run in a circle screaming if he so much as mentioned a chicken stew.

He thought that perhaps he could keep that as a backup plan if she continued obsessing about him.

That reminded him that he needed to have a long talk with Lihuan before things got any more uncomfortable. The last thing he needed while trying to fit in among the camp was more young females believing that he was actively looking, or that he was intending to breed anytime soon. Not that he had any real problem with the idea of random females throwing themselves at him, but the thought that they actually wanted to have children with him after just meeting him left him with a stomachache.

He watched Alafa bound along in front of him and genuinely wondered if he would ever be ready for that. Back in Altis, he had not exactly been given opportunity and so had not given the thought much time. He had been with women...not wildlings...but women nonetheless and had been unmoved by any desire to settle in with a life-mate and have a tent full of little ones, let alone with a perfect stranger.

At that moment, Estin had a sudden thought of ringtailed deer bounding through the trees and very nearly burst out laughing. Thankfully, Alafa must not have heard him choke on the laugh.

They soon came out into the open middle of the village, with its burned-black center where the funeral pyres had been blazing for much of the day. Now, they were large piles of ash that had been wetted down to keep from blowing too far.

"I need a minute," Estin said, prying his hand free of Alafa's.

Without waiting to see her reaction, Estin walked towards the piles of ash, feeling the radiant warmth from them even before he began to feel the heated dust underfoot. Kneeling at the edge of the pile, he lowered his head in reverence before the fallen, feeling the ash and crumbling bits of wood crunch under his knees.

"What are you doing?" hissed Alafa, tugging at his arm. "We need to go."

"Give me a moment to say goodbye," he snapped, refusing to be moved. Every time he managed to work up the images of the deceased, the girl tugged at him again.

"We don't do that!"

Estin lifted his head and glared at her, losing patience quickly. Though most of the other wildlings were ignoring him, a few were staring at him like Alafa, giving her statement some credence. Apparently, he had made some kind of error in the village.

"Why?" he inquired, though he did not stand. "Why do we not mourn the dead?"

Alafa looked to be on the verge of genuinely waving her arms and yelling in some kind of fit.

"We...we just don't. It's not right. They're dead and we need to move on."

"What she means," stated Feanne on Estin's other side, "is that they consider it bad luck. Many of the pack members are superstitious about the dead and believe that acknowledging the dead will inhibit pregnancy."

Alafa squeaked and dove behind Estin, physically using him as a shield between herself and Feanne.

"It's true," Alafa whispered near his ear, her fingers clinging to the back of his vest. "Did you know that she hates males? I heard it from all the females."

"I also eat cubs. Oh, I forgot," Feanne exclaimed, tugging at the leather clothing she wore, "I also skin plant-eaters for my leather and the occasional snack. Estin, could I see you alone near that pile of knives over there?"

Squealing as though she had been struck, Alafa fully hid behind him now, nearly dragging Estin off his knees as he tried to remain at least moderately dignified.

"Make her go away, Estin!"

"Ladies, this is not going to work. Isn't there supposed to be a feast? I can't exactly join in with the two of you bickering."

"Fine, we'll just throw the doe in the stew and have a proper celebration."

Alafa let out a full scream right in his ear, nearly deafening Estin, then raced away.

"I'm guessing that's not approved behavior by your father?"

Feanne snickered and wagged her tail amusedly.

"Rarely do I do things my father would approve of. However, it is all talk. I would not harm another member of the pack. Besides, how can I be faulted? The girl's practically screaming, 'Feanne, come eat me. I'm such a tasty little morsel.' The only way she could make it worse is if she got all her friends together and then ran screaming as a group in front of me after I hadn't eaten for several days."

"Just go easy on her, please?"

Feanne's eyes glittered amusedly, but she said nothing further.

Standing slowly, Estin gave one more sad nod at the piles of ashes, then prepared to follow Feanne. Instead, he found himself staring in surprise as she took a knee, touching some of the ash to her forehead, then rose and walked away.

Estin followed Feanne as she made her way towards a row of large pots, sitting atop small fires. Asrahn, Ulra, and nearly a dozen others were dishing out the stews to each pack member who approached.

His nose twitching as he attempted to identify the contents of the pots, Estin approached the lines of wildlings. It took a moment to determine which end was which, but there were several of the breeds that he knew the diet of, allowing him to guess at which pots contained vegetables and which had meat.

Estin began to move towards the disorganized group that was waiting for vegetable stew, fruits, and other delicacies. As he made for the back of the line, he froze when Alafa approached, two older deer wildlings at her back. He recognized the markings on their fur as most likely her parents. The girl was bouncing about and pointing at him and smiling, then pointing at Feanne and glaring as she talked. He could almost imagine every word she said, based entirely on the erratic gesturing.

For the briefest of moments, he considered putting up with the insanity just long enough to get at the food, but when he saw the doe bounce uncontrollably up and down staring at him, he found himself completely unable to force his feet forward. The girl somehow terrified him, destroying the small amount of self-respect he had left.

"Shall I have someone take your food to your tent?" mocked Feanne, standing at his side. "I do believe you're not making it out of there again this evening. Does put a damper on Asrahn's training, but I do applaud you for at least learning to enjoy yourself around here."

"Let's get in line," he told her, turning left and approaching the other group.

Nearly two dozen wolves, bears, coyotes, foxes, and mountain lion wildlings turned and stared at him. Though he did not want to look, he guessed there was a similar reaction from the other line.

"Not your best choice," Feanne whispered, looking shocked and a little uncomfortable. "Are you somehow trying to make fun of me? If so, I do not get the joke. Please go with the other fruit-eaters."

"I'll eat meat today, until I figure out how to shake off Alafa. It doesn't bother me too much."

Feanne gave him a horrified stare, then frantically looked around at the others milling about them. She grabbed his arm and started to drag him from the line.

"What are you trying to do?" she demanded quietly. "Omnivores get vegetables and ask someone else to grab them some meat. You put yourself in the meat-eaters' line and there really isn't any going back. They're going to think you're some kind of crazy person...it's like a cow eating steak...you just don't do it. It's not right and a lot of the pack members will have a very big issue with it."

"What kind of issue?"

"The kind where you disappear one night and Lihuan gets very angry."

"Why is this such a big deal?"

Feanne seemed genuinely afraid or shocked by the whole situation, glancing over her shoulder at the others, who were starting to go back to what they were doing before.

"Imagine a pack of wolves taking down a buck near a water-hole. They set to feeding, only to realize that another deer has not only walked up and stood among them, but begun eating part of their food. How long do you think that deer would last once the surprise wore off?"

"So that's why you are so willing to attack me to teach me?" he demanded, his temper flaring. The dream of the night before rose to mind and he felt acutely angry at her. "You see me as your prey? Can you even name my breed, because I can't? Maybe my people hunt yours."

Feanne released his arm and took a step away, lowering her eyes slightly.

"Estin, I am sorry, but a predator can always spot prey. You could be as aggressive or brutal as you want, but your breed somehow just announces itself."

She snatched his hand, turning it over so that his claws were pointing upwards. Holding out her other hand, Feanne showed her claws the same way, the sharpened tips shining in the light of nearby fires.

"Yours are for climbing. Strong, but only slightly sharp. Mine are for cutting and tearing. There is no simpler way to show you."

"And just what," he asked, yanking his hand away, "do you intend to teach your prey in the woods tonight?"

Feanne looked hurt, as though he had slapped her.

"I intend to teach you how to be more than your breed. How to protect yourself and others, using the tools you have at your disposal. If that is too much..."

"No. I...I just don't really feel hungry right now."

Estin turned and walked away, his stomach growling in protest, even as he made for the woods. He walked quickly, not bothering to look back for the reaction of others. Right then, he just wanted to be alone with his thoughts.

Striding out of camp, he paced through the dense trees for a little while, trying to cool down before having to confront Feanne and all the hostility she represented.

He knew that Feanne had not been directly trying to insult or attack him—at least not this time. She had meant well, trying to shield him from his social mistakes. Though he fully understood the gravity in her view of what he had done, Estin wanted to learn for himself. He wanted to walk fully into the error and find a way out, if only to better himself. He would never learn how these people—his people—lived with someone sheltering him. No one here seemed to grasp that he had never been around wildlings since he was little more than palm-sized and had to learn everything from scratch.

Angrily kicking a small stone across the woods, where it smacked loudly against a tree, he turned and headed back into camp towards his tent. The whole way, he ranted in his own mind at Feanne's pompous attitude, treating him like he was helpless, when he had fought to save her and had the scars to prove it.

He hopped the supporting rope of another person's tent and came around a turn to face where his tent was...or should have been. Where it had stood just an hour ago, there was a disturbed section of dirt, where it appeared that someone had dragged off his tent.

Estin followed the not-too-subtle drag marks—and the many hoof prints—around through the southern part of the camp, looping around the western edge and up to the start of the northern section. There, his canvas tent had been tossed between two of the wolves' tents. Sitting alongside the jumbled pile of cloth and supporting poles, Feanne had two bowls of stew and a small pile of bread, as well as several partially-crushed apples.

"I am sorry," she said gently, motioning to the ground beside her.

"What happened?"

"Alafa got her family involved. The deer are remarkably aggressive while demurely avoiding any physical conflict, not wanting to face any threat directly, even among their own. I doubt they will ever face you over this little...scuffle. While she yelled at me over by the stew-lines, some other deer were here tossing your tent.

"They consider you a traitor to your breed. Some garbage about me making you into a monster."

Estin knelt at the edge of his battered tent, poking through the remains until he found the middle of the cloth. The small clay sun was still there, but smashed beyond recognition. He picked up the pieces and arranged them in the palm of his hand, trying to see the original shape Ulra had intended, but there were too many lost pieces.

"Have some stew," Feanne offered, holding out a bowl towards him. She also motioned to a stack of dark bread pieces she had set on the ground in front of her. "We will go train when you are done. The gathering can go on without us. I don't think either of us was looking to find a friend there tonight, anyway."

Estin nodded and tossed the clay into the woods, then sat down beside Feanne. Taking the bowl, he hesitated as he realized that the thick broth was filled with chunks of cooked meats, as well as some herbs and vegetables, though they appeared to be mostly for color.

"Thank you," he told her, poking at the stew with a chunk of dense bread. "I'm sorry I dragged you into this."

She watched him from the corner of her eye, then sighed and set down her own bowl and closed her eyes briefly, as if trying to put her thoughts together.

"No, Estin. Do not apologize to me. I am the one who owes you. Back there, if I had stood up for you, none of this would have happened. I could have diffused the whole situation by explaining that you eat both and did not know how wildlings raised outside the city might act, but I froze up. It would have been enough to get you through the night without conflict."

"It's not your fault..."

"Yes, it is. No one in this camp will stand up to me. That is both a blessing and a curse, but in this situation, I could have saved you much heartache by simply defending your actions. The deer would have considered the entire affair my fault and gone about speaking ill of me for weeks, which is fairly normal. They would have never thought to lash out at you.

"The carnivores...they would have been an issue, but would not act behind my back. Any intent they had to attack or harm you would have been something I could address directly.

"Estin, we all have our ways and I must admit mine are not the best. I am a warrior who avoids direct confrontation in battle. I always want to be seen as strong, but we foxes tend to strike from the shadows, then run if things go badly so that we can kill our opponent later. Sometimes that comes to the forefront, as it did today. My hesitation to confront something, based solely on my initial thought that it was someone else's problem, has cost you dearly. I swear this will not happen again."

Estin pulled a bite of venison, stew, and bread into his mouth as he thought of how to reply to Feanne, who simply sat with her own dinner on her lap, growing cold.

"Feanne...," he started, setting down his own bowl.

"Yes?"

"You didn't say how your fight with Alafa ended…please assure me that I'm not eating her."

Feanne laughed herself nearly to tears, shaking her head.

"No. Not today. Though if I had caught her relatives smashing your tent, they might have been cooked. If you hadn't noticed, I have a touch of temper at times."

Estin smiled at her and resumed eating and this time she joined him.

"You will stay with me out in the woods for a day or two…maybe more," she said between bites. "That will give everyone time to cool off and give us more time for your training."

"That isn't…"

"It's not a request," she said sternly. "It actually makes things easier for me to teach you. The more you come back among others, the easier it will be for you to forget some of the lessons."

They drifted from that topic quickly, the banter rather aimless and distracted as they finished eating. It was clear, at least to Estin, that they were both in no mood for any further serious talk and what they did talk of, he barely remembered later that night. What did matter to him was that while the rest of the pack went and celebrated—and whatever else wildlings did amongst themselves—the female who had been the most cruel and uncivil that he had seen was now treating him like a true male, if not an equal. It made his head hurt, but in a good way.

Once they had finished eating, Feanne waited as he gathered some supplies from the ruins of his tent. Most had vanished in the relocation, but he found a small pack of dried food and his belt pouches, which thankfully still contained an assortment of tools and utensils taken from the wagons as well as Varra's goblet, tied to one of the bags.

It did not take long for Estin to gather all that he might bring with him, then they were off.

Pulling her bear skin over her regular outfit, Feanne led the way through the woods, making his ability to track nearly worthless with the amount of backtracking and detours that she seemed to perform out of habit. She kept them traveling until nearly dawn, as the air became its coldest and the moon drifted near the mountain peaks.

Stopping in a rocky and desolate area, Feanne lowered her head and said softly, "This is home."

Estin looked about confusedly, seeing nothing but rocks, dirt, and the ever-present dense tree coverage. There was no tent, no belongings, not even water nearby, though he could hear some running water not too far off.

"Where do you stay?" he asked, double-checking the trees.

"I sleep on the ground," Feanne answered, sitting down on the rocks and laying out the bearskin rug. She then curled, as though for emphasis. "My ancestors slept beneath the stars, warmed only by their own fur. Why should I shelter myself?"

"Because they had no choice. You choose to sleep in the open."

"I do." She finished settling into a tight ball, then flipped her tail over her face. "Sleep now. We'll train in the afternoon."

Estin turned about, trying to find anywhere he could possibly sleep with any degree of comfort. He finally decided on the base of a large old pine, where he settled against it in a seated position. The rough ground made his tail ache almost immediately and he knew he was going to be sore in the morning, but he had little other option without going back to camp.

Closing his eyes, he found himself unable to sleep, or even relax, as the sounds of the woods came upon him swiftly. Howls of wolves—real wolves—as well as coyote echoed off the mountains. Even closer, he heard the frequent patter of feet, but when he would open his eyes and look around, the area was clear.

It was not until the sun had risen that he finally drifted off to sleep, though it was still restless and fitful.

*

When Estin did wake, the sun was just past its peak and the air was warm. His limbs trembled with remembered chill as he tried to sit up and his tail was completely numb, both from the night's cold and the way he had lain.

Groaning, he stood up slowly, working kinks out of every muscle in his body. As he stretched, he looked around for Feanne, but she had vanished in the night. Somehow that did not surprise him.

Estin paced around the area they had bedded down in, trying to find anything to eat. He was unsure how, but Feanne had managed to choose the most remote and lifeless area he could think of. There was no indication of any animals passing, no berries, no fruit trees, nothing at all. It was just pines and rocks as far as he could see. At first he thought that maybe she had bedded here long enough that she might have scared off the resident wildlife, but after some time patrolling the region he decided that it was unlikely anything much lived near here.

As he hunted for fruit or other edibles, he soon recognized at least vaguely where he was. Feanne had actually led him well up into the mountains, where he now stood far above the altitude where most plants grew. Had they gone much farther up, even the trees would be sparse or gone.

"This," he said, mostly to himself as he looked around at the barren landscape. He did not even know what direction camp was from his location. "This is not good."

He paced for an hour, finally resorting to eating the one pack of dried fruits he had brought to settle his stomach. Still, Feanne was nowhere to be seen.

Long after the fruit was gone, Estin sat in the rocky area, waiting for anything. Hours passed, leaving him lying on his back staring in boredom at the sky. The sun had already drifted near the mountains, making him start to wonder if Feanne was alright, wherever she was. He could not smell any trail, so tracking her was out of the question.

At length, Estin got up and began evaluating what to do next.

From the peak he stood on, Estin guessed that Feanne had brought him largely northwest of the camp. That left him with about half a day's trip back towards Altis' lands, not exactly knowing where he was going. His best bet was to aim for the northern roadway, which he could use to get his bearings and come back south. Unfortunately, that put him two to three days from the camp, once all the detours had been figured in.

Grumbling to himself, even as he fought a mild case of worries over whether Feanne was alright, Estin set out towards the northeast, where he had heard the stream earlier. He needed a drink badly and was willing to risk Feanne's wrath to get one.

Traveling through the woods, Estin made good time, finding the edge of the water while the sun still hung about a half hour above the mountains. He strode happily towards the water, licking his chops in victory at having fended for himself for the day.

A sharp howl made Estin come to a dead halt about ten feet from the water.

He looked around frantically, trying to find the source of the howl. If he had to hazard a guess, it was a wolf, though it was louder than he would have expected of the local wolves. Though they rarely got up the nerve to attack a wildling, he had no desire to be mauled. If food were scarce, they very well might attack him.

Estin rushed to the water and scooped a handful of water into his mouth. As he reached for a second, a different type of call cut through the mountains, echoing off the trees.

This was one Estin recognized. He had heard it as he lay dying from wounds received back in Altis. Even Ghohar had said the call was unique. That left him with no doubt.

"Feanne!" he whispered, leaping to his feet.

Acting purely on a guess, he set out at a dash to the south, hoping he had picked the correct direction the sound had come from. Seconds later, another cry helped him adjust his path, turning slightly more southwest. He ran as hard as he could, rapidly tiring as the high altitude sapped his strength.

Just as the sun was fading behind the mountains and the woods began to darken, Estin leapt over a large rock, then took a hard tumble as he tried to stop.

Ahead of him in a rock-strewn clearing lay Feanne, facing away from him, with blood spattered in a fan away from her body. Standing over her was the largest wolf Estin had ever seen. It turned as he entered the area, its eyes level with his own.

Estin's instincts kicked in hard. He scrambled away, checking the trees for escape routes. After a second, he regained his senses and pulled himself to his feet, drawing his sword.

"This is not going to end well," he muttered, drawing the second blade as the wolf paced off to one side, forcing him to turn with it, or else allow it behind him. "Good boy. Sit!"

The wolf's golden eyes flashed angrily and it snarled, revealing fangs that looked to Estin like thin white daggers.

Estin turned with the wolf, allowing it to clear Feanne's body. Once his path was open, he backed towards her, though he never took his eyes off the wolf. He backed away from it, bringing him nearer to Feanne with each step.

"Feanne, can you hear me?" he asked, but heard no reply. He had been hoping at least for a groan.

Using his tail as guidance, Estin continued retreating until the tip touched Feanne. Still the wolf moved around him, watching for an opening.

His tail brushed against warm blood and Estin flinched.

The wolf reacted immediately, leaping across the distance at him. Fist-sized paws slammed into his chest, knocking him over Feanne's body and dazing him as his head thumped into the rocky ground. He rolled away, somehow managing to keep his weapons, despite how badly his head was spinning.

Coming up as swiftly as he could, Estin found that the wolf was once again over Feanne, apparently protecting its kill.

"Not yours, boy. Give her up or we're going to have to have a little fight...and I'll be soiling myself."

As though replying to him, the wolf growled loudly and bared its teeth again.

More howls cut through the woods, letting Estin know more wolves were coming to aid this one. He did not have much time left before he would need to run, or he would be on the ground in the same condition as Feanne.

"We're done here," he announced, leaping at the wolf, swinging both swords.

The wolf dodged the first blade easily, but snarled and fell as the second caught its shoulder. It scooted away and regained its footing, limping only very slightly.

Estin flipped his left-hand weapon point-down as he approached again. This time he was able to get atop Feanne and take a quick glance down at her.

Though her fur covered any wounds, Estin could see blood everywhere. From what he could see, the majority had run from her neck. The fur on her neck and upper chest was completely covered with blood and all of it was sticky and only barely warm.

"Shit, shit, shit," he swore, returning his attention to the wolf.

This time, the beast cocked its head and snarled, as though acknowledging what he had just found in his companion.

"No way am I letting you have her!" Estin shouted, doing his best to snarl back at the wolf, though it appeared unimpressed.

The wolf leapt again, but Estin threw himself backwards to absorb the creature's weight, while driving his primary weapon into its chest. When he rolled away, he used his inverted weapon to slice open its bowels.

With a shriek, the wolf stumbled a short distance and collapsed, though it was still panting for breath.

"Well done," offered Feanne, sitting up. She looked over at the wolf, then back to Estin. "I doubted you had that in you."

Estin was breathing hard and fast, trying to regain his senses as he backed away from Feanne.

"Estin, relax right now."

"No! What is going on?"

Feanne took to her feet and motioned towards the wolf. Instantly, the massive creature fell apart into smoke and sparks. Though it went away, the blood covering Feanne remained.

"This was part of your test," she explained, trying to approach him.

Estin took a quick step away.

"Stop this, Estin."

He backed away once again.

"I am not dead, Estin."

"How do I know that?"

Feanne appeared to reconsider and frowned. She stopped where she was.

"I had given that part no thought. I do not suppose you will trust me?"

Estin shook his head rapidly.

Sighing deeply, Feanne checked her claws and looked back up at Estin.

"I suppose this works. I just had not expected us to move to this stage just yet. I had hoped to give you a break for rest before you had to fight me. As you wish…"

She leapt at him, slapping aside his sword with her claws, as her other hand's claws came dangerously near his throat. She kept pushing the attack as he attempted to parry, but each time she advanced, Estin lost ground and was slower on his defenses.

Exhaustion was rapidly overtaking Estin. He had not realized just how badly the wolf had worn him down, nor had he initially felt the scratches from its claws, but now he was feeling everything. Feanne had not yet caught him with her own claws, but it was only a matter of time and she was fresh, whereas he was nearing collapse. He could barely breathe, which he guessed was mostly from the altitude taking its toll on him.

"Stop using the tools of your oppressor!" she snapped, her claws screeching against the blade of his sword. "Fight me on your own terms!"

Estin swung his sword wide, but she easily danced out of his reach, grinning all the while, shaking her head sadly as he missed her over and over.

"Whether you're alive or dead, I'm not giving up my weapons just because you say to!" he shouted at her.

"Smart."

Feanne hopped sideways, using a tree to bounce past Estin and land behind him. With a sharp kick, she sent him staggering forwards.

"My pack!" she called out, raising her face to the sky. "Come and aid me!"

Estin's ears went flat to his skull as howls echoed through the woods.

"You have but a few minutes to win this fight," she advised him, standing more calmly.

Partially out of fear and only a little out of need to beat her at her own game, Estin leapt in, his leading sword deflected easily by Feanne's claws. His other weapon was ready and following in a guarded strike at her midsection.

With a practiced twist, Feanne took the sword from him and shoved him off balance.

Rolling with the shove, Estin used the momentum to whip his tail out as hard as he could, striking Feanne in the chest and knocking her to the ground. The sword she had held went flying.

"Call them off!" he demanded, dropping his other weapon and pouncing atop her, struggling to grab her hands before she could claw him.

They fought for a short time, her trying to dig her claws into his legs or chest while he grabbed for her wrists. At last he got hold on her arms, only to find that she was considerably stronger than he was. With only a small effort, she turned his grip around and she took control of his arms, using them to flip their positions, with her now on top.

"I can hold you here," Feanne told him, that sly smile creeping back. "The wolves will be here any time now."

"Won't they kill you too?"

"No. That is one of my skills. The wolves cannot see me, no matter how hard they try. I just need to stay out of their way."

Estin struggled, but she pinned him to the ground. Somewhere not too far away, he could hear the pounding feet of many animals.

Using his usual last resort, Estin brought his long tail up, looping it around Feanne's shoulders. With a tug, he yanked her arms to her sides, confining her. She fought, but could not free herself.

"This is not going to work!" she told him, straining to break free of his tail. Each time she relaxed for a moment, he was able to tighten his grip on her. "Estin, they will tear you apart."

"They will tear us both apart. Did you forget you're wrapped in my tail?"

Though still stuck to the ground by her weight with her kneeling over his stomach, Estin used his leverage to pull Feanne down until she lay on his chest, face to face with him.

"Who dies first if you're on top?" he demanded, staring into her angry eyes until she finally blinked.

Feanne closed her eyes and hissed something he could not recognize. The sound of footfalls faded away.

"They are gone. Now let me go."

"And if I don't? Maybe I like this. Maybe I just want to wait and be sure there's no wolves coming to eat my face."

Her eyes went deadly.

"If you do not release me right now, this will turn from training you to self-defense and from that to a lesson about treating cuts."

Estin considered briefly, not really wanting to let her go. He knew he would never admit it to her of all people, but the close contact and physical struggle had been exhilarating. Had she only been his breed, he might have asked...but he knew she would kill him for even suggesting such a thing, so he released the tension in his tail, freeing her.

With a back-roll, Feanne dropped into a defensive crouch, apparently expecting him to strike again. When he only sat up, she eased herself back into a sitting position.

"What was this all about? Why play dead and then try to kill me?"

Feanne smirked and looked over at the blood spatter on the ground.

"I needed to see whether pure instinct would overtake your intentions," she explained. With one hand she picked at the thickening blood on her neck. "Asrahn wants to be sure that you will defend the pack with your life. This is not something we really expect from non-predators. When things go badly, your instinct is to run every time."

She wiped at the blood, then seemed to notice his eyes on her neck.

"Goat blood. You really need to sniff before assuming."

Estin felt foolish, but then checked where the large wolf had fallen.

"And what was that?"

Feanne followed his gaze and answered, "That...is not something you need to understand yet."

"The others?"

"There were no others. It was a trick that a friend helped me with."

"What if I had killed you, Feanne?"

She stopped cleaning herself and cocked her head quizzically at him. With a skillful hop, she was on her feet.

"I have far more tricks at my disposal than you can counter just yet," she told him, picking up the sword near where she had fallen. "Even had you managed to strike me down, I was prepared with magic that would heal the wound and allow me to keep fighting. It is one of the few healing spells I can manage. If that failed...well...I would have been fine."

Feanne threw the sword off to one side.

"Can you fight me with your claws?" she asked, raising her own.

Estin got to his feet. He was still unsteady, but the break had been enough that he felt he could try. Uneasily, he raised his hands, trying to hold them like she held hers during the fight, but found himself wanting to make fists. The harder he tried to act like he knew how to use his claws, the more humor he saw in Feanne's eyes.

"I wouldn't even know how to try," he finally admitted.

Feanne approached him and took his hand in hers. She unfolded his fingers and touched his claws gently, forcing his fingers mostly straight.

"These are weapons, just as surely as the swords are," explained Feanne, moving his hand through motions that he felt resembled those of sword strikes and blocks. "You cannot directly stop a sword, which is our only weakness. Without your swords though, you will move faster and be able to avoid attacks that currently you must deflect.

"In addition, you have more weapons than I do."

She pointed at his tail, which he shifted behind him from where it was drifting aimlessly.

"You use it when you cannot find another weapon," Feanne observed. "This will not do. You need to rely on it. My claws will cut through thin armor and the flesh beyond, but yours will be stopped more easily. Your tail is far heavier and agile than I would have guessed possible in any wildling. Use that as much as you use your claws or swords...I doubt anyone will be ready to deal with a third attack at once."

She taught him slowly, showing him how to defend himself and even sometimes get an attack in with his claws and tail. At times he guessed that it was the same way she taught children to use their bodies as weapons. Thankfully, she was also patient, working with him to refine the basic skills he already possessed.

Only once did things go badly that night, when Estin accidentally thumped her on the nose with the tip of his tail when trying to use it offensively. It had bled horribly and Feanne had to stop teaching to spend an hour with a rag held to her nose. Luckily, they had been able to laugh at the absurdity of it all, their idle talk stretching well into the night, once the mood had been set and her nose had stopped bleeding.

Chapter Six

"Pacts"

The new dream was a distinct replacement for all of the old ones. It was nice to finally have a dream that did not feel like torture.

Each night, I would see the moon begin to rise and it filled me with dread. I knew what was coming. Legions of wolves came down from the mountains, dragging off my friends, my family, anything in their path. Sometimes, the dream would take it one step farther and the wolves would seem to pull the woods away with them as though they could steal the very world from me.

I had purpose now. I still dreamt that I could heal others that were freed from the wolves, but now I was not alone. Always at my side was Feanne, fighting to protect people. I would never equal her skill in combat, but I could try and there were always more of the snarling, snapping wolves to practice against.

Hours of battle in each dream was a jumble of blood and fur, claws and teeth. I felt both pain and exhilaration as I fought to not only save the pack, but to make Feanne proud.

In the dream, she was very proud of my improvement and skill. I saw so much more of her smiles there than I did when waking. They were not the malicious smirks or the evil grins, but rather genuine smiles. She was my truest friend. My ally.

Having spent just over a week with Feanne in the woods—mostly owing to his general incompetence in her eyes with regards to violence—Estin hardly felt the hard ground anymore. He now awoke at the base of one of the field's trees, having slept soundly nestled between its roots. His body hurt, but it was a good hurt in his mind. Muscle pain was part of the training and he was getting that from the moment he woke until he fell asleep each morning. It had become the routine—a painful one, but welcome.

Yawning so hard that his jaw ached, Estin pulled himself upright and blinked away the sleep, trying to determine where Feanne was at. Nearly every time he woke, she was either gone or leaving to set up some new trial for him. Each seemed to have its own purpose, playing off of some inherent weakness she saw in his personality that would weaken him as a warrior.

Today, Feanne sat with a small fire burning in front of her with fish skewered and cooking in the smoke. She did not appear to notice him, focusing instead on turning the fish.

"So what's the game for today?" he asked her.

"Isn't one."

"Just fighting practice?"

"No."

"Running for endurance?"

"No."

"Then what? We go back to the camp?"

Feanne looked up at him and he swore she looked nervous.

"Tonight," she started, then checked the sky, where the sun was nearing the peaks, "you will need to make a decision."

"Regarding what?"

"That is not my place to explain. I put out the call for an old friend to visit. He would like to speak with you before you return to camp."

"Who is this friend?"

Feanne did not answer and in fact did not say another word as they ate and until well after sunset. When they had nothing to occupy their daily preparations, she just sat with her hands folded and that nervous look on her face, staring at the ground.

Having built up his own worry after watching her like this all evening, Estin was jittery by the time Feanne raised her head and sniffed the air.

"It is time," she told him, standing.

"Where are we going?"

Feanne lowered her face so that she stared down at the ground, her ears flattening back as she answered, "Nowhere. He's already here. Stand and present yourself."

Confused, but having learned to obey her directions lest he be "trained" into an early grave, Estin rose and smoothed his battered and torn jacket and adjusted the swords at his sides. He searched the woods for any indication of a newcomer, but turned full-circle, finding nothing. As he returned to face Feanne, he found a pitch-black wolf standing over her, its eyes nearly two heads over the top of her ears.

The wolf seemed to be made entirely of shadow, the wisps of darkness drifting in the breeze as fur would on a normal beast. Unlike the animals of the forest, whose eyes reflected light and seemed to glow one color or another, this one's eyes actually did glow with an eerie purple light. Its jaws were slightly open and a faint mist rose on its breath, washing over Feanne, who continued to stand passively facing Estin, her head lowered, as though if she were to acknowledge the creature, it might strike.

Without so much as a whisper, the wolf stepped around Feanne, carefully moving to avoid touching her. Paws that could have flattened Ulra came down silently, the shimmering claws on them biting inches into the ground.

"This is the one you have been training?" asked the wolf, though its mouth never moved. The voice seemed to come from the woods around Estin in the form of a deep whisper. "He is young."

"I was the same age, if not younger," Feanne observed, still keeping her head low.

"He still has the look of one who does not believe he is an adult. He wishes to be a child. Can he take the responsibility?"

"You asked me to bring him when he was ready. I believe he is ready."

The wolf took another step towards Estin, who felt as though his very soul had frozen to the spot. He was not specifically scared, but he also was not sure he could speak. Or possibly breathe. He just had no idea what this thing might be or why Feanne had called it.

"Wildling, as the people of this world call you," said the wolf, "have you received any training in magic thus far?"

Estin tried to find words, but they just would not come.

"You will speak, or I will snuff out your life and that of the one who called me. I have no patience for fear."

A flush of anger at the idea that this creature could expect that level of obedience brought back Estin's ability to think clearly and speak.

"I have not, though I am to be taught healing magic soon."

Laughter in many different voices echoed through the woods, but somehow felt as though they were all a part of the wolf's being.

"You are an independent warrior. Why would you seek the path of helping others, when you can be so much more than them?"

"I have no pride in what I am. I have a duty to the pack and..."

"You have a duty to what you are. You are an animal, at least in the same sense that I am. With every breath, you know that. The instincts are there and the Keeper has trained you to use them selectively to be far more than your breed could normally hope for. This is both what you are and what you are meant to be by your bloodline.

"The creatures of the woodlands and wilder places are far closer to what I am and what I represent. This is why I sought out the Keeper and why I now approach you. I find your kind endearing and prefer their service over so many others.

"With the power of nature, the elements, and the fae guiding your hand, do you not think you could do more for your people? The Keeper knew that she could and so she chose wisely to accept our offer. Will you, too, be as wise as she has been? Ask questions as you must, but number them no more than three, lest I grow tired of being questioned and instead destroy you both."

Estin stared into the wolf-creature's eyes, feeling the radiating power from the being. It was overwhelming, giving him a feeling of it burning into him.

"What do I have to gain from agreeing?"

"You will be taught more quickly than another could ever learn on their own. The magic will be yours, with all of its power, much of it from the moment you agree without the years of training. You will possess the power of lightning, flame, stones, and water to strike at your foes. You will possess strength and fury to tear at those who would harm the woods...and your people. Even the gift of healing would be accessible to you. Every aspect that magic represents will be at least a small part of what you will be given and many more gifts that I will not reveal to anyone who has not accepted."

"And I must do what for you?"

The wolf's strange scattered laughter echoed around him again.

"This was not a question that the Keeper thought to ask. It is a wise one.

"I will require of you your presence when it is needed. There will be no debate, no hesitation. You belong to me and will act when directed. You will be another of my weapons in this world, striking at those who would harm the glorious life that exists only in the wilds. Should my gaze fall on something that I believe is a threat to the wilds, you would destroy them first."

Estin looked past the wolf to Feanne, who was being careful not to lift her head. Even her tail was still. He kept his eyes firmly on her as he asked his last question.

"Lastly...what can I offer you?"

"You are the apprentice of the Keeper. She has taught you as a warrior, which I find complements my gifts greatly. Her thoughts lately have dwelled on your continued improvement and fine qualities. I could not help but explore the possibility of taking on another of her skill for my ends and her interest in you draws me. Most of all, you would offer another mortal shell to further the needs of the wilds and my people specifically."

As the wolf mentioned Feanne by her title, her ears flinched. It was barely visible and Estin could not even be sure that he had seen it, but he trusted his eyes.

"I decline your offer," he said calmly, returning his gaze to the wolf's glowing eyes. "I am to be a healer for the pack. It was intended for Feanne, I believe, so it would be wrong of me to also choose another path."

"Do not take this offer lightly, mortal. I will not come again. Refuse again and you will have lost your chance for a bargain that would grant you far more power to help...and to harm...than you will learn from any teacher."

"I said that I decline," Estin repeated firmly. "Your offer is appreciated, but unnecessary."

The wolf turned to look at Feanne briefly, then dissipated as though the smoke it was made from had blown apart. Though its form vanished, the voice spoke once more, fading into the night.

"Remember what you have chosen. Nature does not forgive easily."

The clearing went silent. They stood there quietly for what he guessed were minutes before Feanne collapsed to her knees.

Rushing across the space between them, Estin stopped in front of her.

"What was that?" he asked.

Still not looking up, she answered, "That was the Miharon. It is an ancient fae forest spirit."

"What are you doing with the fae? My father taught me as a child that they were not to be trusted and that they seek to control our world, one person at a time through trickery."

"That is not entirely correct," Feanne said, folding her feet under her and bringing her tail around to her lap, where she picked at its fur with trembling fingers...a nervous habit he had seen many of the pack's cubs perform when they were in trouble and one that seemed very out of place on Feanne. "It is also not entirely wrong."

She fidgeted for a time, seemingly searching for words. Estin gave her the time she needed, sitting down facing her. When she did speak again, she made a very clear point of not looking at him.

"The Miharon told me that it watched when I was being trained to be my mother's successor in the camp. It came to me right before I was to begin the magical portion of my training...the same way that it came tonight to see you. Unfortunately, I was not so careful in what I asked it and wound up bound to it for life, which was not as bad as it sounds, but was horrifying for my parents.

"When I asked it if I would still be able to heal others, it said that I could. That is true...but misleading. I have very limited ability to heal. From what the creature told me, I would be able to hurl magic about just like Ghohar, heal like my mother, and do so many more things. It did not lie, but it glossed over how much weaker my ability to heal or harm would be and totally avoided the topic of how I would be bound to serve any command it gave, even so far as to burn down our camp if it came to it. It also left out other things about the power it gave me…things I prefer not to share."

Estin was horrified at that idea that a spirit-being could actually force Feanne's hand in a matter so dear to her as the pack, but he kept quiet and let her continue.

"I was proud of my decision to follow the spirit," she went on. "I still am, though the pain it has caused others is what gets to me and the idea that it may one day demand that I turn on them. When I went back to my mother, proclaiming the power I had been granted, it very nearly killed her. All the preparation she had done for me to take over her position was lost in that moment...I do not believe she has entirely forgiven me these two years later. I know that my father has not.

"Despite the fact that it was my father's attempt to life-mate me without my permission that finally separated my parents, when pushed for answers, both have mentioned my decision to follow the forest spirit as part of the reason that they stopped trusting me. They believe in my ability, but have no trust in what I might choose to do in the wrong situation and abandoning the male that was to be my mate they consider just a reflection of that. This is also why they wanted me to put you through the test, so that they knew if you could be trusted. If you followed my path, Asrahn would not have had any further contact with you."

"And your title?"

Feanne finally looked up at him, her eyes wet and sad.

"It was supposed to be an honor. The forest spirit bestowed the title of Keeper on me when I defended the deeper woods from a trading company that had begun burning the woods to drive the wildlife into traps. The summer was dry and the fires would have burned out of control and destroyed much of the area, had they not been stopped. It was the right thing to do.

"The pack did not see it that way. They saw me meddling in human matters far away from our camp and drawing attention to us. They were correct in that, as the trading company came after me, causing trouble for the pack over the course of months, harming many to get revenge on me.

"To make matters much worse, the Miharon read some of my thoughts and approached our camp, ordering my father to honor me as it did with the title. This was done in front of many of the pack members, some who did not know of my allegiances previously. For whatever reason, the spirit believed that the pack's snubbing of my actions was an insult upon it.

"Lihuan ordered the spirit to leave, refusing to obey orders from a fae. For this, he was struck down and very nearly lost his life that day...again, my fault. Still, he refused to let the pack call me by the title. He felt it was a foreign title that had no place within the pack. Any who enter the pack are just who they are, not who they were before coming in. This extended to his own child.

"When the camp was attacked by the trading company the last time, bringing with them dozens of furriers, it was on my life-mating day, just hours before the ceremony. They came without warning, killing everyone they could reach. Children and elderly were beaten down and skinned right in front of us. I saw...I saw children I had helped raise skinned alive.

"That day, I called on the Miharon for more strength. Everything after that is...hazy. I remember blood and humans dying all around me, but I cannot be sure how long the battle went on. When I came to my senses at last, I was halfway to Altis, with the last of the surviving furriers fleeing from me. Dozens were dead in my path."

"Sounds like you did a wonderful job of protecting the camp," Estin answered, but she shook her head rapidly.

"I got lost in the rage. As much as I need you to learn to suppress fear and find that anger when you need it, I lost control. Though I could have been the savior of the town, with most of our warriors injured or occupied, I went off in all directions, sometimes running for half an hour to hunt down a single fleeing human so I could rip him apart. Many died while I rampaged. Insrin, the male my father had made arrangements with, was one of them. By the time I returned, his surviving pack-mates had collected his body and left. To this day, we have not heard back from them and do not even know if their pack survives still.

"When I came back to camp, several of the older people began calling me Keeper. I thought at first that they were finally honoring me, as the spirit wished. Instead, they were mocking me. Reminding me that I chose to become a savage, rather than stay and help my people. There are some in the camp still who will refuse to use my name, even if commanded by Lihuan."

A tear rolled down her muzzle and she looked away again, putting up a hand to hide the emotion.

"You don't have to be afraid of me knowing that it makes you sad," Estin offered, reaching out to comfort her, but she slapped his hand away, snarling.

"I've shown my weakness to you once already, I really don't care to repeat it."

"Weakness? When? You've been about as weak as a boulder since the moment I met you."

Feanne glared at him, even as another tear ran unhindered.

"As if you don't know. I nearly killed you when I lost hope."

He thought for a moment, remembering more times than he liked when she had been close to killing him. Only once stood out for her feelings on this topic, though.

"When the hunting dogs nearly got us?" he asked.

Feanne nodded and covered her face again, taking slow deep breaths to try and calm herself.

"What was possibly weak about that? You didn't want me to suffer if the dogs reached me."

"I should have had faith that I could protect you," Feanne argued, keeping her face covered. "I was supposed to protect the camp. That is what my mother wanted me to be. I could not even be sure of protecting one person from dogs and so panicked that I nearly slit your throat just to avoid the guilt of you dying under my watch, while I went crazy trying to kill them."

It was hard for Estin to find words to reply to that. He had not even remotely thought of it in that light. That moment had actually been one of his fonder memories of their time together prior to coming out for his training.

"Feanne," he said softly, taking her jaw in his hand and lifting her face to look up at him, "you are the strongest female I've ever met. Why are you letting guilt over things that you cannot change destroy you from inside? If I added up all of my failures, all the people I let down, and all the people who have died when I was physically capable of saving them, I doubt I could ever get out of bed. I might even go hang myself out of grief.

"I remember them all, Feanne. Every face, every life that I could have changed. That doesn't mean I would make myself live in the wilderness to hide from what I've done.

"My father once told me that making mistakes, even painful ones, is what lets us know who we really are. If Ghohar hadn't died, I doubt I would have accepted Asrahn's offer...if she even would have made it. Yet now, despite missing Ghohar fiercely, I would not give up this moment for any reason."

Feanne smiled and gave a single choked laugh. Leaning close, she put her forehead against his so that their muzzles were side-by-side—the wildling equivalent of a tender kiss, what with not having lips. They stayed that way for a time, neither seeming willing to pull away.

"Thank you," she told him, sitting back and laughing weakly. "I knew I let you live for a reason. You're a far better person than I am. I think I need that balance in my life, so I don't end up mauling every person that annoys me. I…"

Feanne stopped talking and looked up at the sky, even as Estin smiled, waiting for her to continue. They sat for more than a minute like that, with Feanne sniffing the air.

Estin shivered as a chill wind whipped through the area. It was strong enough that dust and small rocks pelted them until it died down again. When it did, the air was noticeably much colder.

"The storm," Feanne gasped, standing to look over the line of stones nearby and beyond to the mountain peaks. "I knew one was coming in, but I thought we would be well on our way to camp by then. We need to hurry, or we'll freeze out here. I don't have the supplies we need to survive a bad storm...I didn't think we'd need them for another week or two."

Estin hopped up and turned to the direction Feanne was staring. A white mist seemed to be moving towards them rapidly. He had lived in Altis long enough to know that was a snowstorm coming fast, with snow falling hard enough to create a white-out. Though not uncommon this time of year, such storms could be surprising and dangerous. It was likely an hour or two before the heart of the storm hit them, but if it caught up, they would be unable to see where they were going, even as they froze to death. It was one of the joys of living in the mountains...at least in the city, he always had places to hide.

Grabbing the items they were not wearing, Feanne and Estin took off at a run southeast, racing through the woods. As they went, the air temperature continued to fall, making Estin's breath misty and his skin tremble with chill. By the time they had reached the creek near their campsite, large fluffy flakes had begun to fall all around them, though they were still well-spaced.

"There's a bear cave not too far from here," Feanne called back to him, her voice sounding distant in the winds. She practically had to shout over the roar. "We might be able to weather it there."

He did not even try replying, instead just waving for her to continue.

The air was getting painful and the wind was not getting any weaker. Estin felt as though his back was starting to freeze and he had lost all feeling in his tail. The snow was starting to stick on the ground too, making footing dangerous in places. The large snowflakes were getting much more frequent, greatly diminishing the distance he could see.

Soon, Estin could only see Feanne's red fur in the snowfall where it was not covered by her bear skin, everything else was just gone. If she got more than ten feet out, even the bright red was lost in the white. With the rate the snow was beginning to fall, he was not sure how much longer her fur would even be exposed enough to show.

Estin's feet were barely keeping him upright, his toes numb and unstable. He was even sure that he had ice forming in his ears. From what he could feel, he believed his tail might be dragging in the snow, too cold to lift.

"Right here!" Feanne shouted, though he mostly guessed the words from the movement of her mouth.

Feanne vanished and Estin rushed to catch up, hoping he did not miss a turn.

Thankfully, he found the gaping maw of the cave, where Feanne stood at the entrance, not moving. She put a hand up to stop him and at this point, Estin finally picked up on the nervous tension in her posture.

As Estin's eyes adjusted, he realized that he was facing a large black bear that was very much awake and unhappy at their intrusion. It rose to its feet, filling the cave completely as it roared a challenge.

"Do not move," Feanne whispered, raising her hands to the beast.

Feanne began whispering at the bear, keeping her hands up as she took very short cautious steps in its direction. She was concentrating very hard as she moved, her eyes barely open.

At last, the bear began to calm somewhat, its stance shifting to a more watchful and nervous look. It dropped back to all fours, studying Feanne as she calmly walked by it. It was by no means happy about the intrusion, but it appeared to accept their presence begrudgingly.

"Come quickly," Feanne told Estin, though clearly still concentrating. "We need to be further back in the cave when the spell ends, or she may reconsider."

Estin slipped past the bear as swiftly as he could, though he had second thoughts when it turned and watched him, its eyes filled with hatred. He made a mental note to never upset Ulra.

Feanne led him back into the cave a goodly distance, until neither of them could see very well and they were forced to stop. There, she stopped and examined the cave, as though for any hidden dangers.

"This is the best we'll get," she said softly, glancing back to the entrance of the cave. "I will be able to hide us from her while we rest and then should be able to coax her into letting us go in the morning. By then, the winds should have stopped and hopefully we can get you back to camp to begin Asrahn's portion of training."

Feanne swept the stone floor of any loose rocks and tossed down the bearskin cloak, then settled down to sleep, curling somewhat to expose as little of her body to the cold air as she could. She had taught Estin how to shield his body from the weather two days ago and it had helped him handle the cold nights, but this was far worse.

Turning about in the narrow confines, Estin tried to find a place to lay, but most of the floor was filled with jagged rocks and most of the flat spots were directly visible to the bear. He began to feel around the floor for any place large enough to even sit through the night without stabbing himself.

"Estin," Feanne said firmly, watching him with that coy smirk of hers, "come over here. It's freezing and I'm not in any mood for modesty. It will be better for both of us. I won't bite...I'm too tired to."

He hesitated, staring at her in the near pitch blackness. The thought...or wish, he could not be sure...had crossed his mind more than once during the week alone with her to lay beside her, even if only for friendly comfort. He had brushed the thought away, knowing that even suggesting the idea was likely to get him clawed, if not outright killed. Now, here she was making the offer.

Brushing aside his apprehensions about things he might do wrong, Estin crawled into the narrow space beside her, feeling instantly warmer for both of their body heat and the thick pelt under them. He settled in, putting his arms around her as they curled up in the dark to sleep. Without thinking, he draped his extensive tail over them both for an extra layer of warmth.

"Oh," Feanne whispered, stiffening a moment later. "Maybe this wasn't a good idea."

Estin thought for a moment he had done something wrong, or that he had touched her in a way she was not happy about. He started to move away, but she grabbed his hand, then his tail as he tried to whisk it away.

"Not your fault," she said softly, pulling him back down behind her. "I just hadn't realized how long it'd been since I had...company. It's funny how you can forget wanting something until the moment is just right."

"Just right as in having someone available, or...?"

She pulled his arm back over her, then lay her head down on his tail, using it as a pillow.

"The right person, I should say. There are plenty of others I could bring out into the wilds...none that I would choose to. You, I do not mind sharing bedding with. It is good to not be alone again. You make good company, Estin."

Wrapping himself around her, Estin nuzzled into the back of her neck and breathed in the faint scent of her that was always so elusive at a distance, usually covered with the smells of the woods. It made him feel happy and safe, though he doubted he could tell her that.

"Estin?"

His ears perked and he stopped what he was doing, realizing that he was likely overstepping his bounds. Inside, he screamed at himself for not being able to be satisfied with just being near her. The moment had been so perfect.

Nothing in the world was more important to him at that moment than keeping her near him. A part of him wanted to wake up smelling her this close and feel her near him every morning, but he doubted that would happen if he had just upset her.

"Yes, Feanne?"

"If I were to do something truly awful, at least according to the other predators...would you hold that against me? I don't usually try to be very proper, but I feel I should ask this time. I don't want you to hate me for it."

"Never. What would you do that could ever make me hate you?"

"Several things," she said softly, pulling his hips firmly against hers and turning to nip playfully at his neck. When he flinched a little in surprise, she took his hand and placed it on the knotted leather that held on her loincloth. "All of which I'm sure won't win me any approval back in camp."

*

Having slept that first night through, then having stayed in the back of the cave the whole next day sharing each others' company, the two had said very little the full day. They had gone back to sleep again that next night exhausted.

By the time they had bedded down—for sleep—Estin felt far less guilty for the enjoyment of their time. At first, he had been loath to believe that Feanne wanted him, rather than just some company to keep her warm. She had tried to assure him briefly of being sincere that she wanted him for who he was, not just because he was male, but it had taken him time to believe it. Once he had finally accepted that, he cherished every moment with her, hoping the day could go on forever.

Estin woke slowly the next morning, far more slowly than he had in a long time. His body wanted him to stay where he was, lingering in sleep for a while longer. It was a good exhaustion.

His lapse into dreams came abruptly to a halt when he realized he was alone. He felt around in the dark, but Feanne was nowhere to be found. The bear skin was cold where she had been when he had fallen asleep.

Grabbing his clothing and yanking it on as quickly as he could, Estin moved towards the entrance of the cave, forgetting completely about the bear that had been there the night before. Luckily, the animal was not in the cave any longer and Feanne sat near the entrance, staring out into the snow-covered world beyond.

"Good morning," Estin told her, approaching from one side. "How long have you been up?"

Feanne shrugged and stared at the snow, rubbing her arms for warmth.

"I woke a while ago to check on the bear, but found that we were loud enough to drive her off. At first that made me laugh, but then I began thinking about the reactions of others. Now, I am dreading what will happen when we return," she said, brows furrowing in thought. "They smashed your tent for coming too close to the wrong food. Have you given any thought what all of this would earn you?"

"Don't really care."

"I do. I promised not to let you get hurt by my actions and I intend to carry through on that. Estin, we will not speak of this. Please do not think that is for lack of my feelings, but I do not want harm to come to you over my being...forward. Will you promise me to never speak of this inside the camp?"

Estin blinked as she turned her eyes to him. She seemed genuinely worried, not upset about what they had done, nor even regretting. Just concerned.

"I promise that I will say nothing, at least until I know we're safe," he promised, taking her hand. She shied away slightly, but did not pull her hand free. "That's the most I can offer. I care too much about you to hide it forever. Just so long as you promise this is not an end for us."

Feanne batted her eyes, laughing at him.

"I'll accept that. Just know that I won't be coming to camp any more often...changing my behavior would draw too much attention."

"Then I'll come to the wilds."

She smiled up at him and squeezed his hand happily.

"We need to get back, or Asrahn will believe you failed your trial. I was supposed to have you back days ago."

Estin helped her up, then realized that she had placed something in his hand. Opening his fingers, he found the folded parchment from Asrahn. It was damp and weather-beaten, but recognizable.

"Your next teacher is Asrahn herself," Feanne explained, reminding him that he was supposed to bring that note to each teacher. "There may be more after that, I would not know, but she's next."

"Given how well this training went, I can hardly wait," he said, jokingly. "If all my teachers are female, I may be the happiest member of the pack before long."

Feanne stuck her tongue out at him and gave him a shove that took him off his feet.

"Not funny, Estin. Not funny."

He laughed at her annoyed expression and held up a hand to be helped up. She obliged, pulling him easily from the floor of the cave. She pulled him close, tapping his nose with hers, holding him tight for a while.

"Follow me closely," she told him eventually, glancing out at the snow again. "There will be a lot of areas where an avalanche might occur after a sudden snowfall like that. We need to be careful until we get farther down."

Feanne pulled away and began hopping through the snow, her footing sure as she left the cave.

Grabbing Feanne's bearskin cloak and taking off after her, Estin ran through the deep snow, barely noticing the cold and wet. He was too filled with elation to care.

Whether Feanne said anything publically or not, he knew at that moment that he was hers for as long as she would have him. No one had ever made his heart race the way she did and he had never even considered anyone as more than a night's company. Her, he wanted to be with, no matter the restrictions.

Even the thought of begging her to be his mate crossed his mind briefly, until he realized that she would not risk that anytime soon. In that moment, Estin decided that even if he could not talk with her about being mates, he would treat her as though she were his mate. There would be no other, so long as she was in his life.

Watching Feanne run ahead of him, Estin found himself smiling, no matter the cold.

They ran onward for almost an hour, taking sharp detours through the mountains when Feanne detected a dangerous stretch. This lengthened their return even more than the snow itself did, taking them the better part of a day to reach the first sighting of the camp.

When the camp came into sight, Feanne was first to stop, staring at it.

"I can't go in," she said abruptly, starting to turn to leave. "Just go without me...I can't see my mother right now."

Estin caught her arm and held her.

"If you run off, that'll be more telling, since you're supposed to be returning me to her."

Glowering, Feanne agreed with him, leaning close and nuzzling his face briefly. As she did, Estin looked down at the long scars down her arm, the perfect match for his own. He had begun to think of them the same way Asrahn spoke of the markings she shared with her mate. They at least spoke of a bond that he shared with Feanne, if nothing else.

"I want to see you again, soon," she said softly, licking his cheek, then whispering near his ear, "Come visit me in the grove. I'll try to be there most nights. No one goes there at night anymore but me. We won't need to hide there."

She pulled away then and started towards the camp again, albeit more slowly.

As they neared the western tents, a patrol of younger wolves and a coyote came out to greet them, raising their hands in acknowledgement while still far off.

"Feanne and Estin?" called out one of the wolves, squinting at them in the bright light that reflected off the snow. "You are both wanted immediately. Feanne, Lihuan requests you at his tent. Estin, please go to Asrahn. They have been waiting for your return and grow impatient."

Feanne shot Estin a terrified look, but then put back on her appearance of calm strength and poise, following one of the wolves off towards Lihuan's tent. Another gestured for Estin to follow him, which he did.

Following the wolf through the camp rather more swiftly than he would expect for a casual meeting, Estin tried asking questions and making small talk, but the wolf just grunted a few unhelpful answers and led him onward.

They came around a section of tents that had a tendency to block any easy access to the middle of camp, allowing Estin to see well into the southern section. Near the far edge, his eyes caught sight of five large blue wagons. From where he was, he could not see the occupants or anything else near there.

Now nervous, Estin was happy to see Asrahn's tent in the distance and accelerated his pace, hurrying inside without the wolf having time to announce him.

"What's happened?" he asked as he barged in, finding Asrahn seated on a large cushion with a cup of tea, looking up in surprise as he entered.

"I could ask you the same," Asrahn replied testily. "You were to return well before the storm. As it was, that would have been longer than we could wait in the circumstances. Coming back now is just...difficult."

"And why is that?"

Asrahn gave a curt jerk of her head to Estin's right, drawing his attention to two human men and a woman, who were seated on cushions, also holding tea. All were heavily draped in cold-weather garments, but what he could see through gaps at buttons and elsewhere of their clothing was all silk and embroidered fabrics. All three had deeply-lined faces and dark skin.

"This is the one you seek, Bandoleer Yoska," Asrahn said to the eldest of the humans, raising her teacup towards Estin. "His name is Estin. He was the one who last came from Altis."

The addressed man stood slowly, handing off his cup to the other man.

"You have seen my Varra?" he asked pointedly, his dialect thick, but easily recognizable as the same one Varra had spoke with. "We get description of long-tailed monkey. When we wish to ask little rat man for more information, we find him gone and no one can tell us where he is. This makes me worry about my daughter, yes?"

Estin fumbled for words, not having been prepared for this. He had thought about what he would say for quite a long time, but had finally forgotten about it in the last week. Now, all those pre-planned conversations were gone from his mind, replaced with thoughts of Feanne that were not helping him at the moment.

"I...we...I mean," he stammered, scratching at one of his ears nervously, "Varra was killed by the duke's men."

Asrahn closed her eyes, sighing as she swept the teapot that lay in front of her out of the way as the other two gypsies leapt to their feet and drew weapons.

"This...this is not good news," advised the elder man, clasping his hands behind him. "Tell me now why I should not believe that you killed her and now seek to blame the city humans? Answer wisely, or you risk the wrath of the clan coming down on this camp."

"Bandoleer," interjected Asrahn, "please work with us. We will resolve this, but threatening bloodshed is not wise for either party."

"Simply because there are twenty of us and nearly four times that many of you?" he asked her.

"That would be a starting point."

"Not a concern when it comes to vengeance. I will sacrifice every cousin I have to avenge my child if I must."

The man stepped up to Estin, his eyes intense enough that it felt as though they were boring into Estin's mind.

"Where is my daughter's body?"

Estin thought through half a dozen lies, but then looked into the man's eyes and found that he needed to tell the truth. It was strangely relieving, knowing that he would carry one less secret with him. He only hoped that he would not get himself killed for it. Somehow, he was more worried about Feanne's reaction than his own life.

"Your daughter died trying to escape the keep with me. A Turessian necromancer separated us and was able to strike her down before I could aid. I could not find a way to save her or free her body. The fault is entirely mine."

The gypsy's forehead tightened, but he remained silent at first, studying Estin. He had a feeling the man was looking for any deception. Estin began to think the man could search his very spirit for a lie and was thankful that he had not told one.

"Whether you helped her or not, she is dead, while you are not, no?"

"Yes, sir."

"Cousins," the gypsy bandoleer said, half-turning to the others, "Prepare the caravan for war."

"Please, Bandoleer!" said Asrahn, standing too.

"The guilt is mine," Estin said firmly, standing his ground between the gypsies and the tent's only exit. "The rest of the camp shares no guilt. They did not even know me then, nor were they hiding me from you. If you want vengeance, I am standing right here."

The bandoleer narrowed his eyes, but held up a hand to the others.

"If you lie, you do it well. As you would have it...you alone will face the fate we intended for all of the others. Do not bother to run, we can find you and really do not need to for the fate we will bring down on you and your line."

"There is no line," Estin corrected softly. "I am the last of my kind that I know of. I accept whatever you have in store for me. I will not run. I just ask that you allow me to fulfill Varra's last wish."

The bandoleer waved his hand invitingly.

Estin reached back on his belt and pulled the goblet around to the front to unfasten it.

As he fumbled with the knot, he watched as Varra's father collapsed onto the dirt floor and his "cousins" did nothing to aid him. They were all staring at Estin.

"Is that...that is not!" mumbled the bandoleer, his eyes on the goblet. "This is what Varra was after?"

"Yes. We climbed the duke's keep to get it from one of the top floors."

He finally got the knot loose and held the goblet out to the gypsies.

"Do you know what this is?" asked the gypsy woman, even as the bandoleer took the goblet from his outstretched hand. "Do you understand at all?"

"No idea. Varra never told me. She just sent it with me at the end, when she doubled back to slow the duke's men. All she told me was that it had been stolen from you and that I needed to get out of the keep at any cost, then she stayed behind to ensure my escape."

The bandoleer turned the cup over and over in his hands, his calloused fingers tracing the patterns on it.

"This," he said softly, almost as though speaking to the goblet itself, "is the cup that founded our clan. It represents the unity and family connection that we all share. Among my people, this is beyond worth. A worthwhile thing to die for, no?"

"She told me that it was what she was doing to be recognized as an adult in the clan."

His eyes going wide, the bandoleer stared up at Estin, his hands still stroking the goblet.

"No...no! That is not so. We sent her to find something of worth to the clan. Worth can mean many things, but it does not mean to dive into the enemy's lair and steal a priceless artifact. She could not have made that mistake."

"I will never know what she believed, but that is what she told me."

Estin waited patiently as the bandoleer tied the goblet to his own belt and stood once more.

The man walked up to Estin, facing him with the same stern face he had displayed during their introductions.

"Estin of the wildlings," he said, some of the letters sounding strained through his dialect, "you have cost me a daughter."

"Yes, I have."

"You have also returned to us something that is nearly as valuable as kin to my people."

"Yes."

"If my daughter has been made into one of the...how you say...monsters, undead, abomination, or whatever you say, what will you do about it?"

Estin mulled that over, then answered, "If it is within my power, I will destroy her, no matter who she was. Varra is gone, if that is what she's become. If that is against your ways, I am sorry. I will only tell you the truth."

He waited for the hammer to fall, for some horrific ending to the meeting, but it never came. Instead the bandoleer nodded gravely and motioned for the others to stand.

"I would drink with you someday soon," noted the man, hugging Estin abruptly then kissing both sides of Estin's muzzle in some kind of strange ritual. Yoska then placed a hand on Estin's left shoulder. "You have a spirit I do not see much in those who do not live the roads. Perhaps someday, you may be considered our cousin, if only in name, yes?"

Estin smiled back at him, placing his own hand on the man's left shoulder, hoping that was the correct reply.

"I hope that to be so, one day. You honor me with your forgiveness."

With a curt nod, the bandoleer started out of the tent, then stopped and turned back to Asrahn.

"You have good tea, but is not gypsy tea. We shall drink tomorrow, yes?"

"Tomorrow?" Asrahn asked, looking surprised.

"Yes, unless we have worn out our welcome already?"

"Not at all. Please, stay as long as you like."

The man smiled and departed, the others leaving with him.

"That...was nearly a disaster," gasped Asrahn, burying her face in her hands. "Do you have any idea how badly it could have gone had they decided to harm the camp?"

"No, but that was not their intent. They wanted Varra's killer and vengeance. If they cannot have him, I was willing to accept that fate."

Asrahn looked up at him with a touch of surprise.

"Humility is not something my Feanne teaches," she observed, chuckling. "You've been hiding that trait from me. Well done, child."

Estin sat down across from her, breathing his own sigh of relief.

"I've not dealt with the gypsies directly, other than Varra. I had no idea what to expect."

"You aren't the only one, child. Last gypsy I spent more than a minute around was almost twenty years ago. She was hot-headed and badly-tempered."

Asrahn offered him a steaming cup of tea, which he readily accepted. The warm liquid was not strongly flavored, but the heat was welcome after the freezing run back to camp.

"Now, how did the training go? Judging by the blood on your shirt and vest, I believe my Feanne did not go easy on you."

Estin produced the folded parchment from his pouch, while taking another sip.

"Superb," Asrahn whispered, glancing inside the paper, then closing it back up and tucking it into a pile of loose parchment near the tea kettle. "You have more than surpassed our hopes, Estin. And just in time, too."

"What?" He set down the cup hurriedly. "Just in time for what? Have we been attacked?"

Asrahn's face darkened and she looked her age for the moment.

"The gypsies were not our only visitors while you left. Lihuan is dealing with the others, though they were growing impatient for your return. We should have plenty of time to start your training tonight, though Feanne will not be able to join us..."

"Where is Feanne? What is going on?"

Asrahn froze, eyeing him peculiarly.

"She is hopefully being a responsible daughter, though if I have my guesses, Lihuan will be coming to yell at me later about her running off. If not...well, then he has finally gotten his way. This has been a long-standing quarrel, which we hope will end today."

Estin's heart went cold, even moreso than the storm had managed to chill him. Throwing down the teacup, he took to his feet, racing off into the heart of the camp, jumping tent ropes and sidestepping the other wildlings.

When he finally approached Lihuan's tent, he found a group of six foxes of varying ages and colorings—none of whom he recognized—standing guard out front. At his approach, they all tightened their formation, placing their hands on short axes at their sides.

Estin took a deep breath and started to approach Lihuan's tent, but the nearest two foxes stepped in front of him, physically stopping him.

"I need to see my pack-leader, Lihuan," he told them, but neither budged.

"Our pack-leader is talking to him right now. Until Insrin finishes, the village can burn for all I care. No one's getting inside. If you try, I'm under orders to cut down anyone who approaches."

Estin waited and fumed, pacing about as the tent remained closed to him, mulling over the name. That had been the one Feanne had mentioned long ago as the male who was to be her mate, though she had been sure he was dead. Nowhere along the way had anyone mentioned that he was a pack-leader.

Others from the camp came by to see what was happening, but would usually leave after a minute or two of watching the tent. Eventually, Asrahn joined Estin, walking slowly up beside him and then standing there, her back straight as she watched him, rather than the others.

"Let it be, Estin," she told him, standing quite still, even as he paced. "She made an oath. We had no way to know he had survived. This is the way of making rash promises, which she has a penchant for. Either she will abide by her promise and go with him, or she will be cast out of this camp for the rest of her days. Neither result do I have any say in."

Barely thinking rationally, Estin growled and let out a growl that seemed out of place for his breed, catching himself and even Asrahn by surprise.

"This display will not help matters, child."

"That's hardly my concern," he snarled, his mind racing through ways he might be able to fight off all of the foxes. He knew that was insane to even consider, but he could not help himself.

"Then what is?"

He stopped short, realizing that he was making it very clear how he felt about Feanne, which would earn him—and possibly her—a swift death if the wrong people knew. Fighting down his internal rage, he tried to remain still at Asrahn's side, though he knew his tail was lashing back and forth, beyond his ability to control.

"I am worried about my friend. She put her trust in me and I do not want to see her hurt."

Asrahn raised an eyebrow in regarding him. She leaned close and loudly sniffed once, then cocked her head.

"I am doubting your intent, oh so very much, child. Do be smarter with future indiscretions and at least hop through a creek to hide the scent. I am no fool, Estin, so do not treat me as though I am."

Estin began shaking, fearing he had just doomed Feanne. Rubbing his forehead with the heel of his hand, he whispered, "Asrahn, please. If you value your daughter's life, do not talk to anyone of this. She is afraid of what will happen if the camp learns."

"Who would I tell, child? I'm a half-breed who's been abandoned by her life-mate. Do you think I'm so shocked by anything people do? I did not expect this, but I am hardly surprised. She could have brought far worse home. Your secret is no one's concern but your own."

"Knowing this...what can I do, Asrahn?"

Asrahn shook her head sadly.

"The poor girl agreed when her father made the arrangement two years ago. Just because it was not enacted does not make it any less of an oath. An agreement to a life-mating is not something you can directly back out of. Meeting someone new a couple years later does not make the oath vanish."

"Directly? How does one indirectly get out of it?"

"There are not many ways. He could have died, which apparently he did not, or did not stay that way. He could change his mind, then if she also had changed her mind, it could be forgotten...this also appears not to be the case, or he would not have come. The only other way I know of is if she has found another male she favors, she could call him in to fight for the right to take her instead."

"So if she just calls...someone...out as her preferred, he can fight to win her?"

"Stop right there, child. Just stop. Look around and tell me what you see."

Estin saw little in the area, other than the six foxes, who were watching him as though he were their blood-sworn enemy. They were all on-edge, ready to strike at the slightest reason.

"His honor-guard, I would guess," he answered, staring down one of the armed foxes. The male smiled grimly, his fingers tightening on the grip of his weapon.

"Precisely. Let us assume that Feanne feels strongly enough to choose you as her favored. You attack him and win. What then?"

"Not caring a whole lot right now," he admitted, his fur rising angrily as the foxes laughed at his challenging behavior. Now they entirely ignored him. "If I die, so be it."

Asrahn grabbed his arm, snapping him out of his rage.

"I sent you to her to learn to fight, not to lose yourself in your emotions like this. Estin, you need to compose yourself, or I cannot help you. Anger and fury have their place, but not when it guarantees your death. You are no predator and a week's training will not entirely change what you were born as. They will kill you where you stand and if Feanne cares for you at all, she will see to it that you do not have the opportunity to throw your life away."

He growled deeply, but nodded and forced himself to relax. Nothing had happened yet, so he had to remind himself that he was assuming the worst. Perhaps she could argue her way out, or her father might renege on the deal. He had to believe that something could be done. There was always a way out, that much he had learned in Altis, running from the guardsmen.

They stood there for another hour, with Estin sometimes hearing raised voices from inside the tent, but he could not make out the words. Just when he was beginning to wonder if the meeting was going to last into the night, Lihuan came out of the tent slowly, looking older and more tired than Estin had seen him.

The elder looked around, spotting Asrahn and Estin. He gave a subtle shake of his head when meeting Asrahn's eyes, then started to walk away from the tent. The fox guards blocked him.

"What are you doing?" Lihuan asked one calmly. "You need to move."

The fox shoved Lihuan back towards the tent, drawing muffled whispers from the camp members present and a sudden rise of tension.

"Until Insrin comes out, no one comes or goes."

"Insrin is coming out in a moment," Lihuan said, his tone firming. "We are under treaty, young one. You will remove your hand from my chest and had best learn not to disrespect me in my own camp. There will not be another warning."

The fox grinned broadly and gave Lihuan another push, but froze as Ulra's paw closed over most of his arm, even as Estin was starting to advance on the foxes.

"You do know you were assaulting our pack-leader?" Ulra asked, stepping into the middle of the group, hoisting the male fox an inch off the ground. Estin could only guess she had been sitting near one side of the tent the whole time, out of sight. "Do so again, I return your limbs to your master in a satchel."

The tension held, with the fox guards keeping their weapons to themselves, but not backing down. The only one moving was the held fox, who struggled to free his arm unsuccessfully.

Estin prepared himself to leap into the fight if it broke out...half-hoping it would. He checked around him, seeing many of his pack mates gathering to watch. He guessed at least half would jump to their pack-leader's aid if needed. He met the eyes of as many as he could, securing silent promises of aid from most. Whether the fight was to protect Lihuan or Feanne, he was counting on those others to back him.

"The large one is correct," announced a new voice.

A tall male fox, grey-furred, yet likely seven or eight years old, emerged from the tent. The male wore an elaborate outfit mixed between leather and cloth, as well as a lengthy necklace, covered with feathers and claws. He surveyed the group—taking in even Ulra's handling of his guard—with a complete calm. As his eyes passed over Estin, he paused and sniffed, as though evaluating what and who he was.

"Stand down," the grey said, focusing his attention on his own guards. "You will bring no harm to the members of this pack, so long as they seek no harm against us. The next one of you who lays a hand on anyone from this camp without provocation will face me in battle.

"Lihuan, I am sorry my orders were not more clear."

"No harm was done," Lihuan said gracefully, though Estin saw him size up the fox who had pushed him. That look told him that if Lihuan had his way, the younger wildling would not have left the camp alive. "The young find ways to make themselves feel important and it sometimes gets them in trouble. I could tell you of many who were as hot-headed as this one over the years."

Coming out behind the grey fox—likely Insrin, Estin had to assume—Feanne stepped into the light and stood straight and regal, her eyes on the ground and her hands folded in front of her. She looked at no one, but seemed to specifically avoid looking at Lihuan as he passed her to approach Insrin, going so far as to turn her head away when he stood before her.

"When will you be wishing to have the ceremony?" Lihuan asked. "I can begin preparations within a day or two. Some of our cooks are actually quite excited about serving you and yours some of their finer dishes."

Estin very nearly retched on the spot. His vision blurred and all he could think was to attack, run, or fall down and weep. He did none of them, but had to put a hand on a thin tree between the tents to stay standing. He felt Asrahn close beside him trembling, and he swore he heard a faint feline growl.

"Tomorrow," Insrin said firmly, glancing at Feanne, who did not move or react in any way. "I have already sent a runner to inform my camp to prepare for it."

"What?" Lihuan looked genuinely taken aback. He shot Asrahn a concerned look, but Estin saw that Asrahn was watching Insrin intently, as though waiting for her own chance to strike. "The ceremony is usually with the female's people. Tradition dictates this. I can tell you where that tradition began, if you like, but I must insist on it. When your father began the discussions of Feanne joining your pack, that was quite clear."

"I am not my father," Insrin answered smoothly. He was not condescending, but firm. "Where I choose to have my mating ceremony is none of your concern. For security reasons, I prefer to be surrounded by my kin. That will not change just because my father believed things were more safe years ago."

"The least I can ask is that you bring my people in as well," insisted Lihuan, standing straighter, as if to more directly challenge Insrin, though the younger fox seemed to ignore the action. "We have a right to act as witness to Feanne's life-mating."

"Of course. If you or any other," Insrin paused and looked around at the assembled wildlings, his eyes falling on the few foxes among them, "respectable members of your camp would like to attend, I will see what I can do. I can make no promises, but you would need to have them assembled within the hour. I will leave guides out in the woods to lead appropriate guests in."

Lihuan leaned more heavily on his walking stick for support as he met the angry eyes of the non-foxes in the crowd.

"Very well. Then I must insist that we must take care of the remaining public part of the ceremony. Having it done at your village rather defeats the purpose. She would have no one to call as her chosen in your village."

Insrin sneered, but replied, "Very well. Does anyone have a claim to this female?"

Jabbing his side hard, Asrahn whispered to Estin, "It's a trick. If a male claims her, they will be executed. Female foxes make the claims, not the males. I have seen this trick used to see if the female has friends who simply dislike the would-be mate and wish to speak up for the sake of fighting, rather than winning her."

The area remained silent.

"And," Insrin continued, turning to face Feanne, "do you wish to claim another male as your chosen and have him fight me for the right to be your mate in my place?"

Asrahn's fingers bit into Estin's wrist, holding him firmly. When he tried to move, he felt her claws begin to come out, digging painfully into his skin.

Lifting her eyes for the first time since leaving the tent, Feanne looked directly at Estin, then past him, scanning the whole crowd. She then came back to him, her eyes widening slightly and showing him a moment of fear as she lingered on him just a moment.

"No. I cannot not ask anyone here to fight for me."

"Well then it is settled," announced Insrin, grinning broadly.

"There was far more to our bargain, as I recall," Lihuan reminded him. "Though we are not in so dire a situation as we were when your father negotiated with me originally, I would still expect the deal to be honored. Thus, I must ask when your merchants will be coming here with sufficient supplies for a rough winter."

"When I feel your camp has something beyond a mate to offer me, Lihuan. Until then, why would I send our supplies anywhere near your camp?"

Lihuan looked even more betrayed and turned to Feanne, who stared blankly at the ground, her hands tightening together.

"This was not our deal..."

"My deal was with her. My father's deal was with you. I simply returned to finish the terms that she and I had set forth during my last visit. Whatever deals you made with my father hold no import with me, as I feel he was giving away what we will need, simply to ensure a proper mate for me. I remember distinctly that he said, 'I will have my merchants,' and as you are well aware, I am not him. Take your concerns to my father's grave, if you desire.

"I am well aware of your penchant for twisting the words of others, Lihuan. I will not have you use my father's words against me. I will honor what I have promised and nothing more."

Ulra let out a short rumbling growl and stepped in alongside Lihuan, as Estin pushed forward, ignoring the claws that tore into his wrist.

"No, he is right," Lihuan said, raising a hand. "I overstepped my authority in this matter. The wording was in his favor, I am afraid."

Insrin bowed slightly, then turned towards the southern end of camp, his guards following at his heel and Feanne walking silently with them.

"Send any respectable guests south," said Insrin over his shoulder. "We will do our best to get them to the ceremony."

Estin pulled free from Asrahn, feeling blood running down onto his hand. He moved alongside the other pack's group, trying to catch Feanne's eyes. She would not look up even when he let out a whistle that caught the unhappy notice of one of the guards, though Insrin smirked.

As they exited the camp, Estin stopped, watching the party move quickly away. Feanne's tail hung still, as though she could not muster the strength to wag it at all. Until the moment the last of the fox guards vanished into the woods, he did not see her lift her head once.

Estin turned to go back into camp, his temper getting control over him once more. Yet again, Asrahn was there, waiting for him, blocking his path.

"Move!" he barked at her, trying to step around her, but the older female made a point of being in his way.

"Estin, this is beyond our control. Let her go."

"What would you do if you were my age in this situation?"

Asrahn blinked and thought a second.

"If I believed the one I wanted was being taken from me without a choice...I would have killed every one of them somewhere where their bodies would not be easily found."

He mulled that briefly, then went around Asrahn, bypassing her through the rows of tents.

"Estin!" she called after him, but he took off at a run.

Estin raced through the camp, spotting people he knew and cared about, but who could not help him this time. Ulra would be too slow and easy to spot. Sohan would not keep his mouth shut and was too young for Estin to risk. He went through the whole camp like this, knowing where he had to turn and not liking his options.

Finally reaching the northeast corner of camp, he found himself in front of Ulra's tent. Approaching reluctantly, he announced himself to whoever was inside, if anyone.

"Yes, yes," grumbled Doln, Ulra's mate, as he came to the tent entrance that towered over Estin's head. "What can I help you with?"

"Doln, do you still have that dwarf here?"

The bear chuckled and motioned inside. There, Finth sat on the ground, with a keg in front of him, a cup in his hand, and a lightly-cooked slab of meat in his lap.

"Welcome back, monkey," the dwarf said, grinning as he leaned against a tent post. "I have to say, if this is how the bears raise their young, I really grew up in the wrong town."

"You stayed here for a reason and I have no time for pretend friendship," Estin began, cutting him off. "Did Nyess send you here?"

The dwarf smiled but just sipped at his drink, his eyes glittering.

"I'll guess that he wanted you to find me. When you couldn't, you let yourself be captured. I don't doubt for a second that you could leave here if you wanted to and you probably intend to when you can bring me in more easily."

"And why do I give one ball-scratch what you guess happened?"

"Because right now," Estin said, glancing over at Doln, then lowering his head in agony at what he had to say next, "I need your help."

"This is the part where I tell you to suck me and walk off a bridge. I can give you directions to a good high one."

Doln reached over and smacked Finth across the back of the head.

"We do not speak like that in this home," the bear reminded the dwarf firmly. "Show some degree of politeness, or the ale goes away."

"Right…forgot about that. Will do, boss."

Finth turned his attention to Estin again, his eyes dark with loathing.

"What do I get for helping you?"

"You get my assurance that once this is over, I will go back with you to Nyess, so long as you try your hardest to make this happen. If you complete the task I set, I will go anywhere you wish."

Finth pondered that…far longer than Estin felt comfortable with.

"Decide, or I leave without you. This is time-critical."

"Yes, yes. I'm coming."

Groaning, Finth got to his feet and wandered over, giving Doln a polite wave.

"I'll be back for dinner," he told the wildling, then followed Estin out of the tent.

"What the high hells do you need me for, anyway?"

Estin motioned to the south, saying, "A group of foxes just took Feanne against her will. I intend to bring her back."

"Against her will? That girl can fight. Why do I think you're leaving something out?"

"Her father sold her into an arranged mating…er…marriage. She can't really refuse even if she wants to for her father's sake. From what I've been told, if she flatly refuses they will burn this camp to the ground for breaking an oath."

"That I believe. Where do I fit in?"

"There are six or more of them and they have trackers with them. I won't be able to keep up and even if I do, they will easily overpower me if I'm alone. If I know anything about Nyess' preference in associates, you're likely more than capable."

Finth grinned broadly, revealing beef stuck in one of his teeth.

"Let's go then. Sounds like fun."

Estin led at first, circling the edge of camp with Finth on his heels the whole way. He was impressed the dwarf could keep up with him, but he had hoped this would be the case. They made good time, but even so, it had been close to an hour of head start for Insrin and Feanne by the time he and Finth reached the southern end of camp where they had departed. That made things even more urgent, quickening Estin's pace.

"This way," Finth noted, pointing out a false trail, then redirected them to a nearby section of dry rocks that had been wind-swept clean of any snow. "Looks like they're using a few tricks to keep any pursuit from coming."

"Their pack-leader wants his entire camp hidden from everyone including us. The tricks will get worse."

"Good!" grunted Finth, taking the lead.

They ran on in silence, covering several miles in the intermittently snow-covered and rocky ground on their way roughly southwest into the mountains. Several times, Finth had been forced to stop and double-back, but they had not lost considerable ground. Estin kept thinking each time they reached a hidden fork of the path, that he was dearly thankful for choosing the dwarf to aid him. Without Finth, he would have lost the trail long ago.

Long after the sky dimmed for the evening, Estin nearly tripped over Finth when the dwarf came to a sudden halt.

"What is it?"

Finth knelt, examining the ground carefully.

"They have friends. We must be close."

Just then, a heavy impact knocked Estin off his feet and sent him sliding in the wet snow. He came around as fast as he could, watching as four foxes emerged from hiding places in the trees.

"Insrin sends his greetings," announced the one who held a heavy axe and stood where Estin had been. Judging by the feel of his shoulder blade, it had been the pommel of that weapon that had struck Estin. "Oh, and tell your pack-leader there will be no guests, thanks to you. Insrin will decide later on the trade agreement. No one from your pack is welcome here."

Weapons were drawn then, with three foxes hefting their axes at Finth, who stood there unarmed, his hands up.

Rising back to his feet, Estin drew his own weapons and launched himself at the fox that had knocked him down, parrying the other's leading attack. He drove the fox backwards, pushing his attack until the fox lost his grip and his weapon slid away, disappearing into the snow, the weight of the weapon carrying it deep into the drifts.

"Need help with this one!" the fox called out, diving behind a tree for cover.

Estin started after him, then the air itself thickened and wrenched his swords from his hands, flinging them away into the trees. Half-turning, he saw that one of the foxes was making motions that marked him as a spellcaster. The fox's eyes widened when Estin spotted him.

Calling on the short training he had received from Feanne, Estin went after that one, dropping to all fours and pouncing him with all his weight, kicking and tearing at him with his own claws. The fox screamed as he went down, trying to get Estin off him. Twice he tried to cast something, but Estin drove his elbow into the man's face each time he began to speak, breaking his jaw and bloodying his face.

Strong hands dragged Estin off his target, reminding him that there were more than the two foxes on the field. He spun, trying to get his claws into one of them, but took a kick to the stomach that winded him.

Gasping for air, Estin fell to his knees as another kick to his side rolled him over. Then, they were everywhere, clawed feet pounding into his chest, legs, head…anything they could reach. He was forced to curl up defensively, dearly hoping that Finth might find a way to help, but he was losing faith in that vague chance. Still the beating continued, long after he was unable to hold his arms up protectively anymore.

At last, he found himself alone, unsure how long it had been since they had stopped hitting him. The woods were quiet and dark, with footprints in the snow everywhere he looked.

Estin groaned and sat up, spitting out a mouthful of blood and a small piece of one or more teeth. From what he could see of himself, he had hundreds of scratches from the foxes' claws, though none were deep. It was the bruises from the beating that made it difficult to move. He could not breathe deeply without choking pain in his chest, which told him that some of his ribs were bruised or broken. When he tried to stand, his left leg gave out, the knee and hip flaring with white-hot pain.

Collapsing into the snow, Estin closed his eyes and waited to die.

"Get up, monkey," grunted Finth, running up alongside him. The dwarf was sporting a deep gash across the side of his head that looked as though it had bled profusely and had since dried. "I found out where they went while you were napping."

With the dwarf's help, Estin got to his feet and staggered through the snow, keeping much of his weight on Finth. They moved slowly through the woods, covering little ground before the sun rose.

At last, they came up on a tiny village of mud and clay-packed houses, nestled against a fairly sheer rock cliff that helped hide it from most directions. Finth had brought them around along the rock face, keeping away from any patrols that might be about.

"Can we get closer?" Estin asked when Finth stopped about twenty feet from the first house.

"And do what? Get invited to breakfast?"

"I need this, Finth."

"You need another kick in the head. Fine…c'mon."

They doubled back against the rocks and slipped into the village unseen. Though it was morning, Estin was seeing no one around, even though he could smell the residents still nearby. As they went, he realized that the only breed he could smell was fox, which struck him as decidedly odd.

Finth tapped his arm, then pointed towards the center of town. There, about forty fox-breed wildlings stood in a tight circle around a simple platform, just large enough for two or three people to stand on.

"Get me closer right now!" Estin hissed, testing weight on his leg again. It held for a moment, then gave out again. "Just go."

Obediently, Finth found a path for them to get nearer the stage without being seen. Within minutes, they were as close as they could get without actually mingling with the residents.

"…do you accept my proposal of a life-mating, to bind our fates as one for so long as our hearts beat?" asked Insrin, atop the platform.

Estin looked up as they got into position, seeing Feanne across from Insrin, holding his hands. She lifted her face to the sky, bathing her face in sunlight as she closed her eyes. Lowering her face, she opened her eyes and gave one long look towards the north, then answered.

"I accept as pledged. This life-mating is our oath and bond until our hearts no longer beat."

Estin collapsed on the spot, his strength gone. He only dimly felt Finth tugging at his arm, as the foxes began to scatter and gather things for a celebration. He heard voices everywhere, but nothing existed in his world aside from Feanne's face. He swore she was both sad and happy, giving polite smiles and greeting those who approached her.

"They're going to find us and they'll choke you with your own damn tail if we don't move," Finth swore in his ear. "Move!"

Struggling to find the strength to move, Estin let Finth guide him and mostly carry him, well into the woods. They both fell once they were safely away from the village, in the shelter of a thick cover of trees. There, Finth grumbled and swore to himself, while Estin stared blankly up at the branches above them.

"What the hell was that all about?" demanded Finth, snorting and then spitting. "You almost got me killed and I don't take kindly to dying for a mark."

"Sorry," was the only answer Estin could muster. "I needed to see her again."

"Oh…oh hells. You and the…? Damn it all, monkey. I'm a little slow, but it would have been good to know you were going there to throw your life away trying to save some girl you wanted to mount."

"Why do you think I'd agree to go back to Nyess after?"

Finth chortled, patting Estin's shoulder.

"It's alright. I've done stupid things for girls, too. That one's gone, so it's time for the recovery drinking, whoring, and waking up in a strange alley covered with oil, as my own dad used to say. Assuming Nyess doesn't have me gut you like a fish and hang you in a public square, you'll find another."

Estin nodded weakly. He had no idea what to do and no recourse. He wanted to scream, wanted to run, but most of all, he just wanted to go to Feanne.

Chapter Seven

"The Long Road"

For as long as I had lived, my dreams were a part of me. Not always a good part, but always there, just as surely as my own tail. When I lost Feanne, something died that you do not easily heal from. I have been told that losing your first real love changes you, making you into the person meant for your next love, or the one after that. It is the loss of the first that shapes every relationship you will have from that point onward, though later relationships make far smaller changes to your outlook.

I did not dream anymore. It was the loss of something I dreaded every morning as I lay my head down for most of my life that made me realize why I had dreamed.

When I was young, I had been told that the nightmares were there to help me slowly forget and work past the agony of watching my parents die, without being able to help. If that were true, Feanne's mating ceremony would have haunted me every night thereafter, but it did not. There was only cold silence in my mind.

That was when I realized what dreams really were, at least for me. They were not a reckoning. They were a guide for hope that reminds you of something that you need to grow from and never let happen again. Feanne's loss was not something I could ever fix, could never change, and could never truly recover from, at least in my own mind.

Without those things, even my mind would not torture me...after all, what was the point? I would suffer just fine in my waking hours, knowing that nothing else could ever be. Without another hope in my heart, there was nothing to dream about. Even my old dreams were unneeded without hope.

Thus, each night I slept deeply, which I know some of the others thought meant I was recovering, but in reality I was dying a little more each time my eyes closed. Every night was a bit harder to wake from, but that was not my friends' concern. I hid it from them, just as I hid from them all the times I visited the cliffs northeast of town, letting myself stand on the very edge, looking out at the sheer drops and daring myself to end the pain.

For now, I had given up on all dreams and focused on the tasks Asrahn set before me. These occupied my thoughts and there was no room for anything else. It was easier and it made people proud of me. I was treated more like an adult now, which suited me fine.

It would get better someday, I told myself as rote habit. It had to...

Estin performed the words and motions Asrahn proscribed without error, creating a shimmering barrier of magical energy around a clay cup. He saw the magic form around it, before it faded from vision, though it was still there. From what little Asrahn had told him, the magic was a sort of shield on the target, the spirits he called upon for magic interceding at his request to protect the item.

"Well done, once again," she offered, dropping a rock over the cup. The rock bounced off just a hair from the cup, as the magic flared brightly, then was gone. "You are learning quickly."

Estin said nothing, staring at the cup and the notebook where he had scribbled the symbols and methods of the magics Asrahn was teaching him. The book was getting rather full, having housed six months of his writing. Before long, he would need to rewrite it all to make it more manageable, but he had no desire to do so...he honestly had little desire to do anything that he was not instructed to.

"Again," Asrahn commanded, but raised her hand to stop him as the tent opened. "We have a guest, Estin."

He waited patiently for Asrahn to speak with her guest so that he could get back to his training. Whether she took a minute or an hour did not matter to him, but right now his only task for the pack was this training and he would do it as requested. This was what he lived for...the job he was being molded to take over from her.

"Sorry, Asrahn," came a gruff voice behind Estin. "I came to see him. We were going to head back to the city to restock what we can for Lihuan."

"Ah, I had nearly forgotten that was today. Estin, Finth has come to see you back to Altis. Were you ready for your journey?"

Estin nodded, though he had done little to prepare for the trip. Without telling her that, he pushed his small notebook into his belt pouch and stood to follow Finth out, barely giving the dwarf a second-glance.

"You sure you're ready to go back again?" Finth asked, once they were out of the tent and moving through camp. "I damn near pissed myself last time."

"Of course I am."

They had gone back to Altis two weeks after Feanne's departure, intending to return to Nyess, likely for a quick execution of Estin for running from the city in the first place. Instead, they had been surprised to find Nyess' main building torn apart and bloodied. There had been no bodies to be found and they had returned to camp bewildered by Nyess' disappearance.

Finth had taken it hard. The whole time he had stayed with the wildling camp, he had been vocal of the belief that he would be returning to his old employer when the time was right. Finding the place ransacked had shocked him into a couple days of heavy drinking—aided by Ulra and her mate, who honestly seemed to enjoy the foul-mouthed little man's company—followed by a reasonably heartfelt apology to the camp, even if it did contain several references to male genitals and the phrase "fur-sucking." He had then asked permission to remain in the camp indefinitely, which Lihuan had accepted.

Since then, Finth and Estin had gone back into Altis one more time, attempting to gather information. That trip had been two months prior and had been rather extensive, giving them a better idea of what had transpired between Altis and Lantonne.

As expected, the attack months earlier on the peace treaty wagons had finally gotten back to Lantonne and sparked widespread outrage. Altis claimed they had no stake in the attack and believed Lantonne had staged the entire affair to provoke escalations of the war. With Altis' army already crushed, it had been a short jump to convincing the people to cheer when the Turessians had come forth with the plan to raise Lantonne's fallen soldiers as Altis' new army, sparing the city-state from further losses. A new army was being built, according to all the rumors they heard, made up of skeletons and zombies pulled from Lantonne's graveyards. Though they had little proof, both Estin and Finth agreed that the truth was more likely that the army was being built from both sides' graveyards.

Most of the city guards were long gone during that visit. They had been replaced with shambling skeletons in small groups, with a single Turessian leading each as their guide. Estin had been shocked that the people accepted that, but the ones he talked to had said that it had taken months for the fear to wear off. In the end, the citizens were happier, as the undead and necromancer teams were far more fair and just to the people than the corrupt city guards had ever been. Most had a very high opinion of the Turessian, who had made it publically-known that they were truly sorry that they had no choice but to bring undead inside the city walls for the protection of the people.

Estin had gotten the impression that those he talked with were trying very hard to convince themselves that this was a good thing and only barely managing to do that. Finth had found many rumors about townsfolk going missing if they spoke out against the dead squads. A few people, willing to speak secretly, had even commented on the coincidence that most of the "fresher" undead had severe damage to their faces, making identification impossible.

After they had returned to camp the last time, heavy pre-spring snows had made travel impossible, forcing the whole camp to settle in and ride out the last of winter. Many said it was one of the coldest on record, but Estin no longer really noticed the chill. It was easy to set aside discomfort, while he had a job or task to focus on. Otherwise, there was always sleep, and he had collected enough fur blankets to endure the rough weather.

"Got some new leads this time," Finth told him, donning a long fur jacket that Doln had crafted for him. "Some butt-kisser down in the Grinder used to be a room-cleaner in the duke's keep. Those guys get all the dirt on everyone."

Estin nodded absently, fitting his fur mantle over his shoulders and checking the straps on his hide clothing. He had found himself missing fasteners a lot lately and had to double-check most things he did. Once he was sure those were all in place, he checked again for his swords and his notebook.

"Ready when you are," he said coolly, pulling up his fur-covered hood up and over his ears to help hide his appearance as they moved through the woods. He also fastened on the heavy bearskin that Feanne had long ago brought back from Altis. He had found it among her things that were left behind and often wore it to hide his tail and as a memento of her. "Do you think the snows will slow us too much?"

"We'll be there around dawn tomorrow," Finth answered, checking the sky. "Assuming some lord of snow doesn't decide to drop his pants and shit on us again."

Estin began to lead the way mostly east out of the camp, then stopped, thinking.

"You said the last time we were in town that you could not find your old stash of coin back at Nyess' place."

"Yeah. So?"

"Do you need coin?"

Finth chuckled and answered, "There was a time when I'd have said 'yes' without a thought, monkey. Right now, money doesn't do me much good. If we had it though, I could pick up some extra supplies while we're in town. Ulra's running short on some spices and there's a few items I'd like to get. But, without coin, I'm as likely to get those as I am a free lay from hightown's best whorehouse."

Estin turned and headed north, with Finth following quietly behind. They skirted camp and came up into the thick forest that shielded the pack's north end from both prying eyes and much of the winds. He continued through this section of woods until he came to an open grove-like area.

There he stopped, studying the trees. This had been Feanne and the ogre's grove, where they had entertained the local children and come to commune with the woods...and possibly the Miharon. There were some child-sized footprints, but not many. The place had been all but abandoned after Feanne had left. Estin had heard that some of the pack members had actually thrown a small party in the grove when she was gone, but no one had actually admitted to it.

Even with winter still blowing strongly, Estin would have expected the evergreens to be vibrant and full of life, as this part of the woods had long been the healthiest and greenest. Now, they were limp, with many trees losing their needles in large piles.

"Some kind of tree plague?" asked Finth, kicking a pile of pine needles aside.

"Something like that."

Estin had his guesses. Since talking to Feanne about the Miharon, he had sought out a great deal of knowledge about such creatures. They thrived on whatever they bound themselves to. By all accounts, this one was in some way bound to the woods or the wilds of the mountains. The health of these trees likely had been influenced by its visits to Feanne and the ogre...with them gone, the grove would either die or at least wither back to the same density as the rest of the woods.

Moving through the sickly trees, Estin took a moment to pick out a tree that had once been pointed out to him. The large knotty pine had a distinct 'Y' in it about ten feet up. Below it, he spotted a matted section, where the dead bushes seemed to create a circle of shelter. He would have bet on that being Feanne's bedding place in the grove...where they would have stayed, had she remained. This thought he pushed down quickly, lest it drag him down with it.

Effortlessly, Estin ran up the tree, his hands and feet used to the familiar feel of climbing, using mostly his claws for grip. At the crook he stopped, poking his head into the gap. He was almost surprised to find what he was looking for still tucked in there, though covered with a thick layer of snow. Feanne must have left it there since his arrival and judging by its weight, it still held all the gems and jewelry he had stolen from the duke the previous fall. That seemed so very long ago now.

Hopping down from the tree, Estin tossed his old pouch to Osrinn, who caught the bag with one hand.

"You now have coin for the trip. Let's go."

They had not even gotten out of the clearing before Finth whistled and laughed.

"I could choke a horse with this much loot," he mused and Estin could hear the sounds of the jewels clinking together as Finth sorted through them as they continued on. "Trust me, I've tried to choke a few horses. Who'd you rob?"

"The duke."

"Yeah...that's gonna be fun to sell, monkey."

"Will you please stop calling me that?"

"The day you can tell me what your breed's called, I will. Till then, not a chance."

They traveled mostly in silence, as was their way, covering much of the ground before stopping for food near dusk. Simple trail rations of dried fruit and meat, hard bread, and wine or water were the easiest to carry and so that is what they had in relative abundance. With no interruptions to their evening meal, they soon continued on, the majority of the trip still ahead of them, but made easier by making it at night when fewer city patrols would be far from the walls.

Through the afternoon into evening, Finth led the way, right up until the sun set, at which point Estin's superior night vision meant that they switched positions. This allowed them to continue at full pace no matter how dark it got, as Finth only needed to be able to pick Estin out of the darkness and follow him.

Around first light, they got their first view of the city in the distance, while they were perhaps another hour out. They stopped there as they had during their last few trips to look over the inspiring city visage.

When Estin had lived in the city, he had no idea how big it was, nor how majestic it must appear to invading armies. Inside the city, the monumental spires of the duke's keep were just more stone walls, but out here he could see all four peaks like arrows aimed at the sky, rising far above even the city walls, which were impressive in their own right.

The city itself was nestled in the space between two of the larger peaks on the east end of the mountain range, guarded on either side by the steep stone walls of the mountains, neither of which offered invaders any place to perch above, without the winds sweeping them to their deaths. The east and west were the only approaches to the city, both of which were difficult terrain. Only the east had a road, which serviced all four entrances to the city, after winding its way up from the foothills in the distance.

It was in the foothills Estin now found his gaze drawn, where there appeared to be lightning or similar storms brewing. He could see no clouds, but there were flashes of light every few seconds. He disregarded it quickly, given that it was easily twenty miles away and far down the mountain. That, and the winds were blowing eastward, so the storm would be moving away from them.

"Finth," he said, checking the sky above them, just in case another storm was brewing like the one in the eastern flatlands, "you wanted me to come here to bring me to Nyess originally. What was the plan?"

The dwarf grunted and rubbed at his beard. Unlike when he had first been taken captive, he had begun taking care of the beard recently, brushing it and braiding it into two long strands that he then usually tossed over his shoulders. From what Estin had heard him let slip, the care a dwarf took of his beard was a sign of his respect for himself.

"In all honesty, he wouldn't tell me. If I brought you back, he said he could get me back into my homelands. Knew it was too damned good to be true."

Estin realized that in the many hours they had spent traveling back and forth, as well as several patrols together, he had never once heard Finth mention his home.

"Here I thought you were born in Altis. When did you leave?"

"Who the hells knows? I left our mining town under the peaks when I was a lot younger than I am now, that's about all I know. After I came to the surface, I think I spent at least a year or two unconscious behind bars."

"I take it you did not leave of your own choice?"

Finth spit and the ground and glared at Estin.

"Last year, I would have already slit your throat just for asking, but no…I did not leave of my own choice. I left because they banished me."

"For?"

"What do you bloody think? Murder. They don't banish you to the surface for much less. I could have pissed on our king's throne while singing a ballad about his mother's skills in bed and just gotten a beating and prison."

"If you don't want to…"

"Of course I don't want to talk about it! May as well though. No sense in keeping it a secret up here. I killed my sister's husband. Axe to the forehead, so he could see it coming. I even warned him the day he was going to die. The man had no excuse to look so damned surprised."

Finth squinted at Estin, then added, "He hit my sister. A lot."

"Good for you, Finth," he answered, turning his eyes back to the city. "Sounds like you did the right thing."

"Not when the husband's the nephew of some random noble. They called me an animal…it's only fitting where I ended up."

"Good and bad decisions don't change based on someone's rank."

Glowering, Finth stomped his foot.

"When by the duke's ass did you learn to be understanding?"

"When I got an abundance of free time to do nothing but think on my own life."

Finth spit again, then started them marching onward, ignoring the next few times Estin tried to spark conversation. They moved quickly, Finth apparently in a hurry to put the woods—or the conversation—behind him.

It was starting to warm up with the sun shining brightly on them when they finally reached the southern gate, which was closest to the slums of the city. There, they could disappear as needed, but first was the task of getting through the gate itself, which Estin estimated to be a lot more unlikely than during previous visits.

Whereas last time they had come, at least some shifts at the three less-used gates were still guarded by the slovenly human guards who were more than happy to take bribes of food, trinkets, or sometimes even information in exchange for entrance—this time, twenty rotting corpses stood in front of the open gates, their heads hanging at odd angles, as though they were in some sort of morbid sleep. All showed signs of decay and massive trauma during life, with a few even missing limbs.

"Not going in that way," Finth grumbled, turning them back around and out of sight behind part of the rocky terrain. "You got another way? My next entrance is on the far east side via the sewers."

Estin looked straight up the wall, trying to see if there were any guards posted there, but he could not see from their position.

"Did you see any archers as we came down?"

"No. Kind of strange, really."

"Good."

Estin hoisted Finth and had him hang onto his shoulders and back, despite furious protests. After taking a long slow breath to prepare himself, he set to climbing the wall with the dwarf fighting to get away for the first few feet, then clinging to him. The whole time Finth mumbled oaths to gods Estin had never heard of…and possibly a few whores, judging by the names.

It took him longer to reach the top than he would have liked, but Finth was not exactly light. If he had to guess, Finth outweighed the much taller Feanne by almost half again.

When he did reach the top, Estin stopped, bracing himself for the hardest part of climbing the outer walls.

Just before the battlements, there was a two foot lip that stuck out over the walls. Above that, it was only another foot or two before he could pull them onto the actual walkway of the walls.

"How do we do this?" Finth whispered, his voice shaking. "Or didn't you think this far ahead?"

Estin had no time or breath to argue with Finth, so he just began picking his way more carefully onto the inverted surface, clinging for all he was worth to the larger gaps in the stones. This put Finth between himself and the ground so very far below, leading to whimpers and threats from him.

Soon, he was able to reach over the lip of the stone and feel around for a new grip. The climb was pushing his physical limits, despite all the labor in the wildling camp, so he would need to hurry or he really would drop them both to their deaths.

Finally, Estin found a good handhold and pulled them back to vertical and then swiftly onto the battlements themselves. Once they had the stone under their feet again, he collapsed, exhausted.

"Why would you even think that's a good idea?" demanded Finth, slapping Estin's shoulder. "By the gods' britches that was stupid! Who really stops and thinks, 'I want to scale a really tall wall just for fun…maybe I'll carry a sack of dwarf, too!'"

"Yeah...but it worked."

Estin checked his hands and feet, finding them badly torn up, with deep abrasions on the pads of his fingers and toes. He concentrated on the wounds, summoning the strength of magic that Asrahn had been teaching him, feeling an otherworldly breeze flow through him outwards, then back into the injuries, warming them as vague voices whispered in his mind. When he focused his eyes again, the wounds were all gone.

"Getting good at that, monkey," Finth said admiringly. "Got yourself a good teacher."

"The best."

He stood and looked around. From where they were standing, they could see that the walls were entirely barren of guards, as though there was no further concern for invasion, aside from the gate guards.

Estin looked up, checking the duke's keep for anything that appeared different, but all he saw were large flocks of crows, circling much of the town.

"Something doesn't feel right," he told Finth, sniffing. The breeze was going the wrong way to give him anything.

"Eh, whatever. Get your fuzzy ass moving and we can get down there and see if there's any other clues about Nyess and where he's gotten himself off to. If I can't find him, Ulra suggested raiding the slave pens tonight to see if we can free a few more of your paw-licker friends."

"You make it sound like you hate us."

"Yeah yeah, whatever. My mom was a whore and my dad couldn't tell copper from steel. Happy now? Everyone gets some love."

"Always the sentimental one."

"That's me," Finth said, snorting, then spitting on the stone floor. "Sentimental."

In searching for stairs down, Estin's attention was drawn back to the foothills and plains to the east. From here, he could see far more clearly, though distance still limited the details.

He could see what looked like a vast sea of black moving southeast and it was from this dark mass that bolts of lightning and flame continually erupted, creating the light flashes in the sky he had seen earlier. Spellcasters, he realized. There were a great many of them, waging violent war against their enemies.

The army that he was watching surrounded two enormous figures that made Estin's head spin to even think about. They were massive metal men, standing so tall that even from miles away, he could see that they were crafted to look like enormous dwarves. These were stomping the ground within their foes, sometimes leaning to punch or sweep at the ground.

"What are those?" he asked Finth, pointing out the giants.

"Oh that's not bloody good," noted the dwarf, squinting. "Those are war golems we built a couple centuries ago to clear out a mineshaft that was filled with lesser dragons. That type of golem can handle an army by itself and when it's done, you just have to clean a few hundred pounds of guts off their boots. Two of them could overthrow an entire country. Who in their right mind would set those things into motion? We've got laws against even letting people see those things."

Shaking his head, Estin tried to make out more of the army, but he had no chance to see them at this distance. Judging by the path they had taken, the troops were likely from Altis.

Turning away from the distant battle, Estin finally spotted the nearest stairs down from the wall into the city and led the way to them. Within five minutes, they were down at the edge of the slum district, trying to get an idea of where they were relative to the places they remembered.

"I'll meet you back here in thirty to forty minutes," Finth said, checking the street both directions. "Then we can decide what to do next. I want to check in with my contact before we do too much inside the city."

Estin agreed and went his own way. He had his own investigation he wanted to do while they were in town and people that he had realized he wanted to see again.

Back when he had lived in the city, he had several shopkeepers who had treated him well. Now, he wanted to repay them. Without having told Finth, he had slipped several tiny gemstones from the pouch with the intent of repaying kindnesses. Though none of these people would likely do more than chase him off with a broom publically, he knew they had all had a soft spot for the homeless, no matter their race. For that, he could think of no better way to reward them, since without their aid, he never would have lived to adulthood.

Turning down one of the cross streets, Estin began to realize that he was walking in plain sight without having to avoid anyone. The streets were empty. Not one person of any race was about. This time of day, though a bit early for the Grinder, there should have been dozens of humans, elves, and dwarves opening shops or just wandering around. If nothing else, there should have been the stragglers from the taverns, stumbling off their evening binges.

Estin turned right and hurried up a block, finding one of the popular—though very rough and dangerous—taverns of the district. There were no patrons out front, or in the alley alongside.

Leaning against the door, Estin listened for a time, while keeping his eyes on the street. Both were still and quiet. Only the occasional creak of wood and the cries of the birds far above broke the silence.

Taking another sniff of the air, he began to pick up on a lingering scent of raw meat left in the sun too long. This was not uncommon, especially for this tavern, but it seemed to hang everywhere in the air. Without thinking about it, he looked up again, watching the large flocks of crows. There were a lot more of them than he remembered having seeing before that day. Cities always drew carrion birds, but these flocks were enormous.

Estin eased the tavern door open, even as he pulled his hood farther forward to do what he could to conceal his face. His kind were allowed in this particular tavern, but anyone new to the place was often assaulted by the regulars and he had no desire to provoke a conflict any sooner than necessary. As the door swung outwards, he had to let his eyes adjust to the dark inside. Not a single candle or torch was lit and that same raw meat smell drifted out of the tavern more strongly.

He stepped in cautiously, his bare feet coming down immediately on bits of broken glass and pottery, which he ignored even as they bit into the pads of his feet.

The whole tavern had been sacked by the look of things. Much of the old mugs and pottery plates now lay strewn about, as though nearly every patron had tossed their meals onto the floor. Rotten food lay in the space between tables and several large mugs still sat on the bar, partially drained.

Estin took each step with increasing care as the hair across his neck and arms began to stand on end. The place reeked of decay, but he could not be sure if it was just all from the old food. He approached the first table closest to the door with trepidation, eyeing the plates of food on it with suspicion.

Though the chairs at this table were overturned, there were two plates of potatoes and steamed vegetables—at least he believed that's what they were after this much decay—still sitting on it, with one mug that contained a small amount of liquid. On the floor alongside the table, he saw the remains of a second mug.

On a whim, Estin bent over the plates of food and took a long deep breath. He was sure of what the food had been now, but there was something more. Maybe a spice he did not recognize. He racked his mind for the particular aroma, but could not place it.

He began creeping through the tavern again, this time moving towards the bar. Leaning over it, he checked on the bartender's side for any further clues as to what had happened.

Estin froze as he saw shoes and visually followed them up to a man's body, hidden behind the bar. The man looked as though he had fallen down and just lay there, close enough to the inside of the bar that he could not be seen from the main room.

Cursing his curiosity, he climbed over the bar and dropped alongside of the barkeep. It took no healer's skill to see that the man was quite dead, his skin ashen and face bloated. Estin guessed that the man had likely been dead three or four days.

As he had been taught, Estin lay a hand on the body and let his mind drift free, searching for the man's spirit. The room remained as empty as it had when he entered, letting him know that the spirit had moved on. This man was well beyond any healer's power.

Estin tossed back his hood and the bearskin, freeing him for swift movement. He doubted stealth was really needed at this point.

He hurried outside, searching the streets for any sign of any living being, but aside from the crows there was no one. Not a footprint, not a recent track from wagons or carts, not even the smell of a single person wandering by in the last day or so.

In a blind panic, Estin ran from home to home, kicking in the door of each and searching for humans. Every place he went, he found disheveled rooms that appeared as if the owners had fallen down or knocked something over, then vanished.

At the fifth home, he finally stopped, panting, at yet another overturned table. He dropped to all fours and began sniffing at some rotting food, trying to identify what they had been eating. It had been bread and some vegetables, but again there was that other scent.

He scrambled all over the room, searching for the source of the smell. As he was about to give up, he spotted a large clay pot of water under a counter.

Yanking the pot out into the open, he whipped the cover off of it and put his nose close to the water's surface. There he found the smell at last, a deep earthy scent that made his skin itch. Unable to identify it, he stuck his finger-claw into the pot, then touched the tiny amount of water to his tongue.

Bitterness in the water was his only hint of what was in there, just before his muscles shook and his stomach clenched. Estin struggled against the effect, forcing his body to accept it and deal with it. This was something his parents had always told him was part of what made his people special and different from the humans, but he had rarely had cause to poison himself. Today, that resistance saved him as his muscles eased and his stomach relaxed, the toxin passing as his body fought it off.

"They poisoned everyone?" he said aloud, surprised at the audacity of the killer. "Why would someone even want to?"

Estin went back to the street, finding Finth walking up the middle of the road, his face pale.

"They're all dead," Finth told Estin, glaze-eyed. "Every single one."

Estin opened his mouth to say something, but his sharp hearing picked up the sound of footfalls approaching. He snapped his fingers in front of Finth's eyes, then motioned to the tavern.

Together, they ran inside, but kept the door ajar so that he could watch the street.

It took several minutes, but finally a group appeared in view.

Numbering almost fifty, the group was entirely made up of undead. Shambling zombies groaned and eyed the buildings, while smooth-moving skeletons marched behind silently. The entire morbid group took a long time to pass, seemingly checking for any survivors…or more corpses.

"Never again!" whispered Finth hoarsely. "I'm staying out in the friggin' woods til the day I die! Who turns their citizens into undead?!"

"We need to know if this is just happening in the slums," Estin told him, checking the road again. He could see no more of the abominations in either direction. "One group of them is bad enough, but there are a lot of people in this town...or were. If the Turessians turned them all, we may have a problem."

Finth paled further.

"Twenty-thousand," Finth said softly. "That was the number I always heard. Another ten-thousand in the farms across the region."

Estin thought about the idea of twenty-thousand undead like he had fought marching on the camp and felt briefly sick. Thoughts of the massive army to the far southeast only furthered his dread, wondering how many of them once lived in Altis.

"We will head for the west gate, then. It's near enough to the slums that we can still move freely, but should be close enough to the arts district to give us a feel for how the rest of the town is doing."

Finth nodded, adding, "We can go through the central market on the way. I promised Ulra I'd try to free some fur-suckers. Promise is a promise."

They waited a little longer, then Estin led the mad dash from the tavern, using his sense of smell and keen hearing to watch for further patrols. They ran through the empty streets towards the middle of town, finding no sign of life the whole way.

As they entered the market, Estin began to smell still more death. He looked in all directions, until at last he noticed the tall wooden structure in the center of the market. It was new and still smelled faintly of fresh-cut wood.

The new gallows had four "guests." Hanging by their necks, two orcs, the duke, and a woman Estin guessed to be the duke's wife all swung in the breeze. They were kept swaying by their struggles to free themselves, their tied limbs twitching and tugging at their bonds.

"Should we free them?" asked Finth.

Estin watched the duke as the man's body spun about, finally getting a good look at the man's face. He was grey and bloated, his broken face snarling as he fought to be free.

"They're already dead. Keep going."

Estin moved on, trying to ignore the guttural noises from the gallows above them. Having avoided this part of town for most of his life, it took him a little bit to find the slave pens, but when he did, he wished he had just left the town.

Long cages were inset into the ground, with narrow staircases that led down to them for adding or removing the slaves. With the slavemasters all gone or dead, the slaves still remained in their cages. Wildlings, fae-kin, and even a few halflings lay in the long pens by the dozens, their emaciated bodies lying still and cold.

"They look as though they were left out through the recent storms," he noted, kneeling beside the lip of the drop-off into the cages. He shifted his mind into the spirit-realm, searching for spirits seeking a healer, but the pens were just as dead in the spirit world as in his own. "These ones never got poisoned. They starved and froze."

Even Finth, for all his stalwart belligerence, looked about ready to cry as he looked from one nearly-skeletal body to the next. Some of the bodies were not even recognizable by race.

"This city needs to burn, Estin."

"It's too big for us to deal with. We need to go."

A shrill hiss from the west made Estin look up. There, a robed humanoid figure stood with about twenty shambling zombies right behind it. The Turessian raised a long spear, then pointed at Estin and Finth, setting the undead into lumbering motion.

"Can you do anything about them, Estin?"

He shook his head vigorously, taking to his feet in a hurry.

"Run."

Finth did not argue, taking off at a pace that Estin struggled to match. They did not bother with any semblance of stealth anymore, making for the east gate as fast as they could manage.

As they approached, Estin remembered the groups of undead that they had seen at the various entrances as they had neared the city originally. He checked behind them, finding the group of zombies moving along fairly swiftly, trying to catch up with them.

"This is going to be rough," he warned Finth, as the gate came into sight.

The east gate—the city's largest—was nearly packed with skeletal or mostly skeletal guards, all facing out towards the foothills and plains beyond. Not one looked back towards the inside of the city.

"Follow me!"

Estin rushed the group, shoulder-checking the first zombie as he cleared the gate proper. He turned sharply, hugging the wall as he leapt at the next corpse that started to turn his way, crashing into it with both feet and tipping it over. He recovered from the landing and hopped over its clawing grasp, punching the next zombie to knock it off-balance as he moved past it.

Only a handful of the creatures remained between them and freedom, but Estin could feel the oppressive weight of the monsters closing on them, forcing them nearly flat against the wall to avoid their grabbing hands.

Estin acted as quickly as he could, summoning the only offensive spell Asrahn had taught him thus far. He made the motions, whispered the secret words, then stomped his foot and threw his arms up towards the sky, feeling magic rush through him with the now-familiar whispers of spirits in his head. A rush of power flared outwards, driving back all of the undead at least ten feet.

"Go!"

Finth raced past him, heading for the trees.

Once his companion passed him, Estin dropped the magic, feeling his heart flutter as the power faded and the undead began rushing forward again. He turned from them, running for all he was worth to catch Finth.

They ran together for a long time, stumbling over rocks and zigzagging through trees as they headed in a randomly-chosen direction. Even the cold winter air was ignored as they sweated from the exertion of running.

When at last they collapsed, they had neither seen nor heard the undead for a very long time. They lay there until the rush began to wear off and the damp cold began to finally make its way through their clothes. Estin found himself shaking from the chill, even when he tried to ignore its effect on him.

Estin rolled onto his feet, even though his body begged to stay on the ground.

"Lihuan will want to know," Finth said, still staring up at the sky.

Estin nodded, then squinted at the faint stars in the sky.

"What day is it?"

"How would I...maybe mid-month. Why?"

Searching the sky, Estin finally found the faint outline of the moon. It was nearly full.

"I'm supposed to patrol the western range tomorrow night. If we head back now, I can just head that way and get to work hours early. I can talk to Asrahn when I get back."

"It's Lihuan that needs to know...besides, I'm on the patrol list, too. I don't remember you having a patrol for another week. There isn't even anything out in the bloody west range."

Estin shook his head.

"I don't answer to Lihuan anymore, if I can help it. It's Asrahn's assignment. Part of the training, I think."

Finth looked quite skeptical, but said nothing.

They made the trek back slowly, their feet aching the whole way after having gone both directions in one day. There was not a single bit of conversation on the return, with both watching the woods for signs of the undead horde, but finding none.

As they reached the outer edges of the camp's patrol range, Estin came to a stop.

"This is where I go elsewhere."

Finth turned around and eyed him oddly.

"When will you be back? Gotta tell Lihuan something, or he'll be expecting you to shamble into camp with the rest of the rot-faces."

"I should be back in a day, maybe a day and a half."

"Travel safe then, monkey."

"Always."

Estin turned from the dwarf and began a western path until he knew he was out of sight, then made for the southwest, moving through the woods by memory. The route was certainly not one that Asrahn had told him to take and likely would have forbidden. Even so, he knew that Finth would not question Asrahn about it. Any time questions had come up about the details of his training, the elder had yelled at the asker, shooing them away. That had worked to his advantage when he had wanted to disobey orders.

Guided by instinct and occasionally his nose, Estin moved through the woods like a shadow, avoiding several potential ambushes and at least one pit-trap that he knew about. The route seemed to become more lethal each time he traveled it, but that was not going to change his decision. He had a feeling that those he was avoiding knew he had come through this way, thus the newer traps.

At last, he reached the sheer face of a cliff and went up it, keeping his body flat against the rock. This was not nearly as easy as climbing trees or the badly-fit stones of the Altis walls, but it was not terribly hard, either. The cliff was uneven, giving him many places to grab if he was careful. He just had to be cautious to stay quiet and watch for anyone moving at the bottom of the cliff who might see him.

Once Estin had reached about fifty feet off the ground, he moved sideways until he came to a thin pathway where the rocks had shifted, leaving a narrow ledge. This took him about another mile southwest, until he found his usual hiding place and settled in.

Below him, Insrin's village lay in full display, all their attempts to hide the place unable to conceal it from above. From here, he had watched them many times.

The guards for the village were diligent, that Estin had to give them. When Feanne had first left, he had come day after day, trying to find a way to sneak in and had always wound up running away. Once his ribs and leg had healed fully, he had climbed the cliff and found this location, from which he could watch the whole town, learning more about them. It was in doing so, he had learned the schedule he now followed.

Twice every month, Insrin would go out with his hunters for a night or two. The times were practically set in stone, letting Estin plan around them by simply watching the moon. By his estimate, tonight would be one of those nights, with Insrin returning late the following day or early the morning after.

He lay in waiting, concealed by the shade of the mountain face, as well as the fact that the village guards would never look up. After this many visits, he felt confident that he could probably throw rocks down on the village without fear.

The sun slowly disappearing behind him, Estin waited patiently, until at last he saw Insrin emerge from his mud hut, right at the bottom of the cliff. The pack-leader stopped at the doorway until Feanne joined him, the two embracing and speaking briefly.

Estin had seen this exact exchange over and over and after months it finally no longer hurt him. At first, he had seen the callousness in Feanne's demeanor, the complete indifference for her mate's departure. Slowly, she had warmed to her mate and they appeared fairly happy now. That had been hard at first for Estin, but he dearly wanted her safe and to have a good life, so this was at least a small comfort.

What had been hard for him to cope with had been her pregnancy. He had first been able to spot the change in her about a little more than a month after she left Lihuan's camp and he had felt sick for the whole remaining duration of the pregnancy—about three months of the four the fox-breeds took to have their young. Despite this, he kept coming back as often as he could sneak away, trying to watch her and wishing he could protect her from closer than the cliffs. He had wanted to wish her well during the pregnancy, but had no way to deliver that message.

Still, Insrin appeared to be doing well at caring for her, often escorting her himself when he did not have his personal guard and a female or two watching her. Someone had always been tending to her. She was being well cared for, Estin had to accept, but still wanted to help her, or at least be there for her.

Two months ago, just before the storms had kept him away, Insrin's hunting trip had been canceled. Estin had sat on the cliff throughout the night, hearing Feanne give birth to the other male's children and then wept for days, unable to even face Asrahn. He had stayed in his tent and spoken to no one for almost a full week. It was that night that had finally broken him.

Now, he watched to be sure that the whole family was safe. He knew at last that

Feanne was truly beyond his reach as Insrin was not the monster he had hoped for. Instead, he was a good mate for her, treating Feanne well, which seemed to somehow make everything worse at times. He just had to keep reminding himself that this was a better life for Feanne than he could ever have offered her.

Each time he came here, Estin wondered why he kept doing this to himself. Some part of him needed this, but he could not fathom why. When he had believed that Feanne hated her mate and would want to run away, it was easy to convince himself to endure anything for her, in the vague hope that he could one day win her back. Now, with two young in the hut and her affection clear even to him, he did not know what kept him coming back.

Tonight was proving to be no different. Insrin lingered a while with Feanne, whispering to her in the night, until he finally turned and joined two waiting foxes, who escorted him into the woods, handing him weapons as they went. As they departed, Feanne waited on the doorstep, watching them go, then turned and herded two small shapes back into the hut before closing the door.

Estin struggled to get a look at the little ones, but never quite saw them directly. From what he had been told back at his own camp, at just shy of two months, the little kits were likely running around and might be speaking already. Having spent so much time around the other races, he could only laugh at how much easier his people had it when dealing with children.

Estin closed his eyes and fell back against the cliff face. The sharp rocks against his back—even through his bearskin cloak—were a welcome feeling in the absence of any others.

*

Waking after a good sleep, Estin realized that it was nearing noon. Normally, he tried to be awake the whole time he was at his hiding place, but the exertion at Altis had made that impossible.

He scanned the village, trying to get a feeling for what he had missed.

The village was fairly active, but like his own breed, the foxes tended to be most active at night, so the village still was hours from much activity. He watched idly, munching some of his remaining food, not even knowing what to watch for. This was how it always was, with him watching mostly for the sake of feeling that he was protecting someone, even if he could not point to any actions he had taken that truly helped.

As this was the first time that Estin had come since Feanne had given birth to the twins, it was them he hoped to see, rather than Feanne. Seeing her hurt him to the soul and he had no desire to endure that again just yet, but he really wanted to look on the kits, if only to know what more he had lost out on. The children at his own camp he had begun caring for out of loyalty to the pack, but Feanne's he just wanted to see.

Leaning forward, Estin managed to spot the two kits running around in the trees near the bottom of the cliff, chasing each other and giggling. Without realizing it, he found himself smiling sadly. They were adorable little puffballs, their fur a reddish-black that stood out on the melting snow. Idly, he wondered what the children would have been like if things had been different and he had been able to stay with Feanne.

Movement caught Estin's eye and he shifted on the cliff, trying not to dislodge any of the loose rock. Not far down the edge of the cliff, he could see a mountain lion—not a wildling—creeping through the trees towards the two kits. At first he thought it coincidental, but then saw that it was staring in their direction. The animals were not uncommon in this area, but approaching civilized areas was.

Hopping to his knees, Esitn tried to find Feanne through the trees. He spotted her at last, back near her hut, working over a steaming pot. She was watching the kits, but not the woods. By the time she smelled or saw the cougar, it would be too late. Even if he yelled to her, he guessed that she would spend more time trying to figure out who was shouting than he could afford.

Fear gripping him at the idea of the defenseless kits getting mauled, Estin began trying to find a way to scare off the cougar. He grabbed several small rocks, throwing them as hard as he could in that direction, but the animal was too focused to look up as they hit the trees around it.

Swearing, Estin leaned out over the ledge, scanning the sheer surface below his hiding place. The rocks were rough, but far smoother than he would have liked, giving him no points to easily grab or land on. Worse still, there were no good hiding places between the cougar and the two kits.

He braced himself and flipped around to face the cliff face, then began climbing down as fast as he could manage. It was taking too much time, and a check over his shoulder confirmed that the cougar was within twenty feet of the kits, who still giggled and ran in circles, lost in a game of tag with one another.

Gritting his teeth, Estin released his grip and slid down the cliff face, tumbling as he hit the bottom hard. His joints ached from the impact, but fear for another was far more consuming. He got right to his feet and ran towards the kits, the cougar now within range to jump on either of them at any moment.

Snarling as animalistic rage took over, Estin leapt, catching the cougar mid-jump and crashing to the ground with the growling animal in his grip. They rolled and kicked at each other, each fighting for control over the other. Fangs snapped near Estin's face and he reacted in kind, driving his claws into its neck on one side, even as he bit it from the other. They struggled for a long time, each growling and struggling with the other, until the cougar finally fell silent, collapsing in Estin's arms, its throat torn.

Estin dropped the beast as he knelt there, gagging as he spit blood from his mouth and wiping it from both his jaw and numerous cuts on his torso that had gotten through the thick hides he wore. Numbly, he touched his chest and repeated the magical phrases Asrahn had taught him, closing the injuries and restoring a tiny amount of his strength.

Still dazed and winded from the fight, Estin looked around...then froze as the two kits stared at him from the sides of a tree nearby. Wide-eyed, they clung to the tree's bark, as though expecting him to maul them next.

"I will not hurt you," he told them, trying not to sound like the crazy guy that had just torn apart a cougar with his bare hands. "It would have."

The kits—a male and a female he noted—retreated slightly, cowering behind the edge of the tree.

Somewhere behind the trees, Estin heard Feanne's voice call out, "Atall! Oria! Where are you?"

"You had better go," Estin told the kits, smiling. He held a finger to his mouth. "Please don't tell."

The male, Atall, ran off, but Oria marched up to him, her little face angry.

"Mommy would have protected us," she told him, thumping her tiny paw into his arm. "She says we don't need guards. Tell daddy to stop making mommy mad!"

Estin laughed and ruffled the child's head fur as she continued to glower at him.

"You're right and I'm sorry. Your mommy would be able to protect you from anything."

The little fox nodded vigorously, crossing her arms and glaring at him as though waiting for his departure. She was shivering in the cold snow, but seemed very determined to stay there. The very picture of her mother, thought Estin.

Somewhere nearby, Estin heard Feanne call again. She was getting close now and sounded concerned.

"I'll go," he told the child, pulling the bearskin from his shoulders. He draped it over her shoulders, practically burying the little fox girl. She poked her face out of the long fur, though Estin could only really see her muzzle. "This was your mother's once. It'll keep you warm. Don't tell her where you got it or she'll be mad at us both."

Little Oria pulled up the bottom of the pelt to get it off the ground and hurried off, looking over her shoulder once at him as she scurried back towards the mud hut.

Still kneeling in the snow, Estin smiled sadly as he watched the kit go, amused with her tiny footprints in the snow and black-tipped tail sticking out from under the bearskin. She was utterly adorable and he wanted to go congratulate Feanne on two lovely children...but knew he could not. He then got to his feet and began the long march home.

*

Hours later, Estin approached his own camp, finding the perimeter active and quite mobile. As he neared, half a dozen males of varying breeds rushed out, hesitated, then went past him, scouring the woods.

He watched all this, then continued towards Asrahn's tent to let her know that he had returned. He got almost to the entrance when Ulra came bounding up, panting.

"Lihuan was looking for you," she said, as though that told him what was expected of him.

"Then tell him I have returned. I'll be with Asrahn, studying."

"He wants to see you."

"That is an awful shame, as I have no desire to see him."

Ulra growled at him, standing straighter. Since the embarrassment of Lihuan at Insrin's hands, Lihuan had been treated by most of the camp as too weak to survive as the pack's leader much longer. This had prompted a dramatic change in Ulra's behavior in turn, seeking to enforce his will at every turn, violently if needed. Attitudes like Estin's were tolerated by some, but Ulra rarely would. Estin was willing to bet that Ulra would be just as happy to drag his body before Lihuan, since he had stopped speaking to their pack-leader.

"Fine. Lead the way."

He followed Ulra through the camp to Lihuan's large tent, stepping inside at her urging.

The inside of the tent was not like Estin remembered it. When last he had entered

213

months before, the place had been well-organized and moderately spartan. Now, the place was badly lit, with thin streams of water running through unpatched holes in the tent's cloth. The pile of furs that had once made up Lihuan's bedding were now mostly scattered, with several torn to shreds at one end of the room.

"Sit down," croaked Lihuan, sitting atop the remaining furs, slouching forward and held up mostly by his cane. "You will speak with me."

Estin flopped in the middle of the room and waited, offering nothing.

"My mate tells me I have wronged many people," he continued slowly. Had Estin not met him before, he would have guessed him far older than he was. It was as though the elder had aged a decade over the winter months. "I seek to know how much harm I have caused."

"Then why ask me?"

Lihuan pushed himself upright to look at Estin. It was then that Estin saw that Lihuan had lost considerable weight. The elder looked as though he were wasting away. The camp had been somewhat short on food through the winter, but Estin knew there was enough for everyone to get by.

"I have some who still answer me. I know that you are not one of them."

"Again, then why ask me? You lost your status as my pack-leader long ago."

"We shall start with me wondering how I have wronged you that you hate me so."

Estin fidgeted, trying to find a delicate way to dissuade the direction of the conversation. He felt like he could not escape Lihuan's stare and finally resorted to most of the truth.

"You sold your daughter for the pack's profit. Do I need more reason?"

Leaning hard on his cane, Lihuan sighed softly.

"No. You do not. Asrahn has much the same reason for hating me and I doubt she will ever forgive me. When we first argued over this, I saw no sense in her ranting. Feanne was willing to go along with the arrangement and it was made at a time when this pack was starving and in need of supplies. It was desperation, Estin. It was the best idea I could come up with to save us at the time.

"Insrin's return surprised me...maybe more than it did Feanne. He held me to my word, something I do not break lightly, nor does Feanne. I did not realize then how much he hated the other breeds. Because I am mated to a half-breed and allow any breed to come and go from my pack, he has no respect for me and no intention of allowing me to ever see my child again."

Estin sat silently.

"I need to know how Feanne is doing. Happy or sad, I need to know before...," Lihuan stopped talking and looked down at the floor.

"You're letting yourself die slowly," Estin observed bitterly. The sagging flesh, the lost weight, the dry nose...his healer's instincts saw it all clearly. Had it been anyone else, he would have held them down and force-fed them. Lihuan, he had enough anger towards that he could look the other way. "You want to know what came of your great mistake before you die."

Lihuan nodded, checking the entrance to the tent.

"I do not wish others to know. Already, some are fighting for the right to lead the pack. I will not give them more cause. I have done more than enough to damage this pack."

"Be that as it may, why bring me here?"

"You were her friend," Lihuan said, broaching no debate. "I could see it in how you two interacted. I also know that you watch out for her still."

Estin froze, wondering if Lihuan was just fishing for information.

"Yes, Estin, I know you have been going there. I have spies who obey me still."

"Then what would you have of me?"

Lihuan lifted a shaking hand and picked up a tightly-rolled piece of rough parchment that had been tied off and sealed with wax. He held it out to Estin, who took it from him.

"I am forbidden to approach their village. You will deliver this. You do not need to speak to her. In fact, for your safety, it may be best if you were not seen in that camp. Just ensure she gets the note and then watch from afar. If there is any reply, please bring it back to me. It is the only thing I will ever ask of you again, Estin."

Estin stood, still holding the parchment and began to leave Lihuan, stopping as he reached the entrance. Turning slightly, he caught Lihuan's eyes, debating whether the words on his mind should be uttered. He finally decided that he had to tell Lihuan.

"You have grandchildren," he began, "named Atall and Oria. A boy and a girl. I thought you might want to know, as you might never get to see them."

That said, Estin left the tent quickly, biting back any sympathy as he heard Lihuan's sobs behind him. As much as he did not tell Lihuan to hurt him, knowing that Estin's pain was shared was some degree of relief for him.

Traveling straight to Asrahn's tent, he came inside without announcing himself and took a seat where he usually did for their training sessions, staring at the tiny fire she usually kept smoldering at the center of the tent, surrounded by the circle of stones for bringing the dead back. Now, he just stared at the embers, waiting for Asrahn to approach from the corner where she sat, sipping at tea.

"What has happened, child?" asked the old female, coming over and sitting beside him. "This is not the calm student I had begun to expect. I see anger in you."

"Lihuan wants me to deliver a note to Feanne," he explained, lifting the parchment in front of him. He turned it so that he could see the three scratch lines in the wax that were Lihuan's mark. "He is looking for forgiveness before he dies."

Asrahn's face sunk and she took the note from his hands, setting it near the smoldering embers.

"Would you allow him to be forgiven for what he has done, or would you have him suffer to the last of his days?"

Estin shook his head, unsure.

"I want him to suffer as I have," he admitted. "I want him to know the harm he caused. You teach that I am supposed to help and to heal. This is one topic that makes me want to watch people bleed and die. I think I honestly could watch Lihuan starve to death and not regret a moment."

Asrahn picked up the parchment with her claws and held it to the coals, sparking the end aflame.

Reacting immediately, Estin grabbed the paper from her, snuffing the flames.

"So you do not hate as much as you thought," she said, sitting back. "Will you deliver it, though?"

He mulled that as he let his fingers slide over the rough parchment and the thick seal on it, brushing away the charred bits on the end of the parchment.

"I will find a way. I owe it to her, not him."

They sat there, both staring at the embers for a long time, until Estin looked up at Asrahn.

"You chide me about my anger, but why are you still here?"

"What do you mean, child? I am not angry about being here. I have tea here."

He motioned at the tent.

"You left your life-mate because of anger. He's stopped eating and mostly stopped drinking and will die within the week. Still, you sit here in your own tent, not even telling him he's being foolish. You let the rest of the camp tear itself apart as the younger members argue over his position."

"Some things are more complicated than just loving someone."

Estin shook his head.

"No, you are being selfish, if I may say so. I had a week with the one I loved and it changed my life. You have had a lifetime, only to throw away what may be the last few years together over a disagreement. An awful disagreement, but still just an argument at heart. I would have argued every day for the rest of my life to have Feanne. Why would you let this end your relationship? I just don't understand."

Smoothing her clothing, Asrahn glared at Estin briefly, then stood and picked up a pitcher of water and a loaf of bread. She kicked a leather-bound book into Estin's lap as she left the tent. She also rolled a small cloth-wrapped package over to him from where it had been hidden under a blanket.

"Read all those and study on your own a while," she said, departing. "I need to tend to an idiot that won't do it for himself."

Estin smiled to himself, sliding the parchment into his belt pouch, beside the folded one from Asrahn. He reclined onto his side and opened the book, finding that it was Asrahn's spellbook, filled with her own version of the notes he had taken for months. Just inside the cover, he found a folded piece of paper, which he set aside for the moment.

He paged through the detailed explanations of spells that he had not even seen, sometimes becoming lost in the details of what the spell was even intended to accomplish.

He soon began transcribing much of what he found onto more paper, copying the concepts and needed words and motions for himself. A great deal of what was held within the book was the part of his training that he knew the least about. While Asrahn had been quite verbose in teaching him about how to heal a wound, she had skirted the issue of using healing magic in battle. He was starting to see why as he poured over the book that had likely taken her much of her life to put together in one place.

Aside from the ability to heal, Estin found a wealth of magic that could hinder a foe, snuff out the life of an opponent, or bring back an dead ally who had just fallen. What caught his eye most was the assortment of different ways he could strike at the undead, using the power of the spirits to weaken or break the magic that animated their form. This was exactly the magic he had sought since Ghohar's death.

It was these spells that Estin focused in copying, until he stopped and realized truly why they had been kept from him so long. While a spell that could kill was obvious, magic that would destroy the undead was less clear until he looked over the way the magic flowed through the caster. From what he could see, every spell that harmed a corpse could be easily twisted to destroy the living or even create a new undead. The powers of the two types were so closely interwoven that Estin believed a healer could easily become a necromancer. It was a short step, that in self-defense, might be all too tempting.

Estin stopped after copying all that he could from the old book. He stretched and lamented that it would likely take him weeks or longer to go through the selection of magic to figure out how to cast them all, let alone when surprised or unable to read from his notes. It meant a lot of work.

Sliding the book aside, he stared at the folded parchment, then at the package she had left him. Curiosity getting the better of him, he picked up the paper and began unfolding it, realizing that it was the same one he had once been told to bring to Feanne to start his training.

The note was short, saying just, "You two could learn from each other. Teach him to be more than prey."

Wincing at the emotions that surfaced, he tossed the note aside. At this point, he turned his attention to the little package Asrahn had also moved his way. It was about fist-sized, with a long twine string holding it closed.

Estin untied the knot in the string slowly, trying not to crush the soft package. With the string gone, he lay the bundle flat on the ground and unrolled the cloth, revealing the leather, bone, and feather necklace he had stolen from the duke's keep. When he picked it up, he saw that there were words written on the inside of the cloth.

He picked it up, recognizing the script as Feanne's.

Estin, if you are being allowed to read this, I have likely fallen in battle and cannot give it to you myself. Today, Asrahn or whatever teacher you currently have, is proud enough of your progress to call you a master. You are my equal in all things magical, now. For this I applaud you. You have done what I could not without selling myself to a woodland spirit. If I were still alive, I would have hung this necklace on you myself. You have earned all that it stands for. Wear it proudly.

Estin very nearly broke down as emotion flooded him, but he smiled and whispered his thanks to whatever spirits or gods might listen for such a friend as he had once had in Feanne. When he had finished, he fastened the necklace around his neck, feeling truly happy at the faith the others had shown in him. He touched the beads gently, wondering what the original owner had been like.

Chapter Eight
"New Life"

I had found a new purpose in my life, finally not focused on my own selfish goals and it lent itself to the return of my dreams. Though I did not remember many dreams during that time of my life, the better sleep I received told me that something had changed and I almost never woke in fear.

Before finding Feanne, I was worried about only myself. I did not see it that way at the time, but I do now, looking back on it. I wondered where my next meal would come from, where I would sleep, whether it would rain, all the while ignoring the other wildlings...even the other races...who suffered around me. Had we but worked together, things could have been so very different.

After joining the pack, my focus was still on myself, but more on how to lead a full life. I spent all my time trying to fit in and become one of the pack in spirit as well as word. Part of this was my desire to find a mate, though I had not even realized how badly I had been wanting and looking for this. It was all part of the culture of acceptance that had been dominating me. Other wildlings sought out mates, so I had too. Unfortunately, that had opened me up to the pain of losing Feanne.

With the recognition as a true healer, I was suddenly free. I was free from fear of rejection by the pack. I was free from concern about fitting in through mating, food choices, and my appearance. I had a purpose in my life and it was simply to help and heal. I was the one they would look to for help with sickness and hurt, regardless of their opinion of me.

This is all not to say I was entirely without nightmares. The fear of Altis' undead coming down in legion haunted me many nights over those next two months. I would see that vast army come marching back up the mountain victorious, watching as they marched into our camp, killing mercilessly.

Whether dream or not, at least now I had the tools I needed to stand my ground.

Estin patted the young rabbit wildling on the head as he flexed his leg experimentally. The youth had fallen in the woods, breaking the leg on rocks. As was his duty, Estin mended the leg and sent the child on his way. Within the day, he would be running around again...possibly falling again. It was a cycle Estin could only laugh at as the child yelled his thanks on the way out.

"If there is anyone waiting, I am free now," he said loudly, rubbing his head.

It had been a rough summer so far, with injuries aplenty. High winds and wildfires had ravaged the area, resulting in several fallen trees on the camp itself and many burned residents who went off to stop the fire before it reached the camp. Luckily, no one had died in all the disasters, something Estin was personally thankful for.

The tent opened and this time, Ulra entered, carrying an unconscious human. She set the human down in front of Estin carefully as she tried to squeeze into the small tent without collapsing it atop herself.

"I found him beyond our outer patrols in the south," she said softly. "I believe he was scouting, but was attacked."

Estin noted the silk clothing and fine leather boots, as well as shrouded jewelry—to keep it from making noise as he moved—and had no doubts that it was one of the gypsies. They had returned to the camp when the weather had warmed, claiming that the roads had become too dangerous for travel and they would like to stay with the pack. Lihuan had been skeptical, but Asrahn had convinced him to allow their long-term stay. Now, the camp ran free with both wildlings and humans, sometimes causing conflict, but mostly just creating mayhem.

This had led to weeks of Lihuan absorbing the endless stories of the gypsy people, much to their joy and somewhat to Asrahn's dismay. Most were bawdy and hardly the realm Lihuan had prided himself on all his life, but his deep love of tales made even these irresistible. Just the fact that Asrahn was putting up with the drunken humans in their tent day after day told volumes about her willingness to forgive Lihuan for his past faults.

"He is alive and not too badly injured," Estin said, touching the boy. He saw and felt few major injuries, but it looked as though he had been bludgeoned and rolled down a hill. "I will let you know when he wakes."

Ulra began to squirm out of the small tent, her girth making it difficult without catching herself on the canvas and bringing it down on herself. Once she was outside, she stuck her head back in.

"Lihuan has also asked that you come when you can. Finth returned this morning."

Estin looked up sharply.

"Does that mean he is still considered banished in his homeland, or did they let him in?"

"All I have heard was that the city was closed."

"How does one close a city?"

Ulra shrugged.

"Never been in one. I would not know."

The bear left then, leaving Estin alone with his patient.

Laying a hand on the boy's forehead, Estin concentrated a moment, feeling the spirits begin to flow through him, whispering as they went. The unseen hands touched the wounds, pulling them closed and repairing even the internal wounds. When he opened his eyes again, the boy slept more naturally, breathing slowly.

"Sleep well," he told the gypsy, "I will return soon."

Taking his leave of the tent, Estin smoothed the long doeskin robes that Asrahn had made for him. The outfit had apparently been a favored style by her father's people, though every so often Estin smirked at the thought of what Alafa would have thought of it, had she still been pursuing him.

The robes had been a gift that Asrahn had made quite a big deal of, presenting them to him as a reward for his first time bringing a dead person back. The task had not been difficult as the young female had been dead less than an hour, having cracked her head on a rock during exploration of the mountains, but the praise from Asrahn and Lihuan had been nearly endless. From what Asrahn had told him, restoring life was the pinnacle ability of the healer and was what she had been waiting to see in him as the completion of all of his training.

He walked across the middle space of the camp, where Lihuan's large tent was directly across from his own, smiling at Doln, who was standing guard at the pack-leader's tent. Passing the bear, he slipped inside, where Asrahn and Lihuan were sitting with Finth, who was waving his hands in the air.

"...a keg this large! I swear that wagon driver had never seen a dwarf drink before!"

Asrahn laughed and rolled her eyes and even Lihuan—having mostly recovered from his depression of the previous months—chuckled and shook his head. Though Lihuan had a deep love for even the gypsy stories, Finth's often left him amazed that dwarves had not driven themselves to extinction long ago…a point that Finth had sometimes been vocal in agreeing with.

"Estin!" exclaimed Finth, grinning broadly. "How goes the healing crap? You try lemon juice and salt yet?"

"I have refrained from using your mother's secret cure-all," he admitted, sitting down with the group. "Ulra tells me that you were unable to get into your home city? I thought that you had received word that all banishments were revoked and a request for aid had been called?"

Finth soured, frowning and giving Estin a dirty look.

"You really know how to jump right to the worst of it, like a cheap whore, you damned fur-licker," he grumbled, then looked over at Asrahn. "Sorry, ma'am. Habit, ya'know."

Asrahn inclined her head acknowledging his apology.

"Yeah, that's what I heard. I went all the way back there and found the dwarven equivalent of a sign saying, 'we're closed, go away.'"

"And what would that be?" asked Estin.

"A huge adamantine door sealing the passage, with a twenty-foot golem standing guard. When you get close, it tries to smash you, while shouting 'we're closed, go away.'"

Estin made a mental note to never...ever...visit a dwarven city.

"I was able to catch up with a gal I used to...uh...," Finth looked at Lihuan and Asrahn, then continued, "court, over near one of the human mining towns. She said that the city was called to arms and all combat-worthy dwarves were sent to Lantonne to aid in holding the city. Everyone else stayed in the deeps, waiting it out."

"Since when do the dwarves come during human wars?" asked Lihuan this time. "There are some dwarves in Lantonne, but it is no less a human city than Altis. All the stories tell that the dwarves normally close their border to leave humans to their own battles."

"True, true. I told her that them going to war for a human was about as likely as me selling myself at a whorehouse for an actual profit, but she insisted it was true. She saw the war golems go out first...all ten of them. Two weeks later, the entire dwarven army of our city marched down the road to Lantonne."

Estin found all of this either unlikely, or lacking information that they needed.

"Did she say why the army would mobilize like this?"

Finth nodded, tugging on his beard nervously.

"She says that the undead are winning the war. Things are getting bad out there.

"We were right about Altis, Estin. When the Turessians took over, they poisoned everyone and turned them, one district at a time. By the time the people knew it wasn't a plague it was too late. That, I got from another trustworthy source who owed me a goodly amount of coin.

"Since they left the walls, the undead have been moving from one village to the next, seizing the graveyards and adding to their troops. Even the war golems haven't been able to stop their advance. From what I'm told, the necromancers who lead the army are using their magic on the golems to slow them, while the main force marches on Lantonne.

"If they take that city, they will number over one hundred thousand."

"Well," interjected Asrahn, her mood dark, "at least that tells us why the gypsies came to stay with us. They likely had no desire to be in the path of that army."

"Expect more refugees soon," Lihuan added. "If I know anything about war, they will begin seeking out the remote areas to hide. That will put them in our laps."

All three of them were silent as they considered all the implications involved in a war of this magnitude. Finth, on the other hand, toyed with a small knife, dancing it on his hand.

"Do you want me to tell you what I found down in the dwarven tunnels?" Finth asked absently, his attention fully on the knife. "Or is that enough bad news already?"

"Might I remind you that you said you were stopped at the gate?" asked Asrahn, her tone annoyed and impatient. "I hear enough long-winded and likely exaggerated stories from my mate. I do not need more from you."

"I said the city was closed and there was some crazy-ass golem at the gate. I didn't say that I didn't get in."

Estin groaned. It was always like this dealing with Finth, if he thought he could get away with it.

"All I care about," stated Lihuan, giving Finth a dark glare, "is whether your people are any better prepared to deal with the undead than we are."

"Not even close. The city is lost already," Finth answered, not looking up. "My homeland is now crawling with bearded troops for the dead."

The tent remained silent for a long time, with Lihuan lowering his head in thought, while Estin and Asrahn watched Finth for any emotion. Instead, Finth just kept playing with the knife until he seemed to grow bored and just got up and walked out.

"That man has no feelings," grumbled Asrahn, once Finth was gone. "His people are all dead and he has no concern."

Lihuan shook his head.

"Not true. You both thought me heartless for not showing my feelings about letting Feanne go, but I hope you both know better. Finth is a far better actor than I am. He does not know how to deal with the pain, so he hides it."

Estin had been warned before that part of Asrahn's agreement to return to Lihuan's side was that he was not to speak of Feanne, unless he had better news for her. The brief mention was enough that Asrahn looked ready to storm off after Finth, but she just dug her claws into the ground and said nothing.

"Estin, have you managed to make my delivery yet?" asked Lihuan, seeming to shift the focus of conversation.

"I have not, but tonight is actually the next time I can try."

"I knew it was soon, but was not sure. Please try to also warn their camp after you try, as I know Insrin will want to be aware, even if he does not want you there."

"If you are having him do something this foolish, wouldn't it be better to send one of the foxes?" asked Asrahn, shooting Lihuan an angry glance.

"Yes, but Estin already has business there. I'd rather not send two and regardless of his breed, if he can get inside their patrols he should be able to deliver the message about the war."

"I will go and do what I can," Estin offered. "They have been stepping up patrols recently, so either they know I stop by sometimes, or they are preparing for an attack."

"Just do what you can," implored Lihuan.

*

That evening, Estin changed from his robes to a simple set of cloth pants and sleeveless shirt. With the warmer weather, his leather garments were nearly unbearable, though he would have greatly preferred them for climbing. Even his necklace he left behind, wanting nothing extra that might hinder his movement through the woods or up the cliff side.

Once he had everything—including his swords, which he dearly hoped he would not need, but brought just in case he was attacked while traveling—Estin began the long walk south. The routine was becoming old now, with the path well-known to him.

These last few months, he had continued going to the other village on his usual schedule. It was still a little painful, but watching the children play always lightened his mood. Unfortunately, the task Lihuan had given him before Asrahn and he had gotten their relationship smoothed out was still proving difficult. Between patrols watching the pack-leader's house and Feanne's own instincts to call for aid when she thought someone was near, he had never gotten within fifty feet of the house.

As he walked, he double-checked to be sure the parchment was still in his pouch, which it was. He would hate to get there, only to find it missing.

Estin crossed a little creek, moving ever southwest, but then stopped and listened as something caught the edge of his hearing. Something was not right. Turning sharply, he ducked behind a tree and waited near the stream.

Several minutes later, he heard splashing and obscure swearing.

"So you are Lihuan's spy?" he asked, stepping out in front of Finth, who was waist deep in the water. "I had a feeling, but thought you wouldn't stoop to spying on me."

"You act like you don't know me," Finth grumbled, trying to keep his beard and a handful of knives out of the water. "Though right now, if I stoop, I'll drown. Can I come out of the water?"

The dwarf waded to the shore and shook his boots and squeezed what he could of the water from his beard.

"Were you going to follow me the whole way?"

Finth laughed and answered, "I've followed you right onto that cliff of yours nearly every time you've gone. Figured someone had to watch out for you."

"And how much have you seen?"

"I saw you kill a mountain lion. That was some gory fighting. That kind of thing traumatizes kids and makes them grow up to be like me, you know."

Estin sighed, having hoped that even if a few people knew he was going to the camp occasionally, there would be no one who knew how attached he still was, or how hard he was trying to break himself of that. If Finth knew, then at least Lihuan and Asrahn knew, though it was likely that Ulra did as well.

"Hurry up then, I don't want to be out here all night."

Finth tagged along behind him the rest of the trip, his navigation as routine as Estin's after so many trips. That only added to Estin's annoyance that Finth knew the route so well.

They made good time, arriving just after sunset.

"I need to try to deliver this," Estin told Finth, holding up the parchment roll. "I'll meet you up top shortly."

He did not wait for an answer, moving along the cliff wall, freezing occasionally when a patrol got too close. Once, he was forced to dart up a tree as a small group of foxes wandered through, unaware he was hiding right above them.

Though it took him a while, Estin finally arrived at Feanne's house, holding the note. He had been given very explicit directions by Lihuan recently to ensure Insrin did not receive it, so he remained in the dark a moment, listening for voices. He needed to be sure that Feanne was alone before he could drop off the note and run.

A cry from the east made Estin turn. Shouts were echoing off the woods from that end of the village, but he could not hear the words from where he was. Soon, the sounds of many feet heading his way made him wonder if he had been seen coming in.

Estin checked the cliff and found that from where he was, it would be a long dash before he could have enough handholds to get far off the ground. The trees were his best option, interspersed as they were with the houses.

Up the nearest tree he went, trying to hide among the braches so that even if someone looked up, they might not readily see him.

The calls and shouts came closer quickly, as a group of foxes ran straight to Insrin and Feanne's home, the leader pounding on their door. When it opened, Estin could see Insrin, his grey fur recognizable among the mostly red foxes in the village.

There was a fast conversation, then Insrin went with the others, carrying weapons and trying to pull on a shirt of leather brigandine armor as he ran.

Estin waited another minute, then hopped down, making for the house as fast as he could. He was actually on the doorstep with the note in his hand when the door opened.

Feanne stood in the lit doorway, her eyes wide as she stared at him.

"What are you doing here?" she hissed softly, leaning out the door to look both ways. "Do you really want him to kill you that badly? I can't protect you."

He held the note towards her, which she snatched angrily.

"Your father wanted this put in your hand. That is all I want, Feanne. Goodbye."

Estin started to leave when he heard a more clear cry from the east. A single word. It was a word that could cut through any amount of noise, driving an icicle of fear and uncertainty into Estin's heart.

"Undead!"

He closed his eyes, standing there facing away from Feanne, wishing he had picked any other night. Nothing could complicate his feelings more than this.

"Stay inside," Estin growled, turning to the east.

"I got that from my mate already, thanks."

Rushing through the camp, while trying not to be too obvious, Estin tried to get an eye on the undead attacking. If it was just a few, he would return to Finth and leave. He had to keep telling himself that, trying to convince himself to let Insrin protect his family and not to intrude. They had more warriors in this village than in his own. They would be fine against most attacks.

Everywhere, fox wildlings were racing around, trying to resupply their warriors, or evacuate their homes. The females, elderly, and children were all being sent towards the back of the village near Feanne's home, to ready the front of the village for battle.

Estin easily passed through the homes with everyone so occupied. He was nearly to the thick line of fox warriors, when he stopped, finally able to see what was coming. As he saw it, he felt his ears go flat and his tail flop weakly to the ground.

Down the slope of the mountain, he could see what looked like a dark wave of humanoid shapes moving in the trees. Their mass was wider than the town and at least a quarter mile deep. There could easily be a thousand undead in the group, stretching well down the mountainside.

Even in the deep dark, the front line of the approaching force was visible. Disorganized and stumbling over the rough terrain, a line of undead a hundred wide glared up the hill at the living, their mouths working in groans and silent pleading for warm flesh. Ahead of them, Estin could see small animals fleeing for cover, sometimes getting dragged down by the slavering monsters that approached.

Fighting terror, Estin began surveying the defensive line.

There were about twenty fox warriors, all bearing long spears to brace against the charge. Every one of the warriors had a sword and shield at their feet, ready to be grabbed once the spear had fulfilled its purpose. Behind them, two middle-aged foxes—one male and one female, but both dressed in robes similar to his own back at camp—paced the line. After the healers, another fifteen foxes were kneeling, waiting with bows in-hand for the command to attack.

The village's defenses were impressive, but Estin kept looking back at the undead army, now only a few minutes out, realizing that they were outnumbered at least ten-to-one. This battle would end swiftly.

Turning, Estin ran back towards Feanne's home, hopping anything and anyone in his way as he tried to get to his destination before the first arrow could be fired. He tore up the path to her door, pounding on it as he reached the threshold.

"Feanne!" he called, pounding again. "You need to come out, now!"

The door opened and Insrin stood in front of him, a spear in one hand.

"What are you doing here?" he growled, advancing until he was practically pushing Estin off the doorstep. "This is my home!"

"And you'll die in it with your children!" Estin countered, shoving Insrin back. "I have someone in the woods that can get them to safety."

Insrin hesitated, glancing back into the small home. His shoulders dipped slightly.

"Feanne," he said calmly, but with a faint touch of sadness that Estin could hear. "I want you to take the children and follow this one's directions to escape."

"What?" asked Feanne, stepping into the light. The two kits were in her arms, clinging to her neck. "Why are we running? You said it was just a few undead."

"Do as I say as your pack-leader," Insrin said, more firmly, not looking her in the eyes. "I will come for you in the morning."

Estin turned to the cliff, waving up at the ledge high above. He then pointed to the north, where the easiest climb down would be. He could only hope Finth had seen him.

"Where are we going?" demanded Feanne, pulling the familiar bearskin cloak over her children and herself against the cool night.

"North," Estin told her, beginning to move towards the woods. "Finth is out there and will guide you. He should be just past the dark of the woods."

Feanne began walking that way, then stopped and looked back at Estin and Insrin.

"Are you both staying?"

Insrin hung his head, saying, "Yes. They are my pack. I will stay, no matter what happens."

Feanne's eyes turned to Estin.

"I will come back here after I take you to Finth. This is what I trained for. This is where I need to be, whether they want me here or not."

Saying nothing, Feanne began walking away, whispering to the kits to be calm them as she went.

Estin ran after her, catching up as they reached the edge of the woods. He walked with her, watching the woods for any threat, when he noticed Atall poking his head up from the bear fur, staring at Estin.

He smiled at the child, who stuck out his tongue, then disappeared under the fur again.

"He doesn't like non-foxes," Feanne said without watching the exchange, walking more quickly as they got into the dark. "It's his father's doing."

Estin just laughed and led her towards the edge of the cliffs, where Finth hopped off a small rock and approached them.

"Kidnapping was not the plan. If it was, I would know," the dwarf said, then grinned at Feanne. "Hey lady."

"I see you are not our prisoner anymore."

The dwarf grinned more broadly.

"Good of you to notice. Had a change of heart. My brother always said that once you go fur, you never go back...or was that once you had a taste of fur...oh damnit, I never can remember the really good dirty jokes."

"Finth," Estin said, taking a knee in front of his friend. "The undead are here. I'm going back to help the village defend themselves. No matter what happens, I need you to get Feanne and the kits back to Lihuan. Swear this to me."

Scowling, Finth regarded Estin with a touch of both annoyance and disappointment.

"Gonna go die like a hero, huh? My dad always said that if you can't run away, you should walk after breaking another guy's knees. Standing and fighting seems really stupid."

"It's what I have to do, but Insrin and I need to know that Feanne and the kits are safe."

Finth glared at Feanne, then at the squirming bundle under her cloak.

"Damnit all, Estin. I promise that they will arrive safely if it's within my power to do so."

"Thank you."

Turning to leave, Estin started to say something to Feanne, but she shook her head.

"I'll see you again, Estin. Go and fight. Bring me my mate back."

He ran back towards the village, his burden lightened already. Turning before he reached the first hut though, Estin moved off further into the woods, searching for a dark and quiet area. This part of his plan was not one he felt was properly thought through, but he could not wait.

"Miharon!" he called out at the night. "Miharon, come to me!"

A roar of anger preceded the smoke condensing before him into the shape of the great wolf, its purple eyes gleaming with hatred. Winds pushed and pulled at Estin as the creature reared up in front of him.

"Why would you call me?" roared the forest spirit. "It is death to call upon me again!"

"I have done you a favor and now you will do one for me."

The wolf hesitated, easing back from Estin briefly.

"Explain."

"Your Keeper was lost to you. She had gone to live in a town, which I'm guessing you frown upon. Have you even heard from her in months?"

The wolf's features made its hatred abundantly clear.

"Right now, she is trying to get to safety with her young. You will help them and protect them, by any and all means. If her young die, I will do everything in my power to see your woods burn to the ground and I will drive her to the farthest reaches of this world to keep her from you. Do we have an understanding?"

The forest spirit roared in his face, but did not strike, vanishing as quickly as it had come.

"I really hope that was a good idea," Estin muttered, turning back towards the village.

When he got back, he found Insrin waiting for him at the edge of the first house, his armor and weapons prepared and his stance relaxed as though this battle were no great concern. Estin could only wish he had that amount of calm in the face of what was coming.

In the distance, a call went out and Estin heard the flutter of many bows firing over and over.

"This is not how I expected our next meeting," Insrin admitted, beginning the walk towards the front lines. He swept his spear around onto his shoulders as he checked his armor's straps again, then flipped the weapon back into his hand. "I had always dreamed I would be chasing you down and stabbing you until my arm was tired."

"I always sort of hoped I could do the same to you. Times change and I grew up."

Insrin laughed, with both of them now nearing the chaotic lines of battle, the sound was muffled. The larger male stopped walking as they came in sight of the lines, where the archers fired endlessly and the spearmen stood ready.

Estin could not yet see the enemy from their position, but he could hear the pounding of hundreds of feet and the growls of the dead.

"I hope you know that we cannot stand in the face of this army," Insrin told Estin calmly, unfastening a clasp that held his sword sheathed, even as he hefted the spear in his right hand, as though testing its balance one more time. "They will destroy us long before dawn."

"This is not the full army. Besides, we just need to hold them long enough for the others to escape. I would see your children live to an old age, Insrin. Once they're safe, we can leave the town."

"I cannot run just because my family needs me," Insrin answered, shaking his head. He gave Estin a stern stare. "Either we win or I die with the last of my warriors. Letting any of them die because I called a retreat is no different than letting my children die. You may run when you must to warn your pack, but I stay here, no matter what."

A loud crash, accompanied by screams and snarls let Estin know that the undead had reached the spear line. When he glanced that way, he saw that the whole fox line had dropped their spears and switched to their melee weapons. Even the archers moved into the fray, most carrying light axes and swords.

As he and Insrin watched, the foxes were driven back several steps and blood began appearing as the undead pushed into the line, tearing at the living with their broken hands.

"Time to die like a warrior," Insrin said, softly enough that Estin believed he was speaking to himself. Without another word, Insrin stepped into a gap in the line as one of his warriors was dragged away into the mass of reaching hands and rotting faces. His spear found its way right into the face of a growling corpse, then he pulled it free and spun the weapon over, using the butt to drive three skeletal undead back a step.

Running along the backs of the warriors, who were just barely holding back the onslaught, Estin made for the robed male he had seen earlier, hoping to help with healing. In horror, he watched as two corpses shoved through the line and grabbed the male fox, dragging him screaming into the mass of clawing undead.

Searching the line, Estin found where the injured had been situated and ran over, kneeling beside the first soldier he found near the wounded. He checked around for the other robed fox, but saw no sign of her.

"How bad are they?" he asked a young fox who was rushing between the different wounded.

The other shook his head.

"I have no idea. I'm just tying off to stop the bleeding."

"Where is your healer?"

The fox shrugged, looking around.

"I think the undead got them all. Arro was helping someone in the front line and got grabbed. She couldn't fight back. I haven't seen her since. The others are missing, too."

Estin closed his eyes and uttered a heartfelt prayer to the spirits for help. This was going to be a long night if he was already the last healer.

For hours, Estin ran between the area where they were putting the fallen and the lines where the soldiers continued to fall. It was taxing his strength of both body and mind as his magic began to wear thin. For all his training, he was running out of healing magic and the bodies were piling up faster than ever.

The face of the battle had remained relatively unchanged. Everywhere he looked, the angry and twisted faces of the dead were packed together, trying to get at the remaining warriors. Nearly a hundred of the dead had been dragged back by those untrained in combat and unceremoniously tossed into a waiting bonfire to ensure that they stayed dead. For all that, the undead force seemed just as strong as it had been at the start of the battle.

"Push through!" cried Insrin somewhere nearby, snapping Estin out of his morbid assessment of the fight.

At his command, Insrin's elite guards fell into a V-shaped formation, driving into the undead horde, while the other warriors attempted to close the gap. Though the corpses continued to stand back up, Insrin appeared to be pushing forward towards some target deep in the enemy force. Estin could only guess that Insrin had seen the necromancer controlling the horde. If not, then the pack's leader was making a last-stand that would likely lead to his death if he did not have help.

Racing to catch up before Insrin's group had moved far enough past the main line that the undead would fill back in, Estin dove into the smaller group, shoving his way in behind Insrin. Estin drew his own weapons and covered gaps and blocked what attacks he could, trying to get Insrin's people the best shot they could at this.

Everywhere, grasping hands were trying to catch the living off-guard. More than once, Estin felt the cold fingers try to wrap around his arms and wrists, until an axe severed the creature's arm, setting him free.

At one point, several of the undead grabbed Estin, their claws digging into his flesh as he was pulled away. He stabbed and slashed, but the creatures would not relent. Teeth sank into his shoulder and he began to think that he had failed the group. Death seemed certain. It was a great shock to Estin when the claws let go and he was pulled bodily back into the foxs' group.

Looking up, he realized that the male that had saved him was actually the same one he had broken the nose of when Feanne had first been taken to their village. There was no more anger between them—now there was only survival, which required every living being to keep fighting.

There was no going back, Estin realized as he scrambled to his feet, wiping at the blood that ran down his arm. Already, the undead were so numerous behind them that they faced equally-awful odds both in front and behind them.

Nearby, Insrin called to push harder and the group's pace accelerated, nearly leaving Estin behind with their abrupt rush. He struggled to continue on, doing what he could to aid them, often just providing the smallest of healing to each of the warriors, trying to keep them upright as they went, rather than worrying about fully mending their wounds.

They were moving at a rough pace downhill, the group moving around a denser section of trees when Insrin fell, bleeding from the arms and face. Deep gashes in his armor had been hidden from Estin, who only had seen his back for a long time. His entire front side was covered in blood.

The second Insrin hit the ground, undead grabbed for his ankles, trying to drag him into their ranks, even as more stepped into the gap he had left, trying to divide the group of foxes. Insrin's honor guard was faster, closing the gap and driving the undead off of their leader, closing ranks over top of him.

Estin dropped alongside Insrin as the line of soldiers closed around them, shielding their leader. The whole advance stopped and they fought to hold their ground, giving Estin the chance to do his duty.

Insrin's wounds were not horrible, Estin noted, but he had fought on long after blood loss should have slowed him. Estin honestly could not find any reason Insrin had lasted as long as he had, given the sheer number of cuts. There was at least one artery that had been severed, covering Insrin's fur with more blood than Estin believed anyone could lose and still breathe. Still, he was alive, though barely.

The undead pushed back hard, driving into the line and forcing the soldiers nearly atop Estin as he tried to mend Insrin. He found himself forced to lay over the fallen pack-leader to shield him from his own warriors as the undead crushed in close enough that he could hear that groans and feel the impacts of their hands against the shields of the foxes who were covering him. It felt as though an entire city had come rampaging down on them, trying to crush them underfoot.

Throwing his hands in the air, Estin called out the words and drew the magic to him, driving the undead back with the same spell he had used at the gates of Altis. This created a small bubble that helped hold the undead back while the warriors regained their footing. Still, the shambling corpses were close enough that they could still claw at the warriors, the sea of broken and rotting faces contorted in rage at being stopped by his spell.

"I need you to hold them back long enough that I can heal Insrin!" Estin shouted, struggling to maintain the barrier as the group of twenty fought to hold their ground inside the ten foot wide bubble he had created. The scent of rotting flesh was beginning to make him sick. While they had been moving, he had managed to ignore it, but now his stomach was twisting at the stench.

Estin lay there, half-kneeling, half-lying, as the warriors struggled to regain any ground at all. He could see Insrin bleeding quickly to death, the blood soaking into Estin's own shirt as he was flattened against Insrin by the warriors trying to cover them.

He looked up from Insrin's chest and stared at the face of the male that Estin had long felt had ruined his life. Killing him would be so easy. Estin did not even have to do anything…just by inaction, he could let Insrin die. Those thoughts passed quickly as Estin thought of Feanne and her children.

"Get me some room to heal him!" Estin screamed at the other foxes. "He'll be dead soon!"

Though the legs of his defenders, Estin could occasionally see the village far up the hill. The main line of warriors still held, but he caught glimpses of people still rushing around behind them. The village was far from evacuated. If his position was overrun now, only part of the village would get away safely. Still, Estin knew he could not do anything more than maintain his spell and hope the others could push back against the undead. It was a truly hopeless feeling, knowing that he could only lay there as people died around him. He lay so close to Insrin, that he could feel the fox's breathing slowing.

The undead closed their ranks again, pushing hard against the group, crushing Estin under the warriors as they tried to hold their positions and not be dragged off.

When the group was able to finally push back and give Estin the slightest bit of room again, he lifted his head to check the village in the hopes that the residents might be mostly clear. Instead, from the middle of the village, Estin saw someone coming their way. With the fires silhouetting her the regal stance and poise told him exactly who it was. Feanne was coming to help—minus the children and her cloak—despite his efforts to get her to safety.

Marching straight through the town's defenders, Feanne went from calm to ferocious instantly. Her speed and strength enhanced by her magic, she tore into the undead, ripping them apart with her claws more effectively than many of the warriors with their weapons. She rushed through the dense group of corpses, slipping through their grasping hands and even using one as a step to leap over the last few between herself and Estin's group.

With a grunt, Feanne landed hard beside Estin, the tight quarters making her landing from the jump difficult.

"How badly hurt is he?" she asked, kneeling beside Estin. She started to reach out for Insrin, then recoiled when she looked down at her gore-covered hands. Instead, she began wiping them off on the ground.

"I can help him, but I need to be able to drop the sanctuary against the undead."

Feanne nodded and stood, raising her hands and calling upon her own form of magic. The trees surrounding them began striking at the undead, hampering their movement and driving them back by the dozens. Many more rushed in to fill the gap, but it bought them precious seconds and allowed the warriors to get better footing, finally solidifying their position.

Dropping the barrier, Estin went right to Insrin, guiding the healing magic. The wounds closed swiftly and in seconds, Insrin opened his eyes, even before all the bleeding had stopped. Insrin jerked in surprise as he woke, then blinked and began looking around.

"Not who I wanted to see," he groaned, looking up at Estin. He then turned his head and saw Feanne towering over them both. "Neither of you."

"The children are safe for now," Feanne told him, reaching down to help him and Estin up. "We need to turn this tide, or they will not be safe anywhere in these mountains."

"What would you propose, my mate? My warriors are doing all they can."

Feanne looked out at the raging horde of undead, then turned to Insrin, stepping close to him and putting her hands on his chest.

"I have been very clear that there are some things about my life you do not need to know of," she whispered, though Estin could hear her, as close as their confines were. He looked away, trying not to be a part of their private conversation. "After this battle, if you wish to never see me again, just say it. For now, it is what needs to be done."

"I would never drive you off," answered Insrin immediately.

"Don't say that until you know what I really am."

Feanne turned on Estin, her demeanor hardening again, the warrior in her taking control.

"A certain spirit tracked me down, out there in the woods. I believe you have made an enemy, but he did guide Finth and the children away."

"It was all I could think to do. I am sorry," Estin apologized.

"Don't be. This is the time to call on him and I want you at my side to ensure that I do not do anything foolish. Be ready to save me from myself, Estin. We will not need an army for this."

"As you wish."

Feanne glanced at her mate one more time, then let out a howl like the call for help that he had heard her make months before. This time, she kept the call going, the sound ringing off the trees, where it was answered by dozens more like it. The moment the answering calls came, Feanne collapsed to the ground, clutching at her face and crying out in agony.

"Are you...," Estin began, then saw that her jaw had broken and was shifting, realigning. In seconds, every bone in her body was moving and growing, destroying much of her clothing with the size of the change.

The alteration of her form took only seconds, but when Feanne rose up, she towered over the other foxes. Still vaguely fox-like in appearance, she was a fearsome sight, with immense claws, long fangs, and eyes that glowed a forest green lighting her face. With a roar, she reached over the line of village warriors and tore three zombies to pieces, her hands able to crush their skulls with ease.

"Fall back and protect the village!" cried Insrin to the warriors, though he looked to Estin to be deeply shaken, as did all of the warriors. "Estin and I will guard the charge!"

Estin himself was not faring much better. He had known about the rages, the loss of control, but he had never once considered how extensive the Miharon's gift to her really was. He could only follow behind as she pushed through the warriors and began tearing a path through the undead forces, with Insrin close behind him.

At first, Estin believed his role was to heal Feanne, to keep her going until whatever had answered her from the mountains was able to arrive. He soon saw that was not his duty at all. Every time the undead clawed at her, bit her, slashed at her with weapons, the wounds would close almost instantly. From what he could see, she was nearly unstoppable. The more she was hit, the angrier she became and the faster they tore into the undead army.

Estin drew his weapons, focusing his magic on them to channel energies that might help him against the undead, the healing energies hovering like a mist over his blades. When a creature shambled past Feanne or ducked under her arms, he slashed at it, the magic flaring as the corpse fell lifeless once more. It was more elegant than Feanne's battery of the undead, but also slower.

For quite some time, all that Estin could see were Feanne, Insrin, and the sea of undead. Everything became a blur of gore and reaching hands. Bulging eyes stared blankly at them, then would vanish as Feanne tore the creatures apart. Soon, Estin was covered head to toe in blood and bits of the corpses from the violence Feanne had unleashed, even hiding just behind her left hip for cover. He checked on Insrin every so often, finding him equally spattered, but unharmed as he fought just behind Feanne's other leg.

An inhuman shriek was Estin's first indication of how far they had come into enemy lines. From what he could see around Feanne, they were only about twenty or thirty bodies from the back side of the undead army, where he could only hope their leaders might be directing from. As the cry echoed through the woods, Feanne shuddered and roared, pushing harder into the enemy lines.

Again that shriek let loose, making Estin's body itch and his mind burn. He fought out from one of Feanne's sides, pushing into the undead to get a better idea of what they were up against. This proved easy, as the corpses just moved past him, all focused on the village and not even trying to fight back against him. Soon, he was able to walk beside Feanne, finding that they were now looking down at a little camp, complete with campfire.

"I wondered what I might find out here," hissed a man's airy voice.

The heavily-bundled form of a Turessian eased itself out of the tent.

Feanne let out a howl that shook the trees and was answered from the woods nearby. It sounded as though whatever she had called was already engaged on the undead, the answering cries coming from several different directions. She panted, eyeing her new target and advancing slowly.

"I demand that you turn your troops back!" shouted Insrin, stepping up to Feanne's other side. He had his sword ready and his hand shook anxiously. "Do you think we can't take you too, after going straight through your army?"

The Turessian laughed, kicking out his small campfire.

"One lycanthrope and two overprotective wildlings will not stop an army," the man said calmly. "If these fall, I'll bring thousands more. If you manage to destroy me, my brethren will come in my place."

He flicked his hand and a shape moved through the trees.

"Assuming you can touch me..."

Feanne lunged at the man, grabbing him with both hands and her teeth, bearing him to the ground. She tore at him, ripping away bone and flesh.

It was then that Estin got a look at what was in the woods.

Misty and almost shapeless, a vague human shape approached from the trees. He could hear the whispering voices in his head, the same as he did when there were spirits seeking help returning to their bodies. This time though, the voices were angry and raged at him, demanding he join them.

The ghostly figure wailed just once and Feanne shrieked in pain, but kept fighting.

"Get the ghost!" Estin cried at Insrin, who raced into the woods, his sword slashing harmlessly through the spirit. He continued his attack, trying to at least distract it.

The ghostly figure fled from Insrin at first, then began ignoring him, letting him attack it to no effect. It turned back to Feanne and wailed again.

This time Feanne shook and stopped clawing at the Turessian. She stared blankly at the necromancer, then collapsed atop him. Estin felt the life die within her body and her spirit cry out against the death magic that had driven it out.

"No!" shouted Insrin, rushing at the ghost again, attacking it as effectively as he could the wind itself.

Another scream from the ghost and Insrin stopped in his tracks, wavered, then fell like a rag doll, his own life snuffed out.

Estin found himself at a loss. He had little magic left and it would not last long against both the Turessian and the death spirit. He was going to have to run soon or he would be helpless, but he knew he was not going anywhere without the others.

Uttering the words of one of his more unfamiliar spells—one which, if successful, should have dismissed the creature from the world of the living—Estin motioned at the ghost, watching as it blinked out of existence and reappeared several feet away. His spell unraveled without a clear target of its destructive power, fading away in a flame-like flicker.

"Don't I know you?" asked the Turessian, pulling himself out from under the limp body of Feanne, shoving her such that she flopped onto her back. He snapped his broken bones into place in much the same way a living person would adjust their clothing. "I think I killed your friends in the woods last year."

Estin had too much to worry about with the spirit moving through the woods to bother bantering with the necromancer, so he kept moving, trying to keep the spirit in sight. It moved and darted, trying to keep the trees between it and him.

"She really is antisocial," laughed the Turessian, popping his collarbone back into place. "Banshees rarely enjoy direct combat. Give her a moment to get her voice back and you'll see."

Estin finally got a line on the banshee and threw out another spell, this one a powerful form of healing that he hoped would cause a great deal of harm to the ghost, or possibly disperse it if he was lucky. This one landed and the ghost wept loudly, its form scattering as a whimper drifted from where she had been as white tendrils of light ripped it apart.

"Now that I would say is impressive. Most people die long before they can land a spell on one of those. No matter though, she will reform tomorrow night back where I found her. Annoying, but not a setback."

The Turessian stepped between Estin and his fallen companions.

Time was beginning to be an issue. Estin knew that he had the strength to bring one person back to life within a few minutes of their death. He just needed to reach them. The longer past that point, the harder it would be to heal them even with Asrahn's circle.

Estin shifted his stance, lifting both swords. The magic he had funneled into them was weak, but still present. He hoped it would be enough to get through this man's magic.

"This gets old, wildling. I have lived longer than your cities have had names and yet, you manage to tire me. Your friends' lives are slipping away. You should hurry. Let us be done with this, as I have some other lycanthropes out attacking my troops that must be dealt with."

Estin attacked, wielding both weapons in a flurry of strikes as Feanne had once taught him. She had demanded independent movement of every weapon, always striking, blocking, or setting up for the next attack. As much as she had hated his use of swords, she had taught him much about using them effectively.

The weapons sliced into the Turessian, sending bits of flesh flying away. He knew the swords would not do much, but everything was a setup for the next strike.

His next move was harder, requiring that he drop into a crouch as he spun. He used that momentum to bring his tail around, sweeping the Turessian right off his feet. Coming back up, Estin drove both swords through its chest, impaling it on the ground with a grunt.

"You have improved," the man gasped, his pale face grinning at Estin from under his cowl. For a moment, Estin saw his eyes flash red. "You have stabbed me before though. It will take far more."

With surprising strength, the man kicked Estin away, where he tumbled and came back to his feet. He was back up just in time to see the Turessian pull the first weapon from his chest.

From beyond the Turessian, Estin saw movement. At first he thought it might be another ghost or one of the shambling corpses from the main army, but it was Feanne, her jaw and fingers twitching. Somehow, she was alive again and trying to get up.

Summoning the last spell he could manage other than the power to restore life, Estin called upon the spirits that whispered in his mind and brought down all his might in a magical white fire on the Turessian. The flames would only harm an undead and the man screamed as he burned, still pinned to the ground.

Despite the attack, the Turessian ripped the second sword free and climbed to his feet, patting out the flames as he stood.

"I sense you weakening," he said, though now Estin could see only bare skull and those glowing eyes. There was no more pretense of being a living man. He stepped over beside Insrin's body.

"This one came in with you...he is mine now."

With a lurch, Insrin stood, his eyes blank and his jaw hanging limply. He simply stood there, waiting for a command. What Estin could see though, was Insrin's spirit fleeing the corrupted body in anguish. There would be no way to heal him without Asrahn's circle now.

"Fight the black and white monkey to the best of your ability," ordered the Turessian, pointing at Estin.

Insrin reached down and numbly picked up his sword, then gurgled a challenge as he rushed Estin. The sword went wide, with Estin easily able to side-step and rake his claws across Insrin's arm. In a living opponent, the injury would have forced him to drop his weapon, but Insrin just spun on him, attacking blindly again.

Knowing he might regret his decision later, Estin danced around Insrin's attack and snaked his tail around and behind him, hooking his neck. With a hard twist of his body, he flipped Insrin backwards. Before the zombie could rise again, Estin leapt on him, driving his elbow into Insrin's neck, breaking it loudly. Though the head continued to growl vaguely, the body was still.

"That was less fun than I had expected," lamented the Turessian. "I am a very busy man. We will need to end this here."

Estin tried to run at him as he realized he was casting another spell, but the distance was too far. Vile magic washed over Estin, attempting to rip his spirit from his body as had happened to the others. He reacted as Asrahn had taught him, sacrificing the ability to grant life to shield his own body from death, effectively negating the spell used on him. He felt it was a safe bet, given that Insrin was beyond his magic and Feanne was moving again.

"You have done well. Be proud of the death I'll give you," laughed the undead, already beginning another spell.

A roar filled the wood as Feanne leapt to her feet, grabbing the Turessian and slamming him face-first into the ground. She dropped atop him, grabbing both his shoulders.

"Holding me down won't ever win this," laughed the man, struggling against Feanne's strength, managing to roll over onto his back. "The moment I find a way, I can kill you again and again. No simple lycanthrope can withstand the lure of death forever."

Roaring in the Turessian's skeletal face, Feanne strained until Estin could see her muscles rippling through her fur. With a loud crack, the Turessian was torn in two, his skull bouncing to a stop nearby. The red glow in his eye sockets faded away.

Panting, Feanne stood slowly, her feet unsteady. She looked up at Estin, but her eyes seemed to not recognize him before she turned back towards the main undead forces, growling softly. Taking but a single step, she wavered and collapsed.

Estin dove over Insrin and checked Feanne. She was not breathing. He summoned what little strength he could find in himself, trying to mend any unseen wounds, but the spell fell apart on her lifeless body. Her body then began to break down again, the bones twisting and changing, reverting her to her former self. This went on for almost a full minute, until at last she was as he remembered her.

"There is a price for every demand," spoke the Miharon's voice, coming from several directions, though the creature did not show itself. "You placed restrictions on your request. She did not. I take her life as payment for such power."

Struggling with emotion, Estin pulled Feanne onto his lap and cradled her head as he looked between the two bodies, trying to decide what to do. He needed to get them both to Asrahn's circle in a hurry, but lacked the strength to do so. He was not even sure he could carry one of them in his weakened state. Exhausted, he hung his head in failure.

At that time, Finth appeared from the woods, followed by Ulra. They ran to him, checking to make sure he, at least, was alive.

"You should not be here," Estin said weakly.

"The undead have their orders to attack the village," Finth said quickly, motioning to Insrin. Ulra followed his direction and scooped up the body. "Nearly everyone is out. The undead have no boss, so they'll just tear at that village forever if need be."

"I don't care about that...what about her children?"

Finth smiled and stood beside Estin.

"They're safe. Lihuan sent a party to find us when the corpse-ridden village began to burn. I sent the two little ones with Sohan, who I think is their new best friend."

"Ulra," Estin said, struggling to lift Feanne's body, "can you carry another? We need to get back to our camp."

"Of course," grunted the bear, lifting Feanne with her other arm.

Feeling mentally and physically drained, Estin staggered along with the others, hurrying as best he could northwards. Though time was crucial in saving the two fallen, he lacked the remaining strength to run. Never in his training had he exhausted his mind like this, having used every last trick and spell Asrahn had taught him. Combined with the regular fighting, his body likely would have given out and forced him unconscious had he not felt the undeniable need to save the two foxes.

Hours later, though Estin could have guessed minutes to days, they reached Lihuan's camp. The three moved through as fast as they could, with Finth shoving people aside who were trying to gawk. He cleared them a path straight to Asrahn's old tent.

Since the elder had moved back into Lihuan's tent, the Asrahn's tent had become mostly unused. It was where Estin trained and where the circle was, but those were its only uses anymore. Thus, when they rushed in, Estin was surprised to find both Lihuan and Asrahn waiting.

"The kits arrived two hours ago," Lihuan said, motioning to the circle of stones. "Give them back their parents. I don't have the heart to tell them that both are dead."

Estin had Ulra lay the bodies down, but soon saw that both would not fit within the small circle. He had hoped that between himself and Asrahn, they could begin both at the same time.

"Stop dawdling and save my daughter," ordered Lihuan, his former ability to command respect surfacing out of nowhere. "I expect nothing less of you, Estin."

Sliding Feanne's corpse into the circle, Estin did rapid preparations to guide her spirit back. As he prepped the body and checked for fatal wounds, he shifted his mind, seeing that her spirit was indeed present, hanging limply in the air.

"How long dead is she?" asked Asrahn, handing him the scented oils they used to focus themselves.

"I don't know," he admitted. "She died twice. Banshee killed her with a scream, but she got back up and died again about a minute later."

Asrahn shook her head.

"Her crazy wild magic never makes any sense and makes our job harder. Just do what you can."

Stepping back out of the circle, Asrahn began prepping Insrin's body, tending to his wounds. She gave Estin an annoyed look at one point as she examined his neck and the fur that Estin's tail had left behind, near his shattered spine, but she did not say anything even to Lihuan.

With a deep breath to control his fears, Estin shifted his sight again, looking up at Feanne's hanging spirit, drifting aimlessly over her body.

"Feanne," he said, focusing on speaking to the spirit, rather than the room. "Feanne, you need to come back."

The spirit drifted off to his left, her head still hanging. It was as though she were unconscious, even as a spirit, her shape suspended by a string from the sky that allowed her to float in almost any direction.

"Feanne!"

Slowly, the spirit's face lifted and looked up at him.

"Please come back and join us."

Estin swore he saw her spirit look down at the body below it, then sigh. She turned once more to Estin, her ethereal hand brushing his face as her sad eyes looked through him. Though having no true ability to touch, Feanne brought her face up alongside his, as though nuzzling him.

"Do not apologize or say goodbye to me," he said, temper rising as he moved away from her. "You will not leave. I saw that same look on Ghohar's face when he chose to depart. You have children here. They are safe, but they need their mother!"

Feanne's countenance hardened and she turned to her body again. Even semi-transparent, her eyes were clearly filled with the determination and drive that Estin had always seen in her. This time she sank back into her body. With a choking gasp, the physical form of Feanne lurched and curled into a ball, struggling for breath.

Wasting no time, Asrahn grabbed her daughter and practically dragged her from the circle, as Lihuan unceremoniously kicked Insrin into it.

"Bring him back so I can throw this in his face," growled Lihuan, glaring at the body. "Having my people save his is only so satisfying if I can tell him about it. I hope you won't mind if I embellish your role, Estin. I think I can drag the story out to at least half a day."

Concentrating yet again, Estin looked beyond and saw Insrin sitting calmly beside his own body, his hand on his chin. It was the most relaxed and perhaps annoyed Estin had ever seen a spirit and at first he thought he must have done something wrong. When the spirit did not change or move, he convinced himself that this was somehow just the way Insrin was while dead.

"Insrin, please return to us."

The fox spirit glanced over at him and just shrugged. It opened its mouth and began speaking, but such was the nature of the link Estin had with spirits that he could not hear anything. He could only address them and only within the circle. This was a new twist and not one he was ready for.

"Asrahn," he said, breaking off his attempts to communicate, "can you hear what the spirits are trying to say?"

"No, I cannot and I am not sure anyone can," Asrahn answered. "What is he doing?"

"He's just sitting there...I think he's trying to argue with me or lecture me."

"That sounds like him," said Feanne weakly, pulling a blanket over herself, her ears flat back as she huddled for warmth. "Tell him to get back here, or I'll die again and come after him."

Estin relayed the statement, but Insrin rolled his eyes and continued talking.

"Actually...," mumbled Finth, stroking his beard. "I drank a gypsy under the wagon last month and he kept babbling about some kind of sight and ancestors and some other rubbish. I kicked him a couple times to shut him up, but maybe they know something we don't."

"Get them!" Estin urged.

Ulra and Finth disappeared, leaving Lihuan, Asrahn, Feanne, and Estin sitting there waiting impatiently. Throughout it all, Insrin's spirit glared at Estin, occasionally trying to speak, then becoming angry when he did not answer, usually followed by sulking. After a minute or two, he would start again, as though trying to convince Estin to join the conversation.

Shortly, Finth returned, almost dragging Bandoleer Yoska.

"The short man does not explain the rudeness," the human said, stepping into the tent. "I was having lovely drink with a wife and had he not said who I was to come for, I would have fed him to dogs by now, yes? He just ask, 'you can speak with spirit' and I say 'yes' and he drag me through the camp."

"I apologize, Bandoleer," Estin said, still sitting in the circle. He noted that Insrin was trying to yell at him again, this time gesturing wildling with his hands, though Estin could make no sense of it. "I have a spirit in this circle who is trying to tell me something before letting me bring him back to life."

"Yes, this I see. He is most upset."

"Please find out what he wants, so we can save him before his body has been dead too long."

"Ah, yes. This I do."

The gypsy stepped alongside Estin, squeezing himself into the circle just barely. Sitting as best he could he looked up at the spirit and said, "Yes. Do start over. Tell me why you are mad at the man who wishes to make you less dead."

For the next twenty minutes, Yoska nodded, agreed, chuckled, and said "I see" repeatedly. Meanwhile, Insrin's spirit paced the circle, waving his arms as he ranted. Through it all, Lihuan glowered and Feanne's eyes—the only part of her visible over her blanket—watched nervously.

Finally, Yoska said "yes, I believe so" and turned to Estin.

"The spirit would like to accept your invitation back now, though he is very upset about you being the one to heal him."

Estin looked at Insrin, who was standing over his own body, watching Estin impatiently.

"Insrin, please return to us."

The body coughed and groaned as life flowed back into him.

"Grey fox person," said Yoska, touching Insrin's arm, "do you remember our conversation?"

"No," wheezed Insrin, flinching away from the gypsy. "Who are you and why are you touching me?"

"I am no one of importance to one as important as yourself, pack-leader Insrin," said Yoska humbly. "I just help the gypsy-friend Estin with a difficult task, yes?"

Insrin looked around at the tent and sneered, sitting up as quickly as he could, though he appeared to still be weak and nearly fell over.

"I need to get back to my village," he grumbled, trying to stand.

"Your village is rubble," Estin told him plainly. "The undead are sacking what's left of it and probably will be for days, though there are creatures of the wilds helping reduce their numbers. You helped Feanne and I kill their leader."

Shaking his head, Insrin just shrugged.

"The last thing I remember is...," then stopped and looked at Feanne, whose ears shot up aggressively and her eyes darkened, while still huddling in the blankets. "I remember my mate joining us in battle against my wishes."

"Our camp will welcome any of your people who wish to relocate here until the undead are gone for good," offered Lihuan. "It is the least we can do, given our treaty and our long-standing agreement to be...civil."

"Normally I would lead them all away without considering your offer. Given what you've done for us, I'll present it to my people and any who wish to stay, may."

Insrin finally managed to get his feet under him, staggering over to Feanne.

"As soon as you are well enough," he told her, touching her face gently, "I want you to gather the children so we can get out of these lands."

Feanne's back stiffened.

"You want to run away?"

"I want to keep my family safe and that would not be here."

Feanne looked around at the others, then stood up, wrapping the blanket around herself.

"Excuse me. My mate and I have to discuss matters."

The two departed swiftly and Estin heard hushed arguing before they were a step out the tent's flap. The softly-spoken angry words drifted away into the night.

"This is all very exciting," said Yoska, giving a fake yawn. "However, I must get back to my people. Bandoleer wander too long and everyone drinks up the stores without you."

The man stood, then tapped Estin's shoulder.

"I would have company on the walk. Is dangerous with undead about, no?"

Agreeing, Estin hoisted himself to his feet, accepted the brief thanks of Asrahn and Lihuan, then left with the bandoleer.

They crossed camp slowly, the gypsy taking his time in getting to the blue wagons at the edge of the village. For a time, he kept rubbing at his clean-shaven chin and pursing his lips, but said nothing. From what Estin could see, the man was actually leading him on a longer path towards his camp than necessary.

"The fox...," he said at last, almost absently, "the girl, not the boy and not your pack-leader."

"Feanne."

"Yes. She is wife of grey fox?"

"That she is, though we call them life-mates."

"I see. You have...how you say...rubbed her man a wrong way?"

Estin looked up at the taller man quizzically.

"Just what did he tell you?"

"He say you and this girl, you were close before he marry her. Very close. I do not think she told him this, but he is no fool. This...closeness...is not something my people disapprove of...in fact, I find it funny how angry this man is about the whole thing."

"He needs to get over it. Our people often have mates long before they choose a single mate for life. What her and I did or did not have between us is none of his concern."

"As do ours. He is mad about something else though. He is angry at you...so very angry...because you are no fox. This bothers him that his wife had bedded outside her race."

"Breed."

"Whatever. This is the start of his anger."

"He won her...I lost. There's no reason for him to be mad at me. I could have reasons to hate him, but I've gotten over them."

"Yes, about this." The bandoleer stopped as they passed the last of the tents. "He doubts the children are his. Again, this is not something that bothers my people, but it seems to bother him. That doubt makes him very crazy, so much that his spirit refused to come back unless I said I thought they were his. I do not think he even brings it up to the girl. Is quite funny how much he hated having you be the one to bring him back, no?"

Estin felt deeply sick.

"There is no way. None," Estin stammered, not even sure if he was talking to Yoska or himself. "I've seen the kits. They're foxes, through and through. No grey fur, no long tail, no stripes."

"Like the girl is, yes? Her mother is strange for a fox, I think? Almost look like cat. I must be wrong, though."

Estin sat down hard on the ground, trying to wrap his mind around it. Yoska was right. Sometimes wildlings who mixed breeds had children that looked entirely like one or the other parent. Other times, they would be a strange mix, like Asrahn. The kits could be anyone's. All he could be sure of was that at least one of their parents was a fox-breed wildling.

"Is not said to make you worry," said Yoska, laughing as he pulled Estin back onto his feet. "I tell you this so you can be prepared, if he gets too jealous. Is always better to know the sword is coming. When lady fox is done arguing, you may wish to speak with her."

His head spinning, Estin just nodded, not even realizing at first that Yoska had left him. When he looked around, the man was nowhere to be found.

With effort, Estin managed to keep his feet under him and began walking back into the camp. He crossed the outer tents slowly, finally reaching his own at the middle. There, he found Sohan, darting about and chittering, trying not to be caught by the two kits, who giggled and ran around, as they tried to corner him. At one side of the clear area, Feanne sat on the ground in a fresh skirt and cloth shirt, watching the two children play.

"Why did you come back for us, Feanne?" Estin asked, sitting down a little ways from her, facing the children and trying to keep his voice low so that the they could not hear them talking. "If you had just gone, he would have never seen what the Miharon had gifted to you."

Feanne's ears twitched.

"I came back because I was not about to lose a life-mate, while my apprentice fought to the death to save him. I could turn that tide and I knew it. I just couldn't be sure how high the price would be. Once I read my father's note...I had no choice but to elicit the power the land has given me."

"What did he say that that changed your mind?"

She smiled and answered, "It said, 'Forgive me and seek your own path in life without fear of what I wish.' That was all. It was the most fatherly thing he has said since the day I took the Miharon's boon. It was the call to embrace my gifts that I had always needed. It made me think about letting a friend and my mate die just to hide those gifts...I had to come or I would never be able to forgive myself, even if you both lived."

Trying to force himself to ask the question that was bothering him, Estin found himself having to ask something different. He was not ready to even address the issue of the kits.

"I need to know something, Feanne. For better or worse."

She cocked her head slightly, but said nothing.

"Why did you choose not to let me fight for you? Things worked out...but you couldn't have known that at the time."

Feanne lowered her head, closing her eyes.

"I wanted to, Estin. Believe me. I also knew that you could not win against him. He would have killed you on the spot and that would have hurt me far more than leaving with someone I did not love."

Estin let that be for a time, smiling occasionally as the three wrestling in front of them made an adorable scene. He sometimes wondered if Sohan would ever grow up.

"Will you be leaving soon?"

Sohan noticed Estin and stopped to wave at him, only to be pounced from both directions, raising a plume of dust as he hit the ground hard.

"If Insrin has his way, yes. That is, when he gets done being mad at me for questioning his decision and comes back into camp to speak with me. Could be a day or more, knowing his temper. Hopefully, he will at least give the kits and I time to relax before we must travel."

"Do you know where you'll go?"

Feanne shook her head, not taking her eyes of the kits.

"He will not tell me. I think he fears I'll tell you."

"Would you?"

Feanne smiled and slowly turned to look at him.

"Would it matter? I have this feeling you'll show up anyway. I found the nicest bear skin on Oria a while ago..."

Grinning at first, Estin watched the children for a while with her. Soon, Oria bounded up to him, barely coming up past mid-shin, and stuck her tongue out at him.

"I told you my mommy could protect us."

"That you did."

Feanne's look became annoyed and she raised an eyebrow as the little girl began hooting as she tried to grab Sohan's tail.

"You really could not leave well enough alone, could you?"

"Curiosity was always a problem for me. I had to see them. You were always good with the pack's kids, so I had to meet yours."

"You shouldn't have even known about them, Estin."

He had no good reply for that and so kept his eyes forward, watching them play. He was starting to think that the kits might actually wear down Sohan, as Atall playfully clawed at the ferret with his dull claws, while Oria tried unsuccessfully to wrestle Sohan to the ground.

"Insrin told Yoska that he believes the kits are mine. I'm sure he doesn't remember saying it, but that's what Yoska said the fuss was about in the circle," Estin said at last, deciding against caution. "Is there any truth in that?"

Feanne closed her eyes and took a deep breath.

"That male is a fool and a thorn in my side. His petty worries about other breeds leads to half of our arguments. All it takes is the wrong color fur and he practically loses his mind."

Estin turned from where he was sitting to face her.

"That wasn't actually an answer."

"No, it wasn't."

She would not look at him. Feanne just hugged her knees and watched the children, her ears flat against her head. Estin soon noticed that she had even pulled her tail close to her body. She was terrified, whether she knew it or not.

"Whoever's children they are…," Estin started.

"They are my children," she replied sharply, raising her voice enough that the kits looked towards her. "I have told him that and now I apparently must tell you the same thing. He is their father, in as much as he is my mate. Beyond that, they are my children and no male is about to take them away from me! No one!"

She rose to her feet, confronting Estin, who just looked up at her calmly.

"I suggested no such thing, Feanne."

Feanne put a hand to her head and sat back down, then covered her face in her hands.

"He wants to flee to safer lands and take the children. Whether I go, he's less concerned about."

"Feanne, you are welcome here, as are they. There is no reason to run. If our camp needs to move, it will, but there is no sense in two adults running off in a random direction, toting children. They're safer here, at least for now."

"Try telling him that."

Feanne took a deep breath and then looked back to her children, her eyes wet.

"This is what I've become, Estin. I spend every day worried about them. I don't think you have any idea how scared I've been. I thought when we turned back the attack, things would get better, but I'm still scared of what is coming. I used to think I could face anything…"

"I do understand," he told her. "Fear for another is a lot harder than fear for yourself."

"No, you really don't," she said, wiping tears from her eyes. "When I found out I was pregnant, I was terrified. Four months of nonstop fear at what the children would look like. There were days I almost wished I would lose the pregnancy to avoid the fear, as much as it shames me to say that.

"That is not even just about you, Estin. My mother's heritage could have shown itself. That would have been all it took for Insrin to rage about the other breeds and about mixed-breeding. I had no way of knowing how badly he would react, or if he would hurt the children.

"The night I was to give birth, I tried to sneak out of the village. I wanted to hide somewhere to have them, so that I knew whether they were safe. When I was caught and brought back for my own safety, I kept a knife under the pillow the whole night, ready to fight for them against my own mate."

"Is he really that bad?" Estin asked, wondering if he had gotten things wrong from his spying.

"No…and yes. He loves me and our children. I do not believe he would even try to hurt us. He's a better mate then I could have hoped for, but he has his areas that just eat at him. If he were to go into a rage at delivering another male's children—or even thinking he was—I could not risk their safety.

"When they were born with the right color fur, I felt so much relief that you cannot imagine. I thought the few things in my life that could endanger my mating were behind me."

Estin wanted to go to her, to console her, but that was just compounding the issue. He knotted his fingers together and remained seated where he was. He kept telling himself over and over that she was just his friend, but that he had to respect Insrin in his dealings with her.

"Do you love him? Enough to follow him if he wants you all to run?"

Feanne gave him an amused smirk, then looked back to the children.

"He may not have been my first choice, but things have a way of working themselves out. He is a good mate, Estin, whether you believe it or not. I have learned to love him and would follow him no matter where he wishes to go...assuming he decides that he still trusts his children with a lycanthrope...even one that has control over her changes. So far, that's his best excuse for why he should take them and run without me. The undead are almost an afterthought."

"If there is anything I can do, Feanne, just ask. I'll stay out of the way though."

"Thank you."

She turned away from him, folding her legs under her and staring blankly at the children.

Excusing himself softly, Estin stood and gave the children one more look before heading back to his tent.

*

The next morning, Estin buried his face in his fur blankets and refused to get up. His body hurt from the fight the night before and he had come up with no good solutions to the problem at-hand. Moreover, with the undead aware of their existence, he dreaded another attack. All in all, he had no desire to do anything until he could sort some of it out.

"Estin," called Asrahn. He could see her peeking into the tent from his resting place under all the furs. Grumbling, he tried to dig himself deeper into the blankets in hopes of disappearing. "Are you awake?"

"No."

"You really need to get up, child. Things are getting strange around here."

Groaning, he tossed the blankets aside and sat up slowly.

"What now?"

"Lihuan asked me not to talk of it yet. He wants you at his tent as soon as possible."

Estin rubbed his face and pulled on some pants, while Asrahn tapped her foot impatiently.

"Ok, ok," he mumbled, staggering after her as she led the way.

They wandered through the bright early morning sunlight, with Estin barely conscious as he pardoned himself around a group of elves standing in the center of town. He had almost gotten past them when he stopped and turned around, staring at the group. He tried to follow Asrahn backwards, but ran into two dwarves that had been sitting near the old fire pit.

"Asrahn…," he asked, stopping.

"You haven't seen anything," she called to him, holding open the flap for him. "Go inside."

Estin groaned again and walked into the tent. There sat Lihuan with two fully-armored human soldiers bearing the insignias of Altis' high guard, as well as a middle-aged human in dark robes, his head shaven.

"More refugees?" Estin asked, tiredly blinking at them. "Welcome to the camp. I'm one of the healers here. I'm not really a morning breed, so if you don't mind…"

"Estin, sit down," growled Lihuan, pointing a finger at a cushion. "You are being rude to our guests. They have stories you need to hear and you know how I love stories."

"Right," he said, practically falling on the indicated seat. "Sorry."

"Please repeat for my latecomer what you were just telling me."

The robed man flinched a little, looking around at all of them.

"I am here as an envoy of Turessi," he explained, touching his forehead in some kind of greeting. "I wanted to explain what has happened…"

Estin never even felt his anger rise. The next moment, he found himself being dragged off the man by the two human soldiers.

"Estin, you will behave in my home!" Lihuan chided, motioning to Asrahn. "If he acts out again, restrain him by any means you feel necessary."

"…as I was saying," continued the man, touching several scratches on his throat gingerly, "I am the ambassador of the Turessian clans to this region. Just over a year ago, I was given the orders to attend to the court of the duke of Altis to discuss options for a treaty between our peoples. When I arrived eleven months ago, I was declared an imposter and thrown into a prison cell."

"That is where we found him last month when we grabbed every living person we could find and fled the city," noted the older of the two soldiers, his beard and moustache full enough to make a dwarf envious.

"The Turessians had been advising the duke since I met Feanne," Estin said, shaking his head. "I saw them in the court myself. That was...what...eight or nine months ago? They had been there for some time already at that point."

"Not Turessian," the robed man professed firmly. "Lihuan tells me that you struck at them and they did not die. Is this true?"

"Yes."

"They were not my people, I can assure you. As you can see by the wounds you've given me, I do very much bleed."

"So who are they?"

The man pouted and took a deep breath.

"Years ago, some of my people were experimenting with giving our ancestors the ability to remember their lives. They had believed it would be an even greater honor than simply animating their bodies, to be able to speak to others of the lives they had lived. In theory, it makes a lot of sense..."

"Except for the animating the dead part."

"You are a healer...I understand your hesitation. You must trust that we take great care of our deceased and mean the utmost respect."

Estin growled and the man held up his hands.

"Very well. It is not for everyone. Suffice to say that several of our ancestors were somewhat changed by the experience of waking up as undead and went a little crazy. They began amassing power and had to be restrained indefinitely. We built a barrier of sorts around them."

Estin rolled his eyes.

"You imprisoned them?"

"In a sense, yes. As all magic wears down eventually, the assumption was that since they were created before the barrier and both used the same essential magical arrangement, that they would deanimate before it dropped."

"Let me guess. The barrier dropped recently?"

"No...actually they found a way around it. It would seem that with nearly limitless time on your hands, you can manage to dig your way under a magical wall that extends nearly a hundred feet into the bedrock. They simply walked away."

"So how bad is this?"

Lihuan focused in on the Turessian at that point.

"That was just what we were getting to when you arrived," he explained.

The Turessian nodded and smiled at the others, looking extremely uncomfortable.

"I do not have good news, there. Though most of our animations are like the crude zombies that I saw back in Altis, the ancestors possess the same powers they had in life. Those that were necromancers...they can create more like themselves. What's worse, they no longer appear to care about who they raise. They started with the Altis graveyard, then the slums, then the market, and so on."

Lihuan stood slowly, using his cane to move towards the entrance of the tent.

"There is more," he noted, tapping Estin as he passed. "Come back outside."

The small group went out and Estin counted at least fifteen humans and elves in the area, with two dwarves arguing off to one side of the open area.

"Up there," Lihuan pointed, indicating a plateau to the south, "I have had the human forces set up their dwellings. There are one thousand warriors and many horses."

Again Lihuan turned, this time pointing to the east, beyond the blue wagons of the gypsies.

"Another clan of gypsies arrived just ahead of the humans. They heard from their cousins about us and were the ones who led the humans here."

Estin just shook his head in amazement. Their little hidden camp was now a sizable city, with its own army.

"What do we do, though?" Estin asked, mostly at the human soldiers. "Your city fell despite all your resources. We have nothing here. I don't care how many men you bring, we cannot hold back the entire population of Altis."

"No need," stated the older soldier, pointing briefly towards their camp. "We were able to secure envoys from the elven and dwarven realms, before they reached the city. They brought word from Lantonne and beyond.

"This war isn't just here. It's spread across at least three kingdoms eastward and who knows how many others. The war golems are taking a toll on the undead, keeping them mostly out in the plains. The plan is to drive the undead into one area long enough to sacrifice one war golem to wipe out the entire local army. If the plan works here, we will try the same thing elsewhere."

Estin thought back, remembering the two giant golems, smashing at the countryside with legions of undead for miles around them.

"What can a war golem do to save us, if the ones out on the plains haven't won it yet?"

"That's the new project," the human explained, grinning. "We got the dwarves and elves talking and we think there's a way we can funnel raw eldritch energy into one of the golems, filling it up until it detonates. That much energy should punch a hole in the world large enough to swallow any number of undead."

"An arcane explosion?" asked Asrahn, skeptically. "Do you think that might be overkill?"

That question seemed to anger the human, who puffed up, saying, "Not at all! If you haven't been inside a city where the entire population has turned, you really have no place guessing at how bad it has gotten out there."

"Silence," cut in Lihuan, glaring at both of them. "You say this is already being enacted?"

"In two or three months. That's how long it will take to create the proper magical formulation and get the majority of the undead army in one place. We'll need to get our forces on the ground down there to deliver the charge into the golem. I'm thinking about fifty volunteers, so we can get in and out without the undead army paying much attention to us. I've sent word to Lantonne to ensure they don't prevent us from getting to the golem."

Lihuan nodded gravely.

"Will your troops be remaining here, or do you expect me to move the children and others elsewhere?"

"There is nowhere safe," the man admitted. "Before we came here, we were halfway to the southern border of Lantonne. The same problems were pouring over from the south. I know they're happening to the east."

The Turessian raised his hand meekly, adding, "I hate to say it, but we're struggling with much the same in our homelands to the far north. I believe it was under control when I left, though. Maybe."

"Then I will keep our families here," Lihuan concluded. "If you dispatch anything from here, you will speak with me first and then a path will be determined to get them out of the mountains without leaving a large trail back here. Understood?"

The two soldiers bowed before Lihuan, apparently accepting his decision, then left the tent.

"Pass this along to Feanne, Estin," Lihuan told him as the others began gathering the newcomers outside. "She needs to know before Insrin makes any plans for where to travel."

Estin gave a short bow of his head, then departed, heading back to his tent to get dressed properly. He was still getting dressed when he heard the tent open behind him.

"If that's Alafa, I have not changed my mind," he said, not looking up. The girl had tried once more recently to sneak into his tent after a bad breakup with a suitor.

When he heard nothing, he half-turned, then froze, seeing Feanne standing in the doorway of the tent. She stood there, hugging her bearskin cloak with tears streaming down her face, shaking both with restrained sobs and what looked like fear. She was still dressed in a night garment and her fur was disheveled as though she had run straight here from her bed. Belying that appearance, her feet were covered with dirt and there were pine needles stuck in places to her fur.

"Feanne," Estin asked, trying to get his feet under him. "Feanne, what's wrong?"

"They're gone," she said softly, burying her face in the fur cloak, sobbing softly.

Estin walked towards her, only to have Feanne collapse to the floor in front of him.

"Who's gone, Feanne?"

"The children. Insrin took them during the night."

His head falling in shared pain, he felt the weight of her loss on his own shoulders as he sat down in front of Feanne, trying to determine what he could do.

"I can send trackers..."

"Insrin is a master tracker, Estin. I doubt anyone here could find him if he was trying not to be found. I can't even find him and I would know his scent anywhere.

"Last night he said he was going for a walk to decide if he could return to my bed after finding out what I was. I'd left the kits with Sohan, so that we could be alone and work through it...or fight...or whatever Insrin needed to forgive me.

"When he went out, he went right to Sohan and took them, then left town immediately. It's been hours since he left. I...can't even find their scent in the woods. I don't know what to do. I've tried to track them and it's like they just vanished."

"I will send the trackers, anyway," Estin told her, touching her foot lightly where it poked out from the bear fur. It was as tender as he dared be with her, even though he knew she likely needed a friendly hug right about then. "Everyone we can muster. If there is a force in this world that can bring them back, I will find it. You have my promise on my life. You will have your children back as soon as I am able."

Feanne touched his muzzle in thanks, then buried her face in the furs again.

"I will be right back, Feanne. Please wait for me."

She just nodded in the furs.

Hurrying from the tent, Estin checked to see if Lihuan or Asrahn were in sight, but they had already left. Cursing, he hopped the ropes of his neighbor's tent and ran up to

Sohan's low-hung tent.

"Sohan," he called, running inside. "Where are you?"

The ferret peeked out from a dark corner, where he was curled into a trembling ball.

"Are you alright?"

Sohan shook his head violently.

Coming into the tent on his knees for lack of room, Estin scurried back to his friend, finding that Sohan's face was bloodied and his arm hung weakly. As he approached, Sohan inched away, trying to disappear into the corner, as if Estin was about to strike him.

"He hit me, Estin," crooned Sohan sadly, "I tried to keep the kits like Feanne asked. I really tried! He just kept saying that his children would not be raised by monsters. I'm not a monster..."

"I know," Estin said, taking Sohan's face in his hands. He let his magic take over for a moment, barely noticing the voices anymore. When he opened his eyes, Sohan looked physically better, but still trembled and appeared ready to run and hide. "This is not your fault."

"Find them, Estin. I don't want Feanne to hate me. I really did try!"

"Did you see which way he took them?"

Sohan thought, then shook his head.

"No. My arm hurt so badly..."

Estin nodded and turned to go. As he began to leave the tent, he stayed low to the ground a moment longer, sniffing the dirt, trying to pick up any hint of Insrin or the kits, but he could only smell Sohan, Feanne, and himself.

"Estin...tell Feanne that she's not a horrible mother."

"What?"

Sohan inched towards him.

"Insrin said he was doing what was best for his family by taking them from her. He said that he was protecting them from their bad parent and the monster."

Estin snarled angrily and took off again, this time going to Ulra and Doln's tent. As he had hoped, Finth sat out front, smoking some noxious plant he had managed to stuff into a pipe.

"Let me guess," the dwarf said, blowing a smoke ring. "You need someone with no bloody morals to do something that Lihuan would cut me from balls to nose for even thinking about? Seems like the only reason you come running up like that."

"Can you track Insrin?" he asked quickly. "If not, who here can?"

"No one, lad," Finth said grimly. "I learned that the last time we followed him. I could track one of his guards and sometimes another, but he just vanishes. He's the best I've seen. If he doesn't want to be found, he's gone if he's had more than an hour's head start."

Estin stood there, panting and wondering what to do next. He had already exhausted his options and reluctantly made his way back to his tent.

As he entered, Feanne's eyes popped up from the furs, her ears alert, then her posture sank as she saw him coming in alone.

"You can't track them, can you?" she asked, her voice muffled by the cloak.

"No," Estin admitted, sitting down in front of her. "I made a promise and I intend..."

"A promise that you could not keep!" roared Feanne, leaping forward and slapping him. "I trusted you, Estin! I came here to protect my kits, because I thought the people here might actually try to shield them from the dangers of the world. This is where it leaves me? Alone?

"If you cannot help me, I'll go back to the Miharon and see what he will do. At least I already know that he will betray me for his own ends."

She got to her feet and stormed out of the tent and was gone, heading northward.

Estin sat in the tent alone for a long time, wondering what he had missed, what he could do to help. He felt like he had failed the kits and Feanne, though he could not have known. Finally, he got up and left, going back to Lihuan's tent.

Though Ulra told him not to enter as the pack-leader had already bedded down for the night, Estin pushed past her and walked into the dark tent, finding Lihuan and Asrahn just stirring under several pelt blankets.

"You're becoming as pushy as my daughter," Lihuan groaned, sitting up slowly. "To what do I owe this obnoxious intrusion?"

"I was taught to be a warrior and a healer," he began softly, trying not to think through what he was about to say. "I doubt there are many among the armies that can claim the same. I want you to send me with the soldiers to detonate the war golem. I cannot help here, without losing my focus. Everything I had here is gone. I need to find myself, no matter the risk."

Lihuan sat up and shook his head, even as Asrahn eyed Estin warily.

"That is exactly why you should not go. The generals believe that the chance of the soldiers surviving all the way to the golem is slim. We cannot afford to lose you, Estin. This is a suicide mission you speak of."

"They need to reach that construct alive if they we are to have any chance of succeeding in this war. I'm going, but I want your blessing, pack-leader."

Lihuan looked to Asrahn, who just shrugged.

"Very well, Estin," Lihuan finally conceded, giving Asrahn a gentle hug. "You will go and represent our people in the war. I will send a small contingent with you. Make good with the rest of the pack over the next few months, for when you leave, you might never return."

Chapter Nine

"Martyrdom"

Knowing that you will likely die in a couple months is somewhat liberating. I found most of my concerns and burden lifted more so than I could have imagined. My dreams were mostly of my own death, but they were a good vision of the future.

In them, I walked through our army, helping guide them against the last bastion of the undead forces. We were holding strong against them, driving them back into the valley where they would meet their end. I watched so many die, but it was all in the name of saving our species and many of the others, so I felt no pain at their loss, so long as I did all I could to help.

The ending of every dream was the same. I was standing at the heart of the undead legion, the growling, wheezing, gurgling corpses surrounding me for miles in every direction. I could see the hills surrounding the area and I knew that we were in the valley where the explosion was to be set off.

I falter there in the dream. I held the magical device myself and could find no way out. My breed's instincts cried out to flee or to curl up and let the undead destroy me, but all of my training told me to stand strong. Still, my life was incomplete and I could not utter the words to trigger the weapon, even though it would save thousands of lives.

It would be then that I look up at the hilltops. Atop one, I saw my parents and my sister, Yalla, standing proudly with the sun setting behind them. They were there to see me succeed where others had failed.

Turning, I would see another hilltop, where Feanne, Insrin, and the twins stood with the sun rising beyond the peak. It was this horizon I faced as I lifted the weapon, knowing that they would be safe once and for all if I could do what I had pledged. Their lives could go on, if I found the strength to set aside my own selfish need to find peace in the world.

The claws of the undead tore at me as I began the words...then I would wake.

Estin woke in his tent and lay there for a time, pondering whether he was truly ready. From what he had been told, after these three months, the humans finally had their great weapon ready. It was their only chance to strike back at the undead.

For the whole time they had waited, rumors and messages had arrived detailing the war. Things had only gotten worse as summer wore on, with the undead army decimating much of the lands between Altis and Lantonne, having pushed the war almost to the gates of the other city.

He sat up and stared at the clothing that Feanne had left him the night before, as she was hurrying off towards her routine searchings of the mountains for her children's trail. The garments had been crafted by her hands to be what she felt were the finest that a warrior-healer could garb themselves in. He could hardly guess when she had found time to make it, let alone the presence of mind to design the garment.

Deep chocolate brown leather was ornamented with steel bits that helped reinforce the softer material. The whole thing had been made in layers of plating that had then been lacquered and hardened to the point that Estin guessed it could turn a weapon with ease. She had even thought to include heavy protection for his legs and a thinner lightweight scalloped covering for his tail. He would be the finest armored person on the battlefield and recognizable to anyone looking for him.

Estin ran his fingers over the clothing and saw in it Feanne's worry that dominated her life now. Since the loss of her family, she rarely spoke to anyone, least of all him, yet here her concern was evident. In every layer of protection she had built into the armor, he could see her worrying about a specific attack that could have killed him.

He took his time fitting the armor over his clothing, finally feeling like he might be able to move freely in it. He was truly amazed at the work she had done, especially without ever sizing him for the armor. It would be hot to wear during the summer months, but he would much rather be sweating than dead.

Striding confidently from the tent, Estin nodded greetings to an elf that passed by on his way to the morning meals that now included many non-wildlings who were more comfortable around the animal people than some of their own. The whole camp had become a strange conglomeration of acceptance that Estin would never have imagined and doubted Insrin would have tolerated, had he stayed.

The conflicts between the groups had proven relatively minor, with Lihuan managing to smooth over most of the hard feelings that had occurred. Estin still had no idea how the pack-leader managed to convince almost anyone of anything if given a few minutes to talk, but his gift of speech seemed almost impossible for anyone to refuse. Those few that were not swayed by his words were still intimidated by the fox, even at his age...or were cowed by his mate.

Estin walked through the camp, politely speaking with all who approached him, most coming to offer their concern for his well-being, or to try one last time to talk him out of going with the army. He talked with them all, but reassured them all that he had made his decision and would be leaving that afternoon as planned.

At last he got past the majority of the residents and headed into the woods, traveling north a short distance towards the grove. Despite all the additions to the camp in recent months, the newcomers were forbidden to use this part of the woods, leaving it in its pristine condition. There had been brief debate about leaving so much nearby space unused, but Lihuan had been firm about it and any who disagreed had backed down.

With Feanne's return, the trees had flourished once more, their boughs recreating the heavily-covered grove where she communed with the fae. He had to push his way through the dense trees to enter the clearing where he hoped to find her.

Feanne knelt there, her hands dug into the loose soil, speaking to the ground itself. As he approached, she pounded at the dirt with one fist, crying as she lay her face on the ground.

"No answer," she said, sitting up and vaguely looking at him, though she seemed to stare right through him as she always did during his visits. "It still will not answer me."

"Feanne, please come to see me off this afternoon. You have been trying to call to the Miharon for months. It is time to come back to us."

"No, no, no!" she cried, sounding as though her mind was gone, going back to scratching at the dry ground. "He will answer me! I have to keep trying."

Estin knelt in front of her, grabbing her wrists as she tried to push him away. She whimpered and mumbled the names of her kits over and over.

"Feanne," he said softly, "they are gone."

Weeping openly, Feanne collapsed against him, beating against his armor with her hands.

"Find them, Estin," Feanne begged, as she had a hundred times before. "Look at what he's turned me into. Please find them."

Sadly, Estin held her head against his chest, trying not to join in her tears. They had repeated this scene at least once a day for several weeks. Feanne would go out in the morning, spending hours patrolling the woods for any sign of her lost family, then would return and rage at the grove, trying to elicit the help of the woodland spirits to no avail. She would not eat all day, focusing on trying to get the Miharon to come to her, unless Estin came and set food in front of her, pushing her to eat it. Whether she had eaten or not, come evening, she would leave the grove, going back to her patrol of the woods, sometimes straight through until morning.

Estin had taken to coming several times through the day, trying to get through to her, but he knew he was making no progress. At the least, he kept her from hurting herself and made her sleep every so often. It was all he could do for her and that terrified him, knowing he might not return once he left. He was not sure if she would be alive when he did come back, if he ever did.

"Goodbye Feanne," he told her, stroking the burr and mud-ridden fur of her cheek. "Please take care of yourself while I am gone."

He hesitated a moment, then added, "I love you."

She did not answer him, just mumbling vaguely about failing to take care of her own children.

Estin remained there as long as he could, brushing the matting and burrs out of Feanne's fur with his claws. He knew from Asrahn that this was something he should not be doing for a female that belonged to another male, but he did it anyway. It was at least something he could do beyond feeding her that made him believe he was doing right by his lost friend and love.

Eventually, the time came to go, and Estin pried Feanne off of him, easing her to the ground where she twitched and whispered as she slept. For a little longer, he knelt beside her, his heart crying out against the injustice that had turned the regal female he had known a year earlier into this, even as he was placed in the face of responsibility. Saying the world was cruel was so much of an understatement.

Leaning close, Estin nuzzled Feanne's cheek briefly, then he got up and headed to the east end of the camp, where he was to meet with the human forces, wiping tears off his face most of the way there.

Collected there, he found a large spattering of warriors from every misfit group that had gathered at the camp. Two gypsies sat near the front of the group, drinking heavily with several dwarves, all boasting about the feats they would perform for their people. Beyond them, a dozen elves sat in quiet contemplation of the day, their faces ashen. To one side of the elves, all four of the orcs that had wandered into camp the month prior were girded for battle, their lust for battle driving them to volunteer the moment they had heard of the plan. A group of four fae-kin stood waiting near the elves, their faintly green skin and antlers marking them as woodland-descended. A single halfling lounged off to a side of the gathering, napping with the remains of a pie lying nearby...from what Estin knew, that was likely comfort food for the short man. Standing forefront, a squad of six wolven wildlings stood at attention, watching Estin approach. The remainder of the army was entirely human.

"The general left us with direction to the ambush point," said one of the wolves, approaching Estin, as he produced a rough sketch on parchment. "He says that we will have a week's march to get there, two days at most to complete the task, then...if we can...we come home."

"Who is carrying the weapon?" Estin found himself asking.

"Two of the elven wizards are the designers of the weapon," the wolf answered, lowering his tone. "They wish to keep it close to them, lest we have any traitors in the group. I've already checked their baggage and found it on the brown mare."

Estin followed the wolf's quick glance, spotting a specific horse in a cluster that would carry the humans' gear and food. It had large saddlebags, but carried nothing else.

"Good work," Estin told him. "Might I get your name? I don't believe we've met."

"Greth. We have met, but I was very young at the time."

Estin eyed the wolf, gauging his age at around four years, perhaps less. He studied Greth's markings and soon realized that they were familiar. It had been a while, but he knew both this wolf's markings and those of his father.

"You are Ghohar's child. Are you of age yet? I didn't think Lihuan was letting younger go along."

"No, but I have Lihuan's permission to go. I swore to help you avenge my father's death long ago. I was not going to wait two more months for a ceremony that means little just to join you."

Estin gave him a welcoming clasp on the shoulder, then excused himself and approached a human wearing markings on his steel armor that set him apart from the others.

"You will lead?" Estin asked the man. "Is this your troop?"

The man squinted up at him, then eyed his armor, including Estin's tail snaking behind him. His eyes settled on the necklace Estin wore.

"Yeah. Lieutenant Linn at your service. I presume you're our token healer?"

"Yes. I'll be fighting alongside you, but I can heal your men."

"Then I think we've got everyone," said the human. "We leave in one hour."

*

The long journey across the foothills and down onto the plains had been exhilarating for Estin. He had dreamed much of his life of traveling to other lands, unhindered by his race, but had never left Altis before going to Lihuan's camp. Now, he watched the changing scenery with wide eyes, taking in everything.

The longest portion of the trip had been in descending the mountains, chewing up the first three days of travel. Once they reached the foothills proper, they had made good time, heading across the plains towards the raging battles in the southeast.

The first night on the plains, Estin had lain in his bedroll, listening to explosions that echoed across the land. He could not even fathom a battle so violent that days of travel away he could still hear the actions of the armies. Dim flashes of light made the night sky flicker, as though a thunderstorm were coming, bringing with it lightning of nearly any imaginable color.

By day, they soon began to see the shapes of the huge war golems on the horizon, appearing like tiny mountains in their own right. Had they not been moving, Estin would never have known what they were. In another two days, their dwarven features came steadily into view, even as Lantonne slowly crept onto the horizon.

This city was not as rugged as Altis, but Estin thought it just as marvelous in design. Large smooth walls guarded the tiny village inside, with a single wide keep tower in the middle. From what he could see, the majority of the people in these lands lived outside the walls of their fortress. That put them squarely in harm's way, with the mighty golems fighting against the undead legions just outside of the walls.

Pulling a horse alongside Estin, Lieutenant Linn said, "The plan is to get the golems to drive the undead into an old quarry way to the north of Lantonne. If we can get them down there, the city should be safe from the explosion, as far away as it'll be."

"Lihuan said that there was to be an escape point for us. How far do we need to get out once the weapon is planted?"

Linn frowned, his young features having deepened into lines during their trip.

"The old mining town at the lip of the quarry is abandoned from what I'm told. The buildings are old but sturdy. I was hoping the quarry itself will absorb enough of the explosion to make the top safe. We might get an hour at most. I don't think anyone really knows how bad this will be, even if I keep getting suggestions to get into that mining town or beyond. No promises on safety anywhere, though."

"There's nothing sure about anything we're doing," Estin noted wryly, but the human just stared straight ahead, his expression grim. "Do you fear dying, Linn?"

The human turned slowly, his expression confused and mildly annoyed.

"I do not fear dying with an army at my back against a foe we have a chance of defeating. Tomorrow, we face an enemy that will try to kill us and use our bodies to murder our families. I do not wish to become that which I fight against. That is what I fear, wildling."

Estin nodded at the sentiment.

"Then we should just not die."

*

They stood on the stone edge of the quarry, fifty men and women strong, staring down at a legion that defied imagination. Thousands of undead raged in a sea of death, flinging magical attacks at the war golems, even as zombies and skeletons attempted to climb the golems pointlessly. Deep gouges and cracks in the golems' legs gave some indication of the persistence of the undead in their struggles, as well as burns and other damage where magic had scarred the metal.

The company had arrived late in the morning, just as the fourth war golem had dragged its arms along the ground, driving thousands of undead over the cliffs into the quarry. Estin had watched this amusedly, right up until the entire force of undead got back up at the bottom. He had continued to watch as the golem had thrown itself into the quarry as well, smashing hundreds of the undead, only to have them get right back up shortly after the golem did.

"Now," continued the elf who had been lecturing the company on the explosive weapon's uses for almost an hour, "the explosion will likely disrupt all magic within the region for several minutes. If you are using magical weapons or items, they will cease to work briefly. This applies also to the war golems, which might fall over, of course excluding the one we're blowing up."

Estin squinted at the golems, which were nearly tall enough to reach the top of the immense quarry. Their heavy armored forms were solid everywhere he could see.

"Where does the weapon go?" Estin asked loudly from his perch on the edge of the quarry. "We were told that it just attaches to the golem."

"Excuse me?"

"Where do we put the weapon on the golem? You've left that out."

The elf glanced around at the soldiers nervously, then finally answered, "In the head, please. That is where its power core is."

Estin watched as the two-hundred foot golems twisted and smashed at their small foes. The faces were solid, each with the features of a legendary dwarven hero.

"How by the dragon's scales do you intend us to get onto the head?" demanded Linn, grabbing the elf by the shirt roughly. "You couldn't have mentioned this a week ago? A month, maybe?"

The entire company erupted into blame and shouting, as the humans debated whether to throw the elf over the ledge and then go home.

Eyeing the golems as they moved, Estin saw a faint line of notches on the back of the nearest, like some kind of basic ladder, starting at the boot of one foot. Often, the undead were clinging to it, trying to scale the golem, but their aimless movements made climbing impossible.

"I can show someone where to go. I can see a way up."

The words cut through the many voices that were shouting, drawing all attention to Estin.

"Can you do it?" asked Linn of Estin. "My men will be heavily-armored. We're already covering you anyway as our healer. It would not be a huge change of plan to have you make the climb."

"Can you climb it with a twenty pound weight on your back?" asked the elf, pulling his shirt free of Linn. "The weapon weighs at least that much."

Estin nodded grimly, now studying the ground at the feet of the golem. Hundreds of the undead swarmed each foot, making any approach incredibly dangerous, compounded by the golem's own stomping. Whoever went in would have to time their run, so as not to be killed by the golem itself.

"The Lantonne controllers should have given the golems orders not to attack the living already," Linn noted, following Estin's gaze. "If we can get past the undead, the golem should let you climb it."

From their position, Estin saw that a wagon-wide path ran down the edge of the quarry, looping the whole of it twice before reaching the bottom near one of the golems.

"We go down as a group," he told the human, leaning over the edge to make sure the path was usable. "I think we can control the ramp all the way to the bottom. Once we get down, we need to cut a swath to the nearest golem. That puts our group against no less than one-hundred undead by my guess, though many may be busy with the golem, depending on their orders."

"That we can do," Linn assured him. "My men were prepared to cut through the whole undead army if they had to. Killing a few distracted undead is simple."

"Can you hold that for me for about ten minutes while I place the weapon, then fight all the way out, after the undead have noticed us?"

That rattled the human somewhat, but he nodded grimly.

They spent the next half hour prepping and watering the horses, checking weapons and, for those who had traveled with their heavy armor stowed away attiring themselves in their armor. Those who had managed to keep their appetites ate silently. Once all was set, they began the long trek down the ramp, trying to set a quick yet not tiring pace. They would need all their strength at the bottom.

The farther they descended, the louder the pitched battle below became. Beyond the sound that thousands of the walking dead could make, there were the booms of magical strikes against the golems and the deafening grinding of the golems themselves.

It took them almost a full hour to reach the bottom of the quarry, though their slow pace contributed much to that. Estin could only hope they could manage the return trip far faster, or this truly would be a suicide mission, as Lihuan had predicted. He was tempted to ask the elves to adjust the weapon for a longer time to escape, but doubted they could do it quickly, so he said nothing.

When they did reach the bottom of the quarry, Linn dismounted with many of his men, setting up a group that would guard the horses for the retreat. That cost them ten men before the fighting was even to begin, but without the horses, the odds of making it out in time was non-existent.

During those last preparations, Estin walked calmly out to the edge of the battle, where the undead horde crashed like the ocean against the war golems. Their commands likely not including any option for another target beyond the golems, the undead before him stood patiently, waiting to push forward over their companions to get at the feet of the golem. He got within five feet of the undead, without drawing so much as a glance from them.

Just then, a war golem stomped, shaking the entire quarry. The aftershocks very nearly knocked Estin to the ground and did topple nearly all the undead around him. When they recovered, they went right back to waiting to attack the golem.

"Are you ready?" asked Linn loudly, two elves beside him, dragging a large bag. "Once we go, there's no turning back. If you're not sure about this, I am sure I can find another in the group who can climb it."

"I've got nothing to go back to," Estin told the man as he hoisted the bag onto his back. It was far heavier than he had expected, but he felt he could manage. "If everything goes badly, I want you to take your men and run, rather than waiting for me."

Linn agreed, then signaled the various groups to form up. Within a minute, he had the entire company arrayed at the bottom of the ramp, with Estin several rows back from the front, ready to heal the soldiers the whole way in.

"Charge!" cried Linn, leading the way as he cut into the undead ahead of them with his sword, even as he bashed others aside with his shield.

The world devolved instantly into chaos around Estin as the battle began. The undead were more than willing to fight back once provoked, surrounding the group in seconds. Were the golems not so large, he doubted that the group would ever know if they were moving in the right direction.

Cries of agony and groans of the dead mingled into one loud cacophony of death as the group pushed slowly forward. The distance they had yet to cover was immense, making it hard to feel like they were truly gaining ground. Sometimes the golem would move away from them, making the distance greater.

With a deafening screech, the golem moved its foot, nearly stepping on the company. Linn had to bring them to an abrupt halt to prevent its heel from coming down on the lead ranks.

"Go, go, go!" he cried at Estin, even as he lanced another undead in front of him. The path ahead was relatively clear all the way to the golem's foot.

Estin raced ahead, diving and sliding through the undead that clamored for a grip on him. His armor absorbed most of the impacts, letting him focus on running, rather than having to fight off every creature in his path. Several he cut down swiftly, but did his best to keep moving at all times. More than once, he felt bone claws rake his armor, trying to drag him down, but the creatures fell back as he ran, leaving long scars on the leather.

Finally, he reached the gleaming foot of the golem, leaping as best he could onto the decorative creases of its boot. His claws scraped loudly against the metal, but he clung and began making his way slowly upwards. Those first twenty feet were unbearably difficult, with him sliding nearly as far as he climbed, using mostly damaged metal on the golem to keep his grip. At last, he reached the top of the boot, where the tiny notches began. These sped his pace immensely, allowing him to ascend swiftly, soon reaching the golem's midsection.

Without warning, the golem reached back, trying to swat at Estin. Where he was, it could not reach, but the impact of its finger brushing nearby knocked his feet loose briefly.

He was forced to hold still and ride out the golem's attacks, until at last it went back to smashing the undead.

Estin hurried the remaining distance, scaling the torso rapidly, then reaching the base of the neck, where he was told he could get inside. At first, he thought the long ladder simply ended between the giant's shoulder blades, but then saw a well-hidden door.

Feeling around the edges of the door, Estin found a latch that released it, allowing him to fall inside. As he did, he kicked the door shut behind him, then tried to get his bearings in the shifting dark room. The entire place was sealed, letting no light at all in, rendering even his night-vision useless.

Estin slid across the floor as the golem shifted again, this time slamming into something solid that he grabbed onto to stay where he was. Once he was sure that the golem would not toss him around again, he raised his hand overhead, whispering words of magic to make his hand glow brightly, illuminating the room.

From where he lay, Estin could see that the chamber had been designed to allow dozens of riders to travel with the golem as needed. Long benches of metal were built right into the floor every few feet. The room itself was likely almost as large as Lihuan's entire camp. A staircase nearby led down and from what little Estin could see, the room below was identical.

Estin moved slowly through the golem's upper-chest, trying to find a way up into its head. This took him longer than he liked, until at last he found a ladder near the middle of the room that could be easily reached by standing on one of the benches. Climbing that soon put him at a hatch that he shoved open, clearing the way into the golem's head.

As he pulled himself into the head, Estin was awestruck by the arcing energy that hovered over him. A large stream of bluish-white lightning seemed to flow outwards, feeding into the body of the golem as it crackled and hissed.

Estin hurriedly emptied the bag he had carried all the way up, letting the three heavy pieces clang to the floor. He attached them one to another as he had been taught on the way down into the quarry, receiving a sputtering hum from the device as he locked in the last piece.

He took a deep breath, knowing the moment he activated the device, he would need to be running. With that done, he traced a symbol on the surface of the weapon, lighting a simple sigil on the side of the device. Within seconds, he watched as the energy above drifted towards and into the weapon's end, feeding it and making it hum.

Then he ran, diving into the lower room and racing for the door to the outside. He yanked the door open and started to climb out when the cliff side came up on him swiftly, forcing him back inside as the golem crashed into the side of the quarry. Rocks flew everywhere and Estin's bare feet slid on the metal, driving him almost halfway back across the room.

Digging in and running at the door as he saw sky again, Estin managed to get outside, even as the stone walls approached again. The golem was staggering drunkenly, crashing into everything around it. Though the other golems seemed to continue their fight against the undead, this one was stumbling and putting out its hands, trying to balance itself.

Far below, Estin could see the human troops begin to break and run for the ramp.

Clinging for all he was worth to the doorframe, Estin waited as the cliff neared. He had one chance and it was not going to be an easy one.

Estin leaped as the golem got close, slamming hard into the stones as the golem's shoulder hit the wall nearby. He tried to hang on, but the impact dislodged him, sending him sliding and tumbling down the steep wall of the quarry until he crashed into the ramp twenty feet lower.

Dazed and hurting, Estin began crawling up the ramp, then slowly got to his feet and limped as best he could. The spot he had landed was almost two-thirds of the way up and he was moving far slower than he had planned, giving him only a small head-start over the other soldiers.

Staggering up the rise, he looked down the ramp to where the army was riding up furiously, gaining ground on him. That gave him hope and drive, allowing him to quicken his pace slightly. His leg—the same one that had been so badly injured by Insrin's honor guard months earlier—was just not holding his weight very well, even with some quick healing. He recognized that he would need to devote some time to mending the injury, but it would need to wait.

Estin soon reached the top, beginning to hobble towards the abandoned mining town part way around the lip. Once he was sure that he could reach the buildings soon, Estin leaned over the quarry's edge and checked on the others, finding them more than halfway up. They had slowed considerably as the golem had damaged part of the ramp, forcing the soldiers to go single-file up one section.

The narrow-file of the group gave Estin a chance to see what their losses looked like. From what he could see at that distance, nearly a quarter of the men were still there, in addition to those who had stayed with the horses. They had done extremely well, especially without a healer.

He mentally cheered on his companions, then hurried to close the gap to the mining town. Its large grey wooden buildings loomed ominously, though nearly anything would look inviting to Estin at that moment, knowing what was coming soon. He wanted any form of cover he could find, be it building or a large rock.

Though there were many buildings, one in particular caught his attention. The squat structure was solidly-built, with several iron beams supporting the otherwise wooden walls. It was the only one he had seen that might survive the explosion, if it reached as far as the little town.

A sudden waft of animal scents alerted Estin that something was not right. He sniffed the air, initially thinking he smelled wolf, but the scent quickly changed into fox…and blood. From what he could tell, it came from a two-story building a little farther from the quarry edge. He started to move on, ignoring it, but the scent grew stronger, almost as if the winds were trying to coax him into checking on something important. He finally gave up on his original plan, unable to ignore the smells.

Following his nose cautiously, he approached the tall building and eased the door open. Fly-ridden corpses lay strewn everywhere. Their broken bodies had decayed considerably, but from what he could see, they had likely been dead when they walked in and then cut down after shambling inside. Several of these were draped over a makeshift barricade at the back end of the room, up against a staircase and a few even hung off the sides of the staircase. Aside from the ruins of the battle, there was little in the room, other than some broken furniture and cabinets.

Estin padded slowly into the room, watching the bodies for movement. All appeared to be truly dead, but he could not be too cautious. As he stepped among them, he began to see dried blood near the barricade, pooled and covering much of the floor. In it, he could see dried prints that looked human, as well as wildling…and some that were too large for either and looked faintly wolven.

That was when he began to see the defenders' bodies.

Fox wildlings lay behind the wooden barrier, strewn across the first few steps of the staircase. Several were actually draped over the barricade, as though they had been mauled and dragged onto the small wall to die. One fox body that lay among the zombies had been torn so far beyond recognition that he could not even be sure of gender or coloring anymore.

He eased himself up to the barricade, kneeling slowly to check the nearest wildling body. The male had been beaten until his face was caved in, but Estin did see that his hand still held an ornate weighted axe—one of Insrin's guards' weapons. When he touched the male's hand, he found the skin cold. This had happened hours ago.

Climbing over bodies and the remains of the barricade, Estin hurried up the stairs, finding that the second floor was in no better shape. At the top of the steps, another barricade had been built, with two more foxes and dozens of undead bodies lying in front of it. Beyond the barricade, he could see nothing but a bare wall and ancient cabinets, like the ones downstairs. The mostly-dry blood bore many footprints, again of wildlings and humans.

Moving over the barricade, he found five more bodies. Surrounded by four zombie corpses, the single wildling body's eyes still stared blankly up at the ceiling, the grey fox's throat torn open. His sword was still clutched in his hand and a spear lay near the barricade. His claws and even his mouth were covered with dried gore, as though he had resorted to every weapon at his disposal at the end, but still fell to superior numbers.

"Insrin," Estin said softly, kneeling beside him. The body was cold to the touch and he felt no spirit present. He could only guess that the man had sought safety in Lantonne and never quite made it. "You fool, what did you get yourself into?"

A rustle nearby brought Estin to attention. It was coming from the cabinet. He sniffed the air, trying to identify what else might be in there with him. The scent he recognized instantly—he would known it in his sleep—and did his best to cover Insrin's body with debris from the barricade. Estin then tossed Insrin's weapons away, where they would be less visible.

With trembling hands, Estin opened the cabinet, praying to the newer gods, the dragons, and anything else he could think of that was more powerful than him that the kits were alive. He doubted he could bear the idea of fighting off two tiny zombies. If that was what he found, he began to wonder if he would even be able to stop them from killing him.

Inside the cabinet lay Atall and Oria, staring up at him with tear-filled eyes. They were shaking violently, pressed against the back end of the small space.

"Daddy said we need to stay in here til he comes back," Atall said softly, trying to pull the cabinet closed on Estin.

Estin held the door of the cabinet and did his best to look like nothing was wrong, though he bet he looked as though he had rolled down a mountainside after the run through the quarry.

"Your mom sent me to get you," he told them, making sure his body blocked their view of Insrin's corpse. "We need to go. She's very worried."

Oria was the first to pounce Estin, clinging to his neck with a death grip that impressed Estin. Atall was not far after, running up his knee to grab hold also. They had grown a lot since he had last seen them and were getting big for carrying this way, but he would find a way.

"Close your eyes," he told them, and both buried their faces against his damaged armor. "I will protect you."

Estin hurried down the stairs, not knowing how much time he had left before the explosion. There could not be much, he knew, so when he heard a high-pitched noise growing in intensity, he rushed into the back of the bottom floor, where the beams looked the strongest.

He knelt in the corner, setting the twins on the ground beneath him, using his body to cover them both. As best he could, he covered both of them with the heavier sections of his armor, hoping that even if he died, between his body and the armor, they would survive. As an afterthought, he wrapped his tail around them, using its added armor to help guard the kits against any flying debris.

"Cover your ears," he whispered, then cast a defensive spell that would allow his body to absorb one impact from debris or the roof coming down on them. "This is about to get very loud."

He dearly hoped the kits were fully covered, as the screeching noise grew deafening.

White light washed out his vision as his ears rang. The floor shook and he was tossed about, though he kept himself over the children. Vaguely, he became aware of the ceiling flying away, followed by much of the walls. The next thing he knew, Estin was tumbling across the ground, the twins still clutched in his arms, crying loudly.

For a time, Estin lay there on the soft ground, staring up at the sky. His vision was blurred and his ears throbbed, but he could feel both twins moving. He had managed to keep them both alive.

Footsteps neared as Estin heard voices talking. He was so giddy at having survived that all he heard of the conversation was, "I think the wolf went this way."

Seconds later, a large human leaned in over Estin, checking to see if he was alive, as he just laughed at the craziness of having gotten through anything like he had that day. Estin sat up and put the kits on the ground in front of him, where they clung to each other nervously.

Looking around at the dozen men around him, Estin realized that he had no idea who these humans were. They did not look to be the ones from Linn's company. The armor and even hairstyles were all wrong and every one of them glared at him angrily.

"Do we kill it or throw it in with the others?" asked the man standing over Estin, turning to an older man on horseback. "It's not the wolf, but I still say it doesn't belong here."

That cut through the shock and Estin grabbed the twins again, trying to get to his feet. They screamed and clutched at him again. He had no idea what wolf they were talking about, but he was not about to let these strangers near the kits.

"Throw him in a cage. I'm not worried about trying a beast for murder. Skin the pups."

Estin lost his mind on the spot. With one hand holding the kits to him, he tore into the soldiers as they came up on him, using his free hand and tail and sometimes his teeth. When he came to, he was kneeling on the ground, the kits crying nearby, with a sword in his stomach. He numbly pulled it free and closed the wound with magic, sitting up to see if he had any chance of getting to the kits without being struck again.

Dozens lay bleeding around him, just behind a line of soldiers who had weapons drawn and leveled at his throat. The kits were just a few steps from him and the soldiers appeared nervous about touching them, but the humans had effectively cut Estin off from them.

"Fine, throw them all in the wagon. Damn, I hate cornered vermin."

A heavy blow to Estin's neck dazed him and was swiftly followed by a harder hit to his head that blacked everything out.

*

Estin woke and felt as though the war golem had fallen atop him. His leg was badly twisted, his stomach hurt where he had not finished mending the mortal wound from the sword, and he could tell that after blacking out, he had been beaten. He was deeply thankful that he found himself in the dark when he opened his eyes.

He lay there, listening to a creaking noise and feeling a gentle swaying of his resting place. It felt as though he were in a wagon, but for all he could see, it might have been a cave.

"You thought you could escape?" whispered an airy voice inside Estin's head, startling him wide awake. When it spoke again, Estin realized it was the bodiless voice of the Miharon. "The fae always win in the end. Our bargain is at an end."

Reaching out nervously in the absolute dark, Estin tried to find out what was around him.

The floor was wooden, that much he could be sure. Tightly-fitted boards. He could even feel the holes where nails had them attached.

He reached out to his sides next, feeling vertical metal bars on his left and beyond them, more wood. To his right, he felt nothing at first, but then his hand brushed fur. A little yelp was followed by scurrying.

"Oria? Atall?" he asked of the dark. The scurrying came closer.

"Daddy?" asked Atall, his voice trembling.

"No, it's Estin," he answered, smiling at knowing the child was alive. "Where is your sister?"

"You're not a fox. Why should I tell you?"

Estin sat up and banged his head on more bars overhead.

"I want to know she's safe, Atall."

"I'm here, too," came Oria's little voice, somewhere near where Atall's voice had been.

"Of course, of course, they will put them in here," came another voice, but not one Estin recognized. A female's voice, somewhere on the far side of the dark place they were in. "Always with the children and the men. All just makes you crazy. You might have claws and fangs, or maybe you're just strong. Does it really matter?"

"Who is that?" Estin asked of the darkness.

"Not a person. Just another animal. Another woman in a cage. You know they always throw one of us in the box, right? Always. Can't be fun without a woman..."

Estin began to feel really nervous about staying where he was. He made sure to find the kits in the dark, pulling them close to him, despite Atall's objections and a painful nip at Estin's finger.

"What are you talking about?" he asked the mysterious female.

"Can't be easier to break your toys. Put them in a box and shake it a lot. If they still won't break, put a man in the box, too. He'll break her for you. Just takes a little while. He won't want to, true, true, but he will eventually..."

Estin swallowed hard.

"Then, then comes the best part," continued the raspy voice. "Just having a man abuse the woman out of frustration isn't enough. No, certainly not. You lock them in a box long enough, he'll do just about anything to make himself feel better, then it's breathing in your ear and apologies later. So much pain. That's what they give you in the box, you know.

"But...yes, the best part. Throw in the children. Make them listen to the two fight. Make them listen when the man hurts her. Make them listen when the man overpowers the female and kills her for food, because the others forgot to feed them. Maybe the children get eaten first, maybe not. Either way, one day, they do not know how to leave the cage. For all the pain in the cage the outside might be worse..."

The kits squirmed and whimpered against Estin's bare chest.

"I am not in here to hurt you," Estin said, still not even sure exactly where the voice was coming from. The closed area made things echo weirdly. "Are you the only other one in here?"

"Only one! Last man got taken away...maybe they killed him? Maybe he pulls a plow? Who knows? Maybe he hurts another woman? Oh so many ways to hurt us, there is. You'll hurt us too, it just takes time in the box..."

Estin closed his eyes as she mumbled on, hugging the kits to him. Atall fought to get away at first, but soon both slept. Still the room jostled onward and the demented voice trailed on into the darkness.

In desperation, Estin slid away from the voice, finding the corner of the cage. He had bars on two sides of him. Some protection, at least.

Time passed slowly, though he could not be sure how much was actual time passing and how much was his imagination in the dark quiet. It felt like days that the cage continued to rock, with the female yammering almost constantly about the abuses she had endured. When the kits would wake, Estin would talk to them about almost anything, trying to help them ignore the other voice in the cage.

The twins had begun crying almost constantly, having gone without food for even longer than Estin had. He had searched the floor for his pouches that had been filled with rations, but they were long gone, along with his weapons and armor. His searching fingers had only brushed a patch of bare skin of the mysterious female, eliciting a sharp hiss before she retreated to her side of the cage.

When the movement stopped at last, Estin pulled the children close again, unsure what was coming next. To his amazement, the sides of his prison opened up, revealing wooden panels over a large iron cage on a wagon. He blinked in the restored light, finding that they were in a large camp of humans, with tents as far as he could see.

Estin turned to check the other direction, but froze when he saw the poor creature sharing the cage with them.

She had been human, that much he could be certain of. Her clothing was tattered and stained with both dirt and blood. The woman appeared to have been beaten over and over again, but never so much as washed down after months of captivity. Dark terrified eyes darted around as she cringed at every noise and tried to keep herself curled as small as she could in the corner. She covered her ears and eyes as the cage was opened up to the air, whimpering and still talking to herself.

Estin had never seen a more pitiful creature, even in the slave pits of Altis. Still, he knew that was her origin, based on a small burned mark on her neck that denoted the particular slaving group that had originally sold her. Estin felt such loathing and pity that he had to look away. He had never realized that the long arm of slavery reached even to the humans' own.

"Okay!" shouted a human to the wagon's driver. "I'll just get them all hooked up and you're good to go."

The man approached Estin's side of the cage holding a leather collar.

Holding the kits more tightly, Estin shifted to the middle of the cage, growling and snarling at the man.

"Either you take the collar," the man said, sounding annoyed, "or when you pass out from hunger, I'll take the lil ones from you. Not really in the mood for arguing."

Estin looked down at the two kits, who stared up at him nervously.

He leaned forward to the edge of the cage, struggling to keep from biting the man as the heavy collar closed on his throat, the clasp locking shut.

"Now," the human said, walking around to the lock of the cage, "what manner of work are you used to? Fields? Mines? Cooking, maybe?"

Glaring at the human as he sat down, Estin dragged the forefinger claw of his left hand across his right palm, slicing open the flesh. He then drew magic into the wound, closing it.

"Well I'll be damned," the man said, his eyes wide. "You just saved yourself a lot of training in the fields under a whip, boy. If you can heal, you may just find yourself better off than most."

"The kits stay with me," Estin growled.

"Can't promise that, boy. If someone else needs them on another field..."

"Either they stay with me, or why would I have any reason to let those who need healing live?"

The human's eyes narrowed angrily.

"For now. That's all I can promise. You screw up too bad, they're gone and you go to a mine. Agreed?"

Estin closed his eyes and nodded, trying to shut out the crying of the kits. If he let that get through his defenses, he knew he would try to kill every person here between him and their freedom.

"Alright, c'mon out," the man said, swinging open the cage. "Stop when you get down."

Obediently, Estin carried the kits to the entrance of the cage, then slid down to stand on the ground. His legs were both shaky from being unable to stand so long and the hunger that was making him woozy.

The human snapped a leash onto Estin's collar, but Estin bit down his pride and looked at the kits as a reminder why he needed to be calm. The glance was not lost on the human, who gave him a moment before gesturing towards one of the few semi-permanent structures nearby.

"They say you were found near the old quarry," the man said, leading them into the tent village. "Was the human in the cage with you?"

"No," he answered, following reluctantly as they left the wagon. "She was in the wagon when I woke."

The man nodded knowingly and glanced back at the wagon, where other handlers were trying to get the woman out, as she screamed and clung to the bars, kicking at them and growling like some feral beast.

"That one's just not right. Must be one of the ones from the Altis slave caravans…we've had a few come through like that from time to time, when a caravan got disrupted. The things they did to their slaves makes me wonder why anyone would put up with seeing that done to another living being."

Estin looked at the man in confusion, asking, "How is your slave camp any different?" The man laughed and shook his head.

"Not a slave camp, boy. Slavery is illegal in Lantonne. What you have here is old farmland that we're using to supply the troops while Altis is crushed." He gestured broadly at hundreds of tents, then over at expansive fields, tended by hundreds of people of every race. "You're all from Altis, or lands it controlled. You never paid taxes here, so the law is that you all work to help us win the war against their undead, or you get tossed in the way of Altis' army…that's not where anyone wants to be right now, trust me."

"So you're forcing us to work your fields and your soldiers are threatening to kill children to enforce it…and you don't call that slavery?"

Estin gave the leash a gentle tug to reinforce his point.

The man stopped walking and sighed.

"I didn't say it was right, but it's what we need to do," he confessed, glancing down at the crying kits. "There's a war at our doorstep that's killing thousands. Those who can fight are out there and I don't doubt they're willing to do awful things in the name of saving society from the undead horde. Those of us left here are not fighters…hell, we're not trained to take care of two-hundred refugees.

"I wouldn't hurt you or your kids if I had a choice, but it's not always my call, and not everyone feels the same way."

Estin whispered to the kits, trying to calm them, as the man watched them sadly.

"You were found near the quarry, so I'm guessing the soldiers would have been happy to stick a sword in you," the man admitted. "You're lucky you weren't wearing Altis' colors, or they'd have killed the kids and then seen you hang for murder."

"Murder? Since when is destroying part of the undead forces considered murder?" asked Estin, bewildered. He could have expected nearly any reaction from Altis' enemies, but that was not one that had ever even occurred to him.

"Not that part," the man said, giving Estin another tug on the leash to get him moving again towards the building. "That was actually pretty clever and unexpected…we still don't know why Altis blew up its own soldiers. I was talking about the aftermath."

"I think I was in a cage by that point."

"Great, I get the smart-ass," grumbled the man, stopping Estin at the door of the building. "What I meant was the collapse of the rest of our mines and the magical hole that opened up and ate everything that went down into the quarry. Last word I got was with the driver of your wagon and he says the death toll from that little stunt was over a thousand. They got the Altis soldiers that did it though, so we can at least hang them."

Estin felt sick, thinking that the very men that depended on him to deliver the magical explosive now faced execution for an act that was meant to help everyone. He thought about confessing his own role, then remembered the kits, who were squirming against his chest. He bit down his thoughts of saying anything of what he had done.

The human swung open the door to the building, half-leading and half-pulling Estin after him.

The dimly-lit interior of the building was larger than Estin had expected, the plank floor extending far back and away from him. Several dozen people lay around, many groaning and holding injuries, while others appeared to be gravely ill and barely conscious.

"You're only the second healer we've been graced with," the human explained, leading them inside. "Most get shipped out to the army. They probably didn't even think of the possibility of you using magic…low opinions of wildlings abound in some parts of our city, I'm afraid, though it helps us out.

"You'll stay here and tend to those too sick to work. If you leave without permission, there are taskmasters out in the fields who seem to think they're tending to slaves, rather than prisoners. They'll whip you if you're lucky. Just be smart and stay in here. At least you'll stay warmer than most of the others."

"What about food and water?" Estin asked, as Oria nuzzled his neck. "We haven't had either in more than a day."

The man studied Estin's face a moment, then glowered at the kits.

"I'll get you some water and whatever food I can find. The little ones eat from your rations until they're old enough to work. Not my rules, but I get to enforce them. We just don't have enough to feed everyone properly without depriving the military of needed supplies."

Estin looked at the two kits, who stared back at him, their eyes filled with terror. Feanne had taught him to be killed rather than face enslavement, a distinctly odd mindset for his breed. Between training and instinct, he felt that he should either run, or kill until he himself was killed or had escaped.

Now, looking at the fear and need for someone to care for them that he saw in the kits, he began to see what had taken the rage from Feanne. Dying for freedom and independence was useless if the children died too. For her children, he would do as the taskmasters told him. He would accept what was thrown at him, day by day. It was all he could do.

Chapter Ten

"The Other Side"

What nearly broke my spirit was the leash. Every time someone touched that thing, I felt like I was letting my mother die again. It was an old wound on my mind, made fresh by seeing what my sister had become through years of slavery. Though those who ran the camp were not awful, it was their rule that I had to wear the leash anytime they let me out of the building.

I would be led from my "home" to the latrines or the showers—generally a pair of large men who would dump a bucket of water over you, then send you back in line—by a random human from Lantonne, who would tug that damned leash the whole way out and back. The leash was not just for wildlings, it was for anyone that was not in charge.

Tell me I am not a slave, but put a leash on me and I will call you a liar.

Some pulled us along by those leashes because that was their job and I held no special dislike for them. Others enjoyed it, finding any opportunity to drag those who were larger or more "dangerous" by the leashes to prove something to themselves. Having fangs and claws put me into that category, it would seem. Oria and Atall were also treated this way, often dragged bodily when they tried to resist. I longed to walk over and cut them free, but I knew that all three of us would suffer for that decision.

Over those many months, I saw a great many of the slaves—indebted foreigners, I believe they called us—released to live as citizens of Lantonne, after having worked off their debts. Each time, we were passed over for this honor, owing mostly to my skills. Once a blessing, the ability to heal became an anchor for us, making us too valuable to lose. They were at least kind enough to let the kits stay with me, but there were times I considered sending them on, in hopes of finding a better life without me.

In that year, I learned that dreams do not require sleep. I had daydreamed before, mostly about Feanne in times past, but here my dreams became very much a part of my waking self. Sleep was my body's way of telling me that I had been pushed too far for the day and was my only true escape. It was the only time I could free myself from constant worry about the kits.

The new dream for the daytime was simple, really. I would get Oria and Atall back into the wilds where they belonged, free of leashes and taskmasters. That was all. There was no thought for myself, Feanne, or anyone else. Even my sister was forgotten for a while, so far gone was she. It was these two precious young lives that I needed to save.

That is what it is to be a healer. They always said it was about saving lives and I knew which ones I needed to work to spare.

Thirteen months into his labors at the supply camp, Estin found himself barely able to rouse himself to sit up as the morning began to shine through the slats of the poorly-sealed building. The day would be exactly the same as the last few hundred.

An hour before dawn—an hour or two prior—all the others were herded out of their blankets and herded out to the fields to begin working. Some would work with the cattle, others raising crops or moving water where it was needed. The kits were already out in the fields, helping how they could, while trying not to get trampled by the horses and oxen. Meanwhile, Estin was left in the building to wait and stare at the ceiling until further notice.

Usually around noon, the injured would begin being brought to him. Most were those who had misused a tool and cut themselves badly or twisted a leg wrong, preventing them from doing their duties. Some were severely sick, having finally succumbed to the cold rains that had plagued the area nearly every afternoon for the last month, in anticipation of the upcoming winter. And, just to add some spice to the excitement of his day, nearly half of his patients were actual cattle, being brought to him to ensure they were healthy or to fix broken legs. At least once a week, one of the taskmasters would be brought in, though that was far more rare.

He turned his head, looking towards the front of the building, still not able to motivate himself to stand. What drew his attention there—as it did every day as he woke—was the leash the taskmasters kept near the door. It was the one they put on him, as it was the only one left after everyone else had gone for the day.

Fear over the fate of the kits kept Estin from ever touching that leash unless ordered to do so. If he had his way, it would have found its way into a fire months earlier.

Estin just lay there for a long time, eventually putting his hands above his face as he examined them. When he had lived in Altis, his hands had been rubbed clean of fur in spots from climbing their stone walls. After that, the training to fight properly, followed by magical education had allowed the fur to regrow, but the pads on his palms and fingers had thickened from burns and nicks with claws. Now, his hands were soft, aside from several recent scars. The only notable thing about them was that the claws were all but gone.

This had actually been one of the earlier decisions by the taskmasters after his arrival.

Wildlings and others with horns or claws had them filed down until they bled, for the safety of everyone around them. Every couple weeks, a pair of burly men would hold his arms down as they ground down his claws. It was humiliating and made Estin feel as though it were just one more piece of his self-worth they had taken from him, though like everything else, they did it for the supposed "greater good."

Only once had he fought against the embarrassing ordeal, having reached a breaking-point with the demands of the taskmasters on a day where they had preached yet again about how the workers were not slaves. He had struck out at one of the men, doing no real harm, but earning himself a severe beating. After his claws had been filed, he had been warned that if he resisted again, the kits would be moved somewhere outside of his watch. That had been the last time he even considered fighting back.

Sometime around late morning, the door to the building opened and one of the taskmasters came in, helping a leashed fae-kin woman who was limping badly. Having seen the same injury a thousand times, Estin knew immediately that she had stepped into one of the freshly-dug holes in the fields, twisting her leg or ankle. Given her cloven hooves, he guessed it was her knee that had been wrenched.

"She's getting her papers this afternoon," the taskmaster said, helping the woman sit in front of Estin. "We want to make sure she isn't still limping on her first day as a Lantonne citizen."

"Easily done," he answered numbly, sitting up and rubbing his face to push away the lingering drowsiness. "She should be fine in a few minutes."

The taskmaster offered sincere thanks to Estin—healing was something most of the taskmasters were truly grateful to have, even if they failed to understand how much it was killing Estin to be enslaved just to provide it—then departed, leaving him with his patient.

"How much longer?" the woman asked as Estin examined her leg. The knee was certainly swollen.

"Just a minute or two," he answered, glancing up at her for only a moment. Her human features seemed out of place to him with the long horns that protruded from her forehead—though they were sanded flat like his claws. "It's not too bad."

"I meant, how long until you get your papers?" she asked, studying him. "You were here when they first carted me in, half-dead from an undead attack out east. You should already be gone."

Estin could not remember the woman, her face blurring into the hundreds he had healed and exchanged brief conversation with over the year. That she could remember one person in the camp somewhat amazed him, though given his somewhat unique appearance, he guessed that was easy for most people.

"I don't get to leave. They need healers."

The whispers of the spirits touched the back of Estin's mind as he mended the woman's leg, the swelling fading visibly within seconds.

"Everyone is supposed to be freed," she said sadly, watching him, as if looking for a reaction, even as she flexed her leg experimentally. Her hoof thumped loudly against the floorboards. "Six months of being someone's slave is difficult for me. I cannot imagine not knowing when or if you will be free. I am so sorry. Have you considered escaping? With your skills, I imagine it would be possible. If I could in any way help you…"

"I cannot escape. There are children that I need to watch out for. I swore an oath to someone a long time ago and I won't back down on it, even to save myself."

The woman grabbed his hand and squeezed it reassuringly.

"Then what can I do to help in the meantime?" she asked, glancing around at the dim room. She seemed to be taking in what was or was not in the room. "I have some supplies that they gave me to survive in a tent through last winter that I could sneak to you. I also hear a great many rumors, owing to my work detail cleaning the tents of the taskmasters. Anything I have I consider a small price in thanks for healing me and as apology for how little I can help you beyond today."

"Information would help. I hear nothing in here," Estin admitted, sitting back. This was the first hint in many months that someone might know about things beyond the camp. "What have you heard of the war? Are we close to done with supplying an army?"

"Not even close. The undead number in the hundreds of thousands and are attacking other lands, not just here. I doubt the war will end anytime soon."

"So there is no hope?"

"That is not what I said at all. Since Altis attacked the quarry last year, Lantonne has been duplicating their efforts to strike at the undead. Many days, those of us on the west end of camp can hear the explosions. Since that began during the summer, the ash in the sky has gotten steadily thicker…you have seen it, right?"

Estin had to shake his head. He was only allowed out in the evenings, not having seen the sun in months, except through the walls of the building. As much as he disliked bright sunlight, being denied it was emotionally painful.

"Well…we thought that it was just clouds when it started. Each explosion gets worse and the sunlight we do get now is brief. At least it rains more than it used to…"

"What happened at the quarry?" Estin cut in, hoping to learn more about Lieutenant Linn's soldiers. Greth came to mind instantly. "You mentioned that Altis attacked there."

"Yes, that I did," the woman said excitedly, sitting forward. "They say that Altis saw how well Lantonne was doing in holding back their undead army, so they sent some people down to blow up the north wall of Lantonne. Luckily, they were stopped at the quarry and their weapon went off early, though it did destroy one of our war golems and damaged several others. Most of the undead got away, too, since Altis warned them before it happened. Then all those monsters came out of the quarry...sickening really, that anyone would do this on purpose."

"What happened to the soldiers?"

"Oh, they've been mostly executed," she answered dismissively. "I think I heard that their commander is going to be hung in town in a few days. I might actually get to see that. It will be good to know that the last of them is gone. I just hate that Lantonne felt the need to hold them in prisons for this long. It's no better than sticking people in this camp."

The conversation trailed off for a time and the fae-kin woman glanced back at the door.

"They will come for me soon," she reminded Estin. "Is there anything else I can tell you?"

He thought for a while on that, then finally said, "If you are ever in the mountain wilds, please look for more of my people. Let them know I'm alive."

"You have my pledge," the woman answered, patting his hand as she got up, testing her leg's stability.

"Oh, I almost forgot," she added, turning back to face Estin. "You should know that something flew in from the mountains just the other day. Huge, whatever it was. We all saw it heading towards the warfront. We're hoping it's a new weapon. Anything that large should really do some damage to the undead."

Estin was barely listening anymore, just nodding out of habit.

Out on the porch of the building, the taskmaster had returned, calling inside for the woman to come out.

"I wish you luck," she told Estin, smiling sadly. "I hope to see you in Lantonne soon."

With that, she left, closing the door behind her, leaving Estin in the shadows that always lingered in the building. Alone and wondering at the world outside, Estin hung his head and just waited, having nothing else he really could do.

*

The day was a slow one, leaving Estin with far too many hours of time to himself. That was always the hardest part of his duties, when he could sit with nothing but his thoughts to occupy him. If he were busy, it would have been far easier to let the time pass, but hours of pacing the room, stretching his muscles and trying to keep Feanne's training in the back of his mind was difficult. He wanted to just lay down and sleep until made to do something more, but he forced himself every day to keep himself ready for that one day that they might leave the camp.

At nightfall, those who were lucky enough or important enough among the laborers came back to the building, most collapsing onto their bedding. Food would be delivered to the building soon enough, but some of the laborers were so exhausted each day that they would sleep any extra minute they could manage between working and eating.

Estin waited at his back corner of the room, watching as several dozen people filed in. At last, he saw the kits come in as well, trying to stay out from under people's feet as they hurried back towards him. Though they were now as tall as his waist, in a building full of humans, orcs, and others, the kits were still all too easily trampled.

Both kits ran straight to him, giving his legs a firm hug, as they did most days. They had their routines in the camp and this was one of the better ones in Estin's life.

"How was the day?" he asked them both, sitting them down near their bedding.

"Fine," answered Oria, perhaps a little too quickly, making Estin cock his head.

"She's lying," Atall admitted, watching his sister as though she would claw his eyes out…which her expression said was a distinct possibility. "She got attacked today."

"What?"

Oria shook her head.

"No, not really. I mean…yeah. There was a little fight."

"Explain."

Oria closed her mouth and crossed her arms over her chest, glaring at Estin. Her stubbornness rivaled her mother's when she did not want to do something and thought she could get away with it. That was something Estin both enjoyed about her, as well as dreaded in situations such as this.

"She got in the way of another wildling when he was walking some horses," blurted out Atall, as usual more than happy to tell on his sister. "He was really angry and hit her, then threw her face-down on the ground and said he'd teach her what use little girls are…"

Estin studied Oria's face, now able to see the faint puffiness around one of her eyes. His thoughts darted to what spells he could manage. He could maim the one who touched her, disease him, our outright kill him. Nothing felt off-limits suddenly.

"I'm okay," Oria insisted, looking sheepishly at Estin. "He didn't manage to do anything else after he got on top of me. I clawed up his face pretty bad and he ran off. He didn't…I mean…I'm fine. Please don't look at me like that…I really am okay, Estin."

Atall added, "It was over so fast, I couldn't even get to her before he was gone."

Not concerned about the girl's dislike of him showing any affection for her or her brother, Estin swept her into a hug, holding her close.

"Just tell me who it was," he whispered to her. "If I can't be there to protect you in the fields, I want to at least know that I'm not healing the one who tried to hurt you."

"I don't know his name. He'll be in here tonight or tomorrow, I think."

Oria clung back, clearly more upset than she let on. Estin had not known the girl to willingly accept hugs otherwise. This time, she was practically choking him with how tightly she held to him.

Just as Estin was setting Oria back down, trying to compose himself, he looked up as the next group of laborers came back. Most were ones that had been randomly allowed to sleep in the proper shelter of the building for the night to make use of its fireplace, so the faces were not ones he recognized. One caught his eye though, the large cougar wildling male wiping at thin scratches down his face and nose, starting just below his eye. This one saw Estin staring at him and turned, heading to the far corner of the building.

"Please stay here," he told the kits, pulling his hand away as Oria tried to hold him back. "I need to have a word with someone."

The kits both hissed and whispered, pleading with him to stop, but he knew he could not. Some things just went beyond what he could bear or rationalize. It was all he could do to calm himself as he strode across the room, excusing himself as he pushed through the crowds of laborers.

He took his time, trying to relax as he walked, making a conscious effort to greet the few people he passed that he knew by name. It was a struggle, forcing himself to not rush to judgment, attacking the male that had tried to hurt Oria. The longer he made himself wait to confront him, the more calm he became, finally skirting by the building's front door as he headed for the far corner, where the offender sat, rubbing at the cuts on his face.

In passing, Estin grabbed his leash, not even sure why, but wanting it for some reason. Any weapon was better than his bare hands. He then knotted the thick leather cord around his left hand as he walked, coming up beside the male and sitting down.

"I don't think we've met," Estin said, keeping his voice neutral. The cougar wildling looked up at him, seemingly surprised to be spoken to. "I'm the camp healer, Estin."

The other male smiled, saying as he motioned to his face, "Stendin. Heard we'd gotten a healer, but hadn't needed it. You mind?"

"Not at all. What happened?"

"Some little fox girl got in the way when I was moving some horses to the next field. Nearly got me trampled. When I yelled at her, she clawed me."

Estin inspected the claw marks as he talked. They were very shallow, but having run into Stendin's nose, they were likely stinging quite a lot. The width and depth was right for Oria's hands.

"Just yelled?" asked Estin, trying to manage a smirk. He had to be sure. "Most foxes don't claw you for anything less than a slap."

Stendin shrugged and laughed somewhat.

"She didn't understand the natural order of things. I guess I got a little rough with her."

"What order is that?"

"I'm bigger, meaner, and male. She needed to learn how things work in the real world."

Estin felt his hands begin to shake and quickly took them off Stendin, lest he notice.

"That something you enjoy teaching females?"

Stendin laughed for real this time, nodding.

"Teach them young and often, or they'll think they can boss you around."

The leash dropped from Estin's hand, dangling as he pondered how to reply. He knew the risks and the punishments, but he could not let go this time. All the anger of a year of captivity welled up and centered on this one male. He knew harming him would not change much, but somehow he did not care.

"Have you met my wards?" Estin asked casually, one hand near Stendin's wounds, the other adjusting the length of the leash.

"No, don't really care to, either. Who cares? Just heal me already."

"I believe you met Oria today," Estin added, flicking the leash around Stendin's neck as he went wide-eyed, apparently making the connection, just as the leash went taught. "No one tries to rape a child around me."

Stendin kicked and struggled, then the whole building went alive with shouts and movement, but Estin paid no attention to any of it. He felt Stendin's claws rake him over and over, as he slammed the cougar into the floor repeatedly, still tightening the leash as best he could. Between the impacts to his head and lack of air, Stendin fought less with each second, until Estin was able to properly tighten the makeshift noose to ensure that it would kill Stendin. He managed to get one knee up along the back of Stendin's neck, giving him a brace against which to pull.

"What's going on...?" began a voice somewhere near the door. "You! Drop him!"

Estin recognized the voice as that of one of the taskmasters, but could not concern himself with that. His only focus was Stendin's lolling tongue and bulging eyes. He wanted to see Stendin dead, even if it cost him dearly. There had to be a price for an attack on the kits.

Seconds later, many strong hands grabbed Estin, trying to drag him off of his opponent. He fought against them, knowing Stendin was likely within seconds of death, having not budged in almost a minute. He lashed out with his tail, knocking at least one person aside as he fought to finish the job. Still, they were stronger than he was and soon he found it difficult to keep his grip on the leash. He strained, trying to keep hold on Stendin, but was steadily pulled off of him. In a last-ditch attempt to get his revenge, Estin kicked Stendin in the jaw, feeling bone crack and watching as he bit through his own tongue.

The taskmasters had to work together, three of them dragging Estin through the crowd and outside, where they threw him face-first on the ground.

"What is wrong with you?" demanded one of the humans. "You were one of the calm ones!"

"He tried to hurt Oria," Estin said, pushing himself up onto his knees. "The girl I watch. He tried to hurt her."

"I'm sorry, but that's not something I can do anything about now," the man said, sounding sincere. "Our laws are clear. You just tried to kill someone within Lantonne lands. If he'd been a citizen, you'd already be dead. As it is..."

"Public flogging," Estin finished for him. The punishment was not a rare one in the camp, given the tempers that flared in such a situation. He had cared for many whose whip-marks were threatening their lives. "I am aware."

The taskmasters looked between one another.

"If you knew, why did you attack him?"

Estin shrugged, closing his eyes as he tried to slow his racing heart, answering, "What would you do for your children? I doubt humans are much different from my people."

A leather leash wrapped tightly around Estin's throat, dragging him to his feet. He was somehow amused that it was not the one he had traditionally wore, which he hoped was still around Stendin's neck.

"I'm sorry," the human told him, face-to-face with him. "We didn't catch him hurting her. We did catch you. The law is what it is. This isn't making it any easier for us to release you as a citizen."

"We both know that wasn't going to happen until after the war," said Estin softly, smiling. "Just beat me and get it over with. I think I got my point across to the cougar about touching anyone's children."

The human sighed and offered, "If you'll heal him, I might be able to go easier…"

"He will never receive healing from me," said Estin, smiling at the human and shrugging. "Not even to spare my life. To save those children, I would've torn him apart. I will not cheapen what I did by undoing it."

"As you wish. I'm sorry, boy."

They led him towards a tall pole, used mostly for such punishments. Estin knew he would be strapped to it and beaten until he lost consciousness—or even until he died—but he did not care. Without hesitation, he stepped up to the pole and let them tie him there, pressing his forehead against the thick wood to center himself.

He just hoped that he had done enough for the kits, if this was an ending.

*

Estin finally began to wake, having been unconscious at least the whole night and most of the morning. As he struggled to open his eyes, he could see the midday sunlight coming through the walls, letting him know just how long he had been out.

Drearily, he was thankful that the daylight meant that he would not have to face Oria and Atall for several hours. That would give him the time to at least try to act as though he were fine, though deep down he knew they had likely tended to him during the night and were well aware how badly hurt he was.

Fighting against the pain of the lashes on his back, which felt as though they had torn deeply into the muscles and possibly cracked a rib or two, he tried to sit up, but barely managed to lift his head.

"Stop trying to get up," ordered a familiar voice, as Oria came around in front of him.

"You need to lie still until the bleeding stops."

"I'll be fine. Shouldn't you be out picking turnips or something?"

"Atall and I were excused for the day," she explained, moving behind him again. She tried to cover the sound of a nervous gasp as he felt her hands touching his back, letting him know just how bad the wounds must be. "One of the taskmasters was worried about you and wanted us to stay close, just in case."

"Where's your brother?"

Atall cleared his throat, letting Estin know the boy was sitting near his feet, glowering.

"And this is why we don't get into fights," Estin offered, trying to laugh. Atall glared all the more.

"You need to be quiet," Oria told him, applying a damp cloth to his back. The water stung horribly, but he knew if she did not clean the wounds, they would quickly infect in the filthy building. "This isn't a joke. You could still bleed to death."

Estin had thought time and again that Oria was the spitting image of her mother, with the same temper. He could hear her mother in her bossy orders, even as she tried to care for him. It made him smile absently, until he thought about the idea of her and her brother spending the rest of their childhood here. Given how fast wildlings grew up, there were only about two more years until they reached adulthood.

The idea of them spending what was left of their childhood surrounded by people like Stendin absolutely terrified him. Worse yet, once Oria was no longer a child, he was willing to bet more people like Stendin would appear.

"I'm fine," he said, inadvertently whimpering as he sat up. "Stop babying me."

The gentle brushing on his back turned into a mind-numbingly painful jab to one of the wounds.

"Don't treat me like you can boss me around," Oria growled, finally removing her hand from the cut. "Sit still or this will hurt more."

Estin groaned as he finished getting himself upright, trying to find the motivation to heal himself.

Finding the strength within himself, Estin focused on the spirits and let them touch his wounds briefly. The wounds were far from healed, but he had learned long ago not to fully heal any injury that was intentional, lest the taskmasters just do it again. They could repeat punishments far more than he could heal them.

"Why can't we sneak away some night?" asked Atall after several minutes of brooding. "I want to go back to dad's village."

Oria smacked her brother in the arm.

"The undead burned it, stupid."

"She's right Atall. Oria, don't hit your brother or call him stupid."

Oria frowned and flopped on the pile of ragged sheets that the three of them used, refusing to look at him, batting her tail angrily about.

"Why do you still tell us what to do?" demanded Atall, rubbing his arm and glaring at his sister. "Why do you even stand up for us? You're not our dad and you're not even a fox. Why do you care?"

Estin watched the boy for a minute, trying to figure out how to answer.

"I made your mother a promise. You'll do as I say until she...or your father...come back."

They all sat there for a long time, until the sun had moved far enough across the sky that Estin could see the filtered sunlight through the western wall.

"You slept through a whole day," Atall said finally, no longer looking quite so cross. "You missed a lot."

Oria rolled over and gave Atall a horrified look.

"What did I miss?" Estin asked, watching Oria, rather than Atall. She was frantically trying to signal her brother to be quiet.

"There's a rumor in the fields that some dwarven slave-trader is in from the south and the camp is actually selling people against the law in exchange for weapons. They say he's collecting wildlings for some kind of show for his king. No one's allowed to go out today, so that he can come by and inspect us all. Those already out are being brought back soon."

Estin groaned, wishing that this surprised him at all. Lantonne could preach about not allowing slavery, but whatever name it went by, there was no doubt in Estin's mind about what he was to them.

Laying back down, Estin closed his eyes and took a shuddering breath, trying to calm himself. He could only hope he had the strength to protect the kits if and when someone came for them.

Deciding to sleep until he could regain his strength, Estin curled up on his blankets, trying to block out everything else, at least for a time. As he lay there, the kits crawled onto the bedding beside him, Atall squirming under his arm, while Oria curled up near his head, her face pressed against his ears. This was how most nights had been for a long time, since the kits had finally accepted that Feanne and their father were not coming anytime soon. Once that had set in, despite all their objections to listening to Estin, they had clung to him every chance they got, refusing to be apart from him for any longer than required by the taskmasters.

It did not take long for Estin to fall asleep again, the pain from his lashings fading as his mind drifted.

The next few hours were filled with vague dreams of his childhood and the distant memories of his sister when she was still strong of mind and body. Those memories were sparse and possibly imagined, but he clung to them as long as he could, remembering her how he wished. No one else was left to dispute those memories.

When he did wake, Estin realized that it was dark out and the building was full again. Dozens of snoring people made the structure rumble as he lay there, his eyes still closed as he wrapped his arms around the kits, who were now snuggled close to one another for warmth. The building's fire had already gone out, leaving the place not much warmer than the early winter outdoors.

Estin started to drift back to sleep, but realized that someone was walking around within the building. That was a rarity, as most of the laborers were far too tired to bother getting up after dark. His instinctual first thought was that Stendin was creeping up on them, intending revenge or a second chance at Oria. He prepared himself accordingly, ready to finish the job this time if that male approached him.

After a few seconds, he recognized the sound as one of the elven taskmasters, as well as one or two others, moving through the disorganized group of laborers, whispering as they went.

Listening as best he could over the dripping of the water outside and through the leaky roof, as well as his own shivering, he tried to hear what they were saying as a change of pace. It was not common to have anyone actually enter the building after dark who did not belong there.

"Sir, this is a truly ragged lot," advised the elf's voice. "They were mostly found in areas where the Altisian weapons ravaged the land, so they were brought here for their own protection. There's not much food left out in those areas, so most of these would have starved to death without the farms we're having them work."

"Don't really care, to be honest," laughed a deep voice. "As far as we live below the surface, your weapons aren't doing much more than messing up our ceilings."

"Good to hear, Sir."

"What I'm looking for, I'm betting you don't have. The king wants some exotics. Got a ton of fae-kin in the collection, an orc to show off its muscles for the ladies, and a couple

294

common wildlings just to say he's got the basic's covered...he's looking for something weird."

Estin shifted his tail over the children, then covered it with his arm to hide the color pattern. The last thing he wanted was a slaver to see the long striped tail and think it was "unique."

"How weird do you want, Sir? I have some rather bizarre fae-kin that..."

"He wants animals," the gruff man cut in. "Got wolves, cats...heck, he's even got a lizard or two. He's looking for something different. I dunno, maybe one of those half-breeded paw-lickers...er...wildlings. Sort of looking for a monkey, squirrel, raccoon thing. Saw one once and wanted to get one for the king..."

Estin's eyes popped open. While it was possible more than one dwarf used that expression, he had to wonder. Still, he had no desire to risk himself if this was someone actually collecting sentient beings for show. Safety was more important than curiosity.

"We actually have one that fits that description," the elf said happily. "Though it's...well...an angry one. The darn thing is as wild as any of the wolves or cougars we've caught. Very nearly killed another wildling just the other day. We were actually discussing putting it down for its own sake."

"Angry? How angry? Can I see it?"

The footsteps were creaking on the floorboards his way now. Nervously, Estin tightened his grip on the children, just in case. If this dwarf was not one he knew and thought he could buy Estin without taking them, there would be a fight. Even if it was Finth and he tried to leave the kits, things would get ugly. Estin was willing to strike at his old companion, or abandon his own chance at freedom if it would save the kits.

"Turn it over so I can see it," the gruff man demanded, now just behind Estin. "Damned thing looks like it's been torn to shreds."

The elf's thin fingers grabbed Estin's shoulder and gave him a tug. In another life, Estin would have torn the man's hand off for what he had endured lately, but he just meekly rolled into the light of the elf's torch, blinking against its brightness.

"That's the one I want. Toss the fuzzy little monkey...wait, are those fox kits?"

Estin blinked, trying to make out faces, but the torch was practically in his face.

"Yes, though we're planning to put them down if we sell the striped one. They're too young to be worth the amount they eat."

"I'll take them too," the dwarf said quickly. "Get them on my wagon."

"The foxes aren't really exotic..."

"I said, I will take them."

"Sir, you're not scheduled to be leaving until..."

"Shut your mouth, elf, and do as I say. I don't pay for some butt-licking toady to tell me how to do my job."

Estin finally got a glimpse of the dwarf as the elf raised the torch away from him. It was Finth, his clothing far finer than Estin had ever seen, with gemstones braided into his beard and an ornate axe at his back. The gemstones caught Estin's eye the most...several he recognized as ones he had stolen from the duke's keep in Altis.

"As you wish, sir," the elf offered with a bow. "I'll have them loaded within the hour."

Finth spun on his heel and stormed off, dust rising with each heavy stomp, the elven camp administrator following swiftly behind him.

Within minutes, the elf returned, this time with two burly orcs at his sides.

"Collar and cage them," the man ordered, pointing at Estin and the children, who had just begun to stir. "I want them boxed on the emissary's wagon immediately."

Strong hands grabbed Estin, dragging him from the bedding as the children were caught up by the other orc. He had a good idea what was happening and let the orc slam him face-first to the ground and fasten a heavy collar around his neck and shackles around his wrists. The children did not have that knowledge and screamed and cried, trying to free themselves from the orc, even as the other laborers began sitting up and questioning what was happening.

"Oria, please just do what he wants," Estin hissed at the girl, who was putting up most of the fight.

With a bellow, the orc reeled back, his face bloodied from Oria's raking kick. Atall had bitten down on the man's hand, refusing to let go.

"Get the dwarf a different pair of foxes," the elf ordered angrily. "Put these down and find me something in a hurry."

Estin looked over and saw the orc shake Atall free and reach for a knife at his belt. Despite having the second orc still kneeling on his back, Estin whipped his tail around, cracking his captor in the back of the head to daze him. He used the slight moment of the man's knee lifting to slide free, rolling as he brought his bound hands down past his feet, swinging them easily up in front of him.

He dove into the orc with the knife, slamming his shoulder into the man and barreling him over onto another laborer's bedding.

With both orcs off of them for the moment, Estin slid on his knees to the kits, encircling both in his arms.

"He wanted us," Estin said, growling. "We will go without a fight. They don't need to be leashed. Put us in the box already."

The elf threw his hands up and waved the orcs onward. They practically dragged Estin by his leash, while Atall and Oria clung to his arms. They went the length of the camp this way, finally reaching a series of three wagons that were parked near the entrance to the farm camp.

"That one," the elf told the orcs, pointing to an uncovered wagon, with a large cage in back. "Get them in and I'll let the emissary know."

The orcs became anything if not less gentle once the elf had departed. They literally threw Estin into the cage, while still holding the leash, so that when he tumbled inside, the leash became taught and choked him briefly. The kits they threw as hard as they could at the back of the cage, bouncing them off the far end's bars.

"Are you both alright?" Estin asked them, flipping over in the short cage to examine them.

Both groaned and nodded at him, rubbing at bruises.

Before Estin could get a better look at the kits' injuries, the orcs began locking wooden covers over the cage, blocking out the dim moonlight and all air that did not creep through the floorboards. At least it was dry and warmer than the building had been.

They were stuck in the quiet dark for a long time, both kits shaking nervously as they waited to find out what would happen next. A long time later, voices approached the wagon.

"...and so, I'll be heading back to the king with his new gifts. Thank you for all your bloody cooperation."

"Sir," cut in the elf's voice. Faintly, Estin could hear movement of many people nearby. "You do need to present your king's writ before we just let you go. You know that's procedure. Since we cannot endorse slavery, we need to see your writ to seize these debtors."

A long silence followed.

"Of course. Second wagon back, under a false floor. Wouldn't want just anyone to get their hands on that."

A faint rap on the wood covering of the cage was followed by Finth's voice.

"Monkey, get ready for trouble."

Estin hurriedly lay down in the cage, knowing that if it lurched, he did not want to fall far. He got both of the kits to do the same and then grabbed one of the cage's bars for support.

"Sir," called the elf's voice, "I don't...oh...guards!"

Shouts and cries of pain erupted as Estin heard weapons drawn. It sounded as though a dozen people had broken out into combat in seconds. Snarls mixed in with the din of metal weapons.

"Time to go," called back Finth, as the wagon lumbered into motion.

The bouncing and sharp tilts of the covered cage told Estin that they were riding fast and hard, possibly even off the road. This went on for what seemed like hours, making every inch of Estin hurt from the hard floor and judging by the whimpering of the kits, they were not faring much better.

The bouncing soon slowed and the wagon came to a gradual stop. From what Estin could hear, the driver had gotten down and was walking around the back. Several clicks of locks later, the back wooden panel fell away and Finth stared up at them, his head only slightly above the bottom of the cage.

"You are a pain in my hairy ass to find, monkey," the man grumbled, fitting small metal tools into the cage's lock. "I damn near ran out of the duke's jewels trying to track you down."

"Who is he?" hissed Oria in Estin's ear.

"He's a friend. He helped save your mother and I a few times. You met him very briefly back in your mother's camp."

Finth finally popped the lock and swung the cage open.

"Be quiet coming out," he warned them, glancing around nervously. "This place isn't secure. If they find us, we need to run again."

With the kits hiding behind him as he climbed out, Estin slid out of the cage, easing his feet down until his paws touched cool pavestones. He looked around, finding that they were in a city alley, buildings on either side large enough to shield his view of anything much. With the sky dark above, he doubted anyone would be watching the alley.

Estin looked down at Oria and Atall, who were still watching Finth with suspicion.

"You took long enough," Estin told Finth, smiling weakly. The dwarf just spit on the ground.

He reached up and grabbed the thick leather collar on his neck, digging his blunted claws into it as best he could. It took a lot of effort, straining against the seams, but he managed to rip it free, taking a good bit of fur with it, throwing the hateful object into a corner of the alley.

"Lead the way."

Finth obliged, guiding them from the alley towards a side-door of one of the neighboring buildings. Inside the dark building, he took several flights of steps up, leading them to a back room on the third floor. Finth ushered them in, carefully checking the hallway several times before following them inside and closing the door. He lit a tiny oil lamp near the doorway, giving them a small amount of flickering light.

"This is one of my safe houses," he explained, lighting a small lamp, then kicking his muddy boots into a dingy corner. The massive axe across his back, he dropped onto the floor, where it clattered loudly. "Damned stupid weapon for practical fighting."

The dwelling was anything but regal. Old chipped paint was peeling from the walls and in spots, Estin could see rotting boards. The floor creaked as they moved, actually sinking in some spots. Furniture was sparse, consisting mostly of a few tiny tables, chairs, and piles of dirty woolen blankets piled haphazardly around.

"Does the roof leak?" Estin asked, after peeking around the doorways into the rooms beyond.

"No. It's dry here and it stops the wind. Everything should work, including the running water in the pisser," he said, pointing down a dark hall. "Doesn't work great, but it's enough to wash your hands and face."

The kits' eyes lit up and both ran down the hall, pushing and shoving to be the first into the room. They slammed the door behind them and Estin soon heard water and giggling.

"You look like shit, Estin."

"And you look like you've been spending my gift rather well in my absence."

Finth laughed, flopping down on a small chair that groaned dangerously under his weight.

"Dwarf's gotta do what a dwarf's gotta do. Besides, that gift's all that let me find you."

"When do we go back to the camp?" Estin asked after a moment, easing himself down onto a pile of blankets. The soft fabric made him long to sleep after so long on itchy and filthy blankets, but he needed to know what he had missed first.

"Camp's gone. Lantonne delivered one of those bloody magic weapons to Altis' doorstep, inside a smaller golem. Undead got control of the golem, sent it our way. Most of us got out, but the camp is a small crater.

"When things started to look bad, Lihuan and Asrahn ordered everyone out, while he and a couple of his old friends tried to stop the golem. They kept it from following us, but…we haven't seen them since. To be honest, I think the two of them actually blew the damned thing early to keep it from following us."

Estin felt his hope of returning to him home die. Somehow through all the months of degradation and being ignored, he had managed to hope for seeing the shabby little wildling camp in the mountains one more time.

He glanced down the hallway, making sure the kits were not returning yet.

"The grove," he said, keeping his voice low. "Did it survive?"

"Not even close. Burned to a damned cinder, along with anything and anyone inside. I could have shoveled the ash into a bag for you, but all that sentimental garbage gives me gas. Was there more you wanted to know? I can tell you about the crater and the burned trees…"

Estin glared at Finth, but then just looked away, letting the dwarf trail off. That settled it. His old life was gone now. He double-checked the hallway, listening to the kits splash at the water.

"Icy rains for two straight weeks," he mumbled, "Now they want to play in water. I will never understand children."

"They get to have fun and get all the mud off them," Finth said, putting his bare feet up on a stool and wiggling his toes. "Can't fault 'em for that, after whatever you've been through."

Distantly, a door closed and Finth sat up, his hand pulling a wickedly-curved knife from under the chair. He put a finger to his lips, then stood and slipped from the room, somehow managing to keep the floor from creaking.

Estin was too tired to fight, but he found the strength to get his feet under him. He moved to the hallway, not quite ready to alert the kits, but wanting to be ready to grab them and flee if he had to. Beyond the children's chatter in the water room and the soft sound of the water itself, he could hear voices downstairs, soon followed by multiple people climbing the steps.

Deciding to be overly-cautious, Estin felt under a chair, finding another stashed dagger. He pulled it free and waited for Finth to return, hoping everything was safe.

When the door swung open, Estin tensed, prepared to throw his weapon at the leading figure if it was not Finth. Instead, he dropped the weapon with a loud bang.

Feanne strode in, dressed how he had first seen her more than two years earlier, making his heart skip a beat. She had once told him that the simple leather outfit was her "traveling attire." Now she walked in as though nothing had happened in all this time, aside from a long fresh cut across her upper chest and shoulder that bled into her white fur.

They both stood there for a time, staring at one another, until Finth and Yoska came in and closed the door.

"I see you lived," Feanne said sternly, her eyes drifting over Estin.

"You weren't in the grove when it fell?"

"Never said she was," Finth said, chuckling as he sat back down, hiding his weapon again.

"No, I wasn't in it," Feanne said, striding into the room and sizing up Estin. Her tone was cold. "I had begun to wonder if you had abandoned the pack though. You stopped coming to the grove...that much I could piece together. I assumed you were dead or hiding for a very long time, right up until Finth's sources reported a fae-kin who had seen you just a few days ago."

With a flourish of her tail, she sat down on the floor, while Yoska piled several bags in the corner. As she sat, Estin realized that she was avoiding looking directly at him anymore, as though she were lost in thought.

"Feanne..."

"I am your pack-leader," she corrected coolly. "You will address me as such. There may only be a handful of us left, but the right to lead fell to me when no one else suitable could be found."

"Feanne, please..."

"Stop talking, Estin. I would speak with Finth now about our ongoing plans."

"You might want to listen to the monkey," Finth noted, grinning. "He apparently wants to tell you something."

"Very well. What?"

Estin gave Finth a nod of thanks and walked down the hall. He leaned into the water room, finding Oria and Atall practically soaked, but finally free of all the mud that had caked them for weeks. He got their attention and held a finger to his mouth to keep them quiet, then motioned for them to follow him.

"I am growing old waiting on you," Feanne snapped as Estin came back into view. "Can we please..."

The two kits heard her voice and popped around the corner, staring wide-eyed at her.

"Oria?" Feanne whispered, standing quickly. She looked unsteady on her feet. "Atall?

You're alive?"

The children stood still, little Oria grabbing Estin's hand for support.

"It's her," he told them softly. "Go see your mother."

The two raced across the room, slamming into Feanne's legs with enough force to sit her back down, laughing and pulling them close to her.

"Estin," Feanne finally said, looking up from the wet bundles of fur in her lap, clinging to her as hard as they could, "I would speak with them privately before I speak with you."

Bowing slightly, Estin headed for the door out of the small home, with Finth joining him on his way out and Yoska heading down the hall and out of sight. They wandered down the hall to where Finth checked another door, finding it open and the room beyond uninhabited. They then went inside and into a smaller room than Finth's, with a large hole in the floor, where moisture had rotted out the boards.

"She's not happy with you," Finth explained once they were safely alone. "I know she's got some brains in that head of hers, but I think they got more addled than we thought when she lost the kids. After you left, she was still talking to herself for about a week or two, then up and decided that you had left to go murder Insrin and steal her kids. Craziest damn thing I ever heard, but she was convinced."

"Then she won't be happy with the news I brought her."

"Oh?"

Estin just shook his head.

"The kits are fine, that's what matters."

"When I left...she snapped out of the depression? I was worried she'd starve once I was gone."

Finth snorted.

"Not even close. The first couple days, she wouldn't let anyone else near her. She even clawed Asrahn pretty badly. Kept saying that you would be right back, because you would never leave. They finally had to drag her back to camp and Lihuan had her held down and force-fed. Didn't take long before she at least let her parents care for her."

"Were they able to help?" He felt a little sick to his stomach, thinking about having contributed in any way to Feanne's sadness, even if he could not have prevented it.

"No, monkey, they weren't. She was as nuts as the day you left when they evacuated the camp. I had Ulra carry her out, while she screamed at us about how she needed to go wait at the grove for you and her kids."

"She's stronger than all that," Estin mused aloud. "I can't blame her for going a little crazy. She'll sort it all out and understand that I didn't abandon her. I have to believe that."

Finth's eyebrows lowered as he leaned against the creaking walls.

"Just because she came up fighting for her sanity eventually doesn't mean she's about to think you're entirely innocent, no matter how much you stroke her...uh...ego. We'll go with ego, after all, she has kids, you pervert. If you're going to ride their mom, at least buy the kids a sucker, my mother used to say. It's only right.

"As for Insrin...don't care what you did to him, I'll give you credit for that one if he's gone. That tail-sucker bugged the lice off of me, making Lihuan's camp a downright annoying place to live for a while."

Estin glared at the dwarf for a moment, then resigned himself to the man's dour humor, laughing despite himself. It was so good to be able to relax, though Estin was not quite ready to entirely let go.

"Finth...I can't even attempt to follow your thinking half the time."

"It's easy," the dwarf told him. "Start with a few shots of whatever the tavern sells. Then add a healthy amount of sex, some random lewd remarks, and try to make whoever you're talking to think it's all their fault. Not that hard, really."

They waited for a time, the silence uncomfortable at least to Estin as he stood there, wondering why Feanne had wanted him out of the room. When Finth spoke again, it somewhat startled him as he had been lost in thought.

"You ready to come back, what with her being the pack-leader and all?"

"Just how did that happen, if she was spending all her time pining away, waiting for me to bring back the kits?"

Finth shook his head as though the thought had not settled in for him, either. "When Lihuan died, the pack began to fall apart. Feanne hadn't found all her playing cards yet, if you know what I mean, even when word of her parents got to her, though she was struggling to be her old self. It was the in-fighting and the constant challenges all over the camp that rattled her and got her off her fuzzy butt...that and not having anyone coming to bring her food anymore. Once she began exerting control over those tearing the pack apart, it was like she'd never left us. Every person she put in their place brought her a little closer to who she once was.

"I was there during one of the first fights...over whether one guy was in charge or another, both shouting about whether the rabbit wildlings were food or just camp assets. Feanne marched up out of nowhere and tore them both up real bad, never listening to anything they had to say, and not stopping until they both were cowering. By the end of the day, I think she'd fought just about anyone around who had any itch for leading...and a few who didn't, but got in the way. I really think she was just attacking people to make herself feel better at first.

"She tells me that she just wanted the fighting to stop at the time and to protect those who were going to suffer from the arguments, but in the end, no one really wanted the job anymore, though I think a few of them might try if they see her slip up. She's done fine keeping people working together, but I think it's more out of fear than anything. She just doesn't have Lihuan's poise and respect...or years of fear that he built up, mostly through his stories."

Estin weighed all the questions that came to mind, unsure what would be wise or safe to ask Finth. He had no idea if the dwarf might be obediently reporting back to her, though he had his doubts.

"If she's leading...why is she here? This is about as far from the mountains as you can get and still be in the same lands."

"Honestly?"

"I'd prefer that, yes."

Finth looked around uncomfortably, lowering his voice.

"She thought the kits were dead, Estin. She never said it, but I think she came out here to kill you if she found any reason to believe it was your fault. You were gone more than a year. When you first vanished, she was all tears and moping...then she was depressed for a while, even after taking control of the pack...then she was angry.

"When she heard that I'd found a lead on a big black and white monkey, she put Ulra in charge and packed to go, without even waiting to see if I was really on to something. Crazy girl trusted me to find you. She spent the whole way here sharpening her claws."

"Why did you even come looking for me? For all you knew, I was long dead."

Finth shrugged.

"You people are a bad influence. I could have been spending my time trying to find some sneaky way back into my homeland, but it was almost like I worried about you. Getting to be damned annoying, I might add, especially with how many bloody places thought they had you and didn't."

A knock at the door interrupted them.

"Estin," Feanne said, leaning through the opening door. "Can we speak alone?"

Finth gave Estin a smarmy smile that made him uncomfortable, but excused himself and slipped from the room as Feanne entered. When the door clicked closed, it seemed to still the room for a time.

"Yoska is telling the kits some story about how the gypsies were involved in every major world event...it should give us some time," she told him, sitting down in the corner. "I had to talk with the kits before coming to you. I am sorry I had to do that without really greeting you first. I just had to be sure of how you treated them."

"I understand. I just hope Atall wasn't too harsh on me for being the wrong breed."

Feanne smiled, something in her demeanor saying that she did not do that much these days. She absently wiped at the bleeding cut along her collar, but waved him off when he began to move towards her.

"He was not, though he said he wished his father would return. That is what we need to speak about."

Estin felt his stomach sink. Thoughts of Insrin's body flooded his mind, against his wishes.

"Where did you find them, Estin?"

"Near Lantonne, hidden in a cabinet. Insrin tried to keep them safe from the undead by hiding them."

Feanne's eyes locked onto him, though she looked more sad than angry.

"Where is my mate, Estin? Speak true."

This took a lot longer for him to answer, trying to decide how to break it to her, though he had a feeling she knew the truth in her heart. Her eyes betrayed a keen understanding of what he was going to tell her.

"I...I pretty much stumbled on his last stand," he told her, watching her eyes unfocus and her arms tighten around her chest. "The kits were hidden while his guards fought off the undead army. From what I could tell, Insrin died defending that cabinet. The kits don't know he's gone...it wasn't my place."

Feanne swallowed hard, turning her face from him.

"Estin, I need the truthful answer to two questions. Just this once, no matter what may come of it. Can you please do that for me? Even if it were to mean that we never speak again after this day?"

"Anything you ask, Feanne. I swear it."

She looked up at him from where she sat and asked softly, "Did you kill Insrin?"

"No. Whatever I may have thought of the man, he never gave me cause to even consider harming him. He was good to you and the kits. What then could I justify harming him for? The worst I could ever confront him about was abandoning you, which was not my place to do."

Feanne closed her eyes, asking more firmly, "Did you have the ability to heal him and not do so?"

Estin stood across from her, leaning on the wall as he thought through that day.

"I've second-guessed myself a hundred times," he admitted, trying to find any fault in his actions. For months after arriving at the labor camp, he had questioned himself about whether he had made any mistake. "I sought out his spirit and could not find it. He had been dead a long time, Feanne..."

"Could you have helped in any way? Anything at all?"

"No," he confessed. "For all the reasons I hated the man, I would have done anything to keep him alive, if only so that you could have faced him for taking your children from you. It was not my right to exact your revenge, if any. I would have given my life to put him and the kits in front of you, even if I knew you were just going to kill him anyway, which I did not."

Feanne closed her eyes and nodded.

"Thank you. That is all I needed."

She rose to her feet and walked up to him, standing close enough that he could feel her warmth. Gently, she touched the fresher scars on his arms, moving to his side and letting her fingers brush at the cuts on his back, neck, and shoulders. As she came around him, she took one of his hands and lifted it, examining the blunted claws, her expression sad. Her fingers intertwined with his briefly, her long claws alongside his damaged ones.

"I would have died where you have been, whether out of grief or from fighting my captors," she said, tracing a thick scar across the palm of his hand. "How did you manage to endure?"

"For your children and the hope of seeing...," he cut himself off, as Feanne's eyes darted up to meet his, "...the camp again and those I cared about."

She continued to rub at the scar on his hand absently.

"What made this? I recognize the whip marks, but this one I do not."

Estin held up his other hand, where the scar continued.

"The kits were getting sick," he explained. "There wasn't enough food. One of the guards had a penchant for gambling, so I made him a bet. He said that no wildling could endure more pain than an orc, with the prize being extra rations for the kits, or a day without work for the orc."

"And?"

"These are not the only scars from that day, but all that matters is that the kits were able to fill their bellies. No one argued about their rations after that."

She strayed close to him again, releasing his hand as she looked up at his face. "You're lucky to be alive. I may never understand how you endured and kept my children alive. I know that sooner or later, I would have broken and tried to kill my captors. I never would have lasted a year, even knowing the risk to the kits.

"For this, I owe you my life. Whatever you ever want or need, ask me. Nothing is so valuable as my children to me."

Estin leaned towards her, his face brushing hers briefly, before she pulled away, taking a step back from him and putting her hand on his chest to ensure he stayed back.

"If that's what you want," she said, her voice shaking, "I'm sorry. That time has passed, Estin. I am not about to tell Atall and Oria that their father is dead and I'm interested in someone he despised. I won't do that to them. They've been through too much already. Name anything else I can offer you in reward, but please do not ask for that. If you wish a mate, I will happily search for one that would be better for you than I ever would have been."

Estin lowered his eyes and took one knee before her. She backed away a step, clearly not sure what he was doing.

"I ask nothing of you, pack-leader," he told her, struggling to keep his tone even. "A pack-leader does not owe her pack for doing their duty in protecting other pack members. Your father taught me that. My life is yours and your family's, so long as you lead. I will guard you as your honor guard, until you find another more suited."

Feanne nodded curtly, her expression deeply torn. Putting a hand to her head, she left the room quickly, heading back to Finth's little apartment, stifling a sob as she went.

Estin knelt a while longer, trying to find the energy to stand and return to their lodging. He pondered how it was that Feanne always managed to take his strength away every time they spoke. Just once, he wished that he could endure the heartache that came with every meeting. A year apart and already she pulled at his heart, the very sight of her demanding that he love her.

Pulling himself to his feet, Estin headed back down the hall to the other room, slipping into the room quietly so as not to disturb Yoska's ongoing narrative. Before Estin tuned him out, he heard some rubbish about how the gypsies had once blessed even the great dragons, giving them the power they now possess.

Finth sat in his chair, fiddling with the knife he had drawn earlier, absently ignoring Yoska and the two wide-eyed kits as he lost himself in his own thoughts.

Feanne had settled into a pile of blankets in the far corner of the room, her back to the others.

As he closed the door as softly as he could, Estin got Finth's attention, asking him softly where he was to sleep. Finth motioned at Feanne, shrugging.

Estin shook his head and Finth glared at him, giving him a "what is wrong with you" expression, then pointed to another small pile of dirty blankets in the corner nearest the water room, in much the same way one would banish a disobedient dog. Mouthing a "thank you," Estin trudged to the pile, flopping down onto the mass of cloth appreciatively. Dirty or not, they were better than he had had in months.

Curling up and wrapping himself up in the blankets for warmth, Estin was out cold in seconds.

When he woke next, it was sometime near dawn, though still very dark. The room's oil lamp had been put out, bathing the room in fairly deep darkness, with just a little creeping in through a shuttered window near the back hallway.

Finth lay in his chair as though dead, his arms and legs hanging off the chair limply and his mouth wide open, only his snores giving any clue that he had not been murdered.

Nearby, Yoska had set himself up with a well-made foreign bedroll and pillow that he had placed in front of the entry door, blocking it entirely. The man lay still on his back, breathing softly, but giving the impression of being only just barely asleep. Estin wondered if he could actually listen to his surroundings while sleeping.

Estin began to lay back down when he noticed that one of the kits was staring at him from across the room, where they lay under Feanne's arm and blankets. It was Atall, his eyes gleaming white in the dim lighting.

Upon seeing Estin looking back, Atall slid out of his mother's grasp slowly, managing not to disturb her as he scurried across the room to Estin.

"I can't sleep," the child whispered to Estin, kneeling in front of Estin's bedding. "Can I sleep with you?"

Estin hesitated, but saw no harm in offering part of the blankets to the boy. The kit curled up against him and soon was soundly asleep, holding tight to Estin's arm, as though for reassurance that he was still there.

Smiling at the change of heart in the boy, Estin looked up and saw that Feanne was watching him, her nighttime white eyes unblinking for a long time. Then they closed and the room was dark again.

*

When Estin woke next, the faint light through the window-shade spoke of midday or later. He struggled to sit upright, realizing that Atall was gone already. In fact, everyone but him was out of their bedding and sitting at one of the room's small tables, talking in low tones.

"What'd I miss?" he asked, rubbing his eyes.

"The little fox girl," Yoska began, waving a hand at Oria, "is quite a good story-teller, no? She tells us of your time at the camp. Much heroics on your part. Perhaps someday, you will drink from the cup and join my people, as full of stories as your life is, no?"

Estin smiled at Oria, who was practically bouncing, sitting at the far side of the table. She had always dearly loved being the center of attention and he had no doubts that she would string along her stories as long as she could to maintain that attention. Atall on the other hand was actively searching the room, pulling knives and other weapons...including a small crossbow...from hiding places.

"She also mentioned that you lost your notebook with all of your spells in it," Feanne said, pulling Oria onto her lap. "That would be greatly limiting to your ability to heal, would it not?"

Estin nodded and yawned, his jaw cracking loudly.

"They took everything from me before I got to the slave camp. Spellbook, jewelry, weapons, and that gorgeous armor you made for me...which saved me from about two hundred undead, I might add."

Feanne smiled demurely, appearing embarrassed as the others turned to look at her, then searched through a makeshift backpack that lay on the floor near her. She went through piles of small items, many of which were burned badly. At last, she pulled out a small leather-bound book and tossed it at Estin.

Catching it, he recognized Asrahn's book, though it had been tied closed with a thin leather cord that had not been on it the last time he had held the book.

"It is yours now," she told him, giving Oria a squeeze, making the kit giggle. "She asked me to give it to you."

Estin ran his fingers over the dry old leather cover, remembering the first time Asrahn had let him touch the book. It felt so very long ago. With a touch of regret at the elder's passing, he unfastened the cord and began to open the pages, only to have a small packet fall out in his lap.

"What is that?" Feanne asked, her ears perking. "She told me the contents of a healer's book were none of my business..."

Estin rolled the cloth packet over in his hand, feeling two hard objects inside of it. The packet had been sewn shut but when he thought to cut the strings, he found himself glaring at his useless claws. Ignoring Feanne's offer to help, he bit the edge of the cloth, ripping the seam open.

Two simple rings fell into his lap. They were small and not attention-grabbing in their detail. Both were made from silver and when he picked them up, he saw that each was engraved with two symbols. One was a fox's head, the other was the three scratched lines that Lihuan had used as his signature and seal.

"Why would she leave you rings?" Feanne asked. "Those aren't even ones I recognize as hers."

Estin flicked one of the rings to Finth, who caught it in the air.

"What's that worth, Finth? I'm guessing nothing if someone were to find it in Feanne's bag."

The dwarf squinted at the ring, turning it over in his fat fingers. He shook his head.

"Not even pure silver. It's pretty, but no merchant would look twice at it."

He threw it back to Estin.

Estin turned the rings over and over in his hands, trying to figure out what was not right about them. Something just ate at him about why Asrahn would have included them. She had always been obsessed with predicting others' plans and actions, so he had to assume these played into that somehow.

"Feanne," he said, holding one of the rings up to his eyes again. "Your mother once told me stories about people who could create magical weapons and artifacts of great power. Did the camp have anyone with that skill?"

She shook her head.

"No. That was something that if we really wanted, we would need to steal from the city to get it. We had no members of the pack with such a talent that I am aware of."

He waved a hand over the ring, casting one of the few spells he had managed to hang onto without his spellbook all these months. Asrahn had taught it to him as a simple way to identify a spellcaster or to find magical effects remaining on a location. This time, he used it to find residual magic on the ring. Almost unsurprisingly, it glowed brightly to his eyes, as did the other ring, though the others in the room could not see the effect. With a little more concentration, he became convinced that the magic was healing in origin, but that was all he could determine.

Estin picked up the cloth the two rings had been wrapped in, holding it up to the light, trying to find any writing or indication of what Asrahn had intended by sending the rings.

"You have nice gift from old friend," said Yoska, seemingly unimpressed. "Value of item really does not matter, yes?"

"I think there's more to this," Estin told him, putting the cloth between himself and the lamp, so that the light shown straight through it. When he did so, faint lettering appeared. "The rings have magic. I'm trying to find out what she wanted done with them."

The note was difficult to read, with some letters rubbed off, likely from riding in Feanne's bag for some time. The whole thing had been written in an obscure ink that looked more like a smudge until he held to the light and squinted. Even knowing it was there, he had to study each letter and piece together the words.

"As far as I am concerned, they are yours," he read out loud. "Treasure them. These are for who needs our gift the most."

Estin frowned, trying to make sense of the rambling wording and saw Feanne shaking her head.

"My mother was anything but straightforward," she said, wrapping her arms protectively around Oria. "She knew that the camp was in danger. This may not have been thought through. I doubt they're more than a memento of your time training with her."

Estin turned the rings over in his hands a few more times, trying to grasp at what his teacher had meant for them. Finally, he gave up, wondering if he was reading far more into it than he was meant to. Perhaps Feanne was right and Asrahn had just wanted to leave a gift for Estin, should he ever be found.

"Atall," he said, getting the boy's attention as he was fiddling with a hidden panel on the back side of a cabinet. "This is yours now."

He threw the ring to the boy, who caught it and stared at the fox-head imprinted on it.

"This one's yours, Oria," he told the other kit, throwing her the second ring.

"Are you sure, Estin?" Feanne asked quickly, eyeing the ring in her daughter's hands. "They were meant for you. The note said so."

"The book is more than enough for me. Your children deserve a token of their grandmother, more than someone who she taught. I'd feel better knowing that the kits had them."

Feanne gave him a slight bow of thanks, then helped Oria fit the ring to one of her fingers. It really only fit on her thumb, but the girl beamed as she held it up to the light. Nearby, Atall sat on the floor, just holding his ring and studying the engravings.

"Now," Estin said, setting the spellbook behind him on the blankets, "someone please tell me where we are and what's going on. I would dearly like to know why I was thrown into captivity and held like a rabid dog for months. I heard a little…very little…and most of that was just in the last few days."

"The details took us a while to figure out, too," Finth grumbled. "When your gods-forsaken crew didn't return after the explosion, we did some digging. Turns out our dear commander from Altis never actually sent a letter to Lantonne explaining what we were doing and why. He wanted to show them that we could win the war without them. He actually just intercepted information about the Lantonne plan to drive the undead into the quarry and had a spy keep him informed of the golems' movements.

"Needless to say, Lantonne was not too happy with you for blowing up the war golem. They saw that as an act of war, proving that Altis was behind the whole undead invasion from the start. Now, there's no convincing them otherwise.

"They've executed nearly all the survivors, except for Lieutenant Linn, who's finally up for hanging in the next couple days. They spaced each execution out, so the people would have some entertainment every couple weeks. We actually were coming to free him when some skittish fae-kin started babbling at Feanne about a wildling she'd met. I swear the woman thought all wildlings are related."

"How effective was the weapon, though? I've heard most of the undead got away."

Finth laughed and shrugged.

"Who the hells knows? Getting near that quarry is likely to burn the hair off my ass from a mile out. Everywhere they've set off those crazy explosions, the barriers between our world and the planes weaken."

"At the camp, they said that there are monsters near the sites. Is that true?"

Feanne nodded gravely.

"I can confirm that much," she said. "My curiosity is not something I can always resist. After the explosion near Altis, I went out by myself to look for survivors. What I found were dark winged beasts that absorbed the light pouring out of the flames in the forest. I have never seen anything like them and they just kept coming. They are not elemental creatures, but they do not belong here, either."

"So why is Lantonne using the weapons if it's just making things worse?"

"Eh, that's at an end," Finth added. He paused a second, grunting at Atall to keep the boy away from a hidden panel in one of the walls. That only seemed to incite Atall to investigate it further. "Turns out this area was one of the last to keep using them. Other lands stopped earlier when they saw what was happening. Lantonne's just overly stubborn.

"They finally figured out it wasn't such a good idea after part of the nearest dark elven city's tunnels collapsed and someone sat down and figured out that they were only getting a couple hundred undead out of thousands with each weapon. The worst was when one of the Halfling teams that were supposed to deliver a weapon up on the northern plains got attacked by undead, accidentally setting off the weapon right in the middle of a farming community.

"Since then, Lantonne has had all records of the weapons' designs burned and the wizards who built them executed. Little too damned late, though. Doubt anyone would want to make them again."

Estin got up and walked to the shuttered window, peeking through the slats at the city beyond. It was nowhere he recognized at first, then he saw the large central keep with its single tower.

"We're in Lantonne," he noted.

"Yep. Been here on and off for the last six months, trying to free the people we might be able to trust from the group you took into the quarry. That and hunting rumors of what happened to you, you pain in the ass. If I had a copper for every furrier who claimed to have a giant ringtailed monkey-squirrel, who turned out to have a bunch of raccoon pelts, I'd be at least moderately wealthy right now. I know I was ready to give up a long time ago.

"Trust me, monkey, there were actually worse places you three could have wound up. I know that for a fact after spending this much time poking around in the camps."

"Thank you for coming for me," Estin told the group sincerely. "I don't know how long I could have stayed there without losing my mind. Things were getting…tense."

"Is the least we can do for friend," Yoska told him, grinning. "Besides, children are always worth getting dead for, no? You were good man to have with them."

Estin gave the man a grateful smile. Without warning, Atall latched onto Estin's leg, hugging him.

"What's that for?"

Atall looked up at him and shrugged.

"You kept Oria…both of us, really…safe. You're staying with us…not like dad,

313

right?"

Estin gave Feanne a quick glance, seeing her face harden angrily.

Prying the child off his leg, Estin knelt in front of the boy, holding his shoulders firmly.

"Atall, I want you to understand something. No matter what happened, your father loved you very much. Everything he did was to keep you safe, just like what I do. I'm just trying to do what he wanted...until he comes back. I will always protect you, but if your mother wants to go somewhere safer, I might need to stay behind. Hopefully, your father can catch up then."

Oria glowered at her brother, looking the spitting image of her mother, who continued to eye Estin angrily. Suddenly, Oria pulled free of Feanne and ran from the room, slamming the door as she ran into the hall.

"Someone get her!" Finth said gruffly, even as Feanne ran from the room after the girl. "Can't get found here or we're in a shit-pile of trouble."

Estin waited with Atall for the females to return, the mood of the remaining people in the room worried. It was several minutes before Feanne reappeared, half-dragging Oria into the room by the scruff of her neck.

"No one saw us," she told Finth in passing, returning to her seat with Oria in tow, sitting the girl down beside her.

"What is so bad that it requires running off?" asked Yoska, leaning close to Oria, who glared at him. "Some say the gypsies will steal you away if you do not obey your mother."

The child rolled her eyes, but said nothing, just crossed her arms over her chest and glowered at the table in front of her.

"What then is our plan?" Feanne asked, clearly trying to turn attention away from her children. "Linn's to be executed in two days and only the two of you can show your faces in town without drawing a lot of attention. I know by now, the labor camp has told someone that a fox and...Estin...are running around attacking people."

"Do we need the soldier?" Yoska added, sounding quite serious. "He is good soldier, yes, but do we risk ourselves for someone we do not know? I would ask how this helps us free our people from the undead armies."

"My people are blockaded in their own damned caves for the most part," Finth told them all. "We get no help there. Right now, I just want to get warm bodies that can fight in one place, be that here or half a bloody league away. Those undead are everywhere and I don't wanna be caught with my pants down again...figuratively this time..."

"If we do free him, they will come looking for us. This defeats the purpose of hiding, no?"

"Estin?"

He looked up as Feanne inquired, his attention having been on Atall, who in turn was watching his sister nervously as he twisted the silver ring on his thumb. There was something unsettling in Oria's mood and Estin guessed that Atall was trying to figure it out as well, but was faring no better in finding answers.

"I will do as my pack-leader commands," he answered noncommittally. "I don't even know the full situation anymore."

Feanne's anger visibly deepened, but she said nothing further.

"I say we free him," she told the group at length. "We need every warrior we can get and having a human who is also familiar with military tactics will be useful, if we are to escape the undead commanders' own tactics."

Estin found himself confused and interjected, "Aren't we safe here?"

"Not at all," Feanne answered immediately. "In this region, the undead are marching on this location as we speak. It is the only surface location left to strike at. There may be others underground, such as the dwarven or dark elven cities, but we have lost contact with them. If this city falls, we will be moving as a pack again, seeking shelter in small groups in the woods and mountains."

"Shouldn't we be focusing on helping them defend the walls?"

Feanne got to her feet and walked across the room, grabbing one of his hands and digging her thumb-claw into the scar on his hand.

"That is how they seek our aid," she told him, her stare unwavering. "They've tried to take me four times. Lantonne believes their army cannot fail and expects anyone else to work the fields to support the existing army. They are stockpiling food for a siege, Estin. How long do you believe the living can hide inside a wall before all the food is gone and the undead still wait at the gates? One army needs to eat…the other does not."

Atall's fingers closed around Estin's other hand tightly.

"We will get as many together as we can and leave the city," he agreed. "Just tell me where you need me to be and my role."

Feanne eased her own grip on Estin's hand, placing her other over his palm gently.

"I'm sorry. We're all scared," she admitted, rubbing at the scar with the pad of her thumb. She lowered her voice and added, "And I'm scared of messing this up…"

Estin closed his hand over hers, offering only, "You're doing fine."

"It is decided," Feanne said, raising her voice for the others and pulling her hands free. She wandered back to Oria, this time with Atall close beside her. "We will free Linn and then prepare to leave the town. I already sent word to the others to meet in the southern mountains. No large cities, thus no targets for the undead."

"You mean me and the gypsy get to free him," said Finth dryly. "It's not a big deal, but you two need to stay low, or we're more boned than the ladies two streets over. That said, those ladies do some good business."

"We'll work on an escape plan and gathering of supplies," Estin offered to the group, pointedly ignoring Finth. "Much of that can be done at night. I'm guessing this town's got just as many people willing to sell goods to someone with a deep cloak and purse as Altis did."

"More," Finth chuckled. "Just be careful. They may not be as willing to sell you into slavery, what with having laws against that here, but they'll still toss you back into an 'army aid resource camp' if they get the slightest hint you're not a freeman. It's a fine line that they leap over with ease. If someone asks for your papers, you need to be gone."

"Can you get me clothing?"

Estin motioned to his threadbare, torn, muddy, and bloodied garments that he had been given at the slave camp more than a year prior.

"I have friends in clothing district who will do anything I ask," Yoska announced happily. "They owe clan a favor or two. You will have new clothes, as will our foxes. This I pledge. These clothes might even be stylish."

"Go get yourself cleaned up, monkey," Finth barked, waving towards the water room. "Yoska and I will go do our magic. You just need to be ready to hustle tonight...I really hate farming and I look terrible in a collar."

Estin gave Feanne a long look as she doted on the kits, wondering how he had managed to put her out of his mind for so long. Seeing her again felt like a fresh wound that he had no ability to heal. Still, he reminded himself that he had kept his promise and brought her children back to her. That was what mattered. Keeping that firmly in-mind, he got up and headed down the hall to Finth's water room.

The room itself was no less ancient and battered than the rest of the dwelling, but had once been quite nice. Rotted oak paneling lined the walls, where it had not fallen off. Thick metal pipes across the ceiling brought water down into a basin on the wall, which had rusted rather badly from disuse. Still, it was an extravagance that Estin had never had and for the last year, the ability to clean himself at his own pace without someone using a bucket had been absent as well.

To many wildlings, the care one took of their own fur said much about them. He dreaded how he must look to his own people—to Feanne—with the thick matting of mud and grime that he could see down his arms and legs. He had not even looked at his own tail in a long time and cringed at how much effort it would take to pick all the burs and mud from its long fur.

Estin spent the better part of an hour trying to clean himself. He had never realized how much he depended on his claws for grooming until he tried to clean his fur without them. It was a struggle that made the act of washing up far more difficult than it should have been. As he had guessed, his tail was nearly a lost cause, much of the grunge stubbornly refusing to come out, no matter how much water he applied.

Finally, Estin gave up and resigned himself to living with the remaining burs, at least until he could spend more time grooming himself. He shook off as much of the water as he could, the chill of being wet, even in the moderately-warm building, starting to make him shiver. Accepting that this was the best he would be able to do for himself, he pulled back on his filthy clothing and started down the hall.

Estin almost immediately found himself the target of the children's' play while Yoska and Finth left to begin scouting Linn's predicament. The kits were bouncing back from their experience in the camp far faster than he was, wanting to play-fight and generally tackle and maul him to amuse themselves.

At first, he had tried to get Feanne to play the same way with the kits, but she refused, choosing instead to sit nearby, watching with a coy smile that he had longed to see for quite a while, though as usual, he really wanted to know what she was thinking. There was some relief in seeing her burden ease, even if it required having two children leaping from random directions to pounce and bite him.

The later part of the afternoon was far quieter, with Estin curled in a corner with Asrahn's spellbook, refreshing his memory of the complex formulas that he had been without for months. Some of it made his head spin, trying to remember how he had once thought these were easy.

Feanne meanwhile rounded up Atall and Oria, first grooming their fur until it was smooth, then forcing them to settle and sleep for a little while. They argued and begged a while, then promptly passed out, exhaustion finally catching them. As they slept, Feanne sat beside them, watching every breath, stroking their heads as they snored softly.

"How long before you knew I was gone?" Estin asked her eventually, once he was sure the kits were sound asleep.

"Right away," she replied, never looking back. "It just added one more person to try and find in the woods during my routine. Eventually, I accepted that you were gone...though it was far from easy. A few more months after that, I accepted that my children were gone or dead, as well. Convincing myself of those things nearly killed me, but in the end, I found the strength to come back to the pack."

"I never meant to be gone like this."

"I know."

"If there was any way I could have come..."

"Then you would be dead and I likely would be too, as I'd have fought to my last breath to save them," she said, indicating the children. "As it was, I had nothing keeping me there. When we lost the town, I took any who would go and just left. It was for the best."

"Finth told me that you were angry with me for disappearing...that you thought I'd stolen the children."

"No, that's not quite true. I blamed myself for every bit of it, but you made an easy scapegoat when you left. I felt like you had abandoned me...the same way Insrin had. I was furious for that and wanted to confront you, just as I wanted to confront Insrin. I know better now."

She brushed back the fur from Oria's face, where it had curled down near her eyes.

"Will you ever let me go, Estin?" she asked eventually.

Estin snorted and closed the book.

"I let you go a little every time you mention his name. I let you go every time you left because of him. Even now, you won't be near me because of him. I have let you go as much as I am able while I draw breath. I will never push you...but if you want me to leave you completely alone, please send me away. If I'm with you...I am who I am, Feanne."

Feanne closed her eyes and nodded.

"Things are just too...complicated for this to work."

"There is nothing complicated," he said, reopening the book. "You have your children back and I will be the loyal guard to the new pack-leader. Nothing more, nothing less. I said my feelings just once, Feanne, and I have no intention of hopelessly spouting them every time I see you. You've told me before that our people hold no special loyalties to those they were with before choosing a proper mate and I will abide by that."

"And I'll keep telling you that until at least one of us believes it, Estin."

After an hour of silence, Yoska was the first to arrive, entering quietly and checking the halls outside for any sign of pursuit. He then closed the door and turned to Feanne and Estin, giving a polite bow. He then stopped and studied each of them in turn.

"Had I known I had missed a funeral, I would have brought other clothing. Regardless, I have brought clothing that should hide you well tonight."

"We're fine," Feanne said gruffly, taking the clothing he handed her without looking at it.

"Of course you are," Yoska said, chuckling. "Is a good thing we gypsies have no relationship issues...that way I cannot recognize them in others. I will just go sit in the corner, while you two continue to be angry about something that has nothing to do with one another. Yes, I shall do that..."

True to his word, the man sat down in one of the rickety chairs and closed his eyes and appeared to fall asleep.

"We should go soon," Feanne told Estin soon after that, untying the bundle of clothes she had been handed. "I want to be back before the kits have been up very long."

"They will be cared for," Yoska noted, not opening his eyes. "Do what you must. No need for rushing, but please give my regards at the funeral."

Smiling and shaking his head, Estin opened up his own pile of clothing. It contained a simple human-style outfit, with alterations to fit his slightly different frame, specifically his tail. Yoska had even thought to include leather foot covers that would, at least to a cursory glance, look like he were wearing boots. The whole outfit then could be covered with a bulky hooded cloak, which Estin could only hope would somewhat hide his tail.

Pulling on the outfit and fastening the cloak around his neck, he looked over and saw that Feanne was nearly ready as well. A long pleated skirt covered legs, feet, and tail, making her disguise far simpler than his own. With the hood of her own cloak in place, anyone who missed the long muzzle and wet nose would never guess that she was not human and certainly would be unable to identify her breed.

"You look marvelous," said Yoska, his eyes still closed. "Now go mourn or frolic or whatever it is your people do when you are brooding. And please pick up some proper alcohol while you are out. Is essential travel supplies, no?"

"Do we have any coin?" Estin inquired, even as he had started to head for the door. "I can steal if I have to, but I'd prefer not."

Yoska still did not open his eyes, pulling a small jingling pouch from his shirt. He then reached under the chair and drew out Finth's wicked-looking knife and handed that to

Estin with the pouch.

"The coin is all yours to spend, but please bring the knife back without yours or anyone else's blood on it. Is bad luck for hiding."

Estin took both and almost offered the weapon to Feanne, until he saw her eyes under her hood looking at him like he was an idiot. She held out her hands, reminding him that she still had her claws. He just gave her a weak smile and slid the weapon into his own clothing.

With that settled, Estin led the way from the room, heading down the way he had originally come into the building. At the bottom of the last set of steps, he exited out into an alley, at which point Feanne began whispering occasional directions to him, allowing him to remain slightly in front until they reached a wider road, when Feanne began walking alongside him.

"The main street here will take us to the market district," she told him softly. "The sun should be far enough down by the time we get there. Anyone who's still open usually won't ask any questions. Finth took me down there a few times in the middle of the night...that late you wouldn't need the cloak. They really don't care who you are or how many posters your face is on."

They pressed on, moving through light traffic of people from all walks of life. Unlike in Altis, where Estin had seen the clear difference between the ghetto and the rest of town with regards to which races were allowed to be in the open, here he saw a little of everything, comfortably moving about without regard. He smiled at seeing even wildlings, their faces unconcealed.

Feanne guided him through the market section as they arrived, pointing out which shops specialized in which goods. Their destination was specifically a large squat building that Feanne explained sold most of the large quantities that caravans would need. Since they were trying to stockpile not only for their own travel, but anything else they could get for the others out in the mountains, Feanne had told him this store was the best bet.

Leading the way in, Estin walked into the large storeroom, where a dwarf was arguing loudly with a silent orc about the pricing of the goods. Even before he could get a good look around at the aisles of supplies, a blue-skinned fae-kin with odd spots came hurrying up, stepping right in front of Estin.

"Thank you for coming in tonight, can I...," he seemed to notice Estin's face under the hood, "...help you with anything?"

"We need supplies for a small caravan journey," Feanne cut in, handing him a list of what Finth and Yoska had recommended.

The fae-kin took the note, but stared at her face, clearly recognizing them from somewhere…likely a warning to watch out for them after the escape the day before.

"We don't get a lot of…foreigners in here," the man explained, reading over the list. "I presume you have coin, or something to trade that won't get me arrested for accepting?"

"We have coin, no worries," answered Feanne for him, taking charge of the situation and demanding the full attention of the shop-keep. "Can you meet our needs?"

The man went down the list again, nodding at each item.

"Most of this is not an issue," he said, tapping his pointed teeth with a finger. "It'll take me a few days to get it all together. Most people are coming into the town and wanting stockpiles, what with the undead army on the march. Everything's slower to fulfill. Your pricing on here's a little low, as the food specifically has gone up in the last week. I'll do what I can though."

The man folded the list and put it into his shirt pocket.

"Can you have it inside two days?" Feanne asked him.

"Should be able to. Come back, I'll get you a final price and we can have your wagon loaded by end of day. Just need two silver down and I'll get everything moving. Probably going to come to about a gold on final price, assuming you can afford that?"

Feanne accepted and offered her thanks, taking the coins from Estin to pay the shop-keep. With their business finished, the man hurried off to help the next person, leaving them to depart on their own time.

"That was almost too easy," Feanne whispered as they slipped back out into the darkening streets. "I expected more hassle, once he saw what breeds we were."

As they entered the street, Estin checked the coin purse he had been handed, finding a half dozen copper coins, three more silvers, a pair of gold coins, and two of the little gems he had stolen back in Altis. The money in that pouch once would have been enough for him to live comfortably on for years, but now he wondered just how long it would last, providing for not just their small group, but anyone else they brought along.

"Don't worry about the money," Feanne said, leaning in as she saw him looking through the bag. "Finth has been secreting away coin for years, it would seem. This is what he sends us out with any given day. He says he has ten times as much stashed somewhere. With how much more that he said you gave him, he can hardly complain if you spend some.

"If you need something, now is the time to get it. We may not have another chance.

Coin has little value in the wilds."

After looking sadly at his broken claws again, Estin turned to a nearby building where smoke roiled up from a smithy. He headed for it, with Feanne following a few steps behind him. Inside the open-air shop, an impressively-muscled ogre labored, banging a hammer on hot steel, shaping it to his will slowly.

"Shop is closed," the man grunted as they entered. "City law says I don't sell after dark."

"Even if we ask very little but pay well?"

The ogre tossed aside his hammer, turning to eye them as he wiped his brow.

"Wildlings...that's new," grumbled the ogre, walking right up to Estin and squinting at him. "Don't get much request for weapons from your kind. What'd you need, rodent?"

Estin held back his hatred of being called vermin, motioning instead at the man's stock of blades.

"I need weapons before we travel. Swords first. Balanced as well as you have on-hand."

The ogre chuckled and picked up a rather simple longsword, swinging it expertly as though it weighed nothing.

"Balance is relative to the person," the ogre said, flipping the weapon over and catching the blade with his hand. "To me, some of the greatswords are balanced. To you, something else."

He placed the sword back in a rack and picked up a smaller sword.

"The weighting in this one is likely right for you. I can adjust it slightly."

The sword was offered to Estin, who took it slowly, hoisting the gleaming weapon. The ogre was not wrong, the balance was actually amazing. He had never held a finer weapon.

"Do you have two like this?"

The ogre nodded and picked up a second.

"They don't come cheap," the ogre warned, wiping his sooty hands on his leather apron. "I actually pay an enchanter to hone them so they never dull. Most of my finished works have that feature. Want cheap, go elsewhere."

Estin felt the edge of the weapon, finding that it grazed smoothly through some of his fur, cutting it cleanly.

"How much would they cost me?"

The ogre chuckled, watching him hold the sword.

"Eight silver each, just to get you out of my shop."

Estin reached into his money purse and extracted one of the gems, setting it delicately down on the edge of the forge.

"What's that worth to you?"

The ogre eyed the gem, blinked, and picked it up.

"Probably a little while in the stocks if I'm not careful," he said, turning the gem around in the light of the forge. "This is stolen, that much I know. It's been etched for sale to someone with money. I'm guessing that's not you."

Estin stood firm as the ogre eyed him.

"I can give you the swords for it," the ogre finally agreed, dropping the gem into his apron. "If anyone asks, you stole them from me. Awful shame getting robbed like that."

"I need several more things," Estin said, before the ogre could turn away.

"What? What else so I can go home and be done with crazy travelers?"

Estin left Feanne's side, walking with the ogre briefly around the small shop. They picked out two more weapons—long daggers—the ogre wrapping them in oilcloth for him and happily accepting his silver.

"Thank you and goodbye," Estin finally told the man, but the ogre just grunted and pretended to ignore him.

"They are fine weapons," Feanne told him once they were a good distance from the forge. "I might never use one, but they are well-made. I would hate to stand against someone wielding those in battle."

Estin said nothing, hoping to get back to their lodging before too much more time had passed. It took them almost a half hour, but soon they were coming back into the dark hovel that Finth had claimed as his own.

"Well?" asked Yoska as they came in, the twins sitting in front of him, as though a story had been interrupted. They looked to be nervous, which told Estin the story was likely not something that their mother would approve of. "Were you able to get what we need?"

"We were," Feanne said first, unfastening her cloak just in time to move it away from her as the kits latched onto her legs. Within seconds, the two were exploring the large skirts she was wearing, openly questioning human fashion. "Everything should be ready in two days."

As she explained to Yoska what they had gotten ordered with regard to supplies, Estin lay the two swords on the table, unwrapping the oilcloth that hid and protected them.

Almost instantly, Atall and Oria appeared at his side, eyeing the steel with skepticism.

"Mom says we don't need weapons," Oria said firmly, poking at one of the swords with what Estin could only describe as distrust.

"Feanne," Estin called over his shoulder. "Do me a favor, please."

"Yes?"

"Gouge that table as well as you can with your claws."

Feanne eyed the broken table that he had indicated, then raked it with one hand's claws, leaving half-inch lines in it where her fingers traced. Estin knew that she could do far more damage if she used her magic, but the demonstration was what he had hoped for.

"Your turn, Oria," he told the girl, pointing at the table. "Show me what you can do."

Oria gave him a confused look, then sort of slapped the table, dragging her fingers on it, creating a thin set of lines until she yelped and had to suck her finger.

"I can't," she said sadly, to which Feanne gave Estin a questioning look.

"Not yet, you can't. When you're a little older, your mother will teach you. For now..."

He unwrapped the second bundle, revealing two long hooked daggers that looked like claws.

"These are for you two," Estin told the kits, checking that both daggers were well secured in their sheaths. "Your mother or I can teach you how to use those until your claws are a little stronger."

"Estin, we need to speak about this..."

He half-turned, seeing the annoyed look Feanne was giving him. He knew how much she must hate the idea of her children using human weapons and that somehow made it even better for him.

"Would you rather they be unarmed while we travel?"

"No..."

"Then they will be taught to use these. If I'm to be your guard, I will do so my own way, pack-leader. The kits should not be defenseless in a fight."

Feanne seemed to bite back her thoughts and just nodded, her jaw tight.

"Glad we're agreed," he said, grinning at her. "So are you two ready?"

Both clamored for a weapon, ready to learn.

*

The kits and Estin spent that night and the next two learning how to safely wield the weapons, much to the dismay of their mother, who mostly glowered at all three of them during training. When Finth had lauded the children for learning so quickly, Feanne had actually stormed out of the room briefly to compose herself, before returning in a more neutral mood.

All this, Estin just ate up, knowing he could drive her to want to hit him so easily, without raising his voice or a finger to her. Deep down, he felt that was the least he could do as her newfound "guard," but he had no intention of telling her that he was intentionally poking at her easiest annoyances...though he guessed that she knew. He knew it bordered on the backhanded aggression that he had seen from the deer so long ago, but it was all he had left that he could use to rile her, without actually driving her off. Small victories, he told himself.

By the time the wagons were loaded and preparations to depart were well underway, Estin felt confident that the kits could at least make an effort to protect themselves in a pinch. They would not be winning a war, but if someone tried to grab them, they had enough knowledge and skill to cut the other person, rather than themselves. Another person like Stendin would likely find himself quite dead.

Feanne, the kits, and Estin had dressed in their human clothing disguises, taking their time preparing the pair of fresh horses and gear at the new wagon—a covered one, recently acquired by Finth.

They sat in the wagon throughout much of the afternoon, Estin nervously tapping his feet and twitching his tail impatiently, though this seemed to amuse the kits who had taken to trying to pounce it every so often.

Finth and Yoska had left hours earlier, saying that they might have finally found a way to free Linn before his execution, but by Estin's calculations, the hanging was to happen at any moment. If they had not managed it by now, either they had failed and were now captives too, or the escape through the streets had been slowed for some reason. Neither was a situation Estin was prepared to remedy.

Noise began to erupt from the streets, sounding as though a small riot had broken out somewhere. Whether the shouters were angry or afraid, he could not be sure at that distance.

"They have five minutes, then we leave," Feanne said, climbing into the front seat of the wagon and grabbing the horses' reigns.

"We can't just leave them."

Her stern look even settled the kits behind Estin.

"I did not ask, Estin. That was an order."

Estin lowered his face, acknowledging her command begrudgingly.

The minutes ticked away, with Feanne tightening her grip on the reigns, though it was almost twenty minutes before she flicked the horses into motion. As they neared the end of the alley, Finth came running back to them, arms waving frantically as he entered the alley.

"We're good, we're good!" he laughed, hoisting himself onto the side of the wagon and up beside Feanne, where he held his chest and panted. "Yoska's got Linn in a corpse cart and is heading for the south gate. Get going and we'll meet him there."

"Corpse?" asked Atall, speaking everyone's thoughts aloud. "Why's he dead?"

"Long story, fuzzball. Short version is that the guards have their thumbs so far up their asses that they didn't notice us steal a corpse that they thought was poisoned to death."

"Why do they think he was poisoned?" asked Feanne, urging the horses forward again.

"Because we poisoned him. That's one of the reasons we're hurrying. If I don't get him an antidote in about half an hour, he's just as dead as if they hung him."

Estin chimed in, asking, "And what's the other reason?"

Finth groaned and pointed north.

"Undead are here. The north gates are already overrun. They've closed off all but the south and that won't be open long. Rumors say the army looks to be a hundred-thousand strong and they're trying to lay siege to the city. They even found a way to take out the war golems. This war is over and we're not on the winning side, so long as we're in this city."

Estin did not hesitate, grabbing Feanne as Finth took the reins and pulling her into the covered back of the wagon so that they could proceed with less caution through the city. Feanne and the kits grabbed onto the wagon's frame and the secured barrels of food and water, just as the horses dug in to run.

The wagon lumbered, then accelerated, taking them by the best paths Finth could think of towards the gates.

As the gates themselves came into view, Finth slowed the horses, pulling alongside a hunched figure pulling a cart with a wrapped body in the back. The man looked up at them sharply, then grinned.

"Is good you made it," Yoska said as they came up alongside him. "Get him inside and cure him, or we must leave him here."

Estin and Feanne helped the gypsy hoist the limp body of Lieutenant Linn into the back of the wagon. As soon as he was aboard, Finth got the horses going again as he passed a vial back to Yoska.

"Drink my friend," Yoska whispered to the pale body, pouring the vial's thick liquid into his mouth. "Now we hope that I did not walk too slow, yes?"

Estin hurriedly draped the body with a heavy blanket as they rolled up on the southern gates, hoping that the guards would not notice the shape with so many other people crammed in the back of the wagon.

Surprisingly, Estin found that the guards could not have cared less. They likely would have let Linn walk proudly out, as their concern was for trying to get a mass of humans into the city in some semblance of order. Getting one wagon out of the city while it was about to be attacked proved beyond easy. If anything, the guards implied that their departure was a blessing...less mouths to feed during a siege.

Within a few minutes of reaching the gate, they were out beyond the walls, heading southwest toward the mountains as fast as the horses could take them, with the din of the city fading rapidly into the steady rumble of the wheels and horses hooves.

The wagon began to roll free of the thick city walls, when a horn blast echoed through the area and the great gates started to close behind them. Theirs was one of the last wagons to enter or leave as the city closed its last gate and the people waiting to get in could be seen arguing with and attacking the city guards. Soon, the metal-barred wooden gate had closed completely, cutting off any further view inside.

Finth took that as a dire sign and whipped the horses, trying to speed their escape. It was not five minutes later that Estin could see the first of the undead coming around the walls, broken and bloodied faces staring as the wagon rolled away. Thousands more followed those first few, filling in all space around the walls and enclosing the city in a new wall of death. Not one even attempted to follow their wagon, instead rushing in on the hundreds of living people who still waited at the gates, hoping to get inside.

That first hour was nerve-wracking for Estin, watching the undead pour into the area behind them as the wagon rumbled mostly west. No matter how many times he thought that all of the undead must already be encircling the city, more kept coming, creating a buffer hundreds of yards deep around the walls, while larger crowds buffeted the gates.

All of them watched over the next few hours, as the entire city was wrapped in the zombies of the undead force, completely encasing the city in death. When Lantonne at last began to fade into the distance enough that they could no longer see the attacking force, they began to hear the first explosions. Early on, they were the simple pops and booms of small explosives being dropped on the undead, but soon the resounding crackle of magic accompanied the sounds.

Great waves of magical fire and lightning pounded the horizon as the city struggled to defend itself. From what Estin could see, every wizard in that part of the world was calling down any trick they could think of, bathing the entire eastern part of the plains in every element, as well as raw magical energy.

The eastern plains near the city were the first to darken into night, but it continued to look to Estin like a thunderstorm had settled onto the very walls of Lantonne. He just sat on the back of the wagon with the two kits in his lap, watching as colorful explosions rocked the skyline, right up to the moment the sky began to lighten again with dawn. By then, they were too far away to see the battle, but distant booms still did reach them on occasion.

Just as Feanne was trying to drag the kits to sleep for the daylight hours, a thunderous crack echoed from the direction of Lantonne. Though they could see nothing specific in the distance, dark clouds seemed to spiral over the general area where they believed the city to be. Everyone took turns squinting at the horizon, but Lantonne was just too far gone.

The city far behind them, Estin looked at Linn, finding the man still pale and cold to the touch, but clearly breathing. His pulse was relatively normal, but he trembled and twitched in his sleep. From what Yoska told him during his tending to the man, Linn might wake after a day or two, given the poisons that were used on him. Had they waited much longer, he would not have woken at all.

They rode on in silence, pausing only briefly the next two afternoons for food and to let the horses rest for a time. Rarely were words exchanged, all in the group just watching the east, as though at any moment the legion of undead would appear, ready to sweep down on them. Even the children were quiet, both keeping their knives within reach throughout the journey.

It was early on the third day that they finally reached the foothills, with Finth and Yoska having taken turns guiding the horses. Linn had woken during the night, but said nothing, sitting in the corner wrapped in the blanket he was given. They had passed several small villages along the way, but every one of them had been still as they approached, prompting them to continue on without stopping, out of fear that the undead might still be lurking there, though it was far more likely that the residents were among the creatures attacking Lantonne.

At last, the wagon rattled into the first rises of the foothills. Far ahead, the mountains loomed, their peaks already covered with snow, even a little early in the season.

"The pack will be meeting us there," Feanne told Finth, pointing at a pair of mountain peaks that were recognizable at quite a distance. "There are many good canyons and valleys to hide in at their bases. Ulra should be watching for travelers such as ourselves to guide them in."

Finth leaned back, staring up into the heights she had indicated.

"Seriously, woman? That has got to be the most gods-forsaken ass-end of the world..."

"Where even the undead won't care to search," she finished for him, smiling up at the peaks. "Lihuan took me there once as a kit. It's a hard area to get into and looks like it should not support life. Once you get past the avalanches and a long section of wind, sun, and beetle-damaged trees, it's rather nice. Streams, good soil, lots of wildlife. I'd thought about running away to there when I got old enough to rebel against my father."

"So...was at two years? Three? I do not understand your peoples' aging," noted Yoska, sipping from a small flask. "To me, you say you were young and I think twelve, but I do not think you are that old, even now."

"I'll agree with the gypsy for the first time ever," croaked Linn, one of the first things he had managed to utter since waking. His voice was weak and scratchy. He raised his bloodshot eyes and looked over his companions from the corner he sat in. "My niece can't even walk well yet and she's almost two."

Finth, still staring up at the peaks, tossed in, "For my people, I'm hearing her say she was thirty or so...usual age the snot-noses start wanting to run away from their parents. Then again, those two rugrats in back are about as grown as our twenty year-olds."

Feanne glowered at the two men, glancing back at Estin for some support. He just shrugged and gave Oria a playful shove.

"I am ten and the leader of my pack. My parents were in their thirties when they passed beyond, having been quite old when they had me."

Yoska gave her a surprised look, then leaned back into the wagon to look at Estin. "And you?"

"A few months past eight, I think. Not real sure."

Shaking his head, Yoska let out a low whistle.

"You all confuse me. I am fifty-some winters and feel an old man. I travel with two who are younger than some of my grandchildren, yet are long-since adults, plus one who would likely consider me the child. This is why the gypsies keep to themselves...no one else has the sense to age properly. You could drive a man to drink...I think I shall..."

Atall bounded up onto the front seat, landing between Finth and Yoska, staring at the gypsy intently.

"You're old," the boy said, studying Yoska's face. "I don't think I can even get that old."

"My grandson told me the same, once. I will tell you what I tell him...keep calling your elders old and you will certainly not live to be an elder yourself. Is rude, especially to a gypsy. I am in my prime. Ask any of my wives."

Feanne's eyes went wide and she pulled Atall into the back of the wagon quickly.

"Wives?" she asked, holding the boy.

Estin glanced over at Oria, whose face was crinkled up in confusion. She looked back at him and mouthed, "What's a wife?"

"Yes, of course," the gypsy went on, gesturing to Finth to get the wagon moving again. "Let me tell you about all six of them. There are many stories of each, so this should get us well into mountains..."

As Estin explained to Oria the difference between human marriage and their peoples' life-matings, Feanne listened with a look of horror on her face as Yoska described a series of women, most of whom he had won via contests of wit or drinking. By the time he had finished, Feanne appeared very nearly ready to run screaming into the woods that the wagon was slowly making its way into, slowed by the uneven ground.

"...and that is how to properly bed a gypsy woman," continued the man, leaning in his seat, but waving his arms as though explaining to an expansive group in front of him. "Is about being properly-dressed, show a little flair, then get her truly drunk. What woman can resist a gypsy man sober, let alone after both have been drinking?"

"Now, my fifth wife, she is what you call Halfling. Very fine woman and can cook such wonderful food. That is how you bed a gypsy man...through stomach."

Estin at this point realized that Feanne actually had her hands over Atall's ears.

"Why would any female put up with this, let alone that many?" she demanded, still not quite shaking the horrified expression. "I would kill a male that tried to bring in more females. I've heard a few breeds tolerate this, but not mine. The moment my mate brought home a second female, either her or my mate...or both...would be dying in the mountains somewhere."

"Ah, is not such a big deal for the gypsy ladies either, yes? One of my cousins has three husbands. Is all about keeping the family strong."

Feanne took her hands off Atall's ears and just held up her hands, saying, "Please...just please stop. You are making my head hurt."

"Is not meant to offend," Yoska told her politely, turning around to face her. "I do apologize. Is only meant to make you think."

"Of what? That gypsies don't have any place in my pack?"

"No, that you may not have all the answers yet."

Feanne appeared perplexed at that, shaking her head.

"I don't care to have answers like that when I have no questions that go with them. Just...just help Finth drive."

Yoska obediently went back to talking with Finth, the two sharing the flask as the wagon wandered onwards and upwards.

"That man is insane," Feanne told Estin, closing the flap of cloth between the wagon's bench seat and the living area in back. "I need to be more careful about what he says around these two."

"Oh, mom, they're just different," Oria told Feanne, looking up from scratching random drawings into the floorboards with her finger. "Not everyone's the same breed...who cares how someone else finds their mate?"

"This isn't exactly a conversation for you two to be having," Feanne told the girl, eyeing Atall as well. "No one's talking about or thinking about finding mates for at least two more years, if not a lot longer. Got it?"

The twins nodded vigorously, but remained mischievous-looking...though Estin realized that unless they were sad or scared, the two always looked that way. Something in the breed, he told himself.

It was at this point that Estin finally found himself yawning, having slept less than an hour each day during the trip. The few times he had managed to doze off, sudden shifts in the wagon as it hit rocks would jar him awake, thinking that the undead had caught them. He had always sat right up, usually finding Feanne lazily staring out the back of the wagon as she held the children, who seemed immune to any further anxiety about their predicament. Finth and Yoska were oblivious to it all, often managing to fall into a deep sleep while still in the front seat of the wagon. Linn drifted in and out of sleep continually, the poison's effects still lingering.

This time, Estin curled up near the back of the wagon, flopping his tail over his face to shield himself from the sunlight. Almost immediately, both kits flopped alongside him.

Since the start of the trip, the kits had been quite willing and able to sleep, mostly during the day as was their breed's way, like Estin's. What they would not do is sleep if someone else was not also bedding down. That meant that during the brief shifts with Estin or Feanne driving the wagon, the kits were climbing all over the adults and generally making the horses nervous.

When Feanne or he had been able to manage a few minutes of sleep, the kits always took the chance to "rest," as they put it, usually falling deeply asleep against whichever adult they were using as a pillow. This time was no different, with Oria even going so far as to pick up Estin's tail—surprising him as the sunlight suddenly hit him in the face—and wrapping it around herself and her brother like an oddly-shaped blanket.

Without his tail quite being able to reach his face again, Estin blinked and adjusted his position slightly to move his face out of the sunlight. In doing so, he saw Feanne watching the kits and him, smiling absently as she too fought to stay awake. When Estin looked at her though, she closed her eyes and lay down to sleep.

Estin slept a long time that day, finally giving in after the short bouts of sleep he had managed to get since leaving the city. When he did wake, it was late in the afternoon and Feanne had moved up front to talk to Finth, while Yoska dozed in the back with Estin and the children.

He yawned and started to go back to sleep, but Oria flicked one of his whiskers to get his attention, leaning so that her nose was almost pressed into his ear.

"Shhh," she said so quietly that he could barely hear her, even as close as she was. "Don't wake Atall."

Estin glanced past the girl and saw that Atall was still out cold, Estin's tail clutched tightly across his chest. It was a singularly rare occurrence that one of the kits woke without the other.

"I know," Oria said, still whispering. "Please don't tell."

Blinking and wondering if he had missed a conversation while asleep, Estin asked her, "You know what?"

Oria fidgeted, then winced when her brother moved. She waited until he settled again before saying anything else.

"I know about my dad."

Estin wanted to hide any reaction, but knew his eyes were likely wide and his jaw was hanging.

"What do you think you know, Oria?"

"He's dead," she said softly as she puffed up her chest, as she often did when she was trying to be tough. "I kept Atall from seeing. Mom always told me I needed to be stronger than the males so they didn't push me around. I needed to see what happened."

The girl took a long shaky breath, then added, "Dad fell right in front of the place he hid us and I could see through the lock. If you hadn't come, eventually Atall would have seen him. That's why I made us stay in there, so he wouldn't see. I saw what they did to him and I didn't want Atall to have to, too."

Oria quieted down as Atall sat up, blinking and licking his nose. He looked around tiredly, staring blankly, but clearly struggling to stay awake after seeing his sister was up.

"Your secret is safe with me," Estin whispered in Oria's ear as he gave her a hug.

A rumble in the distance caught Estin's ear and he looked around, trying to find the direction it came from.

Opening the back flap of the wagon's covering, Estin watched as a sheet of flame roared across the horizon from somewhere near Lantonne and extending miles to the south. A moment later, it was gone, the sky blackened by smoke.

"They're getting bloody serious!" shouted Finth from the front of the wagon. "Never seen anything like that."

The wagon rumbled on and for the rest of the afternoon, Estin and the children watched the horizon, but saw nothing else amiss. Eventually, they relaxed and settled in, the kits munching on dried meats and bread. It was hardly tasty or even overly filling, but it kept their stomachs filled. Estin, on the other hand, looked over the food and set his aside, still not quite hungry enough for more meat. The labor camp had served them everything from horse stew to oxen-tongue stew, trying to use up any resource they had available.

As the kits ate, Feanne came back from the front of the wagon, eyeing Estin's uneaten food on the floor of the wagon. She stepped nimbly over Yoska—who managed to sleep through most everything—and Linn, whose dazed expression did not really tell Estin if he was awake or not.

"I have a bit of a surprise for Estin," Feanne said, smiling broadly as she unwrapped a knot in the human skirt that she had donned for their escape and just not bothered to change out of. Both kits hopped almost on top of her, trying to see what she was extracting from the folds in the garment. "You've put up with me and the kits long enough, I feel you earned it."

"Feanne..."

"I insist. If you're going to be my guard, you'll put up with me turning it around and catering to you once in a while."

She finally got the last fold out and produced a massive orange.

"I bought this back in Lantonne," Feanne told him, ignoring the gagging noises the kits made when they saw what it was. "We have no idea when we'll find more, particularly this time of year, so I thought I would save it for you."

Estin was speechless and hesitated to take the fruit from her. Then, his mouth watering and realizing that he was being a touch rude, he took it and held it close to his chest.

"Thank you, Feanne," he murmured. "I haven't exactly been the nicest person to deal with lately."

"I never have been. Enjoy the fruit."

Estin bit into the orange, not bothering to skin it. He had never understood the human fascination with getting rid of part of the fruit and not having had any fresh fruit in many months, he was not about to take the time. Happily, he sunk his teeth into the fruit, feeling pure joy as the juices ran down his jaw. Some instincts never quite fade, he thought to himself, chewing happily.

"In some cultures, you two are now married," mumbled Yoska, rolling over in his sleep, opening his eyes only slightly. "Lady gives man food, he accept, they then have lots of cute pudgy children. Sometimes man must give different food back to lady to show he will care for her, too. Be very careful who you give food to, Estin. Is no room for more children in wagon."

Feanne groaned and pointed angrily at the front of the wagon, sending Yoska up to the bench, as the kits giggled endlessly at her expense. The man grumbled the whole way until Feanne had closed the dividing cloth between the wagon insides and the front.

Estin just chuckled and ate the orange, not terribly concerned about the teasing of children over something as simple as fruit. He only barely noticed the jokingly nauseated faces they gave him, grumbling about how "gross" fruit was.

While he ate, Feanne sat down beside him, carefully picking at his fur, clearing away the matting and burs. At first, Estin froze, startled, but she chided him and continued her work, just as she had the night before with the kits. Though most wildlings would not groom someone they were not close to, it was not unheard of to care for a dear friend in that manner, so he had to convince himself to relax and let her brush out his fur.

By the time he had finished the orange and gotten as much of the juice as he could out of his fur, both kits were already distracted with trying to see if they could pounce a bug that had flown into the wagon without squishing it. Feanne meanwhile had finished most of her work, settling in to fuss with Estin's tail. That made him even more uncomfortable, sitting there, having his tail cleaned and groomed by someone he was trying very hard not to show his feelings for. Just her concern alone made his heart beat more quickly, wishing he could stop pretending.

"Estin," wheezed Linn several minutes later, surprising Estin. "Please come here."

Feanne released Estin's tail, shooing him away as she sat down with the kits and Estin shifted over by Linn, taking a seat at the human's side.

"I owe you an apology," he said, his voice fading until he had to clear his throat to get it back. "My commander never told me what we were starting back in that quarry. I owe you more than my life for what you did, even if the result was unpleasant."

"No need for apologies. You couldn't have known."

Linn closed his eyes for a short time, as though mustering his strength to stay awake.

"Linn, were you with the others right to the end?"

The man opened his eyes again, nodding grimly.

"Most died in the hole. The rest of us barely had time to react when the crossbows unloaded on us from Lantonne's soldiers."

Estin thought through his question carefully.

"I don't want to belittle the deaths of any of your people," he said, fumbling for politeness, "but I need to know..."

"I ordered all of the volunteers to run when I found out what was happening," Linn answered. "Only my soldiers were captured or executed. Most of your people got away from the quarry. Beyond that, I do not know. I am sorry."

Estin thanked him softly, then checked his temperature and pulse, finding that the man's condition had actually worsened since earlier in the day.

"Finth!" Estin called out. "What does your poison do?"

"Old dwarven party trick. Makes you deathly sick if you drink any alcohol. The stuff I gave him had dwarven moonshine mixed into it. In a dwarf, the mix wouldn't do much...in a human, it immediately puts them into a sleep and then slowly kills their body."

Estin winced at the morbidity of the toxin that Finth had so readily given an ally. He made a note never to accept anything from Finth again without sniffing it extensively. At that thought, he realized that he should have already been doing that.

Thinking on poisons, Estin wiped at Linn's heavy sweat, then sniffed his finger. An acrid odor lingered even this long after the poisoning.

"It's not all out of him," Estin said, diving into his baggage. He searched through his things quickly as Finth handed off the reigns to Yoska and came back to join him. "He's still poisoned."

"He shouldn't be," Finth said, sounding helpless. "The antidote should have worked..."

"You knew what the amounts were of the poison for use on a human?"

"Of course."

"Did you also adjust the antidote?"

Finth groaned and looked over at Linn, who just closed his eyes and sighed.

"I can't make any more, Estin," the dwarf admitted. "Maybe if we stop and get very lucky with the plants in the area..."

"No time."

Estin finally found Asrahn's spellbook and paged through it as he rushed back to Linn, nearly trampling Atall in the process. It did not take him but a moment to find the spell he was looking for, but it took him a minute or so to refresh his memory of the exact procedure to cast it.

"Hold still," he warned Linn, who nodded slowly. "I can't wait around, casting one curative after another and then waiting to see if it helped. You'll likely be dead before I get through them all. This is going to get rid of anything and everything that isn't part of your body, but it's not pleasant."

Not about to wait for an answer, Estin cast the spell, hearing the whispers of the spirits that aided his healing as they were channeled through his touch into Linn. At the completion of the spell, Linn seemed unaffected for a second or two, then tensed as his body purged itself.

The man began to sweat horribly, trembling as his temperature shot up and his heart raced. Then as swiftly as the effect began, it was gone and he relaxed, gasping for breath.

"Unpleasant doesn't begin to describe that," he admitted between breaths. "Now, I'm starving and thirsty on top of it all."

"I did say anything and everything. How do you feel, though?"

"Better than I have since the psychotic dwarf fed me poison. Thank you."

Finth let out an audible sigh of relief and hurried back to the front of the wagon with an expression that Estin could only describe as having his tail between his legs.

Intending to return to the back of the wagon with the kits, Estin started to move when Linn grabbed his arm, gripping it with a strength that Estin was surprised by, given the man's recent health.

"I need to tell you something," the man said, his voice low. "Please sit down by me. I don't want the others to hear me."

Estin sat alongside the human, perking his ears attentively.

"I shouldn't probably tell you this, but I will anyway. Where I come from—a little north of Altis, up in the northern foothills—we spend most of our time fighting off the barbarian tribes. My village did not think much more of your people than animals...maybe less. I was taught from an early age that wildlings are savage creatures who would murder your children and eat them, usually just for fun. We thought that Altis' allowance for wildling slaves was giving them too much freedom around our children."

"Why are you telling me this?"

"Because I wanted you to know who I was when you met me. I may have been polite to your face, but when my commander told me that you were joining us and that I should follow your lead in anything beyond battle tactics, I argued with him. I'm not proud of that, but it's the truth. I told him that I would sooner hang as a traitor before following a glorified raccoon into war.

"The point is, you and your family have done more to help me than my own family ever did. I owe you my life many times over, Estin. I very nearly did hang as a traitor, but it was the friends of the very creature I despised that came to my aid. You and the fox have my oath by my blood that whatever you need of me will be done. I am deeply sorry for how I perceived your people and I hope that I can make it up to you. Your family may be the most noble people I have met."

Estin clasped wrists with them man's offered arm, then told him, "Please don't take this wrong, but I have no family. The kits are Feanne's. I am just her guard, so long as she'll have me."

"Family is more than blood, Estin. The family I lost when Altis fell consisted of my dead brother's wife and their children. I would have fought to the death to save that woman out of loyalty, even though she was not mine and I had no desire for her to be. They were my family, just as truly as if they were my own. If you care for Feanne and the little ones, they're family in their own way."

"Thank you," Estin told him, clasping his wrist tightly. "I doubt you even realize how helpful that was for me to finally hear my confused life put to words."

"When gypsy say helpful things," Yoska blurted out, apparently having been listening in, even from several feet away, "you say that I have degenerate life. When city-man says vaguely-helpful thing, you thank him. Is most disheartening."

"That's because no one understands what the hell you're trying to say," Linn countered, his voice weak still. "You're either trying to woo the fox into your bed...or Estin. I can't sort out which."

The kits belted out laughter.

"Bah!" Yoska snorted, reaching for his flask. "Will be cold in a few weeks. You, sir, are not invited to share my bed for warmth, no matter how much you beg. Do not argue...it is done and I will not change my mind."

Linn laughed, though the act turned into a cough.

The remainder of the journey, just until the following morning, left Estin, the kits, Feanne, and Linn in the back, with Finth driving and Yoska navigating. Yoska had tried several times to climb back into the living area, but Feanne had been adamant that she wanted a short time without gypsy advice and he was to stay outside.

By dawn, the wagon was firmly wedged in rocks and trees, having gone about as far as the rough terrain would allow. There was talk about seeing how much of their remaining supplies could be carried, while Yoska patrolled ahead and Feanne walked off towards the west, stopping to crouch on a tall rock.

Linn had remained in the wagon, resting in an attempt to recover more of his lost strength. He had been more lucid since Estin's healing, but he was constantly tired and sore, the poison having drained him far more than he was likely to admit in the near future.

"We carrying all her luggage?" Finth asked Estin as he hefted a large keg of either water or ale. "Even the kids got some of the baggage. What's she doin' anyway?"

Estin glanced back at Feanne, who was sitting in a clear area, taking slow deep breaths. Within seconds, she raised her mouth to the sky and took one more deep breath.

"She's calling for more hands."

Feanne's cry echoed off the mountains, though she cut it shorter than Estin knew she could maintain it. This cry was unlike the ones he had heard her make before, when they had been attacked. It was not the desperate call for aid, but an announcement of her presence. He only hoped that someone they could trust had heard her.

"If all is well, Ulra should be here within an hour," Feanne told them as she sauntered back over, then stopped in front of the rest of the group, glaring down at the outfit she still wore from the city.

"I think I am done with human things for this lifetime," she announced, digging her thumb-claws into the waist of the skirt and soundly shredding it. She still wore her leathers beneath and did not hesitate to destroy every last piece of the shirt and skirt, cutting them into long strips with a smile on her face.

This set the kits to a new game...destroying their human disguises. Estin could only watch in dismay as the kits ran around like crazy-things, half-dressed after ripping up their own clothing.

"Well that's one way to start a day," Finth noted, watching the chaos. "If Yoska weren't scouting, he'd have some smart-assed thing to say about all this. Didn't he say something about one of his wives ripping his clothing off? Hers? I can't bloody remember."

"Thank you for ruining every happy moment I can come up with, Finth," Feanne told the dwarf, poking the tip of his nose with her claw. "Remember your manners when we reach the pack. I will not tolerate you or your pet gypsy lackey making lewd comments at my expense."

"Awful sorry, Lady Tail-Biter...I'll be more careful."

"I don't even know what that is supposed to mean. Fur-licker, paw-licker, wet-nose, reddie, Madam Pounce, Lady Furface...do you spend your time actually working on what to call me, or are these supposed to mean something?"

The dwarf wrinkled his brow.

"Not especially. They're stuff I figure wildlings do...hells, I'd be Finth Ass-Scratcher, I guess...maybe Finth Whore-Chaser. How about Finth Swill-Drinker?"

Estin listened to them bicker while he leaned on the water barrel and waited, the children running around trying to catch an angry squirrel. As he stood there, his ears perked as he heard the telltale sound of several bows being drawn.

"Archers!" he yelled, grabbing Atall as he ran by, shoving him bodily under the wagon. He waved for Oria, who slid in after her bother.

Feanne and Finth stopped arguing and began scanning the trees for attackers, even as Yoska came running back towards them as fast as he could in the rough terrain.

"Everyone stand still and identify yourselves!" called out a gruff voice off to Estin's left, past the wagon.

Yoska skidded to a stop, raising a plume of dust. Finth stopped moving, but his eyes darted around, trying to find those out in the trees. Even Linn was visible inside the wagon from Estin's position, trying to appear unmoving, but actually pulling one of Estin's swords into his lap.

"I am Feanne," she announced loudly, turning in place. "I am pack-leader of my people and would return to them without hindrance. Identify yourselves!"

A heavily-armored orc stepped from the trees just up the rise from them, not more than ten steps from Yoska, an arrow notched in his bow and aimed at the gypsy.

Off to Estin's right, a human came into sight, though his fur and leather clothing was battered and looked as though he had crawled to their current position. He bore a throwing axe and was watching Estin very carefully.

Somewhere behind him, Estin heard yet another bit of movement, picking up the smell of fresh pine needles, though given the season, that seemed odd. That person did not speak.

"Lower your weapons," growled a female voice as Ulra stomped into view, coming around a large bank of rocks. She gave Yoska a pat on the back in greeting that made the man stumble. "She is who she says. She is the leader of our pack."

In the year since Estin had last seen the bear wildling, she had aged considerably. Several jagged scars marred her fur and her left hand was badly burned. Patches of white fur around her muzzle told him of rough times that she had endured.

The orc and the human lowered their weapons, but stayed alert, watching Estin and Feanne for any reason to strike.

"My pack-leader," Ulra said formally, bowing before Feanne. "Welcome home."

"Thank you," said Feanne, eyeing the others that had come with Ulra. "Who are our guests?"

Estin turned around, hoping that they finally were out of danger.

The last member of the scouting party was a somewhat human-looking woman, but with forest-green skin and leaves and vines that seemed a part of her clothing. He recognized her as a fae-kin, but soon began to wonder if the very much living plants were actually a part of her, rather than garbing. He had heard talk among some of the laborers that there were fae-kin who were far closer to their nature-spirit ancestors than others…this woman looked to be one of those.

"They are not exactly guests. They and many others came after you left, with the same hope of the valley being shelter. They have joined us and have agreed to work with us to survive. With us now are the remnants of several other tribes scattered by the undead armies."

Feanne studied the orc, then the human, eyeing each carefully. The two stoically glared back, their weapons kept ready, despite the introductions.

"I greet you," she told them, bowing to each, then to the fae-kin behind Estin. "We brought as much food and water as we could manage, which I hope will dissuade any doubts about our intentions here."

The orc grunted, but the fur-clad human gave a curt nod of acknowledgement and walked over to the wagon. He eyed Estin oddly, but stepped past him and lifted one of the kegs onto his shoulder, walking silently westward with it.

"He is right, we should move before we're found," Ulra told the group, coming over and grabbing most of the remaining supplies on her own.

It was Ulra that wound up leading the way for the small group, despite carrying nearly a wagonload of supplies on her back. Behind her, the newcomers walked slowly, the kits mostly hiding near Estin or Feanne's legs as they watched the orc and human, who had fanned out to the woods nearby to intercept any threats. In the rear, Finth and Yoska were the slowest, aiding Linn to walk, his feet still unsteady on the uneven ground. The fae-kin woman had simply vanished.

Throughout the next three hours, the group was made to move without speaking. Whenever someone did begin to talk, either the orc or the human would rush over, motioning them to be silent. This seemed to disturb the kits more than anything.

The group moved into a narrowing space between the steep rocky walls that led hundreds of feet up to two separate mountain peaks. Where these came together, the woods created the illusion of a high wall of stone, but as they got closer, Estin could see that the mountainsides did not quite meet, forming a gap that led deeper into the mountains, though the opening was only wide enough for perhaps fifteen men wide...far less with the dense trees.

It was into this gap that they traveled, the orc taking point and hurrying ahead, even as the human dropped to the far rear, watching for pursuit and skillfully covering their trail.

The gap itself felt to Estin as though it were closing in on him. The trees furthered that feeling, blocking out the sky, even as the stone walls narrowed. He began to wonder if they were marching into some dead-end, but before long, the walls widened again, opening up until he could no longer see them through the trees.

"Welcome to your pack," Ulra announced as they cleared the trees and entered a large camp.

Unlike the old pack's campsite, Estin was surprised to see fifty or sixty tents of incredibly varied types. Whereas the old had been haphazardly-built shelters of canvas, made to fit whatever occupant it housed, this campsite had nearly any kind of tent or temporary shelter he could imagine.

Large human tents with ornate decoration, some with house or city crests emblazoned on them, were the nearest to the entrance to the valley. A half dozen armored soldiers approached, bearing the insignias of both Lantonne and Altis. When they saw Ulra, they returned to what they had been doing previously, but Estin could tell that they were still on-guard.

Beyond the human tents, there were a few ramshackle structures that could have belonged to almost anyone, though Estin smelled dwarves for the most part. Loud curses and arguments came from that area.

Next came large animal-skin tents that had been treated in some way to withstand the weather. Sitting amongst these were more humans like the one escorting them, all stern and clad in pelts and hides. Every member of this little society eyed his group challengingly and several eyed Estin as though evaluating whether his hide was warmer than their current clothing.

Still farther off to the south, Estin could see several lightweight white tents of the elves from Lantonne. These were muddied and barely recognizable, but he remembered their distinctive look from Lihuan's camp, just before he had left it for the last time.

Behind the last section of tents, up on a rise, Estin spotted the blue wagons of Yoska's clan, though his mind raced at how they could have managed to get the large vehicles into the valley.

The east end of the camp, where they were headed, was packed with a random assortment of wildlings that Estin mostly had never met. They were not all from Lihuan's pack, though several he was quite sure he recognized from Insrin's village. It was in this section of the camp that the most residents stopped to stare at their approach, several of the older members approaching Feanne to whisper polite greetings or bow to her.

At this point, Yoska and Finth led Linn away, with Yoska giving Feanne a quick explanation that they were going to find a place for Linn to rest a while, as well as some warm food.

"We prepared a proper tent for you," Ulra told Feanne, leading the group to a large structure near the back of the grouping of smaller tents. It was readily apparent to him that it was Lihuan's old tent, having been patched and moved. "Will you need me to assign guards for you, or do you already have them?"

Feanne glanced over at Estin, giving him a smile.

"I have a guard," she told the bear as they stepped into the tent, though Ulra had to bend over to slip inside. "Another might not be a bad idea, at least until I've established myself with the newcomers."

Ulra grunted as she set the huge pile of supplies near the door of the tent.

"Very well. I'll have Doln bring in bedding for yourself, the kits, and for Estin. I will take the watch tonight to allow you all to rest and recover."

Both Feanne and Estin balked, which Ulra seemed surprised at.

342

"Have I said something wrong, pack-leader?"

"Estin will not be bedding here...," Feanne said quickly.

"A guard is useless if not present," Ulra countered firmly. "I and your father's other three guards took turns sleeping either in his tent or just outside it for the last ten years.

"I will not have you unguarded, pack-leader. Either Estin stays here, or I will have him replaced, with or without your permission. If your pack is not mature enough to understand his place, then he does not belong at your side."

"I'm still in the room, Ulra. If she wants me to sleep outside..."

At this point, Atall and Oria began whining loudly, demanding that Estin be allowed to stay.

"I will not have you out of reach when our pack-leader is unguarded. With her kits at her side, she is vulnerable and there are those who would take advantage of that. Her guards will need to be ready and close at all times. If she had a mate who was here, I could see an argument for modesty, but with him absent, I will see her guarded at any price to your feelings, Estin."

"Put his bedding in the corner," Feanne conceded at last, pointing to one end of the tent. "We'll manage."

Ulra glowered at Feanne briefly, eyeing the corner that she had indicated, as though even that was too far for her taste. Despite this, she dipped her head in acknowledgement and began unrolling a pile of furs and blankets, first in the area where Feanne and the kits would sleep, then where she had indicated for Estin. Once that was set up, Ulra excused herself, heading out with most of the supplies they had brought to disperse them where they were most needed.

"I see little has changed since I was a child," Feanne said, giving the kits a hug that they struggled against. "Ulra will protect me from myself and the more I fight her, the more trouble she will cause me. She is the only one I ever saw bully my father into a decision."

"It's okay, mom," Atall piped up. "Estin's a good guard. He kept us really safe."

Feanne smiled up at Estin.

"Yes, he did. That's why I want to keep him around, too. I just thought he might want some time away from me. No such luck for him, though."

If Estin could blush through his fur, he would have. Trying to avoid any further scrutiny, he set about piling his belongings in the corner assigned to him, while Feanne spent the afternoon getting the kits settled into the camp and their tent.

Chapter Eleven
"Truths"

The new pack was certainly not the old, though I still dreamt of Lihuan's pack. I would remember the calm happiness in that group, where even the drama that came with conflicts over mates and things as simple as eating habits were just trivial by the standards of the new world I was living in. I almost longed for the simpler days when the worst I had to worry about were a bunch of deer wildlings knocking down my tent, rather than bloodthirsty walking corpses.

Nightmares were prevalent for everyone and it was not uncommon for any of us to wake up screaming, remembering undead murdering a family member, or a city or village burning to the ground as corpses marched in relentlessly. Every cry in the night was met with armed guards from every faction that now dwelt with us. No one could be too careful, lest we find out that something had snuck into the village. Luckily, the night terrors affected so many that there were no hard feelings when it would turn out to only be a dream.

Most of us had become secure long ago in the idea of a pack being a singular race or group. Insrin's people had dreamt of a great fox civilization, led by his father and later by him. Lihuan had dreamt of a gathering of wildlings who would share their different lives to become stronger through being a unified family. The human barbarian tribes of the eastern plains that had joined us told me that their elders had dreamt of the day the tribes would work together. The dwarves had dreamt of riding out the wars in their tunnels, free of intrusions. The gypsies had dreamt of just riding away from it all in their wagons. Orcs had dreamt of facing the undead head-on and winning. The Halflings dreamt of the undead giving up and leaving us all alone.

So many dreams that had failed, just like my own dreams of saving my family so long ago. That, we all had in common.

Now, it was time for someone else's dream.

Feanne's dream was not the one she had grown up with. She once had just wanted to be left alone, expecting only the strong to survive. Time had changed that dream and then she had dreamt of a place where her children could grow to adulthood without being murdered—a fear that had grown into an obsession, I soon learned, as her nightmares were of the many children she had seen killed as she had grown up.

Now, her dream for the future appeared to be a new form of her father's, unifying not just her people, but all survivors, whether they wanted it or not. Survival of the strongest had changed into survival of all those strong enough to have lived this long.

The disorganized rabble that had gathered in the camp needed a leader. They needed someone they could respect, who was not going to drive them off. Feanne did not want this dream, but it was hers, nonetheless.

The races all had their own reasons for following her. If nothing else, there were those who followed her lead simply because the camp was largely held by the wildlings and she was their leader. For others, it took a little more.

These were not happy times. It is hard to think happy thoughts or have actual dreams of a good life when you know that at any time undead might descend upon you, murdering every living being for miles. Still, I had my purpose. I was back with my people...Feanne's people...and I was at her side as she led the way. I could live in her shadow and be happy, knowing that the one I—I could not bring myself to say the word 'love' again, though it was accurate—cared most for was where I could watch to be sure she was safe.

If things went badly, I already had my orders. I was to escape with the kits and find a safe place, leaving Feanne and anyone else to die if necessary. Until then, I could accept Feanne's pack as my home. Here, I could stay.

"I will not be challenged, Bockkan," Feanne barked at the human, who stood close enough that her nose nearly brushed his chin. "You will back down, or I will sit you down."

The human glared darkly at her, the snow blowing across his face, though he did not blink or move back in the slightest. He just stood over her, his hands clear of his weapons, yet the menace of him striking at Feanne was clearly there, making Estin nervous as he stood nearby.

The argument had begun shortly after dawn, two months after Estin and the others had come to the camp. Bockkan was the last of the camp's residents to resist Feanne's commands, despite how few she was willing to give. The man had been firm in his belief that Feanne was some kind of "evil spirit," somehow bent on his people's destruction. This particular day, he had called Oria an evil spirit and made new threats against Ulra. Feanne had finally broken, confronting the man publically.

"The fox is a trickster, a liar, and a coward," the barbarian told her yet again. "We will not follow the fox. The elders taught us to follow the ways of many animal spirits, but the fox and others will doom us. You are the fox-spirit in flesh. Why should I tell my people to follow you, when in the end, you will run and leave us, fox?"

Even a short distance away, Estin could see Feanne's fingers flex as she likely contemplated ripping the man's throat out. He put a hand on Oria, who was trying to sneak up to stand alongside her mother. Atall stood more willingly at Estin's side, watching nervously.

"Bockkan, stand down. I do not want bloodshed."

The barbarian laughed, this time making no pretense of the fact he was placing his hand on his sword's hilt.

"I hear much talk from your mouth, little fox. Other people may listen to wise words from you, but my people believe in actions, not words. Can you back your talk with proof of skill, or will your protectors strike at me?"

Feanne glanced back at Estin, then over to Ulra, who had been growling almost incessantly since the argument had begun, standing over Feanne and Bockkan, ready to strike the man down.

"If I can best you in a fight, you will submit to my leadership?"

Bockkan grinned, checking for the agreement of his clanmates, who cheered loudly.

"If a fox can beat a follower of the bear, then I will obey your order," the man said, nearly tapping her forehead as he leaned down, apparently trying to intimidate her. "If the bear totem is stronger, I will lead you, little fox. My people will decide what becomes of both bear and fox, then."

"If that is the only way you will see sense...agreed. Prepare yourself."

Feanne stormed away from the man, marching directly up to Estin.

"This is not how I planned on spending breakfast," she said softly, rustling Oria's fur and ears with her hand. "Did it really need to be this hard to have him stop threatening to skin Ulra? What honor is there in murdering the animal you claim you serve?"

Estin shook his head.

"Their ways are not ours. I was told that they prove their worthiness to an animal by killing it. Ulra must have looked really dangerous."

Sighing, Feanne knelt in front of the kits.

"Oria...Atall...I want you both to watch. A pack-leader cannot back down if challenged. As soon as I back down, the leadership of this pack is lost."

Oria nodded nervously, eyeing the human as he tossed off his fur mantle, striding around the open field in the snow, bare-chested.

"What if you get hurt?" asked Atall, perhaps a little too loud.

"I will be fine," she told him, then looked up at Estin. "If he somehow wins, then Estin will take care of you and leave the camp."

"As you wish, pack-leader," Estin said, knowing he was not to speak during official matters of the pack leadership unless addressed. "They will come to no harm."

Feanne took Estin's hand and squeezed it thankfully, then cast off her cloak and strode into the area where Bockkan strutted back and forth, drawing cheers from his own people. Already, a crowd had gathered from all ends of the camp, though most looked on with a tense and radiant nervousness. This was the first time anyone had openly challenged Feanne's leadership and many in the camp were likely waiting for the moment to finally arrive so they could see if she could back up her attitude with skill.

"What are our terms?" Feanne asked, flexing her hands and examining her claws.

"Terms? This I do not understand."

"May we use any abilities at our disposal, or just our weapons?"

The human's eyes drifted from Feanne's claws, to her face—likely her fangs.

"You may use any ability you possess that is not magic. I have heard rumors of your skill in magic and this is not something I would willingly face as a true warrior."

Feanne smiled grimly, nodding agreement.

The barbarian drew his sword, tossing aside the sheath as he picked up a simple wooden shield.

"Attack when ready, little fox."

The two paced one another, the human relaxed and waited to see what his opponent could do, while the much smaller Feanne circled him, studying muscle movements and the way he held his weapon. Neither was armored, with Feanne wearing basic leathers and a fur mantle and Bockkan in his thick furred pants.

"You wait to deceive me, fox," Bockkan said, laughing as he turned. "We will wait all day if you do not learn to fight like a true warrior. I will not let you use your trickery on me."

Estin winced as Feanne reacted to the jibe, rushing in recklessly. Her claws glanced off Bockkan's shield and he slashed wildly, very nearly taking Feanne's head off as she dodged out of the way, regaining a safe distance from him.

"Will she get hurt?" Atall asked, tugging at Estin's hand. "I don't want mom to get hurt."

"She'll be fine," Estin told the child, watching as Feanne slapped aside another sweep of the sword, snarling as she kept her distance. "She's the best fighter I've ever met."

"Don't be so sure," whispered Linn, stepping up alongside Estin, giving Atall a playful flick on his ear. "Bockkan's killed more than a hundred men in battle and was the bane of my troop's existence for years. He does not want a woman—no matter what race—to tell him what to do. That's what this is about, have no doubts. His tribe does not allow women to lead."

Estin's mood sunk. He had hoped this was a simple dispute that would be resolved quickly, but that told him it was unlikely. He dearly hoped he would not have to get involved, as Feanne was always cross if he prevented her from getting all the glory in a battle. He had learned that when they had scouted out a small undead outpost several weeks earlier and he had used his magic to destroy many of the creatures, only to have Feanne lecture him for hours about having taken away her opportunities to tear them apart, though she had claimed it had something to do with being the leader.

Some things never change, he thought, watching as another flurry of blade, shield, and claws left both combatants uninjured.

"You spend too much time avoiding being hurt in combat," Bockkan chided as Feanne danced away again. "A true warrior would not be afraid of their enemy. You only prove my point."

Feanne bared her fangs, but continued to watch for an opening, having already tested the human's speed and found it a reasonable match for her own.

She lunged again, this time her claws raked Bockkan's shield as he drove her backwards with a stunning blow to the side of the head with the grip of his weapon. Feanne staggered away, holding her head and when she pulled her hand away, blood ran freely down the side of her face.

"She's in trouble," Oria told Estin, her little claws digging into his hand as she panicked. "Do something!"

"No," he told her, kneeling down so he was at face-level with both of the children. "No matter what happens, I won't go against what she told me to do."

"Because she's the pack-leader?" asked Atall, studying Estin's face.

"Sure," he said with a smile. "Would you cross your mother when she's upset?"

Atall and Oria grinned broadly, even as Feanne avoided Bockkan's weapon again, ducking his shield to rake his lead leg with her claws.

"Foxes are bad luck to my people," repeated Bockkan, swinging yet again and missing as Feanne moved under his weapon, raking his bare chest with her claws. Even that did not slow him. "If you are proven to be a dark spirit, all of the foxes must go."

"This," Estin noted, speaking to the kits, "is where things get ugly."

Feanne roared at Bockkan, her claws missing narrowly as he slashed at her, leaving a bloodied line across her leg with his sword.

"She's losing," Oria whimpered.

"Your mother is fine."

"How many times can she get cut before you think she's in trouble, Estin?"

He looked up at Feanne as she stumbled away, one hand on her leg to slow the bleeding.

"A lot more than that, if she's upset enough."

Feanne stopped backpedaling and held her ground, furiously clawing at Bockkan, until he was forced back, bleeding from dozens of minor wounds. Despite the severity of his injuries, he grinned and laughed, slapping his sword against his shield in challenge, only to have the shield fall to the ground, the straps having been cut by Feanne's claws.

"Clever fox."

This time, Feanne was more cautious in her attack, striking from every odd angle Estin could imagine, but Bockkan was faster, managing to avoid or deflect most of her attacks, then countering with a single slash that caught Feanne across the stomach, sending a spray of blood across the crowd as she collapsed.

Half-crawling, Feanne tried to get some distance from her opponent, only to have him grab her by the scruff of the neck. Unceremoniously, Bockkan drove his weapon through her back, pulling it out and raising it high over his head as Feanne fell to the ground.

"The fox is not so tough without her tricks!" announced Bockkan, waving his sword in the air in victory. "You will all listen to my orders now!"

"Mom!" Oria gasped, as Feanne crawled a foot or two, clutching her chest.

"Trust in her," Estin told both children, holding them to keep them from getting in the way. "She's not done yet."

As he expected—but had hoped would not be needed—Feanne curled up on the ground, letting loose a low growl as her body trembled. The sound of breaking bones drew Bockkan and the childrens' shocked stares, as Feanne's body changed rapidly.

"Mom?" whined Atall, wide-eyed.

"Shhhhh," Estin whispered, smiling. "You need to know what your mother really is. She's a lot stronger than you know."

When Feanne reared back up, she had changed into her huge fox-like lycanthrope form, the rage from her injuries having overtaken her control over the change, though all of her previous wounds had closed. Roaring loudly enough that even Bockkan stumbled away from her, she rushed back into the fray, batting Bockkan aside with one massive hand.

Bockkan reeled from the first hit, his arm hanging limply at his side. Striking back with his sword, he stumbled as Feanne grabbed the weapon and threw it aside, pulling it easily from his grasp.

Backhanding Bockkan, Feanne howled as the man tumbled away, clutching his chest, where deep gouges bled profusely.

"Do you yield?" roared Feanne, shaking as though it were an immense strain to keep from attacking. Even the act of speaking seemed difficult for her in this form.

"This," grunted Bockkan, regaining his footing, "is why I had hoped to fight you, little fox. Nature does not just bless you."

The man let forth a roar of his own, the cry as feral and animalistic as any Estin had heard. Around him, shadows seemed to flow together, creating an illusory form around him that reminded Estin of the way the Miharon had appeared. In this case, the silhouette around Bockkan was that of a massive bear. Into this dark shape Bockkan's human body disappeared and only the shadow-bear remained.

The two crashed together, dissuading any pretense of Bockkan's form being anything less than solid. Claws tore into each with a ferocity that made Estin sick to his stomach, the two ripping at the other without any regard for their own safety. Defense and avoidance was forgotten in favor of brutal devastation.

The cries and howls of the two finally died down as Feanne kicked Bockkan away from her, sending him tumbling to the ground, even as her own massive wounds closed. The bear attempted to stand again, but fell back down, the shadows fading and falling away from Bockkan's human body.

"I yield," groaned Bockkan, struggling back to his knees. Blood ran freely between his fingers as he held his chest. "Nature has blessed you well beyond me. You are my better and I am willing to admit it. You fight as no fox I have seen."

Long beyond reason, Feanne roared and rushed at the human, striking at him and flinging him back almost ten feet, where he hit the ground hard, then collapsed.

"Stay here," Estin ordered the kits, then ran onto the field of battle, stepping in front of Feanne.

"Feanne," he said calmly, wishing that he had some inclination that she might not maul him, too. "Feanne, I need you to stop."

Dark animalistic eyes stared at him as she roared yet again, her fangs dangerously close to his face. She brought back her arms, apparently ready to tear him apart as well.

Estin held his ground, dearly wishing he felt as confident about her self-restraint as he was trying to let the kits believe he was. Fear gripped his stomach, knowing that if she saw him as even a slight threat, there were good odds that she would tear him apart. She had mentioned in passing that such a thing could easily happen if she was far enough into her rage. Now, he had to test that and it did not thrill him to do so.

Feanne eyed him for a long time, growling as she tried to intimidate him so that she could get by and attack Bockkan again. Eventually, the instincts of her lycanthrope form began to waver in the face of exhaustion and she sat down, though in her current state, she was still as tall as Estin.

"Let it go," he ordered her, refusing to look away as she stared angrily into his eyes. "This is over."

Staring right back, Feanne growled, but backed down. She did not even react when others of Bockkan's clan came running to his aid, tending to his injuries.

"Come back to me, Feanne," Estin told her, slowly approaching her. Her white teeth bared briefly as he came near, but she let him get close, until he was able to touch her face. "This is done. Let it go."

Feanne closed her eyes and began to change back, her body wracked by convulsions as her bones reshaped themselves and her body returned to its normal shape and size. When it was over, she lay panting, staring blankly at the ground, just barely conscious.

"Mom!" screamed Atall, racing over and dropping beside her, with Oria a few steps behind. "Are you okay?"

Smiling weakly, Feanne looked up at her children, pulling them to her as she rolled onto her back in the snow. With both kits held to her chest, she gazed up at Estin.

"Thank you," she told him, then passed out.

Estin glanced around at the crowd, waiting until all of them had taken a knee, acknowledging Feanne as the victor. Even the barbarians knelt, aside from Bockkan, who was unconscious and being tended to. Once every last person had given their indication that the fight was over, Estin slid his arms under Feanne and picked her up, carrying her towards her tent, with the kits following at his heels, followed by Ulra.

Once he had gotten her onto her bedding, Estin checked Feanne's remaining wounds, finding little of immediate concern. The change had healed her body almost completely, just as it had the one previous time he had seen it, though this time the price was taken in exhaustion, rather than blood.

"What was that?" Ulra demanded, hunkered down in the tent. "They will demand answers."

"That was your pack-leader," said Estin, unwilling to look away from Feanne. He sent Atall to fetch some cool water, while Oria clung to her mother's hand. "Do not question what she has to do to protect her pack. If you question her, the rest will, too."

Grumbling loudly, Ulra left the tent, even as Atall came back in, carrying a half-spilled bowl of water. He offered this to Estin, then backed away from both Estin and his mother.

Estin lifted Feanne slowly, raising the water to her mouth. At first, the cool water ran off her fur, but she began drinking soon enough, stirring as it soothed her.

"What happened?" Feanne gasped, her eyes still closed, but she pushed the water away. "Are we all right?"

"You are," said Estin, checking the children, who were both looking very much terrified. "The kits I think would like an explanation."

Feanne groaned and opened her eyes weakly.

"Atall...Oria...did you see what happened out there?"

Both kits nodded vigorously.

"Estin, you will leave us. I would explain to my children what I really am."

"As you wish, pack-leader."

He got up and began to leave them alone, but Feanne caught his ankle, holding him firmly.

"Thank you for not interfering," she told him softly, then released his foot.

"Not my place to do so, Feanne."

Walking from the tent, Estin stood guard at the door for the next half hour, as he heard vague discussions inside. He made an active effort to ignore them, instead focusing on those who passed by, trying to keep anyone else from getting close enough to intrude or listen in. The air soon chilled him deeply, but this was his post until further notice.

Eventually, Oria and Atall came out, running past Estin and off into the camp without a word. He watched them go, wondering what to do, when finally Feanne called him back inside.

"I am sorry for sending you out," Feanne told him as he sat down on his bedding on the far side of the tent. "I wanted them to hear it from me first, without anyone else."

Estin nodded and watched Feanne for any sign of lingering harm, but she seemed to be recovering quickly.

"Why did the Miharon let you change?"

Laughing sadly, Feanne shrugged.

"He's probably dead. His woods were where we lost the last camp. I haven't heard his call in a very long time, Estin. The power over the change is mine alone, now."

Estin sat there a long time, just watching Feanne, who stared absently at the floor of the room, occasionally picking at drying blood in her fur.

"Will this happen every time you are angry or in pain?"

That caught her attention and she looked at him, cocking her head.

"I do not think so. As weak as I am now, I doubt much could get me to change again soon. It may just be something that happens every so often, if I am in enough danger. I am quite sure if I tried again, the strain would likely kill me."

Estin noted that the children still had not returned.

"Where did the kits go?"

"They are mad at me for hiding what I am from them. They're afraid that they are like me and just don't know it yet. I did not get the chance to explain to them that this was something given just to me. It would not be a part of them. They mentioned that they would go stay with the gypsies for now, which may be for the best, until they are ready to listen more to me."

"You're probably right. They'll need to come to grips with what they saw. Now, I need to make sure you're not more hurt than you want me to believe."

"Estin..."

Easing himself closer, Estin looked to Feanne's wounds, despite her attempts to shove him away. His duties he knew were clear and so he used her weakness to make sure that she was not hiding any lasting damage from him. Once he had gotten her to lay back down and stop fighting him, he was able to check the various places he had seen her cut, but found only small gashes. Only the sword strike that had passed straight through her chest was still in bad shape, the puncture on her back still bleeding slightly. When he went to check where the sword had come through just below her right breast, Feanne grabbed his hand and stopped him more firmly.

"You are quickly moving past being my guard and healer," she warned, her tone low.

"I can close the wound," he reminded her, touching her shoulder. "Just say the word."

Feanne checked the tent door, where Ulra had taken up a watch, her fur recognizable each time a breeze made the tent flap move. The air was chill, yet not too bad considering that it was far into winter already.

"Do not heal me," she finally told him, taking his hand in hers. "I need to learn from my mistakes."

"Cuts are the least of the mistakes we've made," he answered, pulling his hand free.

He started to move back to his side of the tent, wishing he had kept his mouth shut. He longed to have kept his hand in hers, but knew that what he wanted was not within his right to ask for. Distancing himself was safest.

They were both silent for a long time, Feanne staring blankly at the tent's entrance, as Estin lay down on his bedding, watching the fabric of the tent overhead, wavering from the winds outside. Distantly, he swore he could hear the gypsies singing.

"I deserved that," Feanne said at last, breaking the silence within the tent.

Clutching her chest wound, she walked over to him, lying down on the ground beside his bedding. The proximity was something she had expressly forbidden except when he was healing her, so Estin felt acutely uncomfortable with her presence, but he said nothing. She was his pack-leader and he did not want to tell her what—and what not—to do. Still, he readied himself to move away if she became concerned about their proximity.

"Do you still wish we were together, Estin?"

He closed his eyes and rubbed his face, wishing he could go somewhere else. As her personal guard, running away was generally frowned on.

"What I wish is long gone," he answered eventually, trying not to notice her saddened expression. "You said it yourself. You've told me twice since then that I need to find a female to settle down with. I'm working on that, as you've ordered."

"No, you aren't. I am not an idiot, Estin. Please do not act as though you can convince me that you have moved on. I have sent you away many nights and my eyes and ears in camp tell me that you stay within sight of this tent the whole time."

Feanne put an arm over his chest, pulling herself close to him, actually lying down on part of his bedding. Gently, she lay her head on his shoulder, closing her eyes and relaxing, even as Estin felt poised to run.

"Please just hold me. The kits will be gone a while. I am too tired to keep up this game. Maybe tomorrow, but not today. Perhaps with the morning I can manage to lecture you for letting me this near."

They lay there much of the night, Feanne holding him tightly, while he stared at the ceiling, trying to determine what she really wanted of him. It was awkward and hurt him to expose those feelings again, so he kept them under guard, shielding himself by ignoring that she lay so close. Eventually, even his defenses wore down and he pulled her closer, letting her sleep on his chest. It was so calming, so natural, and that was the first real sleep he had gotten in a very long time, not worrying about whether she was safe.

When Estin woke, Feanne still lay at his side, but something was not right in the tent. He stirred, blinking to get his day-vision back. On the third blink, he realized that Atall and Oria stood over them, both staring with wide eyes. Before he could even open his mouth to speak, Atall took off running, with Oria not far behind.

"What?" Feanne asked, sitting up just in time to look around and see Oria's tail vanish through the tent flap. "What just happened?"

"The kits saw us together."

Feanne groaned and shoved herself away from Estin, covering her face in frustration.

"I really cannot make mistakes like this."

"Feanne, we did not do anything."

She shrugged and got up.

"My children don't know that, Estin. I've made a mistake that I cannot repeat. It will take some time to win back their trust. If I ever believe I need company again, I trust that you will be my strength in refusing. I task you with making sure I never allow another male into my bed again—whether yourself or someone else—if only to keep from having to explain this to the kits. I owe it to them to not let my heart wander."

Biting back his anger at himself, Estin just told her, "I'll go find them and make it right, pack-leader."

Getting to his feet, he hurried from the tent, using the excuse to get some air and vent his own frustrations. He shoved past Ulra, thankful that she had no questions for him as he left.

Estin walked slowly through the camp, not in any particular hurry to find the kits. They knew better than to go far and were likely hiding out at one of their friends' tents, trying to sort out what they had walked in on. Sex was not a taboo topic to wildlings—even as young as they were, the kits probably understood all the fundamentals—but he doubted they had been at all prepared to see their mother with anyone. Seeing her with her guard—practically a servant—was a slap in the face to their memory of their father, he rationalized.

In his own head, the night was just as disturbing as it likely was for the kits. He had been so strong for months, suppressing his feelings, without exposing his need for Feanne even once in his duties as her guard. Deep down, he knew that if he was to truly protect her, he needed to distance himself from those feelings, as they would only make him make mistakes.

Now tonight, it was her that slipped, letting him know that for all her stubborn refusal to allow him near her, she still might hold much the same desires for him. That was not as refreshing as he had once hoped it would be, just serving to muddy his mind and his reactions. These days, he needed her to be strong for the pack, without regard for the feelings he hoped might one day fade. Nights like this only prolonged the time that would take.

He took his time wandering the camp, sniffing every so often to make sure he was still following the twins. Estin had no doubts that they were upset and he wanted to be sure they got enough time to relax before he came walking up on them.

When he did finally reach the end of their scent-trail, Estin was rather surprised to find himself at the gypsy wagons. He had not even thought that the kits might come back here. This area of the camp was always lively and loud, not really the mood he expected the kits wanted after their surprise. Strangely, the usual laughter and singing from this part of the village was replaced with nervous whispers and someone shouting, though the voice was muffled by the wagons themselves.

Nervously, Estin ran into the middle of the ring of wagons.

At one side of the open space where the gypsies held their nightly celebrations and kept their campfire, Atall and Oria were standing in front of Yoska, whose back was to a wagon. A dozen gypsies stood in a half-circle around the kits, weapons drawn on them, even as Atall held his own blade to Yoska's chest.

"This is your fault!" the kit was saying as Estin came up. "You gave him the idea."

Estin froze as he grasped what he had just walked up on. Atall believed that Estin had bedded his mother on the recommendation of Yoska's stories about multiple spouses. The boy had always been more shocked than his sister at the tales. Now, he was looking for someone to be angry with.

"Atall, please put it down," Oria pleaded, watching the other gypsies closely. She looked terrified, which Estin had to think was justified with so many weapons pointed at her brother's back. "This isn't right...just let him go."

"Your sister is wise," Yoska said calmly, though he winced as Atall's knife dug a little deeper into his stomach. "Perhaps you tell me what I have done. Is much easier to decide if I have wronged you if I know why you are stabbing me, no?"

"Atall!" Estin yelled as he walked up, hoping to draw the child's attention to himself. In the past, Atall had been far easier to intimidate into abandoning a course of action than his sister. "Turn over your weapon immediately!"

"I won't listen to you," said the boy, glaring angrily at Estin. "It's this human's fault that mother betrayed father. If you come any closer, I'll stab him, then you!"

Estin looked over at Yoska, who gave him a confused shrug. The man seemed remarkably unconcerned, despite his whole clan being on alert, ready to kill Atall the moment they got the chance.

Walking more slowly, Estin had to almost push his way through the other gypsies, some of whom muttered angry threats at him in passing. As he got closer to Atall, he unbuckled his belt and tossed it aside, along with the swords it bore.

"I'm unarmed," he said to Atall, holding up his hands so that the kit could see that his claws had not even fully regrown. They were usable, but likely could not cause any appreciable damage and were certainly no match for the long knife Atall bore. "We need to talk."

Atall whipped his knife away from Yoska, marching towards Estin with the blade pointed at him. Immediately, gypsies filled the gap between him and Yoska.

"I loved you," the boy told him angrily. "Just because you and mom are friends, doesn't mean you can bed her while father's gone. I should kill you for it, but I want him to do it when he returns."

"Atall," said Oria, her voice shaking. "Stop."

Estin held his hands out at his sides, inviting Atall to strike. If nothing else, he knew that would ensure that no one else was getting hurt. How the boy felt was his fault, after all. His first thought was to prepare magic that would mend his body if Atall got lucky and stabbed him, but he disregarded it as unfair to Atall and likely would be too obvious and slow to work, anyway. If the boy wanted to stab him for what he had done, he could not take that away from him.

"I have never disrespected your mother," Estin said, taking another step forward. Atall's blade was now only a foot away. He began evaluating whether he could snatch the knife away without risking either of them. "My life is hers."

Atall trembled with rage. The boy had always been angry, but had never been good at venting it. Now, he seemed to have found his target in Estin. He raised his knife, ready to strike.

"Atall, father is dead."

The anger practically fell out of Atall as he looked back at his sister, looking terrified.

"You're lying!"

Oria shook her head, telling him, "I saw it, Atall. He died saving us. Please don't hurt Estin."

"If he is dead, you made it happen!" Atall screamed at Estin, waving the knife. "You're trying to take mother from him!"

Estin swallowed hard as the knife skimmed his stomach with Atall's last swing, the fine blade easily slicing through his shirt.

"Your mother is devoted to your father and to you, not to me," he admitted, looking up to see Oria's ears flatten back, her eyes on the cut in his clothing. "If there was anything between us, that was before she met your father."

Atall seemed to struggle for a moment, then tensed as one of the gypsies tried to jump at him. He twisted, trying to stab at his attacker, but the blade glanced across Estin's stomach, brushing firmly enough that Estin felt pressure from the blade.

Trying to get the gypsies to stop wrestling the weapon from Atall's hands, Estin tried to shout, but his voice just would not come. He gasped for breath, then looked down to see that his stomach was pouring blood onto the ground. He had forgotten how sharp the kits' weapons were. Numbly, he tried to apply pressure to the long gash, but blood just poured through his fingers.

Unable to breathe or speak, Estin collapsed, his magic uselessly trapped in his own head.

*

Estin came to slowly, pain flooding his stomach as he became gradually aware of his surroundings. Above him stood Feanne, Oria, and an orc female that he did not know. It was the orc who was applying pressure to his wounds and whispering familiar words over the injuries to slow the bleeding.

"He will live," the green-skinned female stated as Estin opened his eyes, the flickering light of torches dancing off her eyes and white tusks. "The wound was deep, but I have done what I can to close it. Let him rest and keep him away from sharp things."

The orcish woman excused herself and left the tent, leaving Estin alone with Feanne and Oria. Though Oria looked terrified as she knelt beside him, it was Feanne that drew his attention. Her face was wet and she was clutching his hand so tightly that his knuckles ached.

"Is Atall alright?" he asked, surprising himself with his raspy voice.

"Yes," Feanne answered, a tear running into her fur. "He has given up his weapon and demanded that Ulra cage him until you are well enough to properly punish him for attacking you."

Estin tried to sit up, but pain flared through his gut and he fell back, with Feanne applying pressure to his chest to keep him down.

"Don't push yourself," Feanne ordered him. "When I got to you, the gypsies were all that was holding your stomach in. You are lucky to be breathing. Had we not gotten to you soon enough, I doubt we could have found another healer who could mend your injuries in time."

Estin brought his other hand up and squeezed back on Feanne's hand, then reached over and wiped a tear off Oria's cheek.

"Why are you crying?" he asked, smiling at the girl, trying to keep his mood light for her sake. "You weren't the one who got stabbed."

"Atall hates us both right now. I don't think he believes either of us and he thinks I'm lying just to save you. He really doesn't want to believe dad is dead."

"Then he will be angry until he accepts it, but he needs to be mad at the undead, not me and certainly not Yoska."

"You will need to talk to him about that," Feanne added. "Right now, he will not talk to anyone. The last he said after Ulra caged him was that he will wait for you to speak with him. I think he expects you to demand he be punished…he may even think he'll be executed for this. I made some stupid declaration a while back that an attack on my guards would result in execution, after Bockkan first suggested skinning Ulra."

"Then help me go to him. I won't have him sitting in a cage, while I lay here."

Feanne began to argue, but gave in as Estin continued to struggle to sit up. Finally, she gave Oria the order to help and they got under Estin's shoulders, helping him stand.

He was shaky on his feet and as soon as he was upright, his stomach began bleeding slowly, but Estin was unwilling to lay back down. Feanne even tried to order him to wait through the night, but Estin told her that he was fully intending to disobey her, drawing a teary-eyed promise of a flogging once he had recovered.

The woman and child helped him limp his way from the tent, where he found Ulra sitting guard closer to a wooden-framed cage than to the tent. The cage was built much the same way that Finth's cage had been when he was first captured…ironically, Finth also stood guard with Ulra near the cage, giving Estin a dark stare as he approached.

Inside the cage, Atall was curled up in a ball, his face covered by his arms as he lay on his side.

"The kid doesn't need guests," said Finth, stepping in front of them as they neared the cage. "He needs time to think about stabbing people who care about him and what some people might do to him if he ever even thinks about doing it again."

"Move," Estin ordered Finth, who spit on the ground, then stormed away.

Estin had the women ease him to a seated position with his back against the cage, then told them all to leave him.

"I'm not going to leave you out here," Feanne told him, kneeling in front of him and examining his bleeding stomach again. "You'll need help getting back to the tent and it is cold tonight."

"I'll stay here tonight," he replied, pulling her hands away from the wound. "Please, Feanne."

She hesitated, but finally took Oria and Ulra, the three returning to Feanne's tent, though Estin did not doubt that they were listening and possibly watching.

"I understand why you are angry, Atall."

The kit grumbled and curled tighter.

"I'm not trying to take your mother away from you. Your father was a good man, who wanted all of you to be safe. He died trying to make that happen. If I could give my life to give him back to you, I would do it without hesitation."

Atall finally sat up, moving to the edge of the wooden bars so that he could look over Estin.

"Did I hurt you badly?"

"Yes." Estin was too tired to lie or attempt to mislead the child. "I'll heal, though."

The silence between them was palpable for a time, until Atall spoke again.

"My dad told me to never trust you. He said you were trying to destroy our family."

"Do you believe that's true, Atall?"

"No. I just wanted so badly for my dad to come back, I had to believe he was alright somewhere. You saved us so many times, I'd decided that he might have been wrong. Then, when I saw you with mom, I heard all the things dad had said. You were mom's guard though, so I had to lash out at someone."

"Yoska."

"Yep. I really didn't want to hurt anyone. I was just mad."

"I know. Sorry for getting in the way of the knife."

Atall laughed weakly.

"If my dad's really dead, I have no right to do the things I did out there tonight. It wasn't right to stab you. Mom can do what she wants now. I'm sorry."

Estin turned to be able to look at Atall, reaching through the bars to touch his arm gently.

"Your mother only cares about you two. Nothing else matters. I'll resign from her guard as soon as I'm better. I don't want you to ever have to worry again."

Atall looked up, his face angry again.

"Don't! I don't want to see you and mom purring or licking each other or anything, but I don't feel safe without you around. I want you to stay with us, Estin. I won't promise that I won't freak out again, but I'll try..."

Estin chuckled despite his pain.

"I'll stay, then. At least you've only cut me once. You've got a lot of catching up to your mother to do."

"She's cut you?! On purpose?"

"Not always. She taught me to fight, before I learned how to heal people. Your mother beat me senseless so many times..."

Atall giggled and leaned back against Estin through the bars.

"Would you...would you stay and tell me about the things you two have been through? Dad said that you and mom traveled together before the war got going. Will you tell me about it?"

"Anything you ask."

Estin sat through the night, leaning against the bars of Atall's cage, telling him the stories of his first meetings with Feanne, her methods for teaching him how to fight, and even a little about the forest spirit she once served. Towards dawn, Atall even begged to be told about the battle for Insrin's village from Estin's perspective, which Estin saw no reason not to share, now that Feanne had shown her "gift" to the camp.

Atall listened to it all with amazement, asking few questions, but his face bunched up in confusion a few times, seemingly catching Estin when he left out uncomfortable details—such as why Insrin had disliked him so much. Luckily, the boy did not appear to notice Estin's exclusion of the winter storm after his training and the time he and Feanne spent together.

When dawn finally did break, Atall at last had dozed off in the cage, while Estin still sat alongside, stroking the boy's curled fur around his brows. At his touch, Atall began mumbling softly in his sleep.

Estin watched the boy sleep, keeping his free hand pressed against his stomach to slow his bleeding until he had the strength to heal himself properly.

As he brushed the child's face again, Atall caught his hand and stared dully up at him, barely opening his eyes.

"You can stay with her," he whispered, yawning loudly. "I'm sorry."

"I won't do anything to hurt you and your sister."

Atall curled up again, mumbling as he drifted back towards sleep, "If I can't have my dad back, I wish you could be my dad."

Wordless, Estin just stared at the child, trying to find some sense in his suddenly jumbled thoughts. Before he could shake the shock of Atall's words, Feanne's voice startled him into looking away.

"Will he be safe to release?" asked Feanne, sitting down beside him. She hesitated and her ears twitched as she looked at Estin. "What's wrong?"

"Nothing…he'll be fine."

Eyeing him as though she knew he was lying to her, Feanne cut the straps that held the cage closed and picked up her son, carrying him into her tent. Estin could hear some talking inside the tent, then she came back several minutes later, putting one of Estin's arms over her shoulder as she helped him up.

They hobbled into the tent, where Estin stopped as he realized that his bedding had been stolen by the children. They had dragged all of his blankets and furs over near Feanne's, then curled up together on his blankets.

Over where Estin's bedding should have been, Ulra lay curled up, snoring softly.

Estin began to pull towards one of the few empty parts of the tent near the low embers of the fire, intending to at least catch some sleep on the ground, but Feanne would not let him walk away.

"The children insist," she told him, easing him down onto her own bedding. "They said that they want you closer to protect us all, like Ulra suggested. I could not argue...they made me promise. It's nothing more than that, but you will be sharing my bedding at least until you heal, or until the children ask me to move you. Atall was most firm in his demands."

Though uncomfortable—especially with the pain in his stomach—Estin lay down as instructed, feeling somewhat guilty as Feanne lay down beside him, being careful not to bump his wound. He tried to object one more time, but she clamped her fingers over his jaw momentarily, preventing him from opening it to talk.

"I'm tired and you're disturbing the children," she told him, yawning as she lay her head on his chest. She nestled her claws into his chest fur. "Go to sleep. You are no good to me as a guard if you're too tired to heal yourself tomorrow."

"As you wish, pack-leader."

"Shut up, Estin."

Chapter Twelve

"Cold, then Hot"

It always amazed me with how life could change without warning. One day, I had to lie to myself and the world about how I felt towards Feanne. The next, I still had to be just her friend, but even her children knew we meant more to each other than that. Atall practically insisted on his mother and I staying close.

Yoska, I was sure, would never let me live it down. Whenever he saw us, he would remind me of his stories of finding true love after a half-dozen marriages and not regretting a moment of the journey. Early on, I had thought the man mad. I had begun to think of him as conniving, instead.

My dreams were my own again.

I could see the war as a backdrop for the stories in my head, but it was something to be dealt with as required. Feanne and I would lead the children safely through it all, sometimes with the whole pack at our sides, sometimes the dream would take its price on our friends and allies.

Through it all though, I had the feeling of that leash still around my neck. No matter how I tried, I could never seem to figure out who held the other end.

"Healer, we need you now!" came the call outside the tent, as Estin shoved what remained of his breakfast into his mouth, nearly choking on the orange pastry. The obscure breakfast had been made by Alafa's father as an apology for earlier behavior after Estin had helped another member of their family with a badly-broken arm.

He had hoped to grab some sleep with the sun rising, but instead he ran out into the day, finding the camp devolving into chaos. People were running rampant, though everyone was running either towards or away from the west end of camp. Whoever had called him had already disappeared, leaving him to figure out the crisis on his own as he stood shivering in the snow, not having had time to throw on a cloak or other garment to keep him reasonably warm.

Estin took a moment and recognized those who were fleeing versus those who were trying to get to the problem. He joined those running westward, where a wide line had formed, shielding the camp against approach from the outside.

He pushed through the line, finding half a dozen warriors encircling a huge beast.

Scaled and easily as long as ten grown men standing straight end-to-end, the lizard-like monster roared at the armed warriors, trying to snap at those who got too close. Near its clawed front feet lay an orc, her shoulder mauled and bleeding into the trampled snow around her.

"What is that?" Estin asked of one of the nearer warriors, a dwarf who was keeping his pike aimed at the creature. "And where did it come from?"

"Rock dragon," the man answered. "There's a few nests in the mountains. One's in our cozy valley."

Nearby, Feanne directed the warriors, urging them to drive the dragon back far enough that the fallen orc could be retrieved. Though they tried, the animal refused to leave the body.

"Has anyone else ever fought one of these?" Linn called out from one side of the warrior line. This was the first time Estin had seen him armored and about since they had arrived at the campsite. From what he had heard, Linn had leapt right into active duty, aiding the patrols and taking charge of training the newer arrivals in the arts of defending a city.

No one answered the human and he cursed, backing out of the line.

"I need a shield and a sword," demanded Linn, tossing aside the boar-spear he had been wielding, then flicking the clasp on his heavy winter cloak to let it drop onto the ground. He adjusted his belt to hold his chain shirt more snugly. Several of the bystanders ran off, apparently to find him the requested gear. "I'll need two people who can make a lot of noise. No one comes near it but me."

Seconds later, people were throwing shields and various swords at Linn's feet, while the other warriors continued to harass the rock dragon, at least keeping it from dragging off the woman's body.

"Rock dragons aren't very smart," explained Linn to Feanne, who helped him strap on his shield, while Estin dug through the swords and found him one that was in decent condition. "We grew up with a nest near our village. Takes three or more people to bring one down, but only one needs to fight it."

Linn tested the weighting of his gear, taking a couple slashes with the sword to be sure of its feel. Once he had everything the way he wanted it, he marched back into the line, near the middle.

"Lots of noise on either side!" he shouted, the dragon hissing and glaring at him.

The warriors on the far ends of the pike-line began shouting, whistling and making whatever sounds they could. The dragon growled and began looking back and forth between the two sides, backing away slowly, seemingly unable to decide which end of the line was more dangerous.

"Wish me luck," Linn told Estin, raising his sword.

While Estin watched from the sides, Linn dove into the fray, using the slick ground to slide to a stop nearly over top of the fallen orcish woman. The dragon hissed at him, but kept its attention darting between the noisier members of the line.

Linn unleashed a rapid series of strikes at the dragon, though most were deflected by its horns and thick skull. He pressed on, pausing to absorb with his shield the creature's attempts to bite him, then pushing on. Every few attacks, he would get an easy blow to its neck as the creature would look around at the people shouting at it, drawing blood each time.

Twice, some of the other warriors began to step in, but Linn ordered them back. When the warriors who were supposed to be shouting would stop, the dragon would focus in on Linn, driving him back and preventing him from delivering so much as a scratch to the beast. It did not take long before his shield was bent and pieces of the edge were torn away.

Easing his way quietly into the fray, Estin kept his head low and crept towards the body, while Linn continued to push back against the dragon. It took Estin a while, doing everything in his power to look unthreatening as he inched forward, until at last he could touch the fallen woman. When he did finally get close enough, he checked her and found that she was barely breathing. Much longer and she would have died.

Reaching out to the spirits, Estin let the magic flow into the woman, feeling her pulse strengthen almost immediately. Once he was sure she would not die, he grabbed hold of her and began dragging her away, eliciting a roar from the dragon, though Linn intercepted it, holding it back.

Once Estin was far enough back, Feanne grabbed the woman's other arm, helping him get her to safety.

"We're clear, Linn!" Estin called over his shoulder, trying not to be louder than the shouters.

Linn began backing away from the dragon, but it tried to jump on him, belying its size with how swiftly it struck. It bowled Linn over and clawed at his body, while trying to get its jaws onto his head. Through it all, Linn kept the shield on top of himself, struggling against the weight of the beast.

"Tend to her, I've got this," Feanne said, rushing out onto the field.

With a wave of her hands, thick root-like vines reached up from the ground, entangling the dragon and dragging it back off of Linn. Almost as soon as the vines grabbed at the dragon, it started kicking and flailing, tearing the vines to shreds, but this gave Linn enough time to reach his feet.

Linn delivered one final thrust of his weapon as the dragon struggled with the last of the vines, driving the blade into the creature's neck. He held the weapon there as the dragon fought for a few more seconds, then collapsed.

"I hate these things," noted Linn, leaning on his sword. "I'm just so glad I've never had more than one attack at the same time."

With his patient stable, Estin joined Feanne as they approached Linn, who sat down hard on the ground, kicking away his shield.

"So this is a dragon?" Feanne said, touching the still animal. She walked its length, studying it as she went. "Impressive creature."

Linn shook his head.

"Not really. Same type of creature, but barely a dragon. The legends say dragons are a lot bigger, but they haven't been seen in a couple hundred years, if they ever existed. This is more like a tough lizard. If it was a real dragon, I would have been the first one running."

Estin took his own turn admiring the beast, sitting beside Linn. From there, he could stare up at the massive jaws and razor teeth. He realized that if it had managed to get a solid bite on Linn, the fight would have been over immediately. Shaking his head at the idea of going near anything like that, he headed back to find the orcish woman beginning to stir.

Estin knelt beside her, listening as the barely conscious woman groaned one word over and over. At first, he could not quite make it out, but as she got stronger, the word became more clear.

"Undead..."

The word rather surprised Estin. Any other time it would have terrified him, but with the dragon lying dead nearby, he was not expecting it this time.

"You were attacked by a dragon," he said to the woman, checking her for fever or other injuries.

"No," she grunted, shoving Estin away. "Dragon got me coming back. Got sloppy."

"How many?"

The woman groaned and shook her head.

"Ten, or so. Don't think they saw me."

"Were you alone out there?"

"No," she said, shaking her head and trying to sit up. "Left Finth out there. He's making sure they don't get closer."

Estin waved down several of the people who had been standing around.

"Get her back to camp and make sure she's taken to one of the other healers."

The men and women agreed and helped the injured woman to her feet, leading her away.

"Feanne!" Estin called out, catching both her and Linn's attention. "We have a situation."

Feanne seemed to watch his face for just a moment, then her body language tensed and she practically dragged Linn over, with several of the pike-bearing warriors joining them.

"What's going on now?" she asked as she approached him. "Did you find out where the nest is?"

"Not even close. We have an undead incursion on the south end of the valley. She was coming to let us know when she found the dragon the hard way."

Linn whistled softly, shaking his head.

"Why was military service during a war less exciting than spending time with your people? I assume we're going to go save the valley?"

"We are," Feanne said, her voice angry. "Do we have eyes on them, or are we tracking the woman who was attacked?"

"Finth is out there. I can follow the woman's trail to the general area, but then we need to hope he's alive and still following the undead."

Feanne helped Estin to his feet and began towards the south, leading the mad rush for the southern narrow passage through the mountains that led back into the foothills. They were running hard, closing on the start of the south entrance to the valley within minutes.

When Estin checked behind him, they had a group of ten following them through the dense woods, all armed and grim-faced. He doubted that any of them had not lost a loved one or even their home cities to the undead war. It did not take much urging to get as many armed troops as they needed when the dead marched on them, or even the rumors surfaced that they might be.

The trip through the narrowed section of the valley took them more than half an hour, as the walls of the mountains closed in on both sides, but then began widening as they left the valley. They slowed at that point, with Estin and Feanne leading the way, pausing every so often to sniff the ground, check prints in the snow, or check the trees for indications of anyone passing through.

Estin found that the trail was meandering through the patches of trees, as though the woman and Finth had been collecting firewood from fallen branches. Finally, he reached a spot where the path of the woman's scent ended, her scent turning sharply back towards the valley, while Finth's continued onward, now directly southwest.

"We're close," he noted, hurrying his own pace.

The vague smell of death and decay began to grow stronger and when Estin looked to Feanne, her own nose crinkled with the awful scents. The farther they went, the worse the odor became.

"Stop tromping around like a golem with an itch," grumbled Finth, hiding amongst the trees. "Get over here!"

The group diverted into the trees, most of the warriors staying back a good distance so that they could get some cover from the thick trees.

"There's more than a dozen of them, just down the hill," Finth explained, pointing farther down the mountainside. "No directions, so they're just wandering around, trying to eat the squirrels and birds."

"They'll still report back to their masters the moment there's someone with control over them," Feanne reminded him.

Estin ignored them both as they discussed tactics and wondered aloud how the undead had gotten so far into the mountains without any leadership. Instead, he watched the hillside, where he could just make out the humanoid shapes, dark against the light snow-cover. They shambled slowly in various directions, one or another sometimes lurching after something, then groaning and resuming their walk in whatever direction they were then facing.

He could hear Feanne talking about rushing the undead after circling them to prevent any from escaping, but he felt something was not right. Sniffing the air, he picked up the faintest whiff of smoke and flame on the breeze.

"There's more out there than just these," he said to no one in particular, though he was not sure if they heard him. "We need higher ground. I need to see what else is moving in the woods."

Estin realized that Feanne and Finth were arguing and likely no one had heard him even talking. Their bickering over proper tactics for fighting a group of undead was not helping the situation in his opinion, so he just began walking away, heading up the slope of the mountain. In his mind, either they would follow, or they would still be arguing when he returned. Only Linn followed him, falling in at his side.

Though his feet kept slipping on the loose rock, Estin hurried his way up the sand and stone mountainside, until he got to a rock outcropping that would give him a good view overtop of most of the nearby trees. Hoisting himself the rock, he moved out to the edge, awed by the miles he could see to the south and east, with only part of the west blocked by mountains.

Linn came part way up the rise, but stopped and sat down when the path became too steep. He glanced occasionally up at Estin, but said nothing.

The undead just south of his position were not visible from his perch, but what he could see was a trail of smoke a little farther south, snaking its way for miles. Though he could not be sure, it appeared to be moving towards the undead and thus straight towards the valley.

Estin leapt off the rock, taking a nasty tumble on the loose ground. He got back to his feet as fast as he could, running back to where Feanne and Finth had very nearly come to a conclusion about their plans, with Linn trailing him the whole way.

"Stop arguing and shut up," he ordered the two, ignoring Feanne's shocked expression. He knew he would hear about it later, but he did not want to waste time right then. "There's something coming from the south. There's a smoke trail, like someone's burning the woods."

Feanne's annoyance at his interruption vanished in a flash as her ears went straight up in anger. If Estin knew her at all, he knew that the idea of the woods burning would become a priority, regardless of whether she still served the forest spirits.

"Approach cautiously," she told the group, waving them towards the south. "Do not engage until I give the order."

The group moved quickly, with Feanne leading the way as they skirted the group of undead. Even Finth nodded and began stalking southwards, keeping near the trees as he drew a long knife from somewhere in his fur jacket. In the rear of the group, Estin followed the others, his nose high as he tried to gather any extra information.

"Fan out," Feanne commanded softly, waving the warriors far and wide around the edges of the loose group of undead. Linn led the group of warriors, directing them around rougher terrain and open areas where they would be more easily seen.

The shambling corpses groaned softly, several stopping as though they had heard the living approach. Despite Finth's earlier statement that there were about a dozen, Estin could make out nearly twice as many, most scattered nearby and several practically dragging themselves, as their legs were damaged or missing entirely.

Crackling and a wave of smoke washed over their group, forcing them to the ground to avoid choking on the heated air. It was such a change from the icy winter air around that gust, that Estin felt as though his skin had been cooked in that brief moment.

When Estin looked up again, the undead had grouped up, running headlong into a line of blazing figures. The flaming humanoid shapes marched into the area, burning the ground bare behind them as they attacked the undead, the flames igniting the dry corpses as the two types of creatures grabbed at one another. Neither force held any weapons, using claws and flame to destroy their enemies instead.

"What the queen's ass is going on?" Finth asked, sitting down on the ground to watch the battle. "Since when do elementals give a squirrel poop about undead?"

Twenty of the flaming humans remained after burning the undead to ash, having lost only a couple of their own.

"They're likely bound by a wizard, or some other power," Feanne whispered back, motioning to the rest of the group to stay low. "If their orders are to destroy the undead, they'll obey completely and ignore us in the process."

Estin watched the elementals as they milled about, turning towards one larger flame elemental that stood nearly ten feet tall. He guessed that they were receiving new instructions. Seconds later, the whole group began to turn and leave, even as a cool mist fell across his back, dampening his fur.

The mist grew stronger and Estin looked around, even as the flame creatures came to an abrupt halt.

Coming up the eastern slope, more elementals flowed, rather than walked, their watery bodies soaking the ground as they moved. These were just barely humanoid, made entirely of water that shifted their appearance one moment to the next. In their passing, long streams of water steamed and re-froze, coating the mountainside in ice.

"Someone's been busy if they're controlling those, too."

Feanne turned around and followed where he was looking, then gasped.

"Everyone, run!" she exclaimed, getting to her feet and practically dragging Estin along. "This is about to get bad if we're caught in the middle!"

As their group stood, the fire elementals began marching towards them, the woods burning in their wake. The moment they saw the water elementals, the entire group turned, rushing into battle, as the water elementals did the same.

Estin and Feanne led the way, running for all they were worth as explosions rocked the hill behind them. Flames washed over the area, while water splashed into the trees and then instantly froze, shattering them. Every step became hazardous as the heat scalded them and debris flew by, pummeling their backs.

"Don't lead them back!" Feanne called, her voice mostly drowned out by the fires that were rapidly engulfing the woods and the deafening explosions of the breaking ice. "Get to high ground!"

Up they ran, detouring well past the entrance to the valley and up into the mountains proper. The ground became difficult very quickly, both from the steep slope and from the loose snow that coated it, but they pushed on, sometimes dragged upwards by Estin or others. He found himself pulling Feanne and many of the armored soldiers up the steep rise, as they had not been prepared for climbing.

They eventually reached a ledge high above the woods, where Feanne stopped driving them onwards and they all collapsed on the stone ground, gasping for breath.

Estin sat up as soon as he was able and did a head count, finding that they were down three people. A check down the hillside, showed no one. He got to his feet and moved through the group, re-counting one more time.

"They're gone," Linn said, grabbing his shoulder. "If you even think about going down there to find them, I'll knock you out and carry you home. Feanne's orders."

"I know, I know."

As the others rested, Feanne was the first to go out to the edge of the stone precipice, looking out over the nearby lands.

"The war has not gone well," she said, sitting down with her legs hanging off the edge of the rock. "Estin, you need to see this."

Pulling free of Linn's grip, Estin went to her side, then felt his heart sink.

From one section of the plains to another, the war against the undead could be seen even as many miles as they were from the heart of it all.

Vast stretches of land to the southeast were on fire, columns of smoke rising so thick that the sky was like pitch. Where the land was not burning, Estin could see blackened ground that led off as far as he could see. South of where he thought Lantonne stood, he could see a narrow—at least it looked narrow from where he stood—jagged line of flame across the land, belching fire into the sky.

To the east and a little farther north, the land looked as though winter had come hard and fast, blanketing much of the area under a layer of snow that he was willing to bet was ten feet or deeper. Vast sections of the plains were frozen solid, while another part had been turned into a deep blue lake. Snow fell in sheets, cutting how far he could see to the northeast dramatically.

"So that's why they tell us not to play with elementals back in the tunnels," Finth said, shaking his head. "I always thought it was because they didn't want the wizards to burn their hair off. Never thought someone bringing in an elemental would destroy the world."

"I've seen elementals before," answered Feanne, not taking her eyes off the horizon. "Elementals aren't this dangerous. They're a threat to the land, but this is nothing like what I have seen."

Estin squinted, picking out something that stood out against the burned lands.

"Is that?"

He pointed at the small shape. From their distance, it looked to be about the size of a human at the bottom of the mountain. However, they were a great many miles from it, making it potentially hundreds of feet tall. The blazing shape walked across the burned lands and in its wake, flashes of light marked the appearance of legions of tiny sparks.

"Some kind of elemental general?" asked Linn.

"No idea," Feanne told him, turning away. "We need to get back home and stay there. I want everyone to start thinking of ways to block off all entrances to the valley. I doubt there's a way, but if we can, I want every avenue of those things finding us cut off."

From the corner of his eyes, Estin saw a shadow sweeping across the tops of the woods, heading towards the plains. He looked up as a vast winged creature flew down from the deepest parts of the mountains, swooping down from the sky as it raced silently towards the flame-blackened southern lands.

"Now that," Linn said, backing away from the edge, "that is a dragon. By the lords of the realms...that's a real dragon."

Estin was frozen where he stood, unable to stop watching.

"Estin," called Feanne firmly, somewhere behind him.

The dragon swept onto the plains, the land under it frosting in a wide swath, as though its very passing could create ice. It flew low over the land, heading straight towards the distant elementals, gliding on the winds, despite its size.

"Estin," Feanne repeated, taking his arm and pulling him gently away, "we're going now. This is no place for us."

Letting himself be led away from the ledge, Estin found himself looking back repeatedly, watching as the dragon disappeared into the distance. By the time they had reached the bottom of the mountainside, where the fire and water elementals had decimated the area, leaving only burned and wet wreckage of the trees, Estin could hear the distant rumbles of battle.

*

"But mom!"

"I said no, Oria."

Estin sat along the side of the tent, paging through his spellbook as Atall watched over his shoulder, eyeing the scribbled notes. The two had been absorbed in the text from the moment that Oria and Feanne had begun arguing almost half an hour earlier. In fact, the argument had become heated enough that Estin had begun memorizing a spell to quickly staunch bleeding, just in case.

Though Estin was quite sure Atall had no idea what he was looking at, the boy had been unwilling to look up since the shouting had begun. He had been smart enough to stay out of the fight from the start and now was making a good show of feigning interest in magic.

"The other children are going out the north end of the valley, why can't I?"

Feanne growled and stepped between Oria and the entrance to the tent.

"I told you already. I forbid you to go, for your own safety. There are things outside the valley that are extremely dangerous. Collecting a few rabbits is not worth going out there."

"But they're going to teach me how to catch them myself!" the girl practically yelled, stomping her foot. "You're supposed to be one of our best hunters...how can you tell me I can't learn to hunt?"

"I am not refusing to teach you...I am refusing to let you learn outside the valley, especially without my supervision. Your brother understood and stopped arguing a long time ago."

"But the coyotes get to go..."

"You are not a coyote, nor are you going," Feanne reiterated, growling at Oria. Estin winced as he saw her instinctively flex her fingers—it was a natural reaction when Feanne felt as though she were being attacked, or could be, but not one he liked seeing in a family dispute. "It is not safe out there and you will not go. That is final."

"So I can't go, just because it's dangerous?"

"Exactly."

"Then send Estin with me. You trust him to be your guard, so trust him to be mine."

Estin's ears went flat as he heard his name get dragged into the conversation. Even Atall winced a little, giving Estin an apologetic look.

Apparently taken aback by the change of tactic, Feanne blinked and eyed her daughter suspiciously.

"You do have a bit of your grandmother in you, Oria, but that does not change my decision. Estin is my guard, not yours. While I have him protect you, that does not make him yours to command."

"You're right, mom," the girl said, throwing her hands in the air and stalking back towards Estin and Atall. "Since I can't tell him what to do, maybe you should. You say he's not mine, so that means he's yours, right? Tell him to go."

Feanne snarled and Estin started to close his spellbook, half expecting bloodshed to begin. Instead, she calmed herself and walked over to her daughter, kneeling in front of her.

"Oria, no one owns another," she explained, touching her daughter's face. It was possibly the most tender Estin had ever seen Feanne be, made all the more surprising to him, given how angry he knew she likely was. "That's why Estin worked so hard to keep you both safe from slavery. We don't own each other."

"Fine!" Oria stomped to the entrance of the tent, glowering back at her mother. "I'll just go watch the elves make salads. That'll be so exciting!"

Oria ran from the tent, letting in a chilling winter breeze for the moment that the flap was open, spraying everything inside with a light dusting of snow. Once the tent had closed again, the small central fire began to slowly warm the area.

"That girl reminds me too much of myself," Feanne grumbled, sitting down with her knees pulled up to her chin. "So help me, I am beginning to understand why some creatures eat their young."

The tent was quiet for a little while, as Feanne relaxed and Atall and Estin tried to look busy. Finally, Feanne turned to Estin.

"The enchanter from the elves should be here shortly to work on the circle you requested," she told him. "It'll be good to have a working healing circle again."

Estin nodded, thinking back to the battle they had seen on the mountainside. It had been several weeks since then without any further incidents, but the camp had been on alert ever since. Feanne had been insistent on keeping as much of the group's activities within the valley as possible, lest they be found out.

The construction of a circle like the one Asrahn had once had was one of their latest priorities. Officially, Estin and Feanne had decided to search for someone in the camp who could make one just as a precaution, but in reality Estin knew they wanted it because they both feared that there could be a lot more deaths in the near future. This was not something they discussed, even with each other, but the tone was there.

"Are you really mad at Oria?" Atall asked eventually, watching Feanne.

She shook her head, though her tension was still visible.

"No, I am a little disappointed, but I'm not upset with your sister. She saw reason in the end, that's what matters."

"Oh," said Atall, fidgeting with his tail. "Do you think she really went to go watch the elves?"

"That's where she said..."

Feanne stopped and stared at Estin, her eyes widening.

"I wouldn't have done what I was told at her age, Estin. I'd be halfway out of the valley by now. Take anyone you need and find out where she is. I'll stay here with Atall and see to it that your circle is completed."

Hopping to his feet as he grabbed his belt and cloak, Estin rushed out into the cold, pulling his fur mantle over his shoulders as the winds bit through his clothing and his own personal fur. Though still only late afternoon, the storms moving through the mountains were making the area rough to traverse and visibility poor, which had been one of the many reasons Feanne had opposed the journey which would have kept Oria out until evening.

Estin checked around the area near Feanne's tent, but saw no one else he could call on for help. Ulra was off spending some time with her mate at Feanne's command, leaving Estin as the only one of Feanne's guards around that day, at least until nightfall when two of the newer pack members were to stand guard outside the tent. With Estin sharing Feanne's bedding, Ulra had insisted that more guards be brought on to ensure that if he fell asleep, there would be no lapse in her protection.

Finth was taking a small group, including Linn, out into the southern range, looking for extra timber. Even Yoska was unavailable, his clan having a celebration for his niece's wedding that Estin guessed would ensure everyone on that end of camp was too drunk to be useful. That left few that Estin could say that he knew well enough to trust and none that were close enough to call upon.

Still, he reminded himself, he just needed to track the girl, which would prove more difficult the longer he waited. He might not be the best tracker in camp, but he could do the job.

Setting out northward, he paid careful attention to his sense of smell, as Oria was not nearly so good as her mother at hiding her scent. The girl had done well at covering her tracks in the thin layer of snow that had accumulated on the ground where the tents had blocked the winds, but her scent led due north, towards where she was to meet with two other adults and several children for their hunting trip.

Years ago, a trip like this one would have been lauded by the pack-leader, at least for children of breeds like Feanne's, which prided themselves on their ability to track and kill small prey. These days, that traditional first step towards adulthood had been set aside in favor of personal ability to fight, leading to many scuffles within the camp involving young wildlings, dwarves, and the occasional barbarian. Estin himself had been forced to break up several and usually been punched or clawed for doing so.

Oria had already been through her fair share of small fights with other children, many owing to the low opinion that the other predatory breeds had for Estin—in that he was viewed by many to be prey—and the idea that he was the primary protector of their pack-leader. Oria had been staunchly defensive of his name, no matter what he and Feanne had told her and that had gotten her jumped more than once.

Estin was happy that the girl had inherited her mother's sense of loyalty to those she trusted, but not nearly so pleased to see that she had gotten the temper, or the willingness to disobey. He had the feeling that if Feanne kept him around as a guard, he would be making a great many trips like this one over the next few years.

The trail through the snowstorm took him past the tents and wagons, into the northern gap between the mountains. At this point, he found more trails merging into Oria's, where she had met with the others for the trip, who were likely unaware that she had been forbidden to go.

Estin hurried his pace, knowing that at this point, there were limited directions the group could go. If he could catch them before they cleared the far end of the pass, he could not miss them in the narrow channel. Once they were outside the valley, he ran the risk of losing them in the snow if he could not find their trail or scent right away.

Half an hour later, he jogged through the far end of the pass, finding Oria and ten others sitting on rocks near the entrance to the valley, talking about the plans for the hunt. He approached them, whistling to catch the attention of the older feline male that led the group.

"Can I help you?" the male called out to Estin, standing and setting his spear aside. "Is there a new warning from the pack-leader? I have been watchful of any approach from outside the valley."

"No, everything is fine, but she has asked that her daughter return home," Estin said, trying not to sound like Oria was in any kind of trouble, but the girl's face betrayed the truth to her friends. The coyotes that made up most of the group began laughing at her, and one of the two wolf children whispered something to her that made her glower. "No problems that we know of. Please have fun."

The male gave a deep bow and motioned for Oria to go to Estin, which she did reluctantly.

"Your mother is really not happy...and not very surprised," Estin said, once they were a little ways back into the pass. "That wasn't the smartest thing you've ever done."

"I did get her to send you, though," muttered Oria, not looking up at him. "Got half of what I asked for. She may not own you, but she sure can boss you around."

They walked through the pass, taking their time as Oria kicked at the snow most of the way, muttering softly to herself. About the only word Estin could pick out of the rants was "unfair," which he heard a lot as they traveled back.

It took them close to an hour to reach Feanne's tent again, but as they approached the edge of camp, Estin began to sense something was seriously wrong. There were people running around and he could see a large crowd near Feanne's tent. As they got closer, he began to smell blood and could see Ulra at the entrance to the tent, keeping dozens of wildlings away. That was when he started to see spots of blood in the snow, leading towards the tent.

"Oria," he said, stopping the girl by grabbing her arm. "I want you to go to Doln right now."

"But..."

"Oria, I need to protect your mother and I can't do that if I have to watch you, too. Just go."

The girl looked between Estin and the tent, then ran off in the direction he had asked of her.

Estin stopped for a moment in the wind and snow, steeling himself for whatever the latest disaster was. Once he was ready—and both of his swords were ready to be drawn quickly—he strode into the cluster of wildlings, who parted at his approach.

"What is going on?" he demanded of no one in particular, though Ulra rose up in front of him, stopping even him from getting closer to Feanne's tent. "Ulra, what happened?"

The bear growled and then stepped aside, but kept herself between the others and the inside of the tent. She waved him inside, then blocked the doorway again the moment he was in.

The tent was still aside from Atall's soft crying. He followed a thin trail of blood from the doorway right over to Feanne's bedding, where she was curled up, with Atall at her side. In the center of the room, the beginnings of Estin's new circle had been started, but the stones that would make it whole were scattered as though someone had tripped over them.

"What happened?" he asked, getting to Feanne's side as fast as he could.

"Challenged," Feanne gasped, clutching her stomach and refusing to move her hands when Estin tried to get a look at the injury. Still, he could see a large and growing pool of dark blood under her, where it was being swiftly swallowed by the dry ground. "One of the wolves...wants to be leader. Ambushed me outside the tent."

Estin touched her, feeling the agony racking her body as the spirits whispered in his head. He pushed back against the pain and eased it, though Feanne's body had been gravely wounded and would need some time to mend itself properly.

When Feanne relaxed as the pain eased, Estin pulled her hands away from her stomach, finding four pink lines across her abdomen, where claws had torn deeply into the flesh. Given the amount of healing he had already performed and the darkness of the blood remaining on the ground, he guessed that she had been very close to death, having suffered grave internal injuries. It was shocking to him that she had even been conscious, let alone able to get herself back into the tent.

"Who did this?" he asked her, though Feanne was drifting to sleep as her body gave out.

"Olis," she told him, opening her eyes briefly. She seemed to be genuinely fighting the drowsiness that came with healing. "He challenged me. His friends would have hurt Atall while we fought. Had to protect him and fight off the challenge at the same time."

Estin began to ask her why she would not have invoked her ability to change, but looked over at Atall's terrified face and knew the answer. The boy would have been in even more danger if Feanne had gone into a blood-crazed rage, so she had fought as she was, trying to shield him the whole time. She had nearly died to keep him away from the part of herself she could not trust.

"I will go deal with him."

"No!" Feanne hissed, grabbing his wrist. "I will need to fight him. It is not a guard's place to seek revenge. Your job is to protect, not to punish."

"You won't be well enough for days, Feanne. Who can act on your behalf?"

"Only family or kin," she answered, trying to pull him closer by his wrist. "Promise me you won't go. If you fight him for me, I'll be seen as too weak to lead."

Estin pulled her hand off his wrist, then closed his fingers around her hand. The palm of her hand was covered with sticky blood, but he held it tight, studying her face for any indication of what to do.

"So make him your mate," said Atall softly, looking between them both. "Then he can fight for you, right?"

Both Feanne and Estin stared at the boy, who clung to his mother's tail as he sat there, not looking at either of them.

"This is dumb," he added. "Estin loves you...you love him...now you both are stuck with stupid rules just because you won't say you love either other. Why are adults so dumb?"

"It's not that easy," Feanne told him as she tried to reach over and sooth him, but Atall shoved her hand away.

"It is. You ask him, he says 'yes,' then you both say some stuff in public. I've seen others do it. Dad isn't coming back, so why do you two spend all your time looking sad at each other?"

Estin tried to find words, but his mouth was too dry to speak. He focused instead on wiping blood from Feanne's hands, busying himself to keep from feeling more foolish than he already did. To hear a child telling him what he knew he should have been saying for years made his ears itch.

"Just because you love someone, doesn't mean it will work out," Feanne was saying, her voice cracking slightly. "I do love Estin, but the pack will not respect him as my mate. It's also not fair to you and Oria."

"He's with us all the time anyway. We both know you two like each other. Who cares what the rest of the pack thinks? Why do they get to decide who your mate is? You always tell us that we need to make our own decisions so that we aren't like the wildlings enslaved in the cities. How's this different?"

Feanne closed her eyes and sighed as Atall got up and went to the far side of the room, sitting down in a frump and glaring at them both.

"Estin," Feanne said, looking up at him finally, "do I kill my children, or take advice from them?"

"Whatever you want, pack-leader."

The words were hard to get out, but it was all Estin could manage. He wanted to give Atall a hug, but knew that it was not his place to agree with the child. Not on this. Feanne had made it very clear that his place was as her guard and her friend, nothing more. To contradict that might make things worse, at least in his mind.

Sitting up slowly, Feanne reached up, then grabbed Estin by the chest fur, pulling him closer as he winced.

"I don't get sweet and soft, Estin," she growled, her voice low. "Hearing this from my son is hard enough for me, without your mocking remarks."

"Then I should leave," he answered, looking away as she released his fur. "I know what your feelings on this are, and I won't push you. If there is any way I can help you recover to challenge Olis…"

Feanne grabbed his face with both her hands, pressing her muzzle against his. She held him there a moment, then relaxed her grip, but stayed close to him—far closer than she had been for a very long time. It was all he could do to keep himself calm and breathing as she put an arm around him, giving him a hug.

The embrace lasted a long time in Estin's mind, his heart racing as the seconds ticked away. Finally, she sat back, watching him carefully.

"Estin, since we are both far more foolish than my children," she began, her voice shaking, "Pending Oria's approval, will you agree to be my mate, with all the troubles that comes along with that and the pain of putting up with me? If my children back it, I can see no reason to continue as we are."

Estin's heart felt like it would beat out of his chest. He looked over at Atall, who was staring at him expectantly.

"Are you sure?" he asked the boy, rather than Feanne. "I don't ever want to do anything that hurts you or your sister."

Atall nodded vigorously, but said nothing. The boy stared at Estin intently, making him even more nervous than he already was.

"I accept," Estin finally answered, closing his eyes. He had never felt such a burden leave him as he did in that moment.

Exhaling as though she had been holding her breath, Feanne answered, "I hereby declare you my chosen. Once I can be sure of Oria's feelings and I am well again, pledges and challenges can be made. For now, if you will have me, I will pledge that I intend to be your mate."

"What about Olis and his challenge to you?"

Feanne smiled up at him, placing a hand on his chest.

"Your potential life-mate was attacked. This was an attack on your would-be kin and your pack-leader. I will deal with him once I have healed. In the meantime, you will bring him in and Ulra will secure him until I am able to fight properly. You do not have my permission to kill him…if it is to be done, that is my duty, not yours."

Estin started to stand, but Feanne grabbed his belt, holding tight.

"The weapons, Estin. They have no place in this conflict. Either leave them or do not go. His people will see it as a weakness if you bring them."

He gave his swords one sad look, knowing that he was putting himself at a further disadvantage against a warrior who had grown up fighting for his life and place among his people. Though his claws had mostly grown back, they were a poor substitute for swords, especially against a seasoned warrior.

"As you wish," he said, unbuckling his belt and setting the weapons beside her. "I will return as soon as I can."

"Just be sure you return."

Estin held her hand to his forehead briefly, then left the tent, shouldering past Ulra as he marched into the camp. As he went, a small crowd began following behind, whispering vigorously, though Estin refused to look back and see just how many were in that group. It felt good just knowing there were those who would back him—and anyone backing him was supporting Feanne's claim to the leadership of the camp.

Halfway across the campsite, he crossed paths with Yoska, who staggered and stared blankly at the group following Estin, before hurrying to walk alongside him. The man reeked of alcohol and Estin wondered how he was even standing. Estin could pick out half a dozen different kinds of beverage that seemed to emanate from Yoska in a noxious blend.

"You know you have many people behind you, yes?"

"Yes."

"Where do we head, my friend? You look less than happy."

Estin held one of his hands out as he walked, showing Yoska the blood covering his palm.

"This…this is not your blood?"

"No. Feanne's."

"Oh. So a blood-feud it is. Who are we killing or maiming this night? Has been too long since I was involved in a good blood-feud."

"You will just keep his friends off me. Other than that, no one here has a stake in this."

"Estin, she is a friend to my people as well."

"She will live," he snapped, the distraction from his own thoughts frustrating him. "They challenged her as pack-leader, but attacked her by deception and surprise, which is not our way. This was not just another fight."

Yoska nodded knowingly, walking a very short distance with Estin in silence.

"So why do you fight, if I cannot?"

"I am tasked with bringing him back for a proper challenge once she has healed."

"And is nice to soundly beat the man that attacked Feanne, yes?"

Estin kept his mouth shut, as they approached his goal. The tents ahead of him were not much different from any of the other wildling structures—mostly haphazard and thrown together from the materials they could find. What made these particular tents special was the gap between them and their neighbors.

Olis and his friends—who he referred to as his own pack—had separated themselves when they had first arrived months earlier, but Feanne had long hoped that they would eventually integrate at least with the other wildlings. Instead, they had become more isolated, the seven wolves in this corner of the camp often threatening those who came near their area. They had even managed to pull in two other wolves who had been a part of the camp before their arrival. Feanne had corrected their aggressive behavior towards the others, but they had clearly ignored her.

Outside the three tents, two of the wolves sat in a casual watch near a fire, sitting up as Estin and his following approached. Ears perked and eyes bright, they seemed both alert and amused.

"What do we have here?" asked one particular male, grinning at Estin, showing off his sharp teeth. "You're a long way from your pack-mistress, prey."

"I've come for Olis."

The two laughed and the one closest to the central tent gave a quick whistle.

"Hey Olis!" the second wolf called out, laughing again. "The fox's pet just showed up. I think he's upset about something."

All three tents opened up, as the remaining wolves came out to meet him, though most hesitated when they saw how many people were backing Estin. Still, they looked to the largest of their group, then fanned out to keep anyone but Estin from approaching Olis.

Estin had not actually met Olis to this point, having left the negotiations with him to Feanne. Now, he wished he had been better prepared. The male wolf towered over him—a head or more taller than Estin—stretching to flex impressive muscles in a show of might as he came out of the tent. His brown, black, and white patterning was consistent with many of the mountain breeds of normal wolf and his cool blue eyes watched Estin with the same terrifying intensity he had encountered in those beasts.

"To what do I owe this visit?" Olis asked, walking calmly up to the group, then looked down at Estin. "Ah, there you are. Almost missed you."

"You attacked our pack-leader."

Olis grinned and hunkered down, making a show of putting himself at face-level with Estin.

"Yes. That I did. Where were you when I did it, little guard? Nevermind, it doesn't matter. You were not there when it happened and that's all that matters. Your pack-leader—not mine—follows the old ways and won't let you seek revenge on her behalf, will she? Awful shame that…you should have heard how she screamed when I pulled her intestines out."

Estin glanced over at Yoska, who had sat down on the side of a tent, looking too drunk to focus on the situation. Despite this, Estin could see the man slip daggers into both of his palms, clearly not as far gone as he pretended.

"I have come to drag you back for the pack-leader to deal with," he told Olis, trying to remain calm. His hands shook with the effort. Despite that, the wolf's size made him think of Feanne's change…and the way she tore her enemies apart. He wondered if Olis could do the same to him without the gifts from nature that Feanne possessed. "If you will not come willingly, I'll do what I need to."

"No thanks. Your pack-leader failed my challenge. Unless she's going to come here and try again, I have no use for her. It's time for a new leader. You touch me and you make her look even weaker than she already is…sending a guard who failed his duties to attack someone who won a challenge."

Estin braced himself, standing as tall and proud as he could manage. It felt so insufficient, facing this huge male.

"I'm not here to seek revenge. I am here at her request to bring you in for a proper challenge when she has recovered. You failed to kill her, after breaking what few rules we have about challenging a pack-leader. You need to face up to what you've done."

Grinning, Olis shook his head.

"Not good enough, prey. I don't take orders from…whatever you are…and you don't belong in my part of the camp. If your master wants me, she can come herself. I will not give some unmated fruit-eater recognition as having any right to speak for the supposed pack-leader, even if she claims you as her personal guard. Now, run along, or the next time I rip into the fox, I'll strangle you with her guts."

The rustle through the crowd behind Estin made him wonder if they were as willing to back him as he had hoped. There was a general feeling of questioning coming from the group, as though they wondered if it was wise or safe to challenge Olis. He even heard some openly question whether it was time for Feanne to be put aside as leader.

"She remains our pack-leader until she is beaten by a challenger, not an ambush," Estin insisted, as Olis laughed and turned his back to walk away. "Until then, she has asked me to speak for her…"

"You don't get to speak for her," roared Olis, throwing his hands in the air. "Do you not understand? You are a glorified babysitter for her children, nothing more. You have no standing to try and drag me back to her, if you were even able to do so. Stop wasting my time!"

Taking a deep breath, Estin raised his voice and replied, "As our pack-leader's pledged, I speak for her by her request in this matter. Your attack on her was an attack on me. She will challenge you properly when she heals, but until then, I will have you brought before her as she has ordered."

Estin felt the area cool, well beyond the chill brought on by winter. The whispers he could hear behind him were varied. The wildlings were angry, asking those around them how he dared make such a claim. The other races were less concerned, likely unaware of any significance in what he had said. He had no regret for making the announcement, but knew it did not make this situation any easier.

"So, this is how low your pack-leader has sunk?" asked Olis, turning on Estin again. "Not only can she not protect this pack, but she stoops to choosing a rodent as her bed-mate? I should have finished digging my claws around inside her when I had the chance, so I could put her out of her misery. Better it be my claws inside her than any half-bred runts of yours."

He turned to one of his fellow wolves and added, "Make sure the next time we see her that the kits die, too. I don't want her bloodline contaminating my pack."

Estin attacked before he realized that he was even considering it. He leapt at Olis, his claws raking the taller wildling's neck and tearing away a thick clump of fur. When he landed from his attack, he watched Olis stumble away, holding his throat.

"That was impressive," Olis said, chuckling as he wiped the loose fur off of the four thin lines on his neck. "If you were more than prey, I might have lost some skin with all that fur."

All around Estin, wildlings and even humans, elves, halflings, and others dove into the fray as the other wolves attempted to come to Olis' aid. Weapons were drawn and soon the field had been secured, leaving only Estin and Olis near the campfire, while the other wolves were kept at the end of many sword tips.

"Is this just about me trying to kill your sad excuse for a pack-leader?" Olis taunted, eyeing Estin, clearly watching him for impatience or loss of control over this temper. "Or was it the kits? What made you so mad, little rodent? Maybe you are afraid that she would ask me to fight for her before you two are oath-bound? That my challenge might have aroused her…made her realize what she's lacking in her current choice?"

Estin snarled at Olis, barely realizing he was doing it.

"That," said Olis, pointing at Estin. "That right there is why I have no respect for you. You just don't know what you are anymore. The rabbits, deer, rats…they all know they are prey and stay clear of me. I don't hurt them because they know what they are. You think you're one of us, don't you? Would your own breed even recognize you anymore? Is that why you feel the need to bed someone who should know better?"

Walking slow circles around the campfire, with Olis doing the same on the far side, Estin fought to keep his temper under control. Feanne had taught him to let his anger go at a moment's notice, but she had never taught him to control it. He had managed to contain the anger many times when he needed to for protecting others, such as the kits, but this was very different. Now, that was making the wait difficult for him. On one hand, his instincts demanded he run, while Feanne's training told him that he needed to throw himself at his opponent, fighting for every drop of blood he could manage, even to the point of sacrificing himself to get atop the other wildling.

"Do you really think you can match me with your tiny claws?" chided Olis, shaking his head as he laughed.

"No, I really don't."

As Olis looked away, Estin let loose a spell that he had been waiting to use, knowing that opportunity was vital in this fight, as once he was within reach of Olis, he likely would not be able to get another spell off. This one caused airy straps to appear and wrap themselves around Olis, preventing him from moving his arms. Though Estin knew it would not hold, he ran at the fire, jumping through it and across, slamming into Olis and knocking him to the ground. With a roll, Estin got back out of Olis' reach.

By the time Estin was back on his feet, Olis had broken free of the magic and growled loudly, rolling onto all fours as he glared angrily at Estin, blood running from shallow cuts along his chest. The calm hatred in his eyes was gone, replaced by a blind rage. His hands dug into the snow as he charged.

In that moment, Estin saw the wolf that Feanne had called to challenge him during his training. Kicking backwards, he rolled with Olis' impact, digging his feet into the much larger wildling's stomach and throwing him into the nearby tent, which collapsed as he tumbled into it.

At that point, one of Olis' followers broke free of the crowd, rushing at Estin. This threat Estin dismissed immediately with a wave of his hand, paralyzing the younger wildling without so much as a glance. Estin remained where he was as the wolf was dragged away, unable to move any part of his body.

"Little spellcaster thinks he's warrior now," growled Olis, throwing aside pieces of cloth and wood as he stood back up. "Do you think your magic makes you better than me? The moment I get my hands on you, I'll wring your neck and deliver your pelt to your precious pack-leader."

Estin backed up until he could feel the campfire nearing his tail, as Olis moved slowly towards him.

"I could kill you where you stand, Olis," he said, knowing he was telling the truth. The power to grant life came with the opposing power, which he had never even attempted to use. "I will not use my magic like that. Not for this and not for you.

"If you want to prove you're tough enough to take this pack from Feanne, then you'd better be a lot stronger than I am. When you've failed to kill me, I'll drag you to her, as ordered."

Olis panted as he stood in the wreckage of the tent, his breath creating a white fog as he watched Estin carefully.

With a speed Estin could not have guessed at, Olis rushed him, his hands grabbing Estin's shoulders before he could react, trying to drive him to the ground. Estin started to resist, but his legs would not hold him and he collapsed, feeling his face go numb as Olis raked his left side with his claws, blinding him in that eye as blood ran down his cheek.

Hitting the ground hard, Estin reached up and caught Olis by the skin of his neck, using it to maintain some leverage as he swept his foot into the larger male's legs, taking them out from under him. He only had a moment to act as Olis fell atop him, rolling using Olis' throat as his pivot. The two rolled together, with Estin coming out on top as Olis fell into the fire.

Olis' growls turned into screams as he tried to get himself out of the flames, but Estin fought to keep him from getting a firm grip on anything that might allow him to drag himself free. Soon, the fire died out under him, the flames smothered. At this point, Olis grabbed Estin's ear and side of his head and swept him aside, dragging him to his feet as Olis stood fully upright.

"She taught you well," growled Olis, picking Estin off the ground by his ear and part of his neck's scruff. "If I close my eyes, I'd think I was just fighting a cub, rather than some rodent. You want to say anything before I rip your throat out?"

"Yeah," he answered, squirming and trying to focus as his ear rang. "Why does everyone ignore the tail?"

Olis looked around frantically, as Estin hooked his tail around behind Olis, wrapping it around his throat as tightly as he could. Olis' surprise gave Estin the brief opportunity to pull his head free, falling back to the ground alongside the dying fire.

Claws began to dig into Estin's tail as he grabbed for a rock from the edge of the campfire, just before he was yanked off the ground by his tail.

"Enough of this!" bellowed Olis.

Estin swung as hard as he could with the rock, feeling Olis' face practically explode with the impact, just before Estin fell yet again. Recoiling from where Olis stumbled around, Estin got as far away as he could, trying to get his bearings and ready himself for the next attack and wiping at the blood that ran freely down his face, hoping that he could clear his vision.

Staggering, bent over double as he held his broken face, Olis tried to growl, but it just came out as a strangled choke. He took one step, then turned and ran from the area, the crowd letting him pass as he ran off into the woods.

The crowd collapsed on Estin immediately, though he could barely see them as he fell to his knees, pressing his palm into the deep gashes in his face that were bleeding horribly. He began to feel pain throughout his body where he had been struck and not even noticed at the time, but his cheek and eye felt the worst.

As praise for his fight was spoken all around him, he gave vague thanks, really not even knowing what he was saying, or to who. It was taking much of his attention to keep the blood-loss from sending him into shock.

It took Estin a minute or two to get the dizziness down to a manageable level, but when he looked around at last, he realized that everyone nearby was of another race. Not one wildling still stood with the group praising him. The only wildlings that remained in the area were the wolves, still being held by various camp members.

"So this is your great victory, no?" asked Yoska, pulling Estin's hand away, then pressing a thick cloth to Estin's face. "Apply pressure here, not here."

Estin sat down on the frozen ground, barely feeling the chill in his current state.

"Not really much of a victory, if my people want nothing to do with me," he answered, his tongue thick.

Estin realized that he had bit through part of his tongue and several of his teeth were badly chipped. One of the back ones was missing entirely. He pulled the cloth away from his face and saw it was already soaked with blood and bits of his white fur.

"Not true," Yoska answered, pushing Estin's hand back up to his face to keep the cloth on the wounds. "Some of us knew that this was coming and have already accepted the idea. Others, not so. Give them a day or two and you will know how they truly feel. Even if they hate you, would you rather that she never marry you?"

"We're not married yet, Yoska."

"This I would argue," the human said, smiling broadly. "Long as I have known you both, you were married. You just did not know it yet. I thought sometimes I would have to make you both drink yourselves into stupor and just tell you that you had wed while you were unconscious. Worked for two of my cousins. You will have your ceremony and we shall see, yes?"

Yoska helped him stand, guiding him slowly back towards Feanne's tent on the far end of camp.

"Can you heal yourself?" the man asked part way across the camp. "You are still bleeding a lot and I worry. I wish to not deliver you to her half-dead."

Focusing on the whispers of the spirits, Estin felt the wounds close slightly, but then he stopped, leaving much of the deep cuts. His strength was waning and if he pushed himself further, he thought he might pass out, which he could not allow himself to do before reaching the tent.

"I'll let the rest scar," he said, pulling away the cloth. He could still feel the cuts oozing, but they would close soon enough and he could see from that eye, which was his larger concern. "This fight meant enough to leave a mark."

"As you wish."

They soon reached the tent, where Ulra still stood guard, though now she was alone, her fur covered with a growing layer of snow that she seemed oblivious to.

"Do you come back with news?" Ulra asked Estin, eyeing his injuries. "Or will you confirm that our leader has been replaced by that pup?"

"There will be no change. The wolf is aware that many are most unhappy with his decision to challenge the fox," cut in Yoska, still helping Estin stand. "Do open the tent. The boy has had a hard time this night and I would have him tended to by more delicate hands than mine."

Ulra eyed the gypsy, opening the tent as she noted, "Have you met our pack-leader? There are no delicate hands in here, human."

Yoska laughed and patted Ulra's arm as he led Estin inside, setting him near the entrance as Feanne, Oria, and Atall scrambled over.

Half-sitting, Estin barely paid attention to the hands checking his injuries and the nervous talk around him. He just sat there, letting himself be poked and prodded, until he saw Feanne's hand near his face and he took a hold of it, hanging on, trying to cling to her strength.

"So I hear there will be a proper wedding in this village," Yoska said, almost to himself, though Estin saw Feanne's eyes dart his way. "When will I receive my invitation to the festivities?"

"It doesn't work that way," she told him, cradling Estin's face. "There will be a public announcement, followed by the allowance for challengers, if I wish it. After that, there is nothing more. We will be together."

"This will not do at all. I will be sure the gypsies are ready."

"Yoska, do not..."

"Is done! I will await your announcement."

From where he sat, Estin watched Feanne's face fall, even as the cold air from someone leaving hit his back.

"Can we please throw that man off a cliff?" Feanne asked, touching the edges of the wound on his face again. "It would make my duties that much easier."

Estin chuckled, but it hurt to even do that.

"If you are here, looking like this, then what condition is Olis in?" she asked him next, her tone serious. Estin could see both of the children perk up at that, as well. "You were to bring him back alive."

"He ran off. His injuries were far worse than mine."

Feanne nodded grimly, giving him a smile that did little to warm him.

"You've done well. Tomorrow, we will finish all that we've started."

*

The next morning, Feanne was true to her word, surprising Estin—he had figured that no matter what she had pledged the previous night, it would be several days before things moved forward. Despite the injuries they both still bore, she called for the camp to gather in late morning. There had been some dissent in some corners of the village once the rumors had confirmed what was to happen, but most knew that her order to appear was not a request and by noon, nearly the entire camp stood assembled.

Feanne waited in the middle of a hastily-constructed platform that gave them enough height to be seen by those who had come. She had hardly moved since they had arrived, her bear skin cloak moving only slightly in the winds as she watched the villagers gather.

Estin stood just behind Feanne on the platform, with the kits leaning in boredom against his legs. He shivered in the cold winds, thankful that at least the snow had stopped falling for the moment, his fur-covered mantle giving him at least some protection from the chill. He had a suspicion that the kits were so close to him mostly for warmth, rather than out of affection.

"He's going to do something," whispered Feanne nervously, watching the crowd as she held her still-aching stomach. The wounds had closed, but Estin had caught her wincing at times when she moved too quickly. "I can feel it."

"Who?"

She gave him a dark look and answered, "Yoska."

Estin could just laugh, knowing she was likely right, but there was little he could do about it.

Once the majority of the camp had arrived, from every faction and group on the site, Feanne stepped to the front edge of the platform and looked over the collected people.

Finth stood at the front of the crowd, grinning and giving Estin occasional lewd gestures that he was actively trying to ignore or feign ignorance of. He hoped that meant the kits would not understand them, or might not notice, so he just ignored the dwarf.

"I have called all of you here to act as my witnesses," Feanne announced. "Today, I wish to take a new mate and as the leader of this pack, this affects every one of you. I would ask that if anyone challenges my decision to have a mate, they come forward now."

A low murmur through the crowd was all the reply she got.

"Very well. I hereby announce that I have chosen Estin to be my mate, for the duration of our lives. I have asked for no challenger or terms to his acceptance. If there are any concerns, I want to hear them now."

The murmur turned into angry jeers from various points in the crowd where wildlings had gathered. From what Estin could see, most of those groups were largely predatory breeds and none of them looked the least bit happy. Their angry looks were split quite evenly between himself and Feanne. He tightened his jaw and attempted to maintain the look of dignity, even if he did not feel it.

"I object," called out a voice farther back in the crowd. "Will you hear me?"

Estin squinted at the group where the voice had come from, seeing people parting quickly as Olis walked through the crowds. Though he had clearly been healed by someone in the valley, the wolf's face was badly mangled, deep-set creases from the edges of the stone Estin had hit him with creating the look of a dent in the side of his skull.

Not actually turning around to see what was coming, Finth gave Estin a questioning look and pulled out a dagger. Estin shook his head and Finth just sighed and turned to watch with everyone else.

"I will hear anyone who will speak their concerns," Feanne told him, her tone hard. "However, you have issued a different challenge already that bears resolving."

Feanne glanced back at Estin, motioning him to move the children back away from the front of the platform, which he did. He had no idea what Olis might try, so he pushed the kits behind him to shield them.

"I just wanted to show proper respects," Olis said, loud enough for the crowd to hear him clearly as he neared the platform. "It is only right, given the recent...disagreements. Perhaps we can resolve this in a more civil fashion."

Feanne nodded, though from where he stood, Estin could see that she was tense and ready for an attack. He could feel the same tension in the kits through his hands on their shoulders.

"I pledge to serve my better for the good of the pack," said Olis, standing directly in front of Feanne. With the extra height of the platform, she still stood only a breath taller than him.

"Then make your pledge, if it will resolve your earlier challenges."

Olin grinned crookedly, his scars twisting the expression. He began to bow before Feanne, then spit on her feet, turning instead to Estin and completing the bow.

"I pledge my respect to the one worthy of it," he stated, his voice carrying through the camp. "I will not bow my knee to some spoiled pup who thinks she can command me because her father held a pack together. You and your little mutts will find your way into a zombie's mouth if I ever catch you alone."

"You will need to stop talking now, Olis. If you wish to challenge my position with this pack, then say so, otherwise you will need to move away from me."

"Yes," Olis agreed, taking a short step back, though he was still easily within range to strike at Feanne. "I do challenge you. I challenge your right to lead. I challenge your decision to take what should be your prey as your mate, rather than killing and eating him like a proper predator. I challenge anyone who believes you possess the common sense to lead others, when you stand here with your mutts, disgracing this pack with your little ceremony."

Estin tightened his grip on the kits as both tried to run at Olis. He could hear them both growling, but doubted anyone farther away would even notice with the chatter and murmurs in the crowd—at least he hoped Olis could not hear them.

"Do you wish to resolve your challenge now, or later?" Feanne asked calmly, still not backing down. "I am rather busy today…"

Olis grinned again, looking over at the kits.

"I was thinking about grabbing something to eat first, but if the mutts are going to stay so far out of reach, we may as well resolve things now. If all goes well, I can have all the wildlings in-line and all the other races scattered to the hills by nightfall."

The two stood there several more seconds, then Olis made his move, reaching for Feanne. His hand never connected as she moved, darting past him as her cloak fell where she had been standing.

Had Estin not known the gravity of both of their injuries, he would never have guessed by watching them. The two wildlings circled and slashed at each other, moving easily through the combat with no hesitation.

They leapt and bit, slashed and kicked, trying to land a solid hit on each other. Often, Feanne would catch Olis with her far greater speed, but these were glancing hits that did more damage to fur than to flesh. He could not even touch her as she danced about, moving under his swings and outside his reach.

Unfortunately, Estin could see Feanne tiring quickly. Her injuries from the previous night were taking their toll, gradually slowing her. He doubted she could continue to avoid Olis much longer, and judging by the grin on Olis' face, he was aware, too. Each time he lunged at her, he came closer to connecting, still showing signs of endurance that would not fade anytime soon.

Olis rushed Feanne again and she ducked under his arm, his claws raking her back as she stumbled away from him. When she got her feet back under her, she inadvertently put a hand to her stomach, where the earlier wounds had broken open. Red lines stained the thick woolen shirt she was wearing.

Whispers through the crowd were loud enough that Estin heard some expecting that the next time Olis struck, Feanne would die. Not all of them sounded entirely disappointed.

"Come on!" growled Olis, spinning on Feanne again. "You intend to run away until I'm tired? Either stand and fight, or tuck-tail and run from camp."

Rounding on him, Feanne tried to lunge, claws leading, but Olis' greater reach let him catch her mid-jump. He held her off the ground, his large hand clamped over her left shoulder and part of her neck.

"I'll break your neck before you can do your little changing act," he gloated, tightening his grip until Feanne let out a grunt of pain. "You can stop this. Your mutts don't need to see you die. Just say the words and I'll send them away before anything is done."

Feanne brought her legs up quickly, pushing her feet into Olis' chest. With a kick, she dragged the claws of her feet from his upper stomach nearly to his groin, spraying blood as the wolf bellowed in agony, dropping her.

"Now, we're even," hissed Feanne as she got her feet under her again, one hand pressed to her own bleeding stomach.

She reached out swiftly to catch Olis by the throat, digging in her claws as he staggered, clutching his ravaged stomach. With a tug, she hoisted him back to his feet, pulling his face level with hers.

Olis growled, clutching at Feanne's hand, trying unsuccessfully to pull it away and only succeeding in leaving bloody gouges when her claws did move. He then tried to use his weight to pull himself away, but Feanne grabbed his torn stomach with her other hand's claws, keeping him from moving without further injury.

"My father only killed three people in all his time in charge of the pack," Feanne said, her voice low but carrying through the still of the crowd.

"I don't care about your father," snarled Olis, his voice choked somewhat from the pressure on his throat. "His pack and legacy can burn for all I care."

"Two were found guilty of murdering other members of the pack out of anger," continued Feanne, dead-calm as she ignored him. "Those, he had his guards execute publicly. One was his own brother."

Olis twisted and tugged, making feral noises that sounded to Estin as though he were losing his mind, trying to get free of the grip on his throat.

"The third I can still remember. He stood in front of my father the way you stood in front of me. He yelled and he mocked my father. I could not understand why Lihuan let him keep talking. My father's guards were ready to strike him down where he stood, but my father held them back, demanding that he be allowed to speak his mind about any matter regarding my father's leadership."

With a twist of his body that clearly was meant to keep his neck and stomach intact, Olis tried to punch at Feanne's body, but she just moved aside, pinching with both hands to make Olis howl in pain.

"Twice before he had challenged my father's leadership and lost. My father had the right as the victor to kill him, but always refused. It was when the young fool said that the next time my father turned his back, he would have my sister and I skinned and put on display to prove that my father couldn't protect us that my father finally changed his mind. Lihuan had nearly taken his head completely off before he calmed himself again.

"Would you like to reconsider threatening my children, Olis?"

"You couldn't kill me last night," grunted Olis, still trying to pry her hand free. "If you do it now, you'll just rile up all those who think you need to go."

"Maybe I was not clear. Are my kits safe in this village, or are they not?"

Olis reached up and grabbed at Feanne, his hand wrapping nearly around her neck. He was fighting to get a solid grip on her throat.

Feanne released her grip on Olis' stomach and grabbed the thumb of the hand he held her neck with to keep him from tightening his grip, then twisted sharply with her other. Her claws cut cleanly, ripping Olis' throat out. She hardly moved as he collapsed at her feet, choking on his own blood.

"Whether I am the best choice to lead and whether or not I continue to lead," Feanne announced loudly as she stepped over Olis' body, "I will not tolerate anyone in this pack threatening to kill children. I do not care whether those children are my own, those of other wildlings, or those of anyone else who has come into the protection of this valley.

"If anyone cares to challenge me, please do so. I would much rather be raising my children and living out my days with the mate of my choice. Instead, I stand here as your pack-leader, not by my own choosing, but because every single person that has offered to lead has done so either with intentions to drive off any they see as undeserving, or to have the right to harm those they dislike.

"All of us are undeserving of survival. While the lands around us are dying, we live here in relative safety. We survive because we work together. The moment someone like him takes this pack apart for their own ends," she pointed down at Olis for emphasis, "we will all die, scattered across the world like everyone else."

Walking up onto the platform to stand in front of Estin, Feanne just looked at him for a moment, then turned back to the silent crowd. The only sound was Olis, still gasping and squirming on the ground, kicking the reddening snow around as he struggled to breathe.

"I have asked this before today, but some of you were not here when I did. I ask one last time: Who would lead in my place?" she asked, raising her voice so that no one could claim to have not heard her request. "Who here is willing to take this burden? Step forward and tell me why I should step down and let you lead. I will not harm anyone who just wishes to speak their mind."

The camp stood silently, some people looking around, while others watched Feanne to see what would happen next. Not one person moved forward or spoke. The awkward silence was only disturbed for Estin by the kits nervously squeezing his hands as their heads darted back and forth, looking for anyone who might be next to attack their mother, almost daring the crowd to try.

"Very well. I want him removed from my sight," Feanne said more softly. Finth began waving people over, who rushed to the body. "If someone wishes to heal him, he is not welcome in this village anymore. Throw him or his remains outside the valley for the four-legged wolves to feed on."

Feanne stood there as several people dragged off the body, leaving a red trail in the snow. Once Olis was no longer visible, she looked up slowly, sweeping the crowd with her gaze.

"I am and will remain your pack-leader, so long as I can help this pack by doing so."

She turned partially, gazing sidelong at Estin.

"Today was supposed to be a happy day, not one of challenges. Today, I declare my choice of mate. There have been some who question my decision in this. Does anyone wish to say that I am not worthy of this male, or him of I?"

This time the whispers were far quieter. Estin guessed that if there were any objections regarding her being weak for choosing a non-predatory breed as a mate, they died with Olis. He watched the gathered people, seeing a few now giving him far more accepting nods. He could only assume that they had decided to accept whatever Feanne chose as the way it would be.

Feanne eventually turned from the crowd and fully faced Estin, her stern demeanor fading instantly. The rage was gone and her eyes were sad as she approached him, her hand pressed to the bleeding cuts on her stomach. When she got near, Estin could see that she was shaking slightly, as she pulled her cloak from the ground and onto her shoulders.

"I am sorry," she whispered, stepping close to Estin. Nervously, she tried to cover her bloodied hand, even as Oria searched through her own outfit and produced a scrap piece of cloth for Feanne. This, she took readily, wiping her hand as clean as she could. "I did not want there to be bloodshed today, of all days. I've spent more than a year wondering what it would be like to stand here with you, only to have to kill to get here."

Smiling despite the grim moment, Estin freed his hands from the kits, then took Feanne's hand in his. Gently, he touched the scars on her arm with his other hand, tracing the lines with his fingertips. Estin could not help but smile as she shivered.

"We've been stuck with bloodshed since we met," Estin reminded her, meaningfully glancing down at his own matching scars. "Why should today be any different?"

Feanne smiled weakly, then gave both of the kits the most reassuring smile she likely could manage.

"Shall we do this?" she asked, looking back up at Estin.

"Yes," came Yoska's overly-loud answer as he approached the platform. "Is time for this, no?"

Estin felt about as horrified as Feanne had at killing a pack-member. He had entirely forgotten the vague threat of Yoska's attendance, but now felt it acutely. The gypsy had climbed onto the platform just behind Feanne, grinning broadly. Estin could only think that Yoska was about to do something that would make the entire day into a great embarrassment and he wondered how he could spare Feanne from that…or keep her from killing Yoska.

"I have spoken with many about your ceremony and been assured that it is boring," Yoska noted, shaking his head. "This will not do. The death of your enemy before saying vows is good custom, but not quite gypsy way. You will wait for me, yes?"

With that, Yoska ran off, leaving most of the crowd looking between him and the platform in confusion. Only the gypsies in the crowd seemed confident in the outcome, many smiling and giving Estin knowing nods.

"Do we just go ahead, or do we wait?" asked Feanne, standing so still that Estin could not be sure she was breathing. She kept her back to the direction Yoska had left.

"I have no idea."

They just stood there, waiting as the crowd began mumbling about the delays. Soon, the kits were fidgeting and Estin felt Atall trying to steal from his pouches without being caught—one of the child's favorite games when he thought Estin was ignoring him and, he suspected, something he could blame Yoska or Finth for.

At last, Yoska reappeared, this time with his entire clan following him back through the crowds, wheeling carts bearing casks that Estin recognized as the gypsy clan's private stash of alcohol. There was very nearly enough to drown the entire camp. The fact that they had this much left after the loud party the night before for another wedding astounded him.

"Now," announced Yoska, coming back to Estin and Feanne, even as his clanmates began unstopping the casks and forcing cups into every hand they could find, "the camp may begin drinking to toast your marriage. You may begin once the drinks are flowing, but you may not have a drink yourselves until you both say 'yes.' This I must insist on, or I fear one of you will find another excuse to escape."

Feanne thumped her forehead against Estin's chest. Sighing, she looked up a moment later, holding his face near hers as the gypsies began singing and making far too much noise.

"No more distractions and no waiting for that man's rules," she said, touching his face softly, then taking a knee in front of him. She pulled his face closer to hers, giving him a happy lick across the cheek just below his ear, then stepped back and said for everyone else to hear, "Estin, will you accept my proposal of a life-mating, knowing fully who and what I am, to bind our fates as one for so long as our hearts still beat?"

"I accept without hesitation," Estin said, trying to ignore the giggling of the children.

Estin took Feanne's hands and stood her back up, taking his own turn on a knee. He clung to her hands as he knelt, trying to use her to steady his own nerves, while giving Oria a quick glare when she gave his tail a tug. He knew for sure that the kits were definitely trying to unnerve him when Atall managed to steal one of his pouches right off his belt and made no effort to hide it.

"Will you accept me as your only mate, no matter the thoughts of others, to bind our fates as one for so long as our hearts beat?" he asked, barely believing that the words were his own. Just speaking them somewhere other than his own mind took his breath away.

Feanne smiled coyly and hesitated, just staring at him, her eyes glittering with mischief. She waited long enough that Estin could hear a couple of the louder gypsies begin to question whether he had misspoken something. Finth went so far as to loudly suggest that he try repeating himself, in case she had not heard him.

"Of course I accept," she finally said, pulling him back to his feet. "This life-mating is our oath and our bond. Let nothing break it."

An uproar of cheers, cat-calls, and other sounds rushed across the crowd, though it was far more muted among the wildlings. All of this Estin was happily able to ignore, looking between Feanne—his life-mate—and the kits, who were bouncing around, cheering.

Chapter Thirteen

"A Rift Between"

Almost two years after I had met her, I was finally bonded with the person I had always loved more than anything. I could hardly believe it, despite Yoska spending far too much of his time giving me advice that no reasonable being would offer to another that was not their mate.

Those were by far the happiest months of my life, unquestionably. Every moment of them was a blessing, especially given the turmoil in the rest of the world, while we hid in our valley, secure in our defenses, through the rest of the winter and well into summer.

I still was not quite free of the dreams, but they were not the ones I had grown up with anymore, either. Details had warped with time, becoming something new, but I could certainly recognize the dream for what it was.

In this new dream, I found myself outside my home when the attack occurred. Invaders rushed into the village, their grotesque undead faces visible in the distance as they grabbed at the other pack members, attempting to drag them off. The most haunting image of this part of the dream were the children I saw butchered by these creatures.

The cries for help came from every direction and I ran to aid as many as I could, knowing the risk to myself. It was what I did as a healer. I needed to protect the pack, no matter what. I fought against one of the invaders after another, knowing somewhere deep down that these should have been bandits and furriers, but that was not this dream. Now, they were undead, their purpose more direct—they needed more corpses, using us as the raw materials that they required.

I finished off yet another of the monsters, reeling with the injuries I had taken. I had to be sparing with my magic, as I knew so many more people would need healing before the day was out and my own wounds would be by no means fatal. Thus, I pushed on, fighting right up until the moment I heard Feanne's scream.

There is no sound in the world that can cut through your mind's defenses like the person you love crying out in pain. You may believe in your own inner-strength, but when that cry comes, every learned moment of pride and vanity goes away and you are left with the panicked fear of a child, running to their aid and praying that they still live. You will make mistakes, but it cannot be helped.

In this dream, I would burst into our house and find Feanne lying on the floor, bleeding from a head wound. At her side, a black-robed Turessian—I was never really sure what else to call them, given their own people's admission that they were abominations— stood over her, holding a chain leash that I knew would choke her to death if she was not already gone.

Time was short, I knew. If Feanne was still alive, that leash needed to come off quickly, or she would not be. For some reason, I knew I could not bring her back to life— perhaps my magic was consumed already, or perhaps the dream just needed it to be so.

Growling and shouting to get the creature's attention, I rushed at the Turessian. I dodged his first attack, hoping to grab the leash from him. I knew it would take a long time to beat the man in a fight, so I wanted to be sure that Feanne was safe first. Unfortunately, the man was stronger than I was, by a great deal. He held firm as I caught hold of the leash, stopping me from getting it away from him.

Before I could react, he struck me across the side of my head, knocking me to the floor beside Feanne. I could barely think or move from the pain, as I struggled to find those little whispering spirits that would help me heal. My mind just would not focus, would not call out to the powers I needed to save both of our lives.

I looked up then and in the far doorway I could see Atall and Oria, their faces drawn with fear. I knew what was coming, but I did not want them to see it. These children had seen too much already and should not see their parents die. If I could not save myself and my love, I would at least spare the children this.

Praying that the Turessian did not notice them, I mouthed the only thing I could think of.

"Hide!"

"You sure you're okay?" Estin called down from the little perch he had stopped on.

Oria and Atall glared up at him with nearly mirrored expressions as they struggled to make their way up the steep rocks. They pushed on, sometimes gaining a bit of ground, but more often slipping back to where they started.

"It's too steep," Atall told him, having slid back off the rock for at least the fifth time. "We can't do this."

"Yes, you can. Don't listen to what your mother says about climbing. Just take your time and look for the handholds."

The kits continued trying, stopping every so often to grumble and complain about the difficulty of the climb. Each time, their own stubbornness kept them trying, until at last

Atall made it up to Estin, followed very soon after by his sister.

"I told you it wasn't too steep," Estin said, giving Atall a poke. "C'mon. We're almost there."

Estin led the way up the remaining section of mountain, nearing a small plateau where he often went to escape the village...and to hide when Feanne was angry with him, or at least in his general direction. That part he had left out when he had told the kits about the place, prompting their immediate demands that he show it to them.

When the kits had run straight to Feanne, begging her to let them go see the place, she had laughed herself to the point of tears at the idea of the two kits struggling up the steep mountain, but had agreed. Estin figured that she had expected them to give up and come right back.

Now, hours of climbing later, he doubted the kits were nearly as eager as when they had started, but they had toughed through the difficult journey. For that, he was rather impressed and proud of them, though he knew much of their drive to make it up the mountain was related to the stubbornness they had inherited from Feanne.

"Right up here," he told them, hoisting Oria, then Atall up onto the ledge. He slid the rope he had tied to himself and to them mostly onto the ledge, then hopped up himself. "This is where I go to watch the world."

The ledge had been Estin's favorite spot in the area since he had discovered it during his exploration of the peaks earlier in the spring. From where they were sitting, he could see for at least fifty miles out onto the plains and about half as far back into the mountain range. Clear skies like this particular day were always the best, letting him relax in the bright sunlight, while watching the horizons.

"What's that?" Oria began, pointing at some random shape in the distance.

"And that?" added Atall, also fixating on something that Estin could not even hope to identify.

"That," Estin explained, picking things he actually could see clear enough to recognize, "is the new lake from the water elementals, where our scouts think their leader is, or at least where the portal to their lands might be. South of there, that blackened crater was once the largest farmland I had ever seen, until the fire lords began burning the area. Still south of that, you see that shape there?"

"Yeah," mumbled Atall, squinting.

"We think that might be stone elementals, building some kind of city or base or something."

The kits stared off into the distance, trying to make out what he was pointing at.

"And here's my favorite thing to watch," he added, indicating a spot nearly north of them. "There is where the dragons are fighting the elemental lords."

At the location he had shown them, Estin had seen at least half a dozen dragons, their immense winged shapes visible for miles. During all of his visits in the last month, the dragons had been circling that area, as faint explosions of magic could be just barely made out. The warfare would continue day and night, with some of the magical detonations so brightly visible that they made Estin's eyes burn.

They watched for a while, the kits silent—for once—as they stared at the seemingly unending battle in the north. While they watched, one of the dragons flew off, crashing into the mountains.

"They killed a dragon!" whispered Atall, his ears flattening. "I thought the dragons were immortal!"

"That I don't know about, but I've seen the dragons fall several times. They always seem to come back into the fight in an hour or so. I think they just need a rest, sometimes."

Estin sat with the children on the ledge for more than two hours, watching the brightly-colored battle rage on. As it was getting late into the afternoon, the dragon that had fallen flew back into the fray, rejoining its kin, much to the amusement and cheering of the kits.

"Alright, time to head back before your mother thinks I threw you both off a cliff," he told them, standing to begin the climb down. "You'll need to..."

Estin cut himself off as a sound like tearing fabric echoed across the mountains. He began looking around for the source of the sound, but could find nothing that would have made anything like it. As he searched, his eyes did fall on movement far below, near the entrance to the valley. Whatever it was, it was moving quickly, heading straight into the valley.

"We need to hurry," Estin said, grabbing Oria under one arm and snagging Atall with his tail, as he yanked the rope off of them. "Please don't tell your mother about this."

He stepped off the edge of the cliff, catching himself as he fell, then hopped down the side of the rock wall, dropping ten or fifteen feet with each fall. The kits screamed the whole way down, though he was not sure if it was for fear or enjoyment, nor did he have time to find out. Whatever was coming up the valley would likely beat him back to the village if he could not get down fast enough.

The same climb that had taken most of the morning with the kits this time took Estin twenty minutes carrying them, though by the time he reached the bottom, his arms and legs ached and he wondered if he could still run. He stood on the ground for a minute, catching his breath, while the kits looked both ways repeatedly, trying to spot whatever he had seen earlier.

A loud and crisp horn blast echoed through the valley's entrance, the warning signal from the scouts if intruders had been found. Abruptly, the sound faded to a strangled bleating noise and went silent.

"Run!" Estin ordered the kits, pointing the direction. The three of them bolted for the village, Estin hoping that they were well ahead of whatever was coming.

Along the way, both kits faltered at one point or another, but he kept scooping them back onto their feet and hurrying them along. By the time they entered the village proper, dozens of the residents were armed and marching in his direction.

"Large force coming up the valley!" Estin called to the nearest of the barbarians— Bockkan, he realized after he had spoken—who appeared to be in charge of the group. "Secure the entrance to the village. Don't let anything past you that you don't already know belongs here."

Bockkan pounded his chest in acknowledgement, then raised his spear, calling for his men to follow him into battle. As one, the twenty men and women charged northward, disappearing into the trees.

With the kits in tow, Estin ran again, then stopped when he heard another horn cry from the south. This one was cut short, too.

"Children," Estin said nervously, kneeling between them, "where are your daggers? Go get them and meet me at Ulra's tent. Bring your mother if you see her."

They both ran off, going exactly where he told them to. That alone let him know that they understood the severity of what was happening.

The horn cries had done their duty and as Estin made his way towards Ulra and Doln's home, he watched the village rapidly mobilize. The young and elderly were being hurriedly moved towards the west end of the valley by a cluster of younger warriors and hunters, where the valley narrowed and could be defended with a smaller number of warriors. Meanwhile, everywhere else, every able being of any race and breed was being armed and rapidly trained by several dwarven smiths. It was honestly the first time Estin had ever seen some of the wildlings look as though they would fight anything.

Up on the mountainsides, Estin could just make out groups of Halflings, arming massive traps that would either collapse the valley entrances, or hopefully crush whoever was invading. That had been an idea of Feanne's only a week earlier and he hoped that it would pay off.

Within seconds of reaching Ulra's tent, he could hear the first echoed sounds of fighting in the north valley. Bockkan's men were far off, he knew, but their cries and challenges rang through the air, warning everyone that those who had arrived were not friendly and that the battle had begun. The calls to battle were very quickly replaced by the screams of the dying.

"Ulra!" Estin called, spotting the bear with her mate not far off. They were herding a group of young elves towards the west, as Finth sat near their tent, pulling on a suit of rusted chainmaile.

Finth glanced up at him and hurried in fastening his belt, rushing over to join the group as Estin came to a halt near Doln.

"Do we have any defense groups set up?" he asked, though Ulra shook her head immediately. "Where are Linn and Yoska?"

"Arming and meeting us at your tent, along with anyone they can find," Finth told him, motioning back towards Estin and Feanne's tent. "The plan is to guard that location so that you can use your fancy little circle to raise our fallen, or whatever in the planes you do with that thing. If we can hold the damned thing long enough, we might be able to beat off whoever's gotten it in their head to stomp on us. Feanne already knows and is gathering others."

The group took a little while to head back the way Estin had come, having to stop repeatedly to guide smaller groups towards or away from the center of the village, where they intended to hold their ground. By the time they did arrive, nearly forty men and women had formed a giant ring around the single tent. All the nearby structures had been torn down hastily and tossed aside to provide better visibility for when the intruders arrived.

A distant explosion in the north told Estin that things were not going well and the Halflings' trap had been sprung.

"Get inside," Linn barked when he saw Estin. The man was decked head to toe in armor and had managed to find a decent sword and shield somewhere. "We've got two more healers out here with us. Feanne wants you on the circle, until we need you outside."

He rushed through the tight crowd, losing Finth, Ulra, and Doln as they joined the others. Pushing into the tent, he cringed at seeing Oria and Atall still there, sitting beside Feanne at the middle of the tent. Both children looked up nervously as he came in, their hands on their knives.

"We are in trouble, Estin," Feanne whispered, her eyes distant. "The Miharon may be gone, but I can still feel the woods through the gifts he gave me. Something is defiling the land as it comes this way. The woods are screaming out against it."

"Undead?"

Feanne nodded.

"I believe so. I did not feel this when the elementals got close. I cannot think of anything else that would upset nature this gravely. Even so, there are a lot of them."

Estin watched the children's faces, but they were fighting to keep a calm demeanor. Neither reacted at all to their mother's remarks, but he could still see the tension in them.

Sitting down at the edge of the healing circle, Estin touched the stones that made up its border, testing the magic. He had not needed the conduit to the spirits since the circle had been completed, so he wanted to familiarize himself with its feel before the battle began. He only hoped that he would not need to use it.

His fingers passing through the circle harmlessly, Estin felt the familiar openness to the realm of the spirits, the touch of those recently dead passing through his mind, waking him to their calls. It was something Asrahn had taught him to be aware of when he entered such a circle, allowing him to immediately hear the cry of any spirit that sought his aid in returning to the world. This time though, something felt off. The magic was not quite as he remembered it, but he could not find words to describe what was different. He shrugged back the thought and reminded himself that he had not used that particular circle before and it was likely just the newness of it that he was feeling.

"They're here!" came a woman's call outside, just as a crack of magical energy left the air with a scent of ozone. That was soon followed by the twang of many dozens of bows being fired.

Within seconds, Estin could hear the crashes of hundreds of weapons and bodies impacting as the war lines collided. He closed his eyes and cringed at the sounds, trying to block them out, as every new cry and shout made him want to go outside all the more. Some of the screams he recognized, making it all that much more painful.

"You may go," Feanne told him, her gaze still distant as she brushed at both children, almost as though she were reassuring herself they were still there. "If the time comes, I can hold the tent against whatever comes. No one will touch the children or the circle while I draw breath. Just be sure to return if our allies begin dying."

Estin knelt in front of her, cradling her head against his for just a moment. He repeated the affectionate embrace for each of the kits, then left the tent, drawing his swords as he went.

The chaos surrounding him very nearly broke Estin's resolve as he stepped from the tent, stunning him with the violence everywhere. For as far as he could see in all directions, the ghastly faces of the recently dead grinned and mouthed silent words at them, pushing at one another in an attempt to get closer to the living.

Blood was the next thing that sunk into Estin's mind as he began pushing his way to the front lines. It was everywhere, both dried on the corpses and fresh on his companions, who were so overwhelmed by the enemy forces that they could not fall back to tend to their injuries. As he joined them, he had to catch warriors who simply collapsed from their wounds, unable to continue. He had not even gotten to the front of the group before he had exhausted much of his ability to heal for the day, tending to those most grievously wounded.

"Nice of you to join us, fox-mate," grunted Bockkan, nearby. The man's body was savaged, bloody lines marring every inch of his flesh that was not covered with animal hides. He took most of the head off a groaning zombie with his axe, then kicked the body away, giving Estin the space to join him. "Show them what the fox has taught us about being more than we appear. I look forward to dying at your side."

Estin took that to be about as close to complement as the man was capable of and hopped in beside him, deflecting the grasping fingers of the zombies with his swords, cutting into the nearest creatures as best he could. They hardly seemed to notice, pushing forward at him, trying to grab or strike with their remaining fingers.

Estin shut down his mind at that point, knowing that if he thought too much, fear would overwhelm him. It was one of the most stressed points that Feanne had taught him so long ago, that as a breed that would not intentionally face conflict, he needed to distance himself from that instinct to run. That was something he had only used briefly in the time since then, but now was essential as he saw the undead tear each other apart in an attempt to get at him, trying to bury their broken and rotted teeth into his flesh.

Magic proved indispensible in the fight and not just for Estin. Throughout the group, they had scattered some of the more powerful spellcasters that had come to the village for shelter. From them, sprays of flame and lightning, as well as crashing balls of ice and stone flew into the enemy, wreaking gory carnage on their lines and often giving the warriors more time to tend to their wounds or fall back as another took their place.

In addition to Estin, there were also more healers who ran tirelessly through the group, doing what they could to keep the warriors fighting. He rarely saw them spend the time to fully heal anyone, instead conserving their abilities to only mend those who were unable to fight anymore.

To Estin's surprise, he even saw several spellcasters hanging near the tent who were led by the vine-clad fae-kin that had originally led him into the village when they had arrived. That group helped the healers occasionally, but mostly spent their time summoning vines and other hindrances for the undead. Once, he even saw the fae-kin woman raise her face to the sky calling down a massive eagle that was larger than Ulra, which swept through the enemy lines, tearing dozens of the undead apart before it was dragged to the ground and butchered, its screams mingling with those of so many others.

Hours or minutes later, Estin was staggering away from the front lines, his arms torn and barely able to hold his weapons. Deep scratches covered most of his skin and he knew that he was no longer providing enough cover for Bockkan, so he stepped back, letting a dwarven warrior take his place as he checked over his injuries.

The cuts were painful and bled awfully, but Estin assured himself that they were not severe enough to waste what remained of his healing. Instead, he began moving through the crowd of defenders, tending to others.

"Get Estin inside!" came a call that made Estin's ears perk. He did not recognize the voice, but he obeyed anyway, slashing open the canvas wall to get in more quickly.

Inside, Feanne and the kits were tending to several severely injured warriors and one of the other healers. As he moved towards them to help, Feanne waved him towards the circle instead, where seven bodies had been dragged in and lay beside the stones.

"Get them up as fast as you can!" she ordered him, tying off a bandage on an aging elf, whose arm hung weakly, covered in blood. "We need everyone out there."

Estin sat down in the healing circle, pulling the first body in with him. There was no time for ritual or preparation, so he just dragged the corpse onto his lap. With the slightest touch of healing, he restored the body enough that the woman should live if he brought her back to life, then looked around for its spirit. Instantly, he saw the ghostly form of the Halfling woman hovering nearby, gazing sadly at her body.

"Come back to...," he began, then watched as the ghostly shape was battered around, as if by winds. "Come back, please!"

The Halfling's ghost reached for her body, but then was blown away, fading into nothing. The circle was still and empty, aside from Estin.

"Lost her!" he called back to Feanne, setting aside the body.

He grabbed the next corpse, repeating the process of healing it slightly, then looking for the spirit. This time, he found himself entirely unable to even shift his gaze into the spirit realm. There was nothing there, as though the circle was powerless and even Estin's own ability to see the spirits had gone.

In a fearful panic, Estin pulled one body after another into the circle, seeing and feeling nothing. There were nothing there at all. Everything beyond his spells had failed, leaving him with no connection to the dead.

"Feanne," he said, voice trembling, "we just lost the circle. I cannot raise these people."

"How is that even possible?" she demanded.

"I have no idea. We need a new plan."

Feanne got up, motioning for the kits to stay where they were. She paced the edge of the tent and traced the outermost line of the area with her feet. Once she had circled the whole place, she closed her eyes and began tracing runes in the air over the entrance to the tent, the lines that she drew in the air lighting briefly, then fading.

"They cannot enter the tent," she said as she finished. "The others can fall back here and the undead will be blocked. It's the best I can offer until we find out why your circle is not working and fix it."

Feanne leaned out of the tent, shouting as loudly as she could over the din of battle, "If you are injured, come inside. The undead cannot follow you here!"

She came back in, going back to the kits and sitting down between them, then returned to tending to the injured.

Estin got up and walked around his circle, eyeing the pattern of the stones. What he knew of the magic that controlled the circles told him that there was really nothing that could disrupt or break them once they had been created. All of the care was needed in their creation, rather than afterwards. Asrahn had told him it could last for years without even tending to its magic. There seemed to be no reason it was not working. Even as he wondered, two more bodies were dragged inside, which he ignored, unable to do anything to help them.

"Can you raise them without the circle?" asked Feanne.

"I can help two people, but that would use up what little magic I have left. Without the circle, we'll lose the village within the hour. I need to know what's happening and whether the undead managed to do this."

Rushing back outside, Estin watched the raging throng of undead, which was tearing into the defenders, pushing those that remained tight against the tent. Those that fell more often than not were dragged off into the undead horde, screaming as they went. Already, the number of living had dwindled to half of where it had begun.

Finally, Estin spotted a group of black-clad figures deep in the crowd of corpses. This group moved casually through the zombies and skeletons, picking through the wreckage of the camp as though they were looting the place.

"Finth!" Estin called into the crowd, only to have the battered and bloodied dwarf show up a moment later, panting as he picked pieces of zombie off of his face. "I'm going out there. I need you to clear the way if I come running back."

"Just stab yourself in the face with your sword, monkey. It's a cleaner death, with less puss-buckets poking at you."

"I'm not planning on dying just yet."

Estin focused a little of his dwindling strength into raising a magical barrier around himself, then walked into the undead forces. The barrier would not last him terribly long, but he knew it could keep the undead from touching him, giving him the singular opportunity to scout what was happening beyond the immediate battle and possibly find out how the undead were keeping his circle suppressed.

As he stepped into the crowd, the undead wailed and clawed in his direction, many forgetting their other targets as they tried desperately to reach him. The nature of the spell kept these creatures from coming closer than an inch or two to him, but every decayed hand that reached for him made Estin flinch, wondering if that would be the one that got through the barrier.

He moved as swiftly as he could through the crowd of clawing groaning undead, making his way towards what he guessed were Turessians. It was slow-going, but soon he broke free of the back end of the undead line, the zombies and others returning to their task of attacking the other defenders.

Ahead of him, the four black-robed figures moved towards the west end of the camp, seemingly not having noticed him yet.

Estin followed the group, trailing them to the far west end of where the village's structures had been. Most were now in shambles, having been trampled by the undead during their approach. It was here that the Turessians stopped, turning to face him abruptly.

"You risk a lot coming outside of your sad group of allies," noted one. From what little Estin could see of the man under his hood, his face was partially skeletal. "Do you believe we cannot tear down that pesky bit of magical sanctuary you wear like a shield?"

Estin did not reply, but tried to get a look at each of the Turessians. If one of them was suppressing his circle, they would be concentrating to maintain that effect. He just needed to find out which one and somehow interrupt them. It was clearly not the tall one that was speaking, leaving the very short one and the two that looked to be of average build.

"Do you wish to see what has become of your others?"

Estin's ears twitched and he found himself cocking his head. He knew of only one other group and they had run far to the west, where they should have outpaced the undead and escaped into the woods.

The Turessian grinned back at him and waved him to follow, then began heading westward.

Following nervously, Estin made sure to maintain his barrier. He had no idea if it would even slow the Turessians, but he had no intention of making it any easier on them than he had to.

They walked a short time into the woods, Estin trailing far behind the group, until they reached a barren area just before the valley ended at a mountain wall. In one corner of the area, Estin knew there was a barely-visible path up into the mountains, which the young and elderly were supposed to have used to escape. Instead, they were being herded into one corner of the rocky area, surrounded by undead, all of whom bore long wooden spears that they used to block the escape of any living that tried to get away from them.

"We have a proposal," stated the Turessian, stopping and turning back to Estin. "All of these lives in exchange for your healing circle and all of your spellcasters. Every other living being is allowed to leave to be hunted some other day."

"My circle?" Estin asked, shocked. He had no idea that there was even a way for someone to track down a circle without having seen it before. "Why do you want my circle?"

The man laughed, a dry wheezing sound that chilled Estin's blood.

"We can make as many of those," he waved at the zombies standing guard nearby, "as we desire. We will never run out of them, until long after your world has died. What we cannot do without a circle, is make very many more of our own or other intelligent undead. Some of our kind can create one or two like themselves, but if we wish to replace the living, we need circles to do so."

The other three Turessians pulled back their hoods, revealing partially-rotted features of varying races. The two average-height ones were human, though one looked to have been a barbarian tribesman at one time and the other bore the features of a Altis noble. The shortest was the one that made Estin nearly drop his barrier, though.

Varra stared back at him with pale white eyes and a cocked smirk.

"You have met," the speaker said, glancing at Varra. "Then you understand how important it is what you give us what we want, or everyone here will die far more horribly than she did."

Estin swallowed, nervously looking over at the large group of humans, elves, dwarves, Halflings, and nearly every other race and culture, standing in a tight clump nearby. Most watched him intently and he saw many heads shake, warning him not to give in.

"The circle is gone," he admitted, hoping for the best. "Its power faded just before I came out. I thought you had done it, but you wouldn't be asking for it if that was the case. I will turn myself over in exchange for their lives."

The Turessians let out howls of anger, their eyes glowing more brightly in their rage.

"Another! Another circle fallen," roared the barbarian-looking man to the one that had been speaking. "What would you have us do, now?"

"We will need to search for another."

Estin glanced at the captives, then back to the Turessian that seemed to be in charge.

"Will you at least tell me what has happened to make that circle fall?"

The man's hood lifted sharply, as though he had forgotten about Estin.

"Your people happened. The living. So determined to keep us from cleansing this world, that you brought in every form of magic that never should have been considered. The arcane explosions, the dragons, the elemental lords...do you think such things do not have a price?"

Estin inched away, feeling the rage growing from the man, but he kept talking as he advanced on Estin.

"That kind of power breaks things, wildling. It tugs at the threads that hold the world together and separate from all the planes. Eventually, a strand will break and things begin to change. While you were hiding away in your mountain retreat, we saw legions from the elemental planes just walk in with no effort. We saw the skies freeze, the lands blow away, and the seas burn. This world may be dying and unless we reverse it, even our kind will perish when it is torn apart."

The man turned to the zombies holding the captives, as his partners stepped between Estin and the living captives.

"Begin staking one every ten minutes, until the others surrender."

As Estin watched, knowing he was unable to stop so many undead himself, the zombies grabbed a young ogre child, dragging him apart from the others. Estin tried to go to him, but the three Turessians moved with him blocking his path.

"Is not your time, my fuzzy friend," hissed Varra, grinning at him. "You will die when the time is better, no? For now, just watch."

Estin snarled at her, drawing only a giggling laugh from Varra, as he watched the zombies drive a wooden spear into the ogre's chest, then hoist him up into the air. The spear was plunged into the ground, leaving the writhing child screaming high in the air.

"You have ten minutes," hissed the lead Turessian, walking away. "When I run out of these, I will begin with your defenders. Surrender and we may be able to make an agreement. If you keep fighting, every last person under your command will be put on a pike."

Already, the young ogre had stopped struggling and now hung limply on the tall spike.

Estin tried to shift his vision, looking for the spirit of the youth, but he saw nothing. It was as though his own connection to the spirits was fading, just like the circle. There just was nothing there, other than the dangling corpse. Furious and watching for the Turessians to follow him—which they did not—he hurried back to where the undead still milled about the tent, barely held back by the few remaining defenders.

As he pushed through the undead forces, he could see Feanne at the entrance to the tent, calling out orders to the dozen remaining warriors. One after another, they were falling back into the tent as their wounds became too great to continue fighting. By the time he reached the tent, he had begun to feel the claws of the undead brushing him as his barrier faded.

"Get inside!" Feanne called out, rushing out to grab him and shove him past her. "Everyone who's still breathing, get in the tent!"

Estin scrambled in with the others, finding the inside of the large tent entirely packed with injured people. Though the tent could have held ten or fifteen adults standing comfortably, it had gotten packed with nearly three times that. He spotted Oria and Atall on top of Ulra's shoulders, as well as Finth on Doln's, trying not to get trampled. Linn was in a corner of the tent, deep gashes from his face down into the top of his armor being tended to by one of the other healers. Even Yoska looked to be gravely injured, a large bite-mark on his upper chest bleeding profusely, despite the efforts of several of his clan-mates.

"Were you able to find anything?" Feanne asked loudly as she squeezed back inside, even as the undead rushed up to the edge of the tent, clawing at it, as though they were held an inch away from its surface.

"Turessians. Four of them," he told her, trying to keep his voice as low as he could, but in the crowded tent surrounded by groaning undead, that was practically a shout. "They've got the group we sent for the mountain path. They're executing them one at a time until we surrender."

Feanne eyed him, then looked over the others in the tent, settling on Oria and Atall.

"I asked you a long time ago whether you would be able to flee with my children if the valley were to fall," Feanne reminded Estin, her shoulders sagging. She was avoiding looking at him as she continued. "You will take them and break through the enemy lines..."

"I would never make it out of the valley. My magic can't protect the kits that far," he cut in, grabbing her wrist and turning her to face him. "Even if I could, I will not leave you here. Life-mate does not mean you get to run off and die, while we live on. I will not obey you in this, Feanne. If I run, all four of us are going."

Smiling sadly, Feanne touched his cheek.

"Then we die here as a family."

She looked around that those who still stood, clearly evaluating their remaining forces.

"Bockkan, you are with me," Feanne called out, waving down the man. He gave her a confused look, but began making his way over. She waited until the large man was standing over them and continued, "We are going out to negotiate. If they are talking terms of surrender, then we have something they want. I need to know what it is. Will you both stand at my side through this?"

"To the ends of the world," Estin answered immediately.

Bockkan smirked, tossing his hair back as he eyed them both.

"Now this is the time for little fox's tricks," he announced, grinning. "Show me the trick, so that I may follow you."

Feanne gave a thankful nod to Bockkan, then turned to the tent's only exit, taking a steadying breath before stepping through into the mass of undead clawing at the invisible barrier that shielded the tent.

As Feanne left the tent, Estin brought up another spell, blanketing the three of them against the nearby undead, forcing the groaning corpses back a few steps. It was the last such spell he would be able to manage, making him wonder if they would even make it back to the tent. The small bubble they walked within would not last long against so many, but it was all he could manage that would protect them as they emerged into the army of walking dead.

"I would negotiate!" cried out Feanne, as they stood in the clawing throng, all three of them looking around nervously at the creatures that were trying endlessly to reach them.

Seconds passed and Estin began to wonder if the Turessians—or whatever he should call them—would actually come. Then, the undead army began moving away, creating a clear walkway leading from the tent westward. Down this path, three of the Turessians walked triumphantly, unhindered by the undead that now stood silently on either sides.

"You are smarter than I had thought," lauded the nearest of the necromancers, clapping his hands. "I had believed I would get to execute at least a half dozen before you were willing to consider speaking with me."

Feanne's jaw trembled with anger, but she appeared able to control herself this time.

"What is it you want here?" she demanded, as though she were in control of the situation. "I would have your army leave and I want to know what it will take to make this happen."

"Things are not that simple, fox. I wish to speak with all of your spellcasters to present my offer. That is all I ask at this time."

Feanne glanced over at Estin. He shrugged, focusing most of his attention on maintaining the barrier over them, whether useful against the Turessian or not.

"You may speak to only the two of us," she answered a moment later. "There are few enough of us in this camp. I will hear your offer and pass it along to the others."

The Turessian laughed and shook his head, though Estin's attention was drawn to the other two. One he recognized as Varra by size and build. The other was the barbarian. The Altis noble was missing from the group, which set Estin's nerves on edge. He began turning about, trying to spot the missing man.

"I would ask that your healers and elementalists surrender themselves to me," said the Turessian, motioning towards Estin for emphasis. "All of them. I have no use for you and your kind. The others are just fodder and can be used in the future, but I do not need them at this time. If every one of those spellcasters surrenders, I will spare the rest for now."

Feanne turned to Estin, drawing his attention away from the search for the other Turessian.

"Take the offer," Estin urged her, keeping his voice low. "They don't know who can cast magic and who cannot. So far as they know, I'm the only healer here. If it will get you and the kits out of harm's way, I'll gladly surrender."

"What was it you said a few minutes ago?" Feanne asked in reply, smiling half-heartedly. "We all walk out, or none of us. I will not give you to them."

"Don't let the whole pack die for me."

She shook her head.

"I will save everyone, or we all die together. No one gets thrown to these creatures. I would rather my children die free, than watching any part of their family turned to undead."

"This is touching, but what will we do?" asked Bockkan, leaning close to them. "Do we fight, or do you ask that we try to run?"

Feanne kept her eyes on Estin, but answered Bockkan.

"You and I will transform ourselves and strike at the Turessians. Estin will attempt to keep us alive long enough to reach them. If we can bring them down, our families might live until tomorrow."

"This is a plan worthy of my people's sacrifice," Bockkan said, thumping his chest with a bare fist. "There will be stories of this battle, little fox."

"We can hope so," she answered softly, her eyes telling Estin that she was doubting anyone would be able to tell such stories. "Let us either live or die trying to save everyone."

Bockkan was the first to turn on the Turessians, roaring first in his human voice, then his tone changing as the shadowy form of the bear engulphed his physical form. Before he had fully been changed, Feanne had dropped to the ground, her bones loudly snapping and changing, as Estin maintained his barrier over them.

"You wish to do this?" the Turessian demanded, as Bockkan rushed towards him and Feanne rose back to her feet, now in her lycanthrope form. "Very well. I never claimed to fight fairly."

"Is time!" shouted Varra, before backing quickly away.

The undead forces closed in on their group, struggling to grab at Feanne and Bockkan as they pushed forward. Estin did what he could to keep them back, but they posed very little resistance as Feanne and Bockkan tore through the lines, rapidly closing on the three Turessians.

A loud tearing noise, followed by screams was Estin's first true hint of danger.

Spinning, even as Feanne and Bockkan continued their berserk charge, he saw that the tent had collapsed behind them and the undead army was pushing inwards, dragging the other townsfolk from the ruins of the structure. At the far side of the tent, the fourth Turessian stood, guiding the undead into the wreckage.

"Feanne! An enchanter brought down the tent!" he screamed, dropping his barrier as he drew his swords and rushed into the fray, trying to clear a path back towards the mass melee. He cut through one undead after another, barely staggering them as he pushed forward, sometimes going over top of squirming corpses to finally reach the edge of what had been the tent.

Diving over another undead, Estin saw where Ulra was fighting for her life, standing practically on top of the two kits. He rushed towards her, while Feanne leapt over him, landing in the middle of a group of undead, ripping them apart. She took another long stride and was beside Ulra, tearing and slashing at the attackers as she hoisted the two children onto her own back.

Estin slowed his pace, knowing Feanne could handle herself. He focused instead on keeping the undead at bay, trying to find a way to get back to where Bockkan still fought with the Turessians, far out in the sea of corpses. He could not see much, but did get the occasional glimpse of Bockkan's massive form as the man threw bodies into the air to get them out of his way.

A strong hand slammed into Estin's side, ripping his leather vest away, along with a good portion of the fur there. As he stumbled away from the attack, he found himself looking at Varra, who had managed to slip through the crowd right up to him, her broken grin visible even under her hood. She casually tossed aside the ripped vest that she had torn right off of him.

"Is a good time now," she mocked, turning with him as he tried to get his torn side away from her. "You have a family now, my fuzzy friend. Is most unfortunate, yes? You will see them all die today."

Estin thought through what little magic he had remaining. It would not go far against Varra, as he had to assume she was at least as powerful as the other Turessians now. He had maybe four or five spells left that he could manage and he knew that most would not affect her.

"So many lives that look to you," continued Varra, taking cautious steps towards him. "Do you think you will miss all this when you are one of us?"

"Varra, don't do this. You were a good person in life."

The girl laughed, tossing back her hood. Black lines marred her dark skin where veins had clotted. For some reason, despite her ghastly appearance, it was the lack of jewelry or fine garments that struck Estin as being the most surprising change.

"Who I was is not who I am now," she explained, drawing and twirling a dagger in her left hand. "Now, I am free. You must fear dying, but there is no fear for me. No pain, no disease, no worry. I will go on, long after this war has ended and your people are ash in shallow grave."

A second dagger appeared in Varra's right hand, as she moved steadily towards him, sometimes pausing mid-stride to wave off the shambling corpses that reached for Estin.

"You have until your heart stops to tell me you will join us," Varra added, raising her weapons. "Is not long, but is all I can give, no?"

Out of nowhere, Finth appeared, driving his own knives into Varra dozens of times as he dodged and moved around her, cutting and ripping at every joint of her body. She staggered under the attack, clearly surprised, barely managing to block or parry more than a quarter of the strikes.

"This is quite good!" she exclaimed, laughing as Finth slashed open her stomach. "You are very good, yes?"

At a gesture from Varra, Estin found himself shoved back a step, unable to move forward to help his friend. Meanwhile, Finth continued his attack, apparently trying to find a weak point, or at least slow Varra down.

"Let me show you what magic can really do," cooed Varra, raising her hand at Finth, ignoring his weapon as it cut into her hand.

While Estin watched helplessly, unable to get closer to aid Finth, Varra whispered words of magic and Finth's body seemed to erupt in magical fire from within. He collapsed on the spot, burning blood flowing from his ears and mouth.

"No!" Estin cried, fighting against the magic that held him back. "Varra, what is wrong with you?"

"You will understand soon."

Varra turned to face him, grinning wickedly.

"I have learned much in death, no?" she asked, laughing.

Varra's hoarse laughter was cut short as Yoska leapt onto her back, driving a knife into her throat. He rolled away and then stood, pacing around her, eyeing her head to toe, as Varra coughed and tried to speak, one hand fumbling with the gaping hole in her neck.

"This fight is not yours, Estin," Yoska said grimly, moving between Estin and Varra. "She cannot cast if she cannot speak, no? Please find your family and protect them. This is my family and must be dealt with just so."

Estin wasted no more time, letting Yoska seek his own revenge. He ran first to Finth, checking the dwarf's pulse and finding nothing. Hoisting Finth to his shoulder, Estin spun around, trying to find Feanne and the kits. They were not hard to spot, Feanne still towering over the undead as she flung them aside by twos and threes, with both kits on her back, clinging to her fur.

Pushing his way through the undead, Estin made some progress towards Feanne, but stopped as he saw the tall Turessian moving through the crowd. The man seemed to notice Estin and raised his hands, weaving one spell after another, launching the next before the previous had landed.

Struggling to counter the magic buffeting his body, Estin dispelled one painful rush of energy, then another, and then another, until his own abilities were essentially exhausted, barely even noticing that he had been forced to drop Finth. Then, just as he thought he might have gotten a break between magical attacks, Estin felt a cold blast of air strike at him, moving through his clothing and skin, tearing into his body and making him stiffen reflexively.

Estin hung there, his body locked into position for the briefest of seconds, as the death magic tore his life away, every excruciating instant vivid in his mind as he felt his heart stop. Everything went black as he began to fall. Everything was so cold...

*

Pain flashed through his body, then another chill, then finally the faintest of warmth. Estin's mind railed against the changing feelings, until at last he managed to drag himself back to consciousness, vomiting uncontrollably as he tried to breathe. He just lay there, gagging for a long time, struggling to regain control over his body.

At last, Estin began to feel more awake and aware, opening his eyes slowly and trying to take in what was around him. Maddening pain flooded his head, making him slam his eyes shut again. It was a struggle to re-open them, gradually managing to keep them open long enough to see some of his surroundings.

Looking up, he saw Atall sitting over him, watching him with nervous impatience.

"What happened?" Estin croaked, his voice strained from the vomiting.

"You died," the boy said matter-of-factly. "You're better now. Others need healing and I can't help. Mom needs you to hurry."

Estin forced his trembling muscles to push him upright. Once off the ground, he began looking around, seeing that he lay in the middle of a huge pile of unmoving zombies, who all looked as though they had been burned. The only other living being nearby was Atall, who was rubbing at Asrahn's ring as he watched Estin.

"Where is your mother?"

Atall pointed towards the west.

Turning, Estin looked off in that direction, where he could see Feanne's huge shape charging through the undead with Oria on her back, even as the last Turessian pointed at her and called out demands at his minions. The group fought against her, barely slowing her progress as she furiously tore through them, trying to reach the Turessian.

"Oria's protecting her right now," Atall told him, helping Estin stand up. "I don't know how much more she can do. We don't know what we can really do, yet."

"How?" gasped Estin, staring in shock at the child. "How did you get me back up?"

Atall smiled and held up his hand with the ring from Asrahn.

"Grandmother let us know we could help with the rings. Mine blew up all the dead near us, then brought you back without a circle. Hers is stopping the bad man's death magic. I think she's used it all up, but the bad man might be out, too."

Estin shook off the last of his delirium and crawled to his feet, checking around on the ground for his weapons, but there was no sign of them. He looked around, seeing only more and more bodies, including Finth's bloodied corpse.

"Stay close," Estin told Atall, stumbling towards Feanne, trying to hurry his pace as best he could. The kit stayed practically on top of his heels, grabbing onto Estin's tail.

Thankfully, most of the undead were either paying attention to Feanne, or to the few remaining townsfolk. A great many more undead now wandered aimlessly, having no further commands since being told to attack the tent, which was now gone. From what Estin could see, the Turessians were too busy to give their mindless army further commands.

Estin pushed through the groups of undead, many of whom ignored him and Atall completely. The few that looked at them just made half-hearted attempts to grab at him, then went back to wandering. He had gotten more than halfway to Feanne when he saw the Turessian she was fighting with break and run, calling the undead after him. As one, the entire undead army turned and fled, running for the north valley, leaving Feanne and Estin standing in the field, watching them go.

He walked up towards Feanne, wondering at the undead forces' strange behavior, but then noticed that Feanne was not quite well. She ignored his approach, growling and advancing a step at a time after the undead. Even when he spoke, she never looked down at him.

"Feanne," he pushed, stepping in front of her. Her eyes were furious and staring into the distance—he had seen the change enough times now to know that she was raging and there was a good chance she would kill anything in her way to get to her foes. This time though, she looked tired, her eyelids drifting closed, before snapping back open repeatedly. "Let them go. We need to help the town. Let the anger go and help me help the others. The kits need us, not more violence."

Growling loudly, Feanne seemed to force herself to look away from her foes, closing her eyes and dropping to one knee. She waited like that until Oria had climbed down, then the transformation of her body began in reverse, Feanne's body tearing itself apart and rebuilding. When it was finished, Feanne lay still on the ground, breathing, but unconscious.

"Is she okay?" asked Oria, panicking as she patted her mother's hand.

"She'll be fine," Estin told both her and Atall, checking Feanne's pulse. "She's just tired. What she did takes a lot out of her. I don't think she's ever fought this long before."

Carefully, Estin lifted Feanne in his arms and looked around the ruined land that had been their village. Every tent had been flattened, as well as the trees and everything else that had once been there. Nothing remained of the majestic landscape within the valley that had graced the area just a few hours earlier.

To the west, he could see a large group of people approaching. They were the ones who had been held by the undead, consisting mostly of elderly, children, and young parents. Those were among the few he still saw moving. That group quickly rejoined with the survivors, helping to check those who had fallen and help those who could not walk well.

Everywhere else he looked, bodies lay strewn, sometimes in pieces. Hundreds of zombie and skeletal remains were scattered, intermingled with dozens of the townsfolk. He saw faces of so many people he had come to know and respect, now lying torn and mutilated among the equally battered undead.

Among the fallen, he saw Bockkan's dismembered body, surrounded by dozens of shredded corpses. The man had died a good death, taking many down with him and showing the might of the bear totem he served. Estin could only assume that his people would tell stories of him, if any had survived to do so.

Where the last tent had stood, no more than a dozen survivors were checking the fallen to see if any still lived. Among those standing, Estin could see Linn and the vine-wrapped fae-kin woman who had led most of the spellcasters during the battle—Dalania, he remembered having heard somewhere.

Off to the side of the battlefield, Ulra was kneeling near Doln, her head hung. The male's body was still and surrounded by a wide swath of bloody ground. Even from a distance, Estin could see Ulra's shoulders shaking with grief.

"Why did they run, Estin?" asked Atall, not budging from Estin's side. "Will they come back?"

"Probably," he answered without thinking. He was too numb to really think his words through, but Atall appeared to be equally dazed, just nodding at the grim reply.

Estin began searching the southern range, trying to find anything that might have scared off the undead, but all he saw were thick mists filling the south exit from the valley. He watched that mist for a minute as he looked for anything coming out of it, then realized that the cloud-like mists were actually glowing faintly. Without any wind, those mists drifted in random directions, sometimes slowly, but then would lurch farther in one direction, as though reaching out to grab at a target.

"We're heading to the west end of the valley," Estin said, louder than he had been talking previously. As he had hoped, he heard the order passed along through the survivors, until everyone was gradually moving towards the west, except for Ulra, the group following him slowly.

"Will she come, too?" Oria whispered, joining Atall in clinging to Estin's tail as they walked away from the ruins of the village. "Ulra's falling behind."

"She knows the way," he told the girl, not looking back. "When she is done saying goodbye to her mate, she will join us, if she wishes."

Estin's attention was on making sure they were not walking into a horde of undead, rather than the children's occasional questions, or whether very many people were following. His only other concern was watching Feanne for any change in her condition. She lay limply in his arms, her breathing shallow. This was something she had mentioned to him one night several weeks earlier, warning him that the longer she used her gift and the more injuries she shrugged off in that form, the harder it would be for her when it ended. This looked to be a rather bad bout and he had no way of knowing how long she would be out and had no way to speed things along.

"How did you know to use the rings?" Estin asked as they passed four tall wooden poles, hoping to distract the kits from the bodies that hung high above them, already being circled by carrion birds. He rather wanted to distract himself as well.

"The bad man tried to kill mom," Oria said, her eyes on Feanne. "When she was able to take it, he laughed and tried to kill me. It just didn't work. I heard grandmother's voice and she told me how to block the death magic. I did it as much as I could, but mom still got hit sometimes."

"She told me to heal a healer," added Atall, rubbing his own ring. "The rest just kinda happened."

Estin smirked, thinking of all the times Asrahn had been one step ahead of everyone. She must have planned ahead, hoping to protect whoever the rings ended up with. He had to assume she had managed to find an enchanter—likely among the humans or elves that had come to the camp—who had made the items for her before her death.

"You two did very well," he told them, though neither kit really paid much attention to him. Both were very much focused on Feanne, watching her for the smallest movement.

They continued onwards and as they reached the steep and uneven path up into the heights of the mountains. Once there, Estin stopped and waited as the others caught up, gathering into a large mass that fanned out and waited for directions. Most looked to Feanne, still in Estin's arms, then began turning around, looking for new leadership.

"We will follow Estin," announced Linn forcefully, limping to the forefront, apparently noticing the group's search for guidance. The man was severely hurt, blood staining much of his armor and his shield-arm hanging limply at his side. "Until our leader has recovered, her mate can speak for her. Do I have any objections?"

The group weakly mumbled something akin to acceptance, then Linn walked up to Estin, bowing his head ever so slightly.

"I'm not letting a bunch of scared civilians tear the village apart, just because she's unconscious," Linn whispered to Estin, glancing down at Feanne. "She'd hurt us both if they scatter before she wakes. Plus, you know the way...right?"

"Yes, I think I do," answered Estin wishing he could give the man a hug. "I've never taken the path, but few of us have. The scouts briefed me on the route, so I can get us pretty far west before I'm lost. By then, the undead should not be able to find us. I'm hoping zombies can't handle the rough terrain."

"Lead on, then. I will make sure they follow her to the ends of the world, if that's what we need to do to get away. So long as you're carrying her, this group will follow you. I can't make them look to you for more than direction, but I can make them follow her, awake or not. Troops will rally to their commander—conscious or not—on a moment's notice, so long as anyone expresses faith in that commander's leadership."

Estin did not know anything about the military, but he could see the assembled people waiting patiently, watching him and Feanne for guidance. Even the kits were watching him, as though he were expected to have all the answers. Suddenly, Estin did not envy Feanne's job in the slightest.

"Follow me," he called out, his voice shakier than he would have liked. "We'll head west into the mountains, towards the pass, at least until Feanne wakes."

Turning, Estin hoisted Feanne's weight back up against his chest, trying to balance her so that he would be able to handle the rough climb. He braced himself, pushing ahead up the gravel slope that disappeared quickly into the rocky-sided mountains, trying not to slide or fall. Every step of the way, he had to dig his claws into the ground in an attempt to keep his feet from slipping. Behind him, he heard the strained grunts and occasional sounds of someone falling.

That first hour, they made negligible progress, mostly struggling to get off of the first slope and up to where the path curved into the mountains proper, disappearing from sight of the valley. Night had begun to make the path treacherous by the time Estin cleared that first rise, looking down across the uneven and sometimes cliff-lined path through the mountains. It was not somewhere he would have ever willingly taken anyone, knowing that few were comfortable with such drop-offs, but he saw little other option.

A roar from somewhere behind them made Estin stop short. He listened just long enough to recognize it as a bear's growls. The roar came several times, then was cut short. Forcing down any thoughts about what he might be hearing, Estin began moving along again, determined not to stop, knowing he could not do anything to help her.

Squinting in the dimming light at the distant ends of what he knew to be just barely a path, he could see where it began descending between two peaks. From what he had been told, that was the pass and would be their target. Anything beyond that was unexplored, but likely no worse than where they were coming from. Whatever might wait there was probably not a massive undead army bent on their destruction.

At their altitude, Estin could see a little ways to the south, where that strange mist drifted through the mountains, glowing dimly in the twilight. They were now far enough from it that it appeared not to be moving, but he had a strange feeling he wanted nothing to do with it. If the undead were actually running from it, he wanted to get the village as far from it as possible.

"Just got word from Sohan," Linn announced, grunting as he stumbled up alongside Estin. "He's making trips back and forth, trying to get us some eyes on the undead."

"How bad?"

Linn shrugged.

"Hard to say. The undead army is largely intact. They lost maybe a quarter of their number. They're holding the north valley entrance, but seem unwilling to come back into the valley proper. From what Sohan said, he even tried to make them chase him, but the main force would not move.

"He did say that there is one large group headed our way, with one of the Turessians leading it. Ulra did her best..."

"We need to worry about these people right now, rather than all those who've made sacrifices. We can mourn them later," Estin replied, shifting Feanne again, then looking down at the kits, who were both wide-eyed as they stared off into the mountains. "Do you have any idea what that mist is?"

"No clue. My mother raised us on tales of the stranger things in the world, but I've never heard of anything like this."

Estin set Feanne down on the ground, checking her heart again, as well as opening one of her eyelids to look at her eyes, while the kits knelt beside him, watching carefully. Her breathing was still very weak.

"She's not getting any worse," Estin told the kits, squeezing Feanne's hand. What he left off was that she was also not getting any better as far as he could tell.

"We may have more problems," Linn announced, leaning close to Estin. "The main force may not be coming, but pursuit is in sight."

Estin turned and looked back down the mountainside, having to adjust his position to see past the large group from the village. Far down the path behind them, he could make out the tall Turessian that had led the attack, moving slowly up the trail with less than a dozen corpses shambling along with him, as well as a pair of semi-transparent spirits.

"Let's get moving," Estin told the man, hoisting Feanne back into his arms. As he did, he felt the kits hands latch back onto him. "The scouts gave me a few different paths we can take once we're farther out of the valley. We'll lose him in the mountains."

The next few hours were a brutal pace for Estin, pushing his own limits, as well as those of the elderly and injured that followed him. Every few minutes, someone would fall, but the group moved on, dragging those who slowed back to their feet and forcing them onwards. They had not lost anyone yet, but Estin knew that by morning, the entire group would be thinned, some from exhaustion, others as they reached the deadly cliffs ahead. As it was, he was not sure how he would possibly navigate the thin cliff-side path while carrying Feanne and keeping a grip on the kits to ensure they would make it through.

Estin considered his limited options, checking the group that clumsily followed him.

The cliffs would kill at least half their number, no doubt. He knew of a side-path one of the scouts had mentioned, which would take them down into the canyon below on the south side of the cliffs, then back up on the far side. It was hours longer, but also would allow them to hide from pursuit and might provide other avenues of escape. The cliff path was faster, but he knew for a fact that there would be no other ways to travel once they were on it.

Though he knew that it was adding a great deal of time to their trip, Estin silently detoured as they neared the narrow ledge, heading instead down an uneven path that twisted sharply towards the south, hugging the mountainside. If nothing else, he hoped that the trail would take them out of sight of the Turessian long enough that they could get to the bottom and find cover. Most likely, the necromancer would stay on the upper path, heading far away from their group by the time they moved on and increasing the distance between himself and the main undead force.

The loose gravel of the steep hillside was treacherous, forcing Estin to move very slowly on his way down. He picked his path carefully, trying to keep Feanne's weight close enough to his body that he could maintain his balance. About halfway down the long incline, he turned somewhat, trying to look back at the rest of the group to be sure they were making their way down without problem.

The closest to him were Atall and Oria, who were practically skipping down the dangerous slope, clearly unaffected by the difficult footing. As he turned a little farther to see how Linn and others were faring, Estin felt his left foot begin to slide. He tried to dig in, but felt his balance vanish in an instant. He watched Oria's eyes widen as he began to tumble backward and several of the others reached out, as though there were anything they could do to arrest his momentum.

Biting back a cry that would have given away their position, Estin pulled Feanne to his chest as he fell, rolling down the remaining fifty feet to the bottom. With each rolling impact, he felt stones drive into his back and arms, as Feanne came down wrong on his knee and nearly slid out of his grip. Even his swords slashed at his body, trapped against him by his belt, until that broke and the weapons flew away. With a final painful lurch, he slammed into a row of rocks at the bottom of the hill with his hip, as Feanne slid free of his arms and away from the rocks.

Groaning and struggling to stand, Estin looked over at Feanne, visually checking her for any major injuries from the fall. She had been scraped up badly, but appeared otherwise intact. Breathing easier, he let his head fall back to the ground, his head spinning for a while until the kits and several others came running up beside him.

"Estin!" Oria hissed, grabbing his arm and tugging at it. "You need to get up."

"I'll be fine," he lied, shifting his weight and feeling the distinct sensation of a broken leg. He struggled to keep the agony off his face as he looked up at Oria, then Atall. "Have Linn find some shelter for us. We all need some rest. Make sure he gets your mother there as quickly as he can. I'll join you in a few minutes once I'm feeling better."

Atall obediently ran off, heading straight to Linn, who was limping his way towards them as swiftly as he could manage. As the two met, Linn appeared to listen to the child, then looked up at Estin. The human stared long at Estin, his eyes revealing that he understood completely, then led Atall towards several other villagers.

Unlike her brother, Oria watched Atall run off, then turned back to Estin, her fearful look fading into sadness. She reached down and touched his leg, leaning to examine the damage.

"You're sending us away," she said softly, tightening her grip on his hand as she closed her eyes. "How badly does it hurt?"

"I'll be fine in a little while," he insisted, forcing a smile. "I'm just winded. I'll catch up soon."

He knew it was a lie. There was nothing left of his healing without extensive rest and the leg felt as though it were twisted at an odd angle under him. Sharp rocks behind his hip and shoulder had torn through his clothing and into his flesh, covering his back with the warmth of blood. Even his tail was bent sharply under him, at least dislocated, if not broken as well. He could feel a raspy rattle in his right lung that he tried to ignore. Without another healer, he would be dead in hours out in the wilds—sooner with the undead coming.

Oria eyed him nervously, then put her hand on his chest, sitting back on her feet. She waved off two of the villagers who came near, but did not look up at them.

"My real dad put us in a cabinet," Oria said softly, glancing back to her brother, who had stopped to talk to the other villagers, then was pointing at Feanne. "He swore we would be all right and he would join us soon. Why do adults always lie when things are bad? You're hurt really badly. Mother told me how people always want to die alone..."

"I need you both to go and find some shelter," he told her, avoiding any acknowledgement of her observations. Oria knew the truth, so he saw no reason to try and deceive her, but could not bring himself to say how badly hurt he really was. "I'll do what I can to catch up."

Oria nodded, refusing to look him in the eyes. Without another word, she slipped her grandmother's ring off her finger and put it on Estin's chest, then got up and walked away, shoving past Atall as he started back towards Estin.

Giving Estin a confused look, Atall finally seemed to understand as his ears drooped. Without a word, the boy stormed off, heading back to the main group of travelers.

Clutching the ring to his breastbone, Estin closed his eyes and listened as the group moved on past him. To his great joy, he heard several people come over and hoist Feanne from the ground and walk away with the rest of the group. He thought he heard some people speak to him or of him, but he ignored it all, trying to shield himself from the emotional pain of watching his extended family leave him to die, even if it was on his orders.

Soon enough, the last of the torches had moved beyond him and the area lay silent and dark, leaving Estin alone with his thoughts and little else. To keep himself from dropping Oria's ring, he slid it onto his little finger.

Though he could not be sure, Estin thought that he drifted in and out of awareness as the sounds of the group departing fully faded. Estin finally opened his eyes again, surveying the rocks that he had landed against. They were sharp pieces of stone that had probably tumbled down the mountainside, just the way he had. Along the side of one, he could see his own blood.

On a whim, he felt around his pouches, hoping that he had at least brought Asrahn's spellbook, in case he lived long enough to rest and then attempt to heal himself. He chuckled grimly, as he found his pouch open and empty, any contents of it long gone. They could have been lost any time during the day's fighting or during travel. He had no way of knowing where the book had wound up.

The rocks' rough sides bit into Estin's hands as he tried to move himself into a better position to evaluate his injuries. Pain lanced through his leg as he forced himself upright, biting back a scream as he used one hand to pull the broken limb out from under himself. When he relaxed against the rocks, he could see that his hand and leg were covered with dark blood, mostly from where a white protrusion of bone now extended from the skin of his thigh. His vision blurred as he fought against blacking out.

There would be no traveling on the leg, even with a splint, he told himself, tying off a piece of his torn clothing just below the hip to do what he could to slow the bleeding. Even so, the pain from the cuts on his back and the rattling in his lung grew worse with each minute, letting him know that the broken leg was bad, but not even close to the extent of his injuries.

Estin shook his head and leaned back against the rocks, amazed at all he had survived in the last few years, only to die to a clumsy misstep. The world's sense of humor had always surprised him, but this was beyond words.

Though the desire at that point was to close his eyes and let the cold sleep that lingered at the edge of his awareness take him, Estin forced himself to focus, struggling to keep himself awake to the very end. He wanted to know that he had not failed Feanne and the kits and that the undead did not catch them, at least before his last breath. Whether he would know or not, he wanted to watch for as long as he could.

Estin sat there for hours, feeling his body slowly going cold as the bleeding slowed and the night grew darker. His chin dipped every so often, threatening to draw him into sleep that he knew he would likely not wake from. He fought the delirium, shaking his head as he tried to see his life through to its last moments. Only the dark skies told him that not too much time had yet passed. The moon was only halfway through its nighttime arc.

Eventually, Estin realized he was lying on his side again, having fallen over without even realizing it. Closing his eyes reluctantly, he began to accept that the end was nearing rapidly. Wakefulness and half-dreaming delusions began to blur together, giving him a light-headed feeling as the pain finally started to fade away.

He could see his parents suddenly. They were nearby on the steep trail, his father kneeling to remove the collar from his mother's neck. Smiling at one another, they got up, walking out of his sight together. At long last, Estin knew they were safe and he no longer needed to hide under the blankets in terror. They would live. Everything was all right now. They would not die and they would live out their lives together. It was what he had always wanted for them. They could finally go on without him.

Time continued to pass slowly for Estin as he lay there, smiling at the knowledge that his parents were no longer hurting. He knew it was a dream, somewhere deep down, but the sense of self-forgiveness let him lay there, calmly accepting whatever would come. He just knew that he had done whatever was needed of him and now they were safe, which was all that mattered.

Shapes blurred in his sight and Estin saw Feanne and the kits in front of him. They were sad at first, but as he watched, they moved on and were happy again. The kits grew up, moving on and taking on their own lives, as Feanne slowly drifted away from his vision. As they all disappeared, Estin was dimly aware that the kits were the adults now, having gone on to have their own children. Whether he was in their lives or not, they had continued on, their lives happy and complete.

If these things were to be the result of his death, Estin could find no reason to fight any longer. Closing his eyes again, he stopped his struggle, letting sleep embrace him. With it, the pain faded away. His work was done. Everyone was safe, at last. Through those last moments, he could feel Feanne sitting beside him, her hand gentle on his head, soothing away his fears. Whether real or imagined, he welcomed the company.

Everyone was safe, at last.

This was Estin's good death.

Chapter Fourteen

"Breathe"

The dreams of the dying are erratic and rarely remembered if the person recovers. These fleeing images are haunting and seek to soothe the one who approaches death's door with the knowledge that they no longer need worry. The world will move on without them. It puts them at ease, so that their spirits may move on without burden. This is my sincere belief as one who has aided many such spirits both to find a safe path back to life and also watched as many passed beyond my ability to help and been witness to such sights.

Without these final moments of peace, it is the belief of many healers—myself included—that the spirit will become so enraged by its loss of purpose and possibility of revenge or alternate outcome, that it will linger in the world, violently striking at all those who still possess life. This may be out of pure anger for having lost its opportunities in life, or could be as basic as a need to attack everything that comes near it out of a desperate hope that this will bring about an ending to its tormented existence.

I felt that moment of true finality. This was not like when I had been killed by the Turessian on the battlefield. I had truly died, my spirit releasing my mortal body and attempting to move on. I knew that there was no circle to save me, no other healer to draw me back. It was all over and I knew it. I had given up my claim to my own body and accepted my fate, intending to leave the world.

As I felt it all falling away behind me, fingers dug into my very spirit, driving me back into my body. The agony was overwhelming, as I was yanked from peaceful non-existence right back to the brink of death, all of my wounds and pain coming back in a rush.

Estin choked and gagged as his body fought against the sudden agony of having his spirit thrown violently back to where it belonged. His leg still throbbed and his back was burning, but he was awake again, almost like someone had startled him from a deep sleep.

At first, he could only lay there, trembling as he tried to make sense of what was happening. His heart was racing and he could barely see or hear, the pounding in his head making all his senses dull. What little he could make out around him was that there was a small-framed person sitting beside him, a hand on his face, stroking his fur.

A light rain fell over them both and likely had been for some time, as Estin's fur was soaked. Even with the disorientation he felt, he could see that the moon was far along in the sky now. He had been unconscious or dead for at least an hour or two.

"Feanne," he wheezed, trying to focus his eyes, even as the pain throughout his body grew more intense. "How did you bring me back?"

She leaned in and just put a finger up to shush him.

"Why are you here? You should be running," he insisted, praying that she had not put herself in danger to come back for him.

The blurred shape sat up straighter, cocking its head.

"I fell behind," she said, though the voice was hollow in Estin's ears, distorted by a continuous ringing sound. There was a haziness even to the sound, which made her voice sound somehow off. "Which way did the others go?"

Estin opened his mouth then froze, trying to force his vision to clear. He could not make out much, other than that the build of the speaker was about right for Feanne, though she wore a hooded cloak that covered her face. None of his senses could confirm who he was looking at.

Reaching up slowly, Estin grabbed her hand under the pretense of holding it against his face. As he did, he pressed the fingertips into his skin, feeling nothing more than the tips against his flesh. There were no claws.

"Who are you?" Estin demanded, shoving her hand away.

"Always were the clever one, my fuzzy friend," hissed the woman, sitting back to watch him. "Is why I chose you for my climbing partner, no?"

Groaning, Estin pressed his face in the wet dirt, wishing he had the strength to even try to fight. Even at his best, he doubted he could have faced down a Turessian—Varra, he reminded himself—at close range without weapons. With his body broken and on the verge of death, with no magic to back him up, he was as helpless as a newborn.

"My master asked that I bring you back to join us," she went on, stroking his cheek again, despite his attempts to push himself out of her reach. "Is good to be wanted, no? You will be strong like us soon. Not so strong as some of us, but is best we can offer without a circle."

"Just let me die."

Varra laughed, though the sound was dry and empty of emotion, completely unlike how he remembered her. She leaned closer, seemingly inspecting his face as she toyed with him. He could faintly see the dead white eyes watching him, though the woman never blinked.

"This I have nearly done already, as I was slow in finding you. I could have changed you without any effort while you were asleep. Instead, I like to offer it to you first. We are all strong, but those who accept it before dying are so much stronger. If I turn you without a circle and without your wishes, you would be little better than the zombies. With at least your wish to live on, you will make nice person to talk with for a few decades. For this, I give you back just a bit of your life, so you can decide. Your body is still dying, but is strong enough for us to talk a little while...like civilized folk, no?"

Estin tried to push her away again, but his arms would barely move. He knew it would not be long before his body gave in to the blood loss again. When that happened, there was no doubt in his mind that Varra could and likely would change him into a monstrosity like herself. There was nothing he could do to stop her, beyond stalling in the hopes that Feanne and the others could get far enough away that they would not be found.

"Where is your army?" Estin asked her, looking around the base of the slope. The two of them were alone. He half-expected a horde of zombies around him, snarling and waiting for the chance to attack.

"My master is not so bright as he thinks," mused the girl, giggling, though the sound was eerie. "He took our troops and went on high road. I thought, 'Varra, would you take high road?' And here I find you, all alone and waiting for me to come save you.

"I had to be very sneaky to be sure I did not find too many of your people...it seems that battle took a lot out of me. Even as powerful as I am, fighting a hundred of your fellows can be so exhausting. Is lucky for you that I saved a little bit of my strength to bring you back from the brink of death, yes?"

They sat there quietly for another minute or two, Varra picking at dried blood and dirt in Estin's fur, even as she unblinkingly watched his face. He felt as though she were staring into his very spirit, waiting for the moment of death to arrive.

"Will not be so bad," Varra whispered at him, her fingers tracing the thin scars on his cheek from the fight with Olis months earlier, making his skin crawl at the feel. "This life has been very hard on you. Once you are turned, you will understand. If we hurry, you may even be able to keep your lover. I would not deny you this, if I am able. Make me wait too long and she will be beyond my help."

"This isn't help."

Varra shook her head and answered, "Not the turning. She could be dead for yea[r]
I could turn her to one of my kind, though not so strong as I. What I mean is if we [
everything here will be destroyed. I will take you—alive or dead—before that h[

your little fox girl will be lost in what is to come next. If you accept now, we can still reach her. Her and the little ones. They do not need to be lost, my friend. The cute little foxes can stay young forever...if we can get to them in time."

Though his vision was still badly distorted, Estin slid his head along the ground so he could look southwards. No more than about a quarter mile away, the dimly-glowing mists he had seen earlier now floated, gradually drifting closer.

"What is it?" he asked, trying to stall. He had to believe that Feanne could escape if he just gave her enough time. "Where does it come from?"

"We do not know," answered Varra, sounding almost sad, her cold fingers brushing at dirt in his fur absently. "The weapons in the golems...these we think made the mists. After each explosion, then we see large black holes that no magic could touch. A day pass, maybe two, maybe even a week, then the hole would go away and one of these mists appears. There are many now, drifting around, though usually not so many as we have here."

"You actually fear them."

Varra chuckled, the dry raspy noise grating on Estin's ears.

"Yes, is true. We sent so many little skeletons in to find out what the mists were, but only a handful came back. We watched some of our precious children burn to ash as the mists touched them. We may live forever, but magic like this will kill even us.

"In passing, mists leave behind the remains of those they have taken from other places, even sometimes giving us parts of another city. Is like they take what they want from one land and drop it in another, no? If they do not like something they touch, it is destroyed.

"At first, we considered them silly and just avoided them. Now, there are too many to avoid."

Shifting to look behind her, Varra watched the mists herself for a time, then returned her attention to Estin.

"So how does being in a family way suit you?" she asked him, a touch of humor in her

"rdering your own father suit you?"

her dry laugh and said nothing for a time, her hand tracing several

g and the skin beneath. Estin watched the motions, then

she had been by the earlier battles if the wounds had

s and
wait,
ppens, but

nore?" Estin asked her after a few more minutes.

"Who?"

"Your ancestors."

Varra sighed deeply, shaking her head.

"They are upset with me, but they do not understand. Soon, the clans will all be like me and the ancestors will have no choice but to accept us as family again. It will take time, but that is what I have the most of now."

Then Varra leaned over top of Estin, watching him closely again, her hood brushing his face.

"Is time to decide, my friend," she told him, pulling back her hood. A deep bloodless cut ran across her face, having torn partly through one of her cheeks. The skin was closing, but almost slow enough that Estin could not see the movement. He could only imagine how bad the wound had been earlier. "I can hear your body dying and we cannot wait much longer. I can save you and those you wish, but there is no more time to wait. Let me give you our gift, then tell me where I can find your woman, so we can help the others."

"I never wanted or asked for your help," muttered Estin, rolling onto his back, even through the pain of moving himself. "I've spent the last couple years watching your kind tear mine apart. I won't help you, Varra. You're offering to put a different kind of leash on me, but it's still a leash. You're the one who wanted me to find freedom outside the cities...I found it without you."

The rain felt good on his face, the small droplets cooling his skin and taking away the feeling of dirt and blood that covered him. He closed his eyes and let the rain calm him, even while Varra laid her hand on his throat. She was gentle, but he knew that could change easily. A part of his mind drifted back to when Feanne had put her hand on his neck the same way...from her, it had felt merciful, but from Varra, it felt like death waiting to claim him.

"Is not surprise, but I wish you could have joined me as my equal," Varra told him, her hand tightening on his throat, making breathing difficult. "We will talk more once I have turned your body into an immortal one. Perhaps then we can agree to find your woman and all the others together, yes? Your children would make adorable travel companions, once turned."

Varra's grip cut off Estin's breathing as he fumbled against her hand. Nothing he could do would move her one inch. Slowly, he felt the pounding in his head begin to fade as his arms became heavier. Sleep closed in on him again, this time feeling so much more oppressive, knowing what was to come, though he still pawed weakly at Varra's iron grip.

Without warning, Varra snatched her hand away, leaving Estin choking and inhaling much of the falling rain as he tried to get air back into his lungs. That only gagged him further, as only one of his lungs felt as though it were working properly.

"You will not touch him again," growled another voice. This one he had no trouble recognizing, even with the ringing in his ears. "Back away from my mate, creature."

Varra laughed and moved away from Estin very slowly, easing herself onto her feet.

"Here I thought you had run away with tail between your legs," said Varra, still standing somewhat over Estin. "He will live much longer with me than running the length of the world, looking for safety with you, fox lady. Very much longer. You are welcome to join us. If you choose not, I understand...I will keep him for the next few hundred years until I am bored with him. Best hurry…he will die soon even without my help."

Estin forced himself onto his side, using his elbow to shove himself off of the rocks so that he could see both Feanne and Varra.

Standing with a straight back and her fingers extended to better fan out her claws, Feanne was not so much as looking down at him. She never took her eyes off of Varra and from what Estin could see, her leg muscles were tense and ready to leap at any moment. Throughout the wait, her ears twitched, turning every so often to follow nearby sounds as she panted, creating small puffs of steam in the cool air. She looked as though she had run hard to get to this place, her clothing and fur covered with a sheen of water and mud.

Far off in the scrub grass of the canyon they were in, Estin saw the slightest bit of movement in his peripheral vision. The white tips of two tails shifted near the ground, as though someone were crawling through the grass. He quickly shifted his attention back to Varra, hoping she had not followed his gaze.

"You should have gone with your people, no?" asked Varra, stepping even closer to Estin, her cloak shielding him from the light rain. "When I have killed you both, you will lead me to them. Had you stayed away, my little Estin would have been guessing at where you had gone."

"Please try to catch them, creature. I have sent them on through underground paths that only the dwarves from my pack will be able to find."

Laughing, Varra closed her eyes for a moment, then opened them and shook her head while grinning.

"Is not smart moment for you, fox lady. Little secret I wish you to know…my people can talk at great distances without words. My master already knows what you have said and is sending one of ours to the caves, with guidance from a dwarf that has already joined us. Your people are lost to you."

Estin swore he saw Feanne's eyes gleam with mischief, but he could well have been imagining it. Before he could think too hard on that, he began coughing. When he opened his eyes again, a wide swath of blood was running swiftly away in the rainwater. He could already feel the drowsiness taking over again, as he fought to stay awake. Some part of him wanted to see the outcome of this battle, even if the result was death for his family.

Seconds passed. Then as though they had announced to one another that it was time to begin, the two women rushed at each other, slamming together with the sound of claws ripping through flesh and metal sliding across fur and skin. The sickening sounds lasted only a moment, then Varra flung Feanne almost twenty feet away, where she hit the ground roughly, but managed to roll back onto her knees, wincing in pain.

"Is not right," mused Varra, eyeing a tear in her chest that exposed broken bones and blackened lungs beneath. Already it was beginning to mend and she looked annoyed, rather than injured. "My master swore we were not to be hurt by mundane weapons. Your claws should not hurt me."

Bleeding from a series of blade-wounds across her upper body, Feanne smiled weakly, tracing symbols in the air as quickly as she could, even as she stood unsteadily.

"Ahh, this I understand," said Varra, grinning broadly as she waved her hand and dismissed whatever magic Feanne had begun. "I did not know you had magic. This will make things much fun, yes? Is nice to fight someone who can try to harm me."

Estin could only helplessly watch as the two began a series of hand motions, each trying to form a spell to attack the other, only to be countered and have to start over. The battle of whispered magical words, overshadowed by the sound of falling rain, struck him as lovely in its simplicity, though he knew the strain both were dealing with, trying to overcome the other's skills. Throughout the display, he saw flickers of magic over and over as spells began to form, then failed.

Twice, Feanne had to step aside in a hurry as gouts of fire arced past her, coming from Varra. The second of those times, Estin saw her brush away flames on her fur.

With a flourish, Varra ducked away as a wave of acid scorched the area where she had stood, steaming loudly in the rain. From what little Estin could see, Varra had been badly burned, but kept moving. The gypsy girl darted through the high grass, keeping Feanne turning as she covered much of the area, preventing a clear attack with magic.

"You have studied a long time," hissed Varra, vanishing yet again behind some rocks. "I am not so good at sitting in one place long enough to learn so much. This makes you better at magic than I."

Feanne swore loudly as long vine-like tendrils wrapped around open air as Varra slipped away. She waited a moment for Varra to reappear, then relaxed slightly, her feet making soft splashes as she walked to stand beside Estin, while she kept her eyes on the long grass around them.

"Can you stand?" she asked softly.

"No," Estin said, though his own voice sounded like a choked gurgle. Even that word made his lungs ache and he began coughing again.

"He will walk again once he has died!" called out Varra from somewhere nearby. "I would save my little fuzzy friend, if I can. Let me help him, then we talk about your dislike of me, yes? Do not make your lover die just because you hate me, fox lady. We can share him, no?"

Estin struggled to get enough air in to be able to speak, fighting against the fluid that was filling his lungs.

"Feanne," he gasped, "just change and kill her, then run."

"Can't. If I change again the strain would kill me and that doesn't help either of us."

Feanne stepped lightly over Estin, moving away from the rocks and out towards the brush that likely concealed Varra. She kept her hands up, possibly to block an attack, as well as to hasten any spells she needed to cast.

"I am not so strong as you," continued Varra, her voice coming from yet another part of the canyon, then moving as she spoke. "This I know, having seen you breaking my dancing puppets in your village. I have already fought long and hard today, leaving so little of my strength to face you. What is a girl to do when she cannot win with magic or might?"

A sudden rustle in the bushes and a pair of squeals announced Varra's location as she stood back up.

"She will cheat, yes? This is how I win. Tricks!"

One dangling from each hand, Varra held the kits by their necks. Both were fighting as best they could, squirming and kicking, trying to free themselves. Despite their whimpers and struggles, Varra held them firmly, grinning back at Feanne, even as acid continued to burn into her clothing on some exposed flesh.

"We run short on time," observed Varra, nodding towards the glowing mists that had drifted much closer. They now hung no more than twenty feet away. "You fight me, they die and become puppets. Give up and let me have both you and Estin, then you can choose if the children die and become mine, or if they just die. Is fair, no?"

Oria cried out, fighting to reach Varra's hand on her neck, tears running down her face. Atall had managed to twist himself almost upside-down and was tearing at Varra's hand with his claws, though she seemed completely unaware or unconcerned.

"Mom, help!" Atall shouted, his claws glancing harmlessly off of Varra's hand. "Get up, dad!"

Feanne's ears twitched and went back and from where Estin lay—struggling not only with his own agony, but now the emotions of hearing Atall's choice of words—he could see Feanne's hands shaking. With a resigned sigh, she eased out of her tense stance.

"You win," Feanne said softly. "I have no other choices. They would be dead before I could tear your arms off."

"Yes! This is most wise," lauded Varra, walking slowly towards Feanne and Estin, the kits whimpering as they were roughly bounced around. "What shall it be for the children?"

From his prone position, Estin could clearly see Feanne's hands. They were not idle anymore, though she looked as though she had given up. She had already begun tracing symbols in the air, but Estin could not see any indication Varra was even watching, focusing instead on Feanne's face that was a mask of defeat.

"My children are my rock in life. I won't see them changed into monsters," said Feanne, letting her shoulders sag…then brought her hands up swiftly and completed whatever magic she had begun.

Though Varra snarled and tried to break the kits' necks, Feanne's spell had split and the two children had instantly hardened to stone, their bodies petrified by Feanne's magic. In dismay, Varra stared at the small statues, unable to damage them.

"Is most clever trick…"

"Never try to out-clever a fox," roared Feanne as she rushed Varra, her claws ripping half of the gypsy's face off with her first swing. The second knocked Varra over backwards as most of her jaw was torn free, the frozen kits tumbling away.

Varra slammed onto the ground on her back, reaching up to try and put her jaw back into place, as though dazed. As she did, Feanne took the moment to call down lightning bolt after lightning bolt, blasting away at Varra until the place where she lay was scorched and blackened, every bit of moisture boiled away. Still, Varra began to sit back up, her entire body burned and broken.

Feanne leapt across the distance separating them as the last flash of light faded, tackling Varra and sitting down on top of her. Without hesitation, Feanne raked Varra over and over with her claws until Varra finally stopped moving, her torn body going limp on the ground. Feanne continued to strike at her for several more seconds, then let her hands fall to her sides as she panted for breath. Even as she fought to breathe, Varra's feet began to twitch again.

Estin just lay there, feeling his breathing slowing as the sun slowly rose, lighting the field. He closed his eyes and waited for the warmth the light would bring, but it did not come. When he opened his eyes again, he realized the light was from the strange mists that now hung only several steps past Feanne.

Inside those eerie clouds, Estin could see things that made no sense. At first, he believed his delirium was reaching a new level, but the bizarre sights only could be seen in the mists. Anywhere else he looked, things were relatively normal. He could not pick out anything specific, but flashes of faces and places appeared and vanished rapidly.

Looking back to Feanne, Estin watched as she leaned to either side, touching first Oria, then Atall. At her touch, each child returned to flesh and bone, blinking as they tried to figure out what had happened. They both just stared between Feanne, Varra, and Estin.

"Feanne, please take them away," Estin gasped, not even sure the words were coming out in a way that she would understand. "Let me be alone now."

Easing herself up from Varra's mangled body, Feanne took the kits' hands and led them to Estin's side, sitting them down opposite one another. Calmly, as though she had all the time in the world, she took a seat there as well, picking up his hand and cradling it against her cheek.

"You will never die alone, my love," she told him, tracing symbols with her free hand over his chest. "Dalania recently taught me a few things the Miharon did not care that I learned about my own magic. I can heal your body, but there is little else I can do to save us."

As her gestures ceased, Estin immediately began to feel warmth return to his body. Unlike his own magic, which would have repaired anything from a scratch to broken bones instantly, hers was slowly moving things back where they belonged. It was an incredible—and painful—sensation as his bones began to shift, repositioning themselves. The shattered bone in his leg popped back into the flesh, making him gasp in agony.

A tendril of light swept over Feanne's head, startling her enough that she forced the children to the ground to avoid any chance of touching it. Estin's dazed mind took far longer to register what was happening, but when he did, fear for the others took over. Nearby, he saw Varra begin to roll onto her side.

"The mists," he whispered, trying to stand, but his body could not support him and his leg ground painfully where the bones had not yet meshed. "You three need to run!"

"Is time for new lesson. I am far from finished with you," hissed Varra, sitting fully upright. She raised her hands towards Estin, beginning the motions of a spell, then was yanked violently backwards as the cloudy mists touched her.

It took only a moment and the mist had swept Varra up as though the mists were alive, gobbling greedily at her, even as she writhed, trying to pull herself free. While Estin watched, Varra was tossed sideways, then whisked away into the shifting cloud. As the last sight of her vanished, the rocks that had been at her feet were swept away, seemingly weightless.

Feanne shoved the kits towards the hill that Estin had fallen down, pointing at the top. They took off running, as she got up and put her arms under Estin's armpits and lifted him slightly.

"The path down here is blocked. We must go the long way...and this will hurt," she warned, then began pulling, not giving him a chance to argue.

The agony was unimaginable for Estin as his shattered leg dragged and each tug by Feanne wrenched his broken ribs. Even with her magic slowly healing him, her efforts to save him continued to undo much of the spell's efforts.

Not even halfway up the hill, with tears rolling down his face, Estin watched as the mists closed over the spot where they had been, long glowing tendrils sweeping across the ground. Had he watched a living creature do that, Estin would have believed it was looking for prey that had escaped, but in this situation, the sentient-seeming motions were horrific.

"Leave me!" he begged, watching the mists begin to slide up the hillside, reaching and searching for anything it could clutch at. "Don't risk the kits for me."

"You never left through all the foolishness I've done," Feanne grunted, sliding on the loose gravel and landing hard, but kept them from falling back down the hill. Without hesitation, she began pulling him again. "If anyone in this world has taught me what being a proper mate is about, it is you. I will not leave you to that thing and the kits would never forgive me if I did."

Though the climb was slow-going, Estin was finally able to help somewhat by the time they neared the top. Far below, the mists were falling steadily behind. The higher they got, the easier it was to see that the mists now filled the canyon, consuming entire sections of the woods.

Even as Estin marveled at the destructive force of the mists, a tall old watchtower appeared at the far end of the canyon, seemingly forming from nowhere. It did not fall into place, but just suddenly was there, as if it had been built on that spot.

"This way," Feanne told both the kits and Estin, pointing up the narrow cliff-side path. "It should take us over the mists for now."

The group hurried to the two foot wide walkway, turning sidewise as they reached it. Estin was able to hop on one foot up to the edge, but hesitated at the narrow perch, knowing that it would be a long while before his other leg could hold his weight.

"Just go," Feanne insisted, pushing him ahead of her, but clutching his hand tightly. "You will not fall."

Estin took a long breath, then began hobbling onto the ledge, using his free hand to balance himself against the wall. He attempted to counter-balance himself with his tail, but it flopped over the edge of the path, the muscles not responding. For all the healing he had gone through already, his body was still broken and uncooperative.

Hating himself for his weakness at such a crucial moment in saving his family, Estin pushed himself forward, struggling to keep himself going. The pain in his leg made him stumble every step, nearly taking him over the edge. Whenever he got too close to tumbling, Feanne would hold him back, making him stop until he could stand comfortably again. Compounding the difficulty, the stones were damp and every so often, Estin's hand would slip off the cliff wall, making him panic for a moment, until he was sure that he had not fully lost his balance.

"Take your time," offered Feanne, but when Estin looked back at her, the mists were just reaching the top of the hill behind her, flowing up and onto the ledge.

At the far end of the path, the kits stopped where the trail widened then split, offering several different directions. They turned around and watched nervously, flinching each time Estin stumbled.

Though it took a goodly amount of time, Estin finally reached the far side, putting just a touch of weight on his broken leg. It could not hold him up, but he could at least put the foot on the ground and apply some pressure.

"Down that way," Feanne ordered the kits, pointing at the long trail that descended into the wilds. "It will curve, but lead us around this mountain towards where we were taking the rest of the pack."

Oria and Atall ran off, scouting ahead, while Feanne pulled Estin's arm over her shoulders to support him and hurry them both along. Working together, they made good time down the trail, though the kits were far out of sight within seconds, darting in and out of the rocks and sparse trees to check for danger.

Ten minutes down the animal path, Feanne brought them to a stop as Atall came running back with Oria not far behind, waving his hands to warn them.

"Turessian!" he announced, motioning for them to get away. "Coming this way!"

Estin clearly heard Feanne's growl.

"You two, get to the upper path that we passed about five minutes ago," she ordered the kits. "We'll be right behind."

Again, the kits ran past them, this time heading up a side path into the higher parts of the mountain.

"Where are we going, Feanne?"

She shook her head and sped up their pace.

"I'm not even sure anymore," she admitted, slipping a little and nearly tripping them both. "I'm running out of areas I know out here."

They soon reached the upper path, Estin seeing the kits' paw prints clearly in the wet dirt. He turned with Feanne, making their way painstakingly up the narrower trail, only to have the kits come skidding to a halt in front of them.

"We can't go this way, either," Oria said, her voice cracking. "Mists."

Sure enough, as Estin gazed past the kits, he could see far up the trail that the glowing mists were spreading across the path.

"I'll deal with the Turessian," muttered Feanne, turning them around again. "I'd rather die fighting than running around in circles in the mountains."

Moving back down the path, they passed near the end of the cliff ledge, then Feanne stopped and pointed back towards the ledge itself. She gave Estin a nervous look that made him not want to immediately follow her finger. When he finally convinced himself to, he saw the remaining Turessian sitting on the narrow path, his feet dangling in the air, even as the mists closed on him from the far side. Spread out on either side of him, a group of four blankly-staring corpses were sitting similarly.

"You," the man said, pointing at one of the zombies. "Jump."

As Estin watched, the zombie just leaned out over the edge and fell, bouncing once off the side of the cliff before vanishing into the mists. With a puff of the glowing cloud, the creature was gone.

"I know you are there," the Turessian called out, not raising his head. "I doubt you will have any better luck than I in escaping. Fifty years I spent researching magic in Altis, yet today I am beaten by a cloud. I will stay here and do what I do best. Killing you serves no purpose."

He waved his hand again and another zombie fell lazily into the clouds, this time passing far into the mists before it vanished from sight.

"Interesting," mumbled the Turessian, his voice barely carrying to Estin. "One out of eight zombies and zero for two on spirits."

"I'm not staying near that thing, or willing to take the time to fight him right now," Estin warned, pointing back towards the path the Turessian had come up. "It's the only way we haven't tried yet."

Feanne agreed, sending the kits ahead as she helped Estin down the descending path into the trees.

This time they were able to move a little faster, as Estin's leg was supporting a portion of his weight, though it was excruciating to do so. Pain was hardly his concern though, knowing how dangerously close to an abrupt death they were at every turn.

After they had come the rest of the way down the slope and gotten well into the woods, Estin began to feel the ground tilting back up again as dawn broke dimly through the tree cover. From what he could recall of the scouts' directions, they were likely getting into the pass between the next two peaks, which would then lead into another section of the range, where he could only hope the mists would not reach.

Atall was the first back this time, pointing at two different paths through the woods.

"Mists off to the left. No way around," he warned, as Oria came skidding to a stop behind him. "The other way has caves that look pretty deep. They go the right direction."

"Atall, you need to lead the way. Find us a safe path," Feanne ordered, then turned to Oria. "You will watch around your brother for danger. His concern is the route, yours is anything that's trying to catch us. I want you both far enough ahead that we can avoid any threats, but close enough that you can watch for us as well."

The kits agreed and ran ahead, disappearing into the trees. Every so often, Estin would see a flash of red or a white tail, then they would vanish again, leaving him and Feanne alone as they slowly pushed on through the woods.

"The more I have them do, the less they'll worry," Feanne explained to Estin, helping him get over a grouping of fallen trees.

"Why are they even here?" Estin asked back, keeping his voice low. "I can't tell you what to do, but why would you bring them, knowing what we faced out here?"

"I made a mistake in telling them that I was going to come back to try and save you, no matter the risk and that they would need to stay with Linn to be safe. The two little monsters latched onto my legs and refused to let me go, unless they could come too. They were worried about you and used my determination against me. In the time it would have taken me to pry them off, you would have been dead. They're learning quickly how to manipulate people…my mother would have been extremely proud."

Estin laughed and watched as Oria bounded off a tall rock ahead and to his right, where she had been watching over top of Atall, getting a better view from the height.

"If what Varra said was true, the others know where our people are."

"When the twins and I came back, the mists closed between us and the pack. Linn waving goodbye as those damned mists thickened between us was the last I saw of him. If the Turessians want the pack, they will need to go through the mists…let them. It does our work for us. Even if some get through, I do not know where Linn will lead the others. I made him swear to hide that from anyone until they had arrived."

"You shouldn't have come back," he finally told Feanne, as the sheer wall of a mountainside began to become visible through the trees. "You should have saved them and yourself."

"Their choice was their own, they're old enough for me to let them make it. As for myself," she stopped talking for a moment, then added cryptically, "I have reason to keep you around."

"Care to share?"

"No. It's more fun to be vague and make you wonder. It might help convince you to stop trying to be left behind."

Up ahead, the kits were standing guard at the entrance to a fairly narrow cave. The two waited until they could wave at Estin and Feanne, then Atall ran into the cave, as Oria followed more slowly, watching for any threats.

"They'll be good hunters someday," Estin observed, knowing it was something Feanne had worried about before. Raising children in a village had been something she had confided in him as a concern, thinking perhaps they would be too used to civilization to handle themselves in the wilds. Feanne obsessed over their safety, even as she worried that they would be too soft to survive outside of her watchful eye. "They pay attention and watch each other."

Giving him an amused smirk, Feanne answered, "Only if we live to see that someday. Worry about today, then we'll worry about how well our children can hunt rabbits. Man-eating clouds, violent undead armies, the fall of all civilization, and so many other things are somewhat higher on my list of concerns."

Estin started to smile, then turned and gave Feanne a confused look.

"Our? Does that mean that they…"

"No," she said quickly, her expression clear that she had misspoken. "I have no idea whose they are, but they have known you longer than Insrin. You're who they look to as their father now for guidance, knowledge, and to tell me I am being too mean to them. As far as I'm concerned, their acceptance makes you their father. I won't allow any more of my children to lose the father they have waiting for them."

Estin stopped, forcing Feanne to stop with him.

"Any more?"

She gave him a wry smile, then carried him along a little farther before saying, "They'll be born before winter."

Estin was both exhilarated and terrified. The idea of his own children made him sick, thinking about the world they would be born into. Assuming they were given the chance to be born at all, he reminded himself. He could not find words to express his jumbled feelings, but Feanne looked to be more than willing to let him contemplate his thoughts.

Finally, as they reached the foot of the mountainside, Estin managed to suppress his fears and be genuinely thankful for Feanne's honesty. He nuzzled her neck lovingly for a moment, hoping that it would not be the last time.

"Estin," gasped Feanne, glancing back behind them.

Turning as best he could without putting all his weight on his leg, Estin saw that the first tendrils of the mists had begun to appear through the trees, inching their way towards where they stood.

"No time to waste, then."

Giving Feanne a tug to get her moving, Estin hobbled his way into the cave, feeling the temperature plummet as the damp air surrounded him. It took only a moment for his eyes to adjust to the deep darkness of the caves and soon he could make out the kits farther down the passage, moving around quickly as they explored the depths.

Advancing farther into the dark cave, Estin found that even his vision was becoming limited. Feanne seemed to be in a similar predicament, keeping one hand out ahead of her to feel the edges of the walls. They had not gone much father before they practically tripped over the kits, who were standing in the middle of the narrowing passage.

"I can't see," whispered Oria, though her voice echoed faintly.

"None of us can," Feanne admitted, lifting the hand that was not in use propping Estin up. With a word, her hand began to glow faintly, just barely illuminating the dark tunnel.

From what Estin could see, the passage had been some kind of water-hewn tunnel that descended from the higher canyon behind them. That at least gave him some hope that there would be some exit at the far end, but cave-ins or other problems could have easily changed that.

Stretching far ahead of them and well out of the dim light's reach, the passage continued onward, twisting and dipping around harder rock.

"Keep moving," Feanne told them all. "The light won't last too long."

Their group moved slowly, trying to keep their feet from getting caught up on the uneven floor and piles of fallen rocks. Time was impossible to guess at in the dark tunnels, gauged only by how exhausted Estin felt, though his injuries probably contributed more to that than the walk.

Feanne's magic had done wonders to repair the mortal damage that Estin had suffered, but he chose not to tell her that the spell had faded, leaving a fair amount of pain and bone aches. He could move, but not well. More importantly, he knew he would survive his injuries, even if he could not walk on his own yet. A day or two of rest, or a handful of his own spells would remedy that in time.

Winding through the passage, Estin brought Feanne to a sharp halt as his toes crushed something that had slightly more give than the rocks around it. Glancing down, he found himself with one foot on a pile of dried bones, partially-buried under fallen rock. They were broken from the stones, but he could make out clear signs of something having chewed on them, as well.

He looked up at the kits, who were out at the edge of the light, apparently unaware of the remains, though Feanne gave him a nervous look.

"Over by us," he told them, keeping his voice as low as he could. "There's no sense in scouting if we can't see."

As the kits approached, Estin moved forward with Feanne, keeping the bones behind them, where the children would not see them.

The next section of the passage took them far longer than the previous. Deep cracks in the floor and walls made for treacherous footing and created more than one situation where they were forced to quietly inch past sections in which the ceiling crumbled and dropped small rocks and dirt during their passing.

They traveled so long through the tunnels that finally Feanne's magical light began to fade, surprising them all as the light faded into the inky blackness again. They hurried as it dwindled, then came to a sudden stop as the last of the light disappeared.

"Now what?" Feanne asked, sounding annoyed. "I cannot cast another of those today."

Remaining very still so as to maintain his balance on the rough floor, Estin blinking and stared into the darkness. Slowly, shapes began to appear as his eyes picked up a small amount of light from somewhere.

"There's light ahead," he said, now guiding the others. "We should be able to see if we can get a little farther down the tunnel."

Picking each step carefully, knowing that a wrong move could leave him tripping over rocks or even falling into a crevice, Estin did what he could to move them forward. It was taking an incredible amount of time and once he could begin to see the walls and floor again, he was sure that they had traveled no more than a hundred yards over the course of an hour or better.

Grinning happily at the approaching daylight, Estin pushed on, ignoring the pain in his leg as he hurried them towards escape from the dark. One final curve in the tunnel lay ahead, then from the look of the lighting, they would be able to see the other end of the passage.

Rounding the curve, Estin very nearly fell as his legs gave out. The bright light was from the outside, as he had thought, but filtered through a wall of the glowing mists. Their path was entirely blocked by the roiling cloud. Though the mists appeared unwilling or unable to enter the caves, they sealed the end of the tunnel completely.

"What do we do now?" Oria asked, stopping beside Estin, her eyes wide as she stared at the mists.

Estin had to almost tear himself away from the hypnotic patterns of the mists, taking his weight off Feanne and using the wall to support himself as he began back up the tunnel.

"There has to be another passage," he said out loud, limping back into the darkness. "We must have missed something."

"We missed nothing," Feanne told him, sitting at the curve in the tunnel, pulling the kits onto her lap. "There were no other ways. I searched the whole way down. We are trapped."

Estin could not accept that, not even believing his own eyes. Each step he took, he let his hands trace the walls on both sides, trying to find anything usable. Even a smaller tunnel that would allow the kits to escape would have been acceptable.

"Children," Feanne said in the distance, once Estin was already far enough out that he could no longer see. "Please go fetch your father before he hurts himself."

Swearing, Estin punched at the wall, barely aware of the sharp pain as the rocks bit into his knuckles. He could feel tears running down his face as he put his forehead to the tunnel wall, even as Atall took his hand and tried to pull him back towards Feanne.

It just was not fair, Estin could only tell himself, weakly following the kits back to their mother. They all had survived so much and seen more in their short lives than they should have managed. With odds stacked against wildlings where he had grown up, then the whole world becoming a threat to any living being, they had thrived somehow. Through war and fate, they had managed to become a family, even as the world was being swept clean of life. While nearly everyone Estin had ever known had died, the love of his life and the children he considered to be his own lived, only to die trapped in a cave, consumed by the mists, created at least partially due to his mistake.

"How can you be so calm?" he asked, collapsing near Feanne. The kits sat down nearby, clasping hands nervously. "With all this happening, how do you do it, Feanne?"

Hoisting the kits back onto her lap, Feanne motioned Estin closer. He practically crawled to her, the last of his strength fading.

"I am not calm," she said, pulling Estin close to her so that she could embrace him with the children. "I am accepting. If this is the end that the land gives me, so be it. I have known love and been loved. I refuse to regret, Estin. Not one moment. I will find my end when it comes and meet it, ready to fight for every breath for all of us, but I will not let it destroy me if I cannot fight."

Estin nodded gravely, understanding at last what she had meant by a "good death." It had little to do with the perfection of completeness and the fulfillment of one's duties in life. It was in knowing what you had done and found, then letting that be enough. It was not what he had hoped to find in his own heart, but he prayed it would be enough.

One arm still around Feanne and the kits in her lap, Estin gingerly placed the other on Feanne's stomach, wondering what could have been. So many lives lost and so many more he would never know. Biting back the desire to weep, he lifted his head and faced the mists, which were already beginning to creep into the tunnel. He was determined not to shake Feanne's calm in front of the kits again.

As he watched, the mists began inching into the cave, tendrils of cloud-like luminescence reaching around the cracks and rocks. The flickering light within the mists became his focus as he held his family tightly. The calm fluttering glow was not much different than watching the light cast by a candle and was equally hypnotic.

Atall was the first of them to break, crawling onto Estin's lap and openly crying. He dug his hands into Estin's clothing and fur, burying his face against Estin's chest. Seconds later, as the mists reached within an arm's length, Oria began weeping, too.

On a whim, Estin looked back up the way they had come, that little voice in his head begging him to take them all and run into the darkness for even a moment's longer life. In the long passage behind them, he could see the flickers of the mists approaching as well, dashing any hope that might have lingered.

Estin swept his tail around the group, finding some degree of reassurance that whatever would happen to any of them would affect them all. If this was the end, they would die together. No part of his heart would ever allow him to watch the others die even a second before he did.

The mists were close enough that Estin could feel a radiant warmth against his arm and tail, where they were closest to the semi-transparent cloud. He looked up at the mist again, trying to steel himself for what was to come, but found himself mesmerized by what he could see inside.

The flickering he had seen within the mists was not at all like that of a flame. Instead, it was a rapidly-changing view of thousands of places and things. Landscapes he had never imagined flashed past him, interspersed with scenes that he could only imagine being the elemental planes, with their raging flames, endless miles of oceans, and so on. He saw people for the briefest moments, though they all appeared to be in agony. Then there were buildings that darted past, built with designs he had never seen in either of the land's major cities. There were fields, deserts, mountains, and swamps. Between all of the scenes, he saw death and destruction.

A tendril of mist reached out, brushing across Estin's arm gingerly. As it did, the fur all across his arm froze painfully, then began to thaw as the tendril moved away, seeking more substance. The whole ghostly entity moved around haphazardly, seemingly seeking things to snatch away, but when it found something, it would not always move in the right direction. To Estin, it seemed both malicious and entirely mindless, seeking to destroy, while having no concept of how to accomplish that goal.

"Don't let go," whimpered Oria, one fist clutching Estin and the other Feanne. "Whatever happens…"

As Estin watched in horror, the mist seemed to rear up like a wave, then it crashed down on them, covering all four of them at once.

Pain filled his body and he could feel his fur burning, as screams drowned out all other sounds. He recognized the kits and Feanne's voices, then realized his own was part of the chorus of agony. Every inch of his body was lit by pain and he felt as though he had been thrown into a vat of molten metal.

As swiftly as the pain came on, it went away. Then there was nothing more as the mists moved on through the empty tunnel, seeking more to consume.

Epilogue

We had gambled and lost. The mists had won where even an undead army could not. We were the last of our people in the valley. Likely, there was not another living creature there once we were gone.

My parting thoughts had been on how I had spent my life seeking things that I never believed would be mine. In the end of all that, I had all of the things I had ever wanted in my arms. The only love I had ever known was beside me, along with our—that word burned itself into my mind, even as the mists swept over us—children, both born and unborn.

Once, I had said that all I needed in life was a roof over my head and some food in my stomach. When my mind grasped at the last vestiges of thought in that cave, knowing my life was at an end, that singular memory came back to me. Neither of those things mattered anymore to me...they were the same things every man and animal seeks to survive, but were not things that I as a sentient person needed. When the mists took me, I was hungry and homeless, but holding all the wealth I could imagine.

The mist certainly could kill. Of that there was no doubt. Whether the odds are one-in-eight of surviving or worse, I could not say. I was never one for gambling...I was bad at it and had always lost my bets.

Now, at her request, I must add that Feanne truly despises this new land and I think all five of the kits share her feelings. My kind may not be built for desert-living, but I can now certainly say that red foxes belong there even less. Perhaps someday we will find a way back to our old homeland, with its woods and mountains, assuming the mists have moved on and the undead have been defeated. If not, I am not too worried about where I live.

What I do care about is that there is no one bringing leashes out here in the desert. Our children will be free.

Made in the USA
Charleston, SC
20 August 2011